The Same Face: the Very Same

CLEARTYPE EDITION

THE WORKS OF
CHARLES DICKENS

WITH ILLUSTRATIONS

A CHRISTMAS CAROL
THE CHIMES
THE CRICKET ON THE HEARTH
AMERICAN NOTES

BOOKS, INC.
NEW YORK   BOSTON

'A Christmas Carol in Prose' was first published in
1843; *'The Chimes'* in 1844 and *'The Cricket
on the Hearth'* in 1845. This Edition contains all the copyright emendations
made in the text as revised by the
Author in 1867 and 1868

TYPESET, NICKELTYPED, PRINTED, AND BOUND
IN THE UNITED STATES OF AMERICA BY
THE COLONIAL PRESS INC., CLINTON, MASS.

CONTENTS

A CHRISTMAS CAROL

LIST OF ILLUSTRATIONS

A CHRISTMAS CAROL

PREFACE

THE narrow space within which it was necessary to confine these Christmas Stories when they were originally published, rendered their construction a matter of some difficulty, and almost necessitated what is peculiar in their machinery. I could not attempt great elaboration of detail, in the working out of character within such limits. My chief purpose was, in a whimsical kind of masque which the good humour of the season justified, to awaken some loving and forbearing thoughts, never out of season in a Christian land.

A CHRISTMAS CAROL

I have endeavoured, in this ghostly little book, to raise the Ghost of an Idea, which shall not put my readers out of humour with themselves, with each other, with the season, or with me. May it haunt their houses pleasantly and no one wish to lay it!

Their faithful friend and servant,

C. D.

December, 1843.

A Christmas Carol

MARLEY'S GHOST

MARLEY was dead, to begin with. There is no doubt whatever about that. The register of his burial was signed by the clergyman, the clerk, the undertaker, and the chief mourner. Scrooge signed it. And Scrooge's name was good upon 'Change, for anything he chose to put his hand to.

Old Marley was as dead as a door-nail.

Mind! I don't mean to say that I know, of my own knowledge, what there is particularly dead about a door-nail. I might have been inclined, myself, to regard a coffin-nail as the deadest piece of iron-mongery in the trade. But the wisdom of our ancestors is in the simile; and my unhallowed hands shall not disturb it, or the Country's done for. You will therefore permit me to repeat, emphatically, that Marley was as dead as a door-nail.

Scrooge knew he was dead? Of course he did. How could it be otherwise? Scrooge and he were partners for I don't know how many years. Scrooge was his sole executor, his sole administrator, his sole assign, his sole residuary legatee, his sole friend, and sole mourner. And even Scrooge was not so dreadfully cut up by the sad event, but that he was an excellent man of business on the very day of the funeral, and solemnised it with an undoubted bargain.

The mention of Marley's funeral brings me back to the point I started from. There is no doubt that Marley was dead. This must be distinctly understood, or nothing wonderful can come of the story I am going to relate. If we were not perfectly convinced that Hamlet's Father died before the play began, there would be nothing more remarkable in his taking a stroll at night, in an easterly wind, upon his own ramparts, than there would be in any other middle-aged gentleman rashly turning out after dark in a breezy spot— say Saint Paul's Churchyard for instance—literally to astonish his son's weak mind.

Scrooge never painted out Old Marley's name. There it stood, years afterwards, above the warehouse door: Scrooge and Marley. The firm was known as Scrooge and Marley. Sometimes people new to the business called Scrooge Scrooge, and sometimes Marley, but he answered to both names. It was all the same to him.

Oh! But he was a tight-fisted hand at the grindstone, Scrooge! a squeezing, wrenching, grasping, scraping, clutching, covetous, old sinner. Hard and sharp as flint, from which no steel had ever struck out generous fire; secret, and self-contained, and solitary as an oyster. The cold within him froze his old features, nipped his pointed nose, shrivelled his cheek, stiffened his gait; made his eyes red, his thin lips blue; and spoke out shrewdly in his grating voice. A frosty rime was on his head, and on his eyebrows, and his wiry chin. He carried his own low temperature always about with him; he iced his office in the dogdays; and didn't thaw it one degree at Christmas.

External heat and cold had little influence on Scrooge. No warmth could warm, no wintry weather chill him. No wind that blew was bitterer than he, no falling snow was more intent upon its purpose, no pelting rain less open to entreaty. Foul weather didn't know where to have him. The heaviest rain, and snow, and hail, and sleet, could boast of the advantage over him in only one respect. They often "came down" handsomely, and Scrooge never did.

Nobody ever stopped him in the street to say, with gladsome looks, "My dear Scrooge, how are you? When will you come to see me?" No beggars implored him to bestow a trifle, no children asked him what it was o'clock, no man or woman ever once in all his life inquired the way to such and such a place, of Scrooge. Even the blind men's dogs appeared to know him; and when they saw him coming on, would tug their owners into doorways and up courts; and then would wag their tails as though they said, "No eye at all is better than an evil eye, dark master!"

But what did Scrooge care! It was the very thing he liked. To edge his way along the crowded paths of life, warning all human sympathy to keep its distance, was what the knowing ones call "nuts" to Scrooge.

Once upon a time—of all the good days in the year, on Christmas Eve—old Scrooge sat busy in his counting-house. It was cold, bleak, biting weather: foggy withal: and he could hear the people in the court outside, go wheezing up and down, beating their hands upon their breasts, and stamping their feet upon the pavement stones to warm them. The city clocks had only just gone three, but it was quite dark already—it had not been light all day—and candles were flaring in the windows of the neighbouring offices, like ruddy smears upon the palpable brown air. The fog came pouring in at every chink and keyhole, and was so dense without, that although the court was of the narrowest, the houses opposite were mere phantoms. To see the dingy cloud come drooping down, obscuring everything, one might have thought that Nature lived hard by, and was brewing on a large scale.

The door of Scrooge's counting-house was open that he might keep his eye upon his clerk, who in a dismal little cell beyond, a sort of tank, was copying letters. Scrooge had a very small fire, but the clerk's fire was so very much smaller that it looked like one coal. But he couldn't replenish it, for Scrooge kept the coal-box in his own room; and so surely as the clerk came in with the shovel, the master predicted that it would be necessary for them to part. Wherefore the clerk put on his white comforter, and tried to warm himself at the candle; in which effort, not being a man of a strong imagination, he failed.

"A merry Christmas, uncle! God save you!" cried a cheerful voice. It was the voice of Scrooge's nephew, who came upon him so quickly that this was the first intimation he had of his approach.

"Bah!" said Scrooge, "Humbug!"

He had so heated himself with rapid walking in the fog and frost, this nephew of Scrooge's, that he was all in a glow; his face was ruddy and handsome; his eyes sparkled, and his breath smoked again.

"Christmas a humbug, uncle!" said Scrooge's nephew. "You don't mean that, I am sure?"

"I do," said Scrooge. "Merry Christmas! What right have you to be merry? What reason have you to be merry? You're poor enough."

"Come, then," returned the nephew gaily. "What right have you to be dismal? What reason have you to be morose? You're rich enough."

Scrooge having no better answer ready on the spur of the moment, said "Bah!" again; and followed it up with "Humbug."

"Don't be cross, uncle!" said the nephew.

"What else can I be," returned the uncle, "when I live in such a world of fools as this? Merry Christmas! Out upon merry Christmas! What's Christmas time to you but a time for paying bills without money; a time for finding yourself a year older, but not an hour richer; a time for balancing your books and having every item in 'em through a round dozen of months presented dead against you? If I could work my will," said Scrooge indignantly, "every idiot who goes about with 'Merry Christmas' on his lips, should be boiled with his own pudding, and buried with a stake of holly through his heart. He should!"

"Uncle!" pleaded the nephew.

"Nephew!" returned the uncle, sternly, "keep Christmas in your own way, and let me keep it in mine."

"Keep it!" repeated Scrooge's nephew. "But you don't keep it."

"Let me leave it alone, then," said Scrooge. "Much good may it do you! Much good it has ever done you!"

"There are many things from which I might have derived good, by which I have not profited, I dare say," returned the nephew. "Christmas among the rest. But I am sure I have always thought of Christmas time, when it has come round—apart from the veneration due to its sacred name and origin, if anything belonging to it can be apart from that—as a good time; a kind, forgiving, charitable, pleasant time: the only time I know of, in the long calendar of the year, when men and women seem by one consent to open their shut-up hearts freely, and to think of people below them as if they really were fellow-passengers to the grave, and not another race of creatures bound on other journeys. And therefore, uncle, though it has never put a scrap of gold or silver in my pocket, I believe that it *has* done me good, and *will* do me good; and I say, God bless it!"

The clerk in the Tank involuntarily applauded. Becoming immediately sensible of the impropriety, he poked the fire, and extinguished the last frail spark for ever.

"Let me hear another sound from *you*," said Scrooge, "and you'll keep your Christmas by losing your situation! You're quite a powerful speaker, sir," he added, turning to his nephew. "I wonder you don't go into Parliament."

"Don't be angry, uncle. Come! Dine with us tomorrow."

Scrooge said that he would see him—yes, indeed he did. He went the whole length of the expression, and said that he would see him in that extremity first.

"But why?" cried Scrooge's nephew. "Why?"

"Why did you get married?" said Scrooge.

"Because I fell in love."

"Because you fell in love!" growled Scrooge, as if that were the only one thing in the world more ridiculous than a merry Christmas. "Good afternoon!"

"Nay, uncle, but you never came to see me before that happened. Why give it as a reason for not coming now?"

"Good afternoon," said Scrooge.

"I want nothing from you; I ask nothing of you; why cannot we be friends?"

"Good afternoon," said Scrooge.

"I am sorry, with all my heart, to find you so resolute. We have never had any quarrel, to which I have been a party. But I have made the trial in homage to Christmas, and I'll keep my Christmas humour to the last. So A Merry Christmas, uncle!"

"Good afternoon," said Scrooge.

"And A Happy New Year!"

"Good afternoon," said Scrooge.

His nephew left the room without an angry word, notwithstanding. He stopped at the outer door to bestow the greetings of the season on the clerk, who, cold as he was, was warmer than Scrooge; for he returned them cordially.

"There's another fellow," muttered Scrooge, who overheard him: "my clerk, with fifteen shillings a week, and a wife and family, talking about a merry Christmas. I'll retire to Bedlam."

This lunatic, in letting Scrooge's nephew out, had let two other people in. They were portly gentlemen, pleasant to behold, and now stood, with their hats off, in Scrooge's office. They had books and papers in their hands, and bowed to him.

"Scrooge and Marley's, I believe," said one of the gentlemen, referring to his list. "Have I the pleasure of addressing Mr. Scrooge, or Mr. Marley?"

"Mr. Marley has been dead these seven years," Scrooge replied. "He died seven years ago, this very night."

"We have no doubt his liberality is well represented by his surviving partner," said the gentleman, presenting his credentials.

It certainly was; for they had been two kindred spirits. At the ominous word "liberality," Scrooge frowned, and shook his head, and handed the credentials back.

"At this festive season of the year, Mr. Scrooge," said the gentleman, taking up a pen, "it is more than usually desirable that we should make some slight provision for the Poor and destitute, who suffer greatly at the present time. Many thousands are in want of common necessaries; hundreds of thousands are in want of common comforts, sir."

"Are there no prisons?" asked Scrooge.

"Plenty of prisons," said the gentleman, laying down the pen again.

"And the Union workhouses?" demanded Scrooge. "Are they still in operation?"

"They are. Still," returned the gentleman, "I wish I could say they were not."

"The Treadmill and the Poor Law are in full vigour, then?" said Scrooge.

"Both very busy, sir."

"Oh! I was afraid, from what you said at first, that something had occurred to stop them in their useful course," said Scrooge. "I'm very glad to hear it."

"Under the impression that they scarcely furnish Christian cheer of mind or body to the multitude," returned the gentleman, "a few of us are endeavouring to raise a fund to buy the Poor some meat and drink, and means of warmth. We choose this time, because it is a time, of all others, when Want is keenly felt, and Abundance rejoices. What shall I put you down for?"

"Nothing!" Scrooge replied.

"You wish to be anonymous?"

"I wish to be left alone," said Scrooge. "Since you ask me what I wish, gentlemen, that is my answer. I don't make merry myself at Christmas and I can't afford to make idle people merry. I help to support the establishments I have mentioned—they cost enough; and those who are badly off must go there."

"Many can't go there; and many would rather die."

"If they would rather die," said Scrooge, "they had better do it, and decrease the surplus population. Besides—excuse me—I don't know that."

"But you might know it," observed the gentleman.

"It's not my business," Scrooge returned. "It's enough for a man to understand his own business, and not to interfere with other people's. Mine occupies me constantly. Good afternoon, gentlemen!"

Seeing clearly that it would be useless to pursue their point, the gentlemen withdrew. Scrooge resumed his labours with an improved opinion of himself, and in a more facetious temper than was usual with him.

Meanwhile the fog and darkness thickened so, that people ran about with flaring links, proffering their services to go before horses in carriages, and conduct them on their way. The ancient tower of a church, whose gruff old bell was always peeping slily down at Scrooge out of a gothic window in the wall, became invisible, and struck the hours and quarters in the clouds, with tremulous vibrations afterwards as if its teeth were chattering in its frozen head up there. The cold became intense. In the main street at the corner of the court, some labourers were repairing the gas-pipes, and had lighted a great fire in a brazier, round which a party of ragged men and boys were gathered: warming their hands and winking their eyes before the blaze in rapture. The water-plug being left in solitude, its overflowings sullenly congealed, and turned to misanthropic ice. The brightness of the shops where holly sprigs and berries crackled in the lamp heat of the windows, made pale faces ruddy as they passed. Poulterers' and grocers' trades became a splendid joke; a glorious pageant, with which it was next to impossible to believe that such dull principles as bargain and sale had anything to do. The Lord Mayor, in the stronghold of the mighty Mansion House, gave orders to his fifty cooks and butlers to keep Christmas as a Lord Mayor's household should; and even the little tailor, whom he had fined five shillings on the previous Monday for being drunk and bloodthirsty in the streets, stirred up to-morrow's pudding in his garret, while his lean wife and the baby sallied out to buy the beef.

Foggier yet, and colder! Piercing, searching, biting cold. If the good Saint Dunstan had but nipped the Evil Spirit's nose with a touch of such weather as that, instead of using his familiar weapons, then indeed he would have roared to lusty purpose. The owner of one scant young nose, gnawed and mumbled by the hungry cold as bones are gnawed by dogs, stooped down at Scrooge's keyhole to regale him with a Christmas carol: but at the first sound of

> 'God bless you, merry gentleman!
> May nothing you dismay!'

Scrooge seized the ruler with such energy of action, that the singer fled in terror, leaving the keyhole to the fog and even more congenial frost.

At length the hour of shutting up the counting-house arrived. With an ill-will Scrooge dismounted from his stool, and tacitly admitted the fact to the expectant clerk in the Tank, who instantly snuffed his candle out, and put on his hat.

"You'll want all day to-morrow, I suppose?" said Scrooge.

"If quite convenient, sir."

"It's not convenient," said Scrooge, "and it's not fair. If I was to stop half-a-crown for it, you'd think yourself ill-used, I'll be bound?"

The clerk smiled faintly.

"And yet," said Scrooge, "you don't think *me* ill-used, when I pay a day's wages for no work."

The clerk observed that it was only once a year.

"A poor excuse for picking a man's pocket every twenty-fifth of December!" said Scrooge, buttoning his great-coat to the chin. "But I suppose you must have the whole day. Be here all the earlier next morning."

The clerk promised that he would; and Scrooge walked out with a growl. The office was closed in a twinkling, and the clerk, with the long ends of his white comforter dangling below his waist (for he boasted no great-coat), went down a slide on Cornhill, at the end of a lane of boys, twenty times, in honour of its being Christmas Eve, and then ran home to Camden Town as hard as he could pelt, to play at blind-man's-bluff.

Scrooge took his melancholy dinner in his usual melancholy tavern; and having read all the newspapers, and beguiled the rest of the evening with his banker's-book, went home to bed. He lived in chambers which had once belonged to his deceased partner. They were a gloomy suite of rooms, in a lowering pile of building up a yard, where it had so little business to be, that one could scarcely help fancying it must have run there when it was a young house, playing at hide-and-seek with other houses, and forgotten the way out again. It was old enough now, and dreary enough, for nobody lived in it but Scrooge, the other rooms being all let out as offices. The yard was so dark that even Scrooge, who knew its every stone, was fain to grope with his hands. The fog and frost so hung about the black old gateway of the house, that it seemed as if the Genius of the Weather sat in mournful meditation on the threshold.

Now, it is a fact, that there was nothing at all particular about the knocker on the door, except that it was very large. It is also a fact, that Scrooge had seen it, night and morning, during his whole residence in that place; also that Scrooge had as little of what is called fancy about him as any man in the city of London, even including—which is a bold word— the corporation, aldermen, and livery. Let it also be borne in mind that Scrooge had not bestowed one thought on Marley, since his last mention of his seven-years' dead partner that afternoon. And then let any man explain to me, if he can, how it happened that Scrooge, having his key in the lock of the door, saw in the knocker, without its undergoing any intermediate process of change—not a knocker, but Marley's face.

Marley's face. It was not in impenetrable shadow as the other objects in the yard were, but had a dismal light about it, like a bad lobster in a dark cellar. It was not angry or ferocious, but looked at Scrooge as Marley used to look: with ghostly spectacles turned up on its ghostly forehead. The hair was curiously stirred, as if by breath or hot air; and, though the eyes were wide open, they were perfectly motionless. That, and its livid colour, made it horrible; but its horror seemed to be in spite of the face and beyond its control, rather than a part of its own expression.

As Scrooge looked fixedly at this phenomenon, it was a knocker again.

To say that he was not startled, or that his blood was not conscious of a terrible sensation to which it had been a stranger from infancy, would be untrue. But he put his hand upon the key he had relinquished, turned it sturdily, walked in, and lighted his candle.

He *did* pause, with a moment's irresolution, before he shut the door; and he *did* look cautiously behind it first, as if he half-expected to be terrified with the sight of Marley's pigtail sticking out into the hall. But there was nothing on the back of the door, except the screws and nuts that held the knocker on, so he said "Pooh, pooh!" and closed it with a bang.

The sound resounded through the house like thunder. Every room above, and every cask in the wine-merchant's cellars below, appeared to have a separate peal of echoes of its own. Scrooge was not a man to be frightened by echoes. He fastened the door, and walked across the hall, and up the stairs; slowly, too: trimming his candle as he went.

You may talk vaguely about driving a coach-and-six up a good old flight of stairs, or through a bad young Act of Parliament; but I mean to say you might have got a hearse up that staircase, and taken it broadwise, with the splinter-bar towards the wall and the door towards the balustrades: and done it easy. There was plenty of width for that, and room to spare; which is perhaps the reason why Scrooge thought he saw a locomotive hearse going on before him in the gloom. Half a dozen gas-lamps out of the street wouldn't have lighted the entry too well, so you may suppose that it was pretty dark with Scrooge's dip.

Up Scrooge went, not caring a button for that. Darkness is cheap, and Scrooge liked it. But before he shut his heavy door, he walked through his rooms to see that all was right. He had just enough recollection of the face to desire to do that.

Sitting-room, bedroom, lumber-room. All as they should be. Nobody under the table, nobody under the sofa; a small fire in the grate; spoon and basin ready; and the little saucepan of gruel (Scrooge had a cold in his head) upon the hob. Nobody under the bed; nobody in the closet; nobody in his dressing-gown, which was hanging up in a suspicious attitude against the wall. Lumber-room as usual. Old fire-guards, old shoes, two fish-baskets, washing-stand on three legs, and a poker.

Quite satisfied, he closed his door, and locked himself in; double-locked himself in, which was not his custom. Thus secured against surprise, he took off his cravat; put on his dressing-gown and slippers, and his nightcap; and sat down before the fire to take his gruel.

It was a very low fire indeed; nothing on such a bitter night. He was obliged to sit close to it, and brood over it, before he could extract the least sensation of warmth from such a handful of fuel. The fireplace was an old one, built by some Dutch merchant long ago, and paved all round with quaint Dutch tiles, designed to illustrate the Scriptures. There were Cains and Abels, Pharaohs' daughters, Queens of Sheba, Angelic messengers descending through the air on clouds like feather-beds, Abrahams, Belshazzars, Apostles putting off to sea in butter-boats, hundreds of figures to attract his thoughts; and yet that face of Marley, seven years dead, came like the ancient Prophet's rod, and swallowed up the whole. If each smooth tile had been a blank at first, with power to shape some picture on its surface from the disjointed fragments of his thoughts, there would have been a copy of old Marley's head on every one.

"Humbug!" said Scrooge; and walked across the room.

After several turns, he sat down again. As he threw his head back in the chair, his glance happened to rest upon a bell, a disused bell, that hung in the room, and communicated for some purpose now forgotten with a chamber in the highest story of the building. It was with great astonishment, and with a strange, inexplicable dread, that as he looked, he saw this bell begin to swing. It swung so softly in the outset that it scarcely made a sound; but soon it rang out loudly, and so did every bell in the house.

This might have lasted half a minute, or a minute, but it seemed an hour. The bells ceased as they had begun, together. They were succeeded by a clanking noise, deep down below; as if some person were dragging a heavy chain over the casks in the wine merchant's cellar. Scrooge then remembered to have heard that ghosts in haunted houses were described as dragging chains.

The cellar-door flew open with a booming sound, and then he heard the noise much louder, on the floors below; then coming up the stairs; then coming straight towards his door.

"It's humbug still!" said Scrooge. "I won't believe it."

His colour changed though, when, without a pause, it came on through the heavy door, and passed into the room before his eyes. Upon its coming in, the dying flame leaped up, as though it cried "I know him; Marley's Ghost!" and fell again.

The same face: the very same. Marley in his pigtail, usual waistcoat, tights and boots; the tassels on the latter bristling, like his pigtail, and his coat-skirts, and the hair upon his head. The chain he drew was clasped about his middle. It was long, and wound about him like a tail; and it was made (for Scrooge observed it closely) of cash-boxes, keys, padlocks, ledgers, deeds, and heavy purses wrought in steel. His body was transparent; so that Scrooge, observing him, and looking through his waistcoat, could see the two buttons on his coat behind.

Scrooge had often heard it said that Marley had no bowels, but he had never believed it until now.

No, nor did he believe it even now. Though he looked the phantom through and through, and saw it standing before him; though he felt the chilling influence of its death-cold eyes; and marked the very texture of the folded kerchief bound about its head and chin, which wrapper he had not observed before: he was still incredulous, and fought against his senses.

"How now!" said Scrooge, caustic and cold as ever. "What do you want with me?"

"Much!"—Marley's voice, no doubt about it.

"Who are you?"

"Ask me who I *was*."

"Who *were* you then?" said Scrooge, raising his voice. "You're particular, for a shade." He was going to say "*to* a shade," but substituted this, as more appropriate.

"In life I was your partner, Jacob Marley."

"Can you—can you sit down?" asked Scrooge, looking doubtfully at him.

"I can."

"Do it, then."

Scrooge asked the question, because he didn't know whether a ghost so transparent might find himself in a condition to take a chair; and felt that in the event of its being impossible, it might involve the necessity of an embarrassing explanation. But the ghost sat down on the opposite side of the fireplace, as if he were quite used to it.

"You don't believe in me," observed the Ghost.

"I don't," said Scrooge.

"What evidence would you have of my reality beyond that of your senses?"

"I don't know," said Scrooge.

"Why do you doubt your senses?"

"Because," said Scrooge, "a little thing affects them. A slight disorder of the stomach makes them cheats. You may be an undigested bit of beef, a blot of mustard, a crumb of cheese, a fragment of an underdone potato. There's more of gravy than of grave about you, whatever you are!"

Scrooge was not much in the habit of cracking jokes, nor did he feel, in his heart, by any means waggish then. The truth is, that he tried to be smart, as a means of distracting his own attention, and keeping down his terror; for the spectre's voice disturbed the very marrow in his bones.

To sit, staring at those fixed glazed eyes, in silence for a moment, would play, Scrooge felt, the very deuce with him. There was something very awful, too, in the spectre's being provided with an infernal atmosphere of its own. Scrooge could not feel it himself, but this was clearly the case; for though the Ghost sat perfectly motionless, its hair, and skirts, and tassels, were still agitated as by the hot vapour from an oven.

"You see this toothpick?" said Scrooge, returning quickly to the charge, for the reason just assigned; and wishing, though it were only for a second, to divert the vision's stony gaze from himself.

"I do," replied the Ghost.

"You are not looking at it," said Scrooge.

"But I see it," said the Ghost, "notwithstanding."

"Well!" returned Scrooge, "I have but to swallow this, and be for the rest of my days persecuted by a legion of goblins, all of my own creation. Humbug, I tell you! humbug!"

At this the spirit raised a frightful cry, and shook its chain with such a dismal and appalling noise, that Scrooge held on tight to his chair, to save himself from falling in a swoon. But how much greater was his horror, when the phantom taking off the bandage round its head, as if it were too warm to wear indoors, its lower jaw dropped down upon its breast!

Scrooge fell upon his knees, and clasped his hands before his face.

"Mercy!" he said. "Dreadful apparition, why do you trouble me?"

"Man of the worldly mind!" replied the Ghost, "do you believe in me or not?"

"I do," said Scrooge. "I must. But why do spirits walk the earth, and why do they come to me?"

"It is required of every man," the Ghost returned, "that the spirit within him should walk abroad among his fellow-men, and travel far and wide; and if that spirit goes not forth in life, it is condemned to do so after death. It is doomed to wander through the world—oh, woe is me!—and witness what it cannot share, but might have shared on earth, and turned to happiness!"

Again the spectre raised a cry, and shook its chain and wrung its shadowy hands.

"You are fettered," said Scrooge, trembling. "Tell me why?"

"I wear the chain I forged in life," replied the Ghost. "I made it link by link, and yard by yard; I girded it on of my own free will, and of my own free will I wore it. Is its pattern strange to *you?*"

Scrooge trembled more and more.

"Or would you know," pursued the Ghost, "the weight and length of the strong coil you bear yourself? It was full as heavy and as long as this, seven Christmas Eves ago. You have laboured on it, since. It is a ponderous chain!"

Scrooge glanced about him on the floor, in the expectation of finding himself surrounded by some fifty or sixty fathoms of iron cable: but he could see nothing.

"Jacob," he said, imploringly. "Old Jacob Marley, tell me more. Speak comfort to me, Jacob!"

"I have none to give," the Ghost replied. "It comes from other regions, Ebenezer Scrooge, and is conveyed by other ministers, to other kinds of men. Nor can I tell you what I would. A very little more, is all permitted to me. I cannot rest, I cannot stay, I cannot linger anywhere. My spirit never walked beyond our counting-house—mark me!—in life my spirit never roved beyond the narrow limits of our money-changing hole; and weary journeys lie before me!"

It was a habit with Scrooge, whenever he became thoughtful, to put his hands in his breeches pockets. Pondering on what the Ghost had said, he did so now, but without lifting up his eyes, or getting off his knees.

"You must have been very slow about it, Jacob," Scrooge observed, in a business-like manner, though with humility and deference.

"Slow!" the Ghost repeated.

"Seven years dead," mused Scrooge. "And travelling all the time!"

"The whole time," said the Ghost. "No rest, no peace. Incessant torture of remorse."

"You travel fast?" said Scrooge.

"On the wings of the wind," replied the Ghost.

"You might have got over a great quantity of ground in seven years," said Scrooge.

The Ghost, on hearing this, set up another cry, and clanked its chain so hideously in the dead silence of the night, that the Ward would have been justified in indicting it for a nuisance.

"Oh! captive, bound, and double-ironed," cried the phantom, "not to know, that ages of incessant labour, by immortal creatures, for this earth must pass into eternity before the good of which it is susceptible is all developed. Not to know that any Christian spirit working kindly in its little sphere, whatever it may be, will find its mortal life too short for its vast means of usefulness. Not to know that no space of regret can make amends for one life's opportunity misused! Yet such was I! Oh! such was I!"

"But you were always a good man of business, Jacob," faltered Scrooge, who now began to apply this to himself.

"Business!" cried the Ghost, wringing its hands again. "Mankind was my business. The common welfare was my business; charity, mercy, forbearance, and benevolence, were, all, my business. The dealings of my trade were but a drop of water in the comprehensive ocean of my business!"

It held up its chain at arm's length, as if that were the cause of all its unavailing grief, and flung it heavily upon the ground again.

"At this time of the rolling year," the spectre said, "I suffer most. Why did I walk through crowds of fellow-beings with my eyes turned down, and never raise them to that blessed Star which led the Wise Men to a poor abode! Were there no poor homes to which its light would have conducted *me!*"

Scrooge was very much dismayed to hear the spectre going on at this rate, and began to quake exceedingly.

"Hear me!" cried the Ghost. "My time is nearly gone."

"I will," said Scrooge. "But don't be hard upon me! Don't be flowery, Jacob! Pray!"

"How it is that I appear before you in a shape that you

can see, I may not tell. I have sat invisible beside you many and many a day."

It was not an agreeable idea. Scrooge shivered, and wiped the perspiration from his brow.

"That is no light part of my penance," pursued the Ghost. "I am here to-night to warn you, that you have yet a chance and hope of escaping my fate. A chance and hope of my procuring, Ebenezer."

"You were always a good friend to me," said Scrooge. "Thank 'ee!"

"You will be haunted," resumed the Ghost, "by Three Spirits."

Scrooge's countenance fell almost as low as the Ghost's had done.

"Is that the chance and hope you mentioned, Jacob?" he demanded, in a faltering voice.

"It is."

"I—I think I'd rather not," said Scrooge.

"Without their visits," said the Ghost, "you cannot hope to shun the path I tread. Expect the first to-morrow, when the bell tolls One."

"Couldn't I take 'em all at once, and have it over, Jacob?" hinted Scrooge.

"Expect the second on the next night at the same hour. The third upon the next night when the last stroke of Twelve has ceased to vibrate. Look to see me no more; and look that, for your own sake, you remember what has passed between us!"

When it had said these words, the spectre took its wrapper from the table, and bound it round its head, as before. Scrooge knew this, by the smart sound its teeth made, when the jaws were brought together by the bandage. He ventured to raise his eyes again, and found his supernatural visitor confronting him in an erect attitude, with its chain wound over and about its arm.

The apparition walked backward from him; and at every step it took, the window raised itself a little, so that when the spectre reached it, it was wide open.

It beckoned Scrooge to approach, which he did. When they were within two paces of each other, Marley's Ghost held up its hand, warning him to come no nearer. Scrooge stopped.

Not so much in obedience, as in surprise and fear; for on the raising of the hand, he became sensible of confused noises in the air; incoherent sounds of lamentation and regret; wailings inexpressibly sorrowful and self-accusatory. The spectre, after listening for a moment, joined in the mournful dirge; and floated out upon the bleak, dark night.

Scrooge followed to the window: desperate in his curiosity. He looked out.

The air was filled with phantoms, wandering hither and thither in restless haste, and moaning as they went. Every one of them wore chains like Marley's Ghost; some few (they might be guilty governments) were linked together; none were free. Many had been personally known to Scrooge in their lives. He had been quite familiar with one old ghost, in a white waistcoat, with a monstrous iron safe attached to its ankle, who cried piteously at being unable to assist a wretched woman with an infant, whom it saw below, upon a door-step. The misery with them all was, clearly, that they sought to interfere, for good, in human matters, and had lost the power for ever.

Whether these creatures faded into mist, or mist enshrouded them, he could not tell. But they and their spirit voices faded together; and the night became as it had been when he walked home.

Scrooge closed the window, and examined the door by which the Ghost had entered. It was double-locked, as he had locked it with his own hands, and the bolts were undisturbed. He tried to say "Humbug!" but stopped at the first syllable. And being, from the emotion he had undergone, or the fatigues of the day, or his glimpse of the Invisible World, or the dull conversation of the Ghost, or the lateness of the hour, much in need of repose; went straight to bed, without undressing, and fell asleep upon the instant.

Stave Two

THE FIRST OF THE THREE SPIRITS

WHEN Scrooge awoke, it was so dark, that looking out of bed, he could scarcely distinguish the transparent window from the opaque walls of his chamber. He was endeavouring to pierce the darkness with his ferret eyes, when the chimes of a neighbouring church struck the four quarters. So he listened for the hour.

To his great astonishment the heavy bell went on from six to seven and from seven to eight, and regularly up to twelve; then stopped. Twelve! It was past two when he went to bed. The clock was wrong. An icicle must have got into the works. Twelve!

He touched the spring of his repeater, to correct this most preposterous clock. Its rapid little pulse beat twelve; and stopped.

"Why, it isn't possible," said Scrooge, "that I can have slept through a whole day and far into another night. It isn't possible that anything has happened to the sun, and this is twelve at noon!"

The idea being an alarming one, he scrambled out of bed, and groped his way to the window. He was obliged to rub the frost off with the sleeve of his dressing-gown before he could see anything; and could see very little then. All he could make out, was, that it was still very foggy and extremely cold, and that there was no noise of people running to and fro, and making a great stir, as there unquestionably would have been if night had beaten off bright day, and taken possession of the world. This was a great relief, because "three days after sight of this First of Exchange pay to Mr. Ebenezer Scrooge or his order," and so forth, would have become a mere United States security if there were no days to count by.

Scrooge went to bed again, and thought, and thought, and

thought it over and over and over, and could make nothing of it. The more he thought, the more perplexed he was; and the more he endeavoured not to think, the more he thought.

Marley's Ghost bothered him exceedingly. Every time he resolved within himself, after mature inquiry, that it was all a dream, his mind flew back again, like a strong spring released, to its first position, and presented the same problem to be worked all through, "Was it a dream or not?"

Scrooge lay in this state until the chime had gone three quarters more, when he remembered, on a sudden, that the Ghost had warned him of a visitation when the bell tolled one. He resolved to lie awake until the hour was passed; and, considering that he could no more go to sleep than go to Heaven, this was perhaps the wisest resolution in his power.

The quarter was so long, that he was more than once convinced he must have sunk into a doze unconsciously, and missed the clock. At length it broke upon his listening ear.

"Ding, dong!"

"A quarter past," said Scrooge, counting.

"Ding, dong!"

"Half-past!" said Scrooge.

"Ding, dong!"

"A quarter to it," said Scrooge.

"Ding, dong!"

"The hour itself," said Scrooge, triumphantly, "and nothing else!"

He spoke before the hour bell sounded, which it now did with a deep, dull, hollow, melancholy ONE. Light flashed up in the room upon the instant, and the curtains of his bed were drawn.

The curtains of his bed were drawn aside, I tell you, by a hand. Not the curtains at his feet, nor the curtains at his back, but those to which his face was addressed. The curtains of his bed were drawn aside; and Scrooge, starting up into a half-recumbent attitude, found himself face to face with the unearthly visitor who drew them: as close to it as

I am now to you, and I am standing in the spirit at your elbow.

It was a strange figure—like a child: yet not so like a child as like an old man, viewed through some supernatural medium, which gave him the appearance of having receded from the view, and being diminished to a child's proportions. Its hair, which hung about its neck and down its back, was white as if with age; and yet the face had not a wrinkle in it, and the tenderest bloom was on the skin. The arms were very long and muscular; the hands the same, as if its hold were of uncommon strength. Its legs and feet, most delicately formed, were, like those upper members, bare. It wore a tunic of the purest white; and round its waist was bound a lustrous belt, the sheen of which was beautiful. It held a branch of fresh green holly in its hand; and, in singular contradiction of that wintry emblem, had its dress trimmed with summer flowers. But the strangest thing about it was, that from the crown of its head there sprung a bright clear jet of light, by which all this was visible; and which was doubtless the occasion of its using, in its duller moments, a great extinguisher for a cap, which it now held under its arm.

Even this, though, when Scrooge looked at it with increasing steadiness, was *not* its strangest quality. For as its belt sparkled and glittered now in one part and now in another, and what was light one instant, at another time was dark, so the figure itself fluctuated in its distinctness: being now a thing with one arm, now with one leg, now with twenty legs, now a pair of legs without a head, now a head without a body: of which dissolving parts, no outline would be visible in the dense gloom wherein they melted away. And in the very wonder of this, it would be itself again; distinct and clear as ever.

"Are you the Spirit, sir, whose coming was foretold to me?" asked Scrooge.

"I am!"

The voice was soft and gentle. Singularly low, as if instead of being so close beside him, it were at a distance.

"Who, and what are you?" Scrooge demanded.

"I am the Ghost of Christmas Past."

"Long Past?" inquired Scrooge: observant of its dwarfish stature.

"No. Your past."

Perhaps, Scrooge could not have told anybody why, if anybody could have asked him; but he had a special desire to see the Spirit in his cap; and begged him to be covered.

"What!" exclaimed the Ghost, "would you so soon put out, with worldly hands, the light I give? Is it not enough that you are one of those whose passions made this cap, and forced me through whole trains of years to wear it low upon my brow!"

Scrooge reverently disclaimed all intention to offend or any knowledge of having wilfully "bonneted" the Spirit at any period of his life. He then made bold to inquire what business brought him there.

"Your welfare!" said the Ghost.

Scrooge expressed himself much obliged, but could not help thinking that a night of unbroken rest would have been more conducive to that end. The Spirit must have heard him thinking, for it said immediately:

"Your reclamation, then. Take heed!"

It put out its strong hand as it spoke, and clasped him gently by the arm.

"Rise! and walk with me!"

It would have been in vain for Scrooge to plead that the weather and the hour were not adapted to pedestrian purposes; that bed was warm, and the thermometer a long way below freezing; that he was clad but lightly in his slippers, dressing-gown, and nightcap; and that he had a cold upon him at that time. The grasp, though gentle as a woman's hand, was not to be resisted. He rose: but finding that the Spirit made towards the window, clasped his robe in supplication.

"I am a mortal," Scrooge remonstrated, "and liable to fall."

"Bear but a touch of my hand *there*," said the Spirit, laying it upon his heart, "and you shall be upheld in more than this!"

As the words were spoken, they passed through the wall, and stood upon an open country road, with fields on either hand. The city had entirely vanished. Not a vestige of it was to be seen. The darkness and the mist had vanished with it, for it was a clear, cold, winter day, with snow upon the ground.

"Good Heaven!" said Scrooge, clasping his hands together, as he looked about him. "I was bred in this place. I was a boy here!"

The Spirit gazed upon him mildly. Its gentle touch, though it had been light and instantaneous, appeared still present to the old man's sense of feeling. He was conscious of a thousand odours floating in the air, each one connected with a thousand thoughts, and hopes, and joys, and cares long, long, forgotten!

"Your lip is trembling," said the Ghost. "And what is that upon your cheek?"

Scrooge muttered, with an unusual catching in his voice, that it was a pimple; and begged the Ghost to lead him where he would.

"You recollect the way?" inquired the Spirit.

"Remember it?" cried Scrooge with fervour; "I could walk it blindfold."

"Strange to have forgotten it for so many years!" observed the Ghost. "Let us go on."

They walked along the road, Scrooge recognising every gate, and post, and tree; until a little market-town appeared in the distance, with its bridge, its church, and winding river. Some shaggy ponies now were seen trotting towards them with boys upon their backs, who called to other boys in country gigs and carts, driven by farmers. All these boys were in great spirits, and shouted to each other, until the broad fields were so full of merry music, that the crisp air laughed to hear it.

"These are but shadows of the things that have been," said the Ghost. "They have no consciousness of us."

The jocund travellers came on; and as they came, Scrooge knew and named them every one. Why was he rejoiced beyond all bounds to see them! Why did his cold eye glisten, and his heart leap up as they went past! Why was he filled with gladness when he heard them give each other Merry Christmas, as they parted at cross-roads and by-ways, for their several homes! What was merry Christmas to Scrooge? Out upon merry Christmas! What good had it ever done to him?

"The school is not quite deserted," said the Ghost. "A solitary child, neglected by his friends, is left there still."

Scrooge said he knew it. And he sobbed.

They left the high-road, by a well-remembered lane, and soon approached a mansion of dull red brick, with a little weathercock-surmounted cupola, on the roof, and a bell hanging in it. It was a large house, but one of broken fortunes; for the spacious offices were little used, their walls were damp and mossy, their windows broken, and their gates decayed. Fowls clucked and strutted in the stables; and the coach-houses and sheds were overrun with grass. Nor was it more retentive of its ancient state, within; for entering the dreary hall, and glancing through the open doors of many rooms, they found them poorly furnished, cold, and vast. There was an earthy savour in the air, a chilly bareness in the place, which associated itself somehow with too much getting up by candle-light, and not too much to eat.

They went, the Ghost and Scrooge, across the hall, to a door at the back of the house. It opened before them, and disclosed a long, bare, melancholy room, made barer still by lines of plain deal forms and desks. At one of these a lonely boy was reading near a feeble fire: and Scrooge sat down upon a form, and wept to see his poor forgotten self as he used to be.

Not a latent echo in the house, not a squeak and scuffle from the mice behind the panelling, not a drip from the half-thawed water-spout in the dull yard behind, not a sigh among the leafless boughs of one despondent poplar, not the idle swinging of an empty store-house door, no, not a click-ing in the fire, but fell upon the heart of Scrooge with a softening influence, and gave a freer passage to his tears.

The Spirit touched him on the arm, and pointed to his younger self, intent upon his reading. Suddenly a man, in foreign garments: wonderfully real and distinct to look at: stood outside the window, with an axe stuck in his belt, and leading by the bridle an ass laden with wood.

"Why, it's Ali Baba!" Scrooge exclaimed in ecstasy. "It's dear old honest Ali Baba! Yes, yes, I know! One Christmas time, when yonder solitary child was left here all alone, he *did* come, for the first time, just like that. Poor boy! And Valentine," said Scrooge, "and his wild brother, Orson; there they go! And what's his name, who was put down in his drawers, asleep, at the Gate of Damascus; don't you see him! And the Sultan's Groom turned upside down by the Genii; there he is upon his head! Serve him right. I'm glad of it. What business had *he* to be married to the Princess!"

To hear Scrooge expending all the earnestness of his na-ture on such subjects, in a most extraordinary voice between laughing and crying; and to see his heightened and excited face; would have been a surprise to his business friends in the city, indeed.

"There's the Parrot!" cried Scrooge. "Green body and yellow tail, with a thing like a lettuce growing out of the top of his head; there he is! Poor Robin Crusoe, he called him, when he came home again after sailing round the island. "Poor Robin Crusoe, where have you been, Robin Crusoe?" The man thought he was dreaming, but he wasn't. It was the Parrot, you know. There goes Friday, running for his life to the little creek! Halloa! Hoop! Halloo!"

Then, with a rapidity of transition very foreign to his usual character, he said, in pity for his former self, "Poor boy!" and cried again.

"I wish," Scrooge muttered, putting his hand in his pock-et, and looking about him, after drying his eyes with his cuff: "but it's too late now."

"What is the matter?" asked the Spirit.

"Nothing," said Scrooge. "Nothing. There was a boy singing a Christmas Carol at my door last night. I should like to have given him something: that's all."

The Ghost smiled thoughtfully, and waved its hand: saying as it did so, "Let us see another Christmas!"

Scrooge's former self grew larger at the words, and the room became a little darker and more dirty. The panels shrunk, the windows cracked; fragments of plaster fell out of the ceiling, and the naked laths were shown instead; but how all this was brought about, Scrooge knew no more than you do. He only knew that it was quite correct; that everything had happened so; that there he was, alone again, when all the other boys had gone home for the jolly holidays.

He was not reading now, but walking up and down despairingly. Scrooge looked at the Ghost, and with a mournful shaking of his head, glanced anxiously towards the door.

It opened; and a little girl, much younger than the boy came darting in, and putting her arms about his neck, and often kissing him, addressed him as her "Dear, dear brother."

"I have come to bring you home, dear brother!" said the child, clapping her tiny hands, and bending down to laugh. "To bring you home, home, home!"

"Home, little Fan?" returned the boy.

"Yes!" said the child, brimful of glee. "Home, for good and all. Home, for ever and ever. Father is so much kinder than he used to be, that home's like Heaven! He spoke so gently to me one dear night when I was going to bed, that I was not afraid to ask him once more if you might come home; and he said Yes, you should; and sent me in a coach to bring you. And you're to be a man!" said the child, opening her eyes, "and are never to come back here; but first, we're to be together all the Christmas long, and have the merriest time in all the world."

"You're quite a woman, little Fan!" exclaimed the boy.

She clapped her hands and laughed, and tried to touch his head; but being too little, laughed again, and stood on tiptoe to embrace him. Then she began to drag him, in her childish eagerness, towards the door; and he, nothing loth to go, accompanied her.

A terrible voice in the hall cried, "Bring down Master Scrooge's box, there!" and in the hall appeared the school-master himself, who glared on Master Scrooge with a ferocious condescension, and threw him into a dreadful state of mind by shaking hands with him. He then conveyed him and his sister into the veriest old well of a shivering best-parlour that ever was seen, where the maps upon the wall, and the celestial and terrestrial globes in the windows, were waxy with cold. Here he produced a decanter of curiously light wine, and a block of curiously heavy cake, and administered instalments of those dainties to the young people: at the same time, sending out a meagre servant to offer a glass of "something" to the postboy, who answered that he thanked the gentleman, but if it was the same tap as he had tasted before, he had rather not. Master Scrooge's trunk being by this time tied on to the top of the chaise, the children bade the schoolmaster good-bye right willingly; and getting into it, drove gaily down the garden-sweep: the quick wheels dashing the hoar-frost and snow from off the dark leaves of the evergreens like a spray.

"Always a delicate creature, whom a breath might have withered," said the Ghost. "But she had a large heart!"

"So she had," cried Scrooge. "You're right. I will not gainsay it, Spirit. God forbid!"

"She died a woman," said the Ghost, "and had, as I think, children."

"One child," Scrooge returned.

"True," said the Ghost. "Your nephew!"

Scrooge seemed uneasy in his mind; and answered briefly, "Yes."

Although they had but that moment left the school behind them, they were now in the busy thoroughfares of a city, where shadowy passengers passed and repassed; where shadowy carts and coaches battled for the way, and all the strife and tumult of a real city were. It was made plain enough, by the dressing of the shops, that here too it was Christmas time again; but it was evening, and the streets were lighted up.

The Ghost stopped at a certain warehouse door, and asked Scrooge if he knew it.

"Know it!" said Scrooge. "Was I apprenticed here!"

They went in. At sight of an old gentleman in a Welsh wig, sitting behind such a high desk, that if he had been two inches taller he must have knocked his head against the ceiling, Scrooge cried in great excitement:

"Why, it's old Fezziwig! Bless his heart: it's Fezziwig alive again!"

Old Fezziwig laid down his pen, and looked up at the clock, which pointed to the hour of seven. He rubbed his hands; adjusted his capacious waistcoat; laughed all over himself, from his shoes to his organ of benevolence; and called out in a comfortable, oily, rich, fat, jovial voice:

"Yo ho, there! Ebenezer! Dick!"

Scrooge's former self, now grown a young man, came briskly in, accompanied by his fellow-'prentice.

"Dick Wilkins, to be sure!" said Scrooge to the Ghost. "Bless me, yes. There he is. He was very much attached to me, was Dick. Poor Dick! Dear, dear!"

"Yo ho, my boys!" said Fezziwig. "No more work to-night. Christmas Eve, Dick. Christmas, Ebenezer! Let's have the shutters up," cried old Fezziwig, with a sharp clap of his hands, "before a man can say Jack Robinson!"

You wouldn't believe how those two fellows went at it! They charged into the street with the shutters—one, two, three—had 'em up in their places—four, five, six—barred 'em and pinned 'em—seven, eight, nine—and came back before you could have got to twelve, panting like racehorses.

"Hilli-ho!" cried old Fezziwig, skipping down from the high desk, with wonderful agility. "Clear away, my lads, and let's have lots of room here! Hilli-ho, Dick! Chirrup, Ebenezer!"

Clear away! There was nothing they wouldn't have cleared away, or couldn't have cleared away, with Old Fezzi wig looking on. It was done in a minute. Every movable was packed off, as if it were dismissed from public life for evermore; the floor was swept and watered, the lamps were trimmed, fuel was heaped upon the fire; and the warehouse was as snug, and warm, and dry, and bright a ballroom, as you would desire to see upon a winter's night.

In came a fiddler with a music-book, and went up to the lofty desk, and made an orchestra of it, and tuned like fifty stomach-aches. In came Mrs. Fezziwig, one vast substantial smile. In came the three Miss Fezziwigs, beaming and loveable. In came the six young followers whose hearts they broke. In came all the young men and women employed in the business. In came the housemaid, with her cousin, the baker. In came the cook, with her brother's particular friend, the milkman. In came the boy from over the way, who was suspected of not having board enough from his master; trying to hide himself behind the girl from next door but one, who was proved to have had her ears pulled by her mistress. In they all came, one after another; some shyly, some boldly, some gracefully, some awkwardly, some pushing, some pulling; in they all came, anyhow and everyhow. Away they all went, twenty couple at once; hands half round and back again the other way; down the middle and up again; round and round in various stages of affectionate grouping; old top couple always turning up in the wrong place; new top couple starting off again, as soon as they got there; all top couples at last, and not a bottom one to help them! When this result was brought about, old Fezziwig, clapping his hands to stop the dance, cried out, "Well done!" and the fiddler plunged his hot face into a pot of porter, especially provided for that purpose. But scorning rest, upon his reappearance, he instantly began again, though there were no dancers yet, as if the other fiddler had been carried home, exhausted, on a shutter, and he were a bran-new man resolved to beat him out of sight, or perish.

There were more dances, and there were forfeits, and more dances, and there was cake, and there was negus, and

there was a great piece of Cold Roast, and there was a great
piece of Cold Boiled, and there were mince-pies, and plenty
of beer. But the great effect of the evening came after the
Roast and Boiled, when the fiddler (an artful dog, mind!
The sort of man who knew his business better than you or
I could have told it him!) struck up "Sir Roger de Cover-
ley." Then old Fezziwig stood out to dance with Mrs. Fezziwig. Top couple, too; with a good stiff piece of work cut
out for them; three or four and twenty pair of partners;
people who were not to be trifled with; people who *would*
dance, and had no notion of walking.

But if they had been twice as many—ah, four times—old
Fezziwig would have been a match for them, and so would
Mrs. Fezziwig. As to *her*, she was worthy to be his partner
in every sense of the term. If that's not high praise, tell
me higher, and I'll use it. A positive light appeared to issue
from Fezziwig's calves. They shone in every part of the
dance like moons. You couldn't have predicted, at any
given time, what would have become of them next. And when
old Fezziwig and Mrs. Fezziwig had gone all through the
dance; advance and retire, both hands to your partner, bow
and curtsey, corkscrew, thread-the-needle, and back again
to your place; Fezziwig "cut"—cut so deftly, that he appeared to wink with his legs, and came upon his feet again
without a stagger.

When the clock struck eleven, this domestic ball broke
up. Mr. and Mrs. Fezziwig took their stations, one on either
side of the door, and shaking hands with every person in-
dividually as he or she went out, wished him or her a Merry
Christmas. When everybody had retired but the two 'pren-
tices, they did the same to them; and thus the cheerful
voices died away, and the lads were left to their beds; which
were under a counter in the back-shop.

During the whole of this time, Scrooge had acted like a
man out of his wits. His heart and soul were in the scene,
and with his former self. He corroborated everything, remembered everything, enjoyed everything, and underwent
the strangest agitation. It was not until now, when the

bright faces of his former self and Dick were turned from them, that he remembered the Ghost, and became conscious that it was looking full upon him, while the light upon its head burnt very clear.

"A small matter," said the Ghost, "to make these silly folks so full of gratitude."

"Small!" echoed Scrooge.

The Spirit signed to him to listen to the two apprentices, who were pouring out their hearts in praise of Fezziwig: and when he had done so, said,

"Why! Is it not? He has spent but a few pounds of your mortal money: three or four perhaps. Is that so much that he deserves this praise?"

"It isn't that," said Scrooge, heated by the remark, and speaking unconsciously like his former, not his latter, self. "It isn't that, Spirit. He has the power to render us happy or unhappy; to make our service light or burdensome; a pleasure or a toil. Say that his power lies in words and looks; in things so slight and insignificant that it is impossible to add and count 'em up: what then? The happiness he gives, is quite as great as if it cost a fortune."

He felt the Spirit's glance, and stopped.

"What is the matter?" asked the Ghost.

"Nothing particular," said Scrooge.

"Something, I think?" the Ghost insisted.

"No," said Scrooge, "No. I should like to be able to say a word or two to my clerk just now. That's all."

His former self turned down the lamps as he gave utterance to the wish; and Scrooge and the Ghost again stood side by side in the open air.

"My time grows short," observed the Spirit. "Quick!"

This was not addressed to Scrooge, or to any one whom he could see, but it produced an immediate effect. For again Scrooge saw himself. He was older now; a man in the prime of life. His face had not the harsh and rigid lines of later years; but it had begun to wear the signs of care and avarice. There was an eager, greedy, restless motion in the eye, which showed the passion that had taken root, and where the shadow of the growing tree would fall.

He was not alone, but sat by the side of a fair young girl in a mourning-dress: in whose eyes there were tears, which sparkled in the light that shone out of the Ghost of Christmas Past.

"It matters little," she said, softly. "To you, very little. Another idol has displaced me; and if it can cheer and comfort you in time to come, as I would have tried to do, I have no just cause to grieve."

"What Idol has displaced you?" he rejoined.

"A golden one."

"This is the even-handed dealing of the world!" he said. "There is nothing on which it is so hard as poverty; and there is nothing it professes to condemn with such severity as the pursuit of wealth!"

"You fear the world too much," she answered, gently. "All your other hopes have merged into the hope of being beyond the chance of its sordid reproach. I have seen your nobler aspirations fall off one by one, until the master-passion, Gain, engrosses you. Have I not?"

"What then?" he retorted. "Even if I have grown so much wiser, what then? I am not changed towards you."

She shook her head.

"Am I?"

"Our contract is an old one. It was made when we were both poor and content to be so, until, in good season, we could improve our worldly fortune by our patient industry. You *are* changed. When it was made, you were *another* man."

"I was a boy," he said impatiently.

"Your own feeling tells you that you were not what you are," she returned. "I am. That which promised happiness when we were one in heart, is fraught with misery now that we are two. How often and how keenly I have thought of this, I will not say. It is enough that I *have* thought of it, and can release you."

"Have I ever sought release?"

"In words. No. Never."

"In what, then?"

"In a changed nature; in an altered spirit; in another atmosphere of life; another Hope as its great end. In everything that made my love of any worth or value in your sight. If this had never been between us," said the girl, looking mildly, but with steadiness, upon him; "tell me, would you seek me out and try to win me now? Ah, no!"

He seemed to yield to the justice of this supposition, in spite of himself. But he said with a struggle, "You think not."

"I would gladly think otherwise if I could," she answered, "Heaven knows! When *I* have learned a Truth like this, I know how strong and irresistible it must be. But if you were free to-day, to-morrow, yesterday, can even I believe that you would choose a dowerless girl—you who, in your very confidence with her, weigh everything by Gain: or, choosing her, if for a moment you were false enough to your one guiding principle to do so, do I not know that your repentance and regret would surely follow? I do; and I release you. With a full heart, for the love of him you once were."

He was about to speak; but with her head turned from him, she resumed.

"You may—the memory of what is past half makes me hope you will—have pain in this. A very, very brief time, and you will dismiss the recollection of it, gladly, as an unprofitable dream, from which it happened well that you awoke. May you be happy in the life you have chosen!"

She left him, and they parted.

"Spirit!" said Scrooge, "show me no more! Conduct me home. Why do you delight to torture me?"

"One shadow more!" exclaimed the Ghost.

"No more!" cried Scrooge. "No more. I don't wish to see it. Show me no more!"

But the relentless Ghost pinioned him in both his arms, and forced him to observe what happened next.

They were in another scene and place; a room, not very

large or handsome, but full of comfort. Near to the winter fire sat a beautiful young girl, so like that last that Scrooge believed it was the same, until he saw *her*, now a comely matron, sitting opposite her daughter. The noise in this room was perfectly tumultuous, for there were more children there, than Scrooge in his agitated state of mind could count; and, unlike the celebrated herd in the poem, they were not forty children conducting themselves like one, but every child was conducting itself like forty. The consequences were uproarious beyond belief; but no one seemed to care; on the contrary, the mother and daughter laughed heartily, and enjoyed it very much; and the latter, soon beginning to mingle in the sports, got pillaged by the young brigands most ruthlessly. What would I not have given to be one of them! Though I never could have been so rude, no, no! I wouldn't for the wealth of all the world have crushed that braided hair, and torn it down; and for the precious little shoe, I wouldn't have plucked it off, God bless my soul! to save my life. As to measuring her waist in sport, as they did, bold young brood, I couldn't have done it; I should have expected my arm to have grown round it for a punishment, and never come straight again. And yet I should have dearly liked, I own, to have touched her lips; to have questioned her, that she might have opened them; to have looked upon the lashes of her downcast eyes, and never raised a blush; to have let loose waves of hair, an inch of which would be a keepsake beyond price: in short, I should have liked, I do confess, to have had the lightest license of a child, and yet to have been man enough to know its value.

But now a knocking at the door was heard, and such a rush immediately ensued that she with laughing face and plundered dress was borne towards it in the centre of a flushed and boisterous group, just in time to greet the father, who came home attended by a man laden with Christmas toys and presents. Then the shouting and the struggling and the onslaught that was made on the defenceless porter! The scaling him with chairs for ladders to drive into his pockets, despoil him of brown-paper parcels, hold on tight by his cravat, hug him round his neck, pommel his back, and kick his legs in irrepressible affection! The shouts of wonder and delight with which the development of every package was received! The terrible announcement that the baby had been taken in the act of putting a doll's frying-pan into his mouth, and was more than suspected of having swallowed a fictitious turkey, glued on a wooden platter! The immense relief of finding this a false alarm! The joy, and gratitude, and ecstasy! They are all indescribable alike. It is enough that by degrees the children and their emotions got out of the parlour and by one stair at a time, up to the top of the house; where they went to bed, and so subsided.

And now Scrooge looked on more attentively than ever, when the master of the house, having his daughter leaning fondly on him, sat down with her and her mother at his own fireside; and when he thought that such another creature, quite as graceful and as full of promise, might have called him father, and been a spring-time in the haggard winter of his life, his sight grew very dim indeed.

"Belle," said the husband, turning to his wife with a smile, "I saw an old friend of yours this afternoon."

"Who was it?"

"Guess!"

"How can I? Tut, don't I know?" she added in the same breath, laughing as he laughed. "Mr. Scrooge."

"Mr. Scrooge it was. I passed his office window; and as it was not shut up, and he had a candle inside, I could scarcely help seeing him. His partner lies upon the point of death, I hear; and there he sat alone. Quite alone in the world, I do believe."

"Spirit!" said Scrooge in a broken voice, "remove me from this place."

"I told you these were shadows of the things that have been," said the Ghost. "That they are what they are, do not blame me!"

"Remove me!" Scrooge exclaimed, "I cannot bear it!"

He turned upon the Ghost, and seeing that it looked upon him with a face, in which in some strange way there were fragments of all the faces it had shown him, wrestled with it.

"Leave me! Take me back. Haunt me no longer!"

In the struggle, if that can be called a struggle in which the Ghost with no visible resistance on its own part was undisturbed by any effort of its adversary, Scrooge observed that its light was burning high and bright; and dimly connecting that with its influence over him, he seized the extinguisher-cap, and by a sudden action pressed it down upon its head.

The Spirit dropped beneath it, so that the extinguisher covered its whole form; but though Scrooge pressed it down with all his force, he could not hide the light, which streamed from under it, in an unbroken flood upon the ground.

He was conscious of being exhausted, and overcome by an irresistible drowsiness; and, further, of being in his own bedroom. He gave the cap a parting squeeze, in which his hand relaxed; and had barely time to reel to bed, before he sank into a heavy sleep.

Stave Three

THE SECOND OF THE THREE SPIRITS

AWAKING in the middle of a prodigiously tough snore, and sitting up in bed to get his thoughts together, Scrooge had no occasion to be told that the bell was again upon the stroke of One. He felt that he was restored to consciousness in the right nick of time, for the especial purpose of holding a conference with the second messenger despatched to him through Jacob Marley's intervention. But, finding that he turned uncomfortably cold when he began to wonder which of his curtains this new spectre would draw back, he put

them every one aside with his own hands, and lying down
again, established a sharp look-out all round the bed. For,
he wished to challenge the Spirit on the moment of its appearance, and did not wish to be taken by surprise, and
made nervous.

Gentlemen of the free-and-easy sort, who plume themselves on being acquainted with a move or two, and being
usually equal to the time-of-day, express the wide range of
their capacity for adventure by observing that they are good
for anything from pitch-and-toss to manslaughter; between
which opposite extremes, no doubt, there lies a tolerably
wide and comprehensive range of subjects. Without venturing for Scrooge quite as hardily as this, I don't mind calling
on you to believe that he was ready for a good broad field of
strange appearances, and that nothing between a baby and
rhinoceros would have astonished him very much.

Now, being prepared for almost anything, he was not by
any means prepared for nothing; and, consequently, when
the Bell struck One, and no shape appeared, he was taken
with a violent fit of trembling. Five minutes, ten minutes, a
quarter of an hour went by, yet nothing came. All this
time, he lay upon his bed, the very core and centre of a blaze
of ruddy light, which streamed upon it when the clock proclaimed the hour; and which, being only light, was more
alarming than a dozen ghosts, as he was powerless to make
out what it meant, or would be at; and was sometimes ap-
prehensive that he might be at that very moment an interesting case of spontaneous combustion, without having the
consolation of knowing it. At last, however, he began to
think—as you or I would have thought at first; for it is always the person not in the predicament who knows what
ought to have been done in it, and would unquestionably
have done it too—at last, I say, he began to think that the
source and secret of this ghostly light might be in the adjoining room, from whence, on further tracing it, it seemed
to shine. This idea taking full possession of his mind, he
got up softly and shuffled in his slippers to the door.

The moment Scrooge's hand was on the lock, a strange

voice called him by his name, and bade him enter. He obeyed.

It was his own room. There was no doubt about that. But it had undergone a surprising transformation. The walls and ceiling were so hung with living green, that it looked a perfect grove; from every part of which, bright gleaming berries glistened. The crisp leaves of holly, mistletoe, and ivy reflected back the light, as if so many little mirrors had been scattered there; and such a mighty blaze went roaring up the chimney, as that dull petrifaction of a hearth had never known in Scrooge's time, or Marley's, or for many and many a winter season gone. Heaped up on the floor, to form a kind of throne, were turkeys, geese, game, poultry, brawn, great joints of meat, sucking-pigs, long wreaths of sausages, mince-pies, plum-puddings, barrels of oysters, red-hot chestnuts, cherry-cheeked apples, juicy oranges, luscious pears, immense twelfth-cakes, and seething bowls of punch, that made the chamber dim with their delicious steam. In easy state upon this couch, there sat a jolly Giant, glorious to see; who bore a glowing torch, in shape not unlike Plenty's horn, and held it up, high up, to shed its light on Scrooge, as he came peeping round the door.

"Come in!" exclaimed the Ghost. "Come in! and know me better, man!"

Scrooge entered timidly, and hung his head before this Spirit. He was not the dogged Scrooge he had been; and though the Spirit's eyes were clear and kind, he did not like to meet them.

"I am the Ghost of Christmas Present," said the Spirit. "Look upon me!"

Scrooge reverently did so. It was clothed in one simple green robe, or mantle, bordered with white fur. This garment hung so loosely on the figure, that its capacious breast was bare, as if disdaining to be warded or concealed by any artifice. Its feet, observable beneath the ample folds of the garment, were also bare; and on its head it wore no other covering than a holly wreath, set here and there with shining icicles. Its dark brown curls were long and free; free as its genial face, its sparkling eye, its open hand, its cheery voice, its unconstrained demeanour, and its joyful air. Girded round its middle was an antique scabbard; but no sword was in it, and the ancient sheath was eaten up with rust.

"You have never seen the like of me before!" exclaimed the Spirit.

"Never," Scrooge made answer to it.

"Have never walked forth with the younger members of my family; meaning (for I am very young) my elder brothers born in these later years?" pursued the Phantom.

"I don't think I have," said Scrooge. "I am afraid I have not. Have you had many brothers, Spirit?"

"More than eighteen hundred," said the Ghost.

"A tremendous family to provide for!" muttered Scrooge.

The Ghost of Christmas Present rose.

"Spirit," said Scrooge submissively, "conduct me where you will. I went forth last night on compulsion, and I learnt a lesson which is working now. To-night, if you have aught to teach me, let me profit by it."

"Touch my robe!"

Scrooge did as he was told, and held it fast.

Holly, mistletoe, red berries, ivy, turkeys, geese, game, poultry, brawn, meat, pigs, sausages, oysters, pies, puddings, fruit, and punch, all vanished instantly. So did the room, the fire, the ruddy glow, the hour of night, and they stood in the city streets on Christmas morning where (for the weather was severe) the people made a rough, but brisk and not unpleasant kind of music, in scraping the snow from the pavement in front of their dwellings, and from the tops of their houses, whence it was mad delight to the boys to see it come plumping down into the road below, and splitting into artificial little snowstorms.

The house fronts looked black enough, and the windows blacker, contrasting with the smooth white sheet of snow upon the roofs, and with the dirtier snow upon the ground; which last deposit had been ploughed up in deep furrows by the heavy wheels of carts and waggons; furrows that crossed and recrossed each other hundreds of times where the great streets branched off; and made intricate channels, hard to trace in the thick yellow mud and ice water. The sky was gloomy, and the shortest streets were choked up with a dingy mist, half thawed half frozen, whose heavier particles descended in a shower of sooty atoms, as if all the chimneys in Great Britain had, by one consent, caught fire, and were blazing away to their dear hearts' content. There was nothing very cheerful in the climate or the town, and yet was there an air of cheerfulness abroad that the clearest summer air and brightest summer sun might have endeavoured to diffuse in vain.

For, the people who were shovelling away on the house-tops were jovial and full of glee; calling out to one another from the parapets, and now and then exchanging a facetious snowball—better-natured missile far than many a wordy jest—laughing heartily if it went right and not less heartily if it went wrong. The poulterers' shops were still half open, and the fruiterers' were radiant in their glory. There were great, round, pot-bellied baskets of chestnuts, shaped like the waistcoats of jolly old gentlemen, lolling at the doors, and tumbling out into the street in their apoplectic opulence. There were ruddy, brown-faced, broad-girthed Spanish Onions, shining in the fatness of their growth like Spanish Friars, and winking from their shelves in wanton slyness at the girls as they went by, and glanced demurely at the hung-up mistletoe. There were pears and apples, clustered high in blooming pyramids; there were bunches of grapes, made, in the shopkeepers' benevolence, to dangle from conspicuous hooks, that people's mouths might water gratis as they passed; there were piles of filberts, mossy and brown, recalling, in their fragrance, ancient walks among the woods, and pleasant shufflings ankle deep through withered leaves; there were Norfolk Biffins, squab and swarthy, setting off the yellow of the oranges and lemons, and, in the great compactness of their juicy persons, urgently entreating and beseeching to be carried home in paper bags and eaten after dinner. The very gold and silver fish, set forth among these

choice fruits in a bowl, though members of a dull and stag-
nant-blooded race, appeared to know that there was something going on; and, to a fish, went gasping round and round
their little world in slow and passionless excitement.

The Grocers'! oh the Grocers'! nearly closed, with perhaps two shutters down, or one; but through those gaps such
glimpses! It was not alone that the scales descending on the
counter made a merry sound, or that the twine and roller
parted company so briskly, or that the canisters were rattled
up and down like juggling tricks, or even that the blended
scents of tea and coffee were so grateful to the nose, or even
that the raisins were so plentiful and rare, the almonds so
extremely white, the sticks of cinnamon so long and straight,
the other spices so delicious, the candied fruits so caked
and spotted with molten sugar as to make the coldest look-
ers-on feel faint and subsequently bilious. Nor was it that
the figs were moist and pulpy, or that the French plums
blushed in modest tartness from their highly-decorated
boxes, or that everything was good to eat and in its Christmas dress; but the customers were all so hurried and so
eager in the hopeful promise of the day, that they tumbled
up against each other at the door, crashing their wicker
baskets wildly, and left their purchases upon the counter,
and came running back to fetch them, and committed hundreds of the like mistakes, in the best humour possible;
while the Grocer and his people were so frank and fresh
that the polished hearts with which they fastened their
aprons behind might have been their own, worn outside for
general inspection, and for Christmas daws to peck at if they
chose.

But soon the steeples called good people all, to church
and chapel, and away they came, flocking through the
streets in their best clothes, and with their gayest faces. And
at the same time there emerged from scores of by-streets,
lanes, and nameless turnings, innumerable people, carrying
their dinners to the bakers' shops. The sight of these poor
revellers appeared to interest the Spirit very much, for he
stood with Scrooge beside him in a baker's doorway, and

taking off the covers as their bearers passed, sprinkled incense on their dinners from his torch. And it was a very uncommon kind of torch, for once or twice when there were angry words between some dinner-carriers who had jostled each other, he shed a few drops of water on them from it, and their good humour was restored directly. For they said, it was a shame to quarrel upon Christmas Day. And so it was! God love it, so it was!

In time the bells ceased, and the bakers were shut up; and yet there was a genial shadowing forth of all these dinners and the progress of their cooking, in the thawed blotch of wet above each baker's oven; where the pavement smoked as if its stones were cooking too.

"Is there a peculiar flavour in what you sprinkle from your torch?" asked Scrooge.

"There is. My own."

"Would it apply to any kind of dinner on this day?" asked Scrooge.

"To any kindly given. To a poor one most."

"Why to a poor one most?" asked Scrooge.

"Because it needs it most."

"Spirit," said Scrooge, after a moment's thought, "I wonder you, of all the beings in the many worlds about us, should desire to cramp these people's opportunities of innocent enjoyment."

"I!" cried the Spirit.

"You would deprive them of their means of dining every seventh day, often the only day on which they can be said to dine at all," said Scrooge. "Wouldn't you?"

"I!" cried the Spirit.

"You seek to close these places on the Seventh Day?" said Scrooge. "And it comes to the same thing."

"*I* seek!" exclaimed the Spirit.

"Forgive me if I am wrong. It has been done in your name, or at least in that of your family," said Scrooge.

"There are some upon this earth of yours," returned the Spirit, "who lay claim to know us, and who do their deeds of passion, pride, ill-will, hatred, envy, bigotry, and selfishness in our name, who are as strange to us and all our kith and kin, as if they had never lived. Remember that, and charge their doings on themselves, not us."

Scrooge promised that he would; and they went on, invisible, as they had been before, into the suburbs of the town. It was a remarkable quality of the Ghost (which Scrooge had observed at the baker's), that notwithstanding his gigantic size, he could accommodate himself to any place with ease; and that he stood beneath a low roof quite as gracefully and like a supernatural creature, as it was possible he could have done in any lofty hall.

And perhaps it was the pleasure the good Spirit had in showing off this power of his, or else it was his own kind, generous, hearty nature, and his sympathy with all poor men, that led him straight to Scrooge's clerk's; for there he went, and took Scrooge with him, holding to his robe; and on the threshold of the door the Spirit smiled, and stopped to bless Bob Cratchit's dwelling with the sprinklings of his torch. Think of that! Bob had but fifteen "Bob" a week himself; he pocketed on Saturdays but fifteen copies of his Christian name; and yet the Ghost of Christmas Present blessed his four-roomed house!

Then up rose Mrs. Cratchit, Cratchit's wife, dressed out but poorly in a twice-turned gown, but brave in ribbons, which are cheap and make a goodly show for sixpence; and she laid the cloth, assisted by Belinda Cratchit, second of her daughters, also brave in ribbons; while Master Peter Cratchit plunged a fork into the saucepan of potatoes, and getting the corners of his monstrous shirt collar (Bob's private property, conferred upon his son and heir in honour of the day) into his mouth, rejoiced to find himself so gallantly attired, and yearned to show his linen in the fashionable Parks. And now two smaller Cratchits, boy and girl, came tearing in, screaming that outside the baker's they had smelt the goose, and known it for their own; and basking in luxurious thoughts of sage and onion, these young Cratchits danced about the table, and exalted Master Peter

Cratchit to the skies, while he (not proud, although his collars nearly choked him) blew the fire, until the slow potatoes bubbling up, knocked loudly at the saucepan-lid to be let out and peeled.

"What has ever got your precious father then?" said Mrs. Cratchit. "And your brother, Tiny Tim! And Martha warn't as late last Christmas Day by half an hour?"

"Here's Martha, mother!" said a girl, appearing as she spoke.

"Here's Martha, mother!" cried the two young Cratchits. "Hurrah! There's *such* a goose, Martha!"

"Why, bless your heart alive, my dear, how late you are!" said Mrs. Cratchit, kissing her a dozen times, and taking off her shawl and bonnet for her with officious zeal.

"We'd a deal of work to finish up last night," replied the girl, "and had to clear away this morning, mother!"

"Well! Never mind so long as you are come," said Mrs. Cratchit. "Sit ye down before the fire, my dear, and have a warm, Lord bless ye!"

"No, no! There's father coming," cried the two young Cratchits, who were everywhere at once. "Hide, Martha, hide!"

So Martha hid herself, and in came little Bob, the father, with at least three feet of comforter exclusive of the fringe, hanging down before him; and his threadbare clothes darned up and brushed, to look seasonable; and Tiny Tim upon his shoulder. Alas for Tiny Tim, he bore a little crutch, and had his limbs supported by an iron frame!

"Why, where's our Martha?" cried Bob Cratchit, looking round.

"Not coming," said Mrs. Cratchit.

"Not coming!" said Bob, with a sudden declension in his high spirits; for he had been Tim's blood horse all the way from church, and had come home rampant. "Not coming upon Christmas Day!"

Martha didn't like to see him disappointed, if it were only in joke; so she came out prematurely from behind the closet door, and ran into his arms, while the two young Cratchits hustled Tiny Tim, and bore him off into the wash-house, that he might hear the pudding singing in the copper.

"And how did little Tim behave?" asked Mrs. Cratchit, when she had rallied Bob on his credulity, and Bob had hugged his daughter to his heart's content.

"As good as gold," said Bob, "and better. Somehow he gets thoughtful, sitting by himself so much, and thinks the strangest things you ever heard. He told me, coming home, that he hoped the people saw him in the church, because he was a cripple, and it might be pleasant to them to remember upon Christmas Day, who made lame beggars walk, and blind men see."

Bob's voice was tremulous when he told them this, and trembled more when he said that Tiny Tim was growing strong and hearty.

His active little crutch was heard upon the floor, and back came Tiny Tim before another word was spoken, escorted by his brother and sister to his stool before the fire; and while Bob, turning up his cuffs—as if, poor fellow, they were capable of being made more shabby—compounded some hot mixture in a jug with gin and lemons, and stirred it round and round and put it on the hob to simmer; Master Peter, and the two ubiquitous young Cratchits, went to fetch the goose, with which they soon returned in high procession.

Such a bustle ensued that you might have thought a goose the rarest of all birds; a feathered phenomenon, to which a black swan was a matter of course—and in truth it was something very like it in that house. Mrs. Cratchit made the gravy (ready beforehand in a little saucepan) hissing hot; Master Peter mashed the potatoes with incredible vigour; Miss Belinda sweetened up the apple-sauce; Martha dusted the hot plates; Bob took Tiny Tim beside him in a tiny corner at the table; the two young Cratchits set chairs for everybody, not forgetting themselves, and mounting guard upon their posts, crammed spoons into their mouths, lest they should shriek for goose before their turn came to be helped. At last the dishes were set on, and grace was said. It was succeeded by a breathless pause, as Mrs. Cratchit, looking slowly all along the carving-knife, prepared to plunge it in the breast; but when she did, and when the long expected gush of stuffing issued forth, one murmur of delight arose all round the board, and even Tiny Tim, excited by the two young Cratchits, beat on the table with the handle of his knife, and feebly cried Hurrah!

There never was such a goose. Bob said he didn't believe there ever was such a goose cooked. Its tenderness and flavour, size and cheapness, were the themes of universal admiration. Eked out by apple sauce and mashed potatoes, it was a sufficient dinner for the whole family: indeed, as Mrs. Cratchit said with great delight (surveying one small atom of a bone upon the dish), they hadn't ate it all at last! Yet every one had had enough, and the youngest Cratchits in particular, were steeped in sage and onion to the eyebrows. But now, the plates being changed by Miss Belinda, Mrs. Cratchit left the room alone—too nervous to bear witnesses—to take the pudding up and bring it in.

Suppose it should not be done enough! Suppose it should break in turning out! Suppose somebody should have got over the wall of the back-yard, and stolen it, while they were merry with the goose—a supposition at which the two young Cratchits became livid! All sorts of horrors were supposed.

Hallo! A great deal of steam! The pudding was out of the copper. A smell like a washing-day! That was the cloth. A smell like an eating-house and a pastrycook's next door to each other, with a laundress's next door to that! That was the pudding! In half a minute Mrs. Cratchit entered—flushed, but smiling proudly—with the pudding, like a speckled cannon-ball, so hard and firm, blazing in half of half-a-quartern of ignited brandy, and bedight with Christmas holly stuck into the top.

Oh, a wonderful pudding! Bob Cratchit said, and calmly too, that he regarded it as the greatest success achieved by Mrs. Cratchit since their marriage. Mrs. Cratchit said that now the weight was off her mind, she would confess she had

had her doubts about the quantity of flour. Everybody had something to say about it, but nobody said or thought it was at all a small pudding for a large family. It would have been flat heresy to do so. Any Cratchit would have blushed to hint at such a thing.

At last the dinner was all done, the cloth was cleared, the hearth swept, and the fire made up. The compound in the jug being tasted, and considered perfect, apples and oranges were put upon the table, and a shovel-full of chestnuts on the fire. Then all the Cratchit family drew round the hearth, in what Bob Cratchit called a circle, meaning half a one; and at Bob Cratchit's elbow stood the family display of glass. Two tumblers, and a custard-cup without a handle.

These held the hot stuff from the jug, however, as well as golden goblets would have done; and Bob served it out with beaming looks, while the chestnuts on the fire sputtered and cracked noisily. Then Bob proposed:

"A Merry Christmas to us all, my dears. God bless us!"

Which all the family re-echoed.

"God bless us every one!" said Tiny Tim, the last of all.

He sat very close to his father's side upon his little stool. Bob held his withered little hand in his, as if he loved the child, and wished to keep him by his side, and dreaded that he might be taken from him.

"Spirit," said Scrooge, with an interest he had never felt before, "tell me if Tiny Tim will live."

"I see a vacant seat," replied the Ghost, "in the poor chimney-corner, and a crutch without an owner, carefully preserved. If these shadows remain unaltered by the Future, the child will die."

"No, no," said Scrooge. "Oh, no, kind Spirit! say he will be spared."

"If these shadows remain unaltered by the Future, none other of my race," returned the Ghost, "will find him here. What then? If he be like to die, he had better do it, and decrease the surplus population."

Scrooge hung his head to hear his own words quoted by the Spirit, and was overcome with penitence and grief.

"Man," said the Ghost, "if man you be in heart, not adamant, forbear that wicked cant until you have discovered What the surplus is, and Where it is. Will you decide what men shall live, what men shall die? It may be, that in the sight of Heaven, you are more worthless and less fit to live than millions like this poor man's child. Oh God! to hear the Insect on the leaf pronouncing on the too much life among his hungry brothers in the dust!"

Scrooge bent before the Ghost's rebuke, and trembling cast his eyes upon the ground. But he raised them speedily, on hearing his own name.

"Mr. Scrooge!" said Bob; "I'll give you Mr. Scrooge, the Founder of the Feast!"

"The Founder of the Feast indeed!" cried Mrs. Cratchit, reddening. "I wish I had him here. I'd give him a piece of my mind to feast upon, and I hope he'd have a good appetite for it."

"My dear," said Bob, "the children! Christmas Day."

"It should be Christmas Day, I am sure," said she, "on which one drinks the health of such an odious, stingy, hard, unfeeling man as Mr. Scrooge. You know he is, Robert! Nobody knows it better than you do, poor fellow?"

"My dear," was Bob's mild answer, "Christmas Day."

"I'll drink his health for your sake and the Day's," said Mrs. Cratchit, "not for his. Long life to him! A merry Christmas and a happy new year! He'll be very merry and very happy, I have no doubt!"

The children drank the toast after her. It was the first of their proceedings which had no heartiness. Tiny Tim drank it last of all, but he didn't care two-pence for it. Scrooge was the Ogre of the family. The mention of his name cast a dark shadow on the party, which was not dispelled for full five minutes.

After it had passed away, they were ten times merrier than before, from the mere relief of Scrooge the Baleful being done with. Bob Cratchit told them how he had a situation in his eye for Master Peter, which would bring in, if obtained, full five-and-sixpence weekly. The two young

Cratchits laughed tremendously at the idea of Peter's being a man of business; and Peter himself looked thoughtfully at the fire from between his collars, as if he were deliberating what particular investments he should favour when he came into the receipt of that bewildering income. Martha, who was a poor apprentice at a milliner's, then told them what kind of work she had to do, and how many hours she worked at a stretch, and how she meant to lie abed to-morrow morning for a good long rest; to-morrow being a holiday she passed at home. Also how she had seen a countess and a lord some days before, and how the lord "was much about as tall as Peter"; at which Peter pulled up his collars so high that you couldn't have seen his head if you had been there. All this time the chestnuts and the jug went round and round; and by and by they had a song, about a lost child travelling in the snow, from Tiny Tim, who had a plaintive little voice, and sang it very well indeed.

There was nothing of high mark in this. They were not a handsome family; they were not well dressed; their shoes were far from being water-proof; their clothes were scanty; and Peter might have known, and very likely did, the inside of a pawnbroker's. But, they were happy, grateful, pleased with one another, and contented with the time; and when they faded, and looked happier yet in the bright sprinklings of the Spirit's torch at parting, Scrooge had his eye upon them, and especially on Tiny Tim, until the last.

By this time it was getting dark, and snowing pretty heavily; and as Scrooge and the Spirit went along the streets, the brightness of the roaring fires in kitchens, parlours, and all sorts of rooms, was wonderful. Here, the flickering of the blaze showed preparations for a cosy dinner, with hot plates baking through and through before the fire, and deep red curtains, ready to be drawn to shut out cold and darkness. There all the children of the house were running out into the snow to meet their married sisters, brothers, cousins, uncles, aunts, and be the first to greet them. Here, again, were shadows on the window-blind of guests assembling; and there a group of handsome girls, all hooded and fur-

booted, and all chattering at once, tripped lightly off to some
near neighbour's house; where, woe upon the single man who
saw them enter—artful witches, well they knew it—in a
glow!

But, if you had judged from the numbers of people on
their way to friendly gatherings, you might have thought
that no one was at home to give them welcome when they
got there, instead of every house expecting company, and
piling up its fires half-chimney high. Blessings on it, how
the Ghost exulted. How it bared its breadth of breast, and
opened its capacious palm, and floated on, outpouring, with
a generous hand, its bright and harmless mirth on everything
within its reach! The very lamplighter, who ran on before,
dotting the dusky street with specks of light, and who was
dressed to spend the evening somewhere, laughed out loudly
as the Spirit passed, though little kenned the lamplighter
that he had any company but Christmas!

And now, without a word of warning from the Ghost, they
stood upon a bleak and desert moor, where monstrous
masses of rude stone were cast about, as though it were the
burial-place of giants; and water spread itself wheresoever
it listed, or would have done so, but for the frost that held it
prisoner; and nothing grew but moss and furze, and coarse
rank grass. Down in the west the setting sun had left a
streak of fiery red, which glared upon the desolation for an
instant, like a sullen eye, and frowning lower, lower, lower
yet, was lost in the thick gloom of darkest night.

"What place is this?" asked Scrooge.

"A place where Miners live, who labour in the bowels of
the earth," returned the Spirit. "But they know me. See!"

A light shone from the window of a hut, and swiftly they
advanced towards it. Passing through the wall of mud and
stone, they found a cheerful company assembled round a
glowing fire. An old, old man and woman, with their
children, and their children's children, and another generation beyond that, all decked out gaily in their holiday attire.
The old man, in a voice that seldom rose above the howling
of the wind upon the barren waste, was singing them a

Christmas song—it had been a very old song when he was a boy—and from time to time they all joined in the chorus. So surely as they raised their voices, the old man got quite blithe and loud; and so surely as they stopped, his vigour sank again.

The Spirit did not tarry here, but bade Scrooge hold his robe, and passing on above the moor, sped—whither? Not to sea? To sea. To Scrooge's horror, looking back, he saw the last of the land, a frightful range of rocks, behind them; and his ears were deafened by the thundering of water, as it rolled and roared, and raged among the dreadful caverns it had worn, and fiercely tried to undermine the earth.

Built upon a dismal reef of sunken rocks, some league or so from shore, on which the waters chafed and dashed, the wild year through, there stood a solitary lighthouse. Great heaps of sea-weed clung to its base, and storm-birds—born of the wind one might suppose, as sea-weed of the water—rose and fell about it, like the waves they skimmed.

But even here, two men who watched the light had made a fire, that through the loophole in the thick stone wall shed out a ray of brightness on the awful sea. Joining their horny hands over the rough table at which they sat, they wished each other Merry Christmas in their can of grog; and one of them: the elder, too, with his face all damaged and scarred with hard weather, as the figure-head of an old ship might be: struck up a sturdy song that was like a Gale in itself.

Again the Ghost sped on, above the black and heaving sea—on, on—until, being far away, as he told Scrooge, from any shore, they lighted on a ship. They stood beside the helmsman at the wheel, the look-out in the bow, the officers who had the watch; dark, ghostly figures in their several stations; but every man among them hummed a Christmas tune, or had a Christmas thought, or spoke below his breath to his companion of some by-gone Christmas Day, with homeward hopes belonging to it. And every man on board, waking or sleeping, good or bad, had had a kinder word for another on that day than on any day in the year; and had shared to some extent in its festivities; and had remembered those he cared for at a distance, and had known that they delighted to remember him.

It was a great surprise to Scrooge, while listening to the moaning of the wind, and thinking what a solemn thing it was to move on through the lonely darkness over an unknown abyss, whose depths were secrets as profound as Death: it was a great surprise to Scrooge, while thus engaged, to hear a hearty laugh. It was a much greater surprise to Scrooge to recognize it as his own nephew's and to find himself in a bright, dry, gleaming room, with the Spirit standing smiling by his side, and looking at that same nephew with approving affability!

"Ha, ha!" laughed Scrooge's nephew. "Ha, ha, ha!"

If you should happen, by any unlikely chance, to know a man more blest in a laugh than Scrooge's nephew, all I can say is, I should like to know him too. Introduce him to me, and I'll cultivate his acquaintance.

It is a fair, even-handed, noble adjustment of things, that while there is infection in disease and sorrow, there is nothing in the world so irresistibly contagious as laughter and good humour. When Scrooge's nephew laughed in this way: holding his sides, rolling his head, and twisting his face into the most extravagant contortions: Scrooge's niece, by marriage, laughed as heartily as he. And their assembled friends being not a bit behindhand, roared out lustily.

"Ha, Ha! Ha, ha, ha, ha!"

"He said that Christmas was a humbug, as I live!" cried Scrooge's nephew. "He believed it too!"

"More shame for him, Fred!" said Scrooge's niece, indignantly. Bless those women; they never do anything by halves. They are always in earnest.

She was very pretty: exceedingly pretty. With a dimpled, surprised-looking, capital face; a ripe little mouth, that seemed made to be kissed—as no doubt it was; all kinds of good little dots about her chin, that melted into one another when she laughed; and the sunniest pair of eyes you

ever saw in any little creature's head. Altogether she was
what you would have called provoking, you know; but satisfactory, too Oh, perfectly satisfactory.

"He's a comical old fellow," said Scrooge's nephew,
"that's the truth; and not so pleasant as he might be. However, his offences carry their own punishment, and I have
nothing to say against him."

"I'm sure he is very rich, Fred," hinted Scrooge's niece.
"At least you always tell *me* so."

"What of that, my dear!" said Scrooge's nephew. "His
wealth is of no use to him. He don't do any good with it.
He don't make himself comfortable with it. He hasn't the
satisfaction of thinking—ha, ha, ha!—that he is ever going
to benefit Us with it."

"I have no patience with him," observed Scrooge's niece.
Scrooge's niece's sisters, and all the other ladies, expressed
the same opinion.

"Oh, I have!" said Scrooge's nephew. "I am sorry for
him; I couldn't be angry with him if I tried. Who suffers
by his ill whims! Himself, always. Here, he takes it into
his head to dislike us, and he won't come and dine with
us. What's the consequence? He don't lose much of a
dinner."

"Indeed, I think he loses a very good dinner," interrupted
Scrooge's niece. Everybody else said the same, and they
must be allowed to have been competent judges, because
they had just had dinner; and, with the dessert upon the
table, were clustered round the fire, by lamplight.

"Well! I'm very glad to hear it," said Scrooge's nephew,
"because I haven't great faith in these young housekeepers.
What do *you* say, Topper?"

Topper had clearly got his eye upon one of Scrooge's
niece's sisters, for he answered that a bachelor was a
wretched outcast, who had no right to express an opinion on
the subject. Whereat Scrooge's niece's sister—the plump
one with the lace tucker: not the one with the roses—
blushed.

"Do go on, Fred," said Scrooge's niece, clapping her

hands. "He never finishes what he begins to say! He is such a ridiculous fellow!"

Scrooge's nephew revelled in another laugh, and as it was impossible to keep the infection off; though the plump sister tried hard to do it with aromatic vinegar; his example was unanimously followed.

"I was only going to say," said Scrooge's nephew, "that the consequence of his taking a dislike to us, and not making merry with us, is, as I think, that he loses some pleasant moments, which could do him no harm. I am sure he loses pleasanter companions than he can find in his own thoughts, either in his mouldy old office, or his dusty chambers. I mean to give him the same chance every year, whether he likes it or not, for I pity him. He may rail at Christmas till he dies, but he can't help thinking better of it—I defy him—if he finds me going there, in good temper, year after year, and saying 'Uncle Scrooge, how are you?' If it only puts him in the vein to leave his poor clerk fifty pounds, *that's* something; and I think I shook him yesterday."

It was their turn to laugh now at the notion of his shaking Scrooge. But being thoroughly good-natured, and not much caring what they laughed at, so that they laughed at any rate, he encouraged them in their merriment, and passed the bottle joyously.

After tea, they had some music. For they were a musical family, and knew what they were about, when they sung a Glee or Catch, I can assure you: especially Topper, who could growl away in the bass like a good one, and never swell the large veins in his forehead, or get red in the face over it. Scrooge's niece played well upon the harp; and played among other tunes a simple little air (a mere nothing; you might learn to whistle it in two minutes), which had been familiar to the child who fetched Scrooge from the boarding-school, as he had been reminded by the Ghost of Christmas Past. When this strain of music sounded, all the things that Ghost had shown him, came upon his mind; he softened more and more; and thought that if he could have listened to it often, years ago, he might have cultivated the kindnesses of life for his own happiness with his own hands, without resorting to the sexton's spade that buried Jacob Marley.

But they didn't devote the whole evening to music. After a while they played at forfeits; for it is good to be children sometimes, and never better than at Christmas, when its mighty Founder was a child himself. Stop! There was first a game at blind-man's buff. Of course there was. And I no more believe Topper was really blind than I believe he had eyes in his boots. My opinion is, that it was a done thing between him and Scrooge's nephew: and that the Ghost of Christmas Present knew it. The way he went after that plump sister in the lace tucker, was an outrage on the credulity of human nature. Knocking down the fire-irons, tumbling over the chairs, bumping against the piano, smothering himself among the curtains, wherever she went, there went he! He always knew where the plump sister was. He wouldn't catch anybody else. If you had fallen up against him (as some of them did), on purpose, he would have made a feint of endeavouring to seize you, which would have been an affront to your understanding, and would instantly have sidled off in the direction of the plump sister. She often cried out that it wasn't fair; and it really was not. But when at last, he caught her; when, in spite of all her silken rustlings, and her rapid flutterings past him, he got her into a corner, whence there was no escape; then his conduct was the most execrable. For his pretending not to know her; his pretending that it was necessary to touch her headdress, and further to assure himself of her identity by pressing a certain ring upon her finger, and a certain chain about her neck; was vile, monstrous! No doubt she told him her opinion of it, when, another blind man being in office, they were so very confidential together, behind the curtains.

Scrooge's niece was not one of the blind-man's buff party, but was made comfortable with a large chair and a footstool, in a snug corner, where the Ghost and Scrooge were close behind her. But she joined in the forfeits, and loved her love to admiration with all the letters of the alphabet. Likewise at the game of How, When, and Where, she was very great, and to the secret joy of Scrooge's nephew, beat her sisters hollow: though they were sharp girls too, as Topper could have told you. There might have been twenty people there, young and old, but they all played, and so did Scrooge; for wholly forgetting in the interest he had in what was going on, that his voice made no sound in their ears, he sometimes came out with his guess quite loud, and very often guessed quite right, too; for the sharpest needle, best Whitechapel, warranted not to cut in the eye, was not sharper than Scrooge; blunt as he took it in his head to be.

The Ghost was greatly pleased to find him in this mood, and looked upon him with such favour, that he begged like a boy to be allowed to stay until the guests departed. But this the Spirit said could not be done.

"Here is a new game," said Scrooge. "One half-hour, Spirit, only one!"

It is a Game called Yes and No, where Scrooge's nephew had to think of something, and the rest must find out what; he only answering to their questions yes or no, as the case was. The brisk fire of questioning to which he was exposed, elicited from him that he was thinking of an animal, a live animal, rather a disagreeable animal, a savage animal, an animal, that growled and grunted sometimes, and talked sometimes, and lived in London, and walked about the streets, and wasn't made a show of, and wasn't led by anybody, and didn't live in a menagerie, and was never killed in a market, and was not a horse, or an ass, or a cow, or a bull, or a tiger, or a dog, or a pig, or a cat, or a bear. At every fresh question that was put to him, this nephew burst into a fresh roar of laughter; and was so inexpressibly tickled, that he was obliged to get up off the sofa and stamp. At last the plump sister, falling into a similar state, cried out:

"I have found it out! I know what it is, Fred! I know what it is!"

"What is it?" cried Fred.

"It's your Uncle Scro-o-o-o-oge!"

Which it certainly was. Admiration was the universal sentiment, though some objected that the reply to "Is it a bear?" ought to have been "Yes"; inasmuch as an answer in the negative was sufficient to have diverted their thoughts from Mr. Scrooge, supposing they had ever had any tendency that way.

"He has given us plenty of merriment, I am sure," said Fred, "and it would be ungrateful not to drink his health. Here is a glass of mulled wine ready to our hand at the moment; and I say, 'Uncle Scrooge!' "

"Well! Uncle Scrooge!" they cried.

"A merry Christmas and a Happy New Year to the old man, whatever he is!" said Scrooge's nephew. "He wouldn't take it from me, but may he have it, nevertheless. Uncle Scrooge!"

Uncle Scrooge had imperceptibly become so gay and light of heart, that he would have pledged the unconscious company in return, and thanked them in an inaudible speech, if the Ghost had given him time. But the whole scene passed off in the breath of the last word spoken by his nephew; and he and the Spirit were again upon their travels.

Much they saw, and far they went, and many homes they visited, but always with a happy end. The Spirit stood beside sick-beds, and they were cheerful; on foreign lands, and they were close at home; by struggling men, and they were patient in their greater hope; by poverty, and it was rich. In almshouse, hospital, and jail, in misery's every refuge, where vain man in his little brief authority had not made fast the door, and barred the Spirit out, he left his blessing, and taught Scrooge his precepts.

It was a long night, if it were only a night; but Scrooge had his doubts of this, because the Christmas Holidays appeared to be condensed into the space of time they passed together. It was strange, too, that while Scrooge remained unaltered in his outward form, the Ghost grew older, clearly older. Scrooge had observed this change, but never spoke of it, until they left a children's Twelfth Night party, when, looking at the Spirit as they stood together in an open place, he noticed that its hair was grey.

"Are spirits' lives so short?" asked Scrooge.

"My life upon this globe, is very brief," replied the Ghost. "It ends to-night."

"To-night!" cried Scrooge.

"To-night at midnight. Hark! The time is drawing near."

The chimes were ringing the three quarters past eleven at that moment.

"Forgive me if I am not justified in what I ask," said Scrooge, looking intently at the Spirit's robe, "but I see something strange, and not belonging to yourself, protruding from your skirts. Is it a foot or a claw?"

"It might be a claw, for the flesh there is upon it," was the Spirit's sorrowful reply. "Look here."

From the foldings of its robe, it brought two children; wretched, abject, frightful, hideous, miserable. They knelt down at its feet, and clung upon the outside of its garment.

"Oh, Man! look here. Look, look, down here!" exclaimed the Ghost.

They were a boy and girl. Yellow, meagre, ragged, scowling, wolfish; but prostrate, too, in their humility. Where graceful youth should have filled their features out, and touched them with its freshest tints, a stale and shrivelled hand, like that of age, had pinched, and twisted them, and pulled them into shreds. Where angels might have sat enthroned, devils lurked, and glared out menacing. No change, no degradation, no perversion of humanity, in any grade, through all the mysteries of wonderful creation, has monsters half so horrible and dread.

Scrooge started back, appalled. Having them shown to him in this way, he tried to say they were fine children, but the words choked themselves, rather than be parties to a lie of such enormous magnitude.

"Spirit! are they yours?" Scrooge could say no more.

"They are Man's," said the Spirit, looking down upon them. "And they cling to me, appealing from their fathers. This boy is Ignorance. This girl is Want. Beware them both, and all of their degree, but most of all beware this boy, for on his brow I see that written which is Doom, unless the writing be erased. Deny it!" cried the Spirit, stretching out its hand towards the city. "Slander those who tell it ye! Admit it for your factious purposes, and make it worse. And abide the end!"

"Have they no refuge or resource?" cried Scrooge.

"Are there no prisons?" said the Spirit, turning on him for the last time with his own words. "Are there no workhouses?"

The bell struck twelve.

Scrooge looked about him for the Ghost, and saw it not. As the last stroke ceased to vibrate, he remembered the prediction of old Jacob Marley, and lifting up his eyes, beheld a solemn Phantom, draped and hooded, coming, like a mist along the ground, towards him.

Stave Four

THE LAST OF THE SPIRITS

THE Phantom slowly, gravely, silently approached. When it came near him, Scrooge bent down upon his knee; for in the very air through which this Spirit moved it seemed to scatter gloom and mystery.

It was shrouded in a deep black garment, which concealed its head, its face, its form, and left nothing of it visible save one outstretched hand. But for this it would have been difficult to detach its figure from the night, and separate it from the darkness by which it was surrounded.

He felt that it was tall and stately when it came beside him, and that its mysterious presence filled him with a solemn dread. He knew no more, for the Spirit neither spoke nor moved.

"I am in the presence of the Ghost of Christmas Yet to Come?" said Scrooge.

The Spirit answered not, but pointed onward with its hand.

"You are about to show me shadows of the things that

They Were a Boy and Girl—Yellow, Meagre, Ragged

have not happened, but will happen in the time before us," Scrooge pursued. "Is that so, Spirit?"

The upper portion of the garment was contracted for an instant in its folds, as if the Spirit had inclined its head That was the only answer he received.

Although well used to ghostly company by this time, Scrooge feared the silent shape so much that his legs trembled beneath him, and he found that he could hardly stand when he prepared to follow it. The Spirit paused a moment, as observing his condition, and giving him time to recover.

But Scrooge was all the worse for this. It thrilled him with a vague uncertain horror, to know that behind the dusky shroud, there were ghostly eyes intently fixed upon him, while he, though he stretched his own to the utmost, could see nothing but a spectral hand and one great heap of black.

"Ghost of the Future!" he exclaimed, "I fear you more than any spectre I have seen. But as I know your purpose is to do me good, and as I hope to live to be another man from what I was, I am prepared to bear you company, and do it with a thankful heart. Will you not speak to me?"

It gave him no reply. The hand was pointed straight before them.

"Lead on!" said Scrooge. "Lead on! The night is waning fast, and it is precious time to me, I know. Lead on, Spirit!"

The Phantom moved away as it had come towards him. Scrooge followed in the shadow of its dress, which bore him up, he thought, and carried him along.

They scarcely seemed to enter the city; for the city rather seemed to spring up about them, and encompass them of its own act. But there they were, in the heart of it; on 'Change, amongst the merchants; who hurried up and down, and chinked the money in their pockets, and conversed in groups, and looked at their watches, and trifled thoughtfully with their great gold seals; and so forth, as Scrooge had seen them often.

The Spirit stopped beside one little knot of business men. Observing that the hand was pointed to them, Scrooge advanced to listen to their talk.

"No," said a great fat man with a monstrous chin, "I don'τ know much about it, either way. I only know he's dead."

"When did he die?" inquired another.

"Last night, I believe."

"Why, what was the matter with him?" asked a third, taking a vast quantity of snuff out of a vèry large snuff-box. "I thought he'd never die."

"God knows," said the first, with a yawn.

"What has he done with his money?" asked a red-faced gentleman with a pendulous excrescence on the end of his nose, that shook like the gills of a turkey-cock.

"I haven't heard," said the man with the large chin, yawning again. "Left it to his company, perhaps. He hasn't left it to *me*. That's all I know."

This pleasantry was received with a general laugh.

"It's likely to be a very cheap funeral," said the same speaker; "for upon my life I don't know of anybody to go to it. Suppose we make up a party and volunteer?"

"I don't mind going if a lunch is provided," observed the gentleman with the excrescence on his nose. "But I must be fed, if I make one."

Another laugh.

"Well, I am the most disinterested among you, after all," said the first speaker, "for I never wear black gloves, and I never eat lunch. But I'll offer to go, if anybody else will. When I come to think of it, I'm not at all sure that I wasn't his most particular friend; for we used to stop and speak whenever we met. Bye, bye!"

Speakers and listeners strolled away, and mixed with other groups. Scrooge knew the men, and looked towards the Spirit for an explanation.

The Phantom glided on into a street. Its finger pointed to two persons meeting. Scrooge listened again, thinking that the explanation might lie here.

He knew these men, also, perfectly. They were men of business: very wealthy, and of great importance. He had made a point always of standing well in their esteem: in a business point of view, that is; strictly in a business point of view.

"How are you?" said one.

"How are you?" returned the other.

"Well!" said the first. "Old Scratch has got his own at last, hey?"

"So I am told," returned the second. "Cold, isn't it?"

"Seasonable for Christmas time. You 're not a skater, I suppose?"

"No. No. Something else to think of. Good morning!"

Not another word. That was their meeting, their conversation, and their parting.

Scrooge was at first inclined to be surprised that the Spirit should attach importance to conversations apparently so trivial; but feeling assured that they must have some hidden purpose, he set himself to consider what it was likely to be. They could scarcely be supposed to have any bearing on the death of Jacob, his old partner, for that was Past, and this Ghost's province was the Future. Nor could he think of any one immediately connected with himself, to whom he could apply them. But nothing doubting that to whomsoever they applied they had some latent moral for his own improvement, he resolved to treasure up every word he heard, and everything he saw; and especially to observe the shadow of himself when it appeared. For he had an expectation that the conduct of his future self would give him the clue he missed, and would render the solution of these riddles easy.

He looked about in that very place for his own image; but another man stood in his accustomed corner, and though the clock pointed to his usual time of day for being there, he saw no likeness of himself among the multitudes that poured in through the Porch. It gave him little surprise, however; for he had been revolving in his mind a change of life, and thought and hoped he saw his new-born resolutions carried out in this.

Quiet and dark, beside him stood the Phantom, with its outstretched hand. When he roused himself from his

thoughtful quest, he fancied from the turn of the hand, and
its situation in reference to himself, that the Unseen Eyes
were looking at him keenly. It made him shudder, and feel
very cold.

They left the busy scene, and went into an obscure part
of the town, where Scrooge had never penetrated before, although he recognised its situation, and its bad repute. The
ways were foul and narrow; the shops and houses wretched;
the people, half-naked, drunken, slipshod, ugly. Alleys and
archways, like so many cesspools, disgorged their offences
of smell, and dirt, and life, upon the straggling streets;
and the whole quarter reeked with crime, with filth, and
misery.

Far in this den of infamous resort, there was a low-
browed, beetling shop, below a pent-house roof, where iron,
old rags, bottles, bones, and greasy offal, were bought. Upon
the floor within, were piled up heaps of rusty keys, nails,
chains, hinges, files, scales, weights, and refuse iron of all
kinds. Secrets that few would like to scrutinise were bred and
hidden in mountains of unseemly rags, masses of corrupted
fat, and sepulchres of bones. Sitting in among the wares he
dealt in, by a charcoal stove, made of old bricks, was a grey-
haired rascal, nearly seventy years of age; who had screened
himself from the cold air without, by a frousy curtaining of
miscellaneous tatters, hung upon a line; and smoked his pipe
in all the luxury of calm retirement.

Scrooge and the Phantom came into the presence of this
man, just as a woman with a heavy bundle slunk into the
shop. But she had scarcely entered, when another woman,
similarly laden, came in too; and she was closely followed
by a man in faded black, who was no less startled by the
sight of them, than they had been upon the recognition of
each other. After a short period of blank astonishment, in
which the old man with the pipe had joined them, they all
three burst into a laugh.

"Let the charwoman alone to be the first!" cried she who
had entered first. "Let the laundress alone to be the second;
and let the undertaker's man alone to be the third. Look

here, old Joe, here's a chance! If we haven't all three met here without meaning it!"

"You couldn't have met in a better place," said old Joe, removing his pipe from his mouth. "Come into the parlour. You were made free of it long ago, you know; and the other two an't strangers. Stop till I shut the door of the shop. Ah! How it skreeks! There an't such a rusty bit of metal in the place as its own hinges, I believe; and I 'm sure there 's no such old bones here, as mine. Ha, ha! We 're all suitable to our calling, we 're well matched. Come into the parlour. Come into the parlour."

The parlour was the space behind the screen of rags. The old man raked the fire together with an old stair-rod, and having trimmed his smoky lamp (for it was night), with the stem of his pipe, put it in his mouth again.

While he did this, the woman who had already spoken threw her bundle on the floor, and sat down in a flaunting manner on a stool; crossing her elbows on her knees, and looking with a bold defiance at the other two.

"What odds then! What odds, Mrs. Dilber?" said the woman. "Every person has a right to take care of themselves. *He* always did."

"That 's true, indeed!" said the laundress. "No man more so."

"Why then, don't stand staring as if you was afraid, woman; who 's the wiser? We 're not going to pick holes in each other's coats, I suppose?"

"No, indeed!" said Mrs. Dilber and the man together. "We should hope not."

"Very well, then!" cried the woman. "That 's enough. Who 's the worse for the loss of a few things like these? Not a dead man, I suppose."

"No, indeed," said Mrs. Dilber, laughing.

"If he wanted to keep 'em after he was dead, a wicked old screw," pursued the woman, "why wasn't he natural in his lifetime? If he had been, he 'd have had somebody to look after him when he was struck with Death, instead of lying gasping out his last there, alone by himself."

"It 's the truest word that ever was spoke," said Mrs Dilber. "It 's a judgment on him."

"I wish it was a little heavier judgment," replied the woman; "and it should have been, you may depend upon it, if I could have laid my hands on anything else Open that bundle, old Joe, and let me know the value of it. Speak out plain. I 'm not afraid to be the first, nor afraid for them to see it. We knew pretty well that we were helping ourselves, before we met here, I believe. It 's no sin. Open the bundle, Joe."

But the gallantry of her friends would not allow of this; and the man in faded black, mounting the breach first, produced *his* plunder. It was not extensive. A seal or two, a pencil-case, a pair of sleeve-buttons, and a brooch of no great value, were all. They were severally examined and appraised by old Joe, who chalked the sums he was disposed to give for each, upon the wall, and added them up into a total when he found there was nothing more to come.

"That 's your account," said Joe, "and I wouldn't give another sixpence, if I was to be boiled for not doing it. Who 's next?"

Mrs. Dilber was next. Sheets and towels, a little wearing apparel, two old-fashioned silver teaspoons, a pair of sugar-tongs, and a few boots. Her account was stated on the wall in the same manner.

"I always give too much to ladies. It 's a weakness of mine, and that 's the way I ruin myself," said old Joe. "That 's your account. If you asked me for another penny, and made it an open question, I 'd repent of being so liberal and knock off half-a-crown."

"And now undo *my* bundle, Joe," said the first woman.

Joe went down on his knees for the greater convenience of opening it, and having unfastened a great many knots, dragged out a large and heavy roll of some dark stuff.

"What do you call this?" said Joe. "Bed-curtains!"

"Ah!" returned the woman, laughing and leaning forward on her crossed arms. "Bed-curtains!"

"You don't mean to say you took 'em down, rings and all, with him lying there?" said Joe.

"Yes I do," replied the woman. "Why not?"

"You were born to make your fortune," said Joe, "and you'll certainly do it."

"I certainly shan't hold my hand, when I can get anything in it by reaching it out, for the sake of such a man as He was, I promise you, Joe," returned the woman coolly. "Don't drop that oil upon the blankets, now."

"His blankets?" asked Joe.

"Whose else's do you think?" replied the woman. "He isn't likely to take cold without 'em, I dare say."

"I hope he didn't die of anything catching? Eh?" said old Joe, stopping in his work, and looking up.

"Don't you be afraid of that," returned the woman. "I an't so fond of his company that I'd loiter about him for such things, if he did. Ah! you may look through that shirt till your eyes ache; but you won't find a hole in it, nor a threadbare place. It's the best he had, and a fine one too. They'd have wasted it, if it hadn't been for me."

"What do you call wasting of it?" asked old Joe.

"Putting it on him to be buried in, to be sure," replied the woman with a laugh. "Somebody was fool enough to do it, but I took it off again. If calico an't good enough for such a purpose, it isn't good enough for anything. It's quite as becoming to the body. He can't look uglier than he did in that one."

Scrooge listened to this dialogue in horror. As they sat grouped about their spoil, in the scanty light afforded by the old man's lamp, he viewed them with a detestation and disgust, which could hardly have been greater, though they had been obscene demons, marketing the corpse itself.

"Ha, ha!" laughed the same woman, when old Joe, producing a flannel bag with money in it, told out their several gains upon the ground. "This is the end of it, you see! He frightened every one away from him when he was alive, to profit us when he was dead! Ha, ha, ha!"

"Spirit!" said Scrooge, shuddering from head to foot. "I see, I see. The case of this unhappy man might be my own. My life tends that way, now. Merciful Heaven, what is this!"

He recoiled in terror, for the scene had changed, and now he almost touched a bed: a bare, uncurtained bed: on which, beneath a ragged sheet, there lay a something covered up, which, though it was dumb, announced itself in awful language.

The room was very dark, too dark to be observed with any accuracy, though Scrooge glanced round it in obedience to a secret impulse, anxious to know what kind of room it was. A pale light, rising in the outer air, fell straight upon the bed; and on it, plundered and bereft, unwatched, unwept, uncared for, was the body of this man.

Scrooge glanced towards the Phantom. Its steady hand was pointed to the head. The cover was so carelessly adjusted that the slightest raising of it, the motion of a finger upon Scrooge's part, would have disclosed the face. He thought of it, felt how easy it would be to do, and longed to do it; but had no more power to withdraw the veil than to dismiss the spectre at his side.

Oh cold, cold, rigid, dreadful Death, set up thine altar here, and dress it with such terrors as thou hast at thy command: for this is thy dominion! But of the loved, revered, and honoured head, thou canst not turn one hair to thy dread purposes, or make one feature odious. It is not that the hand is heavy and will fall down when released; it is not that the heart and pulse are still; but that the hand WAS open, generous, and true; the heart brave, warm, and tender; and the pulse a man's. Strike, Shadow, strike! And see his good deeds springing from the wound, to sow the world with life immortal!

No voice pronounced these words in Scrooge's ears, and yet he heard them when he looked upon the bed. He thought, if this man could be raised up now, what would be his foremost thoughts? Avarice, hard-dealing, griping cares? They have brought him to a rich end, truly!

He lay, in the dark empty house, with not a man, a woman, or a child, to say that he was kind to me in this or that, and for the memory of one kind word I will be kind to him. A cat was tearing at the door, and there was a sound of gnawing rats beneath the hearth-stone. What *they* wanted in the room of death, and why they were so restless and disturbed, Scrooge did not dare to think.

"Spirit!" he said, "this is a fearful place. In leaving it, I shall not leave its lesson, trust me. Let us go!"

Still the Ghost pointed with an unmoved finger to the head.

"I understand you," Scrooge returned, "and I would do it, if I could. But I have not the power, Spirit. I have not the power."

Again it seemed to look upon him.

"If there is any person in the town, who feels emotion caused by this man's death," said Scrooge quite agonised, "show that person to me, Spirit, I beseech you!"

The Phantom spread its dark robe before him for a moment, like a wing; and withdrawing it, revealed a room by daylight, where a mother and her children were.

She was expecting some one, and with anxious eagerness; for she walked up and down the room; started at every sound; looked out from the window; glanced at the clock; tried, but in vain, to work with her needle; and could hardly bear the voices of the children in their play.

At length the long-expected knock was heard. She hurried to the door, and met her husband; a man whose face was careworn and depressed, though he was young. There was a remarkable expression in it now; a kind of serious delight of which he felt ashamed, and which he struggled to repress.

He sat down to the dinner that had been hoarding for him by the fire; and when she asked him faintly what news (which was not until after a long silence), he appeared embarrassed how to answer.

"Is it good," she said, "or bad?"—to help him.

"Bad," he answered.

"We are quite ruined?"

"No. There is hope yet, Caroline."

"If *he* relents," she said, amazed, "there is! Nothing is past hope if such a miracle has happened."

"He is past relenting," said her husband. "He is dead."

She was a mild and patient creature if her face spoke truth; but she was thankful in her soul to hear it, and she said so, with clasped hands. She prayed forgiveness the next moment, and was sorry; but the first was the emotion of her heart.

"What the half-drunken woman whom I told you of last night, said to me, when I tried to see him and obtain a week's delay; and what I thought was a mere excuse to avoid me; turns out to have been quite true. He was not only very ill, but dying, then."

"To whom will our debt be transferred?"

"I don't know. But before that time we shall be ready with the money; and even though we were not, it would be a bad fortune indeed to find so merciless a creditor in his successor. We may sleep to-night with light hearts, Caroline!"

Yes. Soften it as they would, their hearts were lighter. The children's faces, hushed and clustered round to hear what they so little understood, were brighter; and it was a happier house for this man's death! The only emotion that the Ghost could show him, caused by the event, was one of pleasure.

"Let me see some tenderness connected with a death," said Scrooge; "or that dark chamber, Spirit, which we left just now, will be for ever present to me."

The Ghost conducted him through several streets familiar to his feet; and as they went along, Scrooge looked here and there to find himself, but nowhere was he to be seen. They entered poor Bob Cratchit's house; the dwelling he had visited before; and found the mother and the children seated round the fire.

Quiet. Very quiet. The noisy little Cratchits were as still as statues in one corner, and sat looking up at Peter, who had a book before him. The mother and her daughters were engaged in sewing. But surely they were very quiet!

" 'And He took a child and set him in the midst of them.' "

Where had Scrooge heard those words? He had not dreamed them. The boy must have read them out, as he and the Spirit crossed the threshold. Why did he not go on?

The mother laid her work upon the table, and put her hand up to her face.

"The colour hurts my eyes," she said.

The colour? Ah, poor Tiny Tim!

"They 're better now again," said Cratchit's wife. "It makes them weak by candlelight; and I wouldn't show weak eyes to your father when he comes home, for the world. It must be near his time."

"Past it rather," Peter answered, shutting up his book. "But I think he has walked a little slower than he used, these few last evenings, mother."

They were very quiet again. At last she said, and in a steady, cheerful voice, that only faltered once:

"I have known him walk with—I have known him walk with Tiny Tim upon his shoulder, very fast indeed."

"And so have I," cried Peter. "Often."

"And so have I," exclaimed another. So had all.

"But he was very light to carry," she resumed, intent upon her work, "and his father loved him so, that it was no trouble: no trouble. And there is your father at the door!"

She hurried out to meet him; and little Bob in his comforter—he had need of it, poor fellow—came in. His tea was ready for him on the hob, and they all tried who should help him to it most. Then the two young Cratchits got upon his knees and laid, each child a little cheek, against his face, as if they said, "Don 't mind it, father! Don 't be grieved!"

Bob was very cheerful with them, and spoke pleasantly to all the family. He looked at the work upon the table, and praised the industry and speed of Mrs. Cratchit and the girls. They would be done long before Sunday, he said.

"Sunday! You went to-day, then, Robert?" said his wife.

"Yes, my dear," returned Bob. "I wish you could have gone. It would have done you good to see how green a place it is. But you'll see it often. I promised him that I would walk there on a Sunday. My little, little child!" cried Bob. "My little child!"

He broke down all at once. He couldn't help it. If he could have helped it, he and his child would have been farther apart perhaps than they were.

He left the room, and went upstairs into the room above, which was lighted cheerfully, and hung with Christmas. There was a chair set close beside the child, and there were signs of some one having been there, lately. Poor Bob sat down in it, and when he had thought a little and composed himself, he kissed the little face. He was reconciled to what had happened, and went down again quite happy.

They drew about the fire, and talked; the girls and mother working still. Bob told them of the extraordinary kindness of Mr. Scrooge's nephew, whom he had scarcely seen but once, and who, meeting him in the street that day, and seeing that he looked a little—"just a little down you know," said Bob, inquired what had happened to distress him. "On which," said Bob, "for he is the pleasantest-spoken gentleman you ever heard, I told him. 'I am heartily sorry for it, Mr. Cratchit,' he said, 'and heartily sorry for your good wife.' By the bye, how he ever knew *that*, I don't know."

"Knew what, my dear?"

"Why, that you were a good wife," replied Bob.

"Everybody knows that!" said Peter.

"Very well observed, my boy!" cried Bob. "I hope they do. 'Heartily sorry,' he said, 'for your good wife. If I can be of service to you in any way,' he said, giving me his card, 'that's where I live. Pray come to me.' Now it wasn't," cried Bob, "for the sake of anything he might be able to do for us, so much as for his kind way, that this was quite delightful. It really seemed as if he had known our Tiny Tim and felt with us."

"I'm sure he's a good soul!" said Mrs. Cratchit.

"You would be surer of it, my dear," returned Bob, "if you saw and spoke to him. I shouldn't be at all surprised—mark what I say—if he got Peter a better situation."

"Only hear that, Peter," said Mrs. Cratchit.

"And then," cried one of the girls, "Peter will be keeping company with some one, and setting up for himself."

"Get along with you!" retorted Peter, grinning.

"It's just as likely as not," said Bob, "one of these days; though there's plenty of time for that, my dear. But however and whenever we part from one another, I am sure we shall none of us forget poor Tiny Tim—shall we—or this first parting that there was among us?"

"Never, father!" cried they all.

"And I know," said Bob, "I know, my dears, that when we recollect how patient and how mild he was; although he was a little, little child; we shall not quarrel easily among ourselves, and forget poor Tiny Tim in doing it."

"No, never, father!" they all cried again.

"I am very happy," said little Bob, "I am very happy!"

Mrs. Cratchit kissed him, his daughters kissed him, the two young Cratchits kissed him, and Peter and himself shook hands. Spirit of Tiny Tim, thy childish essence was from God!

"Spectre," said Scrooge, "something informs me that our parting moment is at hand. I know it, but I know not how. Tell me what man that was whom we saw lying dead?"

The Ghost of Christmas Yet To Come conveyed him, as before—though at a different time, he thought: indeed, there seemed no order in these latter visions, save that they were in the Future—into the resorts of business men, but showed him not himself. Indeed, the Spirit did not stay for anything, but went straight on, as to the end just now desired, until besought by Scrooge to tarry for a moment.

"This court," said Scrooge, "through which we hurry now, is where my place of occupation is, and has been for a length of time. I see the house. Let me behold what I shall be, in days to come!"

The Spirit stopped; the hand was pointed elsewhere.

"The house is yonder," Scrooge exclaimed. "Why do you point away?"

The inexorable finger underwent no change.

Scrooge hastened to the window of his office, and looked in. It was an office still, but not his. The furniture was not the same, and the figure in the chair was not himself. The Phantom pointed as before.

He joined it once again, and wondering why and whither he had gone, accompanied it until they reached an iron gate. He paused to look round before entering.

A churchyard. Here, then, the wretched man whose name he had now to learn, lay underneath the ground. It was a worthy place. Walled in by houses; overrun by grass and weeds, the growth of vegetation's death, not life; choked up with too much burying; fat with repleted appetite. A worthy place!

The Spirit stood among the graves, and pointed down to One. He advanced towards it trembling. The Phantom was exactly as it had been, but he dreaded that he saw new meaning in its solemn shape.

"Before I draw nearer to that stone to which you point," said Scrooge, "answer me one question. Are these the shadows of the things that Will be, or are they shadows of things that May be, only?"

Still the Ghost pointed downward to the grave by which it stood.

"Men's courses will foreshadow certain ends, to which, if persevered in, they must lead," said Scrooge. "But if the courses be departed from, the ends will change. Say it is thus with what you show me?"

The Spirit was immovable as ever.

Scrooge crept towards it, trembling as he went; and following the finger, read upon the stone of the neglected grave his own name, EBENEZER SCROOGE.

"Am *I* that man who lay upon the bed?" he cried, upon his knees.

The finger pointed from the grave to him, and back again.

The Spirit Stood Among the Graves

"No, Spirit! Oh no, no!"

The finger still was there.

"Spirit!" he cried, tight clutching at its robe, "hear me! I am not the man I was. I will not be the man I must have been but for this intercourse. Why show me this, if I am past all hope!"

For the first time the hand appeared to shake.

"Good Spirit," he pursued, as down upon the ground he fell before it: "Your nature intercedes for me, and pities me. Assure me that I yet may change these shadows you have shown me, by an altered life!"

The kind hand trembled.

"I will honour Christmas in my heart, and try to keep it all the year. I will live in the Past, the Present, and the Future. The Spirits of all Three shall strive within me. I will not shut out the lessons that they teach. Oh, tell me I may sponge away the writing on this stone!"

In his agony, he caught the spectral hand. It sought to free itself, but he was strong in his entreaty, and detained it. The Spirit, stronger yet, repulsed him.

Holding up his hands in a last prayer to have his fate reversed, he saw an alteration in the Phantom's hood and dress. It shrunk, collapsed, dwindled down into a bedpost.

Stave Five

THE END OF IT

YES! and the bedpost was his own. The bed was his own, the room was his own. Best and happiest of all, the Time before him was his own, to make amends in!

"I will live in the Past, the Present, and the Future!" Scrooge repeated, as he scrambled out of bed. "The Spirits of all Three shall strive within me. Oh Jacob Marley! Heaven, and the Christmas Time be praised for this! I say it on my knees, old Jacob, on my knees!"

He was so fluttered and so glowing with his good intentions, that his broken voice would scarcely answer to his call. He had been sobbing violently in his conflict with the Spirit, and his face was wet with tears.

"They are not torn down," cried Scrooge, folding one of his bed-curtains in his arms, "they are not torn down, rings and all. They are here—I am here—the shadows of the things that would have been, may be dispelled. They will be. I know they will!"

His hands were busy with his garments all this time; turning them inside out, putting them on upside down, tearing them, mislaying them, making them parties to every kind of extravagance.

"I don't know what to do!" cried Scrooge, laughing and crying in the same breath; and making a perfect Laocoön of himself with his stockings. "I am as light as a feather, I am as happy as an angel, I am as merry as a schoolboy. I am as giddy as a drunken man. A merry Christmas to everybody! A happy New Year to all the world. Hallo here! Whoop! Hallo!"

He had frisked into the sitting-room, and was now standing there: perfectly winded.

"There's the saucepan that the gruel was in!" cried Scrooge, starting off again, and going round the fireplace. "There's the door, by which the Ghost of Jacob Marley entered! There's the corner where the Ghost of Christmas Present, sat! There's the window where I saw the wandering Spirits! It's all right, it's all true, it all happened. Ha, ha, ha!"

Really, for a man who had been out of practice for so many years, it was a splendid laugh, a most illustrious laugh. The father of a long, long line of brilliant laughs!

"I don't know what day of the month it is!" said Scrooge. "I don't know how long I've been among the Spirits. I don't know anything. I'm quite a baby. Never mind. I don't care. I'd rather be a baby. Hallo! Whoop! Hallo here!"

He was checked in his transports by the churches ringing

out the lustiest peals he had ever heard. Clash, clang, hammer; ding, dong, bell. Bell, dong, ding; hammer, clang, clash! Oh, glorious, glorious!

Running to the window, he opened it and put out his head. No fog, no mist; clear, bright, jovial, stirring, cold; cold, piping for the blood to dance to; Golden sunlight; Heavenly sky; sweet fresh air; merry bells. Oh, glorious. Glorious!

"What's to-day?" cried Scrooge, calling downward to a boy in Sunday clothes, who perhaps had loitered in to look about him.

"Eh?" returned the boy, with all his might of wonder.

"What's to-day, my fine fellow?" said Scrooge.

"To-day!" replied the boy. "Why, Christmas Day."

"It's Christmas Day!" said Scrooge to himself. "I haven't missed it. The Spirits have done it all in one night. They can do anything they like. Of course they can. Of course they can. Hallo, my fine fellow!"

"Hallo!" returned the boy.

"Do you know the Poulterer's, in the next street but one, at the corner?" Scrooge inquired.

"I should hope I did," replied the lad.

"An intelligent boy!" said Scrooge. "A remarkable boy! Do you know whether they've sold the prize Turkey that was hanging up there?—Not the little prize Turkey: the big one?"

"What, the one as big as me?" returned the boy.

"What a delightful boy!" said Scrooge. "It's a pleasure to talk to him. Yes, my buck!"

"It's hanging there now," replied the boy.

"Is it?" said Scrooge. "Go and buy it."

"Walk-er!" exclaimed the boy.

"No, no," said Scrooge, "I am in earnest. Go and buy it, and tell 'em to bring it here, that I may give them the direction where to take it. Come back with the man, and I'll give you a shilling. Come back with him in less than five minutes and I'll give you half-a-crown!"

The boy was off like a shot. He must have had a steady

hand at a trigger who could have got a shot off half so fast.

"I'll send it to Bob Cratchit's!" whispered Scrooge, rubbing his hands, and splitting with a laugh. "He shan't know who sends it. It's twice the size of Tiny Tim. Joe Miller never made such a joke as sending it to Bob's will be!"

The hand in which he wrote the address was not a steady one, but write it he did, somehow, and went downstairs to open the street door, ready for the coming of the poulterer's man. As he stood there, waiting his arrival, the knocker caught his eye.

"I shall love it, as long as I live!" cried Scrooge, patting it with his hand. "I scarcely ever looked at it before. What an honest expression it has in its face! It's a wonderful knocker!—Here's the Turkey. Hello! Whoop! How are you! Merry Christmas!"

It *was* a Turkey! He could never have stood upon his legs, that bird. He would have snapped 'em short off in a minute, like sticks of sealing-wax.

"Why, it's impossible to carry that to Camden Town," said Scrooge. "You must have a cab."

The chuckle with which he said this, and the chuckle with which he paid for the Turkey, and the chuckle with which he paid for the cab, and the chuckle with which he recompensed the boy, were only to be exceeded by the chuckle with which he sat down breathless in his chair again, and chuckled till he cried.

Shaving was not an easy task, for his hand continued to shake very much; and shaving requires attention, even when you don't dance while you are at it. But if he had cut the end of his nose off, he would have put a piece of sticking-plaster over it, and been quite satisfied.

He dressed himself "all in his best," and at last got out into the streets. The people were by this time pouring forth, as he had seen them with the Ghost of Christmas Present; and walking with his hands behind him, Scrooge regarded every one with a delighted smile. He looked so irresistibly pleasant, in a word, that three or four good-humoured fellows said, "Good-morning, sir! A merry Christmas to you!"

And Scrooge said often afterwards, that of all the blithe sounds he had ever heard, those were the blithest in his ears.

He had not gone far, when coming on towards him he beheld the portly gentleman, who had walked into his counting-house the day before, and said, "Scrooge and Marley's, I believe?" It sent a pang across his heart to think how this old gentleman would look upon him when they met; but he knew what path lay straight before him, and he took it.

"My dear sir," said Scrooge, quickening his pace, and taking the old gentleman by both his hands. "How do you do? I hope you succeeded yesterday. It was very kind of you. A merry Christmas to you, sir!"

"Mr. Scrooge?"

"Yes," said Scrooge. "That is my name, and I fear it may not be pleasant to you. Allow me to ask your pardon. And will you have the goodness"—here Scrooge whispered in his ear.

"Lord bless me!" cried the gentleman, as if his breath were taken away. "My dear Mr. Scrooge, are you serious?"

"If you please," said Scrooge. "Not a farthing less. A great many back-payments are included in it, I assure you. Will you do me that favour?"

"My dear sir," said the other, shaking hands with him. "I don't know what to say to such munifi—"

"Don't say anything, please," retorted Scrooge. "Come and see me. Will you come and see me?"

"I will!" cried the old gentleman. And it was clear he meant to do it.

"Thank 'ee," said Scrooge. "I am much obliged to you. I thank you fifty times. Bless you!"

He went to church, and walked about the streets, and watched the people hurrying to and fro, and patted children on the head, and questioned beggars, and looked down into the kitchens of houses, and up to the windows, and found that everything could yield him pleasure. He had never dreamed that any walk—that anything—could give him so much happiness. In the afternoon he turned his steps towards his nephew's house.

He passed the door a dozen times, before he had the courage to go up and knock. But he made a dash, and did it:

"Is your master at home, my dear?" said Scrooge to the girl. Nice girl! Very.

"Yes, sir."

"Where is he, my love?" said Scrooge.

"He's in the dining-room, sir, along with mistress. I'll show you upstairs, if you please."

"Thank 'ee. He knows me," said Scrooge, with his hand already on the dining-room lock. "I'll go in here, my dear."

He turned it gently, and sidled his face in, round the door. They were looking at the table (which was spread out in great array); for these young housekeepers are always nervous on such points, and like to see that everything is right.

"Fred!" said Scrooge.

Dear heart alive, how his niece by marriage started! Scrooge had forgotten, for the moment, about her sitting in the corner with the footstool, or he wouldn't have done it, on any account.

"Why bless my soul!" cried Fred, "who's that?"

"It's I. Your uncle Scrooge. I have come to dinner. Will you let me in, Fred?"

Let him in! It is a mercy he didn't shake his arm off. He was at home in five minutes. Nothing could be heartier. His niece looked just the same. So did Topper when *he* came. So did the plump sister, when *she* came. So did every one when *they* came. Wonderful party, wonderful games, wonderful unanimity, won-der-ful happiness!

But he was early at the office next morning. Oh, he was early there. If he could only be there first, and catch Bob Cratchit coming late! That was the thing he had set his heart upon.

And he did it; yes he did! The clock struck nine. No Bob. A quarter past. No Bob. He was full eighteen minutes and a half behind his time. Scrooge sat with his door wide open, that he might see him come into the Tank.

His hat was off, before he opened the door; his comforter too. He was on his stool in a jiffy; driving away with his pen, as if he were trying to overtake nine o'clock.

"Hallo!" growled Scrooge, in his accustomed voice, as near as he could feign it. "What do you mean by coming here at this time of day?"

"I am very sorry, sir," said Bob. "I *am* behind my time."

"You are?" repeated Scrooge. "Yes. I think you are. Step this way, sir, if you please."

"It's only once a year, sir," pleaded Bob, appearing from the Tank. "It shall not be repeated. I was making rather merry yesterday, sir."

"Now, I'll tell you what, my friend," said Scrooge, "I am not going to stand this sort of thing any longer. And there-fore," he continued, leaping from his stool, and giving Bob such a dig in the waistcoat that he staggered back into the Tank again: "and therefore I am about to raise your salary!"

Bob trembled, and got a little nearer to the ruler. He had a momentary idea of knocking Scrooge down with it, hold-ing him, and calling to the people in the court for help and a strait-waistcoat.

"A merry Christmas, Bob!" said Scrooge, with an earn-estness that could not be mistaken, as he clapped him on the back. "A merrier Christmas, Bob, my good fellow, than I have given you for many a year! I'll raise your salary, and endeavour to assist your struggling family, and we will dis-cuss your affairs this very afternoon, over a Christmas bowl of smoking bishop, Bob! Make up the fires, and buy an-other coal-scuttle before you dot another i, Bob Cratchit!"

Scrooge was better than his word. He did it all, and in-finitely more; and to Tiny Tim, who did NOT die he was a second father. He became as good a friend, as good a master, and as good a man, as the good old city knew, or any other good old city, town, or borough, in the good old world. Some people laughed to see the alteration in him, but he let them laugh, and little heeded them; for he was wise enough to know that nothing ever happened on this globe, for good, at which some people did not have their fill of laughter in the outset; and knowing that such as these would be blind anyway, he thought it quite as well that they should wrinkle up their eyes in grins, as have the malady in less attractive forms. His own heart laughed: and that was quite enough for him.

He had no further intercourse with Spirits, but lived upon the Total Abstinence Principle, ever afterwards; and it was always said of him, that he knew how to keep Christmas well, if any man alive possessed the knowledge. May that be truly said of us, and all of us! And so, as Tiny Tim observed, God bless Us, Every One!

The Chimes

First Quarter

THERE are not many people—and as it is desirable that a story-teller and a story-reader should establish a mutual understanding as soon as possible, I beg it to be noticed that I confine this observation neither to young people nor to little people, but extend it to all conditions of people: little and big, young and old: yet growing up, or already growing down again—there are not, I say, many people who would care to sleep in a church. I don't mean at sermon-time in warm weather (when the thing has actually been done, once or twice), but in the night, and alone. A great multitude of persons will be violently astonished, I know, by this position, in the broad bold Day. But it applies to Night. It must be argued by night, and I will undertake to maintain it successfully on any gusty winter's night appointed for the purpose, with any one opponent chosen from the rest, who will meet me singly in an old church-yard, before an old church-door; and will previously empower me to lock him in, if needful to his satisfaction, until morning.

For the night-wind has a dismal trick of wandering round and round a building of that sort, and moaning as it goes; and of trying, with its unseen hand, the windows and the doors; and seeking out some crevices by which to enter. And when it has got in; as one not finding what it seeks, whatever that may be, it wails and howls to issue forth again: and not content with stalking through the aisles, and gliding round and round the pillars, and tempting the deep organ, soars up to the roof, and strives to rend the rafters:

1

then flings itself despairingly upon the stones below, and
passes, muttering, into the vaults. Anon, it comes up stealth-
ily, and creeps along the walls, seeming to read, in whispers,
the Inscriptions sacred to the Dead. At some of these, it
breaks out shrilly, as with laughter; and at others, moans
and cries as if it were lamenting. It has a ghostly sound too,
lingering within the altar; where it seems to chaunt, in its
wild way, of Wrong and Murder done, and false Gods worshipped, in defiance of the Tables of the Law, which look
so fair and smooth, but are so flawed and broken. Ugh!
Heaven preserve us, sitting snugly round the fire! It has an
awful voice, that wind at Midnight, singing in a church!

But, high up in the steeple! There the foul blast roars
and whistles! High up in the steeple, where it is free to
come and go through many an airy arch and loophole, and
to twist and twine itself about the giddy stair, and twirl the
groaning weathercock, and make the very tower shake and
shiver! High up in the steeple, where the belfry is, and iron
rails are ragged with rust, and sheets of lead and copper,
shrivelled by the changing weather, crackle and heave beneath the unaccustomed tread; and birds stuff shabby nests
into corners of old oaken joists and beams; and dust grows
old and grey; and speckled spiders, indolent and fat with
long security, swing idly to and fro in the vibration of the
bells, and never loose their hold upon their thread-spun
castles in the air, or climb up sailor-like in quick alarm, or
drop upon the ground and ply a score of nimble legs to save
one life! High up in the steeple of an old church, far above
the light and murmur of the town and far below the flying
clouds that shadow it, is the wild and dreary place at night:
and high up in the steeple of an old church, dwelt the
Chimes I tell of.

They were old Chimes, trust me. Centuries ago, these
Bells had been baptized by bishops: so many centuries ago,
that the register of their baptism was lost long, long before
the memory of man, and no one knew their names. They had
had their Godfathers and Godmothers, these Bells (for my
own part, by the way, I would rather incur the responsibil-

ity of being Godfather to a Bell than a Boy), and had their silver mugs no doubt, besides. But Time had mowed down their sponsors, and Henry the Eighth had melted down their mugs; and they now hung, nameless and mugless, in the church-tower.

Not speechless, though. Far from it. They had clear, loud, lusty, sounding voices, had these Bells; and far and wide they might be heard upon the wind. Much too sturdy Chimes were they, to be dependent on the pleasure of the wind, moreover; for, fighting gallantly against it when it took an adverse whim, they would pour their cheerful notes into a listening ear right royally; and bent on being heard, on stormy nights, by some poor mother watching a sick child, or some lone wife whose husband was at sea, they had been sometimes known to beat a blustering Nor'-Wester; aye, "all to fits," as Toby Veck said;—for though they chose to call him Trotty Veck, his name was Toby, and no-body could make it anything else either (except Tobias) without a special act of parliament; he having been as law-fully christened in his day as the Bells had been in theirs, though with not quite so much of solemnity or public re-joicing.

For my part, I confess myself of Toby Veck's belief, for I am sure he had opportunities enough of forming a correct one. And whatever Toby Veck said, I say. And I take my stand by Toby Veck, although he *did* stand all day long (and weary work it was) just outside the church-door. In fact he was a ticket-porter, Toby Veck, and waited there for jobs.

And a breezy, goose-skinned, blue-nosed, red-eyed, stony-toed, tooth-chattering place it was, to wait in, in the winter-time, as Toby Veck well knew. The wind came tearing round the corner—especially the east wind—as if it had sallied forth, express, from the confines of the earth, to have a blow at Toby. And oftentimes it seemed to come upon him sooner than it had expected, for bouncing round the corner, and passing Toby, it would suddenly wheel round again, as if it cried "Why, here he is!" Incontinently his little white apron would be caught up over his head like a naughty boy's garments, and his feeble little cane would be seen to wrestle and struggle unavailingly in his hand, and his legs would undergo tremendous agitation, and Toby himself all aslant, and facing now in this direction, now in that, would be so banged and buffeted, and touzled, and worried, and hustled, and lifted off his feet, as to render it a state of things but one degree removed from a positive miracle, that he wasn't carried up bodily into the air as a colony of frogs or snails or other very portable creatures sometimes are, and rained down again, to the great astonishment of the natives, on some strange corner of the world where ticket-porters are unknown.

But, windy weather, in spite of its using him so roughly, was, after all, a sort of holiday for Toby. That's the fact. He didn't seem to wait so long for sixpence in the wind, as at other times; the having to fight with that boisterous element took off his attention, and quite freshened him up, when he was getting hungry and low-spirited. A hard frost too, or a fall of snow, was an Event; and it seemed to do him good, somehow or other—it would have been hard to say in what respect though, Toby! So wind and frost and snow, and perhaps a good stiff storm of hail, were Toby Veck's red-letter days.

Wet weather was the worst; the cold, damp, clammy wet, that wrapped him up like a moist great-coat—the only kind of great-coat Toby owned, or could have added to his comfort by dispensing with. Wet days, when the rain came slow-ly, thickly, obstinately down; when the street's throat, like his own, was choked with mist; when smoking umbrellas passed and re-passed, spinning round and round like so many teetotums, as they knocked against each other on the crowded footway, throwing off a little whirlpool of uncomfortable sprinklings; when gutters brawled and waterspouts were full and noisy; when the wet from the projecting stones and ledges of the church fell drip, drip, drip, on Toby, making the wisp of straw on which he stood mere mud in no time; those were the days that tried him. Then indeed, you might see Toby looking anxiously out from his shelter in an angle of the church wall—such a meagre shelter that in summer time it never cast a shadow thicker than a good-sized walking-stick upon the sunny pavement—with a disconsolate and lengthened face. But coming out, a minute afterwards, to warm himself by exercise, and trotting up and down some dozen times, he would brighten even then, and go back more brightly to his niche.

They called him Trotty from his pace, which meant speed if it didn't make it. He could have Walked faster perhaps; most likely; but rob him of his trot, and Toby would have taken to his bed and died. It bespattered him with mud in dirty weather; it cost him a world of trouble; he could have walked with infinitely greater ease; but that was one reason for his clinging to it so tenaciously. A weak, small, spare old man, he was a very Hercules, this Toby, in his good intentions. He loved to earn his money. He delighted to believe—Toby was very poor, and couldn't well afford to part with a delight—that he was worth his salt. With a shilling or an eighteen-penny message or small parcel in hand, his courage, always high, rose higher. As he trotted on, he would call out to fast Postmen ahead of him, to get out of the way; devoutly believing that in the natural course of things he must inevitably overtake and run them down; and he had perfect faith—not often tested—in his being able to carry anything that man could lift.

Thus, even when he came out of his nook to warm himself on a wet day, Toby trotted. Making, with his leaky shoes, a crooked line of slushy footprints in the mire; and blowing on his chilly hands and rubbing them against each other, poorly defended from the searching cold by threadbare mufflers of grey worsted, with a private apartment only for the thumb, and a common room or tap for the rest of the fingers; Toby, with his knees bent and his cane beneath his arm, still trotted. Falling out into the road to look up at the belfry when the Chimes resounded, Toby trotted still.

He made this last excursion several times a day, for they were company to him; and when he heard their voices, he

had an interest in glancing at their lodging-place, and thinking how they were moved, and what hammers beat upon
them. Perhaps he was the more curious about these Bells,
because there were points of resemblance between themselves and him. They hung there, in all weathers, with the
wind and rain driving in upon them; facing only the out-
sides of all those houses; never getting any nearer to the
blazing fires that gleamed and shone upon the windows, or
came puffing out of the chimney tops; and incapable of par-
ticipation in any of the good things that were constantly
being handed, through the street doors and the area railings,
to prodigious cooks. Faces came and went at many windows:
sometimes pretty faces, youthful faces, pleasant faces: sometimes the reverse: but Toby knew no more (though he often
speculated on these trifles, standing idle in the streets)
whence they came, or where they went, or whether, when the
lips moved, one kind word was said of him in all the year,
than did the Chimes themselves.

Toby was not a casuist—that he knew of, at least—and I
don't mean to say that when he began to take to the Bells,
and to knit up his first rough acquaintance with them into
something of a closer and more delicate woof, he passed
through these considerations one by one, or held any formal
review or great field-day in his thoughts. But what I mean
to say, and do say is, that as the functions of Toby's body,
his digestive organs for example, did of their own cunning,
and by a great many operations of which he was altogether
ignorant, and the knowledge of which would have astonished
him very much, arrive at a certain end, so his mental faculties, without his privity or concurrence, set all these wheels
and springs in motion, with a thousand others, when they
worked to bring about his liking for the Bells.

And though I had said his love, I would not have recalled
the word, though it would scarcely have expressed his complicated feeling. For, being but a simple man, he invested
them with a strange and solemn character. They were so
mysterious, often heard and never seen, so high up, so far

Coming Out . . . To Warm Himself By Exercise . . .

off, so full of such a deep strong melody, that he regarded them with a species of awe; and sometimes when he looked up at the dark arched windows in the tower, he half expected to be beckoned to by something which was not a Bell, and yet was what he had heard so often sounding in the Chimes. For all this, Toby scouted with indignation a certain flying rumour that the Chimes were haunted, as implying the possibility of their being connected with any Evil thing. In short, they were very often in his ears, and very often in his thoughts, but always in his good opinion; and he very often got such a crick in his neck by staring with his mouth wide open, at the steeple where they hung, that he was fain to take an extra trot or two, afterwards, to cure it.

The very thing he was in the act of doing one cold day, when the last drowsy sound of Twelve o'clock, just struck, was humming like a melodious monster of a Bee, and not by any means a busy bee, all through the steeple!

"Dinner-time, eh!" said Toby, trotting up and down before the church. "Ah!"

Toby's nose was very red, and his eyelids were very red, and he winked very much, and his shoulders were very near his ears, and his legs were very stiff, and altogether he was evidently a long way upon the frosty side of cool.

"Dinner-time, eh!" repeated Toby, using his right-hand muffler like an infantine boxing-glove, and punishing his chest for being cold. "Ah-h-h-h!"

He took a silent trot, after that, for a minute or two.

"There's nothing," said Toby, breaking forth afresh— but here he stopped short in his trot, and with a face of great interest and some alarm, felt his nose carefully all the way up. It was but a little way (not being much of a nose) and he had soon finished.

"I thought it was gone," said Toby, trotting off again. "It's all right, however. I am sure I couldn't blame it if it was to go It has a precious hard service of it in the bitter weather, and precious little to look forward to; for I don't take snuff myself. It's a good deal tried, poor creetur, at the best of times; for when it *does* get hold of a pleasant whiff or so (which an't too often), it's generally from somebody else's dinner, a-coming home from the baker's."

The reflection reminded him of that other reflection, which he had left unfinished.

"There's nothing," said Toby, "more regular in its coming round than dinner-time, and nothing less regular in its coming round than dinner. That's the great difference between 'em. It's took me a long time to find it out. I wonder whether it would be worth any gentleman's while, now, to buy that obserwation for the Papers; or the Parliament!"

Toby was only joking, for he gravely shook his head in self-depreciation.

"Why! Lord!" said Toby. "The Papers is full of obserwations as it is; and so's the Parliament. Here's last week's paper, now"; taking a very dirty one from his pocket, and holding it from him at arm's length; "full of obserwations! Full of obserwations! I like to know the news as well as any man," said Toby, slowly; folding it a little smaller, and putting it in his pocket again: "but it almost goes against the grain with me to read a paper now. It frightens me almost. I don't know what we poor people are coming to. Lord send we may be coming to something better in the New Year nigh upon us!"

"Why, father, father!" said a pleasant voice, hard by.

But Toby, not hearing it, continued to trot backwards and forwards; musing as he went, and talking to himself.

"It seems as if we can't go right, or do right, or be righted," said Toby. "I hadn't much schooling, myself, when I was young; and I can't make out whether we have any business on the face of the earth, or not. Sometimes I think we must have—a little; and sometimes I think we must be intruding. I get so puzzled sometimes that I am not even able to make up my mind whether there is any good at all in us, or whether we are born bad. We seem to be dreadful things; we seem to give a deal of trouble; we are always being complained of and guarded against. One way or other, we fill the papers. Talk of a New Year!" said Toby, mournfully. "I can bear up as well as another man at most times; better than a good many, for I am as strong as a lion, and all men an't; but supposing it should really be that we have no right to a New Year—supposing we really *are* intruding——"

"Why, father, father!" said the pleasant voice again.

Toby heard it this time; started; stopped; and shortening his sight, which had been directed a long way off as seeking for enlightenment in the very heart of the approaching year, found himself face to face with his own child, and looking close into her eyes.

Bright eyes they were. Eyes that would bear a world of looking in, before their depth was fathomed. Dark eyes, that reflected back the eyes which searched them; not flashingly, or at the owner's will, but with a clear, calm, honest, patient radiance, claiming kindred with that light which Heaven called into being. Eyes that were beautiful and true, and beaming with Hope. With Hope so young and fresh; with Hope so buoyant, vigorous, and bright, despite the twenty years of work and poverty on which they had looked; that they became a voice to Trotty Veck, and said: "I think we have some business here—a little!"

Trotty kissed the lips belonging to the eyes, and squeezed the blooming face between his hands.

"Why, Pet," said Trotty. "What's to do? I didn't expect you to-day, Meg."

"Neither did I expect to come, father," cried the girl, nodding her head and smiling as she spoke. "But here I am! And not alone; not alone!"

"Why you don't mean to say," observed Trotty, looking curiously at a covered basket which she carried in her hand, "that you—"

"Smell it, father dear," said Meg. "Only smell it!"

Trotty was going to lift up the cover at once, in a great hurry, when she gaily interposed her hand.

"No, no, no," said Meg, with the glee of a child. "Lengthen it out a little. Let me just lift up the corner; just the lit-tle ti-ny cor-ner, you know," said Meg, suiting the action to the word with the utmost gentleness, and speaking very softly, as if she were afraid of being overheard by something inside the basket; "there. Now. What's that?"

Toby took the shortest possible sniff at the edge of the basket, and cried out in a rapture:

"Why, it's hot!"

"It's burning hot!" cried Meg. "Ha, ha, ha! It's scalding hot!"

"Ha, ha, ha!" roared Toby, with a sort of kick. "It's scalding hot."

"But what is it, father?" said Meg. "Come. You haven't guessed what it is. And you must guess what it is. I can't think of taking it out, till you guess what it is. Don't be in such a hurry! Wait a minute! A little more of the cover. Now guess!"

Meg was in a perfect fright lest he should guess right too soon; shrinking away, as she held the basket towards him; curling up her pretty shoulders; stopping her ear with her hand, as if by so doing she could keep the right word out of Toby's lips; and laughing softly the whole time.

Meanwhile Toby, putting a hand on each knee, bent down his nose to the basket, and took a long inspiration at the lid; the grin upon his withered face expanding in the process, as if he were inhaling laughing gas.

"Ah! It's very nice," said Toby. "It an't—I suppose it an't Polonies?"

"No, no, no!" cried Meg, delighted. "Nothing like Polonies!"

"No," said Toby, after another sniff. "It's—it's mellower than Polonies. It's very nice. It improves every moment. It's too decided for Trotters. An't it?"

Meg was in an ecstasy. He could not have gone wider of the mark than Trotters—except Polonies.

"Liver?" said Toby, communing with himself. "No. There's a mildness about it that don't answer to liver. Pettitoes? No. It an't faint enough for pettitoes. It wants the stringiness of Cocks' heads. And I know it an't sausages. I'll tell you what it is. It's chitterlings!"

"No, it an't!" cried Meg, in a burst of delight. "No, it an't!"

"Why, what am I a-thinking of!" said Toby, suddenly recovering a position as near the perpendicular as it was possible for him to assume. "I shall forget my own name next. It's tripe!"

Tripe it was; and Meg, in high joy, protested he should say, in half a minute more, it was the best tripe ever stewed.

"And so," said Meg, busying herself exultingly with the basket, "I'll lay the cloth at once, father; for I have brought the tripe in a basin, and tied the basin up in a pocket-handkerchief; and if I like to be proud for once, and spread that for a cloth, and call it a cloth, there's no law to prevent me; is there, father?"

"Not that I know of, my dear," said Toby. "But they're always a-bringing up some new law or other."

"And according to what I was reading you in the paper the other day, father; what the Judge said, you know; we poor people are supposed to know them all. Ha, ha! What a mistake! My goodness me, how clever they think us!"

"Yes, my dear," cried Trotty; "and they'd be very fond of any one of us that *did* know 'em all. He'd grow fat upon the work he'd get, that man, and be popular with the gentlefolks in his neighbourhood. Very much so!"

"He'd eat his dinner with an appetite, whoever he was, if it smelt like this," said Meg, cheerfully. "Make haste, for there's a hot potato besides, and half a pint of fresh-drawn beer in a bottle. Where will you dine, father? On the Post, or on the Steps? Dear, dear, how grand we are. Two places to choose from!"

"The steps to-day, my Pet," said Trotty. "Steps in dry weather. Post in wet. There's a greater conveniency in the steps at all times, because of the sitting down; but they're rheumatic in the damp."

"Then here," said Meg, clapping her hands, after a moment's bustle; "here it is, all ready! And beautiful it looks! Come, father. Come!"

Since his discovery of the contents of the basket, Trotty

had been standing looking at her—and had been speaking too —in an abstracted manner, which showed that though she was the object of his thoughts and eyes, to the exclusion even of tripe, he neither saw nor thought about her as she was at that moment, but had before him some imaginary rough sketch or drama of her future life. Roused, now, by her cheerful summons, he shook off a melancholy shake of the head which was just coming upon him, and trotted to her side. As he was stooping to sit down, the Chimes rang.

"Amen!" said Trotty, pulling off his hat and looking up towards them.

"Amen to the Bells, father?" cried Meg.

"They broke in like a grace, my dear," said Trotty, taking his seat. "They'd say a good one, I am sure, if they could. Many's the kind thing they say to me."

"The Bells do, father!" laughed Meg, as she set the basin, and a knife and fork, before him. "Well!"

"Seem to, my Pet," said Trotty, falling to with great vigour. "And where's the difference? If I hear 'em, what does it matter whether they speak it or not? Why bless you, my dear," said Toby, pointing at the tower with his fork, and becoming more animated under the influence of dinner, "how often have I heard them bells say 'Toby Veck, Toby Veck, keep a good heart, Toby! Toby Veck, Toby Veck, keep a good heart, Toby!' A million times? More!"

"Well, I never!" cried Meg.

She had, though—over and over again. For it was Toby's constant topic.

"When things is very bad," said Trotty; "very bad indeed, I mean; almost at the worst; then it's 'Toby Veck, Toby Veck, job coming soon, Toby! Toby Veck, Toby Veck, job coming soon, Toby!' That way."

"And it comes—at last, father," said Meg, with a touch of sadness in her pleasant voice.

"Always," answered the unconscious Toby. "Never fails."

While this discourse was holding, Trotty made no pause in his attack upon the savoury meat before him, but cut and ate, and cut and drank, and cut and chewed, and dodged about, from tripe to hot potato, and from hot potato back again to tripe, with an unctuous and unflagging relish. But happening now to look all round the street—in case anybody should be beckoning from any door or window, for a porter —his eyes, in coming back again, encountered Meg: sitting opposite to him, with her arms folded: and only busy in watching his progress with a smile of happiness.

"Why, Lord forgive me!" said Trotty, dropping his knife and fork. "My dove! Meg! why didn't you tell me what a beast I was?"

"Father?"

"Sitting here," said Trotty, in penitent explanation, "cramming, and stuffing, and gorging myself; and you before me there, never so much as breaking your precious fast, nor wanting to, when—"

"But I have broken it, father," interposed his daughter, laughing, "all to bits. I have had my dinner."

"Nonsense," said Trotty. "Two dinners in one day! It an't possible! You might as well tell me that two New Year's days will come together, or that I have had a gold head all my life, and never changed it."

"I have had my dinner, father, for all that," said Meg, coming nearer to him. "And if you'll go on with yours, I'll tell you how and where; and how your dinner came to be bought; and—and something else besides."

Toby still appeared incredulous; but she looked into his face with her clear eyes, and laying her hand upon his shoulder, motioned him to go on while the meat was hot. So Trotty took up his knife and fork again, and went to work. But much more slowly than before, and shaking his head, as if he were not at all pleased with himself.

"I had my dinner, father," said Meg, after a little hesitation, "with—with Richard. His dinner-time was early; and as he brought his dinner with him when he came to see me, we—we had it together, father."

Trotty took a little beer, and smacked his lips. Then he said "Oh!"—because she waited.

"And Richard says, father—" Meg resumed. Then stopped.

"What does Richard say, Meg?" asked Toby.

"Richard says, father—" Another stoppage.

"Richard's a long time saying it," said Toby.

"He says then, father," Meg continued, lifting up her eyes at last, and speaking in a tremble, but quite plainly; "another year is nearly gone, and where is the use of waiting on from year to year, when it is so unlikely we shall ever be better off than we are now? He says we are poor now, father, and we shall be poor then, but we are young now, and years will make us old before we know it. He says that if we wait: people in our condition: until we see our way quite clearly, the way will be a narrow one indeed—the common way—the Grave, father."

A bolder man than Trotty Veck must needs have drawn upon his boldness largely, to deny it. Trotty held his peace.

"And how hard, father, to grow old, and die, and think we might have cheered and helped each other! How hard in all our lives to love each other; and to grieve, apart, to see each other working, changing, growing old and grey. Even if I got the better of it, and forgot him (which I never could), oh father dear, how hard to have a heart so full as mine is now, and live to have it slowly drained out every drop, without the recollection of one happy moment of a woman's life, to stay behind and comfort me, and make me better!"

Trotty sat quite still. Meg dried her eyes, and said more gaily: that is to say, with here a laugh, and there a sob, and here a laugh and sob together:

"So Richard says, father; as his work was yesterday made certain for some time to come, and as I love him, and have loved him full three years—ah! longer than that, if he knew it!—will I marry him on New Year's Day; the best and happiest day, he says, in the whole year, and one that is almost sure to bring good fortune with it. "It's a short notice, father—isn't it?—but I haven't my fortune to be settled, or my wedding dresses to be made, like the great

ladies, father, have I? And he said so much, and said it in
his way; so strong and earnest, and all the time so kind and
gentle; that I said I 'd come and talk to you, father. And as
they paid the money for that work of mine this morning
(unexpectedly, I am sure!) and as you have fared very
poorly for a whole week, and as I couldn't help wishing there
should be something to make this day a sort of holiday to
you as well as a dear and happy day to me, father, I made a
little treat and brought it to surprise you."

"And see how he leaves it cooling on the step!" said another voice.

It was the voice of this same Richard, who had come upon
them unobserved, and stood before the father and daughter;
looking down upon them with a face as glowing as the iron on
which his stout sledge-hammer daily rung. A handsome,
well-made, powerful youngster he was; with eyes that
sparkled like the red-hot droppings from a furnace fire;
black hair that curled about his swarthy temples rarely; and
a smile—a smile that bore out Meg's eulogium on his style
of conversation.

"See how he leaves it cooling on the step!" said Richard.
"Meg don't know what he likes. Not she!"

Trotty, all action and enthusiasm, immediately reached
up his hand to Richard, and was going to address him in a
great hurry, when the house-door opened without any warning, and a footman very nearly put his foot into the tripe.

"Out of the vays here, will you! You must always go and
be a-settin' on our steps, must you! You can't go and give
a turn to none of the neighbours never, can't you! *Will*
you clear the road, or won't you?"

Strictly speaking, the last question was irrelevant, as
they had already done it.

"What 's the matter, what 's the matter!" said the gentleman for whom the door was opened; coming out of the
house at that kind of light-heavy pace—that peculiar compromise between a walk and a jog-trot—with which a gentleman upon the smooth down-hill of life, wearing creaking
boots, a watch-chain, and clean linen, *may* come out of his

house; not only without any abatement of his dignity, but with an expression of having important and wealthy engagements elsewhere. "What 's the matter! What 's the matter!"

"You 're always a-being begged, and prayed, upon your bended knees you are," said the footman with great emphasis to Trotty Veck, "to let our door-steps be. Why don't you let 'em be? CAN'T you let 'em be?"

"There! That 'll do, that 'll do!" said the gentleman. "Halloa there! Porter!" beckoning with his head to Trotty Veck. "Come here. What 's that? Your dinner?"

"Yes, sir," said Trotty, leaving it behind him in a corner.

"Don't leave it there," exclaimed the gentleman. "Bring it here, bring it here. So! This is your dinner, is it?"

"Yes, sir," repeated Trotty, looking with a fixed eye and a watery mouth, at the piece of tripe he had reserved for a last delicious tit-bit; which the gentleman was now turning over and over on the end of the fork.

Two other gentlemen had come out with him. One was a low-spirited gentleman of middle age, of a meagre habit, and a disconsolate face; who kept his hands continually in the pockets of his scanty pepper-and-salt trousers, very large and dog's-eared from that custom; and was not particularly well brushed or washed. The other, a full-sized, sleek, well-conditioned gentleman, in a blue coat with bright buttons, and a white cravat. This gentleman had a very red face, as if an undue proportion of the blood in his body were squeezed up into his head; which perhaps accounted for his having also the appearance of being rather cold about the heart.

He who had Toby's meat upon the fork, called to the first one by the name of Filer; and they both drew near together. Mr. Filer being exceedingly short-sighted, was obliged to go so close to the remnant of Toby's dinner before he could make out what it was, that Toby's heart leaped up into his mouth. But Mr. Filer didn't eat it.

"This is a description of animal food, Alderman," said Filer, making little punches in it, with a pencil-case, "commonly known to the labouring population of this country, by the name of tripe."

The Alderman laughed, and winked; for he was a merry fellow, Alderman Cute. Oh, and a sly fellow too! A knowing fellow. Up to everything. Not to be imposed upon. Deep in the people's hearts! He knew them, Cute did. I believe you!

"But who eats tripe?" said Mr. Filer, looking round. "Tripe is without an exception the least economical, and the most wasteful article of consumption that the markets of this country can by possibility produce. The loss upon a pound of tripe has been found to be, in the boiling, seven-eighths of a fifth more than the loss upon a pound of any other animal substance whatever. Tripe is more expensive, properly understood, than the hothouse pine-apple. Taking into account the number of animals slaughtered yearly within the bills of mortality alone; and forming a low estimate of the quantity of tripe which the carcasses of those animals, reasonably well butchered, would yield; I find that the waste on that amount of tripe, if boiled, would victual a garrison of five hundred men for five months of thirty-one days each, and a February over. The Waste, the Waste!"

Trotty stood aghast, and his legs shook under him. He seemed to have starved ⌐ garrison of five hundred men with his own hand.

"Who eats tripe?" said Mr. Filer, warmly. "Who eats tripe?"

Trotty made a miserable bow.

"You do, do you?" said Mr. Filer. "Then I'll tell you something. You snatch your tripe, my friend, out of the mouths of widows and orphans."

"I hope not, sir," said Trotty, faintly. "I'd sooner die of want!"

"Divide the amount of tripe before mentioned, Alderman," said Mr. Filer, "by the estimated number of existing widows and orphans, and the result will be one pennyweight of tripe to each. Not a grain is left for that man. Consequently, he's a robber."

Trotty was so shocked, that it gave him no concern to see the Alderman finish the tripe himself. It was a relief to get rid of it, anyhow.

"And what do you say?" asked the Alderman, jocosely, of the red-faced gentleman in the blue coat. "You have heard friend Filer. What do *you* say?"

"What's it possible to say?" returned the gentleman. "What *is* to be said? Who can take any interest in a fellow like this," meaning Trotty; "in such degenerate times as these? Look at him! What an object! The good old times, the grand old times, the great old times! *Those* were the times for a bold peasantry, and all that sort of thing. Those were the times for every sort of thing, in fact. There's nothing now-a-days. Ah!" sighed the red-faced gentleman, "The good old times, the good old times!"

The gentleman didn't specify what particular times he alluded to; nor did he say whether he objected to the present times, from a disinterested consciousness that they had done nothing very remarkable in producing himself.

"The good old times, the good old times," repeated the gentleman. "What times they were! They were the only times. It's of no use talking about any other times, or discussing what the people are in *these* times. You don't call these, times, do you? I don't. Look into Strutt's Costumes, and see what a Porter used to be, in any of the good old English reigns."

"He hadn't, in his very best circumstances, a shirt to his back, or a stocking to his foot; and there was scarcely a vegetable in all England for him to put into his mouth," said Mr. Filer. "I can prove it, by tables."

But still the red-faced gentleman extolled the good old times, the grand old times. the great old times. No matter what anybody else said, he still went turning round and round in one set form of words concerning them; as a poor squirrel turns and turns in its revolving cage; touching the mechanism, and trick of which, it has probably quite as distinct perceptions, as ever this red-faced gentleman had of his deceased Millennium.

Trotty Stood Aghast, and His
Legs Shook Under Him.

It is possible that poor Trotty's faith in these very vague Old Times was not entirely destroyed, for he felt vague enough, at that moment. One thing, however, was plain to him, in the midst of his distress; to wit, that however these gentlemen might differ in details, his misgivings of that morning, and of many other mornings, were well founded. "No, no. We can't go right or do right," thought Trotty in despair. "There is no good in us. We are born bad!"

But Trotty had a father's heart within him; which had somehow got into his breast in spite of this decree; and he could not bear that Meg, in the blush of her brief joy, should have her fortune read by these wise gentlemen. "God help her," thought poor Trotty. "She will know it soon enough."

He anxiously signed, therefore, to the young smith, to take her away. But he was so busy, talking to her softly at a little distance, that he only became conscious of this desire, simultaneously with Alderman Cute. Now, the Alderman had not yet had his say, but *he* was a philosopher, too—practical, though! Oh, very practical—and, as he had no idea of losing any portion of his audience, he cried "Stop!"

"Now, you know," said the Alderman, addressing his two friends, with a self-complacent smile upon his face which was habitual to him, "I am a plain man, and a practical man; and I go to work in a plain practical way. That's my way. There is not the least mystery or difficulty in dealing with this sort of people if you only understand 'em, and can talk to 'em in their own manner. Now, you Porter! Don't you ever tell me, or anybody else, my friend, that you haven't always enough to eat, and of the best; because I know better. I have tasted your tripe, you know, and you can't 'chaff' me. You understand what 'chaff' means, eh? That's the right word, isn't it? Ha, ha, ha! Lord bless you," said the Alderman, turning to his friends again, "it's the easiest thing on earth to deal with this sort of people, if you understand 'em."

Famous man for the common people, Alderman Cute! Never out of temper with them! Easy, affable, joking, knowing gentleman!

"You see, my friend," pursued the Alderman, "there's a great deal of nonsense talked about Want—'hard up,' you know; that's the phrase, isn't it? ha! ha! ha!—and I intend to Put it Down. There's a certain amount of cant in vogue about Starvation, and I mean to Put it Down. That's all! Lord bless you," said the Alderman, turning to his friends again, "you may Put Down anything among this sort of people, if you only know the way to set about it."

Trotty took Meg's hand and drew it through his arm. He didn't seem to know what he was doing though.

"Your daughter, eh?" said the Alderman, chucking her familiarly under the chin.

Always affable with the working classes, Alderman Cute! Knew what pleased them! Not a bit of pride!

"Where's her mother?" asked that worthy gentleman.

"Dead," said Toby. "Her mother got up linen; and was called to Heaven when She was born."

"Not to get up linen *there*, I suppose," remarked the Alderman pleasantly.

Toby might or might not have been able to separate his wife in Heaven from her old pursuits. But query: If Mrs. Alderman Cute had gone to Heaven, would Mr. Alderman Cute have pictured her as holding any state or station there?

"And you're making love to her, are you?" said Cute to the young smith.

"Yes," returned Richard quickly, for he was nettled by the question. "And we are going to be married on New Year's Day."

"What do you mean!" cried Filer sharply. "Married!"

"Why, yes, we're thinking of it, Master," said Richard. "We're rather in a hurry, you see, in case it should be Put Down first."

"Ah!" cried Filer, with a groan. "Put *that* down, indeed, Alderman, and you'll do something. Married! Married!! The ignorance of the first principles of political economy on the part of these people; their improvidence; their wickedness; is, by Heavens! enough to—Now look at that couple, will you!"

Well? They were worth looking at. And marriage seemed as reasonable and fair a deed as they need have in contemplation.

"A man may live to be as old as Methuselah," said Mr. Filer, "and may labour all his life for the benefit of such people as those; and may heap up facts on figures, facts on figures, facts on figures, mountains high and dry; and he can no more hope to persuade 'em that they have no right or business to be married, than he can hope to persuade 'em that they have no earthly right or business to be born. And *that* we know they haven't. We reduced it to a mathematical certainty long ago!"

Alderman Cute was mightily diverted, and laid his right forefinger on the side of his nose, as much as to say to both his friends, "Observe me, will you! Keep your eye on the practical man!"—and called Meg to him.

"Come here, my girl!" said Alderman Cute.

The young blood of her lover had been mounting, wrathfully, within the last few minutes; and he was indisposed to let her come. But, setting a constraint upon himself, he came forward with a stride as Meg approached, and stood beside her. Trotty kept her hand within his arm still, but looked from face to face as wildly as a sleeper in a dream.

"Now, I'm going to give you a word or two of good advice, my girl," said the Alderman, in his nice easy way. "It's my place to give advice, you know, because I'm a Justice. You know I'm a Justice, don't you?"

Meg timidly said, "Yes." But everybody knew Alderman Cute was a Justice! Oh dear, so active a Justice always! Who such a mote of brightness in the public eye, as Cute!

"You are going to be married, you say," pursued the Alderman. "Very unbecoming and indelicate in one of your sex! But never mind that. After you are married, you'll quarrel with your husband and come to be a distressed wife. You may think not; but you will, because I tell you so. Now, I give you fair warning, that I have made up my mind to

Put distressed wives Down. So, don't be brought before me.
You'll have children—boys. Those boys will grow up bad,
of course, and run wild in the streets, without shoes and
stockings. Mind, my young friend! I'll convict 'em summarily, every one, for I am determined to Put boys without
shoes and stockings, Down. Perhaps your husband will die
young (most likely) and leave you with a baby. Then you'll
be turned out of doors, and wander up and down the streets.
Now, don't wander near me, my dear, for I am resolved to
Put all wandering mothers Down. All young mothers, of all
sorts and kinds, it's my determination to Put Down. Don't
think to plead illness as an excuse with me; or babies as an
excuse with me; for all sick persons and young children (I
hope you know the church-service, but I'm afraid not) I
am determined to Put Down. And if you attempt, desperately, and ungratefully, and impiously, and fraudulently
attempt, to drown yourself, or hang yourself, I'll have no
pity for you, for I have made up my mind to Put all suicide
Down! If there is one thing," said the Alderman, with his
self-satisfied smile, "on which I can be said to have made up
my mind more than on another, it is to Put suicide Down.
So don't try it on. That's the phrase, isn't it? Ha, ha!
now we understand each other."

Toby knew not whether to be agonised or glad, to see that
Meg had turned a deadly white, and dropped her lover's
hand.

"And as for you, you dull dog," said the Alderman, turning with even increased cheerfulness and urbanity to the
young smith, "what are you thinking of being married for?
What do you want to be married for, you silly fellow? If I
was a fine, young, strapping chap like you, I should be
ashamed of being milksop enough to pin myself to a woman's apron-strings! Why, she'll be an old woman before
you're a middle-aged man! And a pretty figure you'll cut
then, with a draggle-tailed wife and a crowd of squalling
children crying after you wherever you go!"

O, he knew how to banter the common people, Alderman
Cute!

"There! Go along with you," said the Alderman, "and repent. Don't make such a fool of yourself as to get married on New Year's Day. You'll think very differently of it, long before next New Year's Day; a trim young fellow like you, with all the girls looking after you. There! Go along with you!"

They went along. Not arm in arm, or hand in hand, or interchanging bright glances; but, she in tears; he, gloomy and down-looking. Were these the hearts that had so lately made old Toby's leap up from its faintness? No, no. The Alderman (a blessing on his head!) had Put *them* Down.

"As you happen to be here," said the Alderman to Toby, "you shall carry a letter for me. Can you be quick? You're an old man."

Toby, who had been looking after Meg, quite stupidly, made shift to murmur out that he was very quick, and very strong.

"How old are you?" inquired the Alderman.

"I'm over sixty, sir," said Toby.

"O! This man's a great deal past the average, you know," cried Mr. Filer, breaking in as if his patience would bear some trying, but this really was carrying matters a little too far.

"I feel I'm intruding, sir," said Toby. "I—I misdoubted it this morning. Oh dear me!"

The Alderman cut him short by giving him the letter from his pocket. Toby would have got a shilling too; but Mr. Filer clearly showing that in that case he would rob a certain given number of persons of ninepence-halfpenny a-piece, he only got sixpence; and thought himself very well off to get that.

Then the Alderman gave an arm to each of his friends, and walked off in high feather; but, he immediately came hurrying back alone, as if he had forgotten something.

"Porter!" said the Alderman.

"Sir!" said Toby.

"Take care of that daughter of yours. She's much too handsome."

"Even her good looks are stolen from somebody or other I suppose," thought Toby, looking at the sixpence in his hand, and thinking of the tripe. "She's been and robbed five hundred ladies of a bloom a-piece, I shouldn't wonder. It's very dreadful!"

"She's much too handsome, my man," repeated the Alderman. "The chances are, that she'll come to no good, I clearly see. Observe what I say. Take care of her!" With which, he hurried off again.

"Wrong every way. Wrong every way!" said Trotty, clasping his hands. "Born bad. No business here!"

The Chimes came clashing in upon him as he said the words. Full, loud, and sounding—but with no encouragement. No, not a drop.

"The tune's changed," cried the old man, as he listened. "There's not a word of all that fancy in it. Why should there be? I have no business with the New Year nor with the old one neither. Let me die!"

Still the Bells, pealing forth their changes, made the very air spin. Put 'em down, Put 'em down! Good old Times, Good old Times! Facts and Figures, Facts and Figures! Put 'em down, Put 'em down. If they said anything they said this, until the brain of Toby reeled.

He pressed his bewildered head between his hands, as if to keep it from splitting asunder. A well-timed action, as it happened; for finding the letter in one of them, and being by that means reminded of his charge, he fell, mechanically, into his usual trot, and trotted off.

The Second Quarter

THE letter Toby had received from Alderman Cute, was addressed to a great man in the great district of the town. The greatest district of the town. It must have been the greatest district of the town, because it was commonly called "the world" by its inhabitants.

The letter positively seemed heavier in Toby's hand, than another letter. Not because the Alderman had sealed it with a very large coat of arms and no end of wax, but because of the weighty name on the superscription, and the ponderous amount of gold and silver with which it was associated.

"How different from us!" thought Toby, in all simplicity and earnestness, as he looked at the direction. "Divide the lively turtles in the bills of mortality, by the number of gentlefolks able to buy 'em; and whose share does he take but his own! As to snatching tripe from anybody's mouth—he'd scorn it!"

With the involuntary homage due to such an exalted character, Toby interposed a corner of his apron between the letter and his fingers.

"His children," said Trotty, and a mist rose before his eyes; "his daughters—Gentlemen may win their hearts and marry them; they may be happy wives and mothers; they may be handsome like my darling M—e—"

He couldn't finish the name. The final letter swelled in his throat, to the size of the whole alphabet.

"Never mind," thought Trotty. "I know what I mean. That's more than enough for me." And with this consolatory rumination, trotted on.

It was a hard frost, that day. The air was bracing, crisp, and clear. The wintry sun, though powerless for warmth, looked brightly down upon the ice it was too weak to melt, and set a radiant glory there. At other times, Trotty might have learned a poor man's lesson from the wintry sun; but, he was past that, now.

The Year was Old, that day. The patient Year had lived through the reproaches and misuses of its slanderers, and faithfully performed its work. Spring, summer, autumn, winter. It had laboured through the destined round, and now laid down its weary head to die. Shut out from hope, high impulse, active happiness, itself, but active messenger of many joys to others, it made appeal in its decline to have its toiling days and patient hours remembered, and to die in peace. Trotty might have read a poor man's allegory in the fading year; but he was past that, now.

And only he? Or has the like appeal been ever made, by seventy years at once upon an English labourer's head, and made in vain!

The streets were full of motion, and the shops were decked out gaily. The New Year, like an Infant Heir to the whole world, was waited for, with welcomes, presents, and rejoicings. There were books and toys for the New Year, glittering trinkets for the New Year, dresses for the New Year, schemes of fortune for the New Year; new inventions to beguile it. Its life was parcelled out in almanacks and pocket-books; the coming of its moons, and stars, and tides, was known beforehand to the moment; all the workings of its seasons in their days and nights, were calculated with as much precision as Mr. Filer could work sums in men and women.

The New Year, the New Year. Everywhere the New Year! The Old Year was already looked upon as dead; and its effects were selling cheap, like some drowned mariner's aboard ship. Its patterns were Last Year's, and going at a sacrifice, before its breath was gone. Its treasures were mere dirt, beside the riches of its unborn successor!

Trotty had no portion, to his thinking, in the New Year or the Old.

"Put 'em down, Put 'em down! Facts and Figures, Facts and Figures! Good old Times, Good old Times! Put 'em down, Put 'em down!"—his trot went to that measure, and would fit itself to nothing else.

But, even that one, melancholy as it was, brought him, in due time, to the end of his journey. To the mansion of Sir Joseph Bowley, Member of Parliament.

The door was opened by a Porter. Such a Porter! Not of Toby's order. Quite another thing. His place was the ticket though; not Toby's.

This Porter underwent some hard panting before he could speak; having breathed himself by coming incautiously out of his chair, without first taking time to think about it and compose his mind. When he had found his voice—which it took him a long time to do, for it was a long way off, and hidden under a load of meat—he said in a fat whisper,

"Who's it from?"

Toby told him.

"You're to take it in, yourself," said the Porter, pointing to a room at the end of a long passage, opening from the hall. "Everything goes straight in, on this day of the year. "You're not a bit too soon: for, the carriage is at the door now, and they have only come to town for a couple of hours, a' purpose."

Toby wiped his feet (which were quite dry already) with great care, and took the way pointed out to him; observing as he went that it was an awfully grand house, but hushed and covered up, as if the family were in the country. Knocking at the room-door, he was told to enter from within; and doing so found himself in a spacious library, where, at a table strewn with files and papers, were a stately lady in a bonnet; and a not very stately gentleman in black who wrote from her dictation; while another, and an older, and a much statelier gentleman, whose hat and cane were on the table, walked up and down, with one hand in his breast, and looked complacently from time to time at his own picture— a full length; a very full length—hanging over the fireplace.

"What is this?" said the last-named gentleman. "Mr. Fish, will you have the goodness to attend?"

Mr. Fish begged pardon, and taking the letter from Toby, handed it, with great respect.

"From Alderman Cute, Sir Joseph."

"Is this all? Have you nothing else, Porter?" inquired Sir Joseph.

Toby replied in the negative.

"You have no bill or demand upon me—my name is Bowley, Sir Joseph Bowley—of any kind from anybody, have you?" said Sir Joseph. "If you have, present it. There is a cheque-book by the side of Mr. Fish. I allow nothing to be carried into the New Year. Every description of account is settled in this house at the close of the old one. So that if death was to—to—"

"To cut," suggested Mr. Fish.

"To sever, sir," returned Sir Joseph, with great asperity, "the cord of existence—my affairs would be found, I hope, in a state of preparation."

"My dear Sir Joseph!" said the lady, who was greatly younger than the gentleman. "How shocking!"

"My lady Bowley," returned Sir Joseph, floundering now and then, as in the great depth of his observations, "at this season of the year we should think of—of—ourselves. We should look into our—our accounts. We should feel that every return of so eventful a period in human transactions, involves a matter of deep moment between a man and his—and his banker."

Sir Joseph delivered these words as if he felt the full morality of what he was saying; and desired that even Trotty should have an opportunity of being improved by such discourse. Possibly he had this end before him in still forbearing to break the seal of the letter, and in telling Trotty to wait where he was, a minute.

"You were desiring Mr. Fish to say, my lady—" observed Sir Joseph.

"Mr. Fish has said that, I believe," returned his lady, glancing at the letter. "But, upon my word, Sir Joseph, I don't think I can let it go after all. It is so very dear."

"What is dear?" inquired Sir Joseph.

"That Charity, my love. They only allow two votes for a subscription of five pounds. Really monstrous!"

"My lady Bowley," returned Sir Joseph, "you surprise me. Is the luxury of feeling in proportion to the number of votes; or is it, to a rightly constituted mind, in proportion to the number of applicants, and the wholesome state of mind to which their canvassing reduces them? Is there no excitement of the purest kind in having two votes to dispose of among fifty people?"

"Not to me, I acknowledge," replied the lady. "It bores one. Besides, one can't oblige one's acquaintance. But you are the Poor Man's Friend, you know, Sir Joseph. You think otherwise."

"I *am* the Poor Man's Friend," observed Sir Joseph, glancing at the poor man present. "As such I may be taunted. As such I have been taunted. But I ask no other title."

"Bless him for a noble gentleman!" thought Trotty.

"I don't agree with Cute here, for instance," said Sir Joseph, holding out the letter. "I don't agree with the Filer party. I don't agree with any party. My friend the Poor Man, has no business with anything of that sort, and nothing of that sort has any business with him. My friend the Poor Man, in my district, is my business. No man or body of men has any right to interfere between my friend and me. That is the ground I take. I assume a—a paternal character towards my friend. I say, 'My good fellow, I will treat you paternally.' "

Toby listened with great gravity, and began to feel more comfortable.

"Your only business, my good fellow," pursued Sir Joseph, looking abstractedly at Toby; "your only business in life is with me. You needn't trouble yourself to think about anything. I will think for you; I know what is good for you; I am your perpetual parent. Such is the dispensation of an all-wise Providence! Now, the design of your creation is—not that you should swill, and guzzle, and associate your enjoyments, brutally, with food"; Toby thought remorsefully of the tripe; "but that you should feel the Dignity of Labour. Go forth erect into the cheerful morning air, and—and stop there. Live hard and temperately, be respectful, exercise your self-denial, bring up your family on next to nothing, pay your rent as regularly as the clock strikes, be punctual in your dealings (I set you a good example; you will find Mr. Fish, my confidential secretary, with a cash-box before him at all times); and you may trust me to be your Friend and Father."

"Nice children, indeed, Sir Joseph!" said the lady, with a shudder. "Rheumatisms, and fevers, and crooked legs, and asthmas, and all kinds of horrors!"

"My lady," returned Sir Joseph, with solemnity, "not the less am I the Poor Man's Friend and Father. Not the less shall he receive encouragement at my hands. Every quarter-day he will be put in communication with Mr. Fish. Every New Year's Day, myself and friends will drink his health. Once every year, myself and friends will address him with the deepest feeling. Once in his life, he may even perhaps receive; in public, in the presence of the gentry; a Trifle from a Friend; And when, upheld no more by these stimulants, and the Dignity of Labour, he sinks into his comfortable grave, then my lady"—here Sir Joseph blew his nose—"I will be a Friend and a Father—on the same terms—to his children."

Toby was greatly moved.

"O! You have a thankful family, Sir Joseph!" cried his wife.

"My lady," said Sir Joseph, quite majestically, "Ingratitude is known to be the sin of that class. I expect no other return."

"Ah! Born bad!" thought Toby. "Nothing melts us."

"What man can do, I do," pursued Sir Joseph. "I do my duty as the Poor Man's Friend and Father; and I endeavour to educate his mind, by inculcating on all occasions the one great moral lesson which that class requires. That is, entire Dependence on myself. They have no business whatever with—with themselves. If wicked and designing persons tell them otherwise, and they become impatient and discontented, and are guilty of insubordinate conduct and black-hearted ingratitude; which is undoubtedly the case; I am their Friend and Father still. It is so Ordained. It is in the nature of things."

With that great sentiment, he opened the Alderman's letter; and read it.

"Very polite and attentive, I am sure!" exclaimed Sir Joseph. "My lady, the Alderman is so obliging as to remind

me that he has had 'the distinguished honour'—he is very
good—of meeting me at the house of our mutual friend
Deedles, the banker; and he does me the favour to inquire
whether it will be agreeable to me to have Will Fern put
down."

"*Most* agreeable!" replied my Lady Bowley. "The worst
man among them! He has been committing a robbery, I
hope?"

"Why no," said Sir Joseph, referring to the letter. "Not
quite. Very near. Not quite. He came up to London, it
seems, to look for employment (trying to better himself—
that's his story), and being found at night asleep in a shed,
was taken into custody, and carried next morning before
the Alderman. The Alderman observes (very properly) that
he is determined to put this sort of thing down; and that if
it will be agreeable to me to have Will Fern put down, he
will be happy to begin with him."

"Let him be made an example of, by all means," returned
the lady. "Last winter, when I introduced pinking and eye-
let-holing among the men and boys in the village, as a nice
evening employment, and had the lines,

> O let us love our occupations,
> Bless the squire and his relations,
> Live upon our daily rations,
> And always know our proper stations,

set to music on the new system, for them to sing the while;
this very Fern—I see him now—touched that hat of his,
and said, 'I humbly ask your pardon, my lady, but *an't* I
something different from a great girl?' I expected it, of
course; who can expect anything but insolence and ingratitude from that class of people! That is not to the purpose,
however. Sir Joseph! Make an example of him!"

"Hem!" coughed Sir Joseph. "Mr. Fish, if you'll have
the goodness to attend—"

Mr. Fish immediately seized his pen, and wrote from Sir
Joseph's dictation.

"Private. My dear Sir. I am very much indebted to you

for your courtesy in the matter of the man William Fern, of whom, I regret to add, I can say nothing favourable. I have uniformly considered myself in the light of his Friend and Father, but have been repaid (a common case I grieve to say) with ingratitude, and constant opposition to my plans. He is a turbulent and rebellious spirit. His character will not bear investigation. Nothing will persuade him to be happy when he might. Under these circumstances, it appears to me, I own, that when he comes before you again (as you informed me he promised to do to-morrow, pending your inquiries, and I think he may be so far relied upon), his committal for some short term as a Vagabond, would be a service to society, and would be a salutary example in a country where—for the sake of those who are, through good and evil report, the Friends and Fathers of the Poor, as well as with a view to that, generally speaking, misguided class themselves—examples are greatly needed. And I am," and so forth.

"It appears," remarked Sir Joseph when he had signed this letter, and Mr. Fish was sealing it, "as if this were Ordained: really. At the close of the year, I wind up my account and strike my balance, even with William Fern!"

Trotty, who had long ago relapsed, and was very low-spirited, stepped forward with a rueful face to take the letter.

"With my compliments and thanks," said Sir Joseph. "Stop!"

"Stop!" echoed Mr. Fish.

"You have heard, perhaps," said Sir Joseph, oracularly, "certain remarks into which I have been led respecting the solemn period of time at which we have arrived, and the duty imposed upon us of settling our affairs, and being prepared. You have observed that I don't shelter myself behind my superior standing in society, but that Mr. Fish—that gentleman—has a cheque-book at his elbow, and is in fact here, to enable me to turn over a perfectly new leaf, and enter on the epoch before us with a clean account. Now, my friend, can you lay your hand upon your heart, and say that you also have made preparations for a New Year?"

"I am afraid, sir," stammered Trotty, looking meekly at him, "that I am a—a—little behind-hand with the world."

"Behind-hand with the world!" repeated Sir Joseph Bowley, in a tone of terrible distinctness.

"I am afraid, sir," faltered Trotty, "that there's a matter of ten or twelve shillings owing to Mrs. Chickenstalker."

"To Mrs. Chickenstalker!" repeated Sir Joseph, in the same tone as before.

"A shop, sir," exclaimed Toby, "in the general line. Also a—a little money on account of rent. A very little, sir. It oughtn't to be owing, I know, but we have been hard put to it, indeed!"

Sir Joseph looked at his lady, and at Mr. Fish, and at Trotty, one after another, twice all round. He then made a despondent gesture with both hands at once, as if he gave the thing up altogether.

"How a man, even among this improvident and impracticable race; an old man; a man grown grey; can look a New Year in the face, with his affairs in this condition; how he can lie down on his bed at night, and get up again in the morning, and—There!" he said, turning his back on Trotty. "Take the letter. Take the letter!"

"I heartily wish it was otherwise, sir," said Trotty, anxious to excuse himself. "We have been tried very hard."

Sir Joseph still repeating "Take the letter, take the letter!" and Mr. Fish not only saying the same thing, but giving additional force to the request by motioning the bearer to the door, he had nothing for it but to make his bow and leave the house. And in the street, poor Trotty pulled his worn old hat down on his head, to hide the grief he felt at getting no hold on the New Year, anywhere.

He didn't even lift his hat to look up at the Bell tower when he came to the old church on his return. He halted there a moment, from habit: and knew that it was growing dark, and that the steeple rose above him, indistinct and faint, in the murky air. He knew, too, that the Chimes would ring immediately; and that they sounded to his fancy,

at such a time, like voices in the clouds. But he only made
the more haste to deliver the Alderman's letter, and get out
of the way before they began; for he dreaded to hear them
tagging "Friends and Fathers, Friends and Fathers," to the
burden they had rung out last.

Toby discharged himself of his commission, therefore,
with all possible speed, and set off trotting homeward. But
what with his pace, which was at best an awkward one in
the street; and what with his hat, which didn't improve it;
he trotted against somebody in less than no time, and was
sent staggering out into the road.

"I beg your pardon, I'm sure!" said Trotty, pulling up
his hat in great confusion, and between the hat and the torn
lining, fixing his head into a kind of bee-hive. "I hope I
haven't hurt you."

As to hurting anybody, Toby was not such an absolute
Samson, but that he was much more likely to be hurt himself: and indeed, he had flown out into the road, like a shut-
tlecock. He had such an opinion of his own strength, however, that he was in real concern for the other party: and
said again,

"I hope I haven't hurt you?"

The man against whom he had run; a sun-browned, sin-
ewy, country-looking man, with grizzled hair, and a rough
chin; stared at him for a moment, as if he suspected him to
be in jest. But, satisfied of his good faith, he answered:

"No, friend. You have not hurt me."

"Nor the child, I hope?" said Trotty.

"Nor the child," returned the man. "I thank you kindly."

As he said so, he glanced at a little girl he carried in his
arms, asleep: and shading her face with the long end of
the poor handkerchief he wore about his throat, went
slowly on.

The tone in which he said "I thank you kindly," penetrated Trotty's heart. He was so jaded and foot-sore, and
so soiled with travel, and looked about him so forlorn and
strange, that it was a comfort to him to be able to thank
any one: no matter for how little. Toby stood gazing after

him as he plodded wearily away, with the child's arm clinging round his neck.

At the figure in the worn shoes—now the very shade and
ghost of shoes—rough leather leggings, common frock, and
broad slouched hat, Trotty stood gazing, blind to the whole
street. And at the child's arm, clinging round its neck.

Before he merged into the darkness the traveller stopped;
and looking round, and seeing Trotty standing there yet,
seemed undecided whether to return or go on. After doing
first the one and then the other, he came back, and Trotty
went half way to meet him.

"You can tell me, perhaps," said the man with a faint
smile, "and if you can I am sure you will, and I'd rather
ask you than another—where Alderman Cute lives."

"Close at hand," replied Toby. "I'll show you his house
with pleasure."

"I was to have gone to him elsewhere to-morrow," said
the man, accompanying Toby, "but I'm uneasy under suspicion, and want to clear myself, and to be free to go and
seek my bread—I don't know where. So, maybe he'll forgive my going to his house to-night."

"It's impossible," cried Toby with a start, "that your
name's Fern!"

"Eh!" cried the other, turning on him in astonishment.

"Fern! Will Fern!" said Trotty.

"That's my name," replied the other.

"Why then," cried Trotty, seizing him by the arm, and
looking cautiously round, "for Heaven's sake don't go to
him! Don't go to him! He'll put you down as sure as ever
you were born. Here! come up this alley, and I'll tell you
what I mean. Don't go to *him*."

His new acquaintance looked as if he thought him mad;
but he bore him company nevertheless. When they were
shrouded from observation, Trotty told him what he knew,
and what character he had received, and all about it.

The subject of his history listened to it with a calmness
that surprised him. He did not contradict or interrupt it,
once. He nodded his head now and then—more in corrob-

oration of an old and worn-out story, it appeared, than in refutation of it; and once or twice threw back his hat, and passed his freckled hand over a brow, where every furrow he had ploughed seemed to have set its image in little. But he did no more.

"It's true enough in the main," he said, "master, I could sift grain from husk here and there, but let it be as 'tis. What odds? I have gone against his plans; to my misfortun'. I can't help it; I should do the like to-morrow. As to character, them gentlefolks will search and search, and pry and pry, and have it as free from spot or speck in us, afore they'll help us to a dry good word!—Well! I hope they don't lose good opinion as easy as we do, or their lives is strict indeed, and hardly worth the keeping. For myself, master, I never took with that hand"—holding it before him —"what wasn't my own; and never held it back from work, however hard, or poorly paid. Whoever can deny it, let him chop it off! But when work won't maintain me like a human creetur; when my living is so bad, that I am Hungry, out of doors and in; when I see a whole working life begin that way, go on that way, and end that way, without a chance or change; then I say to the gentlefolks 'Keep away from me! Let my cottage be. My doors is dark enough without your darkening of 'em more. Don't look for me to come up into the Park to help the show when there's a Birthday, or a fine Speechmaking, or what not. Act your Plays and Games without me, and be welcome to 'em, and enjoy 'em. We've nowt to do with one another. I'm best let alone!'"

Seeing that the child in his arms had opened her eyes, and was looking about her in wonder, he checked himself to say a word or two of foolish prattle in her ear, and stand her on the ground beside him. Then slowly winding one of her long tresses round and round his rough forefinger like a ring, while she hung about his dusty leg, he said to Trotty:

"I'm not a cross-grained man by natur', I believe; and easy satisfied, I'm sure. I bear no ill-will against none of 'em. I only want to live like one of the Almighty's creeturs. I can't—I don't—and so there's a pit dug between me, and them that can and do. There's others like me. You might tell 'em off by hundreds and by thousands, sooner than by ones."

Trotty knew he spoke the Truth in this, and shook his head to signify as much.

"I've got a bad name this way," said Fern; "and I'm not likely, I'm afeared, to get a better. 'Tan't lawful to be out of sorts, and I AM out of sorts, though God knows I'd sooner bear a cheerful spirit if I could. Well! I don't know as this Alderman could hurt *me* much by sending me to gaol; but without a friend to speak a word for me, he might do it; and you see—!" pointing downward with his finger, at the child.

"She has a beautiful face," said Trotty.

"Why yes!" replied the other in a low voice, as he gently turned it up with both his hands towards his own, and looked upon it steadfastly. "I've thought so, many times. I've thought so, when my hearth was very cold, and cupboard very bare. I thought so t'other night, when we were taken like two thieves. But they—they shouldn't try the little face too often, should they, Lilian? That's hardly fair upon a man!"

He sunk his voice so low, and gazed upon her with an air so stern and strange, that Toby, to divert the current of his thoughts, inquired if his wife were living.

"I never had one," he returned, shaking his head. "She's my brother's child: a orphan. Nine year old, though you'd hardly think it; but she's tired and worn out now. They'd have taken care on her, the Union—eight-and-twenty mile away from where we live—between four walls (as they took care of my old father when he couldn't work no more, though he didn't trouble 'em long); but I took her instead, and she's lived with me ever since. Her mother had a friend once, in London here. We are trying to find her, and to find work too; but it's a large place. Never mind. More room for us to walk about in Lilly!"

Meeting the child's eyes with a smile which melted Toby more than tears, he shook him by the hand.

"I don't so much as know your name," he said, "but I've opened my heart free to you, for I'm thankful to you; with good reason. I'll take your advice, and keep clear of this —"

"Justice," suggested Toby.

"Ah!" he said. "If that's the name they give him. This Justice. And to-morrow will try whether there's better fortun' to be met with, somewheres near London. Good-night. A Happy New Year!"

"Stay!" cried Trotty, catching at his hand, as he relaxed his grip. "Stay! The New Year never can be happy to me, if we part like this. The New Year never can be happy to me, if I see the child and you, go wandering away, you don't know where, without a shelter for your heads. Come home with me! I'm a poor man, living in a poor place; but I can give you lodging for one night and never miss it. Come home with me! Here! I'll take her!" cried Trotty, lifting up the child. "A pretty one! I'd carry twenty times her weight, and never know I'd got it. Tell me if I go too quick for you. I'm very fast. I always was!" Trotty said this, taking about six of his trotting paces to one stride of his fatigued companion; and with his thin legs quivering again, beneath the load he bore.

"Why, she's as light," said Trotty, trotting in his speech as well as in his gait; for he couldn't bear to be thanked, and dreaded a moment's pause; "as light as a feather. Lighter than a Peacock's feather—a great deal lighter. Here we are, and here we go! Round this first turning to the right, Uncle Will, and past the pump, and sharp off up the passage to the left, right opposite the public-house. Here we are and here we go! Cross over, Uncle Will, and mind the kidney pieman at the corner! Here we are and here we go! Down the Mews here, Uncle Will, and stop at the black door, with 'T. Veck, Ticket Porter' wrote upon a board; and here we are and here we go, and here we are indeed, my precious Meg, surprising you!"

With which words Trotty, in a breathless state, set the child down before his daughter in the middle of the floor. The little visitor looked once at Meg; and doubting nothing in that face, but trusting everything she saw there; ran into her arms.

"Here we are and here we go!" cried Trotty, running round the room, and choking audibly. "Here, Uncle Will, here's a fire you know! Why don't you come to the fire? Oh here we are and here we go! Meg, my precious darling, where's the kettle? Here it is and here it goes, and it'll bile in no time!"

Trotty really had picked up the kettle somewhere or other in the course of his wild career, and now put it on the fire; while Meg, seating the child in a warm corner, knelt down on the ground before her, and pulled off her shoes, and dried her wet feet on a cloth. Ay, and she laughed at Trotty too —so pleasantly, so cheerfully, that Trotty could have blessed her where she kneeled; for he had seen that, when they entered, she was sitting by the fire in tears.

"Why, father!" said Meg. "You're crazy to-night, I think. I don't know what the Bells would say to that. Poor little feet. How cold they are!"

"Oh, they're warmer now!" exclaimed the child. "They're quite warm now!"

"No, no, no," said Meg. "We haven't rubbed 'em half enough. We're so busy. So busy! And when they're done, we'll brush out the damp hair; and when that's done, we'll bring some colour to the poor pale face with fresh water; and when that's done, we'll be so gay, and brisk, and happy—!"

The child, in a burst of sobbing, clasped her round the neck; caressed her fair cheek with its hand; and said, "Oh Meg! oh dear Meg!"

Toby's blessing could have done no more. Who could do more!

"Why, father!" cried Meg, after a pause.

"Here I am and here I go, my dear!" said Trotty.

"Good Gracious me!" cried Meg. "He's crazy! He's

put the dear child's bonnet on the kettle, and hung the lid behind the door!"

"I didn't go for to do it, my love," said Trotty, hastily repairing this mistake. "Meg, my dear?"

Meg looked towards him and saw that he had elaborately stationed himself behind the chair of their male visitor, where with many mysterious gestures he was holding up the sixpence he had earned.

"I see, my dear," said Trotty, "as I was coming in, half an ounce of tea lying somewhere on the stairs; and I'm pretty sure there was a bit of bacon too. As I don't remember where it was exactly, I'll go myself and try to find 'em."

With this inscrutable artifice, Toby withdrew to purchase the viands he had spoken of, for ready money, at Mrs. Chickenstalker's; and presently came back, pretending he had not been able to find them, at first, in the dark.

"But here they are at last," said Trotty, setting out the tea-things, "all correct! I was pretty sure it was tea, and a rasher. So it is, Meg, my pet, if you'll just make the tea, while your unworthy father toasts the bacon, we shall be ready, immediate. It's a curious circumstance," said Trotty, proceeding in his cookery, with the assistance of the toasting-fork, "curious, but well known to my friends, that I never care, myself, for rashers, nor for tea. I like to see other people enjoy 'em," said Trotty, speaking very loud, to impress the fact upon his guest, "but to me, as food, they're disagreeable."

Yet Trotty sniffed the savour of the hissing bacon—ah! —as if he liked it; and when he poured the boiling water in the tea-pot, looked lovingly down into the depths of that snug cauldron, and suffered the fragrant steam to curl about his nose, and wreathe his head and face in a thick cloud. However, for all this, he neither ate nor drank, except at the very beginning, a mere morsel for form's sake, which he appeared to eat with infinite relish, but declared was perfectly uninteresting to him.

No. Trotty's occupation was, to see Will Fern and Lilian

eat and drink; and so was Meg's. And never did spectators at a city dinner or court banquet find such high delight in seeing others feast: although it were a monarch or a pope: as those two did, in looking on that night. Meg smiled at Trotty, Trotty laughed at Meg. Meg shook her head, and made belief to clap her hands, applauding Trotty; Trotty conveyed, in dumb-show, unintelligible narratives of how and when and where he had found their visitors, to Meg; and they were happy. Very happy.

"Although," thought Trotty, sorrowfully, as he watched Meg's face; "that match is broken off, I see!"

"Now, I'll tell you what," said Trotty after tea. "The little one, she sleeps with Meg, I know."

"With good Meg!" cried the child, caressing her. "With Meg."

"That's right," said Trotty. "And I shouldn't wonder if she kiss Meg's father, won't she? *I*'m Meg's father."

Mightily delighted Trotty was, when the child went timidly towards him, and having kissed him, fell back upon Meg again.

"She's as sensible as Solomon," said Trotty. "Here we come and here we—no, we don't—I don't mean that—I—what was I saying, Meg, my precious?"

Meg looked towards their guest, who leaned upon her chair, and with his face turned from her, fondled the child's head, half hidden in her lap.

"To be sure," said Toby. "To be sure! I don't know what I'm rambling on about, to-night. My wits are wool-gathering, I think. Will Fern, you come along with me. You're tired to death, and broken down for want of rest. You come along with me."

The man still played with the child's curls, still leaned upon Meg's chair, still turned away his face. He didn't speak, but in his rough coarse fingers, clenching and expanding in the fair hair of the child, there was an eloquence that said enough.

"Yes, yes," said Trotty, answering unconsciously what he saw expressed in his daughter's face. "Take her with you,

Meg. Get her to bed. There! Now, Will, I'll show you where you lie. It's not much of a place: only a loft; but, having a loft, I always say, is one of the great conveniences of living in a mews; and till this coach-house and stable gets a better let, we live here cheap. There's plenty of sweet hay up there, belonging to a neighbour; and it's as clean as hands, and Meg, can make it. Cheer up! Don't give way. A new heart for a New Year, always!"

The hand released from the child's hair, had fallen, trembling, into Trotty's hand. So Trotty, talking without intermission, led him out as tenderly and easily as if he had been a child himself.

Returning before Meg, he listened for an instant at the door of her little chamber; an adjoining room. The child was murmuring a simple Prayer before lying down to sleep; and when she had remembered Meg's name, "Dearly, Dearly"—so her words ran—Trotty heard her stop and ask for his.

It was some short time before the foolish little old fellow could compose himself to mend the fire, and draw his chair to the warm hearth. But, when he had done so, and had trimmed the light, he took his newspaper from his pocket, and began to read. Carelessly at first, and skimming up and down the columns; but with an earnest and a sad attention, very soon.

For this same dreaded paper re-directed Trotty's thoughts into the channel they had taken all that day, and which the days' events had so marked out and shaped. His interest in the two wanderers had set him on another course of thinking, and a happier one, for the time; but being alone again, and reading of the crimes and violences of the people, he relapsed into his former train.

In this mood, he came to an account (and it was not the first he had ever read) of a woman who had laid her desperate hands not only on her own life but on that of her young child. A crime so terrible, and so revolting to his soul, dilated with the love of Meg, that he let the journal drop, and fell back in his chair, appalled!

"Unnatural and cruel!" Toby cried. "Unnatural and cruel! None but people who were bad at heart, born bad, who had no business on the earth, could do such deeds. It's too true, all I've heard to-day; too just, too full of proof. We're Bad!"

The Chimes took up the words so suddenly—burst out so loud, and clear, and sonorous—that the Bells seemed to strike him in his chair.

And what was that they said?

"Toby Veck, Toby Veck, waiting for you Toby! Toby Veck, Toby Veck, waiting for you Toby! Come and see us, come and see us, Drag him to us, drag him to us, Haunt and hunt him, haunt and hunt him, Break his slumbers, break his slumbers! Toby Veck Toby Veck, door open wide Toby, Toby Veck Toby Veck, door open wide Toby—" then fiercely back to their impetuous strain again, and ringing in the very bricks and plaster on the walls.

Toby listened. Fancy, fancy! His remorse for having run away from them that afternoon! No, no. Nothing of the kind. Again, again, and yet a dozen times again. "Haunt and hunt him, haunt and hunt him, Drag him to us, drag him to us!" Deafening the whole town!

"Meg," said Trotty softly: tapping at her door. "Do you hear anything?"

"I hear the Bells, father. Surely they're very loud to-night."

"Is she asleep?" said Toby, making an excuse for peeping in.

"So peacefully and happily! I can't leave her yet though, father. Look how she holds my hand!"

"Meg," whispered Trotty. "Listen to the Bells!"

She listened, with her face towards him all the time. But it underwent no change. She didn't understand them.

Trotty withdrew, resumed his seat by the fire, and once more listened by himself. He remained here a little time.

It was impossible to bear it; their energy was dreadful.

"If the tower-door is really open," said Toby, hastily laying aside his apron, but never thinking of his hat, "what's to hinder me from going up into the steeple and satisfying myself? If it's shut, I don't want any other satisfaction. That's enough."

He was pretty certain as he slipped out quietly into the street that he should find it shut and locked, for he knew the door well, and had so rarely seen it open, that he couldn't reckon above three times in all. It was a low arched portal, outside the church, in a dark nook behind a column; and had such great iron hinges, and such a monstrous lock, that there was much more hinge and lock than door.

But what was his astonishment when, coming bare-headed to the church; and putting his hand into this dark nook, with a certain misgiving that it might be unexpectedly seized, and a shivering propensity to draw it back again; he found that the door, which opened outwards, actually stood ajar!

He thought, on the first surprise, of going back; or of getting a light, or a companion; but his courage aided him immediately, and he determined to ascend alone.

"What have I to fear?" said Trotty. "It's a church! Besides, the ringers may be there, and have forgotten to shut the door."

So he went in, feeling his way as he went, like a blind man; for it was very dark. And very quiet, for the Chimes were silent.

The dust from the street had blown into the recess; and lying there, heaped up, made it so soft and velvet-like to the foot, that there was something startling, even in that. The narrow stair was so close to the door, too, that he stumbled at the very first; and shutting the door upon himself, by striking it with his foot, and causing it to rebound back heavily, he couldn't open it again.

This was another reason, however, for going on. Trotty groped his way, and went on. Up, up, up, and round, and round; and up, up, up; higher, higher, higher up!

It was a disagreeable staircase for that groping work; so low and narrow, that his groping hand was always touching something; and it often felt so like a man or ghostly figure standing up erect and making room for him to pass without discovery, that he would rub the smooth wall upward searching for its face, and downward searching for its feet, while a chill tingling crept all over him. Twice or thrice, a door or niche broke the monotonous surface; and then it seemed a gap as wide as the whole church; and he felt on the brink of an abyss, and going to tumble headlong down, until he found the wall again.

Still up, up, up; and round and round, and up, up, up; higher, higher, higher up!

At length, the dull and stifling atmosphere began to freshen: presently to feel quite windy: presently it blew so strong, that he could hardly keep his legs. But, he got to an arched window in the tower, breast high, and holding tight, looked down upon the house-tops, on the smoking chimneys, on the blurr and blotch of lights (towards the place where Meg was wondering where he was and calling to him perhaps), all kneaded up together in a leaven of mist and darkness.

This was the belfry, where the ringers came. He had caught hold of one of the frayed ropes which hung down through apertures in the oaken roof. At first he started, thinking it was hair; then trembled at the very thought of waking the deep Bell. The Bells themselves were higher. Higher, Trotty, in his fascination, or in working out the spell upon him, groped his way. By ladders now, and toilsomely, for it was steep, and not too certain holding for the feet.

Up, up, up; and climb and clamber; up, up, up; higher, higher, higher up!

Until, ascending through the floor, and pausing with his head just raised above its beams, he came among the Bells. It was barely possible to make out their great shapes in the gloom; but there they were. Shadowy, and dark, and dumb.

A heavy sense of dread and loneliness fell instantly upon him, as he climbed into this airy nest of stone and metal. His head went round and round. He listened, and then raised a wild "Holloa!"

Holloa! was mournfully protracted by the echoes.

Giddy, confused, and out of breath, and frightened, Toby looked about him vacantly, and sunk down in a swoon.

Third Quarter

BLACK are the brooding clouds and troubled the deep waters, when the Sea of Thought, first heaving from a calm, gives up its Dead. Monsters uncouth and wild, arise in premature, imperfect resurrection; the several parts and shapes of different things are joined and mixed by chance; and when, and how, and by what wonderful degrees, each separates from each, and every sense and object of the mind resumes its usual form and lives again, no man—though every man is every day the casket of this type of the Great Mystery—can tell.

So, when and how the darkness of the night-black steeple changed to shining light; when and how the solitary tower was peopled with a myriad figures; when and how the whispered "Haunt and hunt him," breathing monotonously through his sleep or swoon, became a voice exclaiming in the waking ears of Trotty, "Break his slumbers"; when and how he ceased to have a sluggish and confused idea that such things were, companioning a host of others that were not; there are no dates or means to tell. But, awake and standing on his feet upon the boards where he had lately lain, he saw this Goblin Sight.

He saw the tower, whither his charmed footsteps had brought him, swarming with dwarf phantoms, spirits, elfin creatures of the Bells. He saw them leaping, flying, dropping, pouring from the Bells without a pause. He saw them, round him on the ground; above him, in the air; clambering from him, by the ropes below; looking down upon him, from the massive iron-girded beams; peeping in upon him, through the chinks and loopholes in the walls; spreading away and away from him in enlarging circles, as the water ripples give way to a huge stone that suddenly comes plashing in among them. He saw them, of all aspects and all shapes. He saw them ugly, handsome, crippled, exquisitely formed. He saw them young, he saw them old, he saw them kind, he saw them cruel, he saw them merry, he saw them grim; he saw them dance, and heard them sing; he saw them tear their hair, and heard them howl. He saw the air thick with them. He saw them come and go, incessantly. He saw them riding downward, soaring upward, sailing off afar, perching near at hand, all restless and all violently active. Stone, and brick, and slate, and tile, became transparent to him as to them. He saw them *in* the houses, busy at the sleepers' beds. He saw them soothing people in their dreams; he saw them beating them with knotted whips; he saw them yelling in their ears; he saw them playing softest music on their pillows; he saw them cheering some with the songs of birds and the perfume of flowers; he saw them flashing awful faces on the troubled rest of others, from enchanted mirrors which they carried in their hands.

He saw these creatures, not only among sleeping men but waking also, active in pursuits irreconcilable with one another, and possessing or assuming natures the most opposite. He saw one buckling on innumerable wings to increase his speed; another loading himself with chains and weights, to retard his. He saw some putting the hands of clocks forward, some putting the hands of clocks backward, some endeavouring to stop the clock entirely. He saw them representing, here a marriage ceremony, there a funeral; in this chamber an election, in that a ball; he saw, everywhere, restless and untiring motion.

Bewildered by the host of shifting and extraordinary figures, as well as by the uproar of the Bells, which all this while were ringing, Trotty clung to a wooden pillar for support, and turned his white face here and there, in mute and stunned astonishment.

As he gazed, the Chimes stopped. Instantaneous change! The whole swarm fainted! their forms collapsed, their speed deserted them; they sought to fly, but in the act of falling died and melted into air. No fresh supply succeeded them. One straggler leaped down pretty briskly from the surface of the Great Bell, and alighted on his feet, but he was dead and gone before he could turn round. Some few of the late company who had gambolled in the tower, remained there, spinning over and over a little longer; but these became at every turn more faint, and few, and feeble, and soon went the way of the rest. The last of all was one small hunchback, who had got into an echoing corner, where he twirled and twirled, and floated by himself a long time; showing such perseverance, that at last he dwindled to a leg and even to a foot, before he finally retired; but he vanished in the end, and then the tower was silent.

Then and not before, did Trotty see in every Bell a bearded figure of the bulk and stature of the Bell—incomprehensibly, a figure and the Bell itself. Gigantic, grave, and darkly watchful of him, as he stood rooted to the ground.

Mysterious and awful figures! Resting on nothing; poised in the night air of the tower, with their draped and hooded heads merged in the dim roof; motionless and shadowy. Shadowy and dark, although he saw them by some light belonging to themselves—none else was there—each with its muffled hand upon its goblin mouth.

He could not plunge down wildly through the opening in the floor; for all power of motion had deserted him. Otherwise he would have done so—aye, would have thrown himself, headforemost, from the steeple-top, rather than have seen them watching him with eyes that would have waked and watched although the pupils had been taken out.

Again, again, the dread and terror of the lonely place, and of the wild and fearful night that reigned there, touched him like a spectral hand. His distance from all help; the long, dark, winding, ghost-beleaguered way that lay between him and the earth on which men lived; his being high, high, high, up there, where it had made him dizzy to see the birds fly in the day; cut off from all good people, who at such an hour were safe at home and sleeping in their beds; all this struck coldly through him, not as a reflection but a bodily sensation. Meantime his eyes and thoughts and fears, were fixed upon the watchful figures; which, rendered unlike any figures of this world by the deep gloom and shade enwrapping and enfolding them, as well as by their looks and forms and supernatural hovering above the floor, were nevertheless as plainly to be seen as were the stalwart oaken frames, cross-pieces, bars and beams, set up there to support the Bells. These hemmed them, in a very forest of hewn timber; from the entanglements, intricacies, and depths of which, as from among the boughs of a dead wood blighted for their phantom use, they kept their darksome and unwinking watch.

A blast of air—how cold and shrill!—came moaning through the tower. As it died away, the Great Bell, or the Goblin of the Great Bell, spoke.

"What visitor is this?" it said. The voice was low and deep, and Trotty fancied that it sounded in the other figures as well.

"I thought my name was called by the Chimes!" said Trotty, raising his hands in an attitude of supplication. "I hardly know why I am here, or how I came. I have listened to the Chimes these many years. They have cheered me often."

"And you have thanked them?" said the Bell.

"A thousand times!" cried Trotty.

"How?"

"I am a poor man," faltered Trotty, "and could only thank them in words."

"And always so?" inquired the Goblin of the Bell. "Have you never done us wrong in words?"

"No!" cried Trotty eagerly.

"Never done us foul, and false, and wicked wrong, in words?" pursued the Goblin of the Bell.

Trotty was about to answer, "Never!" But he stopped, and was confused.

"The voice of Time," said the Phantom, "cries to man, Advance! Time is for his advancement and improvement; for his greater worth, his greater happiness, his better life;

his progress onward to that goal within its knowledge and its view, and set there, in the period when Time and He began. Ages of darkness, wickedness, and violence, have come and gone—millions uncountable, have suffered, lived, and died—to point the way before him. Who seeks to turn him back, or stay him on his course, arrests a mighty engine which will strike the meddler dead; and be the fiercer and the wilder, ever, for its momentary check!"

"I never did so to my knowledge, sir," said Trotty. "It was quite by accident if I did. I wouldn't go to do it, I'm sure."

"Who puts into the mouth of Time, or of its servants," said the Goblin of the Bell, "a cry of lamentation for days which have had their trial and their failure, and have left deep traces of it which the blind may see—a cry that only serves the present time, by showing men how much it needs their help when any ears can listen to regrets for such a past —who does this, does a wrong. And you have done that wrong, to us, the Chimes."

Trotty's first excess of fear was gone. But he had felt tenderly and gratefully towards the Bells, as you have seen; and when he heard himself arraigned as one who had offended them so weightily, his heart was touched with penitence and grief.

"If you knew," said Trotty, clasping his hands earnestly —"or perhaps you do know—if you know how often you have kept me company; how often you have cheered me up when I've been low; how you were quite the plaything of my little daughter Meg (almost the only one she ever had) when first her mother died, and she and me were left alone; you won't bear malice for a hasty word!"

"Who hears in us, the Chimes, one note bespeaking disregard, or stern regard, of any hope, or joy, or pain, or sorrow, of the many-sorrowed throng; who hears us make response to any creed that gauges human passions and affections, as it gauges the amount of miserable food on which humanity may pine and wither; does us wrong. That wrong you have done us!" said the Bell.

"I have!" said Trotty. "Oh forgive me!"

"Who hears us echo the dull vermin of the earth; the Putters Down of crushed and broken natures, formed to be raised up higher than such maggots of the time can crawl or can conceive," pursued the Goblin of the Bell; "who does so, does us wrong. And you have done us wrong!"

"Not meaning it," said Trotty. "In my ignorance. Not meaning it!"

"Lastly, and most of all," pursued the Bell. "Who turns his back upon the fallen and disfigured of his kind; abandons them as vile; and does not trace and track with pitying eyes the unfenced precipice by which they fell from good—grasping in their fall some tufts and shreds of that lost soil, and clinging to them still when bruised and dying in the gulf below; does wrong to Heaven and man, to time and to eternity. And you have done that wrong!"

"Spare me," cried Trotty, falling on his knees; "for Mercy's sake!"

"Listen!" said the Shadow.

"Listen!" cried the other Shadows.

"Listen!" said a clear and childlike voice, which Trotty thought he recognised as having heard before.

The organ sounded faintly in the church below. Swelling by degrees, the melody ascended to the roof, and filled the choir and nave. Expanding more and more, it rose, up, up; up, up; higher, higher, higher up; awakening agitated hearts within the burly piles of oak, the hollow bells, the iron-bound doors, the stairs of solid stone; until the tower walls were insufficient to contain it, and it soared into the sky.

No wonder that an old man's breast could not contain a sound so vast and mighty. It broke from that weak prison in a rush of tears; and Trotty put his hands before his face.

"Listen!" said the Shadow.

"Listen!" said the other Shadows.

"Listen!" said the child's voice.

A solemn strain of blended voices, rose into the tower.

It was a very low and mournful strain—a Dirge—and as he listened, Trotty heard his child among the singers.

"She is dead!" exclaimed the old man. "Meg is dead! Her spirit calls to me. I hear it!"

"The Spirit of your child bewails the dead, and mingles with the dead—dead hopes, dead fancies, dead imaginings of youth," returned the Bell, "but she is living. Learn from her life, a living truth. Learn from the creature dearest to your heart, how bad the bad are born. See every bud and leaf plucked one by one from off the fairest stem, and know how bare and wretched it may be. Follow her! To desperation!"

Each of the shadowy figures stretched its right arm forth, and pointed downward.

"The Spirit of the Chimes is your companion," said the figure. "Go! It stands behind you!"

Trotty turned, and saw—the child! The child Will Fern had carried in the street; the child whom Meg had watched, but now, asleep!

"I carried her myself, to-night," said Trotty. "In these arms!"

"Show him what he calls himself," said the dark figures, one and all.

The tower opened at his feet. He looked down, and beheld his own form, lying at the bottom, on the outside: crushed and motionless.

"No more a living man!" cried Trotty. "Dead!"

"Dead!" said the figures all together.

"Gracious Heaven! And the New Year—"

"Past," said the figures.

"What!" he cried, shuddering. "I missed my way, and coming on the outside of this tower in the dark, fell down— a year ago?"

"Nine years ago!" replied the figures.

As they gave the answer, they recalled their outstretched hands; and where their figures had been, there the Bells were.

And they rung; their time being come again. And once again, vast multitudes of phantoms sprung into existence;

once again, were incoherently engaged, as they had been
before; once again, faded on the stopping of the Chimes;
and dwindled into nothing.

"What are these?" he asked his guide. "If I am not mad,
what are these?"

"Spirits of the Bells. Their sound upon the air," returned the child. "They take such shapes and occupations
as the hopes and thoughts of mortals, and the recollections
they have stored up, give them."

"And you," said Trotty wildly. "What are you?"

"Hush, hush!" returned the child. "Look here!"

In a poor, mean room: working at the same kind of
embroidery which he had often, often seen before her; Meg,
his own dear daughter, was presented to his view. He made
no effort to imprint his kisses on her face; he did not strive
to clasp her to his loving heart; he knew that such endearments were, for him, no more. But, he held his trembling
breath, and brushed away the blinding tears, that he might
look upon her; that he might only see her.

Ah! Changed. Changed. The light of the clear eyes, how
dimmed. The bloom, how faded from the cheek. Beautiful
she was, as she had ever been, but Hope, Hope, Hope, oh
where was the fresh Hope that had spoken to him like a
voice!

She looked up from her work, at a companion. Following
her eyes, the old man started back.

In the woman grown, he recognised her at a glance. In
the long silken hair, he saw the self-same curls; around the
lips, the child's expression lingering still. See! In the eyes,
now turned inquiringly on Meg, there shone the very look
that scanned those features when he brought her home!

Then what was this, beside him!

Looking with awe into its face, he saw a something reigning there: a lofty something, undefined and indistinct, which
made it hardly more than a remembrance of that child—as
yonder figure might be—yet it was the same: the same: and
wore the dress.

Hark. They were speaking!

"Meg," said Lilian, hesitating. "How often you raise your head from your work to look at me!"

"Are my looks so altered, that they frighten you?" asked Meg.

"Nay, dear! But you smile at that, yourself! Why not smile, when you look at me, Meg?"

"I do so. Do I not!" she answered: smiling on her.

"Now you do," said Lilian, "but not usually. When you think I'm busy, and don't see you, you look so anxious and so doubtful, that I hardly like to raise my eyes. There is little cause for smiling in this hard and toilsome life, but you were once so cheerful."

"Am I not now!" cried Meg, speaking in a tone of strange alarm, and rising to embrace her. "Do I make our weary life more weary to you, Lilian!"

"You have been the only thing that made it life," said Lilian, fervently kissing her; "sometimes the only thing that made me care to live so, Meg. Such work, such work! So many hours, so many days, so many long, long nights of hopeless, cheerless, never-ending work—not to heap up riches, not to live grandly or gaily, not to live upon enough, however coarse; but to earn bare bread: to scrape together just enough to toil upon, and want upon, and keep alive in us the consciousness of our hard fate! Oh, Meg, Meg!" she raised her voice and twined her arms about her as she spoke, like one in pain. "How can the cruel world go round, and bear to look upon such lives!"

"Lilly!" said Meg, soothing her, and putting back her hair from her wet face. "Why Lilly! You! So pretty and so young!"

"Oh Meg!" she interrupted, holding her at arm's-length, and looking in her face imploringly. "The worst of all, the worst of all! Strike me old, Meg! Wither me, and shrivel me, and free me from the dreadful thoughts that tempt me in my youth!"

Trotty turned to look upon his guide. But, the Spirit of the child had taken flight. Was gone.

Neither did he himself remain in the same place; for, Sir Joseph Bowley, Friend and Father of the Poor, held a great festivity at Bowley Hall, in honour of the natal day of Lady Bowley. And as Lady Bowley had been born on New Year's Day (which the local newspapers considered an especial pointing of the finger of Providence to number One, as Lady Bowley's destined figure in Creation), it was on a New Year's Day that this festivity took place.

Bowley Hall was full of visitors. The red-faced gentleman was there, Mr. Filer was there, the great Alderman Cute was there—Alderman Cute had a sympathetic feeling with great people, and had considerably improved his acquaintance with Sir Joseph Bowley on the strength of his attentive letter: indeed had become quite a friend of the family since then—and many guests were there. Trotty's ghost was there, wandering about, poor phantom, drearily; and looking for its guide.

There was to be a great dinner in the Great Hall. At which Sir Joseph Bowley, in his celebrated character of Friend and Father of the Poor, was to make his great speech. Certain plum-puddings were to be eaten by his Friends and Children in another Hall first; and, at a given signal, Friends and Children flocking in among their Friends and Fathers, were to form a family assemblage, with not one manly eye therein unmoistened by emotion.

But, there was more than this to happen. Even more than this. Sir Joseph Bowley, Baronet and Member of Parliament, was to play a match at skittles—real skittles—with his tenants!

"Which quite reminds me," said Alderman Cute, "of the days of old King Hal, stout King Hal, bluff King Hal. Ah. Fine character!"

"Very," said Mr. Filer, dryly. "For marrying women and murdering 'em. Considerably more than the average number of wives by the bye."

"You'll marry the beautiful ladies, and not murder 'em, eh?" said Alderman Cute to the heir of Bowley, aged twelve. "Sweet boy! We shall have this little gentleman in

Parliament now," said the Alderman, holding him by the shoulders, and looking as reflective as he could, "before we know where we are. We shall hear of his successes at the poll; his speeches in the House; his overtures from Governments; his brilliant achievements of all kinds; ah! we shall make our little orations about him in the Common Council, I'll be bound; before we have time to look about us!"

"Oh, the difference of shoes and stockings!" Trotty thought. But his heart yearned towards the child, for the love of those same shoeless and stockingless boys, predestined (by the Alderman) to turn out bad, who might have been the children of poor Meg.

"Richard," moaned Trotty, roaming among the company, to and fro; "where is he? I can't find Richard! Where is Richard?"

Not likely to be there, if still alive! But Trotty's grief and solitude confused him; and he still went wandering among the gallant company, looking for his guide, and saying, "Where is Richard? Show me Richard!"

He was wandering thus, when he encountered Mr. Fish, the confidential Secretary: in great agitation.

"Bless my heart and soul!" cried Mr. Fish. "Where's Alderman Cute? Has anybody seen the Alderman?"

Seen the Alderman? Oh dear! Who could ever help seeing the Alderman? He was so considerate, so affable, he bore so much in mind the natural desires of folks to see him, that if he had a fault, it was the being constantly On View. And wherever the great people were, there, to be sure, attracted by the kindred sympathy between great souls, was Cute.

Several voices cried that he was in the circle round Sir Joseph. Mr. Fish made way there; found him; and took him secretly into a window near at hand. Trotty joined them. Not of his own accord. He felt that his steps were led in that direction.

"My dear Alderman Cute," said Mr. Fish. "A little more this way. The most dreadful circumstance has occurred. I have this moment received the intelligence. I think it will be best not to acquaint Sir Joseph with it till the day is over. You understand Sir Joseph, and will give me your opinion. The most frightful and deplorable event!"

"Fish!" returned the Alderman. "Fish! My good fellow, what is the matter? Nothing revolutionary, I hope! No— no attempted interference with the magistrates?"

"Deedles, the banker," gasped the Secretary. "Deedles Brothers—who was to have been here to-day—high in office in the Goldsmiths' Company—"

"Not stopped!" exclaimed the Alderman. "It can't be!"

"Shot himself!"

"Good God!"

"Put a double-barrelled pistol to his mouth, in his own counting-house," said Mr. Fish, "and blew his brains out. No motive. Princely circumstances!"

"Circumstances!" exclaimed the Alderman. "A man of noble fortune. One of the most respectable of men. Suicide, Mr. Fish! By his own hand!"

"This very morning," returned Mr. Fish.

"Oh the brain, the brain!" exclaimed the pious Alderman, lifting up his hands. "Oh the nerves, the nerves; the mysteries of this machine called Man! Oh the little that unhinges it: poor creatures that we are! Perhaps a dinner, Mr. Fish. Perhaps the conduct of his son, who, I have heard, ran very wild, and was in the habit of drawing bills upon him without the least authority! A most respectable man. One of the most respectable men I ever knew! A lamentable instance, Mr. Fish. A public calamity! I shall make a point of wearing the deepest mourning. A most respectable man! But there is One above. We must submit, Mr. Fish. We must submit!"

"What, Alderman! No word of Putting Down? Remember, Justice, your high moral boast and pride. Come, Alderman! Balance those scales. Throw me into this, the empty one, no dinner, and Nature's founts in some poor woman, dried by starving misery and rendered obdurate to claims for which her offspring *has* authority in holy mother Eve. Weigh me the two, you Daniel, going to judgment, when your day shall come! Weigh them, in the eyes of suffering thousands, audience (not unmindful) of the grim farce you play. Or supposing that you strayed from your five wits—it's not so far to go, but that it might be—and laid hands upon that throat of yours, warning your fellows (if you have a fellow) how they croak their comfortable wickedness to raving heads and stricken hearts. What then?"

The words rose up in Trotty's breast, as if they had been spoken by some other voice within him. Alderman Cute pledged himself to Mr. Fish that he would assist him in breaking the melancholy catastrophe to Sir Joseph when the day was over. Then, before they parted, wringing Mr. Fish's hand in bitterness of soul, he said, "The most respectable of men!" And added that he hardly knew (not even he), why such afflictions were allowed on earth.

"It 's almost enough to make one think, if one didn't know better," said Alderman Cute, "that at times some motion of a capsizing nature was going on in things, which affected the general economy of the social fabric. Deedles Brothers!"

The skittle-playing came off with immense success. Sir Joseph knocked the pins about quite skillfully; Master Bowley took an innings at a shorter distance also; and everybody said that now, when a Baronet and the Son of a Baronet played at skittles, the country was coming round again, as fast as it could come.

At its proper time, the Banquet was served up. Trotty involuntarily repaired to the Hall with the rest, for he felt himself conducted thither by some stronger impulse than his own free will. The sight was gay in the extreme; the ladies were very handsome; the visitors delighted, cheerful, and good-tempered. When the lower doors were opened, and the people flocked in, in their rustic dresses, the beauty of the spectacle was at its height; but Trotty only murmured more and more, "Where is Richard! He should help and comfort her! I can't see Richard!"

There had been some speeches made; and Lady Bowley's health had been proposed; and Sir Joseph Bowley had returned thanks, and had made his great speech, showing by

various pieces of evidence that he was the born Friend and
Father, and so forth; and had given as a Toast, his Friends
and Children, and the Dignity of Labour; when a slight
disturbance at the bottom of the Hall attracted Toby's
notice. After some confusion, noise, and opposition, one
man broke through the rest, and stood forward by himself.

Not Richard. No. But one whom he had thought of, and
had looked for, many times. In a scantier supply of light, he
might have doubted the identity of that worn man, so old,
and gray, and bent; but with a blaze of lamps upon his
gnarled and knotted head, he knew Will Fern as soon as he
stepped forth.

"What is this!" exclaimed Sir Joseph, rising. "Who gave
this man admittance? This is a criminal from prison! Mr.
Fish, sir, *will* you have the goodness—"

"A minute!" said Will Fern. "A minute! My Lady, you
was born on this day along with a New Year. Get me a
minute's leave to speak."

She made some intercession for him. Sir Joseph took his
seat again, with native dignity.

The ragged visitor—for he was miserably dressed—
looked round upon the company, and made his homage to
them with a humble bow.

"Gentlefolks!" he said. "You've drunk the Labourer.
Look at me!"

"Just come from jail," said Mr. Fish.

"Just come from jail," said Will. "And neither for the
first time, nor the second, nor the third, nor yet the fourth."

Mr. Filer was heard to remark testily, that four times
was over the average; and he ought to be ashamed of himself.

"Gentlefolks!" repeated Will Fern. "Look at me! You
see I'm at the worst. Beyond all hurt or harm; beyond your
help; for the time when your kind words or kind actions
could have done ME good,"—he struck his hand upon his
breast, and shook his head, "is gone, with the scent of last
year's beans or clover on the air. Let me say a word for
these," pointing to the labouring people in the Hall; "and

when you 're met together, hear the real Truth spoke out for once."

"There 's not a man here," said the host, "who would have him for a spokesman."

"Like enough, Sir Joseph. I believe it. Not the less true, perhaps, is what I say. Perhaps that 's a proof on it. Gentlefolks, I 've lived many a year in this place. You may see the cottage from the sunk fence over yonder. I 've seen the ladies draw it in their books, a hundred times. It looks well in a picter, I 've heerd say; but there an't weather in picters, and maybe 'tis fitter for that, than for a place to live in. Well! I lived there. How hard—how bitter hard, I lived there, I won't say. Any day in the year, and every day, you can judge for your own selves."

He spoke as he had spoken on the night when Trotty found him in the street. His voice was deeper and more husky, and had a trembling in it now and then; but he never raised it passionately, and seldom lifted it above the firm stern level of the homely facts he stated.

" 'Tis harder than you think for, gentlefolks, to grow up decent, commonly decent, in such a place. That I growed up a man and not a brute, says something for me—as I was then. As I am now, there 's nothing can be said for me or done for me. I 'm past it."

"I am glad this man has entered," observed Sir Joseph, looking round serenely. "Don't disturb him. It appears to be Ordained. He is an example: a living example. I hope and trust, and confidently expect, that it will not be lost upon my Friends here."

"I dragged on," said Fern, after a moment's silence, "somehow. Neither me nor any other man knows how; but so heavy, that I couldn't put a cheerful face upon it, or make believe that I was anything but what I was. Now, gentlemen—you gentlemen that sits at Sessions—when you see a man with discontent writ on his face, you says to one another, 'He 's suspicious. I has my doubts,' says you, 'about Will Fern. Watch that fellow!' I don't say, gentlemen, it an't quite nat'ral, but I say 'tis so; and from that hour, whatever Will Fern does, or lets alone—all one—it goes against him."

Alderman Cute stuck his thumbs in his waistcoat-pockets, and leaning back in his chair, and smiling, winked at a neighbouring chandelier. As much as to say, "Of course! I told you so. The common cry! Lord bless you, we are up to all this sort of thing—myself and human nature."

"Now, gentlemen," said Will Fern, holding out his hands, and flushing for an instant in his haggard face, "see how your laws are made to trap and hunt us when we're brought to this. I tries to live elsewhere. And I'm a vagabond. To jail with him! I comes back here. I goes a-nutting in your woods, and breaks—who don't?—a limber branch or two. To jail with him! One of your keepers sees me in broad day, near my own patch of garden, with a gun. To jail with him! I has a nat'ral angry word with that man, when I'm free again! To jail with him! I cuts a stick. To jail with him! I eats a rotten apple or a turnip. To jail with him! It's twenty mile away; and coming back I begs a trifle on the road. To jail with him! At last, the constable, the keeper—anybody—finds me anywhere, a-doing anything. To jail with him, for he's a vagrant, and a jail-bird known; and the jail's the only home he's got."

The Alderman nodded sagaciously, as who should say, "A very good home too!"

"Do I say this to serve MY cause!" cried Fern. "Who can give me back my liberty, who can give me back my good name, who can give me back my innocent niece? Not all the Lords and Ladies in wide England. But gentlemen, gentlemen, dealing with other men like me, begin at the right end. Give us, in mercy, better homes when we're a-lying in our cradles; give us better food when we're a-working for our lives; give us kinder laws to bring us back when we're a-going wrong; and don't set Jail, Jail, Jail, afore us, everywhere we turn. There an't a condescension you can show the Labourer then, that he won't take, as ready and as grateful as a man can be; for, he has a patient, peaceful, willing heart. But you must put his rightful spirit

in him first; for, whether he's a wreck and ruin such as me,
or is like one of them that stand here now, his spirit is
divided from you at this time. Bring it back, gentlefolks,
bring it back! Bring it back, afore the day comes when even
his Bible changes in his altered mind, and the words seem
to him to read, as they have sometimes read in my own eyes
—in Jail: 'Whither thou goest, I can Not go; where thou
lodgest, I do Not lodge; thy people are Not my people; Nor
thy God my God!'"

A sudden stir and agitation took place in the Hall. Trotty
thought at first, that several had risen to eject the man; and
hence this change in its appearance. But, another moment
showed him that the room and all the company had vanished
from his sight, and that his daughter was again before him,
seated at her work. But in a poorer, meaner garret than before; and with no Lilian by her side.

The frame at which she had worked, was put away upon a
shelf and covered up. The chair in which she had sat, was
turned against the wall. A history was written in these little
things, and in Meg's grief-worn face. Oh! who could fail
to read it!

Meg strained her eyes upon her work until it was too dark
to see the threads; and when the night closed in, she lighted
her feeble candle and worked on. Still her old father was
invisible about her; looking down upon her; loving her—
how dearly loving her!—and talking to her in a tender voice
about the old times, and the Bells. Though he knew, poor
Trotty, though he knew she could not hear him.

A great part of the evening had worn away, when a
knock came at her door. She opened it. A man was on the
threshold. A slouching, moody, drunken sloven, wasted by
intemperance and vice, and with his matted hair and un-
shorn beard in wild disorder; but, with some traces on him,
too, of having been a man of good proportion and good
features in his youth.

He stopped until he had her leave to enter; and she, retiring a pace or two from the open door, silently and sorrow-

fully looked upon him. Trotty had his wish. He saw Richard.

"May I come in, Margaret?"

"Yes! Come in. Come in!"

It was well that Trotty knew him before he spoke; for with any doubt remaining on his mind, the harsh discordant voice would have persuaded him that it was not Richard but some other man.

There were but two chairs in the room. She gave him hers, and stood at some short distance from him, waiting to hear what he had to say.

He sat, however, staring vacantly at the floor; with a lustreless and stupid smile. A spectacle of such deep degradation, of such abject hopelessness, of such a miserable downfall, that she put her hands before her face and turned away, lest he should see how much it moved her.

Roused by the rustling of her dress, or some such trifling sound, he lifted his head, and began to speak as if there had been no pause since he entered.

"Still at work, Margaret? You work late."

"I generally do."

"And early?"

"And early."

"So she said. She said you never tired; or never owned that you tired. Not all the time you lived together. Nor even when you fainted, between work and fasting. But I told you that, the last time I came."

"You did," she answered. "And I implored you to tell me nothing more; and you made me a solemn promise, Richard, that you never would."

"A solemn promise," he repeated, with a drivelling laugh and vacant stare. "A solemn promise. To be sure. A solemn promise!" Awakening, as it were, after a time; in the same manner as before; he said with sudden animation:

"How can I help it, Margaret? What am I to do? She has been to me again!"

"Again!" cried Meg, clasping her hands. "O, does she think of me so often! Has she been again!"

"Twenty times again," said Richard. "Margaret, she haunts me. She comes behind me in the street, and thrusts it in my hand. I hear her foot upon the ashes when I'm at my work (ha, ha! that an't often), and before I can turn my head, her voice is in my ear, saying, 'Richard, don't look round. For Heaven's love, give her this!' She brings it where I live; she sends it in letters; she taps at the window and lays it on the sill. What *can* I do? Look at it!"

He held out in his hand a little purse, and chinked the money it enclosed.

"Hide it," said Meg. "Hide it! When she comes again, tell her, Richard, that I love her in my soul. That I never lie down to sleep, but I bless her, and pray for her. That, in my solitary work, I never cease to have her in my thoughts. That she is with me, night and day. That if I died to-morrow, I would remember her with my last breath. But, that I cannot look upon it!'

He slowly recalled his hand, and crushing the purse together, said with a kind of drowsy thoughtfulness:

"I told her so. I told her so, as plain as words could speak. I've taken this gift back and left it at her door, a dozen times since then. But when she came at last, and stood before me, face to face, what could I do?"

"You saw her!" exclaimed Meg. "You saw her! O Lilian, my sweet girl! O, Lilian, Lilian!"

"I saw her," he went on to say, not answering, but engaged in the same slow pursuit of his own thoughts. "There she stood: trembling! 'How does she look, Richard? Does she ever speak of me? Is she thinner? My old place at the table: what's in my old place? And the frame she taught me our old work on—has she burnt it, Richard!' There she was. I heard her say it."

Meg checked her sobs, and with the tears streaming from her eyes, bent over him to listen. Not to lose a breath.

With his arms resting on his knees; and stooping forward in his chair, as if what he said were written on the ground in some half legible character, which it was his occupation to decipher and connect; he went on.

" 'Richard, I have fallen very low; and you may guess how much I have suffered in having this sent back, when I can bear to bring it in my hand to you. But you loved her once, even in my memory, dearly. Others stepped in between you; fears, and jealousies, and doubts, and vanities, estranged you from her; but you did love her, even in my memory!' I suppose I did," he said, interrupting himself for a moment. "I did! That's neither here nor there. 'O Richard, if you ever did: if you have any memory for what is gone and lost, take it to her once more. Once more! Tell her how I laid my head upon your shoulder, where her own head might have lain, and was so humble to you, Richard. Tell her that you looked into my face, and saw the beauty which she used to praise, all gone: all gone: and in its place, a poor, wan, hollow cheek, that she would weep to see. Tell her everything, and take it back, and she will not refuse again. She will not have the heart!' "

So he sat musing, and repeating the last words, until he woke again, and rose.

"You won't take it, Margaret?"

She shook her head, and motioned an entreaty to him to leave her.

"Good-night, Margaret."

"Good-night!"

He turned to look upon her; struck by her sorrow, and perhaps by the pity for himself which trembled in her voice. It was a quick and rapid action; and for the moment some flash of his old bearing kindled in his form. In the next he went as he had come. Nor did this glimmer of a quenched fire seem to light him to a quicker sense of his debasement.

In any mood, in any grief, in any torture of the mind or body, Meg's work must be done. She sat down to her task, and plied it. Night, midnight. Still she worked.

She had a meagre fire, the night being very cold; and rose at intervals to mend it. The Chimes rang half-past twelve while she was thus engaged; and when they ceased she heard a gentle knocking at the door. Before she could so much as wonder who was there, at that unusual hour, it opened.

O Youth and Beauty, happy as ye should be, look at this
O Youth and Beauty, blest and blessing all within your
reach, and working out the ends of your Beneficent Creator
look at this!

She saw the entering figure; screamed its name; cried
"Lilian!"

It was swift, and fell upon its knees before her: clinging
to her dress.

"Up, dear! Up! Lilian! My own dearest!"

"Never more, Meg; never more! Here! Here! Close to
you, holding to you, feeling your dear breath upon my
face!"

"Sweet Lilian! Darling Lilian! Child of my heart—no
mother's love can be more tender—lay your head upon my
breast!"

"Never more, Meg. Never more! When I first looked in
to your face, you knelt before me. On my knees before you
let me die. Let it be here!"

"You have come back. My Treasure! We will live to
gether, work together, hope together, die together!"

"Ah! Kiss my lips, Meg; fold your arms about me; press
me to your bosom; look kindly on me; but don't raise me
Let it be here. Let me see the last of your dear face upon
my knees!"

O Youth and Beauty, happy as ye should be, look at this
O Youth and Beauty, working out the ends of your Benefi
cent Creator, look at this!

"Forgive me, Meg! So dear, so dear! Forgive me!
know you do, I see you do, but say so, Meg!"

She said so, with her lips on Lilian's cheek. And with he
arms twined round—she knew it now—a broken heart.

"His blessing on you, dearest love. Kiss me once more
He suffered her to sit beside His feet, and dry them with he
hair. O Meg, what Mercy and Compassion!"

As she died, the Spirit of the child returning, innocen
and radiant, touched the old man with its hand, and beck
oned him away.

Fourth Quarter

SOME new remembrance of the ghostly figures in the Bell; some faint impression of the ringing of the Chimes; some giddy consciousness of having seen the swarm of phantoms reproduced and reproduced until the recollection of them lost itself in the confusion of their numbers; some hurried knowledge, how conveyed to him he knew not, that more years had passed; and Trotty, with the Spirit of the Child attending him, stood looking on at mortal company.

Fat company, rosy-cheeked company, comfortable company. They were but two, but they were red enough for ten. They sat before a bright fire, with a small low table between them; and unless the fragrance of hot tea and muffins lingered longer in that room than in most others, the table had seen service very lately. But all the cups and saucers being clean, and in their proper places in the corner-cupboard; and the brass toasting-fork hanging in its usual nook and spreading its four idle fingers out as if it wanted to be measured for a glove; there remained no other visible tokens of the meal just finished, than such as purred and washed their whiskers in the person of the basking cat, and glistened in the gracious, not to say greasy, faces of her patrons.

This cosy couple (married, evidently) had made a fair division of the fire between them, and sat looking at the glowing sparks that dropped into the grate; now nodding off into a doze; now waking up again when some hot fragment, larger than the rest, came rattling down, as if the fire were coming with it.

It was in no danger of sudden extinction, however; for it gleamed not only in the little room, and on the panes of window-glass in the door, and on the curtain half drawn across them, but in the little shop beyond. A little shop, quite crammed and choked with the abundance of its stock; a perfectly voracious little shop, with a maw as accommodating and full as any shark's. Cheese, butter, firewood, soap, pickles, matches, bacon, table-beer, peg-tops, sweet-meats, boys' kites, bird-seed, cold ham, birch brooms, hearth-stones, salt, vinegar, blacking, red-herrings, station-ery, lard, mushroom-ketchup, staylaces, loaves of bread, shuttlecocks, eggs, and slate pencil; everything was fish that came to the net of this greedy little shop, and all articles were in its net. How many other kinds of petty merchandise were there, it would be difficult to say; but balls of pack-thread, ropes of onions, pounds of candles, cabbage-nets, and brushes, hung in bunches from the ceiling, like extra-ordinary fruit; while various odd canisters emitting aromatic smells, established the veracity of the inscription over the outer door, which informed the public that the keeper of this little shop was a licensed dealer in tea, coffee, tobacco, pep-per, and snuff.

Glancing at such of these articles as were visible in the shining of the blaze, and the less cheerful radiance of two smoky lamps which burnt but dimly in the shop itself, as though its plethora sat heavy on their lungs; and glancing, then, at one of the two faces by the parlour-fire; Trotty had small difficulty in recognising in the stout old lady, Mrs. Chickenstalker: always inclined to corpulency, even in the days when he had known her as established in the general line, and having a small balance against him in her books.

The features of her companion were less easy to him. The great broad chin, with creases in it large enough to hide a finger in; the astonished eyes, that seemed to expostulate with themselves for sinking deeper and deeper into the yield-ing fat of the soft face, the nose afflicted with that dis-ordered action of its functions which is generally termed The Snuffles; the short thick throat and labouring chest, with other beauties of the like description; though calculated to impress the memory, Trotty could at first allot to nobody he had ever known: and yet he had some recollection of them too. At length, in Mrs. Chickenstalker's partner in the general line, and in the crooked and eccentric line of life, he recognised the former porter of Sir Joseph Bowley; an apoplectic innocent, who had connected himself in Trotty's mind with Mrs. Chickenstalker years ago, by giving him admission to the mansion where he had confessed his obligations to that lady, and drawn on his unlucky head such grave reproach.

Trotty had little interest in a change like this, after the changes he had seen; but association is very strong sometimes; and he looked involuntarily behind the parlour-door, where the accounts of credit customers were usually kept in chalk. There was no record of his name. Some names were there, but they were strange to him, and infinitely fewer than of old; from which he argued that the porter was an advocate of ready money transactions, and on coming into the business had looked pretty sharp after the Chickenstalker defaulters.

So desolate was Trotty, and so mournful for the youth and promise of his blighted child, that it was a sorrow to him, even to have no place in Mrs. Chickenstalker's ledger.

"What sort of a night is it, Anne?" inquired the former porter of Sir Joseph Bowley, stretching out his legs before the fire, and rubbing as much of them as his short arms could reach; with an air that added, "Here I am if it's bad, and I don't want to go out if it's good."

"Blowing and sleeting hard," returned his wife; "and threatening snow. Dark. And very cold."

"I'm glad to think we had muffins," said the former porter, in the tone of one who had set his conscience at rest. "It's a sort of night that's meant for muffins. Likewise crumpets. Also Sally Lunns."

The former porter mentioned each successive kind of eatable, as if he were musingly summing up his good actions. After which he rubbed his fat legs as before, and jerking them at the knees to get the fire upon the yet unroasted parts, laughed as if somebody had tickled him.

"You're in spirits, Tugby, my dear," observed his wife.

The firm was Tugby, late Chickenstalker.

"No," said Tugby. "No. Not particular. I'm a little elevated. The muffins came so pat!"

With that he chuckled until he was black in the face; and

had so much ado to become any other colour, that his fat legs took the strangest excursions into the air. Nor were they reduced to anything like decorum until Mrs. Tugby had thumped him violently on the back, and shaken him as if he were a great bottle.

"Good gracious, goodness, lord-a-mercy bless and save the man!" cried Mrs. Tugby, in great terror. "What 's he doing?"

Mr. Tugby wiped his eyes, and faintly repeated that he found himself a little elewated.

"Then don't be so again, that 's a dear good soul," said Mrs. Tugby, "if you don't want to frighten me to death, with your struggling and fighting!"

Mr. Tugby said he wouldn't; but, his whole existence was a fight, in which, if any judgment might be founded on the constantly-increasing shortness of his breath, and the deepening purple of his face, he was always getting the worst of it.

"So it 's blowing, and sleeting, and threatening snow; and it 's dark, and very cold, is it my dear?" said Mr. Tugby, looking at the fire, and reverting to the cream and marrow of his temporary elevation.

"Hard weather indeed," returned his wife, shaking her head.

"Aye, aye! Years," said Mr. Tugby, "are like Christians in that respect. Some of 'em die hard; some of 'em die easy. This one hasn't many days to run, and is making a fight for it. I like him all the better. There 's a customer, my love!"

Attentive to the rattling door, Mrs. Tugby had already risen.

"Now then!" said that lady, passing out into the little shop. "What 's wanted? Oh! I beg your pardon, sir, I 'm sure. I didn't think it was you."

She made this apology to a gentleman in black, who, with his wristbands tucked up, and his hat cocked loungingly on one side, and his hands in his pockets, sat down astride on the table-beer barrel, and nodded in return.

"This is a bad business upstairs, Mrs. Tugby," said the gentleman. "The man can't live."

"Not the back-attic can't!" cried Tugby, coming out into the shop to join the conference.

"The back-attic, Mr. Tugby," said the gentleman, "is coming downstairs fast, and will be below the basement very soon."

Looking by turns at Tugby and his wife, he sounded the barrel with his knuckles for the depth of beer, and having found it, played a tune upon the empty part.

"The back-attic, Mr. Tugby," said the gentleman: Tugby having stood in silent consternation for some time: "is Going."

"Then," said Tugby, turning to his wife, "he must Go, you know, before he 's Gone."

"I don't think you can move him," said the gentleman, shaking his head. "I wouldn't take the responsibility of saying it could be done, myself. You had better leave him where he is. He can't live long."

"It 's the only subject," said Tugby, bringing the butter-scale down upon the counter with a crash, by weighing his fist on it, "that we 've ever had a word upon; she and me; and look what it comes to! He 's going to die here, after all. Going to die upon the premises. Going to die in our house!"

"And where should he have died, Tugby?" cried his wife.

"In the workhouse," he returned. "What are workhouses made for?"

"Not for that," said Mrs. Tugby, with great energy. "Not for that! Neither did I marry you for that. Don't think it, Tugby. I won't have it. I won't allow it. I 'd be separated first, and never see your face again. When my widow's name stood over that door, as it did for many years: this house being known as Mrs. Chickenstalker's far and wide, and never known but to its honest credit and its good report: when my widow's name stood over that door, Tugby, I knew him as a handsome, steady, manly, independent youth; I knew her as the sweetest-looking, sweetest-tempered girl,

eyes ever saw; I knew her father (poor old creetur, he fell
down from the steeple walking in his sleep, and killed himself), for the simplest, hardest-working, childest-hearted
man, that ever drew the breath of life; and when I turn
them out of house and home, may angels turn me out of
Heaven. As they would! And serve me right!"

Her old face, which had been a plump and dimpled one
before the changes which had come to pass, seemed to shine
out of her as she said these words; and when she dried her
eyes, and shook her head and her handkerchief at Tugby,
with an expression of firmness which it was quite clear was
not to be easily resisted, Trotty said, "Bless her! Bless her!"

Then he listened, with a panting heart, for what should
follow. Knowing nothing yet, but that they spoke of Meg.

If Tugby had been a little elevated in the parlour, he more
than balanced that account by being not a little depressed
in the shop, where he now stood staring at his wife, without
attempting a reply; secretly conveying, however—either in
a fit of abstraction or as a precautionary measure—all the
money from the till into his own pockets, as he looked at her.

The gentleman upon the table-beer cask, who appeared to
be some authorised medical attendant upon the poor, was far
too well accustomed, evidently, to little differences of opinion
between man and wife, to interpose any remark in this instance. He sat softly whistling, and turning little drops of
beer out of the tap upon the ground, until there was a perfect calm: when he raised his head, and said to Mrs. Tugby,
late Chickenstalker:

"There's something interesting about the woman, even
now. How did she come to marry him?"

"Why that," said Mrs. Tugby, taking a seat near him, "is
not the least cruel part of her story, sir. You see they kept
company, she and Richard, many years ago. When they
were a young and beautiful couple, everything was settled,
and they were to have been married on a New Year's Day.
But, somehow, Richard got it into his head, through what
the gentlemen told him, that he might do better, and that
he'd soon repent it, and that she wasn't good enough for

him, and that a young man of spirit had no business to be
married. And the gentlemen frightened her, and made her
melancholy, and timid of his deserting her, and of her children coming to the gallows, and of its being wicked to be
man and wife, and a good deal more of it. And in short, they
lingered and lingered, and their trust in one another was
broken, and so at last was the match. But the fault was his.
She would have married him, sir, joyfully. I've seen her
heart swell, many times afterwards, when he passed her in
a proud and careless way; and never did a woman grieve
more truly for a man, than she for Richard when he first
went wrong."

"Oh! he went wrong, did he?" said the gentleman, pulling
out the vent-peg of the table-beer, and trying to peep down
into the barrel through the hole.

"Well, sir, I don't know that he rightly understood himself, you see. I think his mind was troubled by their having
broke with one another; and that but for being ashamed before the gentlemen, and perhaps for being uncertain too, how
she might take it, he'd have gone through any suffering or
trial to have had Meg's promise and Meg's hand again.
That's my belief. He never said so; more's the pity! He
took to drinking, idling, bad companions: all the fine resources that were to be so much better for him than the
Home he might have had. He lost his looks, his character,
his health, his strength, his friends, his work: everything!"

"He didn't lose everything, Mrs. Tugby," returned the
gentleman, "because he gained a wife; and I want to know
how he gained her."

"I'm coming to it, sir, in a moment. This went on for
years and years; he sinking lower and lower; she enduring,
poor thing, miseries enough to wear her life away. At last,
he was so cast down, and cast out, that no one would employ
or notice him; and doors were shut upon him, go where he
would. Applying from place to place, and door to door; and
coming for the hundredth time to one gentleman who had
often and often tried him (he was a good workman to the
very end); that gentleman, who knew his history, said, 'I

believe you are incorrigible; there is only one person in the
world who has a chance of reclaiming you; ask me to trust
you no more, until she tries to do it.' Something like that, in
his anger and vexation."

"Ah!" said the gentleman. "Well?"

"Well, sir, he went to her, and kneeled to her; said it was
so: said it ever had been so; and made a prayer to her to
save him."

"And she?—Don't distress yourself, Mrs. Tugby."

"She came to me that night to ask me about living here.
'What he was once to me,' she said, 'is buried in a grave, side
by side with what I was to him. But I have thought of this;
and I will make the trial. In the hope of saving him; for
the love of the light-hearted girl (you remember her) who
was to have been married on a New Year's Day; and for the
love of her Richard.' And she said he had come to her from
Lilian, and Lilian had trusted to him, and she never could
forget that. So they were married; and when they came
home here, and I saw them, I hoped that such prophecies as
parted them when they were young, may not often fulfill
themselves as they did in this case, or I wouldn't be the
makers of them for a Mine of Gold."

The gentleman got off the cask, and stretched himself, observing:

"I suppose he used her ill, as soon as they were married?"

"I don't think he ever did that," said Mrs. Tugby, shaking her head, and wiping her eyes. "He went on better for a
short time; but, his habits were too old and strong to be got
rid of; he soon fell back a little; and was falling fast back,
when his illness came so strong upon him. I think he has
always felt for her. I am sure he has. I have seen him, in
his crying fits and tremblings, try to kiss her hand; and I
have heard him call her 'Meg,' and say it was her nineteenth
birthday. There he has been lying, now, these weeks and
months. Between him and her baby, she has not been able to
do her own work; and by not being able to be regular, she
has lost it, even if she could have done it. How they have
lived, I hardly know!"

"*I* know," muttered Mr. Tugby; looking at the till, and round the shop, and at his wife; and rolling his head with immense intelligence. "Like Fighting Cocks!"

He was interrupted by a cry—a sound of lamentation—from the upper story of the house. The gentleman moved hurriedly to the door.

"My friend," he said, looking back, "you needn't discuss whether he shall be removed or not. He has spared you that trouble, I believe."

Saying so, he ran upstairs, followed by Mrs. Tugby; while Mr. Tugby panted and grumbled after them at leisure: being rendered more than commonly short-winded by the weight of the till, in which there had been an inconvenient quantity of copper. Trotty, with the child beside him, floated up the staircase like mere air.

"Follow her! Follow her! Follow her!" He heard the ghostly voices in the Bells repeat their words as he ascended. "Learn it, from the creature dearest to your heart!"

It was over. It was over. And this was she, her father's pride and joy! This haggard, wretched woman, weeping by the bed, if it deserved that name, and pressing to her breast, and hanging down her head upon, an infant. Who can tell how spare, how sickly, and how poor an infant! Who can tell how dear!

"Thank God!" cried Trotty, holding up his folded hands. "O, God be thanked! She loves her child!"

The gentleman, not otherwise hard-hearted or indifferent to such scenes, than that he saw them every day, and knew that they were figures of no moment in the Filer sums—mere scratches in the working of these calculations—laid his hand upon the heart that beat no more, and listened for the breath, and said, "His pain is over. It's better as it is!" Mrs. Tugby tried to comfort her with kindness. Mr. Tugby tried philosophy.

"Come, come!" he said, with his hands in his pockets, "you mustn't give way, you know. That won't do. You must fight up. What would have become of me if *I* had given way when I was porter, and we had as many as six runaway carriage-doubles at our door in one night! But, I fell back upon my strength of mind, and didn't open it!"

Again Trotty heard the voices, saying, "Follow her!" He turned towards his guide, and saw it rising from him, passing through the air. "Follow her!" it said. And vanished.

He hovered round her; sat down at her feet; looked up into her face for one trace of her old self; listened for one note of her old pleasant voice. He flitted round the child: so wan, so prematurely old, so dreadful in its gravity, so plaintive in its feeble, mournful, miserable wail. He almost worshipped it. He clung to it as her only safeguard; as the last unbroken link that bound her to endurance. He set his father's hope and trust on the frail baby; watched her every look upon it as she held it in her arms; and cried a thousand times, "She loves it! God be thanked, she loves it!"

He saw the woman tend her in the night; return to her when her grudging husband was asleep, and all was still; encourage her, shed tears with her, set nourishment before her. He saw the day come, and the night again; the day, the night; the time go by; the house of death relieved of death; the room left to herself and to the child; he heard it moan and cry; he saw it harass her, and tire her out, and when she slumbered in exhaustion, drag her back to consciousness, and hold her with its little hands upon the rack; but she was constant to it, gentle with it, patient with it. Patient! Was its loving mother in her inmost heart and soul, and had its Being knitted up with hers as when she carried it unborn.

All this time, she was in want: languishing away, in dire and pining want. With the baby in her arms, she wandered here and there, in quest of occupation; and with its thin face lying in her lap, and looking up in hers, did any work for any wretched sum; a day and night of labour for as many farthings as there were figures on the dial. If she had quarrelled with it; if she had neglected it; if she had looked upon it with a moment's hate; if, in the frenzy of an instant, she had struck it! No. His comfort was, She loved it always.

She told no one of her extremity, and wandered abroad in

the day lest she should be questioned by her only friend: for any help she received from her hands, occasioned fresh disputes between the good woman and her husband; and it was new bitterness to be the daily cause of strife and discord, where she owed so much.

She loved it still. She loved it more and more. But a change fell on the aspect of her love. One night.

She was singing faintly to it in its sleep, and walking to and fro to hush it, when her door was softly opened, and a man looked in.

"For the last time," he said.

"William Fern!"

"For the last time."

He listened like a man pursued: and spoke in whispers.

"Margaret, my race is nearly run. I couldn't finish it, without a parting word with you. Without one grateful word."

"What have you done?" she asked: regarding him with terror.

He looked at her, but gave no answer.

After a short silence, he made a gesture with his hand, as if he set her question by; as if he brushed it aside; and said:

"It 's long ago, Margaret, now; but that night is as fresh in my memory as ever 'twas. We little thought, then," he added, looking round, "that we should ever meet like this. Your child, Margaret? Let me have it in my arms. Let me hold your child."

He put his hat upon the floor, and took it. And he trembled as he took it, from head to foot.

"Is it a girl?"

"Yes."

He put his hand before its little face.

"See how weak I 'm grown, Margaret, when I want the courage to look at it! Let her be, a moment. I won't hurt her. It 's long ago, but—What 's her name?"

"Margaret," she answered, quickly.

"I 'm glad of that," he said. "I 'm glad of that!"

He seemed to breathe more freely; and after pausing for an instant, took away his hand, and looked upon the infant's face. But covered it again, immediately.

"Margaret!" he said; and gave her back the child. "It's Lilian's."

"Lilian's!"

"I held the same face in my arms when Lilian's mother died and left her."

"When Lilian's mother died and left her!" she repeated, wildly.

"How shrill you speak! Why do you fix your eyes upon me so? Margaret!"

She sunk down in a chair, and pressed the infant to her breast, and wept over it. Sometimes, she released it from her embrace, to look anxiously in its face: then strained it to her bosom again. At those times, when she gazed upon it, then it was that something fierce and terrible began to mingle with her love. Then it was that her old father quailed.

"Follow her!" was sounded through the house. "Learn it, from the creature dearest to your heart!"

"Margaret," said Fern, bending over her, and kissing her upon the brow: "I thank you for the last time. Good-night. Good-bye! Put your hand in mine, and tell me you'll forget me from this hour, and try to think the end of me was here."

"What have you done?" she asked again.

"There'll be a Fire to-night," he said, removing from her. "There'll be Fires this winter-time, to light the dark nights, East, West, North, and South. When you see the distant sky red, they'll be blazing. When you see the distant sky red, think of me no more; or, if you do, remember what a Hell was lighted up inside of me, and think you see its flames reflected in the clouds. Good-night. Good-bye!"

She called to him; but he was gone. She sat down stupefied, until her infant roused her to a sense of hunger, cold, and darkness. She paced the room with it the livelong night, hushing it and soothing it. She said at intervals, "Like Lilian, when her mother died and left her!" Why was her step so quick, her eye so wild, her love so fierce and terrible, whenever she repeated those words?

"But, it is Love," said Trotty. "It is Love. She'll never cease to love it. My poor Meg!"

She dressed the child next morning with unusual care—ah, vain expenditure of care upon such squalid robes!—and once more tried to find some means of life. It was the last day of the Old Year. She tried till night, and never broke her fast. She tried in vain.

She mingled with an abject crowd, who tarried in the snow, until it pleased some officer appointed to dispense the public charity (the lawful charity; not that once preached upon a Mount), to call them in, and question them, and say to this one, "Go to such a place," to that one, "Come next week"; to make a football of another wretch, and pass him here and there, from hand to hand, from house to house, until he wearied and lay down to die; or started up and robbed, and so became a higher sort of criminal, whose claims allowed of no delay. Here, too, she failed.

She loved her child, and wished to have it lying on her breast. And that was quite enough.

It was night: a bleak, dark, cutting night: when, pressing the child close to her for warmth, she arrived outside the house she called her home. She was so faint and giddy, that she saw no one standing in the doorway until she was close upon it, and about to enter. Then she recognised the master of the house, who had so disposed himself—with his person it was not difficult—as to fill up the whole entry.

"O!" he said softly. "You have come back?"

She looked at the child, and shook her head.

"Don't you think you have lived here long enough without paying any rent? Don't you think that, without any money, you've been a pretty constant customer at this shop, now?" said Mr. Tugby.

She repeated the same mute appeal.

"Suppose you try and deal somewhere else," he said. "And suppose you provide yourself with another lodging. Come! Don't you think you could manage it?"

She said in a low voice, that it was very late. To-morrow.

"Now I see what you want," said Tugby; "and what you mean. You know there are two parties in this house about you, and you delight in setting 'em by the ears. I don't want any quarrels; I'm speaking softly to avoid a quarrel; but if you don't go away, I'll speak out loud, and you shall cause words high enough to please you. But you can't come in. That I am determined."

She put her hair back with her hand, and looked in a sudden manner at the sky, and the dark lowering distance.

"This is the last night of an Old Year, and I won't carry ill-blood and quarrellings and disturbances into a New One, to please you nor anybody else," said Tugby, who was quite a retail Friend and Father. "I wonder you an't ashamed of yourself, to carry such practices into a New Year. If you haven't any business in the world, but to be always giving way, and always making disturbances between man and wife, you'd be better out of it. Go along with you."

"Follow her! To desperation!"

Again the old man heard the voices. Looking up, he saw the figures hovering in the air, and pointing where she went, down the dark street.

"She loves it!" he exclaimed, in agonised entreaty for her. "Chimes! she loves it still!"

"Follow her!" The shadows swept upon the track she had taken, like a cloud.

He joined in the pursuit; he kept close to her; he looked into her face. He saw the same fierce and terrible expression mingling with her love, and kindling in her eyes. He heard her say, "Like Lilian! To be changed like Lilian!" and her speed redoubled.

O, for something to awaken her! For any sight, or sound, or scent, to call up tender recollections in a brain on fire! For any gentle image of the Past, to rise before her!

"I was her father! I was her father!" cried the old man, stretching out his hands to the dark shadows flying on above. "Have mercy on her, and on me! Where does she go? Turn her back! I was her father!"

But they only pointed to her, as she hurried on; and said, "To desperation! Learn it from the creature dearest to your heart!"

A hundred voices echoed it. The air was made of breath expended in those words. He seemed to take them in, at every gasp he drew. They were everywhere, and not to be escaped. And still she hurried on; the same light in her eyes, the same words in her mouth, "Like Lilian! To be changed like Lilian!"

All at once she stopped.

"Now, turn her back!" exclaimed the old man, tearing his white hair. "My child! Meg! Turn her back! Great Father, turn her back!"

In her own scanty shawl, she wrapped the baby warm. With her fevered hands, she smoothed its limbs, composed its face, arranged its mean attire. In her wasted arms she folded it, as though she never would resign it more. And with her dry lips, kissed it in a final pang, and last long agony of Love.

Putting its tiny hand up to her neck, and holding it there, within her dress, next to her distracted heart, she set its sleeping face against her: closely, steadily against her: and sped onward to the River.

To the rolling River, swift and dim, where Winter Night sat brooding like the last dark thoughts of many who had sought a refuge there before her. Where scattered lights upon the banks gleamed sullen, red, and dull, as torches that were burning there, to show the way to Death. Where no abode of living people cast its shadow, on the deep, impenetrable, melancholy shade.

To the River! To that portal of Eternity, her desperate footsteps tended with the swiftness of its rapid waters running to the sea. He tried to touch her as she passed him, going down to its dark level; but, the wild distempered form, the fierce and terrible love, the desperation that had left all human check or hold behind, swept by him like the wind.

He followed her. She paused a moment on the brink, be·

fore the dreadful plunge. He fell down on his knees, and in a shriek addressed the figures in the Bells now hovering above them.

"I have learnt it!" cried the old man. "From the creature dearest to my heart! O, save her, save her!"

He could wind his fingers in her dress; could hold it! As the words escaped his lips, he felt his sense of touch return, and knew that he detained her.

The figures looked down steadfastly upon him.

"I have learnt it!" cried the old man. "O, have mercy on me in this hour, if, in my love for her, so young and good, I slandered Nature in the breasts of mothers rendered desperate! Pity my presumption, wickedness, and ignorance, and save her."

He felt his hold relaxing. They were silent still.

"Have mercy on her!" he exclaimed, "as one in whom this dreadful crime has sprung from Love perverted; from the strongest, deepest Love we fallen creatures know! Think what her misery must have been, when such seed bears such fruit! Heaven meant her to be good. There is no loving mother on the earth who might not come to this, if such a life had gone before. O, have mercy on my child, who, even at this pass, means mercy to her own, and dies herself, and perils her immortal soul, to save it!"

She was in his arms. He held her now. His strength was like a giant's.

"I see the Spirit of the Chimes among you!" cried the old man, singling out the child, and speaking in some inspiration, which their looks conveyed to him. "I know that our inheritance is held in store for us by Time. I know there is a sea of Time to rise one day, before which all who wrong us or oppress us will be swept away like leaves. I see it, on the flow! I know that we must trust and hope, and neither doubt ourselves, nor doubt the good in one another. I have learnt it from the creature dearest to my heart. I clasp her in my arms again. O Spirits, merciful and good, I take your lesson to my breast along with her! O Spirits, merciful and good, I am grateful!"

He might have said more; but, the Bells, the old familiar Bells, his own dear, constant, steady friends, the Chimes, began to ring the joy-peals for a New Year: so lustily, so merrily, so happily, so gaily, that he leapt upon his feet, and broke the spell that bound him.

"And whatever you do, father," said Meg, "don't eat tripe again, without asking some doctor whether it's likely to agree with you; for how you *have* been going on, Good gracious!"

She was working with her needle, at the little table by the fire: dressing her simple gown with ribbons for her wedding. So quietly happy, so blooming and youthful, so full of beautiful promise, that he uttered a great cry as if it were an Angel in his house; then flew to clasp her in his arms.

But, he caught his feet in the newspaper, which had fallen on the hearth; and somebody came rushing in between them.

"No!" cried the voice of this same somebody; a generous and jolly voice it was! "Not even you. Not even you. The first kiss of Meg in the New Year is mine. Mine! I have been waiting outside the house, this hour, to hear the Bells and claim it. Meg, my precious prize, a happy year! A life of happy years, my darling wife!"

And Richard smothered her with kisses.

You never in all your life saw anything like Trotty after this. I don't care where you have lived or what you have seen; you never in all your life saw anything at all approaching him! He sat down in his chair and beat his knees and cried; he sat down in his chair and beat his knees and laughed; he sat down in his chair and beat his knees and laughed and cried together; he got out of his chair and hugged Meg; he got out of his chair and hugged Richard; he got out of his chair and hugged them both at once; he kept running up to Meg, and squeezing her fresh face between his hands and kissing it, going from her backwards not to lose sight of it, and running up again like a figure in a magic lantern; and whatever he did, he was constantly sitting himself down in this chair, and never stopping in it for one single moment; being—that's the truth—beside himself with joy.

"And to-morrow's your wedding-day, my pet!" cried Trotty. "Your real, happy wedding-day!"

"To-day!" cried Richard, shaking hands with him. "To-day. The Chimes are ringing in the New Year. Hear them!"

They WERE ringing! Bless their sturdy hearts, they WERE ringing! Great Bells as they were; melodious, deep-mouthed, noble Bells; cast in no common metal; made by no common founder; when had they ever chimed like that before!

"But, to-day, my pet," said Trotty. "You and Richard had some words to-day."

"Because he's such a bad fellow, father," said Meg. "An't you, Richard! Such a headstrong, violent man! He'd have made no more of speaking his mind to that great Alderman, and putting *him* down I don't know where, that he would of—"

"—Kissing Meg," suggested Richard. Doing it too!

"No. Not a bit more," said Meg. "But I wouldn't let him, father. Where would have been the use!"

"Richard my boy!" cried Trotty. "You was turned up Trumps originally; and Trumps you must be, till you die! But, you were crying by the fire to-night, my pet, when I came home! Why did you cry by the fire?"

"I was thinking of the years we've passed together, father. Only that. And thinking that you might miss me, and be lonely."

Trotty was backing off to that extraordinary chair again, when the child who had been awakened by the noise, came running in half-dressed.

"Why, here she is!" cried Trotty, catching her up. "Here's little Lilian! Ha ha ha! Here we are and here we go! O here we are and here we go again! And here we are and here we go! and Uncle Will too!" Stopping in his trot to greet him heartily. "O, Uncle Will, the vision that I've had to-night, through lodging you! O, Uncle Will, the obligations that you 've laid me under, by your coming, my good friend!"

Before Will Fern could make the least reply, a band of music burst into the room, attended by a lot of neighbours, screaming "A Happy New Year, Meg!" "A Happy Wedding!" "Many of 'em!" and other fragmentary good wishes of that sort. The Drum (who was a private friend of Trotty's) then stepped forward, and said:

"Trotty Veck, my boy! It 's got about, that your daughter is going to be married to-morrow. There an't a soul that knows you that don't wish you well, or that knows her and don't wish her well. Or that knows you both, and don't wish you both all the happiness the New Year can bring. And here we are, to play it in and dance it in, accordingly."

Which was received with a general shout. The Drum was rather drunk, by the bye; but, never mind.

"What a happiness it is, I 'm sure," said Trotty, "to be so esteemed! How kind and neighbourly you are! It's all along of my dear daughter. She deserves it!"

They were ready for a dance in half a second (Meg and Richard at the top); and the Drum was on the very brink of leathering away with all his power; when a combination of prodigious sounds was heard outside, and a good-humoured comely woman of some fifty years of age, or thereabouts, came running in, attended by a man bearing a stone pitcher of terrific size, and closely followed by the marrow-bones and cleavers, and the bells; not *the* Bells, but a portable collection on a frame.

Trotty said, "It 's Mrs. Chickenstalker!" And sat down and beat his knees again.

"Married, and not tell me, Meg!" cried the good woman. "Never! I couldn't rest on the last night of the Old Year without coming to wish you joy. I couldn't have done it, Meg. Not if I had been bedridden. So here I am; and as it 's New Year's Eve, and the Eve of your wedding too, my dear, I had a little flip made and brought it with me."

Mrs. Chickenstalker's notion of a little flip, did honour to her character. The pitcher steamed and smoked and reeked like a volcano; and the man who had carried it, was faint.

"Mrs. Tugby!" said Trotty, who had been going round and round her, in an ecstasy.—"I *should* say, Chicken-stalker—Bless your heart and soul! A happy New Year, and many of 'em! Mrs. Tugby," said Trotty when he had saluted her;—"I *should* say, Chickenstalker—This is William Fern and Lilian."

The worthy dame, to his surprise, turned very pale and very red.

"Not Lilian Fern whose mother died in Dorsetshire!" said she.

Her uncle answered "Yes," and meeting hastily, they exchanged some hurried words together; of which the upshot was, that Mrs. Chickenstalker shook him by both hands; saluted Trotty on his cheek again of her own free will; and took the child to her capacious breast.

"Will Fern!" said Trotty, pulling on his righthand muffler. "Not the friend you was hoping to find?"

"Ay!" returned Will, putting a hand on each of Trotty's shoulders. "And like to prove a'most as good a friend, if that can be, as one I found."

"O!" said Trotty. "Please to play up there. Will you have the goodness!"

To the music of the band, the bells, the marrow-bones and cleavers, all at once; and while the Chimes were yet in lusty operation out of doors; Trotty, making Meg and Richard second couple, led off Mrs. Chickenstalker down the dance, and danced it in a step unknown before or since; founded on his own peculiar trot.

Had Trotty dreamed? Or, are his joys and sorrows, and the actors in them, but a dream; himself a dream; the teller of this tale a dreamer, waking but now? If it be so, O listener, dear to him in all his visions, try to bear in mind the stern realities from which these shadows come; and in your sphere—none is too wide, and none too limited for such an end—endeavour to correct, improve, and soften them. So may the New Year be a happy one to you, happy to many more whose happiness depends on you! So may each year be happier than the last, and not the meanest of our brethren or sisterhood debarred their rightful share, in what our Great Creator formed them to enjoy.

The End

THE CRICKET ON THE HEARTH

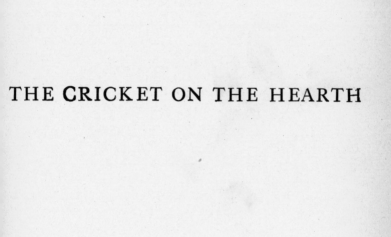

The Cricket on the Hearth

Chirp the First

THE kettle began it! Don't tell me what Mrs. Peerybingle said. I know better. Mrs. Peerybingle may leave it on record to the end of time that she couldn't say which of them began it; but, I say the kettle did. I ought to know, I hope! The kettle began it, full five minutes by the little waxy-faced Dutch clock in the corner, before the Cricket uttered a chirp.

As if the clock hadn't finished striking, and the convulsive little Haymaker at the top of it, jerking away right and left with a scythe in front of a Moorish Palace, hadn't mowed down half an acre of imaginary grass before the Cricket joined in at all!

Why, I am not naturally positive. Every one knows that. I wouldn't set my own opinion against the opinion of Mrs. Peerybingle, unless I were quite sure, on any account whatever. Nothing should induce me. But, this is a question of fact. And the fact is, that the kettle began it, at least five minutes before the Cricket gave any sign of being in existence. Contradict me, and I'll say ten.

Let me narrate exactly how it happened. I should have proceeded to do so in my very first word, but for this plain consideration—if I am to tell a story I must begin at the beginning; and how is it possible to begin at the beginning, without beginning at the kettle?

It appeared as if there were a sort of match, or trial of

skill, you must understand, between the kettle and the Cricket. And this is what led to it, and how it came about.

Mrs. Peerybingle, going out into the raw twilight, and clicking over the wet stones in a pair of pattens that worked innumerable rough impressions of the first proposition in Euclid all about the yard—Mrs. Peerybingle filled the kettle at the water-butt. Presently returning, less the pattens (and a good deal less, for they were tall and Mrs. Peerybingle was but short), she set the kettle on the fire. In doing which she lost her temper, or mislaid it for an instant; for, the water being uncomfortably cold, and in that slippy, slushy, sleety sort of state wherein it seems to penetrate through every kind of substance, patten rings included—had laid hold of Mrs. Peerybingle's toes, and even splashed her legs. And when we rather plume ourselves (with reason too) upon our legs, and keep ourselves particularly neat in point of stockings, we find this for the moment, hard to bear.

Besides, the kettle was aggravating and obstinate. It wouldn't allow itself to be adjusted on the top bar; it wouldn't hear of accommodating itself kindly to the knobs of coal; it *would* lean forward with a drunken air, and dribble, a very Idiot of a kettle, on the hearth. It was quarrelsome, and hissed and spluttered morosely at the fire. To sum up all, the lid, resisting Mrs. Peerybingle's fingers, first of all turned topsy-turvy, and then, with an ingenious pertinacity deserving of a better cause, dived sideways in—down to the very bottom of the kettle. And the hull of the Royal George has never made half the monstrous resistance to coming out of the water, which the lid of that kettle employed against Mrs. Peerybingle, before she got it up again.

It looked sullen and pig-headed enough, even then; carrying its handle with an air of defiance, and cocking its spout pertly and mockingly at Mrs. Peerybingle, as if it said, "I won't boil. Nothing shall induce me!"

But, Mrs. Peerybingle, with restored good humour, dusted her chubby little hands against each other, and sat down before the kettle, laughing. Meantime, the jolly blaze uprose and fell, flashing and gleaming on the little Haymaker at the top of the Dutch clock, until one might have thought he stood stock still before the Moorish Palace, and nothing was in motion but the flame.

He was on the move, however; and had his spasms, two to the second, all right and regular. But, his sufferings when the clock was going to strike, were frightful to behold; and, when a Cuckoo looked out of a trap-door in the Palace, and gave note six times, it shook him, each time, like a spectral voice—or like a something wiry, plucking at his legs.

It was not until a violent commotion and a whirring noise among the weights and ropes below him had quite subsided, that this terrified Haymaker became himself again. Nor was he startled without reason; for these rattling, bony skeletons of clocks are very disconcerting in their operation, and I wonder very much how any set of men, but most of all how Dutchmen, can have had a liking to invent them. There is a popular belief that Dutchmen love broad cases and much clothing for their own lower selves; and they might know better than to leave their clocks so very lank and un-protected, surely.

Now it was, you observe, that the kettle began to spend the evening. Now it was, that the kettle, growing mellow and musical, began to have irrepressible gurglings in its throat, and to indulge in short vocal snorts, which it checked in the bud, as if it hadn't quite made up its mind yet, to be good company. Now it was, that after two or three such vain attempts to stifle its convivial sentiments, it threw off all moroseness, all reserve, and burst into a stream of song so cosy and hilarious, as never maudlin nightingale yet formed the least idea of.

So plain too! Bless you, you might have understood it like a book—better than some books you and I could name, perhaps. With its warm breath gushing forth in a light cloud which merrily and gracefully ascended a few feet, then hung about the chimney-corner as its own domestic Heaven, it trolled its song with that strong energy of cheerfulness, that its iron body hummed and stirred upon the fire; and the lid itself, the recently rebellious lid—such is the influence of a bright example—performed a sort of jig, and clattered like a deaf and dumb young cymbal that had never known the use of its twin brother.

That this song of the kettle's was a song of invitation and welcome to somebody out of doors: to somebody at that moment coming on, towards the snug small home and the crisp fire: there is no doubt whatever. Mrs. Peerybingle knew it, perfectly, as she sat musing before the hearth. It's a dark night, sang the kettle, and the rotten leaves are lying by the way; and, above, all is mist and darkness, and, below, all is mire and clay; and there's only one relief in all the sad and murky air; and I don't know that it is one, for it's nothing but a glare; of deep and angry crimson, where the sun and wind together; set a brand upon the clouds for being guilty of such weather; and the wildest open country is a long dull streak of black; and there's hoar-frost on the finger-post, and thaw upon the track; and the ice it isn't water, and the water isn't free; and you couldn't say that anything is what it ought to be; but he's coming, coming, coming!—

And here, if you like, the Cricket DID chime in! with a Chirrup, Chirrup, Chirrup of such magnitude, by way of chorus; with a voice so astoundingly disproportionate to its size, as compared with the kettle; (size! you couldn't see it!) that if it had then and there burst itself like an over-charged gun, if it had fallen a victim on the spot, and chir-ruped its little body into fifty pieces, it would have seemed a natural and inevitable consequence, for which it had ex-pressly laboured.

The kettle had had the last of its solo performance. It persevered with undiminished ardour; but the Cricket took first fiddle and kept it. Good Heaven, how it chirped! Its shrill, sharp, piercing voice resounded through the house, and seemed to twinkle in the outer darkness like a star. There was an indescribable little trill and tremble in it, at its loudest, which suggested its being carried off its legs, and made to leap again, by its own intense enthusiasm. Yet they went very well together, the Cricket and the kettle. The burden of the song was still the same; and louder, louder, louder still, they sang it in their emulation.

The fair little listener—for fair she was, and young: though something of what is called the dumpling shape; but I don't myself object to that—lighted a candle, glanced at the Haymaker on the top of the clock, who was getting in a pretty average crop of minutes; and looked out of the window, where she saw nothing, owing to the darkness, but her own face imaged in the glass. And my opinion is (and so would yours have been), that she might have looked a long way, and seen nothing half so agreeable. When she came back, and sat down in her former seat, the Cricket and the kettle were still keeping it up, with a perfect fury of competition. The kettle's weak side, clearly being, that he didn't know when he was beat.

There was all the excitement of a race about it. Chirp, chirp, chirp! Cricket a mile ahead. Hum, hum, hum—m —m! Kettle making play in the distance, like a great top. Chirp, chirp, chirp! Cricket round the corner. Hum, hum, hum—m—m! Kettle sticking to him in his own way; no idea of giving in. Chirp, chirp, chirp! Cricket fresher than ever. Hum, hum, hum—m—m! Kettle slow and steady. Chirp, chirp, chirp! Cricket going in to finish him. Hum, hum, hum—m—m! Kettle not to be finished: Until at last they got so jumbled together, in the hurry-skurry, helter-skelter, of the match, that whether the kettle chirped and the Cricket hummed, or the Cricket chirped and the kettle hummed, or they both chirped and both hummed, it would have taken a clearer head than yours or mine to have decided with anything like certainty. But, of this, there is no doubt: that, the kettle and the Cricket, at one and the same moment, and by some power of amalgamation best known to themselves, sent, each, his fireside song of comfort streaming into a ray of the candle that shone out through the window, and a long way down the lane. And this light, bursting on a certain person who, on the instant, approached towards it through the gloom, expressed the whole thing to him, literally in a twinkling, and cried, "Welcome home, old fellow! Welcome home, my boy!"

This end attained, the kettle, being dead beat, boiled over, and was taken off the fire. Mrs. Peerybingle then went running to the door, where, what with the wheels of a cart, the tramp of a horse, the voice of a man, the tearing in and out of an excited dog, and the surprising and mysterious appearance of a baby, there was soon the very What 's-his-name to pay.

Where the baby came from, or how Mrs. Peerybingle got hold of it in that flash of time, *I* don't know. But a live baby there was, in Mrs. Peerybingle's arms; and a pretty tolerable amount of pride she seemed to have in it, when she was drawn gently to the fire, by a sturdy figure of a man, much taller and much older than herself, who had to stoop a long way down, to kiss her. But she was worth the trouble. Six foot six, with the lumbago, might have done it.

"Oh goodness, John!" said Mrs. P. "What a state you are in with the weather!"

He was something the worse for it, undeniably. The thick mist hung in clots upon his eyelashes like candied thaw; and between the fog and fire together, there were rainbows in his very whiskers.

"Why, you see, Dot," John made answer, slowly, as he unrolled a shawl from about his throat; and warmed his hands; "it—it an't exactly summer weather. So, no wonder."

"I wish you wouldn't call me Dot, John. I don't like it," said Mrs. Peerybingle: pouting in a way that clearly showed she *did* like it, very much.

"Why what else are you?" returned John, looking down upon her with a smile, and giving her waist as light a squeeze as his huge hand and arm could give. "A dot and"—here he glanced at the baby—"a dot and carry—I won't say it, for fear I should spoil it; but I was very near a joke. I don't know as ever I was nearer."

He was often near to something or other very clever, by his own account: this lumbering, slow, honest John; this

John so heavy, but so light of spirit; so rough upon the surface, but so gentle at the core; so dull without, so quick within; so stolid, but so good! Oh Mother Nature, give thy children the true poetry of heart that hid itself in this poor Carrier's breast—he was but a Carrier by the way—and we can bear to have them talking prose, and leading lives of prose; and bear to bless thee for their company!

It was pleasant to see Dot, with her little figure, and her baby in her arms: a very doll of a baby: glancing with a coquettish thoughtfulness at the fire, and inclining her delicate little head just enough on one side to let it rest in an odd, half-natural, half-affected, wholly nestling and agreeable manner, on the great rugged figure of the Carrier. It was pleasant to see him, with his tender awkwardness, endeavouring to adapt his rude support to her slight need, and make his burly middle-age a leaning-staff not inappropriate to her blooming youth. It was pleasant to observe how Tilly Slowboy, waiting in the background for the baby, took especial cognizance (though in her earliest teens) of this grouping; and stood with her mouth and eyes wide open, and her head thrust forward, taking it in as if it were air. Nor was it less agreeable to observe how John the Carrier, reference being made by Dot to the aforesaid baby, checked his hand when on the point of touching the infant, as if he thought he might crack it; and bending down, surveyed it from a safe distance, with a kind of puzzled pride, such as an amiable mastiff might be supposed to show, if he found himself, one day, the father of a young canary.

"An't he beautiful, John? Don't he look precious in his sleep?"

"Very precious," said John. "Very much so. He generally 's asleep, an't he?"

"Lor, John! Good gracious no!"

"Oh," said John, pondering. "I thought his eyes was generally shut. Halloa!"

"Goodness, John, how you startle one!"

"It an't right for him to turn 'em up in that way!" said the astonished Carrier, "is it? See how he 's winking with

both of 'em at once! And look at his mouth! Why he'
gasping like a gold and silver fish!"

"You don't deserve to be a father, you don't," said Dot
with all the dignity of an experienced matron. "But how
should you know what little complaints children are trouble
with, John! You wouldn't so much as know their names, yo
stupid fellow." And when she had turned the baby over on
her left arm, and had slapped its back as a restorative, sh
pinched her husband's ear, laughing.

"No," said John, pulling off his outer coat. "It 's ver
true, Dot. I don't know much about it. I only know tha
I 've been fighting pretty stiffly with the wind to-night. It '
been blowing north-east, straight into the cart, the whol
way home."

"Poor old man, so it has!" cried Mrs. Peerybingle, in
stantly becoming very active. "Here! Take the preciou
darling, Tilly, while I make myself of some use. Bless it,
could smother it with kissing it, I could! Hie then, goo
dog! Hie Boxer, boy! Only let me make the tea first, John
and then I 'll help you with the parcels, like a busy bee
'How doth the little'—and all the rest of it, you know
John. Did you ever learn 'how doth the little,' when yo
went to school, John?"

"Not to quite know it," John returned. "I was very nea
it once. But I should only have spoilt it, I dare say."

"Ha ha," laughed Dot. She had the blithest little laugl
you ever heard. "What a dear old darling of a dunce yo
are, John, to be sure!"

Not at all disputing this position, John went out to se
that the boy with the lantern, which had been dancing t
and fro before the door and window, like a Will of the Wisp
took due care of the horse; who was fatter than you woul
quite believe, if I gave you his measure, and so old that hi
birthday was lost in the mists of antiquity. Boxer, feelin,
that his attentions were due to the family in general, an
must be impartially distributed, dashed in and out with be
wildering inconstancy; now, describing a circle of short bark

round the horse, where he was being rubbed down at the stable-door; now, feigning to make savage rushes at his mistress, and facetiously bringing himself to sudden stops; now, eliciting a shriek from Tilly Slowboy, in the low nursing-chair near the fire, by the unexpected application of his moist nose to her countenance; now, exhibiting an obtrusive interest in the baby; now, going round and round upon the hearth, and lying down as if he had established himself for the night; now, getting up again, and taking that nothing of a fag-end of a tail of his, out into the weather, as if he had just remembered an appointment, and was off, at a round trot, to keep it.

"There! There's the teapot, ready on the hob!" said Dot; as briskly busy as a child at play at keeping house. "And there's the cold knuckle of ham; and there's the butter; and there's the crusty loaf, and all! Here's the clothes-basket for the small parcels, John, if you've got any there—where are you, John? Don't let the dear child fall under the grate, Tilly, whatever you do!"

It may be noted of Miss Slowboy, in spite of her rejecting the caution with some vivacity, that she had a rare and surprising talent for getting this baby into difficulties: and had several times imperilled its short life, in a quiet way peculiarly her own. She was of a spare and straight shape, this young lady, insomuch that her garments appeared to be in constant danger of sliding off those sharp pegs, her shoulders, on which they were loosely hung. Her costume was remarkable for the partial development, on all possible occasions, of some flannel vestment of a singular structure; also for affording glimpses, in the region of the back, of a corset or pair of stays, in colour a dead-green. Being always in a state of gaping admiration at everything, and absorbed, besides, in the perpetual contemplation of her mistress's perfections and the baby's, Miss Slowboy, in her little errors of judgment, may be said to have done equal honour to her head and to her heart; and though these did less honour to the baby's head, which they were the occasional means of bringing into contact with deal doors, dressers, stair-rails, bedposts, and other foreign substances, still they were the honest results of Tilly Slowboy's constant astonishment at finding herself so kindly treated, and installed in such a comfortable home. For, the maternal and paternal Slowboy were alike unknown to Fame, and Tilly had been bred by public charity, a foundling; which word, though only differing from fondling by one vowel's length, is very different in meaning, and expresses quite another thing.

To have seen little Mrs. Peerybingle come back with her husband, tugging at the clothes-basket, and making the most strenuous exertions to do nothing at all (for he carried it), would have amused you almost as much as it amused him. It may have entertained the Cricket too, for anything I know; but, certainly, it now began to chirp again, vehemently.

"Heyday!" said John, in his slow way. "It's merrier than ever, to-night, I think."

"And it's sure to bring us good fortune, John! It always has done so. To have a Cricket on the Hearth, is the luckiest thing in all the world!"

John looked at her as if he had very nearly got the thought into his head, that she was his Cricket in chief, and he quite agreed with her. But, it was probably one of his narrow escapes, for he said nothing.

"The first time I heard its cheerful little note, John, was on that night when you brought me home—when you brought me to my new home here; its little mistress. Nearly a year ago. You recollect, John?"

O yes. John remembered. I should think so!

"Its chirp was such a welcome to me! It seemed so full of promise and encouragement. It seemed to say, you would be kind and gentle with me, and would not expect (I had a fear of that, John, then) to find an old head on the shoulders of your foolish little wife."

John thoughtfully patted one of the shoulders, and then the head, as though he would have said No, no; he had had no such expectation; he had been quite content to take them as they were. And really he had reason. They were very comely.

"It spoke the truth, John, when it seemed to say so; for you have ever been, I am sure, the best, the most considerate, the most affectionate of husbands to me. This has been a happy home, John; and I love the Cricket for its sake!"

"Why so do I then," said the Carrier. "So do I, Dot."

"I love it for the many times I have heard it, and the many thoughts its harmless music has given me. Sometimes, in the twilight, when I have felt a little solitary and downhearted, John—before baby was here to keep me company and make the house gay—when I have thought how lonely you would be if I should die; how lonely I should be if I could know that you had lost me, dear; its Chirp, Chirp, Chirp upon the hearth, has seemed to tell me of another little voice, so sweet, so very dear to me, before whose coming sound my trouble vanished like a dream. And when I used to fear—I did fear once, John, I was very young you know—that ours might prove to be an ill-assorted marriage, I being such a child, and you more like my guardian than my husband; and that you might not, however hard you tried, be able to learn to love me, as you hoped and prayed you might; its Chirp, Chirp, Chirp has cheered me up again, and filled me with new trust and confidence. I was thinking of these things to-night, dear, when I sat expecting you; and I love the Cricket for their sake!"

"And so do I," repeated John. "But Dot? *I* hope and pray that I might learn to love you? How you talk! I had learnt that, long before I brought you here, to be the Cricket's little mistress, Dot!"

She laid her hand, an instant, on his arm, and looked up at him with an agitated face, as if she would have told him something. Next moment she was down upon her knees before the basket, speaking in a sprightly voice, and busy with the parcels.

"There are not many of them to-night, John, but I saw some goods behind the cart, just now; and though they give

more trouble, perhaps, still they pay as well; so we have
no reason to grumble, have we? Besides, you have been de-
livering, I dare say, as you came along?"

"Oh yes," John said. "A good many."

"Why what's this round box? Heart alive, John, it's a
wedding-cake!"

"Leave a woman alone to find out that," said John, ad-
miringly. "Now a man would never have thought of it.
Whereas, it's my belief that if you was to pack a wedding-
cake up in a tea-chest, or a turn-up bedstead, or a pickled
salmon keg, or any unlikely thing, a woman would be sure
to find it out directly. Yes; I called for it at the pastrycook's."

"And it weighs I don't know what—whole hundred-
weights!" cried Dot, making a great demonstration of trying
to lift it. "Whose is it, John? Where is it going?"

"Read the writing on the other side," said John.

"Why, John! My Goodness, John!"

"Ah! who'd have thought it!" John returned.

"You never mean to say," pursued Dot, sitting on the
floor and shaking her head at him, "that it's Gruff and
Tackleton the toy-maker!"

John nodded.

Mrs. Peerybingle nodded also, fifty times at least. Not in
assent—in dumb and pitying amazement; screwing up her
lips the while with all their little force (they were never
made for screwing up; I am clear of that), and looking the
good Carrier through and through, in her abstraction. Miss
Slowboy, in the mean time, who had a mechanical power of
reproducing scraps of current conversation for the delecta-
tion of the baby, with all the sense struck out of them, and
all the nouns changed into the plural number, inquired aloud
of that young creature, Was it Gruffs and Tackletons the
toymakers then, and Would it call it Pastry-cooks for wedding cakes, and Did its mothers know the boxes when its
fathers brought them homes; and so on.

"And that is really to come about!" said Dot. "Why, she
and I were girls at school together, John."

He might have been thinking of her, or nearly thinking of her, perhaps, as she was in that same school time. He looked upon her with a thoughtful pleasure, but he made no answer.

"And he's as old! As unlike her!—Why, how many years older than you, is Gruff and Tackleton, John?"

"How many more cups of tea shall I drink to-night at one sitting, than Gruff and Tackleton ever took in four, I wonder!" replied John, good-humouredly, as he drew a chair to the round table, and began at the cold ham. "As to eating, I eat but little; but, that little I enjoy, Dot."

Even this, his usual sentiment at meal times, one of his innocent delusions (for his appetite was always obstinate, and flatly contradicted him), awoke no smile in the face of his little wife, who stood among the parcels, pushing the cake-box slowly from her with her foot, and never once looked, though her eyes were cast down too, upon that dainty shoe she generally was so mindful of. Absorbed in thought, she stood there, heedless alike of the tea and John (although he called to her, and rapped the table with his knife to startle her), until he rose and touched her on the arm; when she looked at him for a moment, and hurried to her place behind the teaboard, laughing at her negligence. But, not as she had laughed before. The manner and the music were quite changed.

The Cricket, too, had stopped. Somehow the room was not so cheerful as it had been. Nothing like it.

"So, these are all the parcels, are they, John?" she said, breaking a long silence, which the honest Carrier had devoted to the practical illustration of one part of his favourite sentiment—certainly enjoying what he ate, if it couldn't be admitted that he ate but little. "So these are all the parcels; are they, John?"

"That's all," said John. "Why—no—I—" laying down his knife and fork, and taking a long breath. "I declare—I've clean forgotten the old gentleman!"

"The old gentleman?"

"In the cart." said John. "He was asleep, among the

straw, the last time I saw him. I 've very nearly remembered him, twice, since I came in; but, he went out of my head again. Holloa! Yahip there! Rouse up! That's my hearty!"

John said these latter words outside the door, whither he had hurried with the candle in his hand.

Miss Slowboy, conscious of some mysterious reference to The Old Gentleman, and connecting in her mystified imagination certain associations of a religious nature with the phrase, was so disturbed, that hastily rising from the low chair by the fire to seek protection near the skirts of her mistress, and coming into contact as she crossed the doorway with an ancient Stranger, she instinctively made a charge or butt at him with the only offensive instrument within her reach. This instrument happening to be the baby, great commotion and alarm ensued, which the sagacity of Boxer rather tended to increase; for, that good dog, more thoughtful than its master, had, it seemed, been watching the old gentleman in his sleep, lest he should walk off with a few young poplar trees that were tied up behind the cart; and he still attended on him very closely, worrying his gaiters in fact, and making dead sets at the buttons.

"You 're such an undeniable good sleeper, sir," said John, when tranquillity was restored; in the mean time the old gentleman had stood, bareheaded and motionless, in the centre of the room; "that I have half a mind to ask you where the other six are—only that would be a joke, and I know I should spoil it. Very near though," murmured the Carrier, with a chuckle; "very near!"

The Stranger, who had long white hair, good features, singularly bold and well defined for an old man, and dark, bright, penetrating eyes, looked round with a smile, and saluted the Carrier's wife by gravely inclining his head.

His garb was very quaint and old—a long, long way behind the time. Its hue was brown, all over. In his hand he held a great brown club or walking-stick; and striking this upon the floor, it fell asunder, and became a chair. On which he sat down, quite composedly.

"There!" said the Carrier, turning to his wife. "That's the way I found him, sitting by the roadside! Upright as a milestone. And almost as deaf."

"Sitting in the open air, John!"

"In the open air," replied the Carrier, "just at dusk. 'Carriage Paid,' he said; and gave me eighteenpence. Then he got in. And there he is."

"He's going, John, I think!"

Not at all. He was only going to speak.

"If you please, I was to be left till called for," said the Stranger, mildly. "Don't mind me."

With that, he took a pair of spectacles from one of his large pockets, and a book from another, and leisurely began to read. Making no more of Boxer than if he had been a house lamb!

The Carrier and his wife exchanged a look of perplexity. The Stranger raised his head; and glancing from the latter to the former, said,

"Your daughter, my good friend?"

"Wife," returned John.

"Niece?" said the Stranger.

"Wife," roared John.

"Indeed?" observed the Stranger. "Surely? Very young!"

He quietly turned over, and resumed his reading. But, before he could have read two lines, he again interrupted himself to say:

"Baby, yours?"

John gave him a gigantic nod; equivalent to an answer in the affirmative, delivered through a speaking trumpet.

"Girl?"

"Bo-o-oy!" roared John.

"Also very young, eh?"

Mrs. Peerybingle instantly struck in. "Two months and three da-ays! Vaccinated just six weeks ago-o! Took very fine-ly! Considered, by the doctor, a remarkably beautiful chi-ld! Equal to the general run of children at five months o-old! Takes notice, in a way quite won-der-ful! May seem impossible to you, but feels his legs al-ready!"

Here the breathless little mother, who had been shrieking these short sentences into the old man's ear, until her pretty face was crimsoned, held up the Baby before him as a stubborn and triumphant fact; while Tilly Slowboy, with a melodious cry of "Ketcher, Ketcher"—which sounded like some unknown words, adapted to a popular Sneeze—performed some cow-like gambols round that all-unconscious Innocent.

"Hark! He's called for, sure enough," said John. "There's somebody at the door. Open it, Tilly."

Before she could reach it, however, it was opened from without; being a primitive sort of door, with a latch, that any one could lift if he chose—and a good many people did choose, for all kinds of neighbours liked to have a cheerful word or two with the Carrier, though he was no great talker himself. Being opened, it gave admission to a little, meagre, thoughtful, dingy-faced man, who seemed to have made himself a great-coat from the sack-cloth covering of some old box; for, when he turned to shut the door, and keep the weather out, he disclosed upon the back of that garment, the inscription G & T in large black capitals. Also the word GLASS in bold characters.

"Good-evening John!" said the little man. "Good-evening Mum. Good-evening Tilly. Good-evening Unbeknown! How's Baby Mum? Boxer's pretty well I hope?"

"All thriving, Caleb," replied Dot. "I am sure you need only look at the dear child, for one, to know that."

"And I'm sure I need only look at you for another," said Caleb.

He didn't look at her though; he had a wandering and thoughtful eye which seemed to be always projecting itself into some other time and place, no matter what he said; a description which will equally apply to his voice.

"Or at John for another," said Caleb. "Or at Tilly, as far as that goes. Or certainly at Boxer."

"Busy just now, Caleb?" asked the Carrier.

"Why, pretty well, John," he returned, with the distraught air of a man who was casting about for the Philosopher's stone, at least. "Pretty much so. There's rather a run on Noah's Arks at present. I could have wished to improve upon the Family, but I don't see how it's to be done at the price. It would be a satisfaction to one's mind, to make it clearer which was Shems and Hams, and which was Wives. Flies an't on that scale neither, as compared with elephants you know! Ah! well! Have you got anything in the parcel line for me, John?"

The Carrier put his hand into a pocket of the coat he had taken off; and brought out, carefully preserved in moss and paper, a tiny flower-pot.

"There it is!" he said, adjusting it with great care. "Not so much as a leaf damaged. Full of buds!"

Caleb's dull eye brightened, as he took it and thanked him.

"Dear, Caleb," said the Carrier. "Very dear at this season."

"Never mind that. It would be cheap to me, whatever it cost," returned the little man. "Anything else, John?"

"A small box," replied the Carrier. "Here you are!"

"'For Caleb Plummer,'" said the little man, spelling out the direction. "'With Cash.' With Cash, John. I don't think it's for me."

"With Care," returned the Carrier, looking over his shoulder. "Where do you make out cash?"

"Oh! To be sure!" said Caleb. "It's all right. With care! Yes, yes; that's mine. It might have been with cash, indeed, if my dear Boy in the Golden South Americas had lived, John. You loved him like a son; didn't you? You needn't say you did. *I* know, of course. 'Caleb Plummer. With care.' Yes, yes, it's all right. It's a box of dolls' eyes for my daughter's work. I wish it was her own sight in a box, John."

"I wish it was, or could be!" cried the Carrier.

"Thank 'ee," said the little man. "You speak very hearty. To think that she should never see the Dolls—and them a-staring at her, so bold, all day long! That's where it cuts. What's the damage, John?"

"I 'll damage you," said John, "if you inquire. Dot! Very near?"

"Well! it 's like you to say so," observed the little man. "It 's your kind way. Let me see. I think that 's all."

"I think not," said the Carrier. "Try again."

"Something for our Governor, eh?" said Caleb, after pondering a little while. "To be sure. That 's what I came for; but my head 's so running on them Arks and things! He hasn't been here, has he?"

"Not he," returned the Carrier. "He 's too busy, courting."

"He 's coming round though," said Caleb; "for he told me to keep on the near side of the road going home, and it was ten to one he 'd take me up. I had better go, by the bye.— You couldn't have the goodness to let me pinch Boxer's tail, Mum, for half a moment, could you?"

"Why, Caleb! what a question!"

"Oh never mind, Mum," said the little man. "He mightn't like it perhaps. There 's a small order just come in, for barking dogs; and I should wish to go as close to Natur' as I could, for sixpence. That 's all. Never mind, Mum."

It happened opportunely, that Boxer, without receiving the proposed stimulus, began to bark with great zeal. But, as this implied the approach of some new visitor, Caleb, postponing his study from the life to a more convenient season, shouldered the round box, and took a hurried leave. He might have spared himself the trouble, for he met the visitor upon the threshold.

"Oh! You are here, are you? Wait a bit. I 'll take you home. John Peerybingle, my service to you. More of my service to your pretty wife. Handsomer every day! Better too, if possible! And younger," mused the speaker, in a low voice; "that 's the Devil of it!"

"I should be astonished at your paying compliments, Mr. Tackleton," said Dot, not with the best grace in the world; "but for your condition."

"You know all about it then?"

"I have got myself to believe it, somehow," said Dot.

"After a hard struggle, I suppose?"

"Very."

Tackleton, the Toy-merchant, pretty generally known as
Gruff and Tackleton—for that was the firm, though Gruff
had been bought out long ago; only leaving his name, and
as some said his nature, according to its Dictionary meaning,
in the business—Tackleton the Toy-merchant, was a man
whose vocation had been quite misunderstood by his Parents
and Guardians. If they had made him a Money Lender, or a
sharp Attorney, or a Sheriff's Officer, or a Broker, he might
have sown his discontented oats in his youth, and, after having had the full run of himself in ill-natured transactions,
might have turned out amiable, at last, for the sake of a
little freshness and novelty. But, cramped and chafing in
the peaceable pursuit of toy-making, he was a domestic
Ogre, who had been living on children all his life, and was
their implacable enemy. He despised all toys; wouldn't have
bought one for the world; delighted, in his malice, to insinuate grim expressions into the faces of brown-paper farmers who drove pigs to market, bellmen who advertised lost
lawyers' consciences, moveable old ladies who darned stockings or carved pies; and other like samples of his stock-in-
trade. In appalling masks; hideous, hairy, red-eyed Jacks
in Boxes; Vampire Kites; demoniacal Tumblers who would-
n't lie down, and were perpetually flying forward, to stare
infants out of countenance; his soul perfectly revelled.
They were his only relief, and safety-valve. He was great in
such inventions. Anything suggestive of a Pony-nightmare,
was delicious to him. He had even lost money (and he took
to that toy very kindly) by getting up Goblin slides for
magic-lanterns, whereon the Powers of Darkness were depicted as a sort of supernatural shell-fish, with human faces.
In intensifying the portraiture of Giants, he had sunk quite
a little capital; and, though no painter himself, he could in-
dicate, for the instruction of his artists, with a piece of chalk,
a certain furtive leer for the countenances of those monsters,

which was safe to destroy the peace of mind of any young
gentleman between the ages of six and eleven, for the whole
Christmas or Midsummer Vacation.

What he was in toys, he was (as most men are) in other
things. You may easily suppose, therefore, that within the
great green cape, which reached down to the calves of his
legs, there was buttoned up to the chin an uncommonly
pleasant fellow; and that he was about as choice a spirit,
and as agreeable a companion, as ever stood in a pair of
bull-headed looking boots with mahogany-coloured tops.

Still, Tackleton, the toy-merchant, was going to be married. In spite of all this, he was going to be married. And
to a young wife too, a beautiful young wife.

He didn't look much like a bridegroom, as he stood in the
Carrier's kitchen, with a twist in his dry face, and a screw
in his body, and his hat jerked over the bridge of his nose,
and his hands tucked down into the bottoms of his pockets,
and his whole sarcastic ill-conditioned self peering out of one
little corner of one little eye, like the concentrated essence
of any number of ravens. But, a Bridegroom he designed to
be.

"In three days' time. Next Thursday. The last day of the
first month in the year. That's my wedding day," said
Tackleton.

Did I mention that he had always one eye wide open, and
one eye nearly shut; and that the one eye nearly shut, was
always the expressive eye? I don't think I did.

"That's my wedding-day!" said Tackleton, rattling his
money.

"Why, it's our wedding-day too," exclaimed the Carrier.

"Ha ha!" laughed Tackleton. "Odd! You're just such
another couple. Just!"

The indignation of Dot at this presumptuous assertion is
not to be described. What next? His imagination would
compass the possibility of just such another Baby, perhaps.
The man was mad.

"I say! A word with you," murmured Tackleton, nudg-
ing the Carrier with his elbow, and taking him a little apart.

"You'll come to the wedding? We're in the same boat, you know."

"How in the same boat?" inquired the Carrier.

"A little disparity, you know"; said Tackleton, with another nudge. "Come and spend an evening with us, beforehand."

"Why?" demanded John, astonished at this pressing hospitality.

"Why?" returned the other. "That's a new way of receiving an invitation. Why, for pleasure—sociability, you know, and all that!"

"I thought you were never sociable," said John, in his plain way.

"Tchah! It's of no use to be anything but free with you I see," said Tackleton. "Why, then, the truth is you have a —what tea-drinking people call a sort of a comfortable appearance together, you and your wife. We know better, you know, but—"

"No, we don't know better," interposed John. "What are you talking about?"

"Well! We *don't* know better, then," said Tackleton. "We'll agree that we don't. As you like; what does it matter? I was going to say, as you have that sort of appearance, your company will produce a favourable effect on Mrs. Tackleton that will be. And, though I don't think your good lady's very friendly to me, in this matter, still she can't help herself from falling into my views, for there's a compactness and cosiness of appearance about her that always tells, even in an indifferent case. You'll say you'll come?"

"We have arranged to keep our Wedding-Day (as far as that goes) at home," said John. "We have made the promise to ourselves these six months. We think, you see, that home—"

"Bah! what's home?" cried Tackleton. "Four walls and a ceiling! (why don't you kill that Cricket! *I* would! I always do. I hate their noise). There are four walls and a ceiling at my house. Come to me!"

"You kill your Crickets, eh?" said John.

"Scrunch 'em, sir," returned the other, setting his heel heavily on the floor. "You'll say you'll come? It's as much your interest as mine, you know, that the women should persuade each other that they're quiet and contented, and couldn't be better off. I know their way. Whatever one woman says, another woman is determined to clinch, always. There's that spirit of emulation among 'em, sir, that if your wife says to my wife, 'I'm the happiest woman in the world, and mine's the best husband in the world, and I dote on him,' my wife will say the same to yours, or more, and half believe it."

"Do you mean to say she don't, then?" asked the Carrier.

"Don't!" cried Tackleton, with a short, sharp laugh. "Don't what?"

The Carrier had some faint idea of adding, "dote upon you." But, happening to meet the half-closed eye, as it twinkled upon him over the turned-up collar of the cape, which was within an ace of poking it out, he felt it such an unlikely part and parcel of anything to be doted on, that he substituted, "that she don't believe it?"

"Ah you dog! You're joking," said Tackleton.

But the Carrier, though slow to understand the full drift of his meaning, eyed him in such a serious manner, that he was obliged to be a little more explanatory.

"I have the humour," said Tackleton: holding up the fingers of his left hand, and tapping the forefinger, to imply "there I am, Tackleton to wit": "I have the humour, sir, to marry a young wife, and a pretty wife": here he rapped his little finger, to express the Bride; not sparingly, but sharply; with a sense of power. "I'm able to gratify that humour and I do. It's my whim. But—now look there!"

He pointed to where Dot was sitting, thoughtfully, before the fire; leaning her dimpled chin upon her hand, and watching the bright blaze. The Carrier looked at her, and then at him, and then at her, and then at him again.

"She honours and obeys, no doubt, you know," said Tackleton; "and that, as I am not a man of sentiment, is quite enough for *me*. But do you think there's anything more in it?"

"I think," observed the Carrier, "that I should chuck any man out of window, who said there wasn't."

"Exactly so," returned the other with an unusual alacrity of assent. "To be sure! Doubtless you would. Of course. I'm certain of it. Good-night. Pleasant dreams!"

The Carrier was puzzled, and made uncomfortable and uncertain, in spite of himself. He couldn't help showing it, in his manner.

"Good-night, my dear friend!" said Tackleton, compassionately. "I'm off. We're exactly alike, in reality, I see. You won't give us to-morrow evening? Well! Next day you go out visiting, I know. I'll meet you there, and bring my wife that is to be. It'll do her good. You're agreeable? Thank 'ee. What's that!"

It was a loud cry from the Carrier's wife: a loud, sharp, sudden cry, that made the room ring, like a glass vessel. She had risen from her seat, and stood like one transfixed by terror and surprise. The Stranger had advanced towards the fire to warm himself, and stood within a short stride of her chair. But quite still.

"Dot!" cried the Carrier. "Mary! Darling! What's the matter?"

They were all about her in a moment. Caleb, who had been dozing on the cake-box, in the first imperfect recovery of his suspended presence of mind, seized Miss Slowboy by the hair of her head, but immediately apologised.

"Mary!" exclaimed the Carrier, supporting her in his arms. "Are you ill! What is it? Tell me, dear!"

She only answered by beating her hands together, and falling into a wild fit of laughter. Then, sinking from his grasp upon the ground, she covered her face with her apron, and wept bitterly. And then she laughed again, and then she cried again, and then she said how cold it was, and suffered him to lead her to the fire, where she sat down as before. The old man standing, as before, quite still.

"I'm better, John," she said. "I'm quite well now—I—"

"John!" But John was on the other side of her. Why turn her face towards the strange old gentleman, as if addressing him! Was her brain wandering?

"Only a fancy, John dear—a kind of shock—a something coming suddenly before my eyes—I don't know what it was. It's quite gone, quite gone."

"I'm glad it's gone," muttered Tackleton, turning the expressive eye all round the room. "I wonder where it's gone, and what it was. Humph! Caleb, come here! Who's that with the grey hair?"

"I don't know, sir," returned Caleb in a whisper. "Never see him before, in all my life. A beautiful figure for a nut-cracker; quite a new model. With a screw jaw opening down into his waistcoat, he'd be lovely."

"Not ugly enough," said Tackleton.

"Or for a firebox, either," observed Caleb, in deep contemplation, "what a model! Unscrew his head to put the matches in; turn him heels up'ards for the light; and what a firebox for a gentleman's mantel-shelf, just as he stands!"

"Not half ugly enough," said Tackleton. "Nothing in him at all! Come! Bring that box! All right now, I hope!"

"Oh quite gone! Quite gone!" said the little woman, waving him hurriedly away. "Good-night!"

"Good-night," said Tackleton. "Good-night, John Peerybingle! Take care how you carry that box, Caleb. Let it fall, and I'll murder you! Dark as pitch, and weather worse than ever, eh? Good-night!"

So, with another sharp look around the room, he went out at the door; followed by Caleb with the wedding-cake on his head.

The Carrier had been so much astounded by his little wife, and so busily engaged in soothing and tending her, that he had scarcely been conscious of the Stranger's presence, until now, when he again stood there, their only guest.

"He don't belong to them, you see," said John. "I must give him a hint to go."

"I beg your pardon, friend," said the old gentleman, advancing to him; "the more so, as I fear your wife has not been well; but the Attendant whom my infirmity," he touched his ears and shook his head, "renders almost indispensable, not having arrived, I fear there must be some mistake. The bad night which made the shelter of your comfortable cart (may I never have a worse!) so acceptable, is still as bad as ever. Would you, in your kindness, suffer me to rent a bed here?"

"Yes, yes," cried Dot. "Yes! Certainly!"

"Oh!" said the Carrier, surprised by the rapidity of this consent. "Well! I don't object; but still I'm not quite sure that—"

"Hush!" she interrupted. "Dear John!"

"Why, he's stone deaf," urged John.

"I know he is, but—Yes sir, certainly. Yes! certainly! I'll make him up a bed, directly, John."

As she hurried off to do it, the flutter of her spirits, and the agitation of her manner, were so strange, that the Carrier stood looking after her, quite confounded.

"Did its mothers make it up a Bed then!" cried Miss Slowboy to the Baby; "and did its hair grow brown and curly, when its caps was lifted off, and frighten it, a precious Pets, a-sitting by the fires!"

With that unaccountable attraction of the mind to trifles, which is often incidental to a state of doubt and confusion, the Carrier, as he walked slowly to and fro, found himself mentally repeating even these absurd words, many times. So many times that he got them by heart, and was still conning them over and over, like a lesson, when Tilly, after administering as much friction to the little bald head with her hand as she thought wholesome (according to the practice of nurses), had once more tied the Baby's cap on.

"And frighten it a precious Pets, a-sitting by the fires. What frightened Dot, I wonder!" mused the Carrier, pacing to and fro.

He scouted, from his heart, the insinuations of the Toy-merchant, and yet they filled him with a vague, indefinite uneasiness. For. Tackleton was quick and sly; and he had

that painful sense, himself, of being a man of slow perception, that a broken hint was always worrying to him. He
certainly had no intention in his mind of linking anything
that Tackleton had said, with the unusual conduct of his
wife, but the two subjects of reflection came into his mind
together, and he could not keep them asunder.

The bed was soon made ready; and the visitor, declining
all refreshment but a cup of tea, retired. Then, Dot—quite
well again, she said, quite well again—arranged the great
chair in the chimney-corner for her husband; filled his pipe
and gave it him; and took her usual little stool beside him
on the hearth.

She always *would* sit on that little stool. I think she must
have had a kind of notion that it was a coaxing, wheedling,
little stool.

She was, out and out, the very best filler of a pipe, I should
say, in the four quarters of the globe. To see her put that
chubby little finger in the bowl, and then blow down the
pipe to clear the tube, and, when she had done so, affect to
think that there was really something in the tube, and blow
a dozen times, and hold it to her eye like a telescope, with
a most provoking twist in her capital little face, as she
looked down it, was quite a brilliant thing. As to the tobacco, she was perfect mistress of the subject; and her lighting of the pipe, with a wisp of paper, when the Carrier had
it in his mouth—going so very near his nose, and yet not
scorching it—was Art, high Art.

And the Cricket and the kettle, turning up again, acknowledged it! The bright fire, blazing up again, acknowledged
it! The little Mower on the clock in his unheeded work
acknowledged it! The Carrier, in his smoothing forehead and
expanding face, acknowledged it, the readiest of all.

And as he soberly and thoughtfully puffed at his old pipe,
and as the Dutch clock ticked, and as the red fire gleamed,
and as the Cricket chirped; that Genius of his Hearth and
Home (for such the Cricket was) came out, in fairy shape,
into the room, and summoned many forms of Home about
him. Dots of all ages, and all sizes, filled the chamber. Dots

who were merry children, running on before him gathering
flowers, in the fields; coy Dots, half shrinking from, half
yielding to, the pleading of his own rough image; newly-
married Dots, alighting at the door, and taking wondering
possession of the household keys; motherly little Dots, attended by fictitious Slowboys, bearing babies to be christened;
matronly Dots, still young and blooming, watching Dots of
Daughters, as they danced at rustic balls; fat Dots, encircled
and beset by troops of rosy grand-children; withered Dots,
who leaned on sticks, and tottered as they crept along. Old
Carriers too, appeared, with blind old Boxers lying at their
feet; and newer carts with younger drivers ("Peerybingle
Brothers" on the tilt); and sick old Carriers, tended by the
gentlest hands; and graves of dead and gone old Carriers,
green in the churchyard. And as the Cricket showed him
all these things—he saw them plainly, though his eyes were
fixed upon the fire—the Carrier's heart grew light and
happy, and he thanked his Household Gods with all his
might, and cared no more for Gruff and Tackleton than you
do.

But, what was that young figure of a man, which the
same Fairy Cricket set so near Her stool, and which remained there, singly and alone? Why did it linger still, so
near her, with its arm upon the chimney-piece, ever repeating "Married! and not to me!"

O Dot! O failing Dot! There is no place for it in all
your husband's visions; why has its shadow fallen on his
hearth!

Chirp the Second

CALEB PLUMMER and his Blind Daughter lived all alone by
themselves, as the Story-books say—and my blessing, with
yours to back it I hope, on the Story-books, for saying anything in this workaday world!—Caleb Plummer and his

Blind Daughter lived all alone by themselves, in a little cracked nutshell of a wooden house, which was, in truth, no better than a pimple on the prominent red-brick nose of Gruff and Tackleton. The premises of Gruff and Tackleton were the great feature of the street; but you might have knocked down Caleb Plummer's dwelling with a hammer or two, and carried off the pieces in a cart.

If any one had done the dwelling-house of Caleb Plummer the honour to miss it after such an inroad, it would have been, no doubt, to commend its demolition as a vast improvement. It stuck to the premises of Gruff and Tackleton, like a barnacle to a ship's keel, or a snail to a door, or a little bunch of toadstools to the stem of a tree. But, it was the germ from which the full-grown trunk of Gruff and Tackleton had sprung; and, under its crazy roof, the Gruff before last, had, in a small way, made toys for a generation of old boys and girls, who had played with them, and found them out, and broken them, and gone to sleep.

I have said that Caleb and his poor Blind Daughter lived here. I should have said that Caleb lived here, and his poor Blind Daughter somewhere else—in an enchanted home of Caleb's furnishing, where scarcity and shabbiness were not, and trouble never entered. Caleb was no sorcerer, but in the only magic art that still remains to us, the magic of devoted, deathless love, Nature had been the mistress of his study; and from her teaching, all the wonder came.

The Blind Girl never knew that ceilings were discoloured, walls blotched and bare of plaster here and there, high crevices unstopped, and widening every day, beams mouldering and tending downward. The Blind Girl never knew that iron was rusting, wood rotting, paper peeling off; the size, and shape, and true proportion of the dwelling, withering away. The Blind Girl never knew that ugly shapes of delf and earthenware were on the board; that sorrow and faint-heartedness were in the house; that Caleb's scanty hairs were turning greyer and more grey, before her sightless face. The Blind Girl never knew they had a master, cold, exacting, and uninterested—never knew that Tackleton was

Tackleton in short; but lived in the belief of an eccentric humourist who loved to have his jest with them, and who while he was the Guardian Angel of their lives, disdained to hear one word of thankfulness.

And all was Caleb's doing; all the doing of her simple father! But he too had a Cricket on his Hearth; and listening sadly to its music when the motherless Blind Child was very young, that Spirit had inspired him with the thought that even her great deprivation might be almost changed into a blessing, and the girl made happy by these little means. For all the Cricket tribe are potent Spirits, even though the people who hold converse with them do not know it (which is frequently the case); and there are not in the unseen world, voices more gentle and more true, that may be so implicitly relied on, or that are so certain to give none but tenderest counsel, as the Voices in which the Spirits of the Fireside and the Hearth address themselves to human kind.

Caleb and his daughter were at work together in their usual working-room, which served them for their ordinary living-room as well; and a strange place it was. There were houses in it, finished and unfinished, for Dolls of all stations in life. Suburban tenements for Dolls of moderate means; kitchens and single apartments for Dolls of the lower classes; capital town residences for Dolls of high estate. Some of these establishments were already furnished according to estimate, with a view to the convenience of Dolls of limited income; others, could be fitted on the most expensive scale, at a moment's notice, from whole shelves of chairs and tables, sofas, bedsteads, and upholstery. The nobility and gentry, and public in general, for whose accommodation these tenements were designed, lay, here and there, in baskets, staring straight up at the ceiling; but, in denoting their degrees in society, and confining them to their respective stations (which experience shows to be lamentably difficult in real life), the makers of these Dolls had far improved on Nature, who is often froward and perverse; for, they, not resting on such arbitrary marks as satin, cotton-print, and bits of rag, had superadded striking personal differences which allowed of no mistake. Thus, the Doll-lady of distinction had wax limbs of perfect symmetry; but, only she and her compeers. The next grade in the social scale being made of leather, and the next of coarse linen stuff. As to the common-people, they had just so many matches out of tinder-boxes, for their arms and legs, and there they were—established in their sphere at once, beyond the possibility of getting out of it.

There were various other samples of his handicraft, besides Dolls, in Caleb Plummer's room. There were Noah's Arks, in which the Birds and Beasts were an uncommonly tight fit, I assure you; though they could be crammed in, anyhow, at the roof, and rattled and shaken into the smallest compass. By a bold poetical licence, most of these Noah's Arks had knockers on the doors; inconsistent appendages, perhaps, as suggestive of morning callers and a Postman, yet a pleasant finish to the outside of the building. There were scores of melancholy little carts which, when the wheels went round, performed most doleful music. Many small fiddles, drums, and other instruments of torture; no end of cannon, shields, swords, spears, and guns. There were little tumblers in red breeches, incessantly swarming up high obstacles of red-tape, and coming down, head first, on the other side; and there were innumerable old gentlemen of respectable, not to say venerable, appearance, insanely flying over horizontal pegs, inserted, for the purpose, in their own street doors. There were beasts of all sorts; horses, in particular, of every breed, from the spotted barrel on four pegs, with a small tippet for a mane, to the thoroughbred rocker on his highest mettle. As it would have been hard to count the dozens upon dozens of grotesque figures that were ever ready to commit all sorts of absurdities on the turning of a handle, so it would have been no easy task to mention any human folly, vice, or weakness, that had not its type, immediate or remote, in Caleb Plummer's room. And not in an exaggerated form, for very little handles will move men and

women to as strange performances, as any Toy was ever
made to undertake.

In the midst of all these objects, Caleb and his daughter
sat at work. The Blind Girl busy as a Doll's dressmaker;
Caleb painting and glazing the four-pair front of a desirable
family mansion.

The care imprinted in the lines of Caleb's face, and his
absorbed and dreamy manner, which would have sat well on
some alchemist or abstruse student, were at first sight an odd
contrast to his occupation, and the trivialities about him.
But, trivial things, invented and pursued for bread, become
very serious matters of fact; and, apart from this consideration, I am not at all prepared to say, myself, that if Caleb
had been a Lord Chamberlain, or a Member of Parliament,
or a lawyer, or even a great speculator, he would have dealt
in toys one whit less whimsical, while I have a very great
doubt whether they would have been as harmless.

"So you were out in the rain last night, father, in your
beautiful new great-coat," said Caleb's daughter.

"In my beautiful new great-coat," answered Caleb, glancing towards a clothes-line in the room, on which the sack-
cloth garment previously described, was carefully hung up
to dry.

"How glad I am you bought it, father!"

"And of such a tailor, too," said Caleb. "Quite a fashionable tailor. It's too good for me."

The Blind Girl rested from her work, and laughed with
delight. "Too good, father! What can be too good for
you?"

"I'm half ashamed to wear it though," said Caleb, watching the effect of what he said, upon her brightening face;
"upon my word! When I hear the boys and people say behind me, 'Halloa. Here's a swell!' I don't know which way
to look. And when the beggar wouldn't go away last night;
and when I said I was a very common man, said 'No, your
Honour! Bless your Honour, don't say that!' I was quite
ashamed. I really felt as if I hadn't a right to wear it."

Happy Blind Girl! How merry she was, in her exultation!

"I see you, father," she said, clasping her hands, "as plainly, as if I had the eyes I never want when you are with me. A blue coat—"

"Bright blue," said Caleb.

"Yes, yes! Bright blue!" exclaimed the girl, turning up her radiant face; "the colour I can just remember in the blessed sky! You told me it was blue before! A bright blue coat—"

"Made loose to the figure," suggested Caleb.

"Made loose to the figure!" cried the Blind Girl, laughing heartily; "and in it, you, dear father, with your merry eye, your smiling face, your free step, and your dark hair—looking so young and handsome!"

"Halloa! Halloa!" said Caleb. "I shall be vain, presently!"

"I think you are, already," cried the Blind Girl, pointing at him, in her glee. "I know you, father! Ha, ha, ha! I've found you out, you see!"

How different the picture in her mind, from Caleb, as he sat observing her! She had spoken of his free step. She was right in that. For years and years, he had never once crossed that threshold at his own slow pace, but with a foot-fall counterfeited for her ear; and never had he, when his heart was heaviest, forgotten the light tread that was to render hers so cheerful and courageous!

Heaven knows! But I think Caleb's vague bewilderment of manner may have half originated in his having confused himself about himself and everything around him, for the love of his Blind Daughter. How could the little man be otherwise than bewildered, after labouring for so many years to destroy his own identity, and that of all the objects that had any bearing on it!

"There we are," said Caleb, falling back a pace or two to form the better judgment of his work; "as near the real thing as sixpenn'orth of halfpence is to sixpence. What a pity that the whole front of the house opens at once! If there was only a staircase in it, now, and regular doors to the rooms to go in at! But that's the worst of my calling, I'm always deluding myself, and swindling myself."

"You are speaking quite softly. You are not tired, father?"

"Tired!" echoed Caleb, with a great burst of animation, "what should tire me, Bertha? *I* was never tired. What does it mean?"

To give the greater force to his words, he checked himself in an involuntary imitation of two half-length stretching and yawning figures on the mantel-shelf, who were represented as in one eternal state of weariness from the waist upwards; and hummed a fragment of a song. It was a Bacchanalian song, something about a Sparkling Bowl. He sang it with an assumption of a Devil-may-care voice, that made his face a thousand times more meagre and more thoughtful than ever.

"What! You're singing, are you?" said Tackleton, putting his head in at the door. "Go it! *I* can't sing."

Nobody would have suspected him of it. He hadn't what is generally termed a singing face, by any means.

"I can't afford to sing," said Tackleton. "I'm glad *you* can. I hope you can afford to work too. Hardly time for both, I should think?"

"If you could only see him, Bertha, how he's winking at me!" whispered Caleb. "Such a man to joke! you'd think, if you didn't know him, he was in earnest—wouldn't you now?"

The Blind Girl smiled and nodded.

"The bird that can sing and won't sing, must be made to sing, they say," grumbled Tackleton. "What about the owl that can't sing, and oughtn't to sing, and will sing; is there anything that *he* should be made to do?"

"The extent to which he's winking at this moment!" whispered Caleb to his daughter. "O, my gracious!"

"Always merry and light-hearted with us!" cried the smiling Bertha.

"O, you're there, are you?" answered Tackleton. "Poor Idiot!"

He really did believe she was an Idiot; and he founded the belief, I can't say whether consciously or not, upon her being fond of him.

"Well! and being there,—how are you?" said Tackleton, in his grudging way.

"Oh! well; quite well. And as happy as even you can wish me to be. As happy as you would make the whole world, if you could!"

"Poor Idiot!" muttered Tackleton. "No gleam of reason. Not a gleam!"

The Blind Girl took his hand and kissed it; held it for a moment in her own two hands; and laid her cheek against it tenderly, before releasing it. There was such unspeakable affection and such fervent gratitude in the act, that Tackleton himself was moved to say, in a milder growl than usual:

"What's the matter now?"

"I stood it close beside my pillow when I went to sleep last night, and remembered it in my dreams. And when the day broke, and the glorious red sun—the *red* sun, father?"

"Red in the mornings and the evenings, Bertha," said poor Caleb, with a woeful glance at his employer.

"When it rose, and the bright light I almost fear to strike myself against in walking, came into the room, I turned the little tree towards it, and blessed Heaven for making things so precious, and blessed you for sending them to cheer me!"

"Bedlam broke loose!" said Tackleton under his breath. "We shall arrive at the strait-waistcoat and mufflers soon. We're getting on!"

Caleb, with his hands hooked loosely in each other, stared vacantly before him while his daughter spoke, as if he really were uncertain (I believe he was) whether Tackleton had done anything to deserve her thanks, or not. If he could have been a perfectly free agent, at that moment, required, on pain of death, to kick the Toy-merchant, or fall at his feet, according to his merits, I believe it would have been an even chance which course he would have taken. Yet, Caleb knew that with his own hands he had brought the little rose-tree home for her. so carefully, and that with his own lips he had forged the innocent deception which should help to keep her from suspecting how much, how very much, he every day denied himself, that she might be the happier.

"Bertha!" said Tackleton, assuming, for the nonce, a little cordiality. "Come here."

"Oh! I can come straight to you! You needn't guide me!" she rejoined.

"Shall I tell you a secret, Bertha?"

"If you will!" she answered, eagerly.

How bright the darkened face! How adorned with light, the listening head!

"This is the day on which little what's-her-name, the spoilt child, Peerybingle's wife, pays her regular visit to you—makes her fantastic Pic-Nic here; an't it?" said Tackleton, with a strong expression of distaste for the whole concern.

"Yes," replied Bertha. "This is the day."

"I thought so," said Tackleton. "I should like to join the party."

"Do you hear that, father!" cried the Blind Girl in an ecstasy.

"Yes, yes, I hear it," murmured Caleb, with the fixed look of a sleep-walker; "but I don't believe it. It's one of my lies, I've no doubt."

"You see I—I want to bring the Peerybingles a little more into company with May Fielding," said Tackleton. "I am going to be married to May."

"Married!" cried the Blind Girl, starting from him.

"She's such a con-founded Idiot," muttered Tackleton, "that I was afraid she'd never comprehend me. Ah, Bertha! Married! Church, parson, clerk, beadle, glass-coach, bells, breakfast, bride-cake, favours, marrow-bones, cleavers, and all the rest of the tom-foolery. A wedding, you know; a wedding. Don't you know what a wedding is?"

"I know," replied the Blind Girl, in a gentle tone. "I understand!"

"Do you?" muttered Tackleton. "It's more than I expected. Well! On that account I want to join the party,

and to bring May and her mother. I 'll send in a little something or other, before the afternoon. A cold leg of mutton,
or some comfortable trifle of that sort. You'll expect
me?"

"Yes," she answered.

She had drooped her head, and turned away; and so stood,
with her hands crossed, musing.

"I don't think you will," muttered Tackleton, looking at
her; "for you seem to have forgotten all about it already.
Caleb!"

"I may venture to say I 'm here, I suppose," thought
Caleb. "Sir!"

"Take care she don't forget what I 've been saying to her."

"*She* never forgets," returned Caleb. "It 's one of the few
things she an't clever in."

"Every man thinks his own geese swans," observed the
Toy-merchant, with a shrug. "Poor devil!"

Having delivered himself of which remark, with infinite
contempt, old Gruff and Tackleton withdrew.

Bertha remained where he had left her, lost in meditation. The gaiety had vanished from her downcast face, and
it was very sad. Three or four times, she shook her head, as
if bewailing some remembrance or some loss; but, her sorrowful reflections found no vent in words.

It was not until Caleb had been occupied, some time, in
yoking a team of horses to a wagon by the summary process
of nailing the harness to the vital parts of their bodies, that
she drew near to his working-stool, and sitting down beside
him, said:

"Father, I am lonely in the dark. I want my eyes, my
patient, willing eyes."

"Here they are," said Caleb. "Always ready. They are
more yours than mine, Bertha, any hour in the four-and-
twenty. What shall your eyes do for you, dear?"

"Look round the room, father."

"All right," said Caleb. "No sooner said than done,
Bertha."

"Tell me about it."

"It's much the same as usual," said Caleb. "Homely, but very snug. The gay colours on the walls; the bright flowers on the plates and dishes; the shining wood, where there are beams or panels; the general cheerfulness and neatness of the building; make it very pretty."

Cheerful and neat it was wherever Bertha's hands could busy themselves. But nowhere else, were cheerfulness and neatness possible, in the old crazy shed which Caleb's fancy so transformed.

"You have your working dress on, and are not so gallant as when you wear the handsome coat?" said Bertha, touching him.

"Not quite so gallant," answered Caleb. "Pretty brisk though."

"Father," said the Blind Girl, drawing close to his side, and stealing one arm round his neck, "tell me something about May. She is very fair?"

"She is indeed," said Caleb. And she was indeed. It was quite a rare thing to Caleb, not to have to draw on his invention.

"Her hair is dark," said Bertha, pensively, "darker than mine. Her voice is sweet and musical, I know. I have often loved to hear it. Her shape—"

"There's not a Doll's in all the room to equal it," said Caleb. "And her eyes!"—

He stopped; for Bertha had drawn closer round his neck, and, from the arm that clung about him, came a warning pressure which he understood too well.

He coughed a moment, hammered for a moment, and then fell back upon the song about the sparkling bowl; his infallible resource in all such difficulties.

"Our friend, father, our benefactor. I am never tired you know of hearing about him.—Now, was I ever?" she said, hastily.

"Of course not," answered Caleb, "and with reason."

"Ah! With how much reason!" cried the Blind Girl. With such fervency, that Caleb, though his motives were so pure, could not endure to meet her face; but dropped his eyes, as if she could have read in them his innocent deceit.

"Then, tell me again about him, dear father," said Bertha. "Many times again! His face is benevolent, kind, and tender. Honest and true, I am sure it is. The manly heart that tries to cloak all favours with a show of roughness and unwillingness, beats in its every look and glance."

"And makes it noble," added Caleb, in his quiet desperation.

"And makes it noble!" cried the Blind Girl. "He is older than May, father."

"Ye-es," said Caleb, reluctantly. "He's a little older than May. But that don't signify."

"Oh father, yes! To be his patient companion in infirmity and age; to be his gentle nurse in sickness, and his constant friend in suffering and sorrow; to know no weariness in working for his sake; to watch him, tend him, sit beside his bed and talk to him awake, and pray for him asleep; what privileges these would be! What opportunities for proving all her truth and devotion to him! Would she do all this, dear father?"

"No doubt of it," said Caleb.

"I love her, father; I can love her from my soul!" exclaimed the Blind Girl. And saying so, she laid her poor blind face on Caleb's shoulder, and so wept and wept, that he was almost sorry to have brought that tearful happiness upon her.

In the mean time, there had been a pretty sharp commotion at John Peerybingle's, for, little Mrs. Peerybingle naturally couldn't think of going anywhere without the Baby; and to get the Baby under weigh, took time. Not that there was much of the Baby, speaking of it as a thing of weight and measure, but, there was a vast deal to do about and about it, and it all had to be done by easy stages. For instance, when the Baby was got, by hook and by crook, to a certain point of dressing, and you might have rationally supposed that another touch or two would finish him off, and turn him out a tip-top Baby challenging the world, he was unexpectedly extinguished in a flannel cap, and hustled off to bed; where he simmered (so to speak) between two blankets for the best part of an hour. From this state of in-action he was then recalled, shining very much and roaring violently, to partake of—well? I would rather say, if you'll permit me to speak generally—of a slight repast. After which, he went to sleep again. Mrs. Peerybingle took advantage of this interval, to make herself as smart in a small way as ever you saw anybody in all your life; and, during the same short truce, Miss Slowboy insinuated herself into a spencer of a fashion so surprising and ingenious, that it had no connection with herself, or anything else in the universe, but was a shrunken, dog's-eared, independent fact, pursuing its lonely course without the least regard to any-body. By this time, the Baby, being all alive again, was invested, by the united efforts of Mrs. Peerybingle and Miss Slowboy, with a cream-coloured mantle for its body, and a sort of nankeen raised-pie for its head; and so in course of time they all three got down to the door, where the old horse had already taken more than the full value of his day's toll out of the Turnpike Trust, by tearing up the road with his impatient autographs; and whence Boxer might be dimly seen in the remote perspective, standing looking back, and tempting him to come on without orders.

As to a chair, or anything of that kind for helping Mrs. Peerybingle into the cart, you know very little of John, if you think *that* was necessary. Before you could have seen him lift her from the ground, there she was in her place, fresh and rosy, saying, "John! How *can* you! Think of Tilly!"

If I might be allowed to mention a young lady's legs, on any terms, I would observe of Miss Slowboy's that there was a fatality about them which rendered them singularly liable to be grazed; and that she never effected the smallest ascent or descent, without recording the circumstance upon them with a notch, as Robinson Crusoe marked the days upon his wooden calendar. But as this might be considered ungenteel, I'll think of it.

"John? You've got the basket with the Veal and Ham-

Pie and things, and the bottles of Beer?" said Dot. "If you haven't, you must turn round again, this very minute."

"You're a nice little article," returned the Carrier, "to be talking about turning round, after keeping me a full quarter of an hour behind my time."

"I am sorry for it, John," said Dot in a great bustle, "but I really could not think of going to Bertha's—I would not do it, John, on any account—without the Veal and Ham-Pie and things, and the bottles of Beer. Way!"

This monosyllable was addressed to the horse, who didn't mind it at all.

"Oh *do* way, John!" said Mrs. Peerybingle. "Please!"

"It'll be time enough to do that," returned John, "when I begin to leave things behind me. The basket's here, safe enough."

"What a hard-hearted monster you must be, John, not to have said so, at once, and save me such a turn! I declared I wouldn't go to Bertha's without the Veal and Ham-Pie and things, and the bottles of Beer, for any money. Regularly once a fortnight ever since we have been married, John, have we made our little Pic-Nic there. If anything was to go wrong with it, I should almost think we were never to be lucky again."

"It was a kind thought in the first instance," said the Carrier: "and I honour you for it, little woman."

"My dear John," replied Dot, turning very red, "Don't talk about honouring *me*. Good Gracious!"

"By the bye—" observed the Carrier. "That old gentle-man,"—

Again so visibly, and instantly embarrassed!

"He's an odd fish," said the Carrier, looking straight along the road before them. "I can't make him out. I don't believe there's any harm in him."

"None at all. I'm—I'm sure there's none at all."

"Yes," said the Carrier, with his eyes attracted to her face by the great earnestness of her manner. "I am glad you feel so certain of it, because it's a confirmation to me. It's curious that he should have taken it into his head to ask leave to go on lodging with us; an't it? Things come about so strangely."

"So very strangely," she rejoined in a low voice, scarcely audible.

"However, he's a good-natured old gentleman," said John, "and pays as a gentleman, and I think his word is to be relied upon, like a gentleman's. I had quite a long talk with him this morning: he can hear me better already, he says, as he gets more used to my voice. He told me a great deal about himself, and I told him a good deal about myself, and a rare lot of questions he asked me. I gave him information about my having two beats, you know, in my business; one day to the right from our house and back again; another day to the left from our house and back again (for he's a stranger and don't know the names of places about here); and he seemed quite pleased. 'Why, then I shall be returning home tonight your way,' he says, 'when I thought you'd be coming in an exactly opposite direction. That's capital! I may trouble you for another lift perhaps, but I'll engage not to fall so sound asleep again.' He *was* sound asleep, sure-ly!—Dot! what are you thinking of?"

"Thinking of, John? I—I was listening to you."

"O! That's all right!" said the honest Carrier. "I was afraid, from the look of your face, that I had gone rambling on so long, as to set you thinking about something else. I was very near it. I'll be bound."

Dot making no reply, they jogged on, for some little time, in silence. But, it was not easy to remain silent very long in John Peerybingle's cart, for, everybody on the road had something to say. Though it might only be "How are you!" and indeed it was very often nothing else, still, to give that back again in the right spirit of cordiality, required, not merely a nod and a smile, but as wholesome an action of the lungs withal, as a long-winded Parliamentary speech. Sometimes, passengers on foot, or horseback, plodded on a little way beside the cart, for the express purpose of having a chat; and then there was a great deal to be said, on both sides.

Then, Boxer gave occasion to more good-natured recognitions of, and by, the Carrier, than half a dozen Christians could have done! Everybody knew him, all along the road especially the fowls and pigs, who when they saw him approaching, with his body all on one side, and his ears pricked up inquisitively, and that knob of a tail making the most of itself in the air, immediately withdrew into remote back settlements, without waiting for the honour of a nearer acquaintance. He had business everywhere; going down all the turnings, looking into all the wells, bolting in and out of all the cottages, dashing into the midst of all the Dame-Schools, fluttering all the pigeons, magnifying the tails of all the cats, and trotting into the public-houses like a regular customer. Wherever he went, somebody or other might have been heard to cry, "Halloa! Here 's Boxer!" and out came that somebody forthwith, accompanied by at least two or three other somebodies, to give John Peerybingle and his pretty wife, Good-Day.

The packages and parcels for the errand cart, were numerous; and there were many stoppages to take them in and give them out, which were not by any means the worst parts of the journey. Some people were so full of expectation about their parcels, and other people were so full of wonder about their parcels, and other people were so full of inexhaustible directions about their parcels, and John had such a lively interest in all the parcels, that it was as good as a play. Likewise, there were articles to carry, which required to be considered and discussed, and in reference to the adjustment and disposition of which, councils had to be holden by the Carrier and the senders: at which Boxer usually assisted, in short fits of the closest attention, and long fits of tearing round and round the assembled sages and barking himself hoarse. Of all these little incidents, Dot was the amused and open-eyed spectatress from her chair in the cart; and as she sat there, looking on—a charming little portrait framed to admiration by the tilt—there was no lack of nudgings and glancings and whisperings and envyings among the younger men. And this delighted John the Carrier, beyond measure;

for he was proud to have his little wife admired, knowing that she didn't mind it—that, if anything, she rather liked it perhaps.

The trip was a little foggy, to be sure, in the January weather; and was raw and cold. But who cared for such trifles? Not Dot, decidedly. Not Tilly Slowboy, for she deemed sitting in a cart, on any terms, to be the highest point of human joys; the crowning circumstance of earthly hopes. Not the Baby, I'll be sworn; for it's not in Baby nature to be warmer or more sound asleep, though its capacity is great in both respects, than that blessed young Peerybingle was, all the way.

You couldn't see very far in the fog, of course: but you could see a great deal! It's astonishing how much you may see, in a thicker fog than that, if you will only take the trouble to look for it. Why, even to sit watching for the Fairy-rings in the fields, and for the patches of hoar-frost still lingering in the shade, near hedges and by trees, was a pleasant occupation: to make no mention of the unexpected shapes in which the trees themselves came starting out of the mist, and glided into it again. The hedges were tangled and bare, and waved a multitude of blighted garlands in the wind; but, there was no discouragement in this. It was agreeable to contemplate; for, it made the fireside warmer in possession, and the summer greener in expectancy. The river looked chilly; but it was in motion, and moving at a good pace—which was a great point. The canal was rather slow and torpid; that must be admitted. Never mind. It would freeze the sooner when the frost set fairly in, and then there would be skating, and sliding; and the heavy old barges, frozen up somewhere near a wharf, would smoke their rusty iron chimney pipes all day, and have a lazy time of it.

In one place, there was a great mound of weeds or stubble burning; and they watched the fire, so white in the day time, flaring through the fog, with only here and there a dash of red in it, until, in consequence as she observed of the smoke "getting up her nose," Miss Slowboy choked—

she could do anything of that sort, on the smallest provocation—and woke the Baby, who wouldn't go to sleep again. But, Boxer, who was in advance some quarter of a mile or so, had already passed the outposts of the town, and gained the corner of the street where Caleb and his daughter lived; and long before they had reached the door, he and the Blind Girl were on the pavement waiting to receive them.

Boxer, by the way, made certain delicate distinctions of his own, in his communication with Bertha, which persuade me fully that he knew her to be blind. He never sought to attract her attention by looking at her, as he often did with other people, but touched her invariably. What experience he could ever have had of blind people or blind dogs, I don't know. He had never lived with a blind master; nor had Mr. Boxer the elder, nor Mrs. Boxer, nor any of his respectable family on either side, ever been visited with blindness, that I am aware of. He may have found it out for himself, perhaps, but he had got hold of it somehow; and therefore he had hold of Bertha too, by the skirt, and kept hold, until Mrs. Peerybingle and the Baby, and Miss Slowboy, and the basket, were all got safely within doors.

May Fielding was already come; and so was her mother—a little querulous chip of an old lady with a peevish face, who, in right of having preserved a waist like a bedpost, was supposed to be a most transcendent figure; and who, in consequence of having once been better off, or of labouring under an impression that she might have been, if something had happened which never did happen, and seemed to have never been particularly likely to come to pass—but it's all the same—was very genteel and patronising indeed. Gruff and Tackleton was also there, doing the agreeable, with the evident sensation of being as perfectly at home, and as unquestionably in his own element, as a fresh young salmon on the top of the Great Pyramid.

"May! My dear old friend!" cried Dot, running up to meet her. "What a happiness to see you."

Her old friend was, to the full, as hearty and as glad as she; and it really was, if you'll believe me, quite a pleasant

sight to see them embrace. Tackleton was a man of taste,
beyond all question. May was very pretty.

You know sometimes, when you are used to a pretty face,
how, when it comes into contact and comparison with another pretty face, it seems for the moment to be homely and
faded, and hardly to deserve the high opinion you have had
of it. Now, this was not at all the case, either with Dot or
May; for May's face set off Dot's, and Dot's face set off
May's, so naturally and agreeably, that, as John Peerybingle was very near saying when he came into the room,
they ought to have been born sisters—which was the only
improvement you could have suggested.

Tackleton had brought his leg of mutton, and, wonderful
to relate, a tart besides—but we don't mind a little dissipa-
tion when our brides are in the case; we don't get married
every day—and in addition to these dainties, there were the
Veal and Ham-Pie, and "things," as Mrs. Peerybingle
called them; which were chiefly nuts and oranges, and cakes,
and such small deer. When the repast was set forth on the
board, flanked by Caleb's contribution, which was a great
wooden bowl of smoking potatoes (he was prohibited, by
solemn compact, from producing any other viands), Tackleton led his intended mother-in-law to the post of honour. For
the better gracing of this place at the high festival, the
majestic old soul had adorned herself with a cap, calculated
to inspire the thoughtless with sentiments of awe. She also
wore her gloves. But let us be genteel, or die!

Caleb sat next his daughter; Dot and her old schoolfellow
were side by side; the good Carrier took care of the bottom
of the table. Miss Slowboy was isolated, for the time being,
from every article of furniture but the chair she sat on, that
she might have nothing else to knock the Baby's head
against.

As Tilly stared about her at the dolls and toys, they stared
at her and at the company. The venerable old gentlemen at
the street-doors (who were all in full action) showed especial
interest in the party, pausing occasionally before leaping,
as if they were listening to the conversation, and then plung-

ing wildly over and over, a great many times, without halting for breath—as in a frantic state of delight with the whole
proceedings.

Certainly, if these old gentlemen were inclined to have a
fiendish joy in the contemplation of Tackleton's discomfiture, they had good reason to be satisfied. Tackleton
couldn't get on at all; and the more cheerful his intended
bride became in Dot's society, the less he liked it, though he
had brought them together for that purpose. For he was a
regular dog in the manger, was Tackleton; and when they
laughed and he couldn't, he took it into his head, immediately, that they must be laughing at him.

"Ah May!" said Dot. "Dear, dear, what changes! To
talk of those merry school-days makes one young again."

"Why, you an't particularly old, at any time; are you?"
said Tackleton.

"Look at my sober plodding husband there," returned
Dot. "He adds twenty years to my age at least. Don't you,
John?"

"Forty," John replied.

"How many *you*'ll add to May's, I'm sure I don't know,"
said Dot, laughing. "But she can't be much less than a
hundred years of age on her next birthday."

"Ha ha!" laughed Tackleton. Hollow as a drum, that
laugh though. And he looked as if he could have twisted
Dot's neck, comfortably.

"Dear dear!" said Dot. "Only to remember how we used
to talk, at school, about the husbands we would choose. I
don't know how young, and how handsome, and how gay,
and how lively, mine was not to be! And as to May's—Ah
dear! I don't know whether to laugh or cry, when I think
what silly girls we were."

May seemed to know which to do; for the colour flushed
into her face, and tears stood in her eyes.

"Even the very persons themselves—real live young men
—were fixed on sometimes," said Dot. "We little thought
how things would come about. I never fixed on John I'm
sure: I never so much as thought of him. And if I had told

you, you were ever to be married to Mr. Tackleton, why you'd have slapped me. Wouldn't you, May?"

Though May didn't say yes, she certainly didn't say no, or express no, by any means.

Tackleton laughed—quite shouted, he laughed so loud. John Peerybingle laughed too, in his ordinary good-natured and contented manner; but his was a mere whisper of a laugh, to Tackleton's.

"You couldn't help yourselves, for all that. You couldn't resist us, you see," said Tackleton. "Here we are! Here we are! Where are your gay young bridegrooms now!"

"Some of them are dead," said Dot; "and some of them forgotten. Some of them, if they could stand among us at this moment, would not believe we were the same creatures; would not believe that what they saw and heard was real, and we *could* forget them so. No! they would not believe one word of it!"

"Why, Dot!" exclaimed the Carrier. "Little woman!"

She had spoken with such earnestness and fire, that she stood in need of some recalling to herself, without doubt. Her husband's check was very gentle, for he merely interfered, as he supposed, to shield old Tackleton; but it proved effectual, for she stopped, and said no more. There was an uncommon agitation, even in her silence, which the wary Tackleton, who had brought his half-shut eye to bear upon her, noted closely, and remembered to some purpose too.

May uttered no word, good or bad, but sat quite still, with her eyes cast down, and made no sign of interest in what had passed. The good lady her mother now interposed, observing, in the first instance, that girls were girls, and byegones byegones, and that so long as young people were young and thoughtless, they would probably conduct themselves like young and thoughtless persons: with two or three other positions of a no less sound and incontrovertible character. She then remarked, in a devout spirit, that she thanked Heaven she had always found in her daughter May, a dutiful and obedient child; for which she took no credit to herself, though she had every reason to believe it was entirely owing

to herself. With regard to Mr. Tackleton she said, That he
was in a moral point of view an undeniable individual, and
That he was in an eligible point of view a son-in-law to be
desired, no one in their senses could doubt. (She was very
emphatic here.) With regard to the family into which he was
so soon about, after some solicitation, to be admitted, she
believed Mr. Tackleton knew that, although reduced in
purse, it had some pretensions to gentility; and if certain
circumstances, not wholly unconnected, she would go so far
as to say, with the Indigo Trade, but to which she would not
more particularly refer, had happened differently, it might
perhaps have been in possession of wealth. She then remarked that she would not allude to the past, and would not
mention that her daughter had for some time rejected the
suit of Mr. Tackleton; and that she would not say a great
many other things which she did say, at great length. Finally, she delivered it as the general result of her observation
and experience, that those marriages in which there was
least of what was romantically and sillily called love, were
always the happiest; and that she anticipated the greatest
possible amount of bliss—not rapturous bliss; but the solid,
steady-going article—from the approaching nuptials. She
concluded by informing the company that to-morrow was
the day she had lived for, expressly; and that when it was
over, she would desire nothing better than to be packed up
and disposed of, in any genteel place of burial.

As these remarks were quite unanswerable—which is the
happy property of all remarks that are sufficiently wide of
the purpose—they changed the current of the conversation,
and diverted the general attention to the Veal and Ham-Pie,
the cold mutton, the potatoes, and the tart. In order that the
bottled beer might not be slighted, John Peerybingle proposed To-morrow: the Wedding-Day; and called upon them
to drink a bumper to it, before he proceeded on his journey.

For you ought to know that he only rested there, and gave
the old horse a bait. He had to go some four or five miles
farther on; and when he returned in the evening, he called
for Dot, and took another rest on his way home. This was

the order of the day on all the Pic-Nic occasions, and had been, ever since their institution.

There were two persons present, beside the bride and bridegroom elect, who did but indifferent honour to the toast. One of these was Dot, too flushed and discomposed to adapt herself to any small occurrence of the moment; the other, Bertha, who rose up hurriedly, before the rest, and left the table.

"Good-bye!" said stout John Peerybingle, pulling on his dreadnought coat. "I shall be back at the old time. Good-bye all!"

"Good-bye, John," returned Caleb.

He seemed to say it by rote, and to wave his hand in the same unconscious manner; for he stood observing Bertha with an anxious wondering face, that never altered its expression.

"Good-bye, young shaver!" said the jolly Carrier, bending down to kiss the child; which Tilly Slowboy, now intent upon her knife and fork, had deposited asleep (and strange to say, without damage) in a little cot of Bertha's furnishing; "good-bye! Time will come, I suppose, when *you*'ll turn out into the cold, my little friend, and leave your old father to enjoy his pipe and his rheumatics in the chimney-corner; eh? Where's Dot?"

"I'm here, John!" she said, starting.

"Come, come!" returned the Carrier, clapping his sounding hands. "Where's the pipe?"

"I quite forgot the pipe, John."

Forgot the pipe! Was such a wonder ever head of! She! Forgot the pipe!

"I'll—I'll fill it directly. It's soon done."

But it was not so soon done, either. It lay in the usual place—the Carrier's dreadnought pocket—with the little pouch, her own work, from which she was used to fill it; but her hand shook so, that she entangled it (and yet her hand was small enough to have come out easily, I am sure), and bungled terribly. The filling of the pipe and lighting it, those little offices in which I have commended her discre-

tion, were vilely done, from first to last. During the whole
process, Tackleton stood looking on maliciously with the
half-closed eye; which, whenever it met hers—or caught it,
for it can hardly be said to have ever met another eye:
rather being a kind of trap to snatch it up—augmented her
confusion in a most remarkable degree.

"Why, what a clumsy Dot you are, this afternoon!" said
John. "I could have done it better myself, I verily believe!"

With these good-natured words, he strode away, and
presently was heard, in company with Boxer, and the old
horse, and the cart, making lively music down the road.
What time the dreamy Caleb still stood, watching his blind
daughter, with the same expression on his face.

"Bertha!" said Caleb, softly. "What has happened? How
changed you are, my darling, n a few hours—since this
morning. *You* silent and and dull all day! What is it?
Tell me!"

"Oh father, father!" cried the Blind Girl, bursting into
tears. "Oh my hard, hard fate!"

Caleb drew his hand across his eyes before he answered
her.

"But think how cheerful and how happy you have been,
Bertha! How good, and how much loved, by many people."

"That strikes me to my heart, dear father! Always so
mindful of me! Always so kind to me!"

Caleb was very much perplexed to understand her.

"To be—to be blind, Bertha, my poor dear," he faltered,
"is a great affliction; but—"

"I have never felt it!" cried the Blind Girl. "I have never
felt it, in its fulness. Never! I have sometimes wished that
I could see you, or could see him—only once, dear father,
only for one little minute—that I might know what it is I
treasure up," she laid her hands upon her breast, "and hold
here! That I might be sure and have it right! And sometimes (but then I was a child) I have wept in my prayers
at night, to think that when your images ascended from my
heart to Heaven, they might not be the true resemblance

of yourselves. But I have never had these feelings long.
They have passed away and left me tranquil and contented."

"And they will again," said Caleb.

"But father! Oh my good, gentle father, bear with me,
if I am wicked!" said the Blind Girl. "This is not the sorrow
that so weighs me down!"

Her father could not choose but let his moist eyes over-
flow; she was so earnest and pathetic, but he did not understand her, yet.

"Bring her to me," said Bertha. "I cannot hold it closed
and shut within myself. Bring her to me, father!"

She knew he hesitated, and said, "May. Bring May!"

May heard the mention of her name, and coming quietly
towards her, touched her on the arm. The Blind Girl turned
immediately, and held her by both hands.

"Look into my face, Dear heart, Sweet heart!" said Bertha. "Read it with your beautiful eyes, and tell me if the
truth is written on it."

"Dear Bertha, Yes!"

The Blind Girl still, upturning the blank sightless face,
down which the tears were coursing fast, addressed her in
these words:

"There is not, in my soul, a wish or thought that is not
for your good, bright May! There is not, in my soul, a
grateful recollection stronger than the deep remembrance
which is stored there, of the many many times when, in the
full pride of sight and beauty, you have had consideration
for Blind Bertha, even when we two were children, or when
Bertha was as much a child as ever blindness can be! Every
blessing on your head! Light upon your happy course!
Not the less, my dear May"; and she drew towards her, in
a closer grasp; "not the less, my bird, because, to-day, the
knowledge that you are to be His wife has wrung my heart
almost to breaking! Father, May, Mary! oh forgive me
that it is so, for the sake of all he has done to relieve the
weariness of my dark life: and for the sake of the belief

you have in me, when I call Heaven to witness that I could not wish him married to a wife more worthy of his goodness!"

While speaking, she had released May Fielding's hands, and clasped her garments in an attitude of mingled supplication and love. Sinking lower and lower down, as she proceeded in her strange confession, she dropped at last at the feet of her friend, and hid her blind face in the folds of her dress.

"Great Power!" exclaimed her father, smitten at one blow with the truth, "have I deceived her from her cradle, but to break her heart at last!"

It was well for all of them that Dot, that beaming, useful, busy little Dot—for such she was, whatever faults she had, and however you may learn to hate her, in good time —it was well for all of them, I say, that she was there: or where this would have ended, it were hard to tell. But Dot, recovering her self-possession, interposed, before May could reply, or Caleb say another word.

"Come come, dear Bertha! come away with me! Give her your arm, May. So! How composed she is, you see, already; and how good it is of her to mind us," said the cheery little woman, kissing her upon the forehead. "Come away, dear Bertha. Come! and here's her good father will come with her; won't you, Caleb? To—be—sure!"

Well, well! she was a noble little Dot in such things, and it must have been an obdurate nature that could have withstood her influence. When she had got poor Caleb and his Bertha away, that they might comfort and console each other, as she knew they only could, she presently came bouncing back,—the saying is, as fresh as any daisy; I say fresher—to mount guard over that bridling little piece of consequence in the cap and gloves, and prevent the dear old creature from making discoveries.

"So bring me the precious Baby, Tilly," said she, drawing a chair to the fire; "and while I have it in my lap, here's Mrs. Fielding, Tilly, will tell me all about the management of Babies, and put me right in twenty points where I 'm as wrong as can be. Won't you, Mrs. Fielding?"

Not even the Welsh Giant, who according to the popular expression, was so "slow" as to perform a fatal surgical operation upon himself, in emulation of a juggling-trick achieved by his arch-enemy at breakfast-time; not even he fell half so readily into the snare prepared for him, as the old lady did into this artful pitfall. The fact of Tackleton having walked out; and furthermore, of two or three people having been talking together at a distance, for two minutes, leaving her to her own resources; was quite enough to have put her on her dignity, and the bewailment of that mysterious convulsion in the Indigo trade, for four-and-twenty hours. But this becoming deference to her experience, on the part of the young mother, was so irresistible, that after a short affectation of humility, she began to enlighten her with the best grace in the world; and sitting bolt upright before the wicked Dot, she did, in half an hour, deliver more infallible domestic recipes and precepts, than would (if acted on) have utterly destroyed and done up that Young Peerybingle, though he had been an Infant Samson.

To change the theme, Dot did a little needlework—she carried the contents of a whole workbox in her pocket; however she contrived it, I don't know—then did a little nursing; then a little more needlework; then had a little whispering chat with May, while the old lady dozed; and so in little bits of bustle, which was quite her manner always, found it a very short afternoon. Then, as it grew dark, and as it was a solemn part of this Institution of the Pic-Nic that she should perform all Bertha's household tasks, she trimmed the fire, and swept the hearth, and set the tea-board out, and drew the curtain, and lighted a candle. Then she played an air or two on a rude kind of harp, which Caleb had contrived for Bertha, and played them very well; for Nature had made her delicate little ear as choice a one for music as it would have been for jewels, if she had had any to wear. By this time it was the established hour for having tea; and Tackleton came back again, to share the meal, and spend the evening.

Caleb and Bertha had returned some time before, and Caleb had sat down to his afternoon's work. But he couldn't settle to it, poor fellow, being anxious and remorseful for his daughter. It was touching to see him sitting idle on his working-stool, regarding her so wistfully, and always saying in his face, "Have I deceived her from her cradle, but to break her heart!"

When it was night, and tea was done, and Dot had nothing more to do in washing up the cups and saucers; in a word—for I must come to it, and there is no use in putting it off—when the time drew nigh for expecting the Carrier's return in every sound of distant wheels, her manner changed again, her colour came and went, and she was very restless. Not as good wives are, when listening for their husbands. No, no, no. It was another sort of restlessness from that.

Wheels heard. A horse's feet. The barking of a dog. The gradual approach of all the sounds. The scratching paw of Boxer at the door!

"Whose step is that!" cried Bertha, starting up.

"Whose step?" returned the Carrier, standing in the portal, with his brown face ruddy as a winter berry from the keen night air. "Why, mine."

"The other step," said Bertha. "The man's tread behind you!"

"She is not to be deceived," observed the Carrier, laughing. "Come along, sir. You'll be welcome, never fear!"

He spoke in a loud tone; and as he spoke, the deaf old gentleman entered.

"He's not so much a stranger, that you haven't seen him once, Caleb," said the Carrier. "You give him house-room till we go?"

"Oh surely, John, and take it as an honour."

"He's the best company on earth, to talk secrets in," said John. "I have reasonable good lungs, but he tries 'em, I can tell you. Sit down, sir. All friends here, and glad to see you!"

When he had imparted this assurance, in a voice that amply corroborated what he had said about his lungs, he added in his natural tone, "A chair in the chimney-corner, and leave to sit quite silent and look pleasantly about him, is all he cares for. He's easily pleased."

Bertha had been listening intently. She called Caleb to her side, when he had set the chair, and asked him, in a low voice, to describe their visitor. When he had done so (truly now: with scrupulous fidelity), she moved, for the first time since he had come in, and sighed, and seemed to have no further interest concerning him.

The Carrier was in high spirits, good fellow that he was, and fonder of his little wife than ever.

"A clumsy Dot she was, this afternoon!" he said, encircling her with his rough arm, as she stood, removed from the rest; "and yet I like her somehow. See yonder, Dot!"

He pointed to the old man. She looked down. I think she trembled.

"He's—ha ha ha!—he's full of admiration for you!" said the Carrier. "Talked of nothing else, the whole way here. Why, he's a brave old boy. I like him for it!"

"I wish he had had a better subject, John"; she said, with an uneasy glance about the room. At Tackleton especially.

"A better subject!" cried the jovial John. "There's no such thing. Come, off with the great-coat, off with the thick shawl, off with the heavy wrappers! and a cosy half-hour by the fire! My humble service, Mistress. A game of cribbage, you and I? That's hearty. The cards and board, Dot. And a glass of beer here, if there's any left, small wife!"

His challenge was addressed to the old lady, who accepting it with gracious readiness, they were soon engaged upon the game. At first, the Carrier looked about him sometimes, with a smile, or now and then called Dot to peep over his shoulder at his hand, and advise him on some knotty point. But his adversary being a rigid disciplinarian, and subject to an occasional weakness in respect of pegging more than she was entitled to, required such vigilance on his part, as left him neither eyes nor ears to spare. Thus, his whole attention gradually became absorbed upon the cards; and he thought of nothing else, until a hand upon his shoulder restored him to a consciousness of Tackleton.

"I am sorry to disturb you—but a word, directly."

"I'm going to deal," returned the Carrier. "It's a crisis."

"It is," said Tackleton. "Come here, man!"

There was that in his pale face which made the other rise immediately, and ask him, in a hurry, what the matter was.

"Hush! John Peerybingle," said Tackleton. "I am sorry for this. I am indeed. I have been afraid of it. I have suspected it from the first."

"What is it?" asked the Carrier, with a frightened aspect.

"Hush! I'll show you, if you'll come with me."

The Carrier accompanied him, without another word. They went across a yard, where the stars were shining, and by a little side-door, into Tackleton's own counting-house, where there was a glass window, commanding the ware-room, which was closed for the night. There was no light in the counting-house itself, but there were lamps in the long narrow ware-room; and consequently the window was bright.

"A moment!" said Tackleton. "Can you bear to look through that window, do you think?"

"Why not?" returned the Carrier.

"A moment more," said Tackleton. "Don't commit any violence. It's of no use. It's dangerous too. You're a strong-made man; and you might do murder before you know it."

The Carrier looked him in the face, and recoiled a step as if he had been struck. In one stride he was at the window, and he saw—

Oh Shadow on the Hearth! Oh truthful Cricket! Oh perfidious Wife!

He saw her, with the old man—old no longer, but erect and gallant—bearing in his hand the false white hair that had won his way into their desolate and miserable home. He saw her listening to him, as he bent his head to whisper in her ear; and suffering him to clasp her round the waist, as they moved slowly down the dim wooden gallery towards the door by which they had entered it. He saw them stop, and saw her turn—to have the face, the face he loved so, so presented to his view!—and saw her, with her own hands, adjust the lie upon his head, laughing, as she did it, at his unsuspicious nature!

He clenched his strong right hand at first, as if it would have beaten down a lion. But opening it immediately again, he spread it out before the eyes of Tackleton (for he was tender of her, even then), and so, as they passed out, fell down upon a desk, and was as weak as any infant.

He was wrapped up to the chin, and busy with his horse and parcels, when she came into the room, prepared for going home.

"Now John, dear! Good night May! Good night Bertha!"

Could she kiss them? Could she be blithe and cheerful in her parting? Could she venture to reveal her face to them without a blush? Yes. Tackleton observed her closely, and she did all this.

Tilly was hushing the Baby, and she crossed and re-crossed Tackleton, a dozen times, repeating drowsily:

"Did the knowledge that it was to be its wifes, then, wring its hearts almost to breaking; and did its fathers deceive it from its cradles but to break its hearts at last!"

"Now Tilly, give me the Baby! Good-night, Mr. Tackleton. Where's John, for goodness' sake?"

"He's going to walk, beside the horse's head," said Tackleton; who helped her to her seat.

"My dear John. Walk? To-night?"

The muffled figure of her husband made a hasty sign in the affirmative; and the false stranger and the little nurse being in their places, the old horse moved off. Boxer, the unconscious Boxer, running on before, running back, running round and round the cart, and barking as triumphantly and merrily as ever.

When Tackleton had gone off likewise, escorting May and her mother home, poor Caleb sat down by the fire beside his daughter; anxious and remorseful at the core; and still saying in his wistful contemplation of her, "Have I deceived her from her cradle, but to break her heart at last!"

The toys that had been set in motion for the Baby, had all stopped, and run down, long ago. In the faint light and silence, the imperturbably calm dolls, the agitated rocking-horses with distended eyes and nostrils, the old gentlemen at the street-doors, standing half doubled up upon their failing knees and ankles, the wry-faced nut-crackers, the very Beasts upon their way into the Ark, in twos, like a Boarding School out walking, might have been imagined to be stricken motionless with fantastic wonder, at Dot being false, or Tackleton beloved, under any combination of circumstances.

Chirp the Third

THE Dutch clock in the corner struck Ten, when the Carrier sat down by his fireside. So troubled and grief-worn, that he seemed to scare the Cuckoo, who, having cut his ten melodious announcements as short as possible, plunged back into the Moorish Palace again, and clapped his little door behind him, as if the unwonted spectacle were too much for his feelings.

If the little Haymaker had been armed with the sharpest of scythes, and had cut at every stroke into the Carrier's heart, he never could have gashed and wounded it, as Dot had done.

It was a heart so full of love for her; so bound up and held together by innumerable threads of winning remembrance, spun from the daily working of her many qualities of endearment; it was a heart in which she had enshrined herself so gently and so closely; a heart so single and so earnest in its Truth, so strong in right, so weak in wrong; that it could cherish neither passion nor revenge at first, and had only room to hold the broken image of its Idol.

But, slowly, slowly, as the Carrier sat brooding on his hearth, now cold and dark, other and fiercer thoughts began to rise within him, as an angry wind comes rising in the night. The Stranger was beneath his outraged roof. Three steps would take him to his chamber-door. One blow would beat it in. "You might do murder before you know it," Tackleton had said. How could it be murder, if he gave the villain time to grapple with him hand to hand! He was the younger man.

It was an ill-timed thought, bad for the dark mood of his mind. It was an angry thought, goading him to some avenging act, that should change the cheerful house into a haunted place which lonely travellers would dread to pass by night; and where the timid would see shadows struggling in the ruined windows when the moon was dim, and hear wild noises in the stormy weather.

He was the younger man! Yes, yes; some lover who had won the heart that *he* had never touched. Some lover of her early choice, of whom she had thought and dreamed, for whom she had pined and pined, when he had fancied her so happy by his side. O agony to think of it!

She had been above-stairs with the Baby, getting it to bed. As he sat brooding on the hearth, she came close beside him, without his knowledge—in the turning of the rack of his great misery, he lost all other sounds—and put her little stool at his feet. He only knew it, when he felt her hand upon his own, and saw her looking up into his face.

With wonder? No. It was his first impression, and he was fain to look at her again, to set it right. No, not with wonder. With an eager and inquiring look; but not with wonder. At first it was alarmed and serious; then, it changed into a strange, wild, dreadful smile of recognition of his thoughts; then, there was nothing but her clasped hands on her brow, and her bent head, and falling hair.

Though the power of Omnipotence had been his to wield at that moment, he had too much of its diviner property of Mercy in his breast, to have turned one feather's weight of it against her. But he could not bear to see her crouching down upon the little seat where he had often looked on her, with love and pride, so innocent and gay; and, when she rose and left him, sobbing as she went, he felt it a relief to have the vacant place beside him rather than her so long cherished presence. This in itself was anguish keener than all, reminding him how desolate he was become, and how the great bond of his life was rent asunder.

The more he felt this, and the more he knew he could have better borne to see her lying prematurely dead before him with their little child upon her breast, the higher and the stronger rose his wrath against his enemy. He looked about him for a weapon.

There was a gun, hanging on the wall. He took it down, and moved a pace or two towards the door of the perfidious Stranger's room. He knew the gun was loaded. Some shadowy idea that it was just to shoot this man like a wild beast, seized him, and dilated in his mind until it grew into a monstrous demon in complete possession of him, casting out all milder thoughts and setting up its undivided empire.

That phrase is wrong. Not casting out his milder thoughts, but artfully transforming them. Changing them into scourges to drive him on. Turning water into blood, love into hate, gentleness into blind ferocity. Her image, sorrowing, humbled, but still pleading to his tenderness and mercy with resistless power, never left his mind; but, staying there, it urged him to the door; raised the weapon to his shoulder; fitted and nerved his finger to the trigger; and cried "Kill him! In his bed!"

He reversed the gun to beat the stock upon the door; he already held it lifted in the air; some indistinct design was in his thoughts of calling out to him to fly, for God's sake, by the window—

When, suddenly, the struggling fire illumined the whole chimney with a glow of light; and the Cricket on the Hearth began to Chirp!

No sound he could have heard, no human voice, not even hers, could so have moved and softened him. The artless words in which she had told him of her love for this same

Cricket, were once more freshly spoken; her trembling, earnest manner at the moment, was again before him; her pleasant voice—O what a voice it was, for making household music at the fireside of an honest man!—thrilled through and through his better nature, and awoke it into life and action.

He recoiled from the door, like a man walking in his sleep, awakened from a frightful dream; and put the gun aside. Clasping his hands before his face, he then sat down again beside the fire, and found relief in tears.

The Cricket on the Hearth came out into the room, and stood in Fairy shape before him.

"'I love it,'" said the Fairy Voice, repeating what he well remembered, "'for the many times I have heard it, and the many thoughts its harmless music has given me.'"

"She said so!" cried the Carrier. "True!"

"'This has been a happy home, John; and I love the Cricket for its sake!'"

"It has been, Heaven knows," returned the Carrier. "She made it happy, always,—until now."

"So gracefully sweet-tempered; so domestic, joyful, busy, and light-hearted!" said the Voice.

"Otherwise I never could have loved her as I did," returned the Carrier.

The Voice, correcting him, said "do."

The Carrier repeated "as I did." But not firmly. His faltering tongue resisted his control, and would speak in its own way, for itself and him.

The Figure, in an attitude of invocation, raised its hand and said:

"Upon your own hearth—"

"The hearth she has blighted," interposed the Carrier.

"The hearth she has—how often!—blessed and brightened," said the Cricket; "the hearth which, but for her, were only a few stones and bricks and rusty bars, but which has been through her, the Altar of your Home; on which you have nightly sacrificed some petty passion, selfishness, or care, and offered up the homage of a tranquil mind, a trusting nature, and an overflowing heart; so that the smoke from this poor chimney has gone upward with a better fragrance than the richest incense that is burnt before the richest shrines in all the gaudy temples of this world!— Upon your own hearth; in its quiet sanctuary; surrounded by its gentle influences and associations; hear her. Hear me! Hear everything that speaks the language of your hearth and home!"

"And pleads for her?" inquired the Carrier.

"All things that speak the language of your hearth and home, *must* plead for her!" returned the Cricket. "For they speak the truth."

And while the Carrier, with his head upon his hands, continued to sit meditating in his chair, the Presence stood beside him, suggesting his reflections by its power, and presenting them before him, as in a glass or picture. It was not a solitary Presence. From the hearthstone, from the chimney, from the clock, the pipe, the kettle, and the cradle; from the floor, the walls, the ceiling, and the stairs; from the cart without, and the cupboard within, and the household implements; from every thing and every place with which she had ever been familiar, and with which she had ever entwined one recollection of herself in her unhappy husband's mind; Fairies came trooping forth. Not to stand beside him as the Cricket did, but to busy and bestir themselves. To do all honour to her image. To pull him by the skirts, and point to it when it appeared. To cluster round it, and embrace it, and strew flowers for it to tread on. To try to crown its fair head with their tiny hands. To show that they were fond of it and loved it; and that there was not one ugly, wicked, or accusatory creature to claim knowledge of it—none but their playful and approving selves.

His thoughts were constant to her image. It was always there.

She sat plying her needle, before the fire, and singing to herself. Such a blithe, thriving, steady little Dot! The fairy figures turned upon him all at once, by one consent, with one prodigious concentrated stare, and seemed to say "Is this the light wife you are mourning for!"

There were sounds of gaiety outside, musical instruments, and noisy tongues, and laughter. A crowd of young merry-makers came pouring in, among whom were May Fielding and a score of pretty girls. Dot was the fairest of them all; as young as any of them too. They came to summon her to join their party. It was a dance. If ever little foot were made for dancing, hers was, surely. But she laughed, and shook her head, and pointed to her cookery on the fire, and her table ready spread: with an exulting defiance that rendered her more charming than she was before. And so she merrily dismissed them, nodding to her would-be partners, one by one, as they passed, but with a comical indifference, enough to make them go and drown themselves immediately if they were her admirers—and they must have been so, more or less; they couldn't help it. And yet indifference was not her character. O no! For presently, there came a certain Carrier to the door; and bless her what a welcome she bestowed upon him!

Again the staring figures turned upon him all at once, and seemed to say "Is this the wife who has forsaken you!"

A shadow fell upon the mirror or the picture: call it what you will. A great shadow of the Stranger, as he first stood underneath their roof; covering its surface, and blotting out all other objects. But the nimble Fairies worked like bees to clear it off again. And Dot again was there. Still bright and beautiful.

Rocking her little Baby in its cradle, singing to it softly, and resting her head upon a shoulder which had its counterpart in the musing figure by which the Fairy Cricket stood.

The night—I mean the real night: not going by Fairy clocks—was wearing now; and in this stage of the Carrier's thoughts, the moon burst out, and shone brightly in the sky. Perhaps some calm and quiet light had risen also, in his mind; and he could think more soberly of what had happened.

Although the shadow of the Stranger fell at intervals upon the glass—always distinct, and big, and thoroughly defined—it never fell so darkly as at first. Whenever it appeared, the Fairies uttered a general cry of consternation, and plied their little arms and legs, with inconceivable activity, to rub it out. And whenever they got at Dot again, and showed her to him once more, bright and beautiful, they cheered in the most inspiring manner.

They never showed her, otherwise than beautiful and bright, for they were Household Spirits to whom falsehood is annihilation; and being so, what Dot was there for them, but the one active, beaming, pleasant little creature who had been the light and sun of the Carrier's Home!

The Fairies were prodigiously excited when they showed her, with the Baby, gossiping among a knot of sage old matrons, and affecting to be wondrous old and matronly herself, and leaning in a staid demure old way upon her husband's arm, attempting—she! such a bud of a little woman—to convey the idea of having abjured the vanities of the world in general, and of being the sort of person to whom it was no novelty at all to be a mother; yet in the same breath, they showed her, laughing at the Carrier for being awkward, and pulling up his shirt-collar to make him smart, and mincing merrily about that very room to teach him how to dance!

They turned, and stared immensely at him when they showed her with the Blind Girl; for, though she carried cheerfulness and animation with her wheresoever she went, she bore those influences into Caleb Plummer's home, heaped up and running over. The Blind Girl's love for her, and trust in her, and gratitude to her; her own good busy way of setting Bertha's thanks aside; her dexterous little arts for filling up each moment of the visit in doing something useful to the house, and really working hard while feigning to make holiday; her bountiful provision of those standing delicacies, the Veal and Ham-Pie and the bottles of Beer; her radiant little face arriving at the door, and taking leave; the wonderful expression in her whole self, from her neat foot to the crown of her head, of being a part of the establishment—a something necessary to it, which it couldn't be without; all this the Fairies revelled in, and loved her for. And once again they looked upon him all at once, appealingly, and seemed to say, while some among them nestled in her dress and fondled her, "Is this the wife who has betrayed your confidence!"

More than once, or twice, or thrice, in the long thoughtful night, they showed her to him sitting on her favourite seat, with her bent head, her hands clasped on her brow, her falling hair. As he had seen her last. And when they found her thus, they neither turned nor looked upon him, but gathered close round her, and comforted and kissed her, and pressed on one another to show sympathy and kindness to her, and forgot him altogether.

Thus the night passed. The moon went down; the stars grew pale; the cold day broke; the sun rose. The Carrier still sat, musing in the chimney corner. He had sat there, with his head upon his hands, all night. All night the faithful Cricket had been Chirp, Chirp, Chirping on the Hearth. All night he had listened to its voice. All night the household Fairies had been busy with him. All night she had been amiable and blameless in the glass, except when that one shadow fell upon it.

He rose up when it was broad day, and washed and dressed himself. He couldn't go about his customary cheerful avocations—he wanted spirit for them—but it mattered the less, that it was Tackleton's wedding-day, and he had arranged to make his rounds by proxy. He thought to have gone merrily to church with Dot. But such plans were at an end. It was their own wedding-day too. Ah! how little he had looked for such a close to such a year!

The Carrier had expected that Tackleton would pay him an early visit; and he was right. He had not walked to and fro before his own door, many minutes, when he saw the Toy-merchant coming in his chaise along the road. As the chaise drew nearer, he perceived that Tackleton was dressed out sprucely for his marriage, and that he had decorated his horse's head with flowers and favours.

The horse looked much more like a bridegroom than Tackleton, whose half-closed eye was more disagreeably expressive than ever. But the Carrier took little heed of this. His thoughts had other occupation.

"John Peerybingle!" said Tackleton, with an air of condolence. "My good fellow, how do you find yourself this morning?"

"I have had but a poor night, Master Tackleton," returned the Carrier shaking his head: "for I have been a good deal disturbed in my mind. But it's over now! Can you spare me half an hour or so, for some private talk?"

"I came on purpose," returned Tackleton, alighting. "Never mind the horse. He'll stand quiet enough, with the reins over this post, if you'll give him a mouthful of hay."

The Carrier having brought it from his stable, and set it before him, they turned into the house.

"You are not married before noon?" he said, "I think?"

"No," answered Tackleton. "Plenty of time. Plenty of time."

Then they entered the kitchen, Tilly Slowboy was rapping at the Stranger's door; which was only removed from it by a few steps. One of her very red eyes (for Tilly had been crying all night long, because her mistress cried) was at the keyhole; and she was knocking very loud; and seemed frightened.

"If you please I can't make nobody hear," said Tilly, looking round. "I hope nobody an't gone and been and died if you please!"

This philanthropic wish, Miss Slowboy emphasised with various new raps and kicks at the door; which led to no result whatever.

"Shall I go?" said Tackleton. "It's curious."

The Carrier, who had turned his face from the door, signed to him to go if he would.

So Tackleton went to Tilly Slowboy's relief; and he too kicked and knocked; and he too failed to get the least reply. But he thought of trying the handle of the door; and as it opened easily, he peeped in, looked in, went in, and soon came running out again.

"John Peerybingle," said Tackleton, in his ear. "I hope there has been nothing—nothing rash in the night?"

The Carrier turned upon him quickly.

"Because he's gone!" said Tackleton; "and the window's open. I don't see any marks—to be sure it's almost on a level with the garden: but I was afraid there might have been some—some scuffle. Eh?"

He nearly shut up the expressive eye altogether; he looked at him so hard. And he gave his eye, and his face, and his whole person, a sharp twist. As if he would have screwed the truth out of him.

"Make yourself easy," said the Carrier. "He went into that room last night, without harm in word or deed from me, and no one has entered it since. He is away of his own free will. I'd go out gladly at that door, and beg my bread from house to house, for life, if I could so change the past, that he had never come. But he has come and gone. And I have done with him!"

"Oh!—Well, I think he has got off pretty easy," said Tackleton, taking a chair.

The sneer was lost upon the Carrier, who sat down too, and shaded his face with his hand, for some little time, before proceeding.

"You showed me last night," he said at length, "my wife; my wife that I love; secretly—"

"And tenderly," insinuated Tackleton.

"Conniving at that man's disguise, and giving him opportunities of meeting her alone. I think there's no sight I wouldn't have rather seen than that. I think there's no man in the world I wouldn't have rather had to show it me."

"I confess to having had my suspicions always," said Tackleton. "And that has made me objectionable here, I know."

"But as you did show it me," pursued the Carrier, not minding him; "and as you saw her, my wife, my wife that I love"—his voice, and eye, and hand, grew steadier and firmer as he repeated these words: evidently in pursuance of a steadfast purpose—"as you saw her at this disadvantage, it is right and just that you should also see with my eyes, and look into my breast, and know what my mind is, upon the subject. For it's settled," said the Carrier, regarding him attentively. "And nothing can shake it now."

Tackleton muttered a few general words of assent, about its being necessary to vindicate something or other; but he was overawed by the manner of his companion. Plain and unpolished as it was, it had a something dignified and noble in it, which nothing but the soul of generous honour dwelling in the man could have imparted.

"I am a plain, rough man," pursued the Carrier, "with very little to recommend me. I am not a clever man, as you very well know. I am not a young man. I loved my little Dot, because I had seen her grow up, from a child, in her father's house; because I knew how precious she was; because she had been my life, for years and years. There's many men I can't compare with, who never could have loved my little Dot like me, I think!"

He paused, and softly beat the ground a short time with his foot, before resuming.

"I often thought that though I wasn't good enough for her, I should make her a kind husband, and perhaps know her value better than another; and in this way I reconciled it to myself, and came to think it might be possible that we should be married. And in the end it came, and we *were* married."

"Hah!" said Tackleton, with a significant shake of the head.

"I had studied myself; I had had experience of myself; I knew how much I loved her, and how happy I should be," pursued the Carrier. "But I had not—I feel it now—sufficiently considered her."

"To be sure," said Tackleton. "Giddiness, frivolity,

fickleness, love of admiration! Not considered! All left out of sight! Hah!"

"You had best not interrupt me," said the Carrier, with some sternness, "till you understand me; and you're wide of doing so. If, yesterday, I'd have struck that man down at a blow, who dared to breathe a word against her, to-day I'd set my foot upon his face, if he was my brother!"

The Toy-merchant gazed at him in astonishment. He went on in a softer tone:

"Did I consider," said the Carrier, "that I took her—at her age, and with her beauty—from her young companions, and the many scenes of which she was the ornament; in which she was the brightest little star that ever shone, to shut her up from day to day in my dull house, and keep my tedious company? Did I consider how little suited I was to her sprightly humour, and how wearisome a plodding man like me must be, to one of her quick spirit? Did I consider that it was no merit in me, or claim in me, that I loved her, when everybody must, who knew her? Never. I took advantage of her hopeful nature and her cheerful disposition; and I married her. I wish I never had! For her sake; not for mine!"

The Toy-merchant gazed at him, without winking. Even the half-shut eye was open now.

"Heaven bless her!" said the Carrier, "for the cheerful constancy with which she tried to keep the knowledge of this from me! And Heaven help me, that, in my slow mind, I have not found it out before! Poor child! Poor Dot! *I* not to find it out, who have seen her eyes fill with tears, when such a marriage as our own was spoken of. I, who have seen the secret trembling on her lips a hundred times, and never suspected it till last night! Poor girl! That I could ever hope she would be fond of me! That I could ever believe she was!"

"She made a show of it," said Tackleton. "She made such a show of it, that to tell you the truth it was the origin of my misgivings."

And here he asserted the superiority of May Fielding,

who certainly made no sort of show of being fond of *him*.

"She has tried," said the poor Carrier, with greater emotion than he had exhibited yet; "I only now begin to know how hard she has tried, to be my dutiful and zealous wife. How good she has been; how much she has done; how brave and strong a heart she has; let the happiness I have known under this roof bear witness! It will be some help and comfort to me, when I am here alone."

"Here alone?" said Tackleton. "Oh! Then you do mean to take some notice of this?"

"I mean," returned the Carrier, "to do her the greatest kindness, and make her the best reparation, in my power. I can release her from the daily pain of an unequal marriage, and the struggle to conceal it. She shall be as free as I can render her."

"Make *her* reparation!" exclaimed Tackleton, twisting and turning his great ears with his hands. "There must be something wrong here. You didn't say that, of course."

The Carrier set his grip upon the collar of the Toy-merchant, and shook him like a reed.

"Listen to me!" he said. "And take care that you hear me right. Listen to me. Do I speak plainly?"

"Very plainly indeed," answered Tackleton.

"As if I meant it?"

"Very much as if you meant it."

"I sat upon that hearth, last night, all night," exclaimed the Carrier. "On the spot where she has often sat beside me, with her sweet face looking into mine. I called up her whole life, day by day. I had her dear self, in its every passage, in review before me. And upon my soul she is innocent, if there is One to judge the innocent and guilty!"

Staunch Cricket on the Hearth! Loyal household Fairies!

"Passion and distrust have left me!" said the Carrier; "and nothing but my grief remains. In an unhappy moment some old lover, better suited to her tastes and years than I; forsaken, perhaps, for me, against her will; returned. In an unhappy moment, taken by surprise, and wanting time to think of what she did, she made herself a party to his treachery, by concealing it. Last night she saw him, in the interview we witnessed. It was wrong. But otherwise than this she is innocent if there is truth on earth!"

"If that is your opinion—" Tackleton began.

"So let her go!" pursued the Carrier. "Go, with my blessing for the many happy hours she has given me, and my forgiveness for any pang she has caused me. Let her go, and have the peace of mind I wish her. She'll never hate me. She'll learn to like me better, when I'm not a drag upon her, and she wears the chain I have riveted, more lightly. This is the day on which I took her, with so little thought for her enjoyment, from her home. To-day she shall return to it, and I will trouble her no more. Her father and mother will be here to-day—we had made a little plan for keeping it together—and they shall take her home. I can trust her, there, or anywhere. She leaves me without blame, and she will live so I am sure. If I should die—I may perhaps while she is still young; I have lost some courage in a few hours—she'll find that I remembered her, and loved her to the last! This is the end of what you showed me. Now, it's over!"

"O no, John, not over. Do not say it's over yet! Not quite yet. I have heard your noble words. I could not steal away, pretending to be ignorant of what has affected me with such deep gratitude. Do not say it's over, till the clock has struck again!"

She had entered shortly after Tackleton, and had remained there. She never looked at Tackleton, but fixed her eyes upon her husband. But she kept away from him, setting as wide a space as possible between them; and though she spoke with most impassioned earnestness, she went no nearer to him even then. How different in this from her old self!

"No hand can make the clock which will strike again for me the hours that are gone," replied the Carrier, with a faint smile. "But let it be so, if you will, my dear. It will strike soon. It's of little matter what we say. I'd try to please you in a harder case than that."

"Well!" muttered Tackleton. "I must be off, for when the clock strikes again, it 'll be necessary for me to be upon my way to church. Good-morning, John Peerybingle. I 'm sorry to be deprived of the pleasure of your company. Sorry for the loss, and the occasion of it too!"

"I have spoken plainly?" said the Carrier, accompanying him to the door.

"Oh quite!"

"And you 'll remember what I have said?"

"Why, if you compel me to make the observation," said Tackleton, previously taking the precaution of getting into his chaise; "I must say that it was so very unexpected that I 'm far from being likely to forget it."

"The better for us both," returned the Carrier. "Good-bye. I give you joy!"

"I wish I could give it to *you*," said Tackleton. "As I can't; thank 'ee. Between ourselves, (as I told you before, eh?) I don't much think I shall have the less joy in my married life, because May hasn't been too officious about me, and too demonstrative. Good-bye! Take care of yourself."

The Carrier stood looking after him until he was smaller in the distance than his horse's flowers and favours near at hand; and then, with a deep sigh, went strolling like a restless, broken man, among some neighbouring elms; unwilling to return until the clock was on the eve of striking.

His little wife, being left alone, sobbed piteously; but often dried her eyes and checked herself, to say how good he was, how excellent he was! and once or twice she laughed; so heartily, triumphantly, and incoherently (still crying all the time), that Tilly was quite horrified.

"Ow if you please don't!" said Tilly. "It's enough to dead and bury the Baby, so it is if you please."

"Will you bring him sometimes, to see his father, Tilly," inquired her mistress, drying her eyes; "when I can't live here, and have gone to my old home?"

"Ow if you please don't!" cried Tilly, throwing back her head, and bursting out into a howl—she looked at the moment uncommonly like Boxer; "Ow if you please don't! Ow, what has everybody gone and been and done with everybody, making everybody else so wretched! Ow-w-w-w!"

The soft-hearted Slowboy trailed off at this juncture, into such a deplorable howl, the more tremendous from its long suppression, that she must infallibly have awakened the Baby, and frightened him into something serious (probably convulsions), if her eyes had not encountered Caleb Plummer, leading in his daughter. This spectacle restoring her to a sense of the proprieties, she stood for some few moments silent, with her mouth wide open; and then, posting off to the bed on which the Baby lay asleep, danced in a weird, Saint Vitus manner on the floor, and at the same time rummaged with her face and head among the bedclothes, apparently deriving much relief from those extraordinary operations.

"Mary!" said Bertha. "Not at the marriage!"

"I told her you would not be there mum," whispered Caleb. "I heard as much last night. Bless you," said the little man, taking her tenderly by both hands, "*I* don't care for what they say. *I* don't believe them. There an't much of me, but that little should be torn to pieces sooner than I'd trust a word against you!"

He put his arms about her and hugged her, as a child might have hugged one of his own dolls.

"Bertha couldn't stay at home this morning," said Caleb. "She was afraid, I know, to hear the bells ring, and couldn't trust herself to be so near them on their wedding-day. So we started in good time, and came here. I have been thinking of what I have done," said Caleb, after a moment's pause; "I have been blaming myself till I hardly knew what to do or where to turn, for the distress of mind I have caused her; and I've come to the conclusion that I'd better, if you'll stay with me, mum, the while, tell her the truth. You'll stay with me the while?" he inquired, trembling from head to foot. "I don't know what effect it may have upon her; I don't know what she'll think of me; I don't know that she'll ever care for her poor father afterwards. But it's best for her that she should be undeceived, and I must bear the consequences as I deserve!"

"Mary," said Bertha, "where is your hand! Ah! Here it is; here it is!" pressing it to her lips, with a smile, and drawing it through her arm. "I heard them speaking softly among themselves, last night, of some blame against you. They were wrong."

The Carrier's Wife was silent. Caleb answered for her.

"They were wrong," he said.

"I knew it!" cried Bertha, proudly. "I told them so. I scorned to hear a word! Blame *her* with justice!" she pressed the hand between her own, and the soft cheek against her face. "No! I am not so blind as that."

Her father went on one side of her, while Dot remained upon the other: holding her hand.

"I know you all," said Bertha, "better than you think. But none so well as her. Not even you, father. There is nothing half so real and so true about me, as she is. If I could be restored to sight this instant, and not a word were spoken, I could choose her from a crowd! My sister!"

"Bertha, my dear!" said Caleb, "I have something on my mind I want to tell you, while we three are alone. Hear me kindly! I have a confession to make to you, my darling."

"A confession, father?"

"I have wandered from the truth and lost myself, my child," said Caleb, with a pitiable expression in his bewildered face. "I have wandered from the truth, intending to be kind to you; and have been cruel."

She turned her wonder-stricken face towards him, and repeated "Cruel!"

"He accuses himself too strongly, Bertha," said Dot. "You'll say so, presently. You'll be the first to tell him so."

"He cruel to me!" cried Bertha, with a smile of incredulity.

"Not meaning it, my child," said Caleb. "But I have been; though I never suspected it, till yesterday. My dear blind daughter, hear me and forgive me! The world you live in, heart of mine, doesn't exist as I have represented it. The eyes you have trusted in, have been false to you."

She turned her wonder-stricken face towards him still; but drew back, and clung closer to her friend.

"Your road in life was rough, my poor one," said Caleb, "and I meant to smooth it for you. I have altered objects, changed the characters of people, invented many things that never have been, to make you happier. I have had concealments from you, put deceptions on you, God forgive me! and surrounded you with fancies."

"But living people are not fancies!" she said hurriedly, and turning very pale, and still retiring from him. "You can't change them."

"I have done so, Bertha," pleaded Caleb. "There is one person that you know, my love—"

"Oh father! why do you say, I know?" she answered, in a term of keen reproach. "What and whom do *I* know! I who have no leader! I so miserably blind!"

In the anguish of her heart, she stretched out her hands, as if she were groping her way; then spread them, in a manner most forlorn and sad, upon her face.

"The marriage that takes place to-day," said Caleb, "is with a stern, sordid, grinding man. A hard master to you and me, my dear, for many years. Ugly in his looks, and in his nature. Cold and callous always. Unlike what I have painted him to you in everything, my child. In everything."

"Oh why," cried the Blind Girl, tortured, as it seemed, almost beyond endurance, "why did you ever do this! Why did you ever fill my heart so full, and then come in like Death, and tear away the objects of my love! O Heaven, how blind I am! How helpless and alone!"

Her afflicted father hung his head, and offered no reply but in his penitence and sorrow.

She had been but a short time in this passion of regret, when the Cricket on the Hearth, unheard by all but her, began to chirp. Not merrily, but in a low, faint, sorrowing way. It was so mournful that her tears began to flow; and when the Presence which had been beside the Carrier all night, appeared behind her, pointing to her father, they fell down like rain.

She heard the Cricket-voice more plainly soon, and was conscious, through her blindness, of the Presence hovering about her father.

"Mary," said the Blind Girl, "tell me what my home is. What it truly is."

"It is a poor place, Bertha; very poor and bare indeed. The house will scarcely keep out wind and rain another winter. It is as roughly shielded from the weather, Bertha," Dot continued in a low, clear voice, "as your poor father in his sack-cloth coat."

The Blind Girl, greatly agitated, rose, and led the Carrier's little wife aside.

"Those presents that I took such care of; that came almost at my wish, and were so dearly welcome to me," she said, trembling; "where did they come from? Did you send them?"

"No."

"Who then?"

Dot saw she knew, already, and was silent. The Blind Girl spread her hands before her face again. But in quite another manner now.

"Dear Mary, a moment. One moment? More this way. Speak softly to me. You are true, I know. You'd not deceive me now; would you?"

"No, Bertha, indeed!"

"No, I am sure you would not. You have too much pity for me. Mary, look across the room to where we were just now—to where my father is—my father, so compassionate and loving to me—and tell me what you see."

"I see," said Dot, who understood her well, "an old man sitting in a chair, and leaning sorrowfully on the back, with his face resting on his hand As if his child should comfort him, Bertha."

"Yes, yes. She will Go on."

"He is an old man worn with care and work. He is a

spare, dejected, thoughtful, grey-haired man. I see him now, despondent and bowed down, and striving against nothing. But, Bertha, I have seen him many times before, and striving hard in many ways for one great sacred object. And I honour his grey head, and bless him!"

The Blind Girl broke away from her; and throwing herself upon her knees before him, took the grey head to her breast.

"It is my sight restored. It is my sight!" she cried. "I have been blind, and now my eyes are open. I never knew him! To think I might have died, and never truly seen the father who has been so loving to me!"

There were no words for Caleb's emotion.

"There is not a gallant figure on this earth," exclaimed the Blind Girl, holding him in her embrace, "that I would love so dearly, and would cherish so devotedly, as this! The greyer, and more worn, the dearer, father! Never let them say I am blind again. There's not a furrow in his face, there's not a hair upon his head, that shall be forgotten in my prayers and thanks to Heaven!"

Caleb managed to articulate "My Bertha!"

"And in my blindness, I believed him," said the girl, caressing him with tears of exquisite affection, "to be so different! And having him beside me, day by day, so mindful of me always, never dreamed of this!"

"The fresh smart father in the blue coat, Bertha," said poor Caleb. "He's gone!"

"Nothing is gone," she answered. "Dearest father, no! Everything is here—in you. The father that I loved so well: the father that I never loved enough, and never knew; the benefactor whom I first began to reverence and love, because he had such sympathy for me; All are here in you. Nothing is dead to me. The soul of all that was most dear to me is here—here, with the worn face, and the grey head. And I am NOT blind, father, any longer!"

Dot's whole attention had been concentrated, during this discourse, upon the father and daughter; but looking, now,

towards the little Haymaker in the Moorish meadow, she
saw that the clock was within a few minutes of striking, and
fell, immediately, into a nervous and excited state.

"Father," said Bertha, hesitating. "Mary."

"Yes my dear," returned Caleb. "Here she is."

"There is no change in *her*. You never told me anything
of *her* that was not true?"

"I should have done it my dear, I am afraid," returned
Caleb, "if I could have made her better than she was. But
I must have changed her for the worse, if I had changed
her at all. Nothing could improve her, Bertha."

Confident as the Blind Girl had been when she asked the
question, her delight and pride in the reply and her renewed
embrace of Dot, were charming to behold.

"More changes than you think for, may happen though,
my dear," said Dot. "Changes for the better, I mean;
changes for great joy to some of us. You mustn't let them
startle you too much, if any such should ever happen, and
affect you. Are those wheels upon the road? You've a
quick ear, Bertha. Are they wheels?"

"Yes. Coming very fast."

"I—I—I know you have a quick ear," said Dot, placing
her hand upon her heart, and evidently talking on, as fast
as she could, to hide its palpitating state, "because I have
noticed it often, and because you were so quick to find out
that strange step last night. Though why you should have
said, as I very well recollect you did say, Bertha, 'Whose
step is that!' and why you should have taken any greater
observation of it than of any other step, I don't know.
Though as I said just now, there are great changes in the
world: great changes: and we can't do better than prepare
ourselves to be surprised at hardly anything."

Caleb wondered what this meant; perceiving that she
spoke to him, no less than to his daughter. He saw her,
with astonishment, so fluttered and distressed that she could
scarcely breathe; and holding to a chair, to save herself
from falling.

"They are wheels indeed!" she panted. "Coming nearer! nearer! Very close! And now you hear them stopping at the garden-gate! And now you hear a step outside the door—the same step, Bertha, is it not!—and now!"—

She uttered a wild cry of uncontrollable delight; and running up to Caleb put her hands upon his eyes, as a young man rushed into the room and flinging away his hat into the air, came sweeping down upon them.

"Is it over?" cried Dot.

"Yes!"

"Happily over?"

"Yes!"

"Do you recollect the voice, dear Caleb? Did you ever hear the like of it before?" cried Dot.

"If my boy in the Golden South Americas was alive"— said Caleb, trembling.

"He is alive!" shrieked Dot, removing her hands from his eyes, and clapping them in ecstasy; "look at him! See where he stands before you, healthy and strong! Your own dear son! Your own dear living, loving brother, Bertha!"

All honour to the little creature for her transports! All honour to her tears and laughter, when the three were lock-ed in one another's arms! All honour to the heartiness with which she met the sunburnt sailor-fellow, with his dark streaming hair, half way, and never turned her rosy little mouth aside, but suffered him to kiss it, freely, and to press her to his bounding heart!

And honour to the Cuckoo too—why not!—for bursting out of the trap-door in the Moorish Palace like a house-breaker, and hiccoughing twelve times on the assembled company, as if he had got drunk for joy!

The Carrier, entering, started back. And well he might, to find himself in such good company.

"Look, John!" said Caleb, exultingly, "look here! My own boy from the Golden South Americas! My own son! Him that you fitted out, and sent away yourself! Him that you were always such a friend to!"

The Carrier advanced to seize him by the hand; but, re-
coiling, as some feature in his face awakened a remembrance of the Deaf Man in the Cart, said:

"Edward! Was it you?"

"Now tell him all!" cried Dot. "Tell him all, Edward;
and don't spare me, for nothing shall make me spare myself in his eyes, ever again."

"I was the man," said Edward.

"And could you steal, disguised, into the house of your
old friend?" rejoined the Carrier. "There was a frank boy
once—how many years is it, Caleb, since we heard that he
was dead, and had it proved, we thought?—who never
would have done that."

"There was a generous friend of mine, once; more a
father to me than a friend"; said Edward, "who never
would have judged me, or any other man, unheard. You
were he. So I am certain you will hear me now."

The Carrier, with a troubled glance at Dot, who still kept
far away from him, replied "Well! that's but fair. I will."

"You must know that when I left here, a boy," said Edward, "I was in love, and my love was returned. She was a
very young girl, who perhaps (you may tell me) didn't
know her own mind. But I knew mine, and I had a passion
for her."

"You had!" exclaimed the Carrier. "You!"

"Indeed I had," returned the other. "And she returned
it. I have ever since believed she did, and now I am sure
she did."

"Heaven help me!" said the Carrier. "This is worse than
all."

"Constant to her," said Edward, "and returning, full of
hope, after many hardships and perils, to redeem my part of
our old contract, I heard, twenty miles away, that she was
false to me; that she had forgotten me; and had bestowed
herself upon another and a richer man. I had no mind to
reproach her; but I wished to see her, and to prove beyond
dispute that this was true. I hoped she might have been
forced into it, against her own desire and recollection. It

would be small comfort, but it would be some, I thought, and on I came. That I might have the truth, the real truth; observing freely for myself, and judging for myself, without obstruction on the one hand, or presenting my own influence (if I had any) before her, on the other; I dressed myself unlike myself—you know how; and waited on the road—you knew where. You had no suspicion of me; neither had—had she," pointing to Dot, "until I whispered in her ear at that fireside, and she so nearly betrayed me."

"But when she knew that Edward was alive, and had come back," sobbed Dot, now speaking for herself, as she had burned to do, all through this narrative; "and when she knew his purpose, she advised him by all means to keep his secret close; for his old friend John Peerybingle was much too open in his nature, and too clumsy in all artifice—being a clumsy man in general," said Dot, half laughing and half crying—"to keep it for him. And when she—that's me, John," sobbed the little woman—"told him all, and how his sweetheart had believed him to be dead; and how she had at last been over-persuaded by her mother into a marriage which the silly, dear old thing called advantageous; and when she—that's me again, John—told him they were not yet married (though close upon it), and that it would be nothing but a sacrifice if it went on, for there was no love on her side; and when he went nearly mad with joy to hear it; then she—that's me again—said she would go between them, as she had often done before in old times, John, and would sound his sweetheart and be sure that what she—me again, John—said and thought was right. And it was right, John! And they were brought together, John. And they were married, John, an hour ago! And here's the Bride! And Gruff and Tackleton may die a bachelor. And I'm a happy little woman, May, God bless you!"

She was an irresistible little woman, if that be anything to the purpose; and never so completely irresistible as in her present transports. There never were congratulations so endearing and delicious, as those she lavished on herself and on the Bride.

Amid the tumult of emotions in his breast, the honest Carrier had stood, confounded. Flying, now, towards her, Dot stretched out her hand to stop him, and retreated as before.

"No, John, no! Hear all! Don't love me any more, John, till you've heard every word I have to say. It was wrong to have a secret from you, John. I'm very sorry. I didn't think it any harm, till I came and sat down by you on the little stool last night. But when I knew by what was written in your face, that you had seen me walking in the gallery with Edward, and when I knew what you thought, I felt how giddy and how wrong it was. But oh, dear John, how could you, could you, think so!"

Little woman, how she sobbed again! John Peerybingle would have caught her in his arms. But no; she wouldn't let him.

"Don't love me yet, please John! Not for a long time yet! When I was sad about this intended marriage, dear, it was because I remembered May and Edward such young lovers; and knew that her heart was far away from Tackleton. You believe that, now. Don't you, John?"

John was going to make another rush at this appeal; but she stopped him again.

"No; keep there, please John! When I laugh at you, as I sometimes do, John, and call you clumsy and a dear old goose, and names of that sort, it's because I love you John, so well, and take such pleasure in your ways, and wouldn't see you altered in the least respect to have you made a King to-morrow."

"Hooroar!" said Caleb with unusual vigour. "My opinion!"

"And when I speak of people being middle-aged, and steady, John, and pretend that we are a humdrum couple, going on in a jog-trot sort of way, it's only because I'm such a silly little thing, John, that I like, sometimes, to act a kind of Play with Baby, and all that: and make believe."

She saw that he was coming; and stopped him again. But she was very nearly too late

"No, don't love me for another minute or two, if you please John! What I want most to tell you, I have kept to the last. My dear, good, generous John, when we were talking the other night about the Cricket, I had it on my lips to say, that at first I did not love you quite so dearly as I do now; that when I first came home here, I was half afraid I mightn't learn to love you every bit as well as I hoped and prayed I might—being so very young, John! But, dear·John, every day and hour I loved you more and more. And if I could have loved you better than I do, the noble words I heard you say this morning, would have made me. But I can't. All the affection that I had (It was a great deal John) I gave you, as you well deserve, long, long ago, and I have no more left to give. Now, my dear husband, take me to your heart again! That's my home, John; and never, never think of sending me to any other!"

You never will derive so much delight from seeing a glorious little woman in the arms of a third party, as you would have felt if you had seen Dot run into the Carrier's embrace. It was the most complete, unmitigated, soul-fraught little piece of earnestness that ever you beheld in all your days.

You may be sure the Carrier was in a state of perfect rapture; and you may be sure Dot was likewise; and you may be sure they all were, inclusive of Miss Slowboy, who wept copiously for joy, and wishing to include her young charge in the general interchange of congratulations, handed round the Baby to everybody in succession, as if it were something to drink.

But, now, the sound of wheels was heard again outside the door; and somebody exclaimed that Gruff and Tackleton was coming back. Speedily that worthy gentleman appeared, looking warm and flustered.

"Why, what the Devil's this, John Peerybingle!" said Tackleton. "There's some mistake. I appointed Mrs. Tackleton to meet me at the church, and I'll swear I passed her on the road, on her way here. Oh! here she is! I beg your pardon, sir; I haven't the pleasure of knowing you;

but if you can do me the favour to spare this young lady, she has rather a particular engagement this morning."

"But I can't spare her," returned Edward. "I couldn't think of it."

"What do you mean, you vagabond?" said Tackleton.

"I mean, that as I can make allowance for your being vexed," returned the other, with a smile, "I am as deaf to harsh discourse this morning, as I was to all discourse last night."

The look that Tackleton bestowed upon him, and the start he gave!

"I am sorry, sir," said Edward, holding out May's left hand, and especially the third finger; "that the young lady can't accompany you to church; but as she has been there once, this morning, perhaps you'll excuse her."

Tackleton looked hard at the third finger, and took a little piece of silver paper, apparently containing a ring, from his waistcoat-pocket.

"Miss Slowboy," said Tackleton. "Will you have the kindness to throw that in the fire? Thank 'ee."

"It was a previous engagement, quite an old engagement, that prevented my wife from keeping her appointment with you, I assure you," said Edward.

"Mr. Tackleton will do me the justice to acknowledge that I revealed it to him faithfully; and that I told him, many times, I never could forget it," said May, blushing.

"Oh, certainly!" said Tackleton. "Oh to be sure. Oh it's all right. It's quite correct. Mrs. Edward Plummer, I infer?"

"That's the name," returned the bridegroom.

"Ah, I shouldn't have known you, sir," said Tackleton, scrutinising his face narrowly, and making a low bow. "I give you joy, sir!"

"Thank 'ee."

"Mrs. Peerybingle," said Tackleton, turning suddenly to where she stood with her husband; "I am sorry. You haven't done me a very great kindness, but, upon my life I am sorry. You are better than I thought you. John Peerybingle, I am sorry. You understand me; that's enough. It's quite correct, ladies and gentlemen all, and perfectly satisfactory. Good-morning!"

With these words he carried it off, and carried himself off too: merely stopping at the door, to take the flowers and favours from his horse's head, and to kick that animal once, in the ribs, as a means of informing him that there was a screw loose in his arrangements.

Of course it became a serious duty now, to make such a day of it, as should mark these events for a high Feast and Festival in the Peerybingle Calendar for evermore. Accordingly, Dot went to work to produce such an entertainment, as should reflect undying honour on the house and on every one concerned; and in a very short space of time, she was up to her dimpled elbows in flour, and whitening the Carrier's coat, every time he came near her, by stopping him to give him a kiss. That good fellow washed the greens, and peeled the turnips, and broke the plates, and upset iron pots full of cold water on the fire, and made himself useful in all sorts of ways: while a couple of professional assistants, hastily called in from somewhere in the neighbourhood, as on a point of life or death, ran against each other in all the doorways and round all the corners, and everybody tumbled over Tilly Slowboy and the Baby, everywhere. Tilly never came out in such force before. Her ubiquity was the theme of general admiration. She was a stumbling-block in the passage at five-and-twenty minutes past two; a man-trap in the kitchen at half-past two precisely; and a pitfall in the garret at five-and-twenty minutes to three. The Baby's head was, as it were, a test and touchstone for every description of matter,—animal, vegetable, and mineral. Nothing was in use that day that didn't come, at some time or other, into close acquaintance with it.

Then, there was a great Expedition set on foot to go and find out Mrs. Fielding; and to be dismally penitent to that excellent gentlewoman; and to bring her back, by force, if needful, to be happy and forgiving. And when the Expedition first discovered her, she would listen to no terms at all, but said, an unspeakable number of times, that ever she should have lived to see the day! and couldn't be got to say anything else, except, "Now carry me to the grave": which seemed absurd, on account of her not being dead, or anything at all like it. After a time, she lapsed into a state of dreadful calmness, and observed, that when that unfortunate train of circumstances had occurred in the Indigo Trade, she had foreseen that she would be exposed, during her whole life, to every species of insult and contumely; and that she was glad to find it was the case; and begged they wouldn't trouble themselves about her,—for what was she? oh, dear! a nobody!—but would forget that such a being lived, and would take their course in life without her. From this bitterly sarcastic mood, she passed into an angry one, in which she gave vent to the remarkable expression that the worm would turn if trodden on; and, after that, she yielded to a soft regret, and said, if they had only given her their confidence, what might she not have had it in her power to suggest! Taking advantage of this crisis in her feelings, the Expedition embraced her, and she very soon had her gloves on, and was on her way to John Peerybingle's in a state of unimpeachable gentility; with a paper parcel at her side containing a cap of state, almost as tall, and quite as stiff, as a mitre.

Then, there were Dot's father and mother to come, in another little chaise; and they were behind their time; and fears were entertained; and there was much looking out for them down the road; and Mrs. Fielding always would look in the wrong and morally impossible direction; and being apprised thereof, hoped she might take the liberty of looking where she pleased. At last they came: a chubby little couple, jogging along in a snug and comfortable little way that quite belonged to the Dot family; and Dot and her mother, side by side, were wonderful to see. They were so like each other.

Then, Dot's mother had to renew her acquaintance with May's mother; and May's mother always stood on her gentility; and Dot's mother never stood on anything but her active little feet. And old Dot—so to call Dot's father, I forgot it wasn't his right name, but never mind—took liberties, and shook hands at first sight, and seemed to think a cap but so much starch and muslin, and didn't defer himself at all to the Indigo Trade, but said there was no help for it now; and in Mrs. Fielding's summing up, was a good-natured kind of man—but coarse, my dear.

I wouldn't have missed Dot, doing the honours in her wedding-gown, my benison on her bright face! for any money. No! nor the good Carrier, so jovial and so ruddy, at the bottom of the table. Nor the brown, fresh, sailor-fellow, and his handsome wife. Nor any one among them. To have missed the dinner would have been to miss as jolly and as stout a meal as man need eat; and to have missed the overflowing cups in which they drank The Wedding-Day, would have been the greatest miss of all.

After dinner, Caleb sang the song about the Sparkling Bowl. As I'm a living man, hoping to keep so, for a year or two, he sang it through.

And, by the bye, a most unlooked-for incident occurred, just as he finished the last verse.

There was a tap at the door; and a man came staggering in, without saying with your leave, or by your leave, with something heavy on his head. Setting this down in the middle of the table, symmetrically in the centre of the nuts and apples, he said:

"Mr. Tackleton's compliments, and as he hasn't got no use for the cake himself, p'raps you'll eat it."

And with those words, he walked off.

There was some surprise among the company, as you may imagine. Mrs. Fielding, being a lady of infinite discernment, suggested that the cake was poisoned, and related a narrative of a cake, which, within her knowledge, had turned a seminary for young ladies, blue. But she was overruled by acclamation; and the cake was cut by May, with much ceremony and rejoicing.

I don't think any one had tasted it, when there came another tap at the door, and the same man appeared again, having under his arm a vast brown-paper parcel.

"Mr. Tackleton's compliments, and he's sent a few toys for the Baby. They ain't ugly."

After the delivery of which expressions, he retired again. The whole party would have experienced great difficulty in finding words for their astonishment, even if they had had ample time to seek them. But, they had none at all; for, the messenger had scarcely shut the door behind him, when there came another tap, and Tackleton himself walked in.

"Mrs. Peerybingle!" said the Toy-merchant, hat in hand. "I'm sorry. I'm more sorry than I was this morning. I have had time to think of it. John Peerybingle! I'm sour by disposition; but I can't help being sweetened, more or less, by coming face to face with such a man as you. Caleb! This unconscious little nurse gave me a broken hint last night of which I have found the thread. I blush to think how easily I might have bound you and your daughter to me, and what a miserable idiot I was, when I took her for one! Friends, one and all, my house is very lonely to-night. I have not so much as a Cricket on my Hearth. I have scared them all away. Be gracious to me; let me join this happy party!"

He was at home in five minutes. You never saw such a fellow. What *had* he been doing with himself all his life, never to have known, before, his great capacity of being jovial! Or what had the fairies been doing with him, to have effected such a change!

"John! you won't send me home this evening; will you?" whispered Dot.

He had been very near it though!

There wanted but one living creature to make the party complete; and, in the twinkling of an eye, there he was, very thirsty with hard running, and engaged in hopeless endeavours to squeeze his head into a narrow pitcher. He had gone with the cart to its journey's end, very much dis-

gusted with the absence of his master, and stupendously
rebellious to the Deputy. After lingering about the stable
for some little time, vainly attempting to incite the old horse
to the mutinous act of returning on his own account, he had
walked into the tap-room and laid himself down before the
fire. But suddenly yielding to the conviction that the
Deputy was a humbug, and must be abandoned, he had got
up again, turned tail, and come home.

There was a dance in the evening. With which general
mention of that recreation, I should have left it alone, if I
had not some reason to suppose that it was quite an original
dance, and one of a most uncommon figure. It was formed
in an odd way; in this way.

Edward, that sailor-fellow—a good free dashing sort of
a fellow he was—had been telling them various marvels
concerning parrots, and mines, and Mexicans, and gold
dust, when all at once he took it in his head to jump up from
his seat and propose a dance; for Bertha's harp was there,
and she had such a hand upon it as you seldom hear. Dot
(sly little piece of affectation when she chose) said her
dancing days were over; *I* think because the Carrier was
smoking his pipe, and she liked sitting by him, best. Mrs.
Fielding had no choice, of course, but to say *her* dancing
days were over, after that; and everybody said the same,
except May; May was ready.

So, May and Edward get up, amid great applause, to
dance alone; and Bertha plays her liveliest tune.

Well! if you 'll believe me, they have not been dancing
five minutes, when suddenly the Carrier flings his pipe
away, takes Dot round the waist, dashes out into the room,
and starts off with her, toe and heel, quite wonderfully.
Tackleton no sooner sees this, than he skims across to Mrs.
Fielding, takes her round the waist, and follows suit. Old
Dot no sooner sees this, than up he is, all alive, whisks off
Mrs. Dot in the middle of the dance, and is the foremost
there. Caleb no sooner sees this, than he clutches Tilly
Slowboy by both hands and goes off at score; Miss Slowboy,
firm in the belief that diving hotly in among the other

couples, and effecting any number of concussions with them, is your only principle of footing it.

Hark! how the Cricket joins the music with its Chirp, Chirp, Chirp; and how the kettle hums!

.   .   .   .   .

But what is this! Even as I listen to them, blithely, and turn towards Dot, for one last glimpse of a little figure very pleasant to me, she and the rest have vanished into air, and I am left alone. A Cricket sings upon the Hearth; a broken child's-toy lies upon the ground; and nothing else remains·

The End

AMERICAN NOTES
FOR GENERAL CIRCULATION

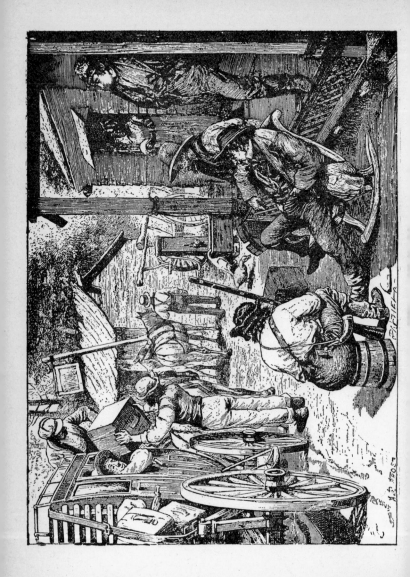

I DEDICATE THIS BOOK

TO

THOSE FRIENDS OF MINE
IN AMERICA,

*who, giving me a welcome I must ever
gratefully and proudly remember,
left my judgment*
FREE;
*and who, loving their country, can bear
the truth, when it is told good
humouredly, and in a
kind spirit.*

CONTENTS

American Notes

CONTENTS

ILLUSTRATIONS

PREFACE

My readers have opportunities of judging for themselves whether the influences and tendencies which I distrusted in America, had, at that time, any existence but in my imagination. They can examine for themselves whether there has been anything in the public career of that country since, at home or abroad, which suggests that those influences and tendencies really did exist. As they find the fact, they will judge me. If they discern any evidences of wrong-going, in any direction that I have indicated, they will acknowledge that I had reason in what I wrote. If they discern no such indications, they will consider me altogether mistaken—but not wilfully.

Prejudiced, I am not, and never have been, otherwise than in favour of the United States. I have many friends in America, I feel a grateful interest in the country, I hope and believe it will successfully work out a problem of the highest importance to the whole human race. To represent me as viewing AMERICA with ill-nature, coldness, or animosity, is merely to do a very foolish thing: which is always a very easy one.

AMERICAN NOTES

CHAPTER I

GOING AWAY

I SHALL never forget the one-fourth serious and three-fourths comical astonishment, with which on the morning of the third of January eighteen hundred and forty-two, I opened the door of, and put my head into, a 'state-room' on board the Britannia steampacket, twelve hundred tons burthen per register, bound for Halifax and Boston, and carrying Her Majesty's mails.

That this state-room had been specially engaged for 'Charles Dickens, Esquire, and Lady,' was rendered sufficiently clear even to my scared intellect by a very small manuscript, announcing the fact, which was pinned on a very flat quilt, covering a very thin mattress, spread like a surgical plaster on a most inaccessible shelf. But that this was the state-room concerning which Charles Dickens, Esquire, and Lady, had held daily and nightly conferences for at least four months preceding: that this could by any possibility be that small snug chamber of the imagination, which Charles Dickens, Esquire, with the spirit of prophecy strong upon him, had always foretold would contain at least one little sofa, and which his lady, with a modest yet most magnificent sense of its limited dimensions, had from the first opined would not hold more than two enormous portmanteaus in some odd corner out of sight (portmanteaus which could now no more be got in at the door, not to say stowed away, than a giraffe could be persuaded or forced into a flower-pot): that this utterly impracticable, thoroughly hopeless, and profoundly preposterous box, had the remotest reference to, or connection with, those chaste and pretty, not to say gorgeous little bowers, sketched by a masterly hand, in the highly varnished lithographic plan hanging up in the agent's counting-house in the city of London: that this room of state, in short, could be anything but a pleasant fiction and cheerful jest of the captain's, invented and

1

put in practice for the better relish and enjoyment of the real state-room presently to be disclosed:—these were truths which I really could not, for the moment, bring my mind at all to bear upon or comprehend. And I sat down upon a kind of horsehair slab, or perch, of which there were two within; and looked, without any expression of countenance whatever, at some friends who had come on board with us, and who were crushing their faces into all manner of shapes by endeavouring to squeeze them through the small doorway.

We had experienced a pretty smart shock before coming below, which, but that we were the most sanguine people living, might have prepared us for the worst. The imaginative artist to whom I have already made allusion, has depicted in the same great work, a chamber of almost interminable perspective, furnished, as Mr. Robins would say, in a style of more than Eastern splendour, and filled (but not inconveniently so) with groups of ladies and gentlemen, in the very highest state of enjoyment and vivacity. Before descending into the bowels of the ship, we had passed from the deck into a long narrow apartment, not unlike a gigantic hearse with windows in the sides; having at the upper end a melancholy stove, at which three of four chilly stewards were warming their hands; while on either side, extending down its whole dreary length, was a long, long table, over each of which a rack, fixed to the low roof, and stuck full of drinking-glasses and cruet-stands, hinted dismally at rolling seas and heavy weather. I had not at that time seen the ideal presentment of this chamber which has since gratified me so much, but I observed that one of our friends who had made the arrangements for our voyage, turned pale on entering, retreated on the friend behind him, smote his forehead involuntarily, and said below his breath, 'Impossible! it cannot be!' or words to that effect. He recovered himself however by a great effort, and after a preparatory cough or two, cried, with a ghastly smile which is still before me, looking at the same time round the walls, 'Ha! the breakfast-room, steward—eh?' We all foresaw what the answer must be: we knew the agony he suffered. He had often spoken of *the saloon;* had taken in and lived upon the pictorial idea; had usually given us to understand, at home, that to form a just conception of it, it would be necessary to multiply the size and furniture of an ordinary drawing-room by seven, and then fall short of the reality. When the man in reply avowed the truth; the blunt, remorseless, naked truth; 'This is the saloon, sir'—he actually reeled beneath the blow.

In persons who were so soon to part, and interpose between their else daily communication the formidable barrier of many thousand miles of stormy space, and who were for that reason anxious to cast no other cloud, not even the passing shadow of a moment's disappointment or discomfiture, upon the short interval of happy companionship that yet remained to them—in persons so situated, the natural transition from these first surprises was obviously into peals of hearty laughter, and I can report that I, for one, being still seated upon the slab or perch before-mentioned, roared outright until the vessel rang again. Thus, in less than two minutes after coming upon it for the first time, we all by common consent agreed that this state-room was the pleasantest and most facetious and capital contrivance possible; and that to have had it one inch larger, would have been quite a disagreeable and deplorable state of things. And with this; and with showing how,—by very nearly closing the door, and twining in and out like serpents, and by counting the little washing slab as standing-room,—we could manage to insinuate four people into it, all at one time; and entreating each other to observe how very airy it was (in dock), and how there was a beautiful port-hole which could be kept open all day (weather permitting), and how there was quite a large bull's-eye just over the looking-glass which would render shaving a perfectly easy and delightful process (when the ship didn't roll too much); we arrived, at last, at the unanimous conclusion that it was rather spacious than otherwise: though I do verily believe that, deducting the two berths, one above the other, than which nothing smaller for sleeping in was ever made except coffins, it was no bigger than one of those hackney cabriolets which have the door behind, and shoot their fares out, like sacks of coals, upon the pavement.

Having settled this point to the perfect satisfaction of all parties, concerned and unconcerned, we sat down round the fire in the ladies' cabin—just to try the effect. It was rather dark, certainly; but somebody said, 'of course it would be light at sea,' a proposition to which we all assented; echoing 'of course, of course'; though it would be exceedingly difficult to say why we thought so. I remember, too, when he had discovered and exhausted another topic of consolation in the circumstance of this ladies' cabin adjoining our state-room, and the consequently immense feasibility of sitting there at all times and seasons, and had fallen into a momentary silence, leaning our faces on our hands and looking at the fire, one of our party said, with the solemn air of a man who had made a discovery, 'What a relish mulled claret will have down here!' which appeared to strike us all most forcibly; as though there were something spicy and high-flavoured in cabins, which essentially improved that composition, and rendered it quite incapable of perfection anywhere else.

There was a stewardess, too, actively engaged in producing clean sheets and tablecloths from the very entrails of the sofas, and from unexpected lockers, of such artful mechanism, that it made one's head ache to see them opened one after another, and rendered it quite a distracting circumstance to follow her proceedings, and to find that every nook and corner and individual piece of furniture was something else besides what it pretended to be, and was a mere trap and deception and place of secret stowage, whose ostensible purpose was its least useful one.

God bless that stewardess for her piously fraudulent account of January voyages! God bless her for her clear recollection of the companion passage of last year, when nobody was ill, and everybody dancing from morning to night, and it was 'a run' of twelve days, and a piece of the purest frolic, and delight, and jollity! And happiness be with her for her bright face and her pleasant Scotch tongue, which had sounds of old Home in it for my fellow traveller: and for her predictions of fair winds and fine weather (all wrong, or I shouldn't be half so fond of her); and for the ten thousand small fragments of genuine womanly tact, by which, without piecing them elaborately together, and pitching them up into shape and form and case and pointed application, she nevertheless did plainly show that all young mothers on one side of the Atlantic were near and close at hand to their little children left upon the other; and that what seemed to the uninitiated a serious journey, was, to those who were in the secret, a mere frolic, to be sung about and whistled at! Light be her heart, and gay her merry eyes, for years!

The state-room had grown pretty fast; but by this time it had expanded into something quite bulky, and almost boasted a bay-window to view the sea from. So we went upon deck again in high spirits; and there, everything was in such a state of bustle and active preparation, that the blood quickened its pace, and whirled through one's veins on that clear frosty morning with involuntary mirthfulness. For every gallant ship was riding slowly up and down, and every little boat was splashing noisily in the water; and knots of people stood upon the wharf, gazing with a kind of 'dread delight' on the far-famed fast American steamer; and one party of men were 'taking in the milk,' or, in other words, getting the cow on board; and another were filling the ice-houses to the very throat with fresh provisions; with butchers'-meat and gardenstuff, pale sucking-pigs, calves' heads in scores, beef, veal, and pork, and poultry out of all proportion; and others were coiling ropes and busy with oakum yarns; and others were lowering heavy packages into the hold; and the purser's head was barely visible as it loomed in a state of exquisite perplexity from the midst of a vast pile of passengers' luggage; and there seemed to be nothing going on anywhere, or uppermost in the mind of everybody, but preparations for this mighty voyage. This, with the bright cold sun, the bracing air, the crisply-curling water, the thin white crust of morning ice upon the decks which crackled with a sharp and cheerful sound beneath the lightest tread, was irresistible. And when, again upon the shore, we turned and saw from the vessel's mast her name signalled in flags of joyous colours, and fluttering by their side the beautiful American banner with its stars and stripes,—the long three thousand miles and more, and, longer still, the six whole months of absence, so dwindled and faded, that the ship had gone out and come home again, and it was broad spring already in the Coburg Dock at Liverpool.

I have not inquired among my medical acquaintance, whether Turtle, and cold Punch, with Hock, Champagne, and Claret, and all the slight et cetera usually included in an unlimited order for a good dinner—especially when it is left to the liberal construction of my faultless friend, Mr. Radley, of the Adelphi Hotel—are peculiarly calculated to suffer a sea-change; or whether a plain mutton-chop, and a glass or two of sherry, would be less likely of conversion into foreign and disconcerting material. My own opinion is, that whether one is discreet or indiscreet in these particulars on the eve of a sea-voyage, is a matter of little consequence; and that, to use a common phrase, 'it comes to very much the same thing in the end.' Be this as it may, I know that the dinner of that day was undeniably perfect; that it comprehended all these items, and a great many more; and that we all did ample justice to it. And I know too, that, bating a certain tacit avoidance of any allusion to to-morrow; such as may be supposed to prevail between delicate-minded turnkeys, and a sensitive prisoner who is to be hanged next morning; we got on very well, and, all things considered, were merry enough.

When the morning—*the* morning—came, and we met at breakfast, it was curious to see how eager we all were to prevent a moment's pause in the conversation, and how astoundingly gay everybody was: the forced spirits of each member of the little party having as much likeness to his natural mirth, as hot-house peas at five guineas the quart, resemble in flavour the growth of the dews, and air, and rain of Heaven. But as one o'clock, the hour for going aboard, drew near, this volubility dwindled away by little and little, despite the most persevering efforts to the contrary, until at last, the matter being now quite desperate, we threw off all disguise; openly speculated upon where we should be this time tomorrow, this time next day, and so forth; and entrusted a vast number of messages to those who intended returning to town that night, which were to be delivered at home and elsewhere without fail, within the very shortest possible space of time after the arrival of the railway train at Euston Square. And commissions and remembrances do so crowd upon one at such a time, that we were still busied with this employment when we found ourselves fused, as it were, into a dense conglomeration of passengers and passengers' friends and passengers' luggage, all jumbled together on the deck of a small steamboat, and panting and snorting off to the packet, which had worked out of dock yesterday afternoon and was now lying at her moorings in the river.

And there she is! all eyes are turned to where she lies, dimly discernible through the gathering fog of the early winter afternoon; every finger is pointed in the same direction; and murmurs of interest and admiration—as 'How beautiful she looks!' 'How trim she is!'—are heard on every side. Even the lazy gentleman with his hat on one side and his hands in his pockets, who has dispensed so much consolation by inquiring with a yawn of another gentleman whether he is 'going across'—as if it were a ferry—even he condescends to look that way, and nod his head, as who should say, 'No mistake about *that*': and not even the sage Lord Burleigh in his nod, included half so much as this lazy gentleman of might who has made the passage (as everybody on board has found out already; it's impossible to say how) thirteen times without a single accident! There is another passenger very much wrapped-up, who has been frowned down by the rest, and morally trampled upon and crushed, for presuming to inquire with a timid interest how long it is since the poor President went down. He is standing close to the lazy gentleman, and says with a faint smile that he believes She is a very strong Ship; to which the lazy gentleman, looking first in his questioner's eye and then very hard in the wind's, answers unexpectedly and ominously, that She need be. Upon this the lazy gentleman instantly falls very low in the popular estimation, and the passengers, with looks of defiance, whisper to each other that he is an ass, and an impostor, and clearly don't know anything at all about it.

But we are made fast alongside the packet, whose huge red funnel is smoking bravely, picking rich promise of serious intentions.

Packing-cases, portmanteaus, carpet-bags, and boxes, are already passed from hand to hand, and hauled on board with breathless rapidity. The officers, smartly dressed, are at the gangway handing the passengers up the side, and hurrying the men. In five minutes' time, the little steamer is utterly deserted, and the packet is beset and over-run by its late freight, who instantly pervade the whole ship, and are to be met with by the dozen in every nook and corner: swarming down below with their own baggage, and stumbling over other people's; disposing themselves comfortably in wrong cabins, and creating a most horrible confusion by having to turn out again; madly bent upon opening locked doors, and on forcing a passage into all kinds of out-of-the-way places where there is no thoroughfare; sending wild stewards, with elfin hair, to and fro upon the breezy decks on unintelligible errands, impossible of execution: and in short, creating the most extraordinary and bewildering tumult. In the midst of all this, the lazy gentleman, who seems to have no luggage of any kind—not so much as a friend, even— lounges up and down the hurricane deck, coolly puffing a cigar; and, as this unconcerned demeanour again exalts him in the opinion of those who have leisure to observe his proceedings, every time he looks up at the masts, or down at the decks, or over the side, they look there too, as wondering whether he sees anything wrong anywhere, and hoping that, in case he should, he will have the goodness to mention it.

What have we here? The captain's boat! and yonder the captain himself. Now, by all our hopes and wishes, the very man he ought to be! A well-made, tight-built, dapper little fellow; with a ruddy face, which is a letter of invitation to shake him by both hands at once: and with a clear, blue honest eye, that it does one good to see one's sparkling image in. 'Ring the bell!' 'Ding, ding, ding!' the very bell is in a hurry. 'Now for the shore—who's for the shore?'—'These gentlemen, I am sorry to say.' They are away, and never said, Good b'ye. Ah! now they wave it from the little boat. 'Good b'ye! Good b'ye!' Three cheers from them; three more from us; three more from them: and they are gone.

To and fro, to and fro, to and fro again a hundred times! This waiting for the latest mail-bags is worse than all. If we could have gone off in the midst of that last burst, we should have started triumphantly: but to lie here, two hours and more in the damp fog, neither staying at home nor going aboard, is letting one gradually down into the very depths of dulness and low spirits. A speck in the mist, at last! That's something. It is the boat we wait for! That's more to the purpose. The captain appears on the paddle-box with his speaking trumpet; the officers take their stations; all hands are on the alert; the flagging hopes of the passengers revive; the cooks pause in their savoury work, and look out with faces full of interest. The boat comes alongside; the bags are dragged in anyhow, and flung down for the moment anywhere. Three cheers more: and as the first one rings upon our ears, the vessel throbs like a strong giant that has just received the breath of life; the two great wheels turn fiercely round for the first time; and the noble ship, with wind and tie astern, breaks proudly through the lashed and foaming water.

CHAPTER II

THE PASSAGE OUT

WE all dined together that day; and a rather formidable party we were: no fewer than eighty-six strong. The vessel being pretty deep in the water, with all her coals on board and so many passengers, and the weather being calm and quiet, there was but little motion; so that before the dinner was half over, even those passengers who were most distrustful of themselves plucked up amazingly; and those who in the morning had returned to the universal question, 'Are you a good sailor?' a very decided negative, now either parried the inquiry with the evasive reply, 'Oh! I suppose I'm no worse than anybody else'; or, reckless of all moral obligations, answered boldly 'Yes': and with some irritation too, as though they would ad, 'I should like to know what you see in *me*, sir, particularly, to justify suspicion!'

Notwithstanding this high tone of courage and confidence, I could not but observe that very few remained long over their wine; and that everybody had an unusual love of the open air; and that the favourite and most coveted seats were invariably those nearest to the door. The tea-table, too, was by no means as well attended as the dinner-table; and there was less whist-playing than might have been expected. Still, with the exception of one lady, who had retired with some precipitation at dinner-time, immediately after being assisted to the finest cut of a very yellow boiled leg of mutton with very green capers, there were no invalids as yet; and walking, and smoking, and drinking of brandy-and-water (but always in the open air), went on with unabated spirit, until eleven o'clock or thereabouts, when 'turning in'—no sailor of seven hours' experience talks of going to bed—became the order of the night. The perpetual tramp of boot-heels on the decks gave place to a heavy silence, and the whole human freight was stowed away below, excepting a very few stragglers, like myself, who were probably, like me, afraid to go there.

To one unaccustomed to such scenes, this is a very striking time on shipboard. Afterwards, and when its novelty had long worn off, it never ceased to have a peculiar interest and charm for me. The gloom through which the great black mass holds its direct and certain course; the rushing water, plainly heard, but dimly seen; the broad, white, glistening track, that follows in the vessel's wake; the men on the look-out forward, who would be scarcely visible against the dark sky, but for their blotting out some score of glistening stars; the helmsman at the wheel, with the illuminated card before him, shining, a speck of light amidst the darkness, like something sentient and of Divine intelligence; the melancholy sighing of the wind through block, and rope, and chain; the gleaming forth of light from every crevice, nook, and tiny piece of glass about the decks, as though the ship were filled with fire in hiding, ready to burst through any outlet, wild with its resistless power of death and ruin. At first, too, and even when the hour, and all the objects it exalts, have come to be familiar, it is difficult, alone and thoughtful, to hold them to their proper shapes and forms. They change with the wandering fancy; assume the semblance of things left far away; put on the well-remembered aspect of favourite places dearly loved; and even people them with shadows. Streets, houses, rooms; figures so like their usual occupants, that they have startled me by their reality, which far exceeded, as it seemed to me, all power of mine to conjure up the absent; have, many and many a time, at such an hour, grown suddenly out of objects with whose real look, and use, and purpose, I was as well acquainted as with my own two hands.

My own two hands, and feet likewise, being very cold, however, on this particular occasion, I crept below at midnight. It was not exactly comfortable below. It was decidedly close; and it was impossible to be unconscious of the presence of that extraordinary compound of strange smells, which is to be found nowhere but on board ship, and which is such a subtle perfume that it seems to enter at every pore of the skin, and whisper of the hold. Two passengers' wives (one of them my own) lay already in silent agonies on the sofa; and one lady's maid (*my* lady's) was a mere bundle on the floor, execrating her destiny, and pounding her cul-papers among the stray boxes. Everything sloped the wrong way: which in itself was an aggravation scarcely to be borne. I had left the door open, a moment before, in the bosom of a gentle declivity, and, when I turned to shut it, it was on the summit of a lofty eminence. Now every plank and timber creaked, as if the ship were made of wicker-work; and now crackled, like an enormous fire of the driest possible twigs. There was nothing for it but bed; so I went to bed.

It was pretty much the same for the next two days, with a tolerable fair wind and dry weather. I read in bed (but to this hour I don't know what) a good deal; and reeled on deck a little; drank cold brandy-and-water with an unspeakable disgust, and ate hard biscuit perseveringly: not ill, but going to be.

It is the third morning. I am awakened out of my sleep by a dismal shriek from my wife, who demands to know whether there's any danger. I rouse myself, and look out of bed. The water-jug is plunging and leaping like a lively dolphin; all the smaller articles are afloat, except my shoes, which are stranded on a carpet-bag, high and dry, like a couple of coal-barges. Suddenly I see them spring into the air, and behold the looking-glass, which is nailed to the wall, sticking fast upon the ceiling. At the same time the door entirely disappears, and a new one is opened in the floor. Then I begin to comprehend that the state-room is standing on its head.

Before it is possible to make any arrangement at all compatible with this novel state of things, the ship rights. Before one can say 'Thank Heaven!' she wrongs again. Before one can cry she *is* wrong, she seems to have started forward, and to be a creature actually running of its own accord, with broken knees and failing legs, through every variety of hole and pitfall, and stumbling constantly. Before one can so much as wonder, she takes a high leap into the air. Before she has well done that, she takes a deep dive into the water. Before she has gained the surface, she throws a summerset. The instant she is on her legs, she rushes backward. And so she goes on staggering, heaving, wrestling, leaping, diving, jumping, pitching, throbbing, rolling, and rocking: and going through all these movements, sometimes by turns, and sometimes altogether: until one feels disposed to roar for mercy.

A steward passes. 'Steward!' 'Sir?' 'What *is* the matter? what *do* you call this?' 'Rather a heavy sea on, sir, and a head-wind.'

A head-wind! Imagine a human face upon the vessel's prow with fifteen thousand Samsons in one bent upon driving her back, and hitting her exactly between the eyes whenever she attempts to advance an inch. Imagine the ship herself, with every pulse and artery of her huge body swollen and bursting under this mal-treatment, sworn to go on or die. Imagine the wind howling, the sea roaring, the rain beating: all in furious array against her. Picture the sky both dark and wild, and the clouds, in fearful sympathy with the waves, making another ocean in the air. Add to all this, the clattering on deck and down below; the tread of hurried feet; the loud hoarse shouts of seamen; the gurgling in and out of water through the scuppers; with, every now and then, the striking of a heavy sea upon the planks above, with the deep, dead, heavy sound of thunder heard within a vault;—and there is the head-wind of that January morning.

I say nothing of what may be called the domestic noises of the ship: such as the breaking of glass and crockery, the tumbling down of stewards, the gambols, overhead, of loose casks and truant dozens of bottled porter, and the very remarkable and far from exhilarating sounds raised in their various state-rooms by the seventy passengers who were too ill to get up to breakfast. I say nothing of them: for although I lay listening to this concert for three or four days, I don't think I heard it for more than a quarter of a minute, at the expiration of which term, I lay down again, excessively sea-sick.

Not sea-sick be it understood, in the ordinary acceptation of the term: I wish I had been: but in a form which I have never seen or heard described, though I have no doubt it is very common. I lay there, all the day long, quite coolly and contentedly; with no sense of weariness, with no desire to get up, or get better, or take the air; with no curiosity, or care, or regret, of any sort or degree, saving that I think I can remember, in this universal indifference having a kind of lazy joy—of fiendish delight, if anything so lethargic can be dignified with the title—in the fact of my wife being too ill to talk to me. If I may be allowed to illustrate my state of mind by such an example, I should say that I was exactly in the condition of the elder Mr. Willet, after the incursion of the rioters into his bar at Chigwell. Nothing would have suprised me. If, in the momentary illumination of any ray of intelligence that may have come upon me in the way of thoughts of Home, a goblin postman, with a scarlet coat and bell, had come into that little kennel before me, broad awake in broad day, and, apoligising for being damp through walking in the sea, had handed me a letter directed to myself, in familiar characters, I am certain I should not have felt one atom of astonishment: I should have been perfectly satisfied. If Neptune himself had walked in, with a toasted shark on his trident, I should have looked upon the event as one of the very commonest everyday occurrences.

Once—once—I found myself on deck. I don't know how I got there, or what possessed me to go there, but there I was; and completely dressed too, with a huge pea-coat on, and a pair of boots such as no weak man in his senses could ever have got into. I found myself standing, when a gleam of consciousness came upon me, holding on to something. I don't know what. I think it was the boatswain: or it may have been the pump: or possibly the cow. I can't say how long I had been there; whether a day or a minute. I recollect trying to think about something (about anything in the whole wide world, I was not particular) without the smallest effect. I could not even make out which was the sea, and which the sky, for the horizon seemed drunk, and was flying wildly about in all directions. Even in that incapable state, however, I recognized the lazy gentleman standing before me: nautically clad in a suit of shaggy blue, with an oilskin hat. But I was too imbecile, although I knew it to be he, to separate him from his dress; and tried to call him, I remember, *Pilot*. After another interval of total unconsciousness, I found he had gone, and recognised another figure in its place. It seemed to wave and fluctuate before me as though I saw it reflected in an unsteady looking-glass; but I knew it for the captain; and such was the cheerful influence of his face, that I tried to smile: yes, even then I tried to smile. I saw by his gesture that he addressed me; but it was a long time before I could make out that he remonstrated against my standing up to my knees in water—as I was; of course, I don't know why. I tried to thank him, but couldn't. I could only point to my boots—or wherever I supposed my boots to be—and say in a plaintive voice, 'Cork soles': at the same time endeavouring, I am told, to sit down in the pool. Finding that I was quite insensible, and for the time a maniac, he humanely conducted me below.

There I remained until I got better: suffering, whenever I was recommended to eat anything, an amount of anguish only second to that which is said to be endured by the apparently drowned, in the process of restoration to life. One gentleman on board had a letter of introduction to me from a mutual friend in London. He sent it below with his card, on the morning of the head-wind; and I was long troubled with the idea that he might be up, and well, and a hundred times a day expecting me to call upon him in the saloon. I imagined him one of those cast-iron images—I will not call them men—who ask, with red faces, and lusty voices, what sea-sickness means, and whether it really is as bad as it is represented to be. This was very torturing indeed; and I don't think I ever felt such perfect gratification and gratitude of heart, as I did when I heard from the ship's doctor that he had been obliged to put a large mustard poultice on this very gentleman's stomach. I date my recovery from the receipt of that intelligence.

It was materially assisted though, I have no doubt, by a heavy gale of wind, which came slowly up at sunset, when we were about ten days out, and raged with gradually increasing fury until morning, saving that it lulled for an hour a little before midnight. There was something in the unnatural repose of that hour, and in the after gathering of the storm, so inconceivably awful and tremendous, that its bursting into full violence was almost a relief.

The labouring of the ship in the troubled sea on this night I shall never forget. 'Will it ever be worse than this?' was a question I had often heard asked, when everything was sliding and bumping about, and when it certainly did seem difficult to comprehend the possibility of anything afloat being more disturbed, without toppling over and going down. But what the agitation of a steam-vessel is, on a bad winter's night in the wild Atlantic, it is impossible for the most vivid imagination to conceive. To say that she is flung down on her side in the waves, with her masts dipping into them, and that, springing up again, she rolls over on the other side, until a heavy sea strikes her with the noise of a hundred great guns, and hurls her back—that she stops, and staggers, and shivers, as though stunned, and then, with a violent throbbing at her heart, darts onward like a monster goaded into madness, to be beaten down, and battered, and crushed, and leaped on by the angry sea—that thunder, lightning, hail, and rain, and wind, are all in fierce contention for the mastery—that every plank has its groan, every nail its shriek, and every drop of water in the great ocean its howling voice—is nothing. To say that all is grand, and all appalling and horrible in the last degree, is nothing. Words cannot express it. Thoughts cannot convey it. Only a dream can call it up again, in all its fury, rage, and passion.

And yet, in the very midst of these terrors, I was placed in a situation so exquisitely ridiculous, that even then I had as strong a sense of its absurdity as I have now, and could no more help laughing than I can at any other comical incident, happening under circumstances the most favourable to its enjoyment. About midnight we shipped a sea, which forced its way through the sky-

lights, burst open the doors above, and came raging and roaring
down into the ladies' cabin, to the unspeakable consternation of
my wife and a little Scotch lady—who, by the way, had previously sent a message to the captain by the stewardess, request-
ing him, with her compliments, to have a steel conductor immediately attached to the top of every mast, and to the chimney,
in order that the ship might not be struck by lightning. They
and the handmaid before-mentioned, being in such ecstasies of
fear that I scarcely knew what to do with them, I naturally
bethought myself of some restorative or comfortable cordial;
and nothing better occurring to me, at the moment, than hot
brandy-and-water, I procured a tumblerfull without delay. It
being impossible to stand or sit without holding on, they were
all heaped together in one corner of a long sofa—a fixture extending entirely across the cabin—where they clung to each
other in momentary expectation of being drowned. When I
approached this place with my specific, and was about to admin-
ister it with many consolatory expressions to the nearest sufferer,
what was my dismay to see them all roll slowly down to the other
end! And when I staggered to that end, and held out the glass
once more, how immensely baffled were my good intentions by
the ship giving another lurch, and their all rolling back again! I
suppose I dodged them up and down this sofa for at least a
quarter of an hour, without reaching them once; and by the
time I did catch them, the brandy-and-water was diminished,
by constant spilling, to a teaspoonful. To complete the group,
it is necessary to recognise in this disconcerted dodger, an individual very pale from sea-sickness, who had shaved his beard
and brushed his hair, last, at Liverpool: and whose only article
of dress (linen not included) were a pair of dreadnought
trousers; a blue jacket, formerly admired upon the Thames at
Richmond; no stockings; and one slipper.

Of the outrageous antics performed by that ship next morning; which made bed a practical joke, and getting up, by process
short of falling out, an impossibility; I say nothing. But anything like the utter dreariness and desolation that met my eyes
when I literally 'tumbled up' on deck at noon, I never saw.
Ocean and sky were all of one dull, heavy, uniform, lead colour.
There was no extent of prospect even over the dreary waste that
lay around us, for the sea ran high, and the horizon encompassed
us like a large black hoop. Viewed from the air, or some tall
bluff on shore, it would have been imposing and stupendous,
no doubt; but seen from the wet and rolling decks, it only im-

pressed one giddily and painfully. In the gale of last night the life-boat had been crushed by one blow of the sea like a walnut-shell; and there it hung dangling in the air: a mere faggot of crazy boards. The planking of the paddle-boxes had been torn sheer away. The wheels were exposed and bare: and they whirled and dashed their spray about the decks at random. Chimney, white with crusted salt; topmasts struck; stormsails set; rigging all knotted, tangled, wet, and drooping: a gloomier picture it would be hard to look upon.

I was now comfortably established by courtesy in the ladies' cabin, where, besides ourselves, there were only four other passengers. First, the little Scotch lady before mentioned, on her way to join her husband at New York, who had settled there three years before. Secondly and thirdly, an honest young Yorkshireman, connected with some American house; domiciled in that same city, and carrying thither his beautiful young wife to whom he had been married but a fortnight, and who was the fairest specimen of a comely English country girl I have ever seen. Fourthly, fifthly, and lastly, another couple: newly married too, if one might judge from the endearments they frequently interchanged: of whom I know no more than that they were rather a mysterious, run-away kind of couple; that the lady had great personal attractions also; and that the gentleman carried more guns with him than Robinson Crusoe, wore a shooting-coat, and had two great dogs on board. On further consideration, I remember that he tired hot roast pig and bottled ale as a cure for sea-sickness; and that he took these remedies (usually in bed) day after day, with astonishing perseverance. I may add, for the information of the curious, that they decidedly failed.

The weather continuing obstinately and almost unprecedently bad, we usually straggled into this cabin, more or less faint and miserable, about an hour before noon, and lay down on the sofas to recover; during which interval, the captain would look in to communicate the state of the wind, the moral certainty of its changing to-morrow (the weather is always going to improve to-morrow, at sea), the vessel's rate of sailing, and so forth. Observations there were none to tell us of, for there was no sun to take them by. But a description of one day will serve for all the rest. Here it is.

The captain being gone, we compose ourselves to read, if the place be light enough; and if not, we doze and talk alternately. At one, a bell rings, and the stewardess comes down with a steaming dish of baked potatoes, and another of roasted apples; and plates of pig's face, cold ham, salt beef; or perhaps a smoking mess of rare hot collops. We fall to upon these dainties; eat as much as we can (we have great appetites now); and are as long as possible about it. If the fire will burn (it *will* sometimes) we are pretty cheerful. If it won't, we all remark to each other that it's very cold, rub our hands, cover ourselves with coats and cloaks, and lie down again to doze, talk, and read (provided as aforesaid), until dinner-time. At five, another bell rings, and the stewardess reappears with another dish of potatoes—boiled this time—and store of hot meat of various kinds: not forgetting the roast pig, to be taken medicinally. We sit down at table again (rather more cheerfully than before); prolong the meal with a rather mouldy dessert of apples, grapes, and oranges; and drink our wine and brandy-and-water. The bottles and glasses are still upon the table, and the oranges and so forth are rolling about according to their fancy and the ship's way, when the doctor comes down, by special nightly invitation, to join our evening rubber: immediately on whose arrival we make a party at whist, and as it is a rough night and the cards will not lie on the cloth, we put the tricks in our pockets as we take them. At whist we remain with exemplary gravity (deducting a short time for tea and toast) until eleven o'clock, or thereabouts; when the captain comes down again, in a sou'-wester hat tied under his chin, and a pilot-coat; making the ground wet where he stands. By this time the card-playing is over, and the bottles and glasses are again upon the table; and after an hour's pleasant conversation about the ship, the passengers, and things in general, the captain (who never goes to bed, and is never out of humour) turns up his coat collar for the deck again; shakes hands all around; and goes laughing out into the weather as merrily as to a birthday party.

As to daily news, there is no dearth of that commodity. This passenger is reported to have lost fourteen pounds at Vingt-et-un in the saloon yesterday; and that passenger drinks his bottle of champagne every day, and how he does it (being only a clerk), nobody knows. The head engineer has distinctly said that there never was such times—meaning weather—and four good hands are ill, and have given in, dead beat. Several berths are full of water, and all the cabins are leaky. The ship's cook, secretly swigging damaged whiskey, has been found drunk; and has been played upon by the fire-engine until quite sober. All the stewards have fallen downstairs at various dinner-times, and go about with plasters in various places. The baker is ill, and so is the pastry cook. A new man, horribly indisposed, has been required to fill the place of the latter officer; and has been propped and jammed up with empty casks in a little house upon deck, and commanded to roll out pie-crust, which he protests (being highly bilious) it is death to him to look at. News! A dozen murders on shore would lack the interest of these slight incidents at sea.

Divided between our rubber and such topics as these, we were running (as we thought) into Halifax Harbour, on the fifteenth night, with little wind and a bright moon—indeed, we had made the Light at its outer entrance, and put the pilot in charge—when suddenly the ship struck upon a bank of mud. An immediate rush on deck took place of course; the sides were crowded in an instant; and for a few minutes we were in as lively as state of confusion as the greatest lover of disorder would desire to see. The passengers, and guns, and water-casks, and other heavy matters, being all huddled together aft, however, to lighten her in the head, she was soon got off; and after some driving on towards an uncomfortable line of objects (whose vicinity had been announced very early in the disaster by a loud cry of 'Breakers a-head!') and much backing of paddles and heaving of the lead into a constantly decreasing depth of water, we dropped anchor in a strange outlandish-looking nook which nobody on board could recognise, although there was land all about us, and so close that we could plainly see the waving branches of the trees.

It was strange enough, in the silence of midnight, and the dead stillness that seemed to be created by the sudden and unexpected stoppage of the engine which had been clanking and blasting in our ears incessantly for so many days, to watch the look of blank astonishment expressed in every face: beginning with the officers, tracing it through all the passengers, and descending to the very stokers and furnacemen, who emerged from below, one by one, and clustered together in a smoky group about the hatchway of the engine-room, comparing notes in whispers. After throwing up a few rockets and firing signal guns in the hope of being hailed from the land, or at least of seeing a light—but without any other sight or sound presenting itself—it was determined to send a boat on shore. It was amusing to observe how very kind some of the passengers were, in volunteering to go ashore in this same boat: for the general good, of course:

not by any means because they thought the ship in an unsafe position, or contemplated the possibility of her heeling over in case the tide were running out. Nor was it less amusing to remark how desperately unpopular the poor pilot became in one short minute. He had had his passage out from Liverpool, and during the whole voyage had been quite a notorious character, as a teller of anecdotes and cracker of jokes. Yet here were the very men who had laughed the loudest at his jests, now flourishing their fists in his face, loading him with imprecations, and defying him to his teeth as a villain!

The boat soon shoved off, with a lantern and sundry blue lights on board; and in less than an hour returned; the officer in command bringing with him a tolerably tall young tree, which he had plucked up by the roots, to satisfy certain distrustful passengers whose minds misgave them that they were to be imposed upon and shipwrecked, and who would on no other terms believe that he had been ashore, or had done anything but fraudulently row a little way into the mist, specially to deceive them and compass their deaths. Our captain had foreseen from the first that we must be in a place called the Eastern passage; and so we were. It was about the last place in the world in which we had any business or reason to be, but a sudden fog, and some error on the pilot's part, were the cause. We were surrounded by banks, and rocks, and shoals of all kinds, but had happily drifted, it seemed, upon the only safe speck that was to be found thereabouts. Eased by this report, and by the assurance that the tide was past the ebb, we turned in at three o'clock in the morning.

I was dressing about half-past nine next day, when the noise above hurried me on deck. When I had left it over-night, it was dark, foggy, and damp, and there were bleak hills all round us. Now, we were gliding down a smooth, broad stream, at the rate of eleven miles an hour: our colours flying gaily: our crew rigged out in their smartest clothes; our officers in uniform again; the sun shining as on a brilliant April day in England; the land stretched out on either side, streaked with light patches of snow; white wooden houses; people at their doors; telegraphs working; flags hoisted; wharfs appearing; ships; quays crowded with people; distant noises; shouts; men and boys running down steep places towards the pier; all more bright and gay and fresh to our unused eyes than words can paint them. We came to a wharf, paved with uplifted faces; got alongside, and were made fast, after some shouting and straining of cables; darted, a score of us along the gangway, almost as soon as it was thrust out to meet us, and before it had reached the ship—and leaped upon the firm glad earth again!

I suppose this Halifax would have appeared an Elysium, though it had been a curiosity of ugly dulness. But I carried away with me a most pleasant impression of the town and its inhabitants, and have preserved it to this hour. Nor was it without regret that I came home, without having found an opportunity of returning thither, and once more shaking hands with the friends I made that day.

It happened to be the opening of the Legislative Council and General Assembly, at which ceremonial the forms observed on the commencement of a new Session of Parliament in England were so closely copied, and so gravely presented on a small scale, that it was like looking at Westminster through the wrong end of a telescope. The governor, as her Majesty's representative, delivered what may be called the Speech from the Throne. He said what he had to say manfully and well. The military band outside the building struck up 'God save the Queen' with grea: vigour before his Excellency had quite finished; the people shouted; the in's rubbed their hands; the out's shook their heads; the Government party said there never was such a good speech; the Opposition declared there never was such a bad one; the Speaker and members of the House of Assembly withdrew from the bar to say a great deal among themselves and do a little; and, in short, everything went on, and promised to go on, just as it does at home upon the like occasions.

The town is built on the side of a hill, the highest point being commanded by a strong fortress, not yet quite finished. Several streets of good breadth and appearance extend from its summit to the waterside, and are intersected by cross streets running parallel with the river. The houses are chiefly of wood. The market is abundantly supplied; and provisions are exceedingly cheap. The weather being unusually mild at that time for the season of the year, there was no sleighing: but there were plenty of those vehicles in yards and by-places, and some of them, from the gorgeous quality of their decorations, might have 'gone on' without alteration as triumphal cars in a melodrama at Astley's. The day was uncommonly fine; the air bracing and healthful; the whole aspect of the town cheerful, thriving, and industrious.

We lay there seven hours, to deliver and exchange the mails. At length. having collected all our bags and all our passengers (including two or three choice spirits, who, having indulged too freely in oysters and champagne, were found lying insensible on their backs in unfrequented streets), the engines were again put in motion, and we stood off for Boston.

Encountering squally weather again in the Bay of Fundy, we tumbled and rolled about as usual all that night and all next day. On the next afternoon, that is to say, on Saturday, the twenty-second of January, an American pilot-boat came alongside, and soon afterwards the Britannia steam-packet, from Liverpool, eighteen days out, was telegraphed at Boston.

The indescribable interest with which I strained my eyes, as the first patches of American soil peeped like molehills from the green sea, and followed them, as they swelled, by slow and almost imperceptible degrees, into a continuous line of coast, can hardly be exaggerated. A sharp keen wind blew dead against us; a hard frost prevailed on shore; and the cold was most severe. Yet the air was so intensely clear, and dry, and bright, that the temperature was not only endurable, but delicious.

How I remained on deck, staring about me, until we came alongside the dock, and how, though I had had as many eyes as Argus, I should have had them all wide open, and all employed on new objects—are topics which I will not prolong this chapter to discuss. Neither will I more than hint at my foreigner-like mistake, in supposing that a party of most active persons, who scrambled on board at the peril of their lives as we approached the wharf, were newsmen, answering to that industrious class at home; whereas, despite the leathern wallets of news slung about the necks of some, and the broad sheets in the hands of all, they were Editors, who boarded ships in person (as one gentleman in a worsted comforter informed me), 'because they liked the excitement of it.' Suffice it in this place to say, that one of these invaders, with a ready courtesy for which I thank him here most gratefully, went on before to order rooms at the hotel; and that when I followed, as I soon did, I found myself rolling through the long passages with an involuntary imitation of the gait of Mr. T. P. Cooke, in a new nautical melodrama.

'Dinner, if you please,' said I to the waiter.

'When?' said the waiter.

'As quick as possible,' said I.

'Right away?' said the waiter.

After a moment's hesitation, I answered 'No,' at hazard.

'*Not* right away?' cried the waiter, with an amount of surprise that made me start.

I looked at him doubtfully, and returned, 'No; I would rather have it in this private room. I like it very much.'

At this, I really thought the waiter must have gone out of his mind: as I believe he would have done, but for the interposition of another man, who whispered in his ear, 'Directly.'

'Well! and that's a fact!' said the waiter, looking helplessly at me: 'Right away.'

I saw now that 'Right away' and 'Directly' were one and the same thing. So I reversed my previous answer, and sat down to dinner in ten minutes afterwards; and a capital dinner it was.

The hotel (a very excellent one) is called the Tremont House. It has more galleries, colonnades, piazzas, and passages than I can remember, or the reader would believe.

CHAPTER III

BOSTON

IN all the public establishments of America, the utmost courtesy prevails. Most of our Departments are susceptible of considerable improvement in this respect, but the Custom-house above all others would do well to take example from the United States and render itself somewhat less odious and offensive to foreigners. The servile rapacity of the French officials is sufficiently contemptible; but there is a surly boorish incivility about our men, alike disgusting to all persons who fall into their hands, and discreditable to the nation that keeps such ill-conditioned curs snarling about its gates.

When I landed in America, I could not help being strongly impressed with the contrast their Custom-house presented, and the attention, politeness, and good humour with which its officers discharged their duty.

As we did not land at Boston, in consequence of some detention at the wharf, until after dark, I received my first impressions of the city in walking down to the Custom-house on the morning after our arrival, which was Sunday. I am afraid to say, by the way, how many offers of pews and seats in church for that morning were made to us, by formal note of invitation, before we had half finished our first dinner in America, but if

I may be allowed to make a moderate guess, without going into nicer calculation, I should say that at least as many sittings were proffered us, as would have accommodated a score or two of grown-up families. The number of creeds and forms of religion to which the pleasure of our company was requested, was in very fair proportion.

Not being able, in the absence of any change of clothes, to go to church that day, we were compelled to decline these kindnesses, one and all; and I was reluctantly obliged to forego the delight of hearing Dr. Channing, who happened to preach that morning for the first time in a very long interval. I mention the name of this distinguished and accomplished man (with whom I soon afterwards had the pleasure of becoming personally acquainted), that I may have the gratification of recording my humble tribute of admiration and respect for his high abilities and character; and for the bold philanthropy with which he has ever opposed himself to that most hideous blot and foul disgrace—Slavery.

To return to Boston. When I got into the streets upon this Sunday morning, the air was so clear, the houses were so bright and gay; the signboards were painted in such gaudy colours; the gilded letters were so very golden; the bricks were so very red, the stone was so very white, the blinds and area railings were so very green, the knobs and plates upon the street doors so marvellously bright and twinkling; and all so slight and unsubstantial in appearance—that every thoroughfare in the city looked exactly like a scene in a pantomime. It rarely happens in the business streets that a tradesman, if I may venture to call anybody a tradesman, where everybody is a merchant, resides above his store; so that many occupations are often carried on in one house, and the whole front is covered with boards and inscriptions. As I walked along, I kept glancing up at these boards, confidently expecting to see a few of them change into something; and I never turned a corner suddenly without looking out for the clown and pantaloon, who, I had no doubt, were hiding in a doorway or behind some pillar close at hand. As to Harlequin and Columbine, I discovered immediately that they lodged (they are always looking after lodgings in a pantomime) at a very small clock-maker's one story high, near the hotel; which, in addition to various symbols and devices, almost covering the whole front, had a great dial hanging out—to be jumped through, of course.

The suburbs are, if possible, even more unsubstantial-looking than the city. The white wooden houses (so white that it makes one wink to look at them), with their green jalousie blinds, are so sprinkled and dropped about in all directions, without seeming to have any root at all in the ground; and the small churches and chapels are so prim, and bright, and highly varnished; that I almost believed the whole affair could be taken up piecemeal like a child's toy, and crammed into a little box.

The city is a beautiful one, and cannot fail, I should imagine, to impress all strangers very favourably. The private dwelling-houses are, for the most part, large and elegant; the shops extremely good; and the public buildings handsome. The State House is built upon the summit of a hill, which rises gradually at first, and afterwards by a steep ascent, almost from the water's edge. In front is a green enclosure, called the Common. The site is beautiful: and from the top there is a charming panoramic view of the whole town and neighborhood. In addition to a variety of commodious offices, it contains two handsome chambers; in one the House of Representatives of the State hold their meetings: in the other, the Senate. Such proceedings as I saw here, were conducted with perfect gravity and decorum; and were certainly calculated to inspire attention and respect.

There is no doubt that much of the intellectual refinement and superiority of Boston, is referable to the quiet influence of the University of Cambridge, which is within three or four miles of the city. The resident professors at that university are gentlemen of learning and varied attainments; and are, without one exception that I can call to mind, men who would shed a grace upon, and do honour to, any society in the civilised world. Many of the resident gentry in Boston and its neighbourhood, and I think I am not mistaken in adding, a large majority of those who are attached to the liberal professions there, have been educated at this same school. Whatever the defects of American universities may be, they disseminate no prejudices; rear no bigots; dig up the buried ashes of no old superstitions; never interpose between the people and their improvement; exclude no man because of his religious opinions; above all, in their whole course of study and instruction, recognise a world, and a broad one too, lying beyond the college walls.

It was a source of inexpressible pleasure to me to observe the almost imperceptible, but not less certain effect, wrought by this institution among the small community of Boston; and

to note at every turn the humanising tastes and desires it has en-
gendered; the affectionate friendships to which it has given
rise; the amount of vanity and prejudice it has dispelled. The
golden calf they worship at Boston is a pigmy compared with
the giant effigies set up in other parts of that vast counting-house
which lies beyond the Atlantic; and the almighty dollar sinks
into something comparatively insignificant, amidst a whole
Pantheon of better gods.

Above all, I sincerely believe that the public institutions and
charities of this capital of Massachusetts are as nearly perfect,
as the most considerate wisdom, benevolence, and humanity,
can make them. I never in my life was more affected by the
contemplation of happiness, under circumstances of privation
and bereavement, than in my visits to these establishments.

It is a great pleasant feature of all such institutions in
America, that they are either supported by the State or assisted
by the State; or (in the event of their not needing its helping
hand) that they act in concert with it, and are emphatically the
people's. I cannot but think, with a view to the principle and
its tendency to elevate or depress the character of the industrious
classes, that a Public Charity is immeasurably better than a
Private Foundation, no matter how munificiently the latter may
be endowed. In our own country, where it has not, until within
these later days, been a very popular fashion with governments
to display any extraordinary regard for the great mass of the
people or to recognise their existence as improvable creatures,
private charities, unexampled in the history of the earth, have
arisen, to do an uncalculable amount of good among the destitute and afflicted. But the government of the country, having
neither act nor part in them, is not in the receipt of any portion
of the gratitude they inspire; and, offering very little shelter
or relief beyond that which is to be found in the workhouse and
the jail, has come, not unnaturally, to be looked upon by the
poor rather as a stern master, quick to correct and punish, than
a kind protector, merciful and vigilant in their hour of need.

The maxim that out of evil cometh good, is strongly illustrated
by these establishments at home; as the records of the Preroga-
tive Office in Doctors' Commons can abundantly prove. Some
immensely rich old gentleman or lady, surrounded by needy
relatives, makes, upon a low average, a will a week. The old
gentleman or lady, never very remarkable in the best times for
good temper, is full of aches and pains from head to foot; full
of fancies and caprices; full of spleen, distrust, suspicion, and

dislike. To cancel old wills, and invent new ones, is at last the sole business of such a testator's existence; and relations and friends (some of whom have been bred up distinctly to inherit a large share of the property, and have been, from their cradles, specially disqualified from devoting themselves to any useful pursuit, on that account) are so often and so unexpectedly and summarily cut off, and re-instated, and cut off again, that the whole family, down to the remotest cousin, is kept in a perpetual fever. At length it becomes plain that the old lady or gentleman has not long to live; and the plainer this becomes, the more clearly the old lady or gentleman perceives that everybody is in a conspiracy against their poor old dying relative; wherefore the old lady or gentleman makes another last will—positively the last this time—conceals the same in a china tea-pot, and expires next day. Then it turns out, that the whole of the real and personal estate is divided between half a dozen charities; and that the dead and gone testator has in pure spite helped to do a great deal of good, at the cost of an immense amount of evil passion and misery.

The Perkins Institution and Massachusetts Asylum for the Blind, at Boston, is superintended by a body of trustees who make an annual report to the corporation. The indigent blind of that state are admitted gratuitously. Those from the adjoining state of Connecticut, or from the states of Maine, Vermont, or New Hampshire, are admitted by a warrant from the state to which they respectively belong; or, failing that, must find security among their friends, for the payment of about twenty pounds English for their first year's board and instruction. and ten for the second. 'After the first year,' say the trustees. 'an account current will be opened with each pupil; he will be charged with the actual cost of his board, which will not exceed two dollars per week'; a trifle more than eight shillings English; and he will be credited with the amount paid for him by the state, or by his friends; also with his earnings over and above the cost of the stock which he uses; so that all his earnings over one dollar per week will be his own. By the third year it will be known whether his earnings will more than pay the actual cost of his board; if they should, he will have it at his option to remain and receive his earnings, or not. Those who prove unable to earn their own livelihood will not be retained; as it is not desirable to convert the establishment into an almshouse, or to retain any but working bees in the hive. Those who by physical or mental imbecility are disqualified from work, are thereby disqualified from being members of an industrious community; and they can be better provided for in establishments fitted for the infirm.

I went to see this place one very fine winter morning: an Italian sky above, and the air so clear and bright on every side, that even my eyes, which are none of the best, could follow the minute lines and scraps of tracery in distant buildings. Like most other public institutions in America, of the same class, it stands a mile or two without the town, in a cheerful healthy spot; and is an airy, spacious, handsome edifice. It is built upon a height, commanding the harbour. When I paused for a moment at the door, and marked how fresh and free the whole scene was—what sparkling bubbles glanced upon the waves, and welled up every moment to the surface, as though the world below, like that above, were radiant with the bright day, and gushing over in its fulness of light: when I gazed from sail to sail away upon a ship at sea, a tiny speck of shining white, the only cloud upon the still, deep, distant blue—and, turning, saw a blind boy with his sightless face addressed that way, as though he too had some sense within him of the glorious distance: I felt a kind of sorrow that the place should be so very light, and a strange wish that for his sake it were darker. It was but momentary, of course, and a mere fancy, but I felt it keenly for all that.

The children were at their daily tasks in different rooms, except a few who were already dismissed, and were at play. Here, as in many institutions, no uniform is worn; and I was very glad of it, for two reasons. Firstly, because I am sure that nothing but senseless custom and want of thought would reconcile us to the liveries and badges we are so fond of at home. Secondly, because the absence of these things presents each child to the visitor in his or her own proper character, with its individuality unimpaired; not lost in a dull, ugly, monotonous repetition of the same unmeaning garb: which is really an important consideration. The wisdom of encouraging a little harmless pride in personal appearance even among the blind, or the whimsical absurdity of considering charity and leather breeches inseparable companions, as we do, require no comment.

Good order, cleanliness, and comfort, pervaded every corner of the building. The various classes, who were gathered round their teachers, answered the questions put to them with readiness and intelligence, and in a spirit of cheerful contest for precedence which pleased me very much. Those who were at play, were gleesome and noisy as other children. More spiritual and affectionate friendships appeared to exist among them, than would be found among other young persons suffering under no deprivation; but this I expected and was prepared to find. It is a part of the great scheme of Heaven's merciful consideration for the afflicted.

In a portion of the building, set apart for that purpose, are workshops for blind persons whose education is finished, and who have acquired a trade, but who cannot pursue it in an ordinary manufactory because of their deprivation. Several people were at work here; making brushes, mattresses, and so forth; and the cheerfulness, industry, and good order discernible in every other part of the building, extended to this department also.

On the ringing of a bell, the pupils all repaired, without any guide or leader, to a spacious music-hall, where they took their seats in an orchestra erected for that purpose, and listened with manifest delight to a voluntary on the organ, played by one of themselves. At its conclusion, the performer, a boy of nineteen or twenty, gave place to a girl; and to her accompaniment they sang a hymn, and afterwards a sort of chorus. It was very sad to look upon and hear them, happy though their condition unquestionably was; and I saw that one blind girl, who (being for the time deprived of the use of her limbs, by illness) sat close beside me with her face towards them, wept silently the while she listened.

It is strange to watch the faces of the blind, and see how free they are from all concealment of what is passing in their thoughts; observing which, a man with eyes may blush to contemplate the mask he wears. Allowing for one shade of anxious expression which is never absent from their countenances, and the like of which we may readily detect in our own faces if we try to feel our way in the dark, every idea, as it rises within them, is expressed with the lightning's speed and nature's truth. If the company at a rout, or drawing-room at court, could only for one time be as unconscious of the eyes upon them as blind men and women are, what secrets would come out, and what a worker of hypocrisy this sight, the loss of which we so much pity, would appear to be!

The thought occurred to me as I sat down in another room, before a girl, blind, deaf, and dumb; destitute of smell! and nearly so of taste; before a fair young creature with every human faculty, and hope, and power of goodness and affection, inclosed within her delicate frame, and but one outward sense—the sense of touch. There she was, before me; built up, as it were, in a marble cell, impervious to any ray of light, or particle of sound; with her poor white hand peeping through a chink in the wall, beckoning to some good man for help, that an Immortal soul might be awakened.

Long before I looked upon her, the help had come. Her face was radiant with intelligence and pleasure. Her hair, braided by her own hands, was bound about a head, whose intellectual capacity and development were beautifully expressed in its graceful outline, and its broad open brow; her dress, arranged by herself, was a pattern of neatness and simplicity; the work she had knitted, lay beside her; her writing-book was on the desk she leaned upon.—From the mournful ruin of such bereavement, there had slowly risen up this gentle, tender, guileless, grateful-hearted being.

Like other inmates of that house, she had a green ribbon bound round her eyelids. A doll she had dressed lay near upon the ground. I took it up, and saw that she had made a green fillet such as she wore herself, and fastened it about its mimic eyes.

She was seated in a little enclosure, made by school-desks and forms, writing her daily journal. But soon finishing this pursuit, she engaged in an animated communication with a teacher who sat beside her. This was a favourite mistress with the poor pupil. If she could see the face of her fair instructress, she would not love her less, I am sure.

I have extracted a few disjointed fragments of her history, from an account, written by that one man who has made her what she is. It is a very beautiful and touching narrative; and I wish I could present it entire.

Her name is Laura Bridgman. 'She was born in Hanover, New Hampshire, on the twenty-first day of December, 1829. She is described as having been a very sprightly and pretty infant, with bright blue eyes. She was, however, so puny and feeble until she was a year and a half old, that her parents hardly hoped to rear her. She was subject to severe fits, which seemed to rack her frame almost beyond her power of endurance: and life was held by the feeblest tenure: but when a year and a half old, she seemed to rally; the dangerous symptoms subsided; and at twenty months old, she was perfectly well.

'Then her mental powers, hitherto stinted in their growth, rapidly developed themselves; and during the four months of

health which she enjoyed, she appears (making due allowance
for a fond mother's account) to have displayed a considerable
degree of intelligence.

'But suddenly she sickened again; her disease raged with
great violence during five weeks, when her eyes and ears were
inflamed, suppurated, and their contents were discharged. But
though sight and hearing were gone for ever, the poor child's
sufferings were not ended. The fever raged during seven weeks;
for five months she was kept in bed in a darkened room; it was
a year before she could walk unsupported, and two years before
she could sit up all day. It was now observed that her sense
of smell was almost entirely destroyed; and, consequently, that
her taste was much blunted.

'It was not until four years of age that the poor child's bodily
health seemed restored, and she was able to enter upon her
apprenticeship of life and the world.

'But what a situation was hers! The darkness and the silence
of the tomb were around her: no mother's smile called forth
her answering smile, no father's voice taught her to imitate his
sounds:—they, brothers and sisters, were but forms of matter
which resisted her touch, but which differed not from the furniture of the house, save in warmth, and in the power of locomo-
tion; and not even in these respects from the dog and the cat.

'But the immortal spirit which had been implanted within her
could not die, nor be maimed nor mutilated; and though most
of its avenues of communication with the world were cut off, it
began to manifest itself through the others. As soon as she
could walk, she began to explore the room, and then the house;
she became familiar with the form, density, weight, and heat,
of every article she could lay her hands upon. She followed her
mother, and felt her hands and arms, as she was occupied about
the house; and her disposition to imitate, led her to repeat everything herself. She even learned to sew a little, and to knit.'

The reader will scarcely need to be told, however, that the opportunities of communicating with her, were very, very limited; and that the moral effects of her wretched state soon began
to appear. Those who cannot be enlightened by reason, can only
be controlled by force; and this, coupled with her great priva-
tions, must soon have reduced her to a worse condition than that
of the beasts that perish, but for timely and unhoped-for aid.

'At this time, I was so fortunate as to hear of the child, and
immediately hastened to Hanover to see her. I found her with
a well-formed figure; a strongly-marked, nervous-sanguine tem-

perament; a large and beautifully-shaped head; and the whole system in healthy action. The parents were easily induced to consent to her coming to Boston, and on the 4th of October, 1837, they brought her to the Institution.

'For a while, she was much bewildered; and after waiting about two weeks, until she became acquainted with her new locality, and somewhat familiar with the inmates, the attempt was made to give her knowledge of arbitrary signs, by which she could interchange thoughts with others.

'There was one of two ways to be adapted: either to go on to build up a language of signs on the basis of the natural language which she had already commenced herself, or to teach her the purely arbitrary language in common use: that is, to give her a sign for every individual thing, or to give her a knowledge of letters by combination of which she might express her idea of the existence, and the mode and condition of existence, of anything. The former would have been easy, but very ineffectual; the latter seemed very difficult, but, if accomplished, very effectual. I determined therefore to try the latter.

'The first experiments were made by taking articles in common use, such as knives, forks, spoons, keys, etc., and pasting upon them labels with their names printed in raised letters. These she felt very carefully, and soon, of course, distinguished that the crooked lines *s p o o n,* differed as much from the crooked line *k e y,* as the spoon differed from the key in form.

'Then small detached labels, with the same words printed upon them, were put into her hands; and she soon observed that they were similar to the ones pasted on the articles. She showed her perception of this similarity by laying the label *k e y* upon the key, and the label *s p o o n* upon the spoon. She was encouraged here by the natural sign of approbation, patting on the head.

'The same process was then repeated with all the articles which she could handle; and she very easily learned to place the proper label upon them. It was evident, however, that the only intellectual exercise was that of imitation and memory. She recollected that the label *b o o k* was placed upon a book, and she repeated the process first from imitation, next from memory, with only the motive of love of approbation, but apparently without the intellectual perception of any relation between the things.

'After a while, instead of labels, the individual letters were

given to her on detached bits of paper: they were arranged side
by side so as to spell *b o o k*, *k e y*, etc.; then they were
mixed up in a heap and a sign was made for her to arrange them
herself so as to express the words *b o o k*, *k e y*, etc.; and
she did so.

'Hitherto, the process had been mechanical, and the success
about as great as teaching a very knowing dog a variety of
tricks. The poor child had sat in mute amazement, and patiently
imitated everything her teacher did; but now the truth began
to flash upon her: her intellect began to work: she perceived
that here was a way by which she could herself make up a
sign of anything that was in her own mind, and show it to another
mind; and at once her countenance lighted up with a human expression: it was no longer a dog, or parrot: it was an immortal
spirit, eagerly seizing upon a new link of union with other
spirits! I could almost fix upon the moment when this truth
dawned upon her mind, and spread its light to her countenance;
I saw that the great obstacle was overcome; and that hence-
forward, nothing but patient and persevering, but plain and
straightforward, efforts were to be used.

'The result thus far, is quickly related, and easily conceived;
but not so was the process; for many weeks of apparently unprofitable labour were passed before it was effected.

'When it was said above, that a sign was made, it was intended to say, that the action was performed by her teacher,
she feeling his hands, and then imitating the motion.

'The next step was to procure a set of metal types, with the
different letters of the alphabet cast upon their ends; also a
board, in which were square holes, into which holes she could
set the types; so that the letters on their ends could alone be
felt above the surface.

'Then, on any article being handed to her, for instance, a
pencil, or a watch, she would select the component letters, and
arrange them on her board, and read them with apparent
pleasure.

'She was exercised for several weeks in this way, until her vocabulary became extensive; and then the important step was
taken of teaching her how to represent the different letters by
the position of her fingers, instead of the cumbrous apparatus
of the board and types. She accomplished this speedily and
easily, for her intellect had begun to work in aid of her teacher,
and her progress was rapid.

'This was the period, about three months after she had commenced, that the first report of her case was made, in which it was stated that "she has just learned the manual alphabet, as used by the deaf mutes, and it is a subject of delight and wonder to see how rapidly, correctly, and eagerly, she goes on with her labours. Her teacher gives her a new object, for instance, a pencil, first lets her examine it, and get an idea of its use, then teaches her how to spell it by making the signs for the letters with her own fingers: the child grasps her hand, and feels her fingers, as the different letters are formed; she turns her head a little on one side like a person listening closely; her lips are apart; she seems scarcely to breathe; and her countenance, at first anxious, gradually changes to a smile, as she comprehends the lesson. She then holds up her tiny fingers, and spells the word in the manual alphabet; next, she takes her types and arranges her letters; and last, to make sure that she is right, she takes the whole of the types composing the words, and places them upon or in contact with the pencil, or whatever the object may be."

'The whole of the succeeding year was passed in gratifying her eager inquiries for the names of every object which she could possibly handle; in exercising her in the use of the manual alphabet; in extending in every possible way her knowledge of the physical relation of things; and in proper care of her health.

'At the end of the year a report of her case was made, from which the following is an extract.

' "It has been ascertained beyond the possibility of doubt, that she cannot see a ray of light, cannot hear the least sound, and never exercises her sense of smell, if she have any. Thus her mind dwells in darkness and stillness, as profound as that of a closed tomb at midnight. Of beautiful sights, and sweet sounds, and pleasant odours, she has no conception; nevertheless, she seems as happy and playful as a bird or a lamb; and the employment of her intellectual faculties, or the acquirement of a new idea, gives her a vivid pleasure, which is plainly marked in her expressive features. She never seems to repine, but has all the buoyancy and gaiety of childhood. She is fond of fun and frolic, and when playing with the rest of the children, her shrill laugh sounds loudest of the group.

' "When left alone, she seems very happy if she have her knitting or sewing, and will busy herself for hours; if she have no occupation, she evidently amuses herself by imaginary dialogues, or by recalling past impressions; she counts with her fingers, or spells out names of things which she has recently

learned, in the manual alphabet of the deaf mutes. In this
lonely self-communion she seems to reason, reflect, and argue; if
she spell a word wrong with the fingers of her right hand, she
instantly strikes it with her left, as her teacher does, in sign of
disapprobation; if right, then she pats herself upon the head,
and looks pleased. She sometimes purposely spells a word
wrong with the left hand, looks roguish for a moment and laughs,
and then with the right hand strikes the left, as if to correct it.

' "During the year she has attained great dexterity in the use
of the manual alphabet of the deaf mutes; and she spells out
the words and sentences which she knows, so fast and so deftly,
that only those accustomed to this language can follow with the
eye the rapid motions of her fingers.

' "But wonderful as is the rapidity with which she writes her
thoughts upon the air, still more so is the ease and accuracy
with which she reads the words thus written by another; grasping their hands in hers, and following every movement of their
fingers, as letter after letter conveys their meaning to her mind.
It is in this way that she converses with her blind playmates,
and nothing can more forcibly show the power of mind in
forcing matter to its purpose than a meeting between them.
For if great talent and skill are necessary for two pantomimes
to paint their thoughts and feelings by the movements of the
body, and the expression of the countenance, how much greater
the difficulty when darkness shrouds them both, and the one
can hear no sound.

' "When Laura is walking through a passage-way, with her
hands spread before her, she knows instantly every one she
meets, and passes them with a sign of recognition: but if it be a
girl of her own age, and especially if it be one of her favourites,
there is instantly a bright smile of recognition, a twining of
arms, a grasping of hands, and a swift telegraphing upon the
tiny fingers; whose rapid evolutions convey the thoughts and
feelings from the outposts of one mind to those of the other.
There are questions and answers, exchanges of joy or sorrow,
there are kissings and partings, just as between little children
with all their senses."

'During this year, and six months after she had left home,
her mother came to visit her, and the scene of their meeting was
an interesting one.

'The mother stood some time, gazing with overflowing eyes
upon her unfortunate child, who, all unconscious of her presence, was playing about the room. Presently Laura ran against

her, and at once began feeling her hands, examining her dress, and trying to find out if she knew her; but not succeeding in this, she turned away as from a stranger, and the poor woman could not conceal the pang she felt, at finding that her beloved child did not know her.

'She then gave Laura a string of beads which she used to wear at home, which were recognised by the child at once, who, with much joy, put them around her neck, and sought me eagerly to say she understood the string was from her home.

'The mother now sought to caress her, but poor Laura repelled her, preferring to be with her acquaintances.

'Another article from home was now given her, and she began to look much interested; she examined the stranger much closer, and gave me to understand that she knew she came from Hanover; she even endured her caresses, but would leave her with indifference at the slightest signal. The distress of the mother was now painful to behold; for, although she had feared that she should not be recognised, the painful reality of being treated with cold indifference by a darling child, was too much for woman's nature to bear.

'After a while, on the mother taking hold of her again, a vague idea seemed to flit across Laura's mind, that this could not be a stranger; she therefore felt her hands very eagerly, while her countenance assumed an expression of intense interest; she became very pale; and then suddenly red; hope seemed struggling with doubt and anxiety, and never were contending emotions more strongly painted upon the human face: at this moment of painful uncertainty, the mother drew her close to her side, and kissed her fondly, when at once the truth flashed upon the child, and all mistrust and anxiety disappeared from her face, as with an expression of exceeding joy she eagerly nestled to the bosom of her parent, and yielded herself to her fond embraces.

'After this, the beads were all unheeded; the playthings which were offered to her were utterly disregarded; her playmates, for whom but a moment before she gladly left the stranger, now vainly strove to pull her from her mother; and though she yielded her usual instantaneous obedience to my signal to follow me, it was evidently with painful reluctance. She clung close to me, as if bewildered and fearful; and when, after a moment, I took her to her mother, she sprang to her arms, and clung to her with eager joy.

'The subsequent parting between them, showed alike the affection, the intelligence, and the resolution of the child.

'Laura accompanied her mother to the door, clinging close to her all the way, until they arrived at the threshold, where she paused, and felt around, to ascertain who was near her. Perceiving the matron, of whom she is very fond, she grasped her with one hand, holding on convulsively to her mother with the other; and thus she stood for a moment: then she dropped her mother's hand; put her handkerchief to her eyes; and turning round, clung sobbing to the matron; while her mother departed, with emotions as deep as those of the child.

* * * * * * * * *

'It has been remarked in former reports, that she can distinguish different degrees of intellect in others, and that she soon regarded almost with contempt, a new comer, when, after a few days, she discovered her weakness of mind. This unamiable part of her character has been more strongly developed during the past year.

'She chooses for her friends and companions, those children who are intelligent, and can talk best with her; and she evidently dislikes to be with those who are deficient in intellect, unless, indeed, she can make them serve her purposes, which she is evidently inclined to do. She takes advantage of them, and makes them wait upon her, in a manner that she knows she could not exact of others; and in various ways shows her Saxon blood.

'She is fond of having other children noticed and caressed by the teachers, and those whom she respects; but this must not be carried too far, or she becomes jealous. She wants to have her share, which, if not the lion's, is the greater part; and if she does not get it, she says, *"My mother will love me."*

'Her tendency to imitation is so strong, that it leads her to actions which must be entirely incomprehensible to her, and which can give her no other pleasure than the gratification of an internal faculty. She has been known to sit for half an hour, holding a bood before her sightless eyes, and moving her lips, as she has observed seeing people do when reading.

'She one day pretended that her doll was sick; and went through all the motions of tending it, and giving it medicine; she then put it carefully to bed, and placed a bottle of hot water to its feet, laughing all the time most heartily. When I came home, she insisted upon my going to see it, and feel its pulse; and when I told her to put a blister on its back, she seemed to enjoy it amazingly, and almost screamed with delight.

'Her social feelings, and her affections, are very strong; and when she is sitting at work, or at her studies, by the side of one of her little friends, she will break off from her task every few moments, to hug and kiss them with an earnestness and warmth that is touching to behold.

'When left alone, she occupies and apparently amuses herself, and seems quite contented; and so strong seems to be the natural tendency of thought to put on the garb of language, that she often soliloquises in the *finger language*, slow and tedious as it is. But it is only when alone, that she is quiet; for if she becomes sensible of the presence of any one near her, she is restless until she can sit close beside them, hold their hand, and converse with them by signs.

'In her intellectual character it is pleasing to observe an insatiable thirst for knowledge, and a quick perception of the relations of things. In her moral character, it is beautiful to behold her continual gladness, her keen enjoyment of existence, her expansive love, her unhesitating confidence, her sympathy with suffering, her conscientiousness, truthfulness, and hopefulness.'

Such are a few fragments from the simple but most interesting and instructive history of Laura Bridgman. The name of her great benefactor and friend, who writes it, is Doctor Howe. There are not many persons, I hope and believe, who, after reading these passages, can ever hear that name with indifference.

A further account has been published by Dr. Howe, since the report from which I have just quoted. It describes her rapid mental growth and improvement during twelve months more, and brings her little history down to the end of last year. It is very remarkable, that as we dream in words, and carry on imaginary conversations, in which we speak both for ourselves and for the shadows who appear to us in those visions of the night, so she, having no words, uses her finger alphabet in her sleep. And it has been ascertained that when her slumber is broken, and is much disturbed by dreams, she expresses her thoughts in an irregular and confused manner on her fingers: just as we should murmur and mutter them indistinctly, in the like circumstances.

I turned over the leaves of her Diary, and found it written in a fair legible square hand, and expressed in terms which were quite intelligible without any explanation. On my saying that I should like to see her write again, the teacher who sat beside her, bade her, in their language, sign her name upon a slip of paper, twice or thrice. In doing so, I observed that she kept her left hand always touching, and following up, her right, in which, of course, she held the pen. No line was indicated by any contrivance, but she wrote straight and freely.

She had, until now, been quite unconscious of the presence of visitors; but, having her hand placed in that of the gentleman who accompanied me, she immediately expressed his name upon her teacher's palm. Indeed her sense of touch is now so exquisite, that having been acquainted with a person once, she can recognize him or her after almost any interval. This gentleman had been in her company, I believe, but very seldom, and certainly had not seen her for many months. My hand she rejected at once, as she does that of any man who is a stranger to her. But she retained my wife's with evident pleasure, kissed her, and examined her dress with a girl's curiosity and interest.

She was merry and cheerful, and showed much innocent playfulness in her intercourse with her teacher. Her delight on recognising a favourite playfellow and companion—herself a blind girl—who silently, and with an equal enjoyment of the coming surprise, took a seat beside her, was beautiful to witness. It elicited from her at first, as other slight circumstances did twice or thrice during my visit, an uncouth noise which was rather painful to hear. But on her teacher touching her lips, she immediately desisted, and embraced her laughingly and affectionately.

I had previously been into another chamber, where a number of blind boys were swinging, and climbing, and engaged in various sports. They all clamoured, as we entered, to the assistant-master, who accompanied us, 'Look at me, Mr. Hart! Please, Mr. Hart, look at me!' evincing, I thought, even in this, an anxiety peculiar to their condition, that their little feats of agility should be *seen*. Among them was a small laughing fellow, who stood aloof, entertaining himself with a gymnastic exercise for bringing the arms and chest into play; which he enjoyed mightily; especially when, in thrusting out his right arm, he brought it into contact with another boy. Like Laura Bridgman, this young child was deaf, and dumb, and blind.

Dr. Howe's account of this pupil's first instruction is so very striking, and so intimately connected with Laura herself, that I cannot refrain from a short extract. I may premise that the poor boy's name is Oliver Caswell; that he is thirteen years of age; and that he was in full possession of all his faculties, until three years and four months old. He was then attacked by scarlet fever; in four weeks became deaf; in a few weeks more, blind; in six months, dumb. He showed his anxious sense of this last deprivation, by often feeling the lips of other persons when they were talking, and then putting his hand upon his own, as if to assure himself that he had them in the right position.

'His thirst for knowledge,' says Dr. Howe, 'proclaimed itself as soon as he entered the house, by his eager examination of everything he could feel or smell in his new location. For instance, treading upon the register of a furnace, he instantly stooped down, and began to feel it, and soon discovered the way in which the upper plate moved upon the lower one; but this was not enough for him, so lying down upon his face, he applied his tongue first to one, then to the other, and seemed to discover that they were of different kinds of metal.

'His signs were expressive: and the strictly natural language, laughing, crying, sighing, kissing, embracing, etc., was perfect.

'Some of the analogical signs which (guided by his faculty of imitation) he had contrived, were comprehensible; such as the waving motion of his hand for the motion of a boat, the circular one for a wheel, etc.

'The first object was to break up the use of these signs and to substitute for them the use of purely arbitrary ones.

'Profiting by the experience I had gained in the other cases, I omitted several steps of the process before employed, and commenced at once with the finger language. Taking therefore, several articles having short names, such as key, cup, mug, etc., and with Laura for an auxiliary, I sat down, and taking his hand, placed it upon one of them, and then with my own, made the letters *key*. He felt my hands eagerly with both of his, and on my repeating the process, he evidently tried to imitate the motions of my fingers. In a few minutes he contrived to feel the motions of my fingers with one hand, and holding out the other he tried to imitate them, laughing most heartily when he succeeded. Laura was by, interested even to agitation; and the two presented a singular sight: her face was flushed and anxious, and her fingers twining in among ours so closely as to follow every motion, but so lightly as not to embarrass them; while Oliver stood attentive, his head a little aside, his face turned up, his left hand grasping mine, and his right held out: at every motion of my fingers his countenance betokened keen attention; there was an expression of anxiety as he tried to imitate the motions; then a smile came stealing out as he thought he could do so, and spread into a jovous laugh the moment he succeeded, and felt me pat his head, and Laura clap him heartily upon the back, and jump up and down in her joy.

'He learned more than a half-dozen letters in half an hour, and seemed delighted with its success, at least in gaining approbation. His attention then began to flag and I commenced playing with him. It was evident that in all this he had merely been imitating the motions of my fingers, and placing his hand upon the key, cup, etc., as part of the process, without any perception of the relation between the sign and the object.

'When he was tired with play I took him back to the table, and he was quite ready to begin again his process of imitation. He soon learned to make the letters for *key, pen, pin;* and by having the object repeatedly placed in his hand, he at last perceived the relation I wished to establish between them. This was evident, because, when I made the letters *p i n,* or *p e n,* or *c u p,* he would select the article.

'The perception of this relation was not accompanied by that radiant flash of intelligence, and that glow of joy, which marked the delightful moment when Laura first perceived it. I then placed all the articles on the table, and going away a little distance with the children, placed Oliver's fingers in the positions to spell *key,* on which Laura went out and brought the article: the little fellow seemed much amused by this, and looked very attentive and smiling. I then caused him to make the letters *b r e a d,* and in an instant Laura went and brought him a piece: he smelled at it; put it to his lips; cocked up his head with a most knowing look; seemed to reflect a moment; and then laughed outright, as much as to say, "Aha! I understand now how something may be made out of this."

'It was now clear that he had the capacity and inclination to learn, that he was a proper subject for instruction, and needed only persevering attention. I therefore put him in the hands of an intelligent teacher, nothing doubting of his rapid progress.'

Well may this gentleman call that a delightful moment, in which some distant promise of her present state first gleamed upon the darkened mind of Laura Bridgman. Throughout his life, the recollection of that moment will be to him a source of pure, unfading happiness; nor will it shine less brightly on the evening of his days of Noble Usefulness.

The affection which exists between these two—the master and the pupil—is as far removed from all ordinary care and regard, as the circumstances in which it has had its growth, are apart from the common occurrences of life. He is occupied now, in de-

vising means of imparting to her, higher knowledge; and of conveying to her some adequate idea of the Great Creator of that
universe in which, dark and silent and scentless though it be to
her, she has such deep delight and glad enjoyment.

Ye who have eyes and see not, and have ears and hear not; ye
who are as the hypocrites of sad countenances, and disfigure your
faces that ye may seem unto men to fast; learn healthy cheerfulness, and mild contentment, from the deaf, and dumb, and
blind! Self-elected saints with gloomy brows, this sightless, ear-
less, voiceless child may teach you lessons you will do well to
follow. Let that poor hand of hers lie gently on your hearts; for
there may be something in its healing touch akin to that of the
Great Master whose precepts you misconstrue, whose lessons you
pervert, of whose charity and sympathy with all the world, not
one among you in his daily practice knows as much as many of
the worst among those fallen sinners, to whom you are liberal in
nothing but the preachment of perdition!

As I rose to quit the room, a pretty little child of one of the
attendants came running in to greet its father. For the moment,
a child with eyes, among the sightless crowd, impressed me almost as painfully as the blind boy in the porch had done, two
hours ago. Ah! how much brighter and more deeply blue, glowing and rich though it had been before, was the scene without,
contrasting with the darkness of so many youthful lives within!

At SOUTH BOSTON, as it is called, in a situation excellently
adapted for the purpose, several charitable institutions are clustered together. One of these, is the State Hospital for the insane;
admirably conducted on those enlightened principles of concilia-
tion and kindness, which twenty years ago would have been worse
than heretical, and which have been acted upon with so much
success in our own pauper Asylum at Hanwell. 'Evince a desire
to show some confidence, and repose some trust, even in mad
people, said the resident physician, as we walked along the galleries, his patients flocking round us unrestrained. Of those who
deny or doubt the wisdom of this maxim after witnessing its effects, if there be such people still alive, I can only say that I hope
I may never be summoned as a Juryman on a Commission of
Lunacy whereof they are the subjects; for I should certainly find
them out of their senses, on such evidence alone.

Each ward in this institution is shaped like a long gallery or
hall, with the dormitories of the patients opening from it on
either hand. Here they work, read, play at skittles, and other

games; and when the weather does not admit of their taking exercise out of doors, pass the day together. In one of these rooms,
seated, calmly, and quite as a matter of course, among a throng
of madwomen, black and white, were the physician's wife and
another lady, with a couple of children. These ladies were graceful and handsome; and it was not difficult to perceive at a
glance that even their presence there, had a highly beneficial influence on the patients who were grouped about them.

Leaning her head against the chimney-piece, with a great assumption of dignity and refinement of manner, sat an elderly
female, in as many scraps of finery as Madge Wildfire herself.
Her head in particular was so strewn with scraps of gauze and
cotton and bits of paper, and had so many queer odds and ends
stuck all about it, that it looked like a bird's-nest. She was radiant with imaginary jewels; wore a rich pair of undoubted gold
spectacles; and gracefully dropped upon her lap, as we approached, a very old greasy newspaper, in which I dare say she had
been reading an account of her own presentation at some Foreign
Court.

I have been thus particular in describing her, because she will
serve to exemplify the physician's manner of acquiring and re-
taining the confidence of his patients.

'This,' he said aloud, taking me by the hand, and advancing
to the fantastic figure with great politeness—not raising her suspicions by the slightest look or whisper, or any kind of aside, to
me: 'This lady is the hostess of this mansion, sir. It belongs to
her. Nobody else has anything whatever to do with it. It is a
large establishment, as you see, and requires a great number of
attendants. She lives, you observe, in the very first style. She is
kind enough to receive my visits, and to permit my wife and
family to reside here; for which it is hardly necessary to say, we
are much indebted to her. She is exceedingly courteous, you perceive,' on this hint she bowed condescendingly, 'and will permit
me to have the pleasure of introducing you: a gentleman from
England, Ma'am: newly arrived from England, after a very tem-
pestuous passage: Mr. Dickens,—the lady of the house!'

We exchanged the most dignified salutations with profound
gravity and respect, and so went on. The rest of the madwomen
seemed to understand the joke perfectly (not only in this case,
but in all the others, except their own), and be highly amused by
it. The nature of their several kinds of insanity was made known
to me in the same way, and we left each of them in high good
humour. Not only is a thorough confidence established, by those

means, between the physician and patient, in respect of the nature and extent of their hallucinations, but it is easy to understand that opportunities are afforded for seizing any moment of reason, to startle them by placing their own delusion before them in its most incongruous and ridiculous light.

Every patient in this asylum sits down to dinner every day with a knife and fork; and in the midst of them sits the gentleman, whose manner of dealing with his charges, I have just described. At every meal, moral influence alone restrains the more violent among them from cutting the throats of the rest; but the effect of that influence is reduced to an absolute certainty, and is found, even as a means of restraint, to say nothing of it as a means of cure, a hundred times more efficacious than all the strait-waistcoats, fetters, and hand-cuffs, that ignorance, prejudice, and cruelty have manufactured since the creation of the world.

In the labour department, every patient is as freely trusted with the tools of his trade as if he were a sane man. In the garden, and on the farm, they work with spades, rakes, and hoes. For amusement, they walk, run, fish, paint, read, and ride out to take the air in carriages provided for the purpose. They have among themselves a sewing society to make clothes for the poor, which holds meetings, passes resolutions, never comes to fisty-cuffs or bowie-knives as sane assemblies have been known to do elsewhere; and conducts all its proceedings with the greatest decorum. The irritability, which would otherwise be expended on their own flesh, clothes, and furniture, is dissipated in these pursuits. They are cheerful, tranquil, and healthy.

Once a week they have a ball, in which the Doctor and his family, with all the nurses and attendants, take an active part. Dances and marches are performed alternately, to the enlivening strains of a piano; and now and then some gentleman or lady (whose proficiency has been previously ascertained) obliges the company with a song; nor does it ever degenerate, at a tender crisis, into a screech or howl; wherein, I must confess, I should have thought the danger lay. At an early hour they all meet together for these festive purposes; at eight o'clock refreshments are served; and at nine they separate.

Immense politeness and good breeding are observed throughout. They all take their tone from the Doctor; and he moves a very Chesterfield among the company. Like other assemblies, these entertainments afford a fruitful topic of conversation among the ladies for some days; and the gentlemen are so anxious to

shine on these occasions, that they have been sometimes found
'practising their steps' in private, to cut a more distinguished
figure in the dance.

It is obvious that one great feature of this system, is the incul-
cation and encouragement, even among such unhappy persons,
of a decent self-respect. Something of the same spirit pervades
all the Institutions at South Boston.

There is the House of Industry. In that branch of it, which is
devoted to the reception of old or otherwise helpless paupers,
these words are painted on the walls: 'WORTHY OF NOTICE.
SELF-GOVERNMENT, QUIETUDE, AND PEACE, ARE BLESSINGS.' It
is not assumed and taken for granted that being there they must
be evil-disposed and wicked people, before whose vicious eyes it
is necessary to flourish threats and harsh restraints. They are
met at the very threshold with this mild appeal. All within-doors
is very plain and simple, as it ought to be, but arranged with a
view to peace and comfort. It costs no more than any other plan
of arrangement, but it speaks an amount of consideration for
those who are reduced to seek a shelter there, which puts them at
once upon their gratitude and good behaviour. Instead of being
parcelled out in great, long, rambling wards, where a certain
amount of weazen life may mope, and pine, and shiver, all day
long, the building is divided into separate rooms, each with its
share of light and air. In these, the better kind of paupers live.
They have a motive for exertion and becoming pride, in the desire to make these little chambers comfortable and decent.

I do not remember one but it was clean and neat, and had its
plant or two upon the window-sill, or row of crockery upon the
shelf, or small display of coloured prints upon the whitewashed
wall, or, perhaps, its wooden clock behind the door.

The orphans and young children are in an adjoining building;
separate from this, but a part of the same Institution. Some are
such little creatures, that the stairs are of Lilliputian measurement, fitted to their tiny strides. The same consideration for
their years and weakness is expressed in their very seats, which
are perfect curiosities, and look like articles of furniture for a
pauper doll's-house. I can imagine the glee of our Poor Law
Commissioners at the notion of these seats having arms and
backs; but small spines being of older date than their occupation
of the Board-room at Somerset House, I thought even this provision very merciful and kind.

Here again, I was greatly pleased with the inscriptions on the
wall, which were scraps of plain morality, easily remembered and

understood: such as 'Love one another'—'God remembers the
smallest creature in His creation': and straightforward advice of
that nature. The books and tasks of these smallest of scholars,
were adapted, in the same judicious manner, to their childish
powers. When we had examined these lessons, four morsels of
girls (of whom one was blind) sang a little song, about the merry
month of May, which I thought (being extremely dismal) would
have suited an English November better. That done, we went to
see their sleeping-rooms on the floor above, in which the arrangements were no less excellent and gentle than those we had seen
below. And after observing that the teachers were of a class and
character well suited to the spirit of the place, I took leave of the
infants with a lighter heart than ever I have taken leave of pauper infants yet.

Connected with the House of Industry, there is also an Hospital, which was in the best order, and had, I am glad to say,
many beds unoccupied. It had one fault, however, which is common to all American interiors: the presence of the eternal, accursed, suffocating redhot demon of a stove, whose breath would
blight the purest air under Heaven.

There are two establishments for boys in this same neighbourhood. One is called the Boylston school, and is an asylum for neglected and indigent boys who have committed no crime, but who
in the ordinary course of things would very soon be purged of that
distinction if they were not taken from the hungry streets and sent
here. The other is a House of Reformation for Juvenile Offenders.
They are both under the same roof, but the two classes of boys
never come in contact.

The Boylston boys, as may be readily supposed, have very much
the advantage of the others in point of personal appearance. They
were in their schoolroom when I came upon them, and answered
correctly, without book, such questions as where was England;
how far was it; what was its population; its capital city; its form
of government; and so forth. They sang a song too, about a farmer sowing his seed: with corresponding action at such parts as
' 'tis thus he sows,' 'he turns him round,' 'he claps his hands';
which gave it greater interest for them, and accustomed them to
act together, in an orderly manner. They appeared exceedingly
well taught, and not better taught then fed; for a more chubby-
looking, full-waistcoated set of boys, I never saw.

The juvenile offenders had not such pleasant faces by a great
deal, and in this establishment there were many boys of colour. I
saw them first at their work (basket-making, and the manufacture

of palm-leaf hats), afterwards in their school, where they sang a chorus in praise of Liberty: an odd, and, one would think, rather aggravating, theme for prisoners. These boys are divided into four classes, each denoted by a numeral, worn on a badge upon the arm. On the arrival of a new comer, he is put into the fourth or lowest class, and left, by good behaviour, to work his way up into the first. The design and object of this Institution is to reclaim the youthful criminal by firm but kind and judicious treatment; to make his prison a place of purification and improvement, not of demoralisation and corruption; to impress upon him that there is but one path, and that one sober industry, which can ever lead him to happiness; to teach him how it may be trodden, if his footsteps have never yet been led that way; and to lure him back to it if they have strayed: in a word, to snatch him from destruction, and restore him to society a penitent and useful member. The importance of such an establishment, in every point of view, and with reference to every consideration of humanity and social policy, requires no comment.

One other establishment closes the catalogue. It is the House of Correction for the State, in which silence is strictly maintained, but where the prisoners have the comfort and mental relief of seeing each other, and of working together. This is the improved system of Prison Discipline which we have imported into England, and which has been in successful operation among us for some years past.

America, as a new and not over-populated country, has in all her prisons, the one great advantage, of being enabled to find useful and profitable work for the inmates; whereas, with us, the prejudice against prison labour is naturally very strong, and almost insurmountable, when honest men who have not offended against the laws are frequently doomed to seek employment in vain. Even in the United States, the principle of bringing convict labour and free labour into a competition which must obviously be to the disadvantage of the latter, has already found many opponents, whose number is not likely to diminish with access of years.

For this very reason though, our best prisons would seem at the first glance to be better conducted than those of America. The tread-mill is conducted with little or no noise; five hundred men may pick oakum in the same room, without a sound; and both kinds of labour admit of such keen and vigilant superintendence, as will render even a word of personal communication amongst the prisoners almost impossible. On the other hand, the noise of the loom, the forge, the carpenter's hammer, or the stonemason's saw, greatly favour those opportunities of intercourse—hurried and brief no doubt, but opportunities still—which these several kinds of work, by rendering it necessary for men to be employed very near to each other, and often side by side, without any barrier or partition between them, in their very nature present. A visitor, too, requires to reason and reflect a little, before the sight of a number of men engaged in ordinary labour, such as he is accustomed to out of doors, will impress him half as strongly as the contemplation of the same persons in the same place and garb would, if they were occupied in some task, marked and degraded everywhere as belonging only to felons in jails. In an American state prison or house of correction, I found it difficult at first to persuade myself that I was really in a jail: a place of ignominious punishment and endurance. And to this hour I very much question whether the humane boast that it is not like one, has its root in the true wisdom or philosophy of the matter.

I hope I may not be misunderstood on this subject, for it is one in which I take a strong and deep interest. I incline as little to the sickly feeling which makes every canting lie or maudlin speech of a notorious criminal a subject of newspaper report and general sympathy, as I do to those good old customs of the good old times which made England, even so recently as in the reign of the Third King George, in respect of her criminal code and her prison regulations, one of the most bloody-minded and barbarous countries on the earth. If I thought it would do any good to the rising generation, I would cheerfully give my consent to the disinterment of the bones of any genteel highwayman (the more genteel, the more cheerfully), and to their exposure, piecemeal, on any sign-post, gate, or gibbet, that might be deemed a good elevation for the purpose. My reason is as well convinced that these gentry were as utterly worthless and debauched villains, as it is that the laws and jails hardened them in their evil courses, or that their wonderful escapes were effected by the prison-turnkeys who, in those admirable days, had always been felons themselves, and were, to the last, their bosom friends and pot-companions. At the same time I know, as all men do or should, that the subject of Prison Discipline is one of the highest importance to any community; and that in her sweeping reform and bright example to other countries on this head, America has shown great wisdom, great benevolence, and exalted policy. In contrasting her system with that which we have modelled upon it, I merely seek to show that with all its drawbacks, ours has some advantages of its own.

The House of Correction which has led to these remarks, is not walled, like other prisons, but is palisaded round about with tall rough stakes, something after the manner of an enclosure for keeping elephants in, as we see it represented in Eastern prints and pictures. The prisoners wear a parti-coloured dress; and those who are sentenced to hard labour, work at nail-making, or stone-cutting. When I was there, the latter class of labourers were employed upon the stone for a new custom-house in course of erection at Boston. They appeared to shape it skilfully and with expedition, though there were very few among them (if any) who had not acquired the art within the prison gates.

The women, all in one large room, were employed in making light clothing, for New Orleans, and the Southern States. They did their work in silence like the men; and like them were overlooked by the person contracting for their labour, or by some agent of his appointment. In addition to this, they are every moment liable to be visited by the prison officers appointed for that purpose.

The arrangements for cooking, washing of clothes, and so forth, are much upon the plan of those I have seen at home. Their mode of bestowing the prisoners at night (which is of general adoption) differs from ours, and is both simple and effective. In the centre of a lofty area, lighted by windows in the four walls, are five tiers of cells, one above the other; each tier having before it a light iron gallery, attainable by stairs of the same construction and material: excepting the lower one, which is on the ground. Behind these, back to back with them and facing the opposite wall, are five corresponding rows of cells, accessible by similar means: so that supposing the prisoners locked up in their cells, an officer stationed on the ground, with his back to the wall, has half their number under his eye at once; the remaining half being equally under the observation of another officer on the opposite side; and all in one great apartment. Unless this watch be corrupted or sleeping on his post, it is impossible for a man to escape; for even in the event of his forcing the iron door of his cell without noise (which is exceedingly improbable), the moment he appears outside, and steps into that one of the galleries on which it is situated, he must be plainly and fully visible to the officer below. Each of these cells holds a small truckle bed, in which one prisoner sleeps; never more. It is small, of course; and the door being not solid, but grated, and without blind or curtain, the prisoner within is at all times exposed to the observation and inspection of any guard who may pass along that tier at any hour or minute of the night. Every day, the prisoners receive their dinner, singly, through a trap in the kitchen wall; and each man carries his to his sleeping cell to eat it, where he is locked

up, alone, for that purpose, one hour. The whole of this arrangement struck me as being admirable: and I hope that the next new
prison we erect in England may be built on this plan.

I was given to understand that in this prison no swords or fire-
arms or even cudgels, are kept; nor is it probable that, so long as
its present excellent management continues, any weapon, offensive
or defensive, will ever be required within its bounds.

Such are the Institutions at South Boston! In all of them, the
unfortunate or degenerate citizens of the State are carefully in-
structed in their duties both to God and man; are surrounded by
all reasonable means of comfort and happiness that their condition
will admit of; are appealed to, as members of the great human
family, however afflicted, indigent, or fallen; are ruled by the
strong Heart, and not by the strong (though immeasurably weak-
er) Hand. I have described them at some length; firstly, because
their worth demanded it; and secondly, because I mean to take
them for a model, and to content myself with saying of others we
may come to, whose design and purpose are the same, that in this
or that respect they practically fail, or differ.

I wish by this account of them, imperfect in its execution, but in
its just intention, honest, I could hope to convey to my readers
one-hundredth part of the gratification, the sights I have described,
afforded me.

To an Englishman, accustomed to the paraphernalia of Westminster Hall, an American Court of Law is as odd a sight as, I
suppose, an English Court of Law would be to an American. Except in the Supreme Court at Washington (where the judges wear
a plain black robe), there is no such thing as a wig or gown connected with the administration of justice. The gentlemen of the
bar being barristers and attorneys too (for there is no division of
those functions as in England) are no more removed from their
clients than attorneys in our Court for the Relief of Insolvent
Debtors are, from theirs. The jury are quite at home, and make
themselves as comfortable as circumstances will permit. The witness is so little elevated above, or put aloof from, the crowd in the
court, that a stranger entering during a pause in the proceedings
would find it difficult to pick him out from the rest. And if it
chanced to be a criminal trial, his eyes, in nine cases out of ten,
would wander to the dock in search of the prisoner, in vain; for
that gentleman would most likely be lounging among the most distinguished ornaments of the legal profession, whispering sugges-

tions in his counsel's ear, or making a toothpick out of an old quill with his penknife.

I could not but notice these differences, when I visited the courts at Boston. I was much surprised at first, too, to observe that the counsel who interrogated the witness under examination at the time, did so *sitting*. But seeing that he was also occupied in writing down the answers, and remembering that he was alone and had no 'junior,' I quickly consoled myself with the reflection that law was not quite so expensive an article here, as at home; and that the absence of sundry formalities which we regard as indispensable, had doubtless a very favourable influence upon the bill of costs.

In every Court, ample and commodious provision is made for the accommodation of the citizens. This is the case all through America. In every Public Institution, the right of the people to attend, and to have an interest in the proceedings, is most fully and distinctly recognised. There are no grim doorkeepers to dole out their tardy civility by the six-penny-worth; nor is there, I sincerely believe any insolence of office of any kind. Nothing national is exhibited for money; and no public officer is a showman. We have begun of late years to imitate this good example. I hope we shall continue to do so; and that in the fulness of time, even deans and chapters may be converted.

In the civil court an action was trying, for damages sustained in some accident upon a railway. The witness had been examined, and counsel was addressing the jury. The learned gentleman (like a few of his English brethren) was desperately long-winded, and had a remarkable capacity of saying the same thing over and over again. His great theme was 'Warren the en*gine* driver,' whom he pressed into the service of every sentence he uttered. I listened to him for about a quarter of an hour; and, coming out of court at the expiration of that time, without the faintest ray of enlightenment as to the merits of the case, felt as if I were at home again.

In the prisoner's cell, waiting to be examined by the magistrate on a charge of theft, was a boy. This lad, instead of being committed to a common jail, would be sent to the asylum at South Boston, and there taught a trade; and in the course of time he would be bound apprentice to some respectable master. Thus, his detection in this offence, instead of being the prelude to a life of infamy and a miserable death, would lead, there was a reasonable hope, to his being reclaimed from vice, and becoming a worthy member of society.

I am by no means a wholesale admirer of our legal solemnities, many of which impress me as being exceedingly ludicrous. Strange

as it may seem to, there is undoubtedly a degree of protection in
the wig and gown—a dismissal of individual responsibility in
dressing for the part—which encourages that insolent bearing and
language, and that gross perversion of the office of a pleader for
The Truth, so frequent in our courts of law. Still, I cannot help
doubting whether America, in her desire to shake off the absurdities and abuses of the old system, may not have gone too far into
the opposite extreme; and whether it is not desirable, especially in
the small community of a city like this, where each man knows the
other, to surround the administration of justice with some artificial
barriers against the 'Hail fellow, well met' deportment of everyday
life. All the aid it can have in the very high character and ability
of the Bench, not only here but elsewhere, it has, and well deserves
to have; but it may need something more: not to impress the
thoughtful and the well-informed, but the ignorant and heedless; a
class which includes some prisoners and many witnesses. These
institutions were established, no doubt, upon the principle that
those who had so large a share in making the laws, would certainly
respect them. But experience has proved this hope to be falla-
cious; for no men know better than the Judges of America, that
on the occasion of any great popular excitement the law is powerless, and cannot, for the time, assert its own supremacy.

The tone of society in Boston is one of perfect politeness, courtesy, and good breeding. The ladies are unquestionably very beautiful—in face: but there I am compelled to stop. Their education
is much as with us; neither better nor worse. I had heard some
very marvellous stories in this respect; but not believing them, was
not disappointed. Blue ladies there are, in Boston; but like philosophers of that colour and sex in most other latitudes, they rather
desire to be thought superior than to be so. Evangelical ladies
there are, likewise, whose attachment to the forms of religion, and
horror of theatrical entertainments, are most exemplary. Ladies
who have a passion for attending lectures are to be found among
all classes and all conditions. In the kind of provincial life which
prevails in cities such as this, the Pulpit has great influence. The
peculiar province of the Pulpit in New England (always excepting
the Unitarian ministry) would appear to be the denouncement of
all innocent and rational amusements. The church, the chapel, and
the lecture-room, are the only means of excitement excepted; and
to the church, the chapel, and the lecture-room, the ladies resort in
crowds.

Wherever religion is resorted to, as a strong drink, and as an escape from the dull monotonous round of home, those of its minis-

ters who pepper the highest will be the surest to please. They who strew the Eternal Path with the greatest amount of brimstone, and who most ruthlessly tread down the flowers and leaves that grow by the wayside, will be voted the most righteous; and they who enlarge with the greatest pertinacity on the difficulty of getting into heaven, will be considered by all true believers certain of going there: though it would be hard to say by what process of reasoning this conclusion is arrived at. It is so at home, and it is so abroad. With regard to the other means of excitement, the Lecture, it has at least the merit of being always new. One lecture treads so quickly on the heels of another, that none are remembered; and the course of this month may be safely repeated next, with its charm of novelty unbroken, and its interest unabated.

The fruits of the earth have their growth in corruption. Out of the rottenness of these things, there has sprung up in Boston a sect of philosophers known as Transcendentalists. On inquiring what this appellation might be supposed to signify, I was given to understand that whatever was unintelligible would be certainly transcendental. Not deriving much comfort from this elucidation, I pursued the inquiry still further, and found that the Transcendentalists are followers of my friend Mr. Carlyle, or I should rather say, of a follower of his, Mr. Ralph Waldo Emerson. This gentleman has written a volume of Essays, in which, among much that is dreamy and fanciful (if he will pardon me for saying so), there is much more that is true and manly, honest and bold. Transcendentalism has its occasional vagaries (what school has not?), but it has good healthful qualities in spite of them; not least among the number a hearty disgust of Cant, and an aptitude to detect her in all the million varieties of her everlasting wardrobe. And therefore if I were a Bostonian, I think I would be a Transcendentalist.

The only preacher I heard in Boston was Mr. Taylor, who addresses himself peculiarly to seamen, and who was once a mariner himself. I found his chapel down among the shipping, in one of the narrow, old, water-side streets, with a gay blue flag waving freely from its roof. In the gallery opposite to the pulpit were a little choir of male and female singers, a violoncello, and a violin. The preacher already sat in the pulpit, which was raised on pillars, and ornamented behind him with painted drapery of a lively and somewhat theatrical appearance. He looked a weather-beaten hard-featured man, of about six or eight and fifty; with deep lines graven as it were into his face, dark hair, and a stern, keen eye. Yet the general character of his countenance was pleasant and

agreeable. The service commenced with a hymn, to which succeeded an extemporary prayer. It had the fault of frequent repetition, incidental to all such prayers; but it was plain and comprehensive in its doctrines, and breathed a tone of general sympathy and charity, which is not so commonly a characteristic of
this form of address to the Deity as it might be. That done he
opened his discouse, taking for his text a passage from the Song of
Solomon, laid upon the desk before the commencement of the service by some unknown member of the congregation: 'Who is this
coming up from the wilderness, leaning on the arm of her beloved!'

He handled his text in all kinds of ways, and twisted it into all
manner of shapes; but always ingeniously, and with a rude eloquence, well adapted to the comprehension of his hearers. Indeed
if I be not mistaken, he studied their sympathies and understand-
ings much more than the display of his own powers. His imagery
was all drawn from the sea, and from the incidents of a seaman's
life; and was often remarkably good. He spoke to them of 'that
glorious man, Lord Nelson,' and of Collingwood; and drew nothing in, as the saying is, by the head and shoulders, but brought it
to bear upon his purpose, naturally, and with a sharp mind to its
effect. Sometimes, when much excited with his subject, he had an
odd way—compounded of John Bunyan, and Balfour of Burley—
of taking his great quarto Bible under his arm and pacing up and
down the pulpit with it; looking steadily down, meantime, into
the midst of the congregation. Thus, when he applied his text to
the first assemblage of his hearers, and pictured the wonder of the
church at their presumption in forming a congregation among
themselves, he stopped short with his Bible under his arm in the
manner I have described, and pursued his discourse after this
manner:

'Who are these—who are they—who are these fellows? where
do they come from? Where are they going to?—Come from!
What's the answer?'—leaning out of the pulpit, and pointing
downward with his right hand: 'From below!'—starting back
again, and looking at the sailors before him: 'From below, my
brethren. From under the hatches of sin, battened down above
you by the evil one. That's where you came from!'—a walk up
and down the pulpit: 'and where are you going'—stopping abruptly: 'where are you going? Aloft!'—very softly, and pointing upward: 'Aloft!'—louder: 'aloft!'—louder still: 'That's where you
are going—with a fair wind,—all taut and trim, steering direct for
Heaven in its glory, where there are no storms or foul weather, and
where the wicked cease from troubling, and the weary are at rest.'

—Another walk: 'That's where you're going to, my friends. That's it. That's the place. That's the port. That's the haven. It's a blessed harbour—still water there, in all changes of the winds and tides; no driving ashore upon the rocks, or slipping your cables and running out to sea, there: Peace—Peace—Peace—all peace!' —Another walk, and patting the Bible under his left arm: 'What! These fellows are coming from the wilderness, are they? Yes. From the dreary, blighted wilderness of Iniquity, whose only crop is Death. But do they lean upon anything—do they lean upon nothing, these poor seamen?'—Three raps upon the Bible: 'Oh yes.—Yes.—They lean upon the arm of their Beloved'—three more raps: 'upon the arm of their Beloved'—three more, and a walk: 'Pilot, guiding-star, and compass, all in one, to all hands— here it is'—three more: 'Here it is. They can do their seaman's duty manfully, and be easy in their minds in the utmost peril and danger, with this'—two more: 'They can come, even these poor fellows can come, from the wilderness leaning on the arm of their Beloved, and go up—up—up!' raising his hand higher, and higher, at every repetition of the word, so that he stood with it at last stretched above his head, regarding them in a strange, rapt manner, and pressing the book triumphantly to his breast, until he gradually subsided into some other portion of his discourse.

I have cited this, rather as an instance of the preacher's eccentricities than his merits, though taken in connection with his look and manner, and the character of his audience, even this was striking. It is possible, however, that my favourable impression of him may have been greatly influenced and strengthened, firstly, by his impressing upon his hearers that the true observance of religion was not inconsistent with a cheerful deportment and an exact discharge of the duties of their station, which, indeed, is scrupulously required of them; and secondly, by his cautioning them not to set up any monopoly in Paradise and its mercies. I never heard these two points so wisely touched (if indeed I have ever heard them touched at all), by any preacher of that kind before.

Having passed the time I spent in Boston, in making myself acquainted with these things, in settling the course I should take in my future travels, and in mixing constantly with its society, I am not aware that I have any occasion to prolong this chapter. Such of its social customs as I have not mentioned, however, may be told in a very few words.

The usual dinner-hour is two o'clock. A dinner party takes place at five; and at an evening party, they seldom sup later than eleven; so that it goes hard but one gets home, even from a rout, by

midnight. I never could find out any difference between a party at
Boston and a party in London, saving that at the former place all
assemblies are held at more rational hours; that the conversation
may possibly be a little louder and more cheerful; and a guest is
usually expected to ascend to the very top of the house to take his
cloak off; that he is certain to see, at every dinner, an unusual
amount of poultry on the table; and at every supper, at least two
mighty bowls of hot stewed oysters, in any one of which a half-
grown Duke of Clarence might be smothered easily.

There are two theatres in Boston, of good size and construction,
but sadly in want of patronage. The few ladies who resort to
them, sit, as of right, in the front rows of the boxes.

The bar is a large room with a stone floor, and there people
stand and smoke, and lounge about, all the evening; dropping in
and out as the humour takes them. There too the stranger is ini-
tiated into the mysteries of Gin-sling, Cock-tail, Sangaree, Mint
Julep, Sherry-cobbler, Timber Doodle, and other rare drinks. The
house is full of boarders, both married and single, many of whom
sleep upon the premises, and contract by the week for their board
and lodging: the charge for which diminishes as they go nearer the
sky to roost. A public table is laid in a very handsome hall for
breakfast, and for dinner, and for supper. The party sitting down
together to these meals will vary in number from one to two hundred: sometimes more. The advent of each of these epochs in the
day is proclaimed by an awful gong, which shakes the very win-
dow-frames as it reverberates through the house, and horribly dis-
turbs nervous foreigners. There is an ordinary for ladies, and an
ordinary for gentlemen.

In our private room the cloth could not, for any earthly consideration, have been laid for dinner without a huge glass dish of
cranberries in the middle of the table; and breakfast would have
been no breakfast unless the principal dish were a deformed beef-
steak with a great flat bone in the centre, swimming in hot butter,
and sprinkled with the very blackest of all possible pepper. Our
bedroom was spacious and airy, but (like every bedroom on this
side of the Atlantic) very bare of furniture, having no curtains to
the French bedstead or to the window. It had one unusual luxury, however, in the shape of a wardrobe of painted wood, something smaller than an English watch-box; or if this comparison
should be insufficient to convey a just idea of its dimensions, they
may be estimated from the fact of my having lived for fourteen
days and nights in the firm belief that it was a shower-bath.

CHAPTER IV

AN AMERICAN RAILROAD. LOWELL AND ITS FACTORY SYSTEM

BEFORE leaving Boston, I devoted one day to an excursion to Lowell. I assign a separate chapter to this visit; not because I am about to describe it at any great length, but because I remember it as a thing by itself, and am desirous that my readers should do the same.

I made acquaintance with an American railroad, on this occasion, for the first time. As these works are pretty much alike all through the States, their general characteristics are easily described.

There are no first and second class carriages as with us: but there is a gentlemen's car and a ladies' car: the main distinction between which is that in the first, everybody smokes; and in the second, nobody does. As a black man never travels with a white one, there is also a negro car; which is a great blundering clumsy chest, such as Gulliver put to sea in, from the kingdom of Brobdingnag. There is a great deal of jolting, a great deal of noise, a great deal of wall, not much window, a locomotive engine, a shriek, and a bell.

The cars are like shabby omnibuses, but larger, holding thirty, forty, fifty people. The seats, instead of stretching from end to end, are placed crosswise. Each seat holds two persons. There is a long row of them on each side of the caravan, a narrow passage up the middle, and a door at both ends. In the centre of the carriage there is usually a stove, fed with charcoal or anthracite coal; which is for the most part red-hot. It is insufferably close; and you see the hot air fluttering between yourself and any other object you may happen to look at, like the ghost of smoke.

In the ladies' car, there are a great many gentlemen who have ladies with them. There are also a great many ladies who have nobody with them: for any lady may travel alone, from one end of the United States to the other, and be certain of the most courteous and considerate treatment everywhere. The conductor or check-taker, or guard, or whatever he may be, wears no uniform. He walks up and down the car, and in and out of it, as his fancy dictates; leans against the door with his hands in his pockets and stares at you, if you chance to be a stranger; or enters into conversation with the passengers about him. A great many newspapers are pulled out, and a few of them are read. Everybody talks to you, or to anybody else who hits his fancy. If you are an Englishman, he expects that that railroad is pretty much like an English railroad. If you say 'No,' he says 'Yes?' (interrogatively), and asks in what respect they differ. You enumerate the heads of difference, one by one, and he says 'Yes?' (still interrogatively) to each. Then he guesses that you don't travel faster in England; and on your replying that you do, says 'Yes?' again (still interrogatively), and it is quite evident, don't believe it. After a long pause he remarks, partly to you, and partly to the knob on the top of his stick, that 'Yankees are reckoned to be considerable of a go-ahead people too'; upon which *you* say 'Yes,' and then *he* says 'Yes' again (affirmatively this time); and upon your looking out of window, tells you that behind that hill, and some three miles from the next station, there is a clever town in a smart lo-ca-tion, where he expects you have con-cluded to stop. Your answer in the negative naturally leads to more questions in reference to your intended route (always pronounced rout); and wherever you are going, you invariably learn that you can't get there without immense difficulty and danger, and that all the great sights are somewhere else.

If a lady take a fancy to any male passenger's seat, the gentleman who accompanies her gives him notice of the fact, and he immediately vacates it with great politeness. Politics are much discussed, so are banks, so is cotton. Quiet people avoid the question of the Presidency, for there will be a new election in three years and a half, and party feeling runs very high; the great constitutional feature of this institution being, that directly the acrimony of the last election is over, the acrimony of the next one begins; which is an unspeakable comfort to all strong politicians and true lovers of their country: that is to say, to ninety-nine men and boys out of every ninety-nine and a quarter.

Except when a branch road joins the main one, there is seldom more than one track of rails; so that the road is very narrow, and the view, where there is a deep cutting, by no means extensive. When there is not, the character of the scenery is always the same. Mile after mile of stunted trees: some hewn down by the axe, some blown down by the wind, some half fallen and resting on their neighbours, many mere logs half-hidden in the swamp, others mouldered away to spongy chips. The very soil of the earth is made up of minute fragments such as these, each pool of stagnant water has its crust of vegetable rottenness; on every side there are the boughs, and trunks and stumps of trees, in every possible stage of decay, decomposition, and neglect. Now you emerge for a few brief minutes on an open country, glittering with some bright lake or pool, broad as many an English river, but so small here that it scarcely has a name; now catch hasty glimpses of a distant town with its clean white houses and their cool piazzas, its prim New England church and schoolhouse; when whir-r-r-r! almost before you have seen them, comes the same dark screen: the stunted trees, the stumps, the logs, the stagnant water—all so like the last that you seem to have been transported back again by magic.

The train calls at stations in the woods, where the wild impossibility of anybody having the smallest reason to get out, is only to be equalled by the apparently desperate hopelessness of there being anybody to get in. It rushes across the turnpike road, where there is no gate, no policeman, no signal: nothing but a rough wooden arch, on which is painted 'WHEN THE BELL RINGS, LOOK OUT FOR THE LOCOMOTIVE.' On it whirls headlong, dives through the woods again, emerges in the light, clatters over frail arches, rumbles upon the heavy ground, shoots beneath a wooden bridge which intercepts the light for a second like a wink, suddenly awakens all the slumbering echoes in the main street of a large town, and dashes on haphazard, pellmell, neck-or-nothing, down the middle of the road. There—with mechanics working at their trades, and people leaning from their doors and windows, and boys flying kites and playing marbles, and men smoking, and women talking, and children crawling, and pigs burrowing, and unaccustomed horses plunging and rearing, close to the very rails—there—on, on, on—tears the mad dragon of an engine with its train of cars; scattering in all directions a shower of burning sparks from its wood fire; screeching, hissing, yelling, panting; until at last the thirsty monster stops beneath a covered way to drink, the people cluster round, and you have time to breathe again.

I was met at the station at Lowell by a gentleman intimately connected with the management of the factories there; and gladly putting myself under his guidance, drove off at once to that quarter of the town in which the works, the object of my visit, were situated. Although only just of age—for if my recollection serve me, it has been a manufacturing town barely one-and-twenty years— Lowell is a large, populous, thriving place. Those indications of its youth which first attract the eye, give it a quaintness and oddity of character which, to a visitor from the old country, is amusing enough. It was a very dirty winter's day, and nothing in the whole town looked old to me, except the mud, which in some parts was almost knee-deep, and might have been deposited there, on the subsiding of the waters after the Deluge. In one place, there was a new wooden church, which, having no steeple, and being yet unpainted, looked like an enormous packing-case without any direction upon it. In another there was a large hotel, whose walls and colonnades were so crisp, and thin, and light, that it had exactly the appearance of being built with cards. I was careful not to draw my breath as we passed, and trembled when I saw a workman come out upon the roof, lest with one thoughtless stamp of his foot he should crush the structure beneath him, and bring it rattling down. The very river that moves the machinery in the mills (for they are all worked by water power), seems to acquire a new character from the fresh buildings of bright red brick and painted wood among which it takes its course; and to be as light-headed, thoughtless, and brisk a young river, in its murmurings and tumblings, as one would desire to see. One would swear that every 'Bakery,' 'Grocery,' and 'Bookbindery,' and other kind of store, took its shutters down for the first time, and started in business yesterday. The golden pestles and mortars fixed as signs upon the sun-blind frames outside the Druggists', appear to have been just turned out of the United States' Mint; and when I saw a baby of some week or ten days old in a woman's arms at a street corner, I found myself unconsciously wondering where it came from: never supposing for an instant that it could have been born in such a young town as that.

There are several factories in Lowell, each of which belongs to what we should term a Company of Proprietors, but what they call in America a Corporation. I went over several of these; such as a woollen factory, a carpet factory, and a cotton factory: examined them in every part; and saw them in their ordinary working aspect, with no preparation of any kind, or departure from their ordinary everyday proceedings. I may add that I am well acquainted with our manufacturing towns in England, and have visited many mills in Manchester and elsewhere in the same manner.

I happened to arrive at the first factory just as the dinner hour was over, and the girls were returning to their work; indeed the stairs of the mill were thronged with them as I ascended. They were all well dressed, but not to my thinking above their condition; for I like to see the humbler class of society careful of their dress and appearance, and even, if they please, decorated with such little trinkets as come within the compass of their means. Supposing it confined within reasonable limits, I would always encourage this kind of pride, as a worthy element of self-respect, in any person I employed; and should no more be deterred from doing so, because some wretched female referred her fall to a love of dress, than I would allow my construction of the real intent and meaning of the Sabbath to be influenced by any warning to the well-disposed, founded on his backslidings on that particular day, which might emanate from the rather doubtful authority of a murderer in Newgate.

These girls, as I have said, were all well dressed: and that phrase necessarily includes extreme cleanliness. They had serviceable bonnets, good warm cloaks, and shawls; and were not above clogs and pattens. Moreover, there were places in the mill in which they could deposit these things without injury; and there were conveniences for washing. They were healthy in appearance, many of them remarkably so, and had the manners and deportment of young women: not of degraded brutes of burden. If I had seen in one of those mills (but I did not, though I looked for something of this kind with a sharp eye), the most lisping, mincing, affected, and ridiculous young creature that my imagination could suggest, I should have thought of the careless, moping, slatternly, degraded, dull reverse (I *have* seen that), and should have been still well pleased to look upon her.

The rooms in which they worked, were as well ordered as themselves. In the windows of some, there were green plants, which were trained to shade the glass; in all, there was as much fresh air, cleanliness, and comfort, as the nature of the occupation would possibly admit of. Out of so large a number of females, many of whom were only then just verging upon womanhood, it may be reasonably supposed that some were delicate and fragile in appearance: no doubt there were. But I solemnly declare, that from all the crowd I saw in the different factories that day, I cannot recall or separate one young face that gave me a painful impression; not one young girl whom, assuming it to be matter of necessity that she should gain her daily bread by the labour of her hands, I would have removed from those works if I had had the power.

They reside in various boarding-houses near at hand. The owners of the mills are particularly careful to allow no persons to enter upon the possession of these houses, whose characters have not undergone the most searching and thorough inquiry. Any complaint that is made against them, by the boarders, or by any one else, is fully investigated; and if good ground of complaint be shown to exist against them, they are removed, and their occupation is handed over to some more deserving person. There are a few children employed in these factories, but not many. The laws of the State forbid their working more than nine months in the year, and require that they be educated during the other three. For this purpose there are schools in Lowell; and there are churches and chapels of various persuasions, in which the young women may observe that form of worship in which they have been educated.

At some distance from the factories, and on the highest and pleasantest ground in the neighbourhood, stands their hospital, or boarding-house for the sick: it is the best house in those parts, and was built by an eminent merchant for his own residence. Like that institution at Boston, which I have before described, it is not parcelled out into wards, but is divided into convenient chambers, each of which has all the comforts of a very comfortable home. The principal medical attendant resides under the same roof; and were the patients members of his own family, they could not be better cared for, or attended with greater gentleness and consideration. The weekly charge in this establishment for each female patient is three dollars, or twelve shillings English; but no girl employed by any of the corporations is ever excluded for want of the means of payment. That they do not very often want the means, may be gathered from the fact, that in July, 1841, no fewer than nine hundred and seventy-eight of these girls were depositors in the Lowell Savings Bank: the amount of whose joint savings was estimated at one hundred thousand dollars, or twenty thousand English pounds.

I am now going to state three facts, which will startle a large class of readers on this side of the Atlantic, very much.

Firstly, there is a joint-stock piano in a great many of the boarding-houses. Secondly, nearly all these young ladies subscribe to circulating libraries. Thirdly, they have got up among themselves a periodical called THE LOWELL OFFERING, 'A repository of original articles, written exclusively by females actively employed in the mills,'—which is duly printed, published, and sold; and whereof I brought away from Lowell four hundred good solid pages, which I have read from beginning to end.

The large class of readers, startled by these facts, will exclaim, with one voice, 'How very preposterous!' On my deferentially inquiring why, they will answer, 'These things are above their station.' In reply to that objection, I would beg to ask what their station is.

It is their station to work. And they *do* work. They labour in these mills, upon an average, twelve hours a day, which is unquestionably work, and pretty tight work too. Perhaps it is above their station to indulge in such amusements, on any terms. Are we quite sure that we in England have not formed our ideas of the 'station' of working people, from accustoming ourselves to the contemplation of that class as they are, and not as they might be? I think that if we examine our own feelings, we shall find that the pianos, and the circulating libraries, and even the Lowell Offering, startle us by their novelty, and not by their bearing upon any abstract question of right or wrong.

For myself, I know no station in which, the occupation of to-day cheerfully done and the occupation of to-morrow cheerfully looked to, any one of these pursuits is not most humanising and laudable. I know no station which is rendered more endurable to the person in it, or more safe to the person out of it, by having ignorance for its associate. I know no station which has a right to monopolise the means of mutual instruction, improvement, and rational entertainment; or which has ever continued to be a station very long, after seeking to do so.

Of the merits of the Lowell Offering as a literary production, I will only observe, putting entirely out of sight the fact of the articles having been written by these girls after the arduous labours of the day, that it will compare advantageously with a great many English Annuals. It is pleasant to find that many of its Tales are of the Mills and of those who work in them; that they inculcate habits of self-denial and contentment, and teach good doctrines of enlarged benevolence. A strong feeling for the beauties of nature, as displayed in the solitudes the writers have left at home, breathes through its pages like wholesome village air; and though a circulating library is a favourable school for the study of such topics, it has very scant allusion to fine clothes, fine marriages, fine houses, or fine life. Some persons might object to the papers being signed occasionally with rather fine names, but this is an American fashion. One of the provinces of the state legislature of Massachusetts is to alter ugly names into pretty ones, as the children improve upon the tastes of their parents. These changes costing little or nothing, scores of Mary Annes are solemnly converted into Bevelinas every session.

It is said that on the occasion of a visit from General Jackson or General Harrison to this town (I forget which, but it is not to the purpose), he walked through three miles and a half of these young ladies all dressed out with parasols and silk stockings. But as I am not aware that any worse consequences ensued, than a sudden looking-up of all the parasols and silk stockings in the market; and perhaps the bankruptcy of some speculative New Englander who bought them all up at any price, in expectation of a demand that never came; I set no great store by the circumstance.

In this brief account of Lowell, and inadequate expression of the gratification it yielded to me, and cannot fail to afford any foreigner to whom the condition of such people at home is a subject of interest and anxious speculation, I have carefully abstained from drawing a comparison between these factories and those of our own land. Many of the circumstances whose strong influence has been at work for years in our manufacturing towns have not arisen here; and there is no manufacturing population in Lowell, so to speak: for these girls (often the daughters of small farmers) come from other States, remain a few years in the mills, and then go home for good.

The contrast would be a strong one, for it would be between the Good and Evil, the living light and deepest shadow. I abstain from it, because I deem it just to do so. But I only the more earnestly adjure all those whose eyes may rest on these pages, to pause and reflect upon the difference between this town and those great haunts of desperate misery: to call to mind, if they can in the midst of party strife and squabble, the efforts that must be made to purge them of their suffering and danger: and last, and foremost, to remember how the precious Time is rushing by.

I returned at night by the same railroad and in the same kind of car. One of the passengers being exceedingly anxious to expound at great length to my companion (not to me, of course) the true principles on which books of travel in America should be written by Englishmen, I feigned to fall asleep. But glancing all the way out at window from the corners of my eyes, I found abundance of entertainment for the rest of the ride in watching the effects of the wood fire, which had been invisible in the morning but were now brought out in full relief by the darkness: for we were travelling in a whirlwind of bright sparks, which showered about us like a storm of fiery snow.

CHAPTER V

WORCESTER. THE CONNECTICUT RIVER. HARTFORD. NEW HAVEN. TO NEW YORK

LEAVING Boston on the afternoon of Saturday the fifth of February, we proceeded by another railroad to Worcester: a pretty New England town, where we had arranged to remain under the hospitable roof of the Governor of the State, until Monday morning.

These towns and cities of New England (many of which would be villages in Old England), are as favourable specimens of the rural America, as their people are of rural Americans. The well-trimmed lawns and green meadows of home are not there; and the grass, compared with our ornamental plots and pastures, is rank, and rough, and wild: but delicate slopes of land, gently-swelling hills, wooded valleys, and slender streams, abound. Every little colony of houses has its church and school-house, peeping from among the white roofs and shady trees; every house is the whitest of the white; every Venetian blind the greenest of the green; every fine day's sky the bluest of the blue. A sharp dry wind and a slight frost had so hardened the roads when we alighted at Worcester, that their furrowed tracks were like ridges of granite. There was the usual aspect of newness on every object, of course. All the buildings looked as if they had been built and painted that morning, and could be taken down on Monday with very little trouble. In the keen evening air, every sharp outline looked a hundred times sharper than ever. The clean cardboard colonnades had no more perspective than a Chinese bridge on a tea-cup, and appeared equally well calculated for use. The razor-like edges of the detached cottages seemed to cut the very wind as it whistled against them, and to send it smarting on its way with a shriller cry than before. Those slightly-built wooden dwellings behind which the sun was setting with a brilliant lustre, could be so looked through and through, that the idea of any inhabitant being able to hide himself from the public gaze, or to have any secrets from the public eye, was not entertainable for a moment. Even where a blazing fire shone through the uncurtained window of some distant house, it had the air of being newly lighted, and of lacking warmth; and instead of awakening thoughts of a snug chamber, bright with faces that first saw the light round that same hearth, and ruddy with warm hangings, it came upon one suggestive of the smell of new mortar and damp walls.

So I thought, at least, that evening. Next morning when the sun was shining brightly, and the clear church bells were ringing, and sedate people in their best clothes enlivened the pathway near at hand and dotted the distant thread of road, there was a pleasant Sabbath peacefulness on everything, which it was good to feel. It would have been the better for an old church; better still for some old graves; but as it was, a wholesome repose and tranquillity pervaded the scene, which after the restless ocean and the hurried city, had a doubly grateful influence on the spirits.

We went on next morning, still by railroad, to Springfield. From that place to Hartford, whither we were bound, is a distance of only five-and-twenty miles, but at that time of the year the roads were so bad that the journey would probably have occupied ten or twelve hours. Fortunately, however, the winter having been unusually mild, the Connecticut River was 'open,' or in other words, not frozen. The captain of a small steamboat was going to make his first trip for the season that day (the second February trip, I believe, within the memory of man), and only waited for us to go on board. Accordingly, we went on board, with as little delay as might be. He was as good as his word, and started directly.

It certainly was not called a small steamboat without reason, I omitted to ask the question, but I should think it must have been of about half a pony power. Mr. Paap, the celebrated Dwarf, might have lived and died happily in the cabin, which was fitted with common sash-windows like an ordinary dwelling-house. These windows had bright-red curtains, too, hung on slack strings across the lower panes; so that it looked like the parlour of a Lilliputian public-house, which had got afloat in a flood or some other water accident, and was drifting nobody knows where. But even in this chamber there was a rocking-chair. It would be impossible to get on anywhere, in America, without a rocking-chair.

I am afraid to tell how many feet short this vessel was, or how many feet narrow: to apply the words length and width to such measurement would be a contradiction in terms. But I may state that we all kept the middle of the deck, lest the boat should unexpectedly tip over; and that the machinery, by some surprising process of condensation, worked between it and the keel: the whole forming a warm sandwich, about three feet thick.

It rained all day as I once thought it never did rain anywhere, but in the Highlands of Scotland. The river was full of floating blocks of ice, which were constantly crunching and cracking under us; and the depth of water, in the course we took to avoid the larger masses, carried down the middle of the river by the current, did not exceed a few inches. Nevertheless, we moved onward, dexterously; and being well wrapped up, bade defiance to the weather, and enjoyed the journey. The Connecticut River is a fine stream; and the banks in summer-time are, I have no doubt, beautiful: at all events, I was told so by a young lady in the cabin; and she should be a judge of beauty, if the possession of a quality include the appreciation of it, for a more beautiful creature I never looked upon.

After two hours and a half of this odd travelling (including a stoppage at a small town, where we were saluted by a gun considerably bigger than our own chimney), we reached Hartford, and straightway repaired to an extremely comfortable hotel: except, as usual, in the article of bed-rooms, which, in almost every place we visited, were very conducive to early rising.

We tarried here, four days. The town is beautifully situated in a basin of green hills; the soil is rich, well-wooded, and carefully improved. It is the seat of the local legislature of Connecticut, which sage body enacted, in bygone times, the renowned code of 'Blue Laws,' in virtue whereof, among other enlightened provisions, any citizen who could be proved to have kissed his wife on Sunday, was punishable, I believe, with the stocks. Too much of the old Puritan spirit exists in these parts to the present hour; but its influence has not tended, that I know, to make the people less hard in their bargains, or more equal in their dealings. As I never heard of its working that effect anywhere else, I infer that it never will, here. Indeed, I am accustomed, with reference to great professions and severe faces, to judge of the goods of the other world pretty much as I judge of the goods of this; and whenever I see a dealer in such commodities with too great a display of them in his window, I doubt the quality of the article within.

In Hartford stands the famous oak in which the charter of King Charles was hidden. It is now inclosed in a gentleman's garden. In the State House is the charter itself. I found the courts of law here, just the same as at Boston; the public institutions almost as good. The Insane Asylum is admirably conducted, and so is the Institution for the Deaf and Dumb.

I very much questioned within myself, as I walked through the Insane Asylum, whether I should have known the attendants from the patients, but for the few words which passed between the former, and the Doctor, in reference to the persons under their charge. Of course I limit this remark merely to their looks; for the conversation of the mad people was mad enough.

There was one little prim old lady, of very smiling and good-humoured appearance, who came sidling up to me from the end of a long passage, and with a curtsey of inexpressible condescension, propounded this unaccountable inquiry:

'Does Pontefract still flourish, sir, upon the soil of England?'

'He does, ma'am,' I rejoined.

'When you last saw him, sir, he was—'

'Well, ma'am,' said I, 'extremely well. He begged me to present his compliments. I never saw him looking better.'

At this the old lady was very much delighted. After glancing at me for a moment, as if to be quite sure that I was serious in my respectful air, she sidled back some paces; sidled forward again; made a sudden skip (at which I precipitately retreated a step or two); and said:

'*I* am an antediluvian, sir.'

I thought the best thing to say was, that I had suspected as much from the first. Therefore I said so.

'It is an extremely proud and pleasant thing, sir, to be an antediluvian,' said the old lady.

'I should think it was, ma'am,' I rejoined.

The old lady kissed her hand, gave another skip, smirked and sidled down the gallery in a most extraordinary manner, and ambled gracefully into her own bed-chamber.

In another part of the building, there was a male patient in bed; very much flushed and heated.

'Well,' said he, starting up, and pulling off his night-cap: 'It's all settled at last. I have arranged it with Queen Victoria.'

'Arranged what?' asked the Doctor.

'Why, that business,' pressing his hand wearily across his forehead, 'about the siege of New York.'

'Oh!' said I, like a man suddenly enlightened. For he looked at me for an answer.

'Yes. Every house without a signal will be fired upon by the British troops. No harm will be done to the others. No harm at all. Those that want to be safe, must hoist flags. That's all they'll have to do. They must hoist flags.'

Even while he was speaking he seemed, I thought, to have some faint idea that this talk was incoherent. Directly he had said these words, he lay down again; gave a kind of a groan; and covered his hot head with the blankets.

There was another: a young man, whose madness was love and music. After playing on the accordion a march he had composed, he was very anxious that I should walk into his chamber, which I immediately did.

By way of being very knowing, and humouring him to the top of his bent, I went to the window, which commanded a beautiful prospect, and remarked, with an address upon which I greatly plumed myself:

'What a delicious country you have about these lodgings of yours.'

'Poh!' said he, moving his fingers carelessly over the notes of his instrument: *'Well enough for such an Institution as this!'*

I don't think I was ever so taken aback in all my life.

'I have come here just for a whim,' he said coolly. 'That's all.'

'Oh! That's all!' said I.

'Yes. That's all. The Doctor's a smart man. He quite enters into it. It's a joke of mine. I like it for a time. You needn't mention it, but I think I shall go out next Tuesday!'

I assured him that I would consider our interview perfectly confidential; and rejoined the Doctor. As we were passing through a gallery on our way out, a well-dressed lady, of quiet and composed manners, came up, and proffering a slip of paper and a pen, begged that I would oblige her with an autograph. I complied, and we parted.

'I think I remember having had a few interviews like that, with ladies out of doors. I hope *she* is not mad?'

'Yes.'

'On what subject? Autographs?'

'No. She hears voices in the air.'

'Well!' though I, 'it would be well if we could shut up a few false prophets of these later times, who have professed to do the same; and I should like to try the experiment on a Mormonist or two to begin with.'

In this place, there is the best Jail for untried offenders in the world. There is also a very well-ordered State prison, arranged upon the same plans as that at Boston, except that here, there is always a sentry on the wall with a loaded gun. It contained at that time about two hundred prisoners. A spot was shown me in the sleeping ward, where a watchman was murdered some years since in the dead of night, in a desperate attempt to escape, made by a prisoner who had broken from his cell. A woman, too, was pointed out to me, who, for the murder of her husband, had been a close prisoner for sixteen years.

'Do you think,' I asked of my conductor, 'that after so very long an imprisonment, she has any thought or hope of ever regaining her liberty?'

'Oh dear yes,' he answered. 'To be sure she has.'

'She has no chance of obtaining it, I suppose?'

'Well, I don't know': which, by the bye, is a national answer. 'Her friends mistrust her.'

'What have *they* to do with it?' I naturally inquired.

'Well, they won't petition.'

'But if they did, they couldn't get her out, I suppose?'

'Well, not the first time, perhaps, nor yet the second, but tiring and wearying for a few years might do it.'

'Does that ever do it?'

'Why yes, that'll do it sometimes. Political friends'll do it sometimes. It's pretty often done, one way or another.'

I shall always entertain a very pleasant and grateful recollection of Hartford. It is a lovely place, and I had many friends there, whom I can never remember with indifference. We left it with no little regret on the evening of Friday the 11th ,and travelled that night by railroad to New Haven. Upon the way, the guard and I were formally introduced to each other (as we usually were on such occasions), and exchanged a variety of small-talk. We reached New Haven at about eight o'clock, after a journey of three hours, and put up for the night at the best inn.

New Haven, known also as the City of Elms, is a fine town. Many of its streets (as its *alias* sufficiently import) are planted with rows of grand old elm-trees; and the same natural ornaments surround Yale College, an establishment of considerable eminence and reputation. The various departments of this Institution are erected in a kind of park or common in the middle of the town, where they are dimly visible among the shadowing trees. The effect is very like that of an old cathedral yard in England; and when their branches are in full leaf, must be extremely picturesque. Even in the winter time, these groups of well-grown trees, clustering among the busy streets and houses of a thriving city, have a very quaint appearance; seeming to bring about a kind of compromise between town and country; as if each had met the other half-way, and shaken hands upon it; which is at once novel and pleasant.

After a night's rest, we rose early, and in good time went down to the wharf, and on board the packet New York *for* New York. This was the first American steamboat of any size that I had seen; and certainly to an English eye it was infinitely less like a steamboat than a huge floating bath. I could hardly persuade myself, indeed, but that the bathing establishment off Westminster Bridge, which I left a baby, had suddenly grown to an enormous size; run away from home; and set up in foreign parts as a steamer. Being in America, too, which our vagabonds do so particularly favour, it seemed the more probable.

The great difference in appearance between these packets and ours, is that there is so much of them out of the water: the main-deck being enclosed on all sides, and filled with casks and goods, like any second or third floor in a stock of warehouses; and the promenade or hurricane-deck being a-top of that again. A part of the machinery is always above this deck; where the connecting-rod, in a strong and lofty frame, is seen working away like an iron top-sawyer. There is seldom any mast or tackle: nothing aloft but two tall black chimneys. The man at the helm is shut up in a little house in the fore part of the boat (the wheel being connected with the rudder by iron chains, working the whole length of the deck); and the passengers, unless the weather be very fine indeed, usually congregate below. Directly you have left the wharf, all the life, and stir, and bustle of a packet ceases. You wonder for a long time how she goes on, for there seems to be nobody in charge of her: and when another of these dull machines comes splashing by, you feel quite indignant with it, as a sullen, cumbrous, ungraceful, unshiplike leviathan: quite forgetting that the vessel you are on board of, is its very counterpart.

There is always a clerk's office on the lower deck, where you pay your fare; a ladies' cabin; baggage and stowage rooms; engineer's room; and in short a great variety of perplexities which render the discovery of the gentlemen's cabin, a matter of some difficulty. It often occupies the whole length of the boat (as it did in this case), and has three or four tiers of berths on each side. When I first descended into the cabin of the New York, it looked, in my unaccustomed eyes, about as long as the Burlington Arcade.

The Sound, which has to be crossed on this passage, is not always a very safe or pleasant navigation, and has been the scene of some unfortunate accidents. It was a wet morning, and very misty, and we soon lost sight of land. The day was calm, however, and brightened towards noon. After exhausting (with good help from a friend) the larder, and the stock of bottled beer, I lay down to sleep: being very much tired with the fatigues of yesterday. But I awoke from my nap in time to hurry up, and see Hell Gate, the Hog's Back, the Frying Pan, and other notorious localities, attractive to all readers of famous Diedrich Knickerbocker's History. We were now in a narrow channel, with sloping banks on either side, besprinkled with pleasant villas, and made refreshing to the sight by turf and trees. Soon we shot in quick succession, past a lighthouse; a madhouse (how the lunatics flung up their caps and roared in sympathy with the headlong engine and the driving tide!); a jail; and other buildings: and so emerged into a noble bay, whose waters sprakled in the now cloudless sunshine like Nature's eyes turned up to Heaven.

Then there lay stretched out before us, to the right, confused heaps of buildings, with here and there a spire or steeple, looking

down upon the herd below; and here and there, again, a cloud of
lazy smoke; and in the foreground a forest of ships' masts, cheery
with flapping sails and waving flags. Crossing from among them
to the opposite shore, were steam ferryboats laden with people,
coaches, horses, waggons, baskets, boxes: crossed and recrossed by
other ferryboats: all travelling to and fro: and never idle. Stately
among these restless Insects, were two or three large ships, moving
with slow majestic pace, as creatures of a prouder kind, disdainful
of their puny journeys, and making for the broad sea. Beyond,
were shining heights, and islands in the glancing river, and a
distance scarcely less blue and bright than the sky it seemed to
meet. The city's hum and buzz, the clinking of capstans, the ringing of bells, the barking of dogs, the clattering of wheels,
tingled in the listening ear. All of which life and stir, coming
across the stirring water, caught new life and animation from its
free companionship; and, sympathising with its buoyant spirits,
glistened as it seemed in sport upon its surface, and hemmed the
vessel round, and plashed the water high about her sides, and,
floating her gallantly into the dock, flew off again to welcome
other comers, and speed before them to the busy port.

CHAPTER VI

NEW YORK

THE beautiful metropolis of America is by no means so clean a
city as Boston, but many of its streets have the same characteristics; except that the houses are not quite so fresh-coloured, the
sign-boards are not quite so gaudy, the gilded letters not quite
so golden, the bricks not quite so red, the stone not quite so
white, the blinds and area railings not quite so green, the knobs
and plates upon the street doors not quite so bright and twinkling.
There are many by-streets, almost as neutral in clean colours,
and positive in dirty ones, as by-streets in London; and there is
one quarter, commonly called the Five Points, which, in respect
to filth and wretchedness, may be safely backed against Seven
Dials, or any other part of famed St. Giles's.

The great promenade and thoroughfare, as most people know,
is Broadway; a wide and bustling street, which, from the Battery
Gardens to its opposite termination in a country road, may be
four miles long. Shall we sit down in an upper floor of the Carlton

House Hotel (situated in the best part of this main artery of New York), and when we are tired of looking down upon the life below, sally forth arm-in-arm, and mingle with the stream?

Warm weather! The sun strikes upon our heads at this open window, as though its rays were concentrated through a burning glass; but the day is in its zenith, and the season an unusual one. Was there ever such a sunny street as this Broadway! The pavement stones are polished with the tread of feet until they shine again; the red bricks of the houses might be yet in the dry, hot kilns; and the roofs of those omnibuses look as though, if water were poured on them, they would hiss and smoke, and smell like half-quenched fires. No stint of omnibuses here! Half a dozen have gone by within as many minutes. Plenty of hackney cabs and coaches too; gigs, phaetons, large-wheeled tilburies, and private carriages—rather of a clumsy make, and not very different from the public vehicle, but built for the heavy roads beyond the city pavement. Negro coachmen and white; in straw hats, black hats, white hats, glazed caps, fur caps; in coats of drab, black, brown, green, blue, nankeen, striped jean and linen; and there, in that one instance (look while it passes, or it will be too late), in suits of livery. Some southern republican that, who puts his blacks in uniform, and swells with Sultan pomp and power. Yonder, where that phaeton with the well-clipped pair of grays has stopped—standing at their heads now—is a Yorkshire groom, who has not been very long in these parts, and looks sorrowfully round for a companion pair of top-boots, which he may traverse the city half a year without meeting. Heaven save the ladies, how they dress! We have seen more colours in these ten minutes, than we should have seen elsewhere, in as many days. What various parasols! what rainbow silks and satins! what pinking of thin stockings, and pinching of thin shoes, and fluttering of ribbons and silk tassels, and display of rich cloaks with gaudy hoods and lining! The young gentlemen are fond, you see, of turning down their shirt-collars and cultivating their whiskers, especially under the chin; but they cannot approach the ladies in their dress or bearing, being, to say the truth, humanity of quite another sort. Byrons of the desk and counter, pass on, and let us see what kind of men those are behind ye: those two labourers in holiday clothes, of whom one carries in his hand a crumpled scrap of paper from which he tries to spell out a hard name, while the other looks about for it on all the doors and windows.

Irishmen both! You might know them, if they were masked, by their long-tailed blue coats and bright buttons, and their drab trousers, which they wear like men well used to working dresses, who are easy in no others. It would be hard to keep your model republics going, without the countrymen and countrywomen of those two labourers. For who else would dig, and delve, and drudge, and do domestic work, and make canals and roads, and execute great lines of Internal Improvements! Irishmen both, and sorely puzzled too, to find out what they seek. Let us go down, and help them, for the love of home, and that spirit of liberty which admits of honest service to honest men, and honest work for honest bread, no matter what it be.

That's well! We have got at the right address at last, though it is written in strange characters truly, and might have been scrawled with the blunt handle of the spade the writer better knows the use of, than a pen. Their way lies yonder, but what business takes them there? They carry savings: to hoard up? No. They are brothers, those men. One crossed the sea alone, and working very hard for one half-year, and living harder, saved funds enough to bring the other out. That done, they worked together side by side, contentedly sharing hard labour and hard living for another term, and then their sisters came, and then another brother, and lastly, their old mother. And what now? Why, the poor old crone is restless in a strange land, and yearns to lay her bones, she says, among her people in the old graveyard at home: and so they go to pay her passage back: and God help her and them, and every simple heart, and all who turn to the Jerusalem of their younger days, and have an altar-fire upon the cold hearth of their fathers.

This narrow thoroughfare, baking and blistering in the sun, is Wall Street: the Stock Exchange and Lombard Street of New York. Many a rapid fortune has been made in this street, and many a no less rapid ruin. Some of these very merchants whom you see hanging about here now, have locked up money in their strong-boxes, like the man in the Arabian Nights, and opening them again, have found but withered leaves. Below, here by the water-side, where the bowsprits of ships stretch across the footway, and almost thrust themselves into the windows, lie the noble American vessels which have made their Packet Service the finest in the world. They have brought hither the foreigners who abound in all the streets: not, perhaps, that there are more here, than in other commercial cities; but elsewhere, they have particular haunts, and you must find them out; here, they pervade the town.

We must cross Broadway again; gaining some refreshment from

the heat, in the sight of the great blocks of clean ice which are being carried into shops and bar-rooms; and the pine-apples and water-melons profusely displayed for sale. Fine streets of spacious houses here, you see!—Wall Street has furnished and dismantled many of them very often—and here a deep green leafy square. Be sure that this is a hospitable house with inmates to be affectionately remembered always, where they have the open door and pretty show of plants within, and where the child with laughing eyes is peeping out of window at the little dog below. You wonder what may be the use of this tall flagstaff in the by-street, with something like Liberty's head-dress on its top: so do I. But there is a passion for tall flagstaffs hereabouts and you may see its twin brother in five minutes, if you have a mind.

Again across Broadway, and so—passing from the many-coloured crowd and glittering shops—into another long main street, the Bowery. A railroad yonder, see where two stout horses trot along, drawing a score or two of people and a great wooden ark, with ease. The stores are poorer here; the passengers less gay. Clothes ready-made, and meat ready-cooked, are to be bought in these parts; and the lively whirl of carriages is exchanged for the deep rumble of carts and waggons. These signs which are so plentiful, in shape like river buoys, or small balloons, hoisted by cords to poles, and dangling there, announce, as you may see by looking up, 'OYSTERS IN EVERY STYLE. They tempt the hungry most at night, for then dull candles glimmering inside, illuminate these dainty words, and make the mouths of idlers water, as they read and linger.

What is this dismal-fronted pile of bastard Egyptian, like an enchanter's palace in a melodrama!—a famous prison, called The Tombs. Shall we go in?

So. A long narrow lofty building, stove-heated as usual, with four galleries, one above the other, going round it, and communicating by stairs. Between the two sides of each gallery, and in its centre, a bridge, for the greater convenience of crossing. On each of these bridges sits a man: dozing or reading, or talking to an idle companion. On each tier, are two opposite rows of small iron doors. They look like furnace-doors, but are cold and black, as though the fires within had all gone out. Some two or three are open, and women, with drooping heads bent down, are talking to the inmates. The whole is lighted by a skylight, but it is fast closed; and from the roof there dangle, limp and drooping, two useless windsails.

A man with keys appears, to show us round. A good-looking fellow, and, in his way, civil and obliging.

'Are those black doors the cells?'

'Yes.'

'Are they all full?'

'Well, they's pretty nigh full, and that's a fact, and no two ways about it.'

'Those at the bottom are unwholesome, surely?'

'Why, we *do* only put coloured people in 'em. That's the truth.'

'When do the prisoners take exercise?'

'Well, they do without it pretty much.'

'Do they never walk in the yard?'

'Considerable seldom.'

'Sometimes, I suppose?'

'Well, it's rare they do. They keep pretty bright without it.'

'But suppose a man were here for a twelvemonth. I know this is only a prison for criminals who are charged with grave offences, while they are awaiting their trial, or under remand, but the law here, affords criminals many means of delay. What with motions for new trials, and in arrest of judgment, and what not, a prisoner might be here for twelve months, I take it, might he not?'

"Well, I guess he might.'

'Do you mean to say that in all that time he would never come out at that little iron door, for exercise?'

'He might walk some, perhaps—not much.'

'Will you open one of the doors?'

'All, if you like.'

The fastenings jar and rattle, and one of the doors turns slowly on its hinges. Let us look in. A small bare cell, into which the light enters through a high chink in the wall. There is a rude means of washing, a table, and a bedstead. Upon the latter, sits a man of sixty; reading. He looks up for a moment; gives an impatient dogged shake; and fixes his eyes upon his book again. As we withdrew our heads, the door closes on him, and is fastened as before. This man has murdered his wife, and will probably be hanged.

'How long has he been here?'

'A month.'

'When will he be tried?'

'Next term.'

'When is that?'

'Next month.'

'In England, if a man be under sentence of death, even he has air and exercise at certain periods of the day.'

'Possible?'

With what stupendous and untranslatable coolness he says this, and how loungingly he leads on to the women's side: making, as he goes, a kind of iron castanet of the key and the stair-rail!

Each cell door on this side has a square aperture in it. Some of the women peep anxiously through it at the sound of footsteps; others shrink away in shame.—For what offence can that lonely child, of ten or twelve years old, be shut up here? Oh! that boy? He is the son of the prisoner we saw just now; is a witness against his father; and is detained here for safe keeping, until the trial; that's all.

But it is a dreadful place for the child to pass the long days and nights in. This is rather hard treatment for a young witness, is it not?—What says our conductor?

'Well, it an't a very rowdy life, and *that's* a fact!'

Again he clinks his metal castanet, and leads us leisurely away. I have a question to ask him as we go.

'Pray, why do they call this place The Tombs?'

'Well, it's the cant name.'

'I know it is. Why?'

'Some suicides happened here, when it was first built. I expect it come about from that.'

'I saw just now, that that man's clothes were scattered about the floor of his cell. Don't you oblige the prisoners to be orderly, and put such things away?'

'Where should they put 'em?'

'Not on the ground surely. What do you say to hanging them up?'

He stops and looks round to emphasise his answer:

'Why, I say that's just it. When they had hooks they *would* hang themselves, so they're taken out of every cell, and there's only the marks left where they used to be!'

The prison-yard in which he pauses now, has been the scene of terrible performances. Into this narrow, grave-like place, men are brought out to die. The wretched creature stands beneath the gibbet on the ground; the rope about his neck; and when the sign is given, a weight at its other end comes running down, and swings him up into the air—a corpse.

The law requires that there be present at this dismal spectacle, the judge, jury, and citizens to the amount of twenty-five. From the community it is hidden. To the dissolute and bad, the thing remains a frightful mystery. Between the criminal and them, the prison-wall is interposed as a thick gloomy veil. It is the curtain to his bed of death, his winding-sheet, and grave. From him it shuts out life, and all the motives to unrepenting hardihood in that last hour, which its mere sight and presence is often all-sufficient to sustain. There are no bold eyes to make him bold; no ruffians to uphold a ruffian's name before. All beyond the pitiless stone wall, is unknown space.

Let us go forth again into the cheerful streets.

Once more in Broadway! Here are the same ladies in bright colours, walking to and fro, in pairs and singly; yonder the very same light blue parasol which passed and repassed the hotel-window twenty times while we were sitting there. We are going to cross here. Take care of the pigs. Two portly sows are trotting up behind this carriage, and a select party of half a dozen gentlemen hogs have just now turned the corner.

Here is a solitary swine lounging homeward by himself. He has only one ear; having parted with the other to vagrant-dogs in the course of his city rambles. But he gets on very well without it; and leads a roving, gentlemanly, vagabond kind of life, somewhat answering to that of our club-men at home. He leaves his lodgings every morning at a certain hour, throws himself upon the town, gets through his day in some manner quite satisfactory to himself, and regularly appears at the door of his own house again at night, like the mysterious master of Gil Blas. He is a free-and-easy, careless, indifferent kind of pig, having a very large acquaintance among other pigs of the same character, whom he rather knows by sight than conversation, as he seldom troubles himself to stop and exchange civilities, but goes grunting down the kennel, turning up the news and small-talk of the city in the shape of cabbage-stalks and offal, and bearing no tails but his own: which is a very short one, for his old enemies, the dogs, have been at that too, and have left him hardly enough to swear by. He is in every respect a republican pig, going wherever he pleases, and mingling with the best society, on an equal, if not superior footing, for every one makes way when he appears, and the haughtiest give him the wall, if he prefer it. He is a great philosopher, and seldom moved, unless by the dogs before mentioned. Sometimes, indeed, you may see his small eye twinkling on a slaughtered friend, whose carcase garnishes a butcher's door-post, but he grunts out 'Such is life: all flesh is pork!' buries his nose in the mire again, and waddles down the gutter: comforting himself with the reflection that there is one snout the less to anticipate stray cabbage-stalks, at any rate.

They are the city scavengers, these pigs. Ugly brutes they are; having, for the most part, scanty brown backs, like the lids of old horsehair trunks: spotted with unwholesome black blotches. They have long, gaunt legs, too, and such peaked snouts, that if one of them could be persuaded to sit for his profile, nobody would recognise it for a pig's likeness. They are never attended upon, or fed, or driven, or caught, but are thrown upon their own resources in early life, and become preternaturally knowing in consequence. Every pig knows where he lives, much better than anybody could tell him. At this hour, just as evening is closing in, you will see them roaming towards bed by scores, eating their way to the last. Occasionally, some youth among them who has over-eaten himself, or has been worried by dogs, trots shrinkingly homeward, like a prodigal son: but this a rare case: perfect self-possession and self-reliance, and immovable composure, being their foremost attributes.

The streets and shops are lighted now; and as the eye travels down the long thoroughfare, dotted with bright jets of gas, it is reminded of Oxford Street, or Piccadilly. Here and there a flight of broad stone cellar-steps appears, and a painted lamp directs you to the Bowling Saloon, or Ten-Pin alley; Ten-Pins being a game of mingled chance and skill, invented when the legislature passed an act forbidding Nine-Pins. At other downward flights of steps, are other lamps, marking the whereabouts of oyster-cellars—pleasant retreats, say I: not only by reason of their wonderful cookery of oysters, pretty nigh as large as cheese-plates (or for thy dear sake, heartiest of Greek Professors!), but because of all kinds of eaters of fish, or flesh, or fowl, in these latitudes, the swallowers of oysters alone are not gregarious; but subduing themselves, as it were, to the nature of what they work in, and copying the coyness of the thing they eat, do sit apart in curtained boxes, and consort by twos, not by two hundreds.

But how quiet the streets are! Are there no itinerant bands; no wind or stringed instruments? No, not one. By day, are there no Punches, Fantoccini, Dancing-dogs, Jugglers, Conjurers, Orchestrinas, or even Barrel-organs? No, not one. Yes, I remember one. One barrel-organ and a dancing-monkey—sportive by nature, but fast fading into a dull, lumpish monkey, of the Utilitarian school. Beyond that, nothing lively; no, not so much as a white mouse in a twirling cage.

Are there no amusements? Yes. There is a lecture-room across

the way, from which that glare of light proceeds, and there may
be evening service for the ladies thrice a week, or oftener. For
the young gentlemen, there is the counting-house, the store, the
bar-room: the latter, as you see through these windows, pretty
full. Hark! to the clinking sound of hammers breaking lumps
of ice, and to the cool gurgling of the pounded bits, as, in the
process of mixing, they are poured from glass to glass! No amusements? What are these suckers of cigars and swallowers of
strong drinks, whose hats and legs we see in every possible variety
of twist, doing, but amusing themselves? What are the fifty newspapers, which those precocious urchins are bawling down the
street, and which are kept filed within, what are they but amusements? Not vapid waterish amusements, but good strong stuff;
dealing in round abuse and blackguard names; pulling off the
roofs of private houses, as the Halting Devil did in Spain; pimp-
ing and pandering for all degrees of vicious taste, and gorging
with coined lies the most voracious maw; imputing to every man
in public life the coarsest and the vilest motives; scaring away
from the stabbed and prostrate body-politic, every Samaritan of
clear conscience and good deeds; and setting on, with yell and
whistle and the clapping of foul hands, the vilest vermin and worst
birds of prey.—No amusements!

Let us go on again; and passing this wilderness of an hotel with
stores about its base, like some Continental theatre, or the London
Opera House shorn of its colonnade, plunge into the Five Points.
But it is needful, first, that we take as our escort these two heads
of the police, whom you would know for sharp and well-trained
officers if you met them in the Great Desert. So true it is, that certain pursuits, wherever carried on, will stamp men with the same
character. These two might have been begotten, born, and bred, in
Bow Street.

We have seen no beggars in the streets by night or day; but of
other kinds of strollers, plenty. Poverty, wretchedness, and vice,
are rife enough where we are going now.

This is the place: these narrow ways, diverging to the right
and left, and reeking everywhere with dirt and filth. Such lives
as are led here, bear the same fruits here as elsewhere. The coarse
and bloated faces at the doors, have counterparts at home, and all
the wide world over. Debauchery has made the very houses prematurely old. See how the rotten beams are tumbling down, and
how the patched and broken windows seem to scowl dimly, like
eyes that have been hurt in drunken frays. Many of those pigs live
here. Do they ever wonder why their masters walk upright in

lieu of going on all-fours? and why they talk instead of grunting?

So far, nearly every house is a low tavern; and on the bar-room walls, are coloured prints of Washington, and Queen Victoria of England, and the American Eagle. Among the pigeon-holes that hold the bottles, are pieces of plate-glass and coloured paper, for there is, in some sort, a taste for decoration, even here. And as seamen frequent these haunts, there are maritime pictures by the dozen: of partings between sailors and their lady-loves, portraits of William, of the ballad, and his Black-Eyed Susan; of Will Watch, the Bold Smuggler; of Paul Jones the Pirate, and the like: on which the painted eyes of Queen Victoria, and of Washington to boot, rest in as strange companionship, as on most of the scenes that are enacted in their wondering presence.

What place is this, to which the squalid street conducts us? A kind of square of leprous houses, some of which are attainable only by crazy wooden stairs without. What lies beyond this tottering flight of steps, that creak beneath our tread?—a miserable room, lighted by one dim candle, and destitute of all comfort, save that which may be hidden in a wretched bed. Beside it, sits a man: his elbows on his knees: his forehead hidden in his hands. 'What ails that man?' asks the foremost officer. 'Fever,' he sullenly replies, without looking up. Conceive the fancies of a fevered brain, in such a place as this!

Ascend these pitch-dark stairs, heedful of a false footing on the trembling boards, and grope your way with me into this wolfish den, where neither ray of light nor breath of air, appears to come. A negro lad, startled from his sleep by the officer's voice—he knows it well—but comforted by his assurance that he has not come on business, officiously bestirs himself to light a candle. The match flickers for a moment, and shows great mounds of dusky rags upon the ground; then dies away and leaves a denser darkness than before, if there can be degrees in such extremes. He stumbles down the stairs and presently comes back, shading a flaring taper with his hand. Then the mounds of rags are seen to be astir, and rise slowly up, and the floor is covered with heaps of negro women, waking from their sleep: their white teeth chattering, and their bright eyes glistening and winking on all sides with surprise and fear, like the countless repetition of one astonished African face in some strange mirror.

Mount up these other stairs with no less caution (there are traps and pitfalls here, for those who are not so well escorted as ourselves) into the housetop; where the bare beams and rafters meet overhead, and calm night looks down through the crevices

in the roof. Open the door of one of these cramped hutches full
of sleeping negroes. Pah! They have a charcoal fire within; there
is a smell of singeing clothes, or flesh, so close they gather round
the brazier; and vapours issue forth that blind and suffocate.
From every corner, as you glance about you in these dark retreats, some figure crawls half-awakened, as if the judgment-hour
were near at hand, and every obscene grave were giving up its dead.
Where dogs would howl to lie, women, and men, and boys slink
off to sleep, forcing the dislodged rats to move away in quest
of better lodgings.

Here too are lanes and alleys, paved with mud knee-deep, un-
derground chambers, where they dance and game; the walls be-
decked with rough designs of ships, and forts, and flags, and American eagles out of number: ruined houses, open to the street,
whence, through wide gaps in the walls, other ruins loom upon the
eye, as though the world of vice and misery had nothing else to
show: hideous tenements which take their name from robbery and
murder: all that is loathsome, drooping, and decayed is here.

Our leader has his hand upon the latch of 'Almack's,' and
calls to us from the bottom of the steps; for the assembly-room
of the Five Point fashionables is approached by a descent. Shall
we go in? It is but a moment.

Heydey! the landlady of Almack's thrives! A buxom fat
mulatto woman, with sparkling eyes, whose head is daintily ornamented with a handkerchief of many colours. Nor is the landlord
much behind her in his finery, being attired in a smart blue jacket,
like a ship's steward, with a thick gold ring upon his little finger,
round his neck a gleaming golden watchguard. How glad he is
to see us! What will we please to call for? A dance? It shall
be done directly, sir: 'a regular breakdown.'

The corpulent black fiddler, and his friend who plays the tambourine, stamp upon the boarding of the small raised orchestra in
which they sit, and play a lively measure. Five or six couple
come upon the floor, marshalled by a lively young negro, who is
the wit of the assembly, and the greatest dancer known. He never
leaves off making queer faces, and is the delight of all the rest,
who grin from ear to ear incessantly. Among the dancers are two
young mulatto girls, with large, black, drooping eyes, and head-
gear after the fashion of the hostess, who are as shy, or feign
to be, as though they never danced before, and so look down before the visitors, that their partners can see nothing but the long
fringed lashes.

But the dance commences. Every gentleman sets as long as he

likes to the opposite lady, and the opposite lady to him, and all are so long about it that the sport begins to languish, when suddenly the lively hero dashes in to the rescue. Instantly the fiddler grins, and goes at it tooth and nail; there is new energy in the tambourine; new laughter in the dancers; new smiles in the landlady; new confidence in the landlord; new brightness in the very candles. Single shuffle, double shuffle, cut and cross-cut; snapping his fingers, rolling his eyes, turning in his knees, presenting the backs of his legs in front, spinning about on his toes and heels like nothing but the man's fingers on the tambourine; dancing with two left legs, two right legs, two wooden legs, two wire legs, two spring legs—all sorts of legs and no legs—what is this to him? And in what walk of life, or dance of life, does man ever get such stimulating applause as thunders about him, when, having danced his partner off her feet, and himself too, he finishes by leaping gloriously on the bar-counter, and calling for something to drink, with the chuckle of a million of counterfeit Jim Crows, in one inimitable sound!

The air, even in these distempered parts, is fresh after the stifling atmosphere of the houses; and now, as we emerge into a broader street, it blows upon us with a purer breath, and the stars look bright again. Here are The Tombs once more. The city watchhouse is a part of the building. It follows naturally on the sights we have just left. Let us see that, and then to bed.

What! do you thrust your common offenders against the police discipline of the town, into such holes as these? Do men and women, against whom no crime is proved, lie here all night in perfect darkness, surrounded by the noisome vapours which encircle that flagging lamp you light us with, and breathing this filthy and offensive stench! Why, such indecent and disgusting dungeons as these cells, would bring disgrace upon the most despotic empire in the world! Look at them, man—you, who see them every night, and keep the keys. Do you see what they are? Do you know how drains are made below the streets, and wherein these human sewers differ, except in being always stagnant?

Well, he don't know. He has had five-and-twenty young women locked up in this very cell at one time, and you'd hardly realise what handsome faces there were among 'em.

In God's name! shut the door upon the wretched creature who is in it now, and put its screen before a place, quite unsurpassed in all the vice, neglect, and devilry, of the worst old town in Europe.

Are people really left all night, untried, in those black sties?— Every night. The watch is set at seven in the evening. The magistrate opens his court at five in the morning. That is the earliest hour at which the first prisoner can be released; and if an officer appear against him, he is not taken out till nine o'clock or ten.— But if any one among them die in the interval, as one man did, not long ago? Then he is half-eaten by the rats in an hour's time; as that man was; and there an end.

What is this intolerable tolling of great bells, and crashing of wheels, and shouting in the distance? A fire. And what that deep red light in the opposite direction? Another fire. And what these charred and blackened walls we stand before? A dwelling where a fire has been. It was more than hinted, in an official report, not long ago, that some of these conflagrations were not wholly accidental, and that speculation and enterprise found a field of exertion, even in flames: but be this as it may, there was a fire last night, there are two to-night, and you may lay an even wager there will be at least one, to-morrow. So, carrying that with us for our comfort, let us say, Good-night, and climb upstairs to bed.

One day, during my stay in New York, I paid a visit to the different public institutions on Long Island, or Rhode Island: I forget which. One of them is a Lunatic Asylum. The building is handsome; and is remarkable for a spacious and elegant staircase. The whole structure is not yet finished, but it is already one of considerable size and extent, and is capable of accommodating a very large number of patients.

I cannot say that I derived much comfort from the inspection of this charity. The different wards might have been cleaner and better ordered; I saw nothing of that salutary system which had impressed me so favourably elsewhere; and everything had a lounging, listless, madhouse air, which was very painful. The moping idiot, cowering down with long dishevelled hair; the gibbering maniac, with his hideous laugh and pointed finger; the vacant eye, the fierce wild face, the gloomy picking of the hands and lips, and munching of the nails: there they were all, without disguise, in naked ugliness and horror. In the dining-room, a bare, dull, dreary place, with nothing for the eye to rest on but the empty walls, a woman was locked up alone. She was bent, they told me, on committing suicide. If anything could have strengthened her in her resolution, it would certainly have been the insupportable monotony of such an existence.

The terrible crowd with which these halls and galleries were filled, so shocked me, that I abridged my stay within the shortest limits, and declined to see that portion of the building in which the refractory and violent were under closer restraint. I have no doubt that the gentleman who presided over this establishment at the time I write of, was competent to manage it, and had done all in his power to promote its usefulness: but will it be believed that the miserable strife of Party feeling is carried even into this sad refuge of afflicted and degraded humanity? Will it be believed that the eyes which are to watch over and control the wanderings of minds on which the most dreadful visitation to which our nature is exposed has fallen, must wear the glasses of some wretched side in Politics? Will it be believed that the governor of such a house as this, is appointed, and deposed, and changed perpetually, as Parties fluctuate and vary, and as their despicable weathercocks are blown this way or that? A hundred times in every week, some new most paltry exhibition of that narrow-minded and injurious Party Spirit, which is the Simoom of America, sickening and blighting everything of wholesome life within its reach, was forced upon my notice; but I never turned my back upon it with feelings of such deep disgust and measureless contempt, as when I crossed the threshold of this madhouse.

At a short distance from this building is another called the Alms House, that is to say, the workhouse of New York. This is a large Institution also: lodging, I believe, when I was there, nearly a thousand poor. It was badly ventilated, and badly lighted; was not too clean; and impressed me, on the whole, very uncomfortably. But it must be remembered that New York, as a great emporium of commerce, and as a place of general resort, not only from all parts of the States, but from most parts of the world, has always a large pauper population to provide for; and labours, therefore, under peculiar difficulties in this respect. Nor must it be forgotten that New York is a large town, and that in all large towns a vast amount of good and evil is intermixed and jumbled up together.

In the same neighbourhood is the Farm, where young orphans are nursed and bred. I did not see it, but I believe it is well conducted; and I can the more easily credit it, from knowing how mindful they usually are, in America, of that beautiful passage in the Litany which remembers all sick persons and young children.

I was taken to these Institutions by water, in a boat belonging to the Island jail, and rowed by a crew of prisoners, who were dressed in a striped uniform of black and buff, in which they looked like faded tigers. They took me, by the same conveyance, to the Jail itself.

It is an old prison, and quite a pioneer establishment, on the plan I have already described. I was glad to hear this, for it is unquestionably a very indifferent one. The most is made, however, of the means it possesses, and it is as well regulated as such a place can be.

The women work in covered sheds, erected for that purpose. If I remember right, there are no shops for the men, but be that as it may, the greater part of them labour in certain stone-quarries near at hand. The day being very wet indeed, this labour was suspended, and the prisoners were in their cells. Imagine these cells, some two or three hundred in number, and in every one a man locked up; this one at his door for air, with his hands thrust through the grate; this one in bed (in the middle of the day, remember); and this one flung down in a heap upon the ground, with his head against the bars, like a wild beast. Make the rain pour down, outside, in torrents. Put the everlasting stove in the midst; hot, and suffocating, and vaporous, as a witch's caldron. Add a collection of gentle odours, such as would arise from a thousand mildewed umbrellas, wet through, and a thousand buck-baskets, full of half-washed linen—and there is the prison, as it was that day.

The prison for the State at Sing Sing, is, on the other hand, a model jail. That, and Auburn, are, I believe, the largest and best examples of the silent system.

In another part of the city, is the Refuge for the Destitute: an Institution whose object is to reclaim youthful offenders, male and female, black and white, without distinction; to teach them useful trades, apprentice them to respectable masters, and make them worthy members of society. Its design, it will be seen, is similar to that at Boston; and it is a no less meritorious and admirable establishment. A suspicion crossed my mind during my inspection of this noble charity, whether the superintendent had quite sufficient knowledge of the world and wordly characters; and whether he did not commit a great mistake in treating some young girls, who were to all intents and purposes, by their years and their past lives, women, as though they were little children; which certainly had a ludicrous effect in my eyes, and, or I am much mistaken, in theirs also. As the Institution, however, is always under the vigilant examination of a body of gentlemen of great intelligence and experience, it cannot fail to be well conducted; and whether I am right or wrong in this slight particular, is unimportant to its deserts and character, which it would be difficult to estimate too highly.

In addition to these establishments, there are in New York, excellent hospitals and schools, literary institutions and libraries;

an admirable fire department (as indeed it should be, having constant practice), and charities of every sort and kind. In the suburbs there is a spacious cemetery; unfinished yet, but every day improving. The saddest tomb I saw there was 'The Strangers' Grave. Dedicated to the different hotels in this city.'

There are three principal theatres. Two of them, the Park and the Bowery, are large, elegant, and handsome buildings, and are, I grieve to write it, generally deserted. The third, the Olympic, is a tiny show-box for vaudevilles and burlesques. It is singularly well conducted by Mr. Mitchell, a comic actor of great quiet humour and originality, who is well remembered and esteemed by London playgoers. I am happy to report of this deserving gentleman, that his benches are usually well filled, and that his theatre rings with merriment every night. I had almost forgotten a small summer theatre, called Niblo's, with gardens and open-air amusements attached; but I believe it is not exempt from the general depression under which Theatrical Property, or what is humorously called by that name, unfortunately labours.

The country round New York, is surpassingly and exquisitely picturesque. The climate, as I have already intimated, is somewhat of the warmest. What it would be, without the sea breezes which come from its beautiful Bay in the evening time, I will not throw myself or my readers into a fever by inquiring.

The tone of the best society in this city, is like that of Boston; here and there, it may be, with a greater infusion of the mercantile spirit, but generally polished and refined, and always most hospitable. The houses and tables are elegant; the hours later and more rakish; and there is, perhaps, a greater spirit of contention in reference to appearances, and the display of wealth and costly living. The ladies are singularly beautiful.

Before I left New York I made arrangements for securing a passage home in the George Washington packet ship, which was advertised to sail in June: that being the month in which I had determined, if prevented by no accident in the course of my ramblings, to leave America.

I never thought that going back to England, returning to all who are dear to me, and to pursuits that have insensibly grown to be a part of my nature, I could have felt so much sorrow as I endured, when I parted at last, on board this ship, with the friends who had accompanied me from this city. I never thought the name of any place, so far away and so lately known, could ever associate itself in my mind with the crowd of affectionate remembrances that now cluster about it. There are those in this city who would brighten, to me, the darkest winter-day that ever glimmered and went out in Lapland; and before whose presence even Home grew dim, when they and I exchanged that painful word which mingles with our every thought and deed; which haunts our cradleheads in infancy, and closes up the vista of our lives in age.

CHAPTER VII

PHILADELPHIA, AND ITS SOLITARY PRISON

THE journey from New York to Philadelphia, is made by railroad, and two ferries; and usually occupies between five and six hours. It was a fine evening when we were passengers in the train: and watching the bright sunset from a little window near the door by which we sat, my attention was attracted to a remarkable appearance issuing from the windows of the gentlemen's car immediately in front of us, which I supposed for some time was occasioned by a number of industrious persons inside, ripping open feather-beds, and giving the feathers to the wind. At length it occurred to me that they were only spitting, which was indeed the case; though how any number of passengers which it was possible for that car to contain, could have maintained such a playful and incessant shower of expectoration, I am still at a loss to understand: notwithstanding the experience in all salivatory phenomena which I afterwards acquired.

I made acquaintance, on this journey, with a mild and modest young quaker, who opened the discourse by informing me, in a grave whisper, that his grandfather was the inventor of cold-drawn castor oil. I mention the circumstance here, thinking it probable that this is the first occasion on which the valuable medicine in question was ever used as a conversational aperient.

We reached the city, late that night. Looking out of my chamber-window, before going to bed, I saw, on the opposite side of the way, a handsome building of white marble, which had a mournful ghost-like aspect, dreary to behold. I attributed this to the sombre influence of the night, and on rising in the morning looked out again, expecting to see its steps and portico thronged with groups of people passing in and out. The door was still tight shut, however; the same cold cheerless air prevailed; and the building looked as if the marble statue of Don Guzman could alone have any business to transact within its gloomy walls. I hastened to inquire its name and purpose, and then my surprise vanished. It was the Tomb of many fortunes; the Great Catacomb of investment; the memorable United States Bank.

The stoppage of this bank, with its all ruinous consequences, had cast (as I was told on every side) a gloom on Philadelphia, under the depressing effect of which it yet laboured. It certainly did seem rather dull and out of spirits.

It is a handsome city, but distractingly regular. After walking about it for an hour or two, I felt that I would have given the world for a crooked street. The collar of my coat appeared to stiffen, and the brim of my hat to expand, beneath its quakery influence. My hair shrunk into a sleek short crop, my hands folded themselves upon my breast of their own calm accord, and thoughts of taking lodgings in Mark Lane over against the Market Place, and of making a large fortune by speculations in corn, came over me involuntarily.

Philadelphia is most bountifully provided with fresh water, which is showered and jerked about, and turned on, and poured off, everywhere. The Waterworks, which are on a height near the city, are no less ornamental than useful, being tastefully laid out as a public garden, and kept in the best and neatest order. The river is dammed at this point, and forced by its own power into certain high tanks or reservoirs, whence the whole city, to the top stories of the houses, is supplied at a very trifling expense.

There are various public institutions. Among them a most excellent Hospital—a quaker establishment, but not sectarian in the great benefits it confers; a quiet, quaint old Library, named after Franklin; a handsome Exchange and Post Office; and so forth. In connection with the quaker Hospital, there is a picture by West, which is exhibited for the benefit of the funds of the institution. The subject is, our Saviour healing the sick, and it is, perhaps, as favourable a specimen of the master as can be seen anywhere. Whether this be high or low praise, depends upon the reader's taste.

In the same room, there is a very characteristic and lifelike portrait by Mr. Sully, a distinguished American artist.

My stay in Philadelphia was very short, but what I saw of its society, I greatly liked. Treating of its general characteristics, I should be disposed to say that it is more provincial than Boston or New York, and that there is afloat in the fair city, an assumption of taste and criticism, savouring rather of those genteel discussions upon the same themes, in connection with Shakespeare and the Musical Glasses, of which we read in the Vicar of Wakefield. Near the city, is a most splendid unfinished marble structure for the Girard College, founded by a deceased gentleman of that name, and of enormous wealth, which, if completed according to the original design, will be perhaps the richest edifice of modern times. But the bequest is involved in legal disputes, and pending them the work has stopped; so that like many other great undertakings in America, even this is rather going to be done one of these days, than doing now.

In the outskirts, stands a great prison, called the Eastern Penitentiary: conducted on a plan peculiar to the state of Pennsylvania. The system here, is rigid, strict, and hopeless solitary confinement. I believe it, in its effects, to be cruel and wrong.

In its intention, I am well convinced that it is kind, humane, and meant for reformation; but I am persuaded that those who devised this system of Prison Discipline, and those benevolent gentlemen who carry it into execution, do not know what it is that they are doing. I believe that very few men are capable of estimating the immense amount of torture and agony which this dreadful punishment, prolonged for years, inflicts upon the sufferers; and in guessing at it myself, and in reasoning from what I have seen written upon their faces, and what to my certain knowledge they feel within, I am only the more convinced that there is a depth of terrible endurance in it which none but the sufferers themselves can fathom, and which no man has a right to inflict upon his fellow-creature. I hold this slow and daily tampering with the mysteries of the brain, to be immeasurably worse than any torture of the body: and because its ghastly signs and tokens are not so palpable to the eye and sense of touch as scars upon the flesh; because its wounds are not upon the surface, and it extorts few cries that human ears can hear; therefore I the more denounce it, as a secret punishment which slumbering humanity is not roused up to stay. I hesitated once, debating with myself, whether, if I had the power of saying 'Yes' or 'No,' I would allow it to be tried in certain cases, where the terms of imprisonment were short; but now, I solemnly declare, that with no rewards or honours could I walk a happy man beneath the open sky by day, or lay me down upon my bed at night, with the consciousness that one human creature, for any length of time, no matter what, lay suffering this unknown punishment in his silent cell, and I the cause, or I consenting to it in the least degree.

I was accompanied to this prison by two gentlemen officially connected with its management, and passed the day in going from cell to cell; and talking with the inmates. Every facility was afforded me, that the utmost courtesy could suggest. Nothing was concealed or hidden from my view, and every piece of information that I sought, was openly and frankly given. The perfect order of the building cannot be praised too highly, and of the excellent motives of all who are immediately concerned in the administration of the system, there can be no kind of question.

Between the body of the prison and the outer wall, there is a spacious garden. Entering it, by a wicket in the massive gate, we pursued the path before us to its other termination, and passed into a large chamber, from which seven long passages radiate. On either side of each, is a long, long row of low cell doors, with a certain number over every one. Above, a gallery of cells like those below, except that they have no narrow yard attached (as those in the ground tier have), and are somewhat smaller. The possession of two of these, is supposed to compensate for the absence of so much air and exercise as can be had in the dull strip attached to each of the others, in an hour's time every day; and therefore every prisoner in this upper story has two cells, adjoining and communicating with each other.

Standing at the central point, and looking down these dreary passages, the dull repose and quiet that prevails, is awful. Occasionally, there is a drowsy sound from some lone weaver's shuttle, or shoemaker's last, but it is stifled by the thick walls and heavy dungeon-door, and only serves to make the general stillness more profound. Over the head and face of every prisoner who comes into this melancholy house, a black hood is drawn; and in this dark shroud, an emblem of the curtain dropped between him and the living world, he is led to the cell from which he never again comes forth, until his whole term of imprisonment has expired. He never hears of wife and children; home or friends; the life or death of any single creature. He sees the prison-officers, but with that exception he never looks upon human countenance, or hears a human voice. He is a man buried alive; to be dug out in the slow round of years; and in the mean time dead to everything but torturing anxieties and horrible despair.

His name, and crime, and term of suffering, are unknown, even to the officer who delivers him his daily food. There is a number over his cell-door, and in a book of which the governor of the prison has one copy, and the moral instructor another: this is the index of his history. Beyond these pages the prison has no record of his existence; and though he live to be in the same cell ten weary years, he has no means of knowing, down to the very last hour, in what part of the building it is situated; what kind of men there are about him; whether in the long winter nights there are living people near, or he is in some lonely corner of the great jail, with walls, and passages, and iron doors between him and the nearest sharer in its solitary horrors.

Every cell has double doors: the outer one of sturdy oak, the other of grated iron, wherein there is a trap through which his food is handed. He has a Bible, and a slate and pencil, and under certain restrictions, has sometimes other books, provided for the purpose, and pen and ink and paper. His razor, plate, and can, and basin, hang upon the wall, or shine upon the little shelf. Fresh water is laid on in every cell, and he can draw it at his pleasure. During the day, his bedstead turns up against the wall, and leaves more space for him to work in. His loom, or bench, or wheel, is there; and there he labours, sleeps and wakes, and counts the seasons as they change, and grows old.

The first man I saw, was seated at his loom, at work. He had been there six years, and was to remain, I think, three more. He had been convicted as a receiver of stolen goods, but even after his long imprisonment, denied his guilt, and said he had been hardly dealt by. It was his second offence.

He stopped his work when we went in, took off his spectacles, and answered freely to everything that was said to him, but always with a strange kind of pause first, and in a low, thoughtful voice. He wore a paper hat of his own making, and was pleased to have it noticed and commended. He had very ingeniously manufactured a sort of Dutch clock from some disregarded odds and ends; and his vinegar bottle served for the pendulum. Seeing me interested in this contrivance, he looked up at it with a great deal of pride, and said that he had been thinking of improving it, and that he hoped the hammer and a little piece of broken glass beside it 'would play music before long.' He had extracted some colours from the yarn with which he worked, and painted a few poor figures on the wall. One, of a female, over the door, he called 'The Lady of the Lake.'

He smiled as I looked at these contrivances to wile away the time; but when I looked from them to him, I saw that his lip trembled, and could have counted the beating of his heart. I forget how it came about, but some allusion was made to his having a wife. He shook his head at the word, turned aside, and covered his face with his hands.

'But you are resigned now!' said one of the gentlemen after a short pause, during which he had resumed his former manner. He answered with a sign that seemed quite reckless in its hopelessness, 'Oh yes, oh yes! I am resigned to it.' 'And are a better man, you think?' 'Well, I hope so: I'm sure I hope I may be.' 'And time goes pretty quickly?' 'Time is very long, gentlemen, within these four walls!'

He gazed about him—Heaven only knows how wearily!—as he said these words; and in the act of doing so, fell into a strange stare as if he had forgotten something. A moment afterwards he sighed heavily, put on his spectacles, and went about his work again.

In another cell, there was a German, sentenced to five years' imprisonment for larceny, two of which had just expired. With colours procured in the same manner, he had painted every inch of the walls and ceiling quite beautifully. He had laid out the few feet of ground, behind, with exquisite neatness, and had made a little bed in the centre, that looked by the bye like a grave. The taste and ingenuity he had displayed in everything were most extraordinary; and yet a more dejected, heart-broken, wretched creature, it would be difficult to imagine. I never saw such a picture of forlorn affliction and distress of mind. My heart bled for him; and when the tears ran down his cheeks, and he took one of the visitors aside, to ask, with his trembling hands nervously clutching at his coat to detain him, whether there was no hope of his dismal sentence being commuted, the spectacle was really too painful to witness. I never saw or heard of any kind of misery that impressed me more than the wretchedness of this man.

In a third cell, was a tall strong black, a burglar, working at his proper trade of making screws and the like. His time was nearly out. He was not only a very dexterous thief, but was notorious for his boldness and hardihood, and for the number of his previous convictions. He entertained us with a long account of his achievements, which he narrated with such infinite relish, that he actually seemed to lick his lips as he told us racy anecdotes of stolen plate, and of old ladies whom he had watched as they sat at windows in silver spectacles (he had plainly had an eye to their metal even from the other side of the street) and had afterwards robbed. This fellow, upon the slightest encouragement, would have mingled with his professional recollections the most detestable cant; but I am very much mistaken if he could have surpassed the unmitigated hypocrisy with which he declared that he blessed the day on which he came into that prison, and that he never would commit another robbery as long as he lived.

There was one man who was allowed, as an indulgence, to keep rabbits. His room having rather a close smell in consequence, they called to him at the door to come out into the passage. He compiled of course, and stood shading his haggard face in the unwonted sunlight of the great window, looking as wan and unearthly as if he had been summoned from the grave. He had a white rabbit in his breast; and when the little creature, getting down upon the ground, stole back into the cell, and he, being dismissed, crept timidly after it, I thought it would have been very hard to say in what respect the man was the nobler animal of the two.

There was an English thief, who had been there but a few days out of seven years: a villainous, low-browed, thin-lipped fellow, with a white face; who had as yet no relish for visitors, and who, but for the additional penalty, would have gladly stabbed me with his shoemaker's knife. There was another German who had entered the jail but yesterday, and who started from his bed when we looked in, and pleaded, in his broken English, very hard for work. There was a poet, who after doing two days' work in every four-and-twenty hours, one for himself and one for the prison, wrote verses about ships (he was by trade a mariner), and 'the maddening wine-cup,' and his friends at home. There were very many of them. Some reddened at the sight of visitors, and some turned very pale. Some two or three had prisoner nurses with them, for they were very sick; and one, a fat old negro whose leg had been taken off within the jail, had for his attendant a classical scholar and an accomplished surgeon, himself a prisoner likewise. Sitting upon the stairs, engaged in some slight work, was a pretty coloured boy. 'Is there no refuge for young criminals in Philadelphia, then? said I. 'Yes, but only for white children.' Noble aristocracy in crime!

There was a sailor who had been there upwards of eleven years, and who in a few months' time would be free. Eleven years of solitary confinement!

'I am very glad to hear your time is nearly out.' What does he say? Nothing. Why does he stare at his hands, and pick the flesh upon his fingers, and raise his eyes for an instant, every now and then, to those bare walls which have seen his head turn grey? It is a way he has sometimes.

Does he never look men in the face, and does he always pluck at those hands of his, as though he were bent on parting skin and bone? It is his humour; nothing more.

It is his humour too, to say that he does not look forward to going out; that he is not glad the time is drawing near; that he did look forward to it once, but that was very long ago; that he has lost all care for everything. It is his humour to be a helpless, crushed, and broken man. And, Heaven be his witness that he has his humour thoroughly gratified!

There were three young women in adjoining cells, all convicted at the same time of a conspiracy to rob their prosecutor. In the silence and solitude of their lives they had grown to be quite beautiful. Their looks were very sad, and might have moved the sternest visitor to tears, but not to that kind of sorrow which the contemplation of the men awaken. One was a young girl; not twenty, as I recollect; whose snow-white room was hung with the work of some former prisoner, and upon whose downcast face the sun in all its splendour shone down through the high chink in the wall, where one narrow strip of bright blue sky was visible. She was very penitent and quiet; had come to be resigned, she said (and I believe her); and had a mind at peace. 'In a word, you are happy here?' said one of my companions. She struggled—she did struggle very hard—to answer, Yes; but raising her eyes, and meeting that glimpse of freedom overhead, she burst into tears, and said, 'She tried to be; she uttered no complaint; but it was natural that she should sometimes long to go out of that one cell: she could not help *that*,' she sobbed, poor thing!

I went from cell to cell that day; and every face I saw, or word I heard, or incident I noted, is present to my mind in all its painfulness. But let me pass them by, for one, more pleasant, glance of a prison on the same plan which I afterwards saw at Pittsburg.

When I had gone over that, in the same manner, I asked the governor if he had any person in his charge who was shortly going out. He had one, he said, whose time was up next day; but he had only been a prisoner two years.

Two years! I looked back through two years of my own life—out of jail, prosperous, happy, surrounded by blessings, comforts, good fortune—and thought how wide a gap it was, and how long those two years passed in solitary captivity would have been. I have the face of this man, who was going to be released next day, before me now. It is almost more memorable in its happiness than the other faces in their misery. How easy and how natural it was for him to say that the system was a good one; and that the time went 'pretty quick—considering'; and that when a man once felt that he had offended the law, and must satisfy it, 'he got along, somehow': and so forth!

'What did he call you back to say to you, in that strange

flutter?' I asked of my conductor, when he had locked the door and joined me in the passage.

'Oh! That he was afraid the soles of his boots were not fit for walking, as they were a good deal worn when he came in; and that he would thank me very much to have them mended, ready.'

Those boots had been taken off his feet, and put away with the rest of his clothes, two years before!

I took that opportunity of inquiring how they conducted themselves immediately before going out; adding that I presumed they trembled very much.

'Well, it's not so much a trembling,' was the answer—'though they do quiver—as a complete derangement of the nervous system. They can't sign their names to the book; sometimes can't even hold the pen; look about 'em without appearing to know why, or where they are; and sometimes get up and sit down again, twenty times in a minute. This is when they're in the office, where they are taken with the hood on, as they were brought in. When they get outside the gate, they stop, and look first one way and then the other; not knowing which to take. Sometimes they stagger as if they were drunk, and sometimes are forced to lean against the fence, they're so bad:—but they clear off in course of time.'

As I walked among these solitary cells, and looked at the faces of the men within them, I tried to picture to myself the thoughts and feelings natural to their condition. I imagined the hood just taken off, and the scene of their captivity disclosed to them in all its dismal monotony.

At first, the man is stunned. His confinement is a hideous vision; and his old life a reality. He throws himself upon his bed, and lies there abandoned to despair. By degrees the insupportable solitude and barrenness of the place rouses him from his stupor, and when the trap in his grated door is opened, he humbly begs and prays for work. 'Give me some work to do, or I shall go raving mad!'

He has it; and by fits and starts applies himself to labour; but every now and then there comes upon him a burning sense of the years that must be wasted in that stone coffin, and an agony so piercing in the recollection of those who are hidden from his view and knowledge, that he starts from his seat, and striding up and down the narrow room with both hands clasped on his uplifed head, hears spirits tempting him to beat his brains out on the wall.

Again he falls upon his bed, and lies there, moaning. Suddenly he starts up, wondering whether any other man is near; whether there is another cell like that on either side of him: and listens keenly.

There is no sound, but other prisoners may be near for all that He remembers to have heard once, when he little thought of coming here himself, that the cells were so constructed that the prisoners could not hear each other, though the officers could hear them. Where is the nearest man—upon the right, or on the left? or is there one in both directions? Where is he sitting now—with his face to the light? or is he walking to and fro? How is he dressed? Has he been here long? Is he much worn away? Is he very white and spectre-like? Does *he* think of his neighbour too?

Scarcely venturing to breathe, and listening while he thinks, he conjures up a figure with his back towards him, and imagines it moving about in this next cell. He has no idea of the face, but he is certain of the dark form of a stooping man. In the cell upon the other side, he puts another figure, whose face is hidden from him also. Day after day, and often when he wakes up in the middle of the night, he thinks of these two men until he is almost distracted. He never changes them. There they are always as he first imagined them—an old man on the right; a younger man upon the left—whose hidden features torture him to death, and have a mystery that makes him tremble.

The weary days pass on with solemn pace, like mourners at a funeral; and slowly he begins to feel that the white walls of the cell have something dreadful in them: that their colour is horrible: that their smooth surface chills his blood: that there is one hateful corner which torments him. Every morning when he wakes, he hides his head beneath the coverlet, and shudders to see the ghastly ceiling looking down upon him. The blessed light of day itself peeps in, an ugly phantom face, through the unchangeable crevice which is his prison window.

By slow but sure degrees, the terrors of that hateful corner swell until they beset him at all times; invade his rest, make his dreams hideous, and his nights dreadful. At first, he took a strange dislike to it; feeling as though it gave birth in his brain to something of corresponding shape, which ought not to be there, and racked his head with pains. Then he began to fear it, then to dream of it, and of men whispering its name and pointing to it. Then he could not bear to look at it, nor yet to turn his back upon it. Now, it is every night the lurking-place of a ghost: a shadow:—a silent something, horrible to see, but whether bird, or beast, or muffled human shape, he cannot tell.

When he is in his cell by day, he fears the little yard without. When he is in the yard, he dreads to re-enter the cell. When night comes, there stands the phantom in the corner. If he have the courage to stand in its place, and drive it out (he had once: being desperate), it broods upon his bed. In the twilight, and always at the same hour, a voice calls to him by name; as the darkness thickens, his Loom begins to live; and even that, his comfort, is a hideous figure, watching him till daybreak.

Again, by slow degrees, these horrible fancies, depart from him one by one: returning sometimes, unexpectedly, but at longer intervals, and in less alarming shapes. He has talked upon religious matters with the gentleman who visits him, and has read his Bible, and has written a prayer upon his slate, and hung it up as a kind of protection, and an assurance of Heavenly companionship. He dreams now, sometimes, of his children or his wife, but is sure that they are dead, or have deserted him. He is easily moved to tears; is gentle, submissive, and broken-spirited. Occasionally, the old agony comes back: a very little thing will revive it; even a familiar sound, or the scent of summer flowers in the air; but it does not last long, now: for the world without, has come to be the vision, and this solitary life, the sad reality.

If his term of imprisonment be short—I mean comparatively, for short it cannot be—the last half-year is almost worst than all; for then he thinks the prison will take fire and he be burnt in the ruins, or that he is doomed to die within the walls, or that he will be detained on some false charge and sentenced for another term: or that something, no matter what, must happen to prevent his going at large. And this is natural, and impossible to be reasoned against, because, after his long separation from human life, and his great suffering, any event will appear to him more probable in the contemplation, than the being restored to liberty and his fellow-creatures.

If his period of confinement had been very long, the prospect of release bewilders and confuses him. His broken heart may flutter for a moment, when he thinks of the world outside, and what it might have been to him in all those lonely years, but that is all. The cell-door has been closed too long on all its hopes and cares. Better to have hanged him in the beginning than bring him to this pass, and send him forth to mingle with his kind, who are his kind no more.

On the haggard face of every man among these prisoners, the same expression sat. I know not what to liken it to. It had something of that strained attention which we see upon the faces of the blind and deaf, mingled with a kind of horror, as though they had all been secretly terrified. In every little chamber that I entered, and at every grate through which I looked, I seemed to see the same appalling countenance. It lives in my memory, with the fascination of a remarkable picture. Parade before my eyes, a hundred men, with one among them newly released from this solitary suffering, and I would point him out.

The faces of the women, as I have said, it humanises and refines. Whether this be because of their better nature, which is elicited in solitude, or because of their being gentler creatures, of greater patience and longer suffering, I do not know; but so it is. That the punishment is nevertheless, to my thinking, fully as cruel and as wrong in their case, as in that of the men, I need scarcely add.

My firm conviction is that, independent of the mental anguish it occasions—an anguish so acute and so tremendous, that all imagination of it must fall far short of the reality—it wears the mind into a morbid state, which renders it unfit for the rough contact and busy action of the world. It is my fixed opinion that those who have undergone this punishment, MUST pass into society again morally unhealthy and diseased. There are many instances on record, of men who have chosen, or have been condemned, to lives of perfect solitude, but I scarcely remember one, even among sages of strong and vigourous intellect, where its effect has not become apparent, in some disordered train of thought, or some gloomy hallucination. What monstrous phantoms, bred of despondency and doubt, and born and reared in solitude, have stalked upon the earth, making creation ugly, and darkening the face of Heaven!

Suicides are rare among these prisoners: are almost, indeed, unknown. But no argument in favour of the system, can reasonably be deduced from this circumstance, although it is very often urged. All men who have made diseases of the mind their study, know perfectly well that such extreme depression and despair as will change the whole character, and beat down all its powers of elasticity and self-resistance, may be at work within a man, and yet stop short of self-destruction. This is a common case.

That it makes the senses dull, and by degrees impairs the bodily faculties, I am quite sure. I remarked to those who were with me in this very establishment at Philadelphia, that the criminals who had been there long, were deaf. They, who were in the habit of seeing these men constantly, were perfectly amazed at the idea, which they regarded as groundless and fanciful. And yet the very first prisoner to whom they appealed—one of their own selection—confirmed my impression (which was unknown to him) instantly, and said, with a genuine air it was impossible to doubt, that he couldn't think how it happened, but he *was* growing very dull of hearing.

That it is a singularly unequal punishment, and affects the worst man least, there is no doubt. In its superior efficiency as a means of reformation, compared with that other code of regulations which allows the prisoners to work in company without communicating together, I have not the smallest faith. All the instances of reformation that were mentioned to me, were of a kind that might have been—and I have no doubt whatever, in my own mind, would have been—equally well brought about by the Silent System. With regard to such men as the negro burglar and the English thief, even the most enthusiastic have scarcely any hope of their conversion.

It seems to me that the objection that nothing wholesome or good has ever had its growth in such unnatural solitude, and that even a dog or any of the more intelligent among beasts, would pine, and mope, and rust away, beneath its influence, would be in itself a sufficient argument against this system. But when we recollect, in addition, how very cruel and severe it is, and that a solitary life is always liable to peculiar and distinct objections of a most deplorable nature, which have arisen here, and call to mind, moreover, that the choice is not between this system, and a bad or ill-considered one, but between it and another which has worked well, and is, in its whole design and practice, excellent; there is surely more than sufficient reason for abandoning a mode of punishment attended by so little hope or promise, and fraught, beyond dispute, with such a host of evils.

As a relief to its contemplation, I will close this chapter with a curious story arising out of the same theme, which was related to me, on the occasion of this visit, by some of the gentlemen concerned.

At one of the periodical meetings of the inspectors of this prison, a working man of Philadelphia presented himself before the Board, and earnestly requested to be placed in solitary confinement. On being asked what motive could possibly prompt him to make this strange demand, he answered that he had an irristible propensity to get drunk; that he was constantly indulging it, to his great misery and ruin; that he had no power of resistance; that he wished to be put beyond the reach of temptation; and that he could think of no better way than this. It was pointed out to him, in reply, that the prison was for criminals who had been tried and sentenced by the law, and could not be made available for any such fanciful purposes; he was exhorted to abstain from intoxicating drinks, as he surely might if he would; and received other very good advice, with which he retired, exceedingly dissatisfied with the result of his application.

He came again, and again, and again, and was so very earnest and importunate, that at last they took counsel together, and said, 'He will certainly qualify himself for admission, if we reject him any more. Let us shut him up. He will soon be glad to go away, and then we shall get rid of him.' So they made him sign a statement which would prevent his ever sustaining an action for false imprisonment, to the effect that his incarceration was voluntary, and of his own seeking; they requested him to take notice that the officer in attendance had orders to release him at any hour of the day or night, when he might knock upon his door for that purpose; but desired him to understand, that once going out, he would not be admitted any more. These conditions agreed upon, and he still remaining in the same mind, he was conducted to the prison, and shut up in one of the cells.

In this cell, the man, who had not the firmness to leave a glass of liquor standing untasted on a table before him—in this cell, in solitary confinement, and working every day at his trade of shoemaking, this man remained nearly two years. His health beginning to fail at the expiration of that time, the surgeon recommended that he should work occasionally in the garden; and as he liked the notion very much, he went about this new occupation with great cheerfulness.

He was digging here, one summer day, very industriously, when the wicket in the outer gate chanced to be left open: showing, beyond, the well-remembered dusty road and sunburnt fields. The way was as free to him as to any man living, but he no sooner raised his head and caught sight of it, all shining in the light, than, with the involuntary instinct of a prisoner, he cast away his spade, scampered off as fast as his legs would carry him, and never once looked back.

CHAPTER VIII

WASHINGTON. THE LEGISLATURE. AND THE PRESIDENT'S HOUSE

WE left Philadelphia by steamboat, at six o'clock one very cold morning, and turned our faces towards Washington.

In the course of this day's journey, as on subsequent occasions, we encountered some Englishmen (small farmers, perhaps, or country publicans at home) who were settled in America, and were travelling on their own affairs. Of all grades and kinds of men that jostle one in the public conveyances of the States, these are often the most intolerable and the most insufferable companions. United to every disagreeable characteristic that the worst kind of American travellers possess, these countrymen of ours display an amount of insolent conceit and cool assumption of superiority, quite monstrous to behold. In the coarse familiarity of their approach, and the effrontery of their inquisitiveness (which they are in great haste to assert, as if they panted to revenge themselves upon the decent old restraints of home), they surpass any native specimens that came within my range of observation: and I often grew so patriotic when I saw and heard them, that I would cheerfully have submitted to a reasonable fine, if I could have given any other country in the whole world, the honour of claiming them for its children.

As Washington may be called the head-quarters of tobacco-tinctured saliva, the time is come when I must confess, without any disguise, that the prevalence of those two odious practices of chewing and expectorating began about this time to be anything but agreeable, and soon became most offensive and sickening. In all the public places of America, this filthy custom is recognised. In the courts of law, the judge has his spittoon, the crier his, the witness his, and the prisoner his; while the jurymen and spectators are provided for, as so many men who in the course of nature must desire to spit incessantly. In the hospitals, the students of medicine are requested, by notices upon the wall, to eject their tobacco juice into the boxes provided for that purpose, and not to discolour the stairs. In public buildings, visitors are implored, through the same agency, to squirt the essence of their quids, or 'plugs,' as I have heard them called by gentlemen learned in this kind of sweet-meat, into the national spittoons, and not about the bases of the marble columns. But in some parts, this custom is inseparably mixed up with every meal and morning call, and with all the transactions of social life. The stranger, who follows in the track I took myself, will find it in its full bloom and glory, luxuriant in all its alarming recklessness, at Washington. And let him not persuade himself (as I once did, to my shame) that previous tourists have exaggerated its extent. The thing itself is an exaggeration of nastiness, which cannot be outdone.

On board this steamboat, there were two young gentlemen, with shirt-collars reversed as usual, and armed with very big walking-sticks; who planted two seats in the middle of the deck, at a distance of some four paces apart; took out their tobacco-boxes; and sat down opposite each other, to chew. In less than a quarter of an hour's time, these hopeful youths had shed about them on the clean boards, a copious shower of yellow rain; clearing, by that means, a kind of magic circle, within whose limits no intruders dared to come, and which they never failed to refresh and re-refresh before a spot was dry. This being before breakfast, rather disposed me, I confess, to nausea; but looking attentively at one of the expectorators, I plainly saw that he was young in chewing, and felt inwardly uneasy, himself. A glow of delight came over me at this discovery; and as I marked his face turn paler and paler, and saw the ball of tobacco in his left cheek, quiver with his suppressed agony, while yet he spat, and chewed, and spat again, in emulation of his older friend, I could have fallen on his neck and implored him to go on for hours.

We all sat down to a comfortable breakfast in the cabin below, where there was no more hurry or confusion than at such a meal in England, and where there was certainly greater politeness exhibited than at most of our stage-coach banquets. At about nine o'clock we arrived at the railroad station, and went on by the cars. At noon we turned out again, to cross a wide river in another steamboat; landed at a continuation of the railroad on the opposite shore; and went on by other cars; in which, in the course of the next hour or so, we crossed by wooden bridges, each a mile in length, two creeks, called respectively Great and Little Gunpowder. The water in both was blackened with flights of canvas-backed ducks, which are most delicious eating, and abound hereabouts at that season of the year.

These bridges are of wood, have no parapet, and are only just wide enough for the passage of the trains; which, in the event of the smallest accident, would inevitably be plunged into the river.

They are startling contrivances, and are most agreeable when passed.

We stopped to dine at Baltimore, and being now in Maryland, were waited on, for the first time, by slaves. The sensation of exacting any service from human creatures who are bought and sold, and being, for the time, a party as it were to their condition, is not an enviable one. The institution exists, perhaps, in its least repulsive and most mitigated form in such a town as this; but it *is* slavery; and though I was, with respect to it, an innocent man, its presence filled me with a sense of shame and self-reproach.

After dinner, we went down to the railroad again, and took our seats in the cars for Washington. Being rather early, those men and boys who happened to have nothing particular to do, and were curious in foreigners, came (according to custom) round the carriage in which I sat; let down all the windows; thrust in their heads and shoulders; hooked themselves on conveniently, by their elbows; and fell to comparing notes on the subject of my personal appearance, with as much indifference as if I were a stuffed figure. I never gained so much uncompromising information with reference to my own nose and eyes, and various impressions wrought by my mouth and chin on different minds, and how my head looks when it is viewed from behind, as on these occasions. Some gentlemen were only satisfied by exercising their sense of touch; and the boys (who are surprisingly precocious in America) were seldom satisfied, even by that, but would return to the charge over and over again. Many a budding president has walked into my room with his cap on his head and his hands in his pockets, and stared at me for two whole hours: occasionally refreshing himself with a tweak of his nose, or a draught from the water-jug; or by walking to the windows and inviting other boys in the street below, to come up and do likewise: crying, 'Here he is!' 'Come on!' 'Bring all your brothers!' with other hospitable entreaties of that nature.

We reached Washington at about half-past six that evening, and had upon the way a beautiful view of the Capitol, which is a fine building of the Corinthian order, placed upon a noble and commanding eminence. Arrived at the hotel, I saw no more of the place that night; being very tired, and glad to get to bed.

Breakfast over next morning, I walk about the streets for an hour or two, and, coming home, throw up the window in the front and back, and look out. Here is Washington, fresh in my mind and under my eye.

Take the worst parts of the City Road and Pentonville, or the straggling outskirts of Paris, where the houses are smallest, preserving all their oddities, but especially the small shops and dwellings, occupied in Pentonville (but not in Washington) by furniture-brokers, keepers of poor eating-houses, and fanciers of birds. Burn the whole down; build it up again in wood and plaster; widen it a little: throw in part of St. John's Wood; put green blinds outside all the private houses, with a red curtain and a white one in every window; plough up all the roads; plant a great deal of coarse turf in every place where it ought *not* to be; erect three handsome buildings in stone and marble, anywhere, but the more entirely out of everybody's way the better; call one the Post Office, one the Patent Office, and one the Treasury; make it scorching hot in the morning, and freezing cold in the afternoon, with an occasional tornado of wind and dust; leave a brick-field without the bricks, in all central places where a street may naturally be expected: and that's Washington.

The hotel in which we live, is a long row of small houses fronting on the street, and opening at the back upon a common yard, in which hangs a great triangle. Whenever a servant is wanted, somebody beats on this triangle from one stroke up to seven, according to the number of the house in which his presence is required; and as all the servants are always being wanted, and none of them ever come, this enlivening engine is in full performance the whole day through. Clothes are drying in the same yard; female slaves, with cotton handkerchiefs twisted round their heads, are running to and fro on the hotel business; black waiters cross and recross with dishes in their hands; two great dogs are playing upon a mound of loose bricks in the centre of the little square; a pig is turning up his stomach to the sun, and grunting 'that's comfortable!'; and neither the men, nor the women, nor the dogs, nor the pig, nor any created creature, takes the smallest notice of the triangle, which is tingling madly all the time.

I walk to the front window, and look across the road upon a long, straggling row of houses, one story high, terminating, nearly opposite, but a little to the left, in a melancholy piece of waste ground with frowzy grass, which looks like a small piece of country that has taken to drinking, and has quite lost itself. Standing anyhow and all wrong, upon this open space, like something meteoric that has fallen down from the moon, is an odd, lop-sided, one-eyed kind of wooden building, that looks like a church, with a flag-staff as long as itself sticking out of a steeple something larger than a tea-chest. Under the window, is a small stand of

coaches, whose slave-drivers are sunning themselves on the steps
of our door, and talking idly together. The three most obtrusive
houses near at hand, are the three meanest. On one—a shop,
which never has anything in the window, and never has the door
open—is painted in large characters, 'THE CITY LUNCH.' At another, which looks like a backway to somewhere else, but is an
independent building in itself, oysters are procurable in every
style. At the third, which is a very, very little tailor's shop, pants
are fixed to order; or in other words, pantaloons are made to
measure. And that is our street in Washington.

It is sometimes called the City of Magnificent Distances, but
it might with greater propriety be termed the City of Magnificent Intentions; for it is only on taking a bird's-eye view of it
from the top of the Capitol, that one can at all comprehend the
vast designs of its projector, an aspiring Frenchman. Spacious
avenues, that begin in nothing, and lead nowhere; streets, mile-
long, that only want houses, roads, and inhabitants; public buildings that need but a public to be complete; and ornaments of great
thoroughfares, which only lack great thoroughfares to ornament—
are its leading features. One might fancy the season over, and
most of the houses gone out of town for ever with their masters.
To the admirers of cities it is a Barmecide Feast; a pleasant field
for the imagination to rove in; a monument raised to a deceased
project, with not even a legible inscription to record its departed
greatness.

Such as it is, it is likely to remain. It was originally chosen for
the seat of Government, as a means of averting the conflicting
jealousies and interests of the different States; and very probably, too, as being remote from mobs: a consideration not to be
slighted, even in America. It has no trade or commerce of its
own: having little or no population beyond the President and his
establishment; the members of the legislature who reside there
during the session; the Government clerks and officers employed
in the various departments; the keepers of the hotels and boarding-houses; and the tradesmen who supply their tables. It is very
unhealthy. Few people would live in Washington, I take it, who
were not obliged to reside there; and the tides of emigration and
speculation, those rapid and regardless currents, are little likely to
flow at any time towards such dull and sluggish water.

The principal features of the Capitol, are, of course, the two
houses of Assembly. But there is, besides, in the centre of the
building, a fine rotunda, ninety-six feet in diameter, and ninety-
six high, whose circular wall is divided into compartments, orna-

mented by historical pictures. Four of these have for their subjects prominent events in the revolutionary struggle. They were
painted by Colonel Trumbull, himself a member of Washington's
staff at the time of their occurrence; from which circumstance
they derive a peculiar interest of their own. In this same hall
Mr. Greenough's large statue of Washington has been lately placed.
It has great merits of course, but it struck me as being rather
strained and violent for its subject. I could wish, however, to
have seen it in a better light than it can ever be viewed in, where
it stands.

There is a very pleasant and commodious library in the Capitol;
and from a balcony in front, the bird's-eye view, of which I have
just spoken, may be had, together with a beautiful prospect of
the adjacent country. In one of the ornamented portions of the
building, there is a figure of Justice; whereunto the Guide Book
says, 'the artist at first contemplated giving more of nudity, but
he was warned that the public sentiment in this country would
not admit of it, and in his caution he has gone, perhaps, into the
opposite extreme.' Poor Justice! she has been made to wear much
stranger garments in America than those she pines in, in the
Capitol. Let us hope that she has changed her dress-maker since
they were fashioned, and that the public sentiment of the country did not cut out the clothes she hides her lovely figure in,
just now.

The House of Representatives is a beautiful and spacious hall,
of semicircular shape, supported by handsome pillars. One part
of the gallery is appropriated to the ladies, and there they sit in
front rows, and come in, and go out, as at a play or concert.
The chair is canopied, and raised considerably above the floor of
the House; and every member has an easy chair and a writing
desk to himself: which is denounced by some people out of doors
as a most unfortunate and injudicious arrangement, tending to
long sittings and prosaic speeches. It is an elegant chamber
to look at, but a singularly bad one for all purposes of hearing.
The Senate, which is smaller, is free from this objection, and is
exceedingly well adapted to the uses for which it is designed.
The sittings, I need hardly add, take place in the day; and the
parliamentary forms are modelled on those of the old country.

I was sometimes asked, in my progress through other places,
whether I had not been very much impressed by the *heads* of the
law-makers at Washington; meaning not their chiefs and leaders,
but literally their individual and personal heads, whereon their
hair grew, and whereby the phrenological character of each leg-

islator was expressed: and I almost as often struck my questioner dumb with indignant consternation by answering 'No, that I didn't remember being at all overcome.' As I must, at whatever hazard, repeat the avowal here, I will follow it up by relating my impressions on this subject in as few words as possible.

In the first place—it may be from some imperfect development of my organ of veneration—I do not remember having ever fainted away, or having been moved to tears of joyful pride, at sight of any legislative body. I have borne the House of Commons like a man, and have yielded to no weakness, but slumber, in the House of Lords. I have seen elections for borough and county, and have never been impelled (no matter which party won) to damage my hat by throwing it up into the air in triumph, or to crack my voice by shouting forth any reference to our Glorious Constitution, to the noble purity of our independent voters, or the unimpeachable integrity of our independent members. Having withstood such strong attacks upon my fortitude, it is possible that I may be of a cold and insensible temperament, amounting to iciness, in such matters; and therefore my impressions of the live pillars of the Capitol at Washington must be received with such grains of allowance as this free confession may seem to demand.

Did I see in this public body an assemblage of men, bound together in the sacred names of Liberty and Freedom, and so asserting the chaste dignity of those twin goddesses, in all their discussions, as to exalt at once the Eternal Principles to which their names are given, and their own character and the character of their countrymen, in the admiring eyes of the whole world?

It was but a week, since an aged, grey-haired man, a lasting honour to the land that gave him birth, who has done good service to his country, as his forefathers did, and who will be remembered scores upon scores of years, after the worms bred in its corruption, are but so many grains of dust—it was but a week, since this old man had stood for days upon his trial before this very body, charged with having dared to assert the infamy of that traffic, which has for its accursed merchandise men and women, and their unborn children. Yes. And publicly exhibited in the same city all the while; gilded, framed and glazed; hung up for general admiration; shown to strangers not with shame, but pride; its face not turned towards the wall, itself not taken down and burned; is the Unanimous Declaration of the Thirteen United States of America which solemnly declares that All Men are created Equal; and are endowed by their Creator with the Inalienable Rights of Life, Liberty, and the Pursuit of Happiness!

It was not a month, since this same body had sat calmly by, and heard a man, one of themselves, with oaths which beggars in their drink reject, threaten to cut another's throat from ear to ear. There he sat, among them; not crushed by the general feeling of the assembly, but as good a man as any.

There was but a week to come, and another of that body, for doing his duty to those who sent him there; for claiming in a Republic the Liberty and Freedom of expressing their sentiments, and making known their prayer; would be tried, found guilty, and have strong censure passed upon him by the rest. His was a grave offence indeed; for years before, he had risen up and said, 'A gang of male and female slaves for sale, warranted to breed like cattle, linked to each other by iron fetters, are passing now along the open street beneath the windows of your Temple of Equality! Look!' But there are many kinds of hunters engaged in the Pursuit of Happiness, and they go variously armed. It is the Inalienable Right of some among them, to take the field after *their* Happiness equipped with cat and cart-whip, stocks, and iron collar, and to shout their view halloa! (always in praise of Liberty) to the music of clanking chains and bloody stripes.

Where sat the many legislators of coarse threats; of words and blows such as coalheavers deal upon each other, when they forget their breeding? On every side. Every session had its anecdotes of that kind, and the actors were all there.

Did I recognize in this assembly, a body of men, who, applying themselves in a new world to correct some of the falsehoods and vices of the old, purified the avenues to Public Life, paved the dirty ways to Place and Power, debated and made laws for the Common Good, and had no party but their Country?

I saw in them, the wheels that move the meanest perversion of virtuous Political Machinery that the worst tools ever wrought. Despicable trickery at elections; under-handed tamperings with public officers; cowardly attacks upon opponents, with scurrilous newspapers for shields, and hired pens for daggers; shameful trucklings to mercenary knaves, whose claim to be considered, is, that every day and week they sow new crops of ruin with their venal types, which are the dragon's teeth of yore, in everything but sharpness; aidings and abettings of every bad inclination in the popular mind and artful suppressions of all its good influences: such things as these, and in a word, Dishonest Faction in its most depraved and most unblushing form, stared out from every corner of the crowded hall.

Did I see among them, the intelligence and refinement: the true, honest, patriotic heart of America? Here and there, were drops of its blood and life, but they scarcely coloured the stream of desperate adventurers which sets that way for profit and for pay. It is the game of these men, and of their profligate organs, to make the strife of politics so fierce and brutal, and so destructive of all self-respect in worthy men, that sensitive and delicate-minded persons shall be kept aloof, and they, and such as they, be left to battle out their selfish views unchecked. And thus this lowest of all scrambling fights goes on, and they who in other countries would, from their intelligence and station, most aspire to make the laws, do here recoil the farthest from that degradation.

That there are, among the representatives of the people in both Houses, and among all parties, some men of high character and great abilities, I need not say. The foremost among those politicians who are known in Europe, have been already described, and I see no reason to depart from the rule I have laid down for my guidance, of abstaining from all mention of individuals. It will be sufficient to add, that to the most favourable accounts that have been written of them, I more than fully and most heartily subscribe; and that personal intercourse and free communication have bred within me, not the result predicted in the very doubtful proverb, but increased admiration and respect. They are striking men to look at, hard to deceive, prompt to act, lions in energy, Crichtons in varied accomplishments, Indians in fire of eye and gesture, Americans in strong and generous impulse; and they as well represent the honour and wisdom of their country at home, as the distinguished gentleman who is now its minister at the British Court sustains its highest character abroad.

I visited both houses nearly every day, during my stay in Washington. On my initiatory visit to the House of Representatives, they divided against a decision of the chair; but the chair won. The second time I went, the member who was speaking, being interrupted by a laugh, mimicked it, as one child would in quarrelling with another, and added, 'that he would make honourable gentlemen opposite, sing out a little more on the other side of their mouths presently.' But interruptions are rare; the speaker being usually heard in silence. There are more quarrels than with us, and more threatenings than gentlemen are accustomed to exchange in any civilised society of which we have record: but farm-yard imitations have not as yet been imported from the Parliament of the United Kingdom. The feature in oratory which appears to be the most practised, and most relished, is the constant repetition of the same idea or shadow of an idea in fresh words; and the inquiry out of doors is not, 'What did he say?' but, 'How long did he speak?' These, however, are but enlargements of a principle which prevails elsewhere.

The Senate is a dignified and decorous body, and its proceedings are conducted with much gravity and order. Both houses are handsomely carpeted; but the state to which these carpets are reduced by the universal disregard of the spittoon with which every honourable member is accommodated, and the extraordinary improvements on the pattern which are squirted and dabbled upon it in every direction, do not admit of being described. I will merely observe, that I strongly recommend all strangers not to look at the floor; and if they happen to drop anything, though it be their purse, not to pick it up with an ungloved hand on any account.

It is somewhat remarkable, too, at first, to say the least, to see so many honourable members with swelled faces; and it is scarcely less remarkable to discover that this appearance is caused by the quantity of tobacco they contrive to stow within the hollow of the cheek. It is strange enough too, to see an honourable gentleman leaning back in his tilted chair with his legs on the desk before him, shaping a convenient 'plug' with his penknife, and when it is quite ready for use, shooting the old one from his mouth, as from a pop-gun, and clapping the new one in its place.

I was surprised to observe that even steady old chewers of great experience, are not always good marksmen, which has rather inclined me to doubt that general proficiency with the rifle, of which we have heard so much in England. Several gentlemen called upon me who, in the course of conversation, frequently missed the spittoon at five paces; and one (but he was certainly short-sighted) mistook the closed sash for the open window, at three. On another occasion, when I dined out, and was sitting with two ladies and some gentlemen round a fire before dinner, one of the company fell short of the fireplace, six distinct times. I am disposed to think, however, that this was occasioned by his not aiming at that object; as there was a white marble hearth before the fender, which was more convenient, and may have suited his purpose better.

The Patent Office at Washington, furnishes an extraordinary example of American enterprise and ingenuity; for the immense number of models it contains. are the accumulated inventions of only five years; the whole of the previous collection having been destroyed by fire. The elegant structure in which they are arranged, is one of design rather than execution, for there is but one side erected out of four, though the works are stopped. The Post Office is a very compact and very beautiful building. In one of the departments, among a collection of rare and curious articles, are deposited the presents which have been made from time to time to the American ambassadors at foreign courts by the various potentates to whom they were the accredited agents of the Republic; gifts which by the law they are not permitted to retain. I confess that I looked upon this as a very painful exhibition, and one by no means flattering to the national standard of honesty and honour. That can scarcely be a high state of moral feeling which imagines a gentleman of repute and station, likely to be corrupted, in the discharge of his duty, by the present of a snuff-box, or a richly-mounted sword, or an Eastern shawl; and surely the Nation who reposes confidence in her appointed servants, is likely to be better served, than she who makes them the subject of such very mean and paltry suspicions.

At George Town, in the suburbs, there is a Jesuit College; delightfully situated, and, so far as I had an opportunity of seeing, well managed. Many persons who are not members of the Romish Church, avail themselves, I believe, of these institutions, and of the advantageous opportunities they afford for the education of their children. The heights of this neighbourhood, above the Potomac River, are very picturesque; and are free, I should conceive, from some of the insalubrities of Washington. The air, at that elevation, was quite cool and refreshing, when in the city it was burning hot.

The President's mansion is more like an English club-house, both within and without, than any other kind of establishment with which I can compare it. The ornamental ground above it has been laid out in garden walks; they are pretty, and agreeable to the eye; though they have that uncomfortable air of having been made yesterday, which is far from favourable to the display of such beauties.

My first visit to this house was on the morning after my arrival, when I was carried thither by an official gentleman, who was so kind as to charge himself with my presentation to the President.

We entered a large hall, and having twice o rthrice rung a bell which nobody answered, walked without further ceremony through the rooms on the ground floor, as divers other gentlemen (mostly with their hats on, and their hands in their pockets) were doing very leisurely. Some of these had ladies with them, to whom they were showing the premises; others were lounging on the chairs and sofas; others, in a perfect state of exhaustion from listlessness, were yawning drearily. The greater portion of this assemblage were rather asserting their supremacy than doing anything else, as they had no particular business there, that anybody knew of. A few were closely eyeing the moveables, as if to make quite sure that the President (who was far from popular) had not made away with any of the furniture, or sold the fixtures for his private benefit.

After glancing at these loungers; who were scattered over a pretty drawing-room, opening upon a terrace which commanded a beautiful prospect of the river and the adjacent country; and who were sauntering, too, about a larger state-room called the Eastern Drawing-room; we went upstairs into another chamber, where were certain visitors waiting for audiences. At sight of my conductor, a black in plain clothes and yellow slippers who was gliding noiselessly about, and whispering messages in the ears of the more impatient, made a sign of recognition, and glided off to announce him.

We had previously looked into another chamber fitted all round with a great bare wooden desk or counter, whereon lay files of newspapers, to which sundry gentlemen were referring. But there were no such means of beguiling the time in this apartment, which was as unpromising and tiresome as any waiting-room in one of our public establishments, or any physician's dining-room during his hours of consultation at home.

There were some fifteen or twenty persons in the room. One, a tall, wiry, muscular old man, from the west; sunburnt and swarthy; with a brown white hat on his knees, and a giant umbrella resting between his legs; who sat bolt upright in his chair, frowning steadily at the carpet, and twitching the hard lines about his mouth, as if he had made up his mind 'to fix' the President on what he had to say, and wouldn't bate him a grain. Another, a Kentucky farmer, six-feet-six in height, with his hat on, and his hands under his coat-tails, who leaned against the wall and kicked the floor with his heel, as though he had Time's head under his shoe, and were literally 'killing' him. A third, an over-faced, bilious-looking man, with sleek black hair cropped close, and whiskers and beard shaved down to blue dots, who sucked the head of a thick stick, and from time to time took it out of his mouth, to see how it was getting on. A fourth did nothing but whistle. A fifth did nothing but spit. And indeed all these gentlemen were so very persevering and energetic in this latter particular, and bestowed their favours so abundantly upon the carpet, that I take it for granted the Presidential housemaids have high wages, or, to speak more genteelly, an ample amount of 'compensation': which is the American word for salary, in the case of all public servants.

We had not waited in this room many minutes, before the black messenger returned, and conducted us into another of smaller dimensions, where, at a business-like table covered with papers, sat the President himself. He looked somewhat worn and anxious, and well he might; being at war with everybody— but the expression of his face was mild and pleasant, and his manner was remarkably unaffected, gentlemanly, and agreeable. I thought that in his whole carriage and demeanour, he became his station singularly well.

Being advised that the sensible etiquette of the republican court, admitted of a traveller, like myself, declining, without any impropriety, an invitation to dinner, which did not reach me until I had concluded my arrangements for leaving Washington some days before that to which it referred, I only returned to this house once. It was on the occasion of one of those general assemblies which are held on certain nights, between the hours of nine and twelve o'clock, and are called, rather oddly, Levees.

I went, with my wife, at about ten. There was a pretty dense crowd of carriages and people in the court-yard, and so far as I could make out, there were no very clear regulations for the taking up or setting down of company. There were certainly no policemen to soothe startled horses, either by sawing at their bridles or flourishing truncheons in their eyes; and I am ready to make oath that no inoffensive persons were knocked violently on the head, or poked acutely in their backs or stomachs; or brought to a stand-still by any such gentle means, and then taken into custody for not moving on. But there was no confusion or disorder. Our carriage reached the porch in its turn, without any blustering, swearing, shouting, backing, or other disturbance: and we dismounted with as much ease and comfort as though we had been escorted by the whole Metropolitan Force from A to Z inclusive.

The suite of rooms on the ground-floor, were lighted up; and a military band was playing in the hall. In the smaller drawing-room, the centre of a circle of company, were the President and his daughter-in-law, who acted as the lady of the mansion; and a very interesting, graceful, and accomplished lady too. One gentleman who stood among this group, appeared to take upon himself the functions of a master of ceremonies. I saw no other officers or attendants, and none were needed.

The great drawing-room, which I have already mentioned, and the other chambers on the ground-floor, were crowded to excess. The company was not, in our sense of the term, select, for it comprehended persons of very many grades and classes; nor was there any great display of costly attire: indeed, some of the costumes may have been, for aught I know, grotesque enough. But the decorum and propriety of behaviour which prevailed, were unbroken by any rude or disagreeable incident; and every man, even among the miscellaneous crowd in the hall who were admitted without any orders or tickets to look on, appeared to feel that he was a part of the Institution, and was responsible for its preserving a becoming character, and appearing to the best advantage.

That these visitors, too, whatever their station, were not without some refinement of taste and appreciation of intellectual gifts, and gratitude to those men who, by the peaceful exercise of great abilities, shed new charms and associations upon the homes of their countrymen, and elevate their character in other lands, was most earnestly testified by their reception of Washington Irving, my dear friend, who had recently been appointed Minister at the court of Spain, and who was among them that night, in his new character, for the first and last time before going abroad. I sincerely believe that in all the madness of American politics, few public men would have been so earnestly, devotedly, and affectionately caressed, as this most charming writer: and I have seldom respected a public assembly more, than I did this eager throng, when I saw them turning with one mind from noisy orators and officers of state, and flocking with a generous and honest impulse round the man of quiet pursuits: proud in his promotion as reflecting back upon their country: and grateful to him with their whole hearts for the store of graceful fancies he had poured out among them. Long may he dispense such treasures with unsparing hand; and long may they remember him as worthily!

The term we had assigned for the duration of our stay in Washington, was now at an end, and we were to begin to travel; for the railroad distances we had traversed yet, in journeying among these older towns, are on that great continent looked upon as nothing.

I had at first intended going South—to Charleston. But when I came to consider the length of time which this journey would occupy, and the premature heat of the season, which even at Washington had been often very trying; and weighed moreover, in my own mind, the pain of living in the constant contemplation of slavery, against the more than doubtful chances of my ever seeing it, in the time I had to spare, stripped of the disguises in which it would certainly be dressed, and so adding any item to the host of facts already heaped together on the subject; I began to listen to old whisperings which had often been present to me at home in England, when I little thought of ever being here; and to dream again of cities growing up, like palaces in fairy tales, among the wilds and forests of the west.

The advice I received in most quarters when I began to yield to my desire of travelling towards that point of the compass was, according to custom, sufficiently cheerless: my companion being threatened with more perils, dangers, and discomforts, than I can remember or would catalogue if I could; but of which it will be sufficient to remark that blowing-up in steamboats and breakings down in coaches were among the least. But, having a western route sketched out for me by the best and kindest authority to which I could have resorted, and putting no faith in these discouragements, I soon determined on my plan of action.

This was to travel south, only to Richmond in Virginia; and then to turn, and shape our course for the Far West; whither I beseech the reader's company, in a new chapter.

CHAPTER IX

A NIGHT STEAMER ON THE POTOMAC RIVER. VIRGINIA ROAD. AND A BLACK DRIVER. RICHMOND. BALTIMORE. THE HARRISBURG MAIL, AND A GLIMPSE OF THE CITY. A CANAL BOAT

WE were to proceed in the first instance by steamboat; and as it is usual to sleep on board, in consequence of the starting-hour being four o'clock in the morning, we went down to where she lay, at that very uncomfortable time for such expeditions when slippers are most valuable, and a familiar bed, in the perspective of an hour or two, looks uncommonly pleasant.

It is ten o'clock at night: say half-past ten: moonlight, warm, and dull enough. The steamer (not unlike a child's Noah's ark in form, with the machinery on the top of the roof) is riding lazily up and down, and bumping clumsily against the wooden pier, as the ripple of the river trifles with its unwieldy carcase. The wharf is some distance from the city. There is nobody down here; and one or two dull lamps upon the steamer's decks are the only signs of life remaining, when our coach has driven away. As soon as our footsteps are heard upon the planks, a fat negress, particularly favoured by nature in respect of bustle, emerges from some dark stairs, and marshals my wife towards the ladies' cabin, to which retreat she goes, followed by a mighty bale of cloaks and great-coats. I valiantly resolve not to go to bed at all, but to walk up and down the pier till morning.

I begin my promenade—thinking of all kinds of distant things and persons, and of nothing near—and pace up and down for half an hour. Then I go on board again; and getting into the light of one of the lamps, look at my watch and think it must have stopped; and wonder what has become of the faithful secretary whom I brought along with me from Boston. He is supping with our late landlord (a Field Marshal, at least, no doubt) in honour of our departure, and may be two hours longer. I walk again, but it gets duller and duller: the moon goes down: next June seems farther off in the dark, and the echoes of my footsteps make me nervous. It has turned cold too; and walking up and down without my companion in such lonely circumstances is but poor amuse-ment. So I break my staunch resolution, and think it may be, per-haps, as well to go to bed.

I go on board again; open the door of the gentlemen's cabin; and walk in. Somehow or other—from its being so quiet I suppose —I have taken it into my head that there is nobody there. To my horror and amazement it is full of sleepers in every stage, shape, attitude, and variety of slumber: in the berths, on the chairs, on the floors, on the tables, and particularly round the stove, my de-tested enemy. I take another step forward, and slip on the shining face of a black steward, who lies rolled in a blanket on the floor. He jumps up, grins, half in pain and half in hospitality; whispers my own name in my ear; and groping among the sleepers, leads me to my berth. Standing beside it, I count these slumbering pas-sengers, and get past forty. There is no use in going further, so I begin to undress. As the chairs are all occupied, and there is noth-ing else to put my clothes on, I deposit them upon the ground: not without soiling my hands, for it is in the same condition as the carpets in the Capitol, and from the same cause. Having but parti-ally undressed, I clamber on my shelf, and hold the curtain open for a few minutes while I look round on all my fellow travellers again. That done, I let it fall on them, and on the world: turn round: and go to sleep.

I wake, of course, when we get under weigh, for there is a good deal of noise. The day is then just breaking. Everybody wakes at the same time. Some are self-possessed directly, and some are much perplexed to make out where they are until they have rubbed their eyes, and leaning on one elbow, looked about them. Some yawn, some groan, nearly all spit, and a few get up. I am among the risers: for it is easy to feel, without going into the fresh air, that the atmosphere of the cabin is vile in the last degree. I huddle on my clothes, go down into the fore-cabin, get shaved by the barber, and wash myself. The washing and dressing apparatus for the passengers generally, consists of two jack-towels, three small wooden basins, a keg of water and a ladle to serve it out with, six square inches of looking-glass, two ditto ditto of yellow soap, a comb and brush for the head, and nothing for the teeth. Everybody uses the comb and brush, except myself. Everybody stares to see me using my own; and two or three gentlemen are strongly disposed to banter me on my prejudices, but don't. When I have made my toilet, I go upon the hurricane-deck, and set in for two hours of hard walking up and down. The sun is rising brilliantly; we are passing Mount Vernon, where Washington lies buried; the river is wide and rapid; and its banks are beautiful. All the glory and splendour of the day are coming on, and growing brighter every minute.

At eight o'clock, we breakfast in the cabin where I passed the night, but the windows and doors are all thrown open, and now it is fresh enough. There is no hurry or greediness apparent in the despatch of the meal. It is longer than a travelling breakfast with us; more orderly, and more polite.

Soon after nine o'clock we come to Potomac Creek, where we are to land; and then comes the oddest part of the journey. Seven stage-coaches are preparing to carry us on. Some of them are ready, some of them are not ready. Some of the drivers are blacks, some whites. There are four horses to each coach, and all the horses, harnessed or unharnessed, are there. The passengers are getting out of the steamboat, and into the coaches; the luggage is being transferred in noisy wheelbarrows; the horses are frightened, and impatient to start; the black drivers are chattering to them like so many monkeys; and the white ones whooping like so many drovers: for the main thing to be done in all kinds of hostling here, is to make as much noise as possible. The coaches are something like the French coaches, but not nearly so good. In lieu of springs, they are hung on bands of the strongest leather. There is very little choice or difference between them; and they may be likened to the car portion of the swings at an English fair, roofed, put upon axle-trees and wheels, and curtained with painted canvas. They are covered with mud from the roof to the wheel-tire, and have never been cleaned since they were first built.

The tickets we have received on board the steamboat are marked No. 1, so we belong to coach No. 1. I throw my coat on the box, and hoist my wife and her maid into the inside. It has only one step, and that being about a yard from the ground, is usually approached by a chair: when there is no chair, ladies trust in Providence. The coach holds nine inside, having a seat across from door to door, where we in England put our legs: so that there is only one feat more difficult in the performance than getting in, and that is, getting out again. There is only one outside passenger, and he sits upon the box. As I am that one, I climb up; and while they are strapping the luggage on the roof, and heaping it into a kind of tray behind, have a good opportunity of looking at the driver.

He is a negro—very black indeed. He is dressed in a coarse pepper-and-salt suit excessively patched and darned (particularly at the knees), grey stockings, enormous unblacked high-low shoes, and very short trousers. He has two odd gloves: one of parti-coloured worsted, and one of leather. He has a very short whip, broken in the middle and bandaged up with string. And yet he wears a low-crowned, broad-brimmed, black hat: faintly shadowing forth a kind of insane imitation of an English coachman! But somebody in authority cries 'Go ahead!' as I am making these observations. The mail takes the lead in a four-horse waggon, and all the coaches follow in procession: headed by No. 1.

By the way, whenever an Englishman would cry 'All right!' an American cries 'Go ahead!' which is somewhat expressive of the national character of the two countries.

The first half-mile of the road is over bridges made of loose planks laid across two parallel poles, which tilt up as the wheels roll over them; and IN the river. The river has a clayey bottom and is full of holes, so that half a horse is constantly disappearing unexpectedly, and can't be found again for some time.

But we get past even this, and come to the road itself, which is a series of alternate swamps and gravel-pits. A tremendous place is close before us, the black driver rolls his eyes, screws his mouth up very round, and looks straight between the two leaders, as if he were saying to himself, 'We have done this often before, but *now* I

think we shall have a crash.' He takes a rein in each hand; jerks
and pulls at both; and dances on the splashboard with both feet
(keeping his seat, of course) like the late lamented Ducrow on two
of his fiery courses. We come to the spot, sink down in the mire
nearly to the coach windows, tilt on one side at an angle of forty-
five degrees, and stick there. The insides scream dismally; the
coach stops; the horses flounder; all the other six coaches stop;
and their four-and-twenty horses flounder likewise: but merely for
company, and in sympathy with ours. Then the following circumstances occur.

BLACK DRIVER (to the horses). 'Hi!'

Nothing happens. Insides scream again.

BLACK DRIVER (to the horses). 'Ho!'

Horses plunge, and splash the black driver.

GENTLEMEN INSIDE (looking out). 'Why, what on airth—'

Gentleman receives a variety of splashes and draws his head in
again, without finishing his question or waiting for an answer.

BLACK DRIVER (still to the horses). 'Jiddy! Jiddy!'

Horses pull violently, drag the coach out of the hole, and draw
it up a bank; so steep, that the black driver's legs fly up into the
air, and he goes back among the luggage on the roof. But he immediately recovers himself, and cries (still to the horses),

'Pill!'

No effect. On the contrary, the coach begins to roll back upon
No. 2, which rolls back upon No. 3, which rolls back upon No. 4,
and so on, until No. 7 is heard to curse and swear, nearly a quarter
of a mile behind.

BLACK DRIVER (louder than before). 'Pill!'

Horses make another struggle to get up the bank, and again the
coach rolls backward.

BLACK DRIVER (louder than before). 'Pe-e-e-ill!'

Horses make a desperate struggle.

BLACK DRIVER (recovering spirits). 'Hi, Jiddy, Jiddy, Pill!'

Horses make another effort.

BLACK DRIVER (with great vigour). 'Ally Loo! Hi. Jiddy,
Jiddy. Pill. Ally Loo!'

Horses almost do it.

BLACK DRIVER (with his eyes starting out of his head). 'Lee,
den. Lee, dere. Hi. Jiddy, Jiddy. Pill. Ally Loo. Lee-e-e-e-e!'

They run up the bank, and go down again on the other side at a
fearful pace. It is impossible to stop them, and at the bottom there
is a deep hollow, full of water. The coach rolls frightfully. The insides scream. The mud and water fly about us. The black driver

dances like a madman. Suddenly we are all right by some extraordinary means, and stop to breathe.

A black friend of the black driver is sitting on a fence. The black driver recognises him by twirling his head round and round like a harlequin, rolling his eyes, shrugging his shoulders, and grinning from ear to ear. He stops short, turns to me, and says:

'We shall get you through sa, like a fiddle, and hope a please you when we get you through sa. Old 'ooman at home sa': chuckling very much. 'Outside gentleman sa, he often remember old 'ooman at home sa,' grinning again.

'Ay, ay, we'll take care of the old woman. Don't be afraid.'

The black driver grins again, but there is another hole, and beyond that, another bank, close before us. So he stops short: cries (to the horses again) 'Easy. Easy den. Ease. Steady. Hi. Jiddy. Pill. Ally. Loo,' but never 'Lee!' until we are reduced to the very last extremity, and are in the midst of difficulties, extrication from which appears to be all but impossible.

And so we do the ten miles or thereabouts in two hours and a half; breaking no bones, though bruising a great many; and in short getting through the distance, 'like a fiddle.'

This singular kind of coaching terminates at Fredericksburgh, whence there is a railway to Richmond. The tract of country through which it takes its course was once productive; but the soil has been exhausted by the system of employing a great amount of slave labour in forcing crops, without strengthening the land: and it is now little better than a sandy desert overgrown with trees. Dreary and uninteresting as its aspect is, I was glad to the heart to find anything on which one of the curses of this horrible institution has fallen; and had greater pleasure in contemplating the withered ground, than the richest and most thriving cultivation in the same place could possibly have afforded me.

In this district, as in all others where slavery sits brooding, (I have frequently heard this admitted, even by those who are its warmest advocates:) there is an air of ruin and decay abroad, which is inseparable from the system. The barns and outhouses are mouldering away; the sheds are patched and half-roofless; the log cabins (built in Virginia with external chimneys made of clay or wood) are squalid in the last degree. There is no look of decent comfort anywhere. The miserable stations by the railway side; the great wild wood-yards, whence the engine is supplied with fuel; the negro children rolling on the ground before the cabin doors, with dogs and pigs; the biped beasts of burden slinking past: gloom and dejection are upon them all.

In the negro car belonging to the train in which we made this journey, were a mother and her children who had just been purchased; the husband and father being left behind with their old owner. The children cried the whole way, and the mother was misery's picture. The champion of Life, Liberty, and the Pursuit of Happiness, who had bought them, rode in the same train; and, every time we stopped, got down to see that they were safe. The black in Sinbad's Travels with one eye in the middle of his forehead which shone like a burning coal, was nature's aristocrat compared with this white gentleman.

It was between six and seven o'clock in the evening, when we drove to the hotel: in front of which, and on the top of the broad flight of steps leading to the door, two or three citizens were balancing themselves on rocking chairs, and smoking cigars. We found it a very large and elegant establishment, and were as well entertained as travellers need desire to be. The climate being a thirsty one, there was never, at any hour of the day, a scarcity of loungers in the spacious bar, or a cessation of the mixing of cool liquors: but they were a merrier people here, and had musical instruments playing to them o' nights, which it was a treat to hear again.

The next day, and the next, we rode and walked about the town, which is delightfully situated on eight hills, overhanging James River; a sparkling stream, studded here and there with bright islands, or brawling over broken rocks. Although it was yet but the middle of March, the weather in this southern temperature was extremely warm; the peach-trees and magnolias were in full bloom; and the trees were green. In a low ground among the hills, is a valley known as 'Bloody Run,' from a terrible conflict with the Indians which once occurred there. It is a good place for such a struggle, and, like every other spot I saw associated with any legend of that wild people now so rapidly fading from the earth, interested me very much.

The city is the seat of the local parliament of Virginia; and in its shady legislative halls, some orators were drowsily holding forth to the hot noonday. By dint of constant repetition, however, these constitutional sights had very little more interest for me than so many parochial vestries; and I was glad to exchange this one for a lounge in a well-arranged public library of some ten thousand volumes, and a visit to a tobacco manufactory, where the workmen were all slaves.

I saw in this place the whole process of picking, rolling, pressing, drying, packing in casks, and branding. All the tobacco thus dealt

BLACK AND WHITE

with, was in course of manufacture for chewing; and one would have supposed there was enough in that one store-house to have filled even the comprehensive jaws of America. In this form, the weed looks like the oil-cake on which we fatten cattle; and even without reference to its consequences, is sufficiently uninviting.

Many of the workmen appeared to be strong men, and it is hardly necessary to add that they were all labouring quietly, then. After two o'clock in the day, they are allowed to sing, a certain number at a time. The hour striking while I was there, some twenty sang a hymn in parts, and sang it by no means ill; pursuing their work meanwhile. A bell rang as I was about to leave, and they all poured forth into a building on the opposite side of the street to dinner. I said several times that I should like to see them at their meal; but as the gentleman to whom I mentioned this desire appeared to be suddenly taken rather deaf, I did not pursue the request. Of their appearance I shall have something to say, presently.

On the following day, I visited a plantation or farm, of about twelve hundred acres, on the opposite bank of the river. Here again, although I went down with the owner of the estate, to 'the quarter,' as that part of it in which the slaves live is called, I was not invited to enter into any of their huts. All I saw of them, was, that they were very crazy, wretched cabins, near to which groups of half-naked children basked in the sun, or wallowed on the dusty ground. But I believe this gentleman is a considerate and excellent master, who inherited his fifty slaves, and is neither a buyer nor a seller of human stock; and I am sure, from my own observation and conviction, that he is a kind-hearted, worthy man.

The planter's house was an airy rustic dwelling, that brought Defoe's description of such places strongly to my recollection. The day was very warm, but the blinds being all closed, and the windows and doors set wide open, a shady coolness rustled through the rooms, which was exquisitely refreshing after the glare and heat without. Before the windows was an open piazza, where, in what they call the hot weather—whatever that may be—they sling hammocks, and drink and doze luxuriously. I do not know how their cool refections may taste within the hammocks, but, having experience, I can report that, out of them, the mounds of ices and the bowls of mint-julep and sherry-cobbler they make in these latitudes, are refreshments never to be thought of afterwards, in summer, by those who would preserve contented minds.

There are two bridges across the river: one belongs to the railroad, and the other, which is a very crazy affair, is the private property of some old lady in the neighbourhood, who levies tolls upon the towns-people. Crossing this bridge, on my way back, I saw a notice painted on the gate, cautioning all persons to drive slowly: under a penalty, if the offender were a white man, of five dollars; if a negro, fifteen stripes.

The same decay and gloom that overhang the way by which it is approached, hover above the town of Richmond. There are pretty villas and cheerful houses in its streets, and Nature smiles upon the country round; but jostling its handsome residences, like slavery itself going hand in hand with many lofty virtues, are deplorable tenements, fences unrepaired, walls crumbling into ruinous heaps. Hinting gloomily at things below the surface, these, and many other tokens of the same description, force themselves upon the notice, and are remembered with depressing influence, when livelier features are forgotten.

To those who are happily accustomed to them, the countenances in the streets and labouring-places, too, are shocking. All men who know that there are laws against instructing slaves, of which the pains and penalties greatly exceed in their amount the fines imposed on those who maim and torture them, must be prepared to find their faces very low in the scale of intellectual expression. But the darkness—not of skin, but mind—which meets the stranger's eye at every turn; the brutalising and blotting out of all fairer characters traced by Nature's hand; immeasurably outdo his worst belief. That travelled creation of the great satirist's brain, who fresh from living among horses, peered from a high casement down upon his own kind with trembling horror, was scarcely more repelled and daunted by the sight, than those who look upon some of these faces for the first time must surely be.

I left the last of them behind me in the person of a wretched drudge, who, after running to and fro all day till midnight, and moping in his stealthy winks of sleep upon the stairs between-whiles, was washing the dark passages at four o'clock in the morning; and went upon my way with a grateful heart that I was not doomed to live where slavery was, and had never had my senses blunted to its wrongs and horrors in a slave-rocked cradle.

It had been by intention to proceed by James River and Chesapeake Bay to Baltimore; but one of the steamboats being absent from her station through some accident, and the means of conveyance being consequently rendered uncertain, we returned to Washington by the way we had come (there were two constables on board the steamboat, in pursuit of runaway slaves), and halt-

ing there again for one night went on to Baltimore next afternoon.

The most comfortable of all the hotels of which I had any experience in the United States, and they were not a few, is Bar-
num's, in that city: where the English traveller will find curtains
to his bed, for the first and probably the last time in America
(this is a disinterested remark, for I never use them); and where
he will be likely to have enough water for washing himself, which
is not at all a common case.

This capital of the State of Maryland is a bustling busy town,
with a great deal of traffic of various kinds, and in particular of
water commerce. That portion of the town which it most favours
is none of the cleanest, it is true; but the upper part is of a very
different character, and has many agreeable streets and public
buildings. The Washington Monument, which is a handsome
pillar with a statue on its summit; the Medical College; and the
Battle Monument in memory of an engagement with the British
at North Point; are the most conspicuous among them.

There is a very good prison in this city, and the State Penitentiary is also among its institutions. In this latter establishment there were two curious cases.

One, was that of a young man, who had been tried for the
murder of his father. The evidence was entirely circumstantial,
and was very conflicting and doubtful; nor was it possible to assign any motive which could have tempted him to the commission
of so tremendous a crime. He had been tried twice; and on the
second occasion the jury felt so much hesitation in convicting
him, that they found a verdict of manslaughter, or murder in the
second degree; which it could not possibly be, as there had, beyond all doubt, been no quarrel or provocation, and if he were
guilty at all, he was unquestionably guilty of murder in its broadest
and worst signification.

The remarkable feature in the case was, that if the unfortunate deceased were not really murdered by this own son of his,
he must have been murdered by his own brother. The evidence
lay, in a most remarkable manner, between those two. On all the
suspicious points, the dead man's brother was the witness: all the
explanations for the prisoner (some of them extremely plausible)
went, by construction and inference, to inculcate him as plotting
to fix the guilt upon his nephew. It must have been one of them:
and the jury had to decide between two sets of suspicions, almost
equally unnatural, unaccountable, and strange.

The other case, was that of a man who once went to a certain distiller's and stole a copper measure containing a quantity of liquor. He was pursued and taken with the property in his possession, and was sentenced to two years' imprisonment. On coming out of jail, at the expiration of that term, he went back to the same distiller's, and stole the same copper measure containing the same quantity of liquor. There was not the slightest reason to suppose that the man wished to return to prison: indeed everything, but the commission of the offence, made directly against that assumption. There are only two ways of accounting for this extraordinary proceeding. One is, that after undergoing so much for this copper measure he conceived he had established a sort of claim and right to it. The other that, by dint of long thinking about, it had become a monomania with him, and had acquired a fascination which he found it impossible to resist: swelling from an Earthly Copper Gallon into an Ethereal Golden Vat.

After remaining here a couple of days I bound myself to a rigid adherence to the plan I had laid down so recently, and resolved to set forward on our western journey without any more delay. Accordingly, having reduced the luggage within the smallest possible compass (by sending back to New York, to be afterwards forwarded to us in Canada, so much of it as was not absolutely wanted); and having procured the necessary credentials to banking-houses on the way; and having moreover looked for two evenings at the setting sun, with as well-defined an idea of the country before us as if we had been going to travel into the very centre of that planet; we left Baltimore by another railway at half-past eight in the morning, and reached the town of York, some sixty miles off, by the early dinner-time of the Hotel which was the starting-place of the four-horse coach, wherein we were to proceed to Harrisburg.

This conveyance, the box of which I was fortunate enough to secure, had come down to meet us at the railroad station, and was as muddy and cumbersome as usual. As more passengers were waiting for us at the inn-door, the coachman observed under his breath, in the usual self-communicative voice, looking the while at his mouldly harness as if it were to that he was addressing himself,

'I expect we shall want *the big* coach.'

I could not help wondering within myself what the size of this big coach might be, and how many persons it might be designed to hold; for the vehicle which was too small for our purpose was something larger than two English heavy night coaches, and might have been the twin-brother of a French Diligence. My

speculations were speedily set at rest, however, for as soon as
we had dined, there came rumbling up the street, shaking its
sides like a corpulent giant, a kind of barge on wheels. After
much blundering and backing, it stopped at the door: rolling
heavily from side to side when its other motion had ceased, as if
it had taken cold in its damp stable, and between that, and the
having been required in its dropsical old age to move at any
faster pace than a walk, were distressed by shortness of wind.

'If here ain't the Harrisburg mail at last, and dreadful bright
and smart to look at too,' cried an elderly gentleman in some
excitement, 'darn my mother!'

I don't know what the sensation of being darned may be, or
whether a man's mother has a keener relish or disrelish of the
process than anybody else; but if the endurance of this mysterious ceremony by the old lady in question had depended on the
accuracy of her son's vision in respect to the abstract brightness
and smartness of the Harrisburg mail, she would certainly have
undergone its infliction. However, they booked twelve people
inside; and the luggage (including such trifles as a large rocking-chair and a good-sized dining-table) being at length made fast
upon the roof, we started off in great state.

At the door of another hotel, there was another passenger to be
taken up.

'Any room, sir?' cries the new passenger to the coachman.

'Well, there's room enough,' replies the coachman, without
getting down, or even looking at him.

'There ain't no room at all, sir,' bawls a gentleman inside. Which
another gentleman (also inside) confirms, by predicting that the
attempt to introduce any more passengers 'won't fit nohow.'

The new passenger, without any expression of anxiety, looks
into the coach, and then looks up at the coachman: 'Now, how
do you mean to fix it?' says he, after a pause: 'for I *must* go.'

The coachman employs himself in twisting the lash of his whip
into a knot, and takes no more notice of the question: clearly
signifying that it is anybody's business but his, and that the passengers would do well to fix it, among themselves. In this state
of things, matters seem to be approximating to a fix of another
kind, when another inside passenger in a corner, who is nearly
suffocated, cries faintly, 'I'll get out.'

This is no matter of relief or self-congratulation to the driver,
for his immovable philosophy is perfectly undisturbed by anything that happens in the coach. Of all things in the world, the
coach would seem to be the very last upon his mind. The exchange

is made, however, and then the passenger who has given up his seat makes a third upon the box, seating himself in what he calls the middle; that is, with half his person on my legs, and the other half on the driver's.

'Go ahead, cap'en,' cries the colonel, who directs.

'Gŏ-lāng!' cries the cap'en to his company, the horses and away we go.

We took up at a rural bar-room, after we had gone a few miles, an intoxicated gentleman who climbed upon the roof among the luggage, and subsequently slipping off without hurting himself, was seen in the distant perspective reeling back to the grog-shop where we had found him. We also parted with more of our freight at different times, so that when we came to change horses, I was again alone outside.

The coachmen always change with the horses, and are usually as dirty as the coach. The first was dressed like a very shabby English baker; the second like a Russian peasant: for he wore a loose purple camlet robe, with a fur collar, tied round his waist with a parti-coloured worsted sash; grey trousers; light blue gloves: and a cap of bearskin. It had by this time come on to rain very heavily, and there was a cold damp mist besides, which penetrated to the skin. I was glad to take advantage of a stoppage and get down to stretch my legs, shake the water off my great-coat, and swallow the usual anti-temperance recipe for keeping out the cold.

When I mounted to my seat again, I observed a new parcel lying on the coach roof, which I took to be a rather large fiddle in a brown bag. In the course of a few miles, however, I discovered that it had a glazed cap at one end and a pair of muddy shoes at the other; and further observation demonstrated it to be a small boy in a snuff-coloured coat, with his arms quite pinioned to his sides, by deep forcing into his pockets. He was, I presume, a relative or friend of the coachman's, as he lay a-top of the luggage with his face towards the rain; and except when a change of position brought his shoes in contact with my hat, he appeared to be asleep. At last, on some occasion of our stopping, this thing slowly upreared itself to the height of three feet six, and fixing its eyes on me, observed in piping accents, with a complaisant yawn, half quenched in an obliging air of friendly patronage, 'Well now, stranger, I guess you find this a'most like an English arternoon, hey?'

The scenery, which had been tame enough at first, was, for the last ten or twelve miles, beautiful. Our road wound through the pleasant valley of the Susquehanna; the river, dotted with innumerable green islands, lay upon our right: and on the left, a steep ascent, craggy with broken rock, and dark with pine trees. The mist, wreathing itself into a hundred fantastic shapes, moved solemnly upon the water; and the gloom of evening gave to all an air of mystery and silence which greatly enhanced its natural interest.

We crossed this river by a wooden bridge, roofed and covered in on all sides, and nearly a mile in length. It was profoundly dark; perplexed, with great beams, crossing and recrossing it at every possible angle; and through the broad chinks and crevices in the floor, the rapid river gleamed, far down below, like a legion of eyes. We had no lamps; and as the horses stumbled and floundered through this place, towards the distant speck of dying light, it seemed interminable. I really could not at first persuade myself as we rumbled heavily on, filling the bridge with hollow noises, and I held down my head to save it from the rafters above, but that I was in a painful dream; for I have often dreamed of toiling through such places, and as often argued, even at the time, 'this cannot be reality.'

At length, however, we emerged upon the streets of Harrisburg, whose feeble lights, reflected dismally from the wet ground, did not shine out upon a very cheerful city. We were soon established in a snug hotel, which though smaller and far less splendid than many we put up at, is raised above them all in my remembrance, by having for its landlord the most obliging, considerate, and gentlemanly person I ever had to deal with.

As we were not to proceed upon our journey until the afternoon, I walked out, after breakfast the next morning, to look about me; and was duly shown a model prison on the solitary system, just erected, and as yet without an inmate; the trunk of an old tree to which Harris, the first settler here (afterwards buried under it), was tied by hostile Indians, with his funeral pile about him, when he was saved by the timely appearance of a friendly party on the opposite shore of the river; the local legislature (for there was another of those bodies here again, in full debate); and the other curiosities of the town.

I was very much interested in looking over a number of treaties made from time to time with the poor Indians, signed by the different chiefs at the period of their ratification, and preserved in the office of the Secretary to the Commonwealth. These signatures, traced of course by their own hands, are rough drawings of the creatures or weapons they were called after. Thus, the Great Turtle makes a crooked pen-and-ink outline of a great turtle;

the Buffalo sketches a buffalo; the War Hatchet sets a rough image of that weapon for his mark. So with the Arrow, the Fish, the Scalp, the Big Canoe, and all of them.

I could not but think—as I looked at these feeble and tremulous productions of hands which could draw the longest arrow to the head in a stout elkhorn bow, or split a bead or feather with a rifle-ball—of Crabbe's musings over the Parish Register, and the irregular scratches made with a pen, by men who would plow a lengthy furrow straight from end to end. Nor could I help bestowing many sorrowful thoughts upon the simple warriors whose hands and hearts were set there, in all truth and honesty; and who only learned in course of time from white men how to break their faith, and quibble out of forms and bonds. I wondered, too, how many times the credulous Big Turtle, or trusting Little Hatchet, had put his mark to treaties which were falsely read to him; and had signed away, he knew now what, until it went and cast him loose upon the new possessors of the land, a savage indeed.

Our host announced, before our early dinner, that some members of the legislative body proposed to do us the honour of calling. He had kindly yielded up to us his wife's own little parlour, and when I begged that he would show them in, I saw him look with painful apprehension at its pretty carpet; though, being otherwise occupied at the time, the cause of his uneasiness did not occur to me.

It certainly would have been more pleasant to all parties concerned, and would not, I think, have compromised their independence in any material degree, if some of these gentlemen had not only yielded to the prejudice in favour of spittoons, but had abandoned themselves, for the moment, even to the conventional absurdity of pocket-handkerchiefs.

It still continued to rain heavily, and when we went down to the Canal Boat (for that was the mode of conveyance by which we were to proceed) after dinner, the weather was as unpromising and obstinately wet as one would desire to see. Nor was the sight of this canal boat, in which we were to spend three or four days, by any means a cheerful one; as it involved some uneasy speculations concerning the disposal of the passengers at night, and opened a wide field of inquiry touching the other domestic arrangements of the establishment, which was sufficiently disconcerting.

However, there it was—a barge with a little house in it, viewed from the outside; and a caravan at a fair, viewed from within: the gentlemen being accommodated, as the spectators usually are, in one of those locomotive museums of penny wonders; and the ladies being partitioned off by a red curtain, after the manner of the dwarfs and giants in the same establishment, whose private lives are passed in rather close exclusiveness.

We sat here, looking silently at the row of little tables, which extended down both sides of the cabin, and listening to the rain as it dripped and pattered on the boat, and plashed with a dismal merriment in the water, until the arrival of the railway train, for whose final contribution to our stock of passengers our departure was alone deferred. It brought a great many boxes, which were bumped and tossed upon the roof, almost as painfully as if they had been deposited on one's own head, without the intervention of a porter's knot; and several damp gentlemen, whose clothes, on their drawing round the stove, began to steam again. No doubt it would have been a thought more comfortable if the driving rain, which now poured down more soakingly than ever, had admitted of a window being opened, or if our number had been something less than thirty; but there was scarcely time to think as much, when a train of three horses was attached to the tow-rope, the boy upon the leader smacked his whip, the rudder creaked and groaned complainingly, and we had begun our journey.

CHAPTER X

SOME FURTHER ACCOUNT OF THE CANAL BOAT, ITS DOMESTIC ECONOMY, AND ITS PASSENGERS. JOURNEY TO PITTSBURG ACROSS THE ALLEGHANY MOUNTAINS. PITTSBURG

As it continued to rain most perseveringly, we all remained below: the damp gentlemen round the stove, gradually becoming mildewed by the action of the fire; and the dry gentlemen lying at full length upon the seats, or slumbering uneasily with their faces on the tables, or walking up and down the cabin, which it was barely possible for a man of the middle height to do, without making bald places on his head by scraping it against the roof. At about six o'clock, all the small tables were put together to form one long table, and everybody sat down to tea, coffee, bread, butter, salmon, shad, liver, steaks, potatoes, pickles, ham, chops, black-puddings, and sausages.

'Will you try,' said my opposite neighbour, handing me a dish of potatoes, broken up in milk and butter, 'will you try some of these fixings?'

There are few words which perform such various duties as this word 'fix.' It is the Caleb Quotem of the American vocabulary. You call upon a gentleman in a country town, and his help informs you that he is 'fixing himself' just now, but will be down directly: by which you are to understand that he is dressing. You inquire, on board a steamboat, of a fellow-passenger, whether breakfast will be ready soon, and he tells you he should think so, for when he was last below, they were 'fixing the tables': in other words, laying the cloth. You beg a porter to collect your luggage, and he entreats you not to be uneasy, for he'll 'fix it presently': and if you complain of indisposition, you are advised to have recourse to Doctor So-and-so, who will 'fix you' in no time.

One night, I ordered a bottle of mulled wine at an hotel where I was staying, and waited a long time for it; at length it was put upon the table with an apology from the landlord that he feared it wasn't 'fixed properly.' And I recollect once, at a stage-coach dinner, overhearing a very stern gentleman demand of a waiter who presented him with a plate of under-done roast-beef, 'whether he called *that,* fixing God A'mighty's vittles?'

There is no doubt that the meal, at which the invitation was tendered to me which has occasioned this digression, was disposed of somewhat ravenously; and that the gentlemen thrust the broad-bladed knives and the two-pronged forks further down their throats than I ever saw the same weapons go before, except in the hands of a skilful juggler: but no man sat down until the ladies were seated; or omitted any little act of politeness which could contribute to their comfort. Nor did I ever once, on any occasion, anywhere, during my rambles in America, see a woman exposed to the slightest act of rudeness, incivility, or even inattention.

By the time the meal was over, the rain, which seemed to have worn itself out by coming down so fast, was nearly over too; and it became feasible to go on deck: which was a great relief, notwithstanding its being a very small deck, and being rendered still smaller by the luggage, which was heaped together in the middle under a tarpaulin covering; leaving, on either side, a path so narrow, that it became a science to walk to and fro without tumbling overboard into the canal. It was somewhat embarrassing at first, too, to have to duck nimbly every five minutes whenever the man at the helm cried 'Bridge!' and sometimes, when the cry was 'Low Bridge,' to lie down nearly flat. But custom familiarises one to anything, and there were so many bridges that it took a very short time to get used to this. As night came on, and we drew in sight of the first range of hills, which are the outposts of the Alleghany Mountains, the scenery, which had been uninteresting hitherto, became more bold and striking. The wet ground reeked and smoked, after the heavy fall of rain; and the croaking of the frogs (whose noise in these parts is almost incredible) sounded as though a million of fairy teams with bells, were travelling through the air, and keeping pace with us. The night was cloudy yet, but moonlight too: and when we crossed the Susquehanna river—over which there is an extraordinary wooden bridge with two galleries, one above the other, so that even there, two boat teams meeting, may pass without confusion —it was wild and grand.

I have mentioned my having been in some uncertainty and doubt, at first, relative to the sleeping arrangements on board this boat. I remained in the same vague state of mind until ten o'clock or thereabouts, when going below, I found suspended on either side of the cabin, three long tiers of hanging book-shelves, designed apparently for volumes of the small octavo size. Looking with greater attention at these contrivances (wondering to find such literary preparations in such a place), I described on each shelf a sort of microscopic sheet and blanket; then I began dimly to comprehend that the passengers were the library, and that they were to be arranged, edge-wise, on these shelves, till morning.

I was assisted to this conclusion by seeing some of them gathered round the master of the boat, at one of the tables, drawing lots with all the anxieties and passions of gamesters depicted in their countenances; while others, with small pieces of cardboard in their hands, were groping among the shelves in search of numbers corresponding with those they had drawn. As soon as any gentleman found his number, he took possession of it by immediately undressing himself and crawling into bed. The rapidity with which an agitated gambler subsided into a snoring slumberer, was one of the most singular effects I have ever witnessed. As to the ladies, they were already abed, behind the red curtain, which was carefully drawn and pinned up the centre: though as every cough, or sneeze, or whisper, behind this curtain, was perfectly audible before it, we had still a live consciousness of their society.

The politeness of the person in authority had secured to me a shelf in a nook near this red curtain, in some degree removed from the great body of sleepers: to which place I retired, with many acknowledgments to him for his attention. I found it, on after-measurement, just the width of an ordinary sheet of Bath post letter-paper; and I was at first in some uncertainty as to the best means of getting into it. But the shelf being a bottom one, I finally determined on lying upon the floor, rolling gently in, stopping immediately I touched the mattress, and remaining for the night with that side uppermost, whatever it might be. Luckily, I came upon my back at exactly the right moment. I was much alarmed on looking upward, to see, by the shape of his half yard of sacking (which his weight had bent into an exceedingly tight bag), that there was a very heavy gentleman above me, whom the slender cords seemed quite incapable of holding; and I could not help reflecting upon the grief of my wife and family in the event of his coming down in the night. But as I could not have got up again without a severe bodily struggle, which might have alarmed the ladies; and as I had nowhere to go to, even if I had; I shut my eyes upon the danger, and remained there.

One of two remarkable circumstances is indisputably a fact, with reference to that class of society who travel in these boats. Either they carry their restlessness to such a pitch that they never sleep at all; or they expectorate in dreams, which would be a remarkable mingling of the real and ideal. All night long, and every night, on this canal, there was a perfect storm and tempest of spitting; and once my coat, being in the very centre of the hurricane sustained by five gentlemen (which moved vertically, strictly carrying out Reid's Theory of the Law of Storms), I was fain the next morning to lay it on the deck, and rub it down with fair water before it was in a condition to be worn again.

Between five and six o'clock in the morning we got up, and some of us went on deck, to give them an opportunity of taking the shelves down; while others, the morning being very cold, crowded round the rusty stove, cherishing the newly kindled fire, and filling the grate with those voluntary contributions of which they had been so liberal all night. The washing accommodations were primitive. There was a tin ladle chained to the deck, with which every gentleman who thought it necessary to cleanse himself (many were superior to this weakness), fished the dirty water out of the canal, and poured it into a tin basin, secured in like manner. There was also a jack-towel. And, hanging up before a little looking-glass in the bar, in the immediate vicinity of the bread and cheese and biscuits, were a public comb and hair-brush.

At eight o'clock, the shelves being taken down and put away and the tables joined together, everybody sat down to the tea, coffee, bread, butter, salmon, shad, liver, steak, potatoes, pickles, ham, chops, black-puddings, and sausages, all over again. Some were fond of compounding this variety, and having it all on their plates at once. As each gentleman got through his own personal amount of tea, coffee, bread, butter, salmon, shad, liver, steak, potatoes, pickles, ham, chops, black-puddings, and sausages, he rose up and walked off. When everybody had done with everything, the fragments were cleared away: and one of the waiters appearing anew in the character of a barber, shaved such of the company as desired to be shaved; while the remainder looked on, or yawned over their newspapers. Dinner was breakfast again, without the tea and coffee; and supper and breakfast were identical.

There was a man on board this boat, with a light fresh-coloured face, and a pepper-and-salt suit of clothes, who was the most inquisitive fellow that can possibly be imagined. He never spoke otherwise than interrogatively. He was an embodied inquiry. Sitting down or standing up, still or moving, walking the deck or taking his meals, there he was, with a great note of interrogation in each eye, two in his cocked ears, two more in his turned-up nose and chin, at least half a dozen more about the corners of his mouth, and the largest one of all in his hair, which was brushed pertly off his forehead in a flaxen clump. Every button in his clothes said, 'Eh? What's that? Did you speak? Say that again, will you?' He was always wide awake, like the enchanted bride who drove her husband frantic; always restless; always thirsting for answers; perpetually seeking and never finding. There never was such a curious man.

I wore a fur great-coat at that time, and before we were well clear of the wharf, he questioned me concerning it, and its price, and where I bought it, and when, and what fur it was, and what it weighed, and what it cost. Then he took notice of my watch, and asked me what *that* cost, and whether it was a French watch, and where I got it, and how I got it, and whether I bought it or had it given me, and how it went, and where the key-hole was, and when I wound it, every night or every morning and whether I ever forgot to wind it at all, and if I did, what then? Where had I been to last, and where was I going next, and where was I going after that, and had I seen the President, and what did he say, and what did I say, and what did he say when I had said that? Eh? Lor now! do tell!

Finding that nothing would satisfy him, I evaded his questions after the first score or two, and in particular pleaded ignorance respecting the name of the fur whereof the coat was made. I am unable to say whether this was the reason, but that coat fascinated him afterwards; he usually kept close behind me as I walked, and moved as I moved, that he might look at it the better; and he frequently dived into narrow places after me at the risk of his life, that he might have the satisfaction of passing his hand up the back, and rubbing it the wrong way.

We had another odd specimen on board, of a different kind. This was a thin-faced, spare-figured man of middle age and stature, dressed in a dusty drabbish-coloured suit, such as I never saw before. He was perfectly quiet during the first part of the journey: indeed I don't remember having so much as seen him until he was brought out by circumstances, as great men often are. The conjunction of events which made him famous, happened, briefly, thus.

The canal extends to the foot of the mountain, and there, of course, it stops; the passengers being conveyed across it by land carriage, and taken on afterwards by another canal boat, the counterpart of the first, which awaits them on the other side. There are two canal lines of passage-boats; one is called The Express, and one (a cheaper one) The Pioneer. The Pioneer gets first to the mountain, and waits for the Express people to come up; both sets of passengers being conveyed across it at the same time. We were the Express company; but when we had crossed the mountain, and had come to the second boat, the proprietors took it into their heads to draft all the Pioneers into it likewise, so that we were five-and-forty at least, and the accession of passengers was not at all of that kind which improved the prospect of sleeping at night. Our people grumbled at this, as people do in such cases; but suffered the boat to be towed off with the whole freight aboard nevertheless; and away we went down the canal. At home, I should have protested lustily, but being a foreigner here, I held my peace. Not so this passenger. He cleft a path among the people on deck (we were nearly all on deck), and without addressing anybody whomsoever, soliloquised as follows:

'This may suit *you,* this may, but it don't suit *me.* This may be all very well with Down Easters, and men of Boston raising, but it won't suit my figure nohow; and no two ways about *that;* and so I tell you. Now! I'm from the brown forests of the Mississippi, *I* am, and when the sun shines on me, it does shine— a little. It don't glimmer where *I* live, the sun don't. No. I'm a brown forester, I am. I an't a Johnny Cake. There are no smooth skins where I live. We're rough men there. Rather. If

Down Easters and men of Boston raising like this, I'm glad of it, but I'm none of that raising nor of that breed. No. This company wants a little fixing, *it* does. I'm the wrong sort of man for 'em, *I* am. They won't like me, *they* won't. This is piling of it up, a little too moŭntaĭnoŭs, this is.' At the end of every one of these short sentences he turned upon his heel, and walked the other way; checking himself abruptly when he had finished another short sentence, and turning back again.

It is impossible for me to say what terrific meaning was hidden in the words of this brown forester, but I know that the other passengers looked on in a sort of admiring horror, and that presently the boat was put back to the wharf, and as many of the Pioneers as could be coaxed or bullied into going away, were got rid of.

When we started again, some of the boldest spirits on board, made bold to say to the obvious occasion of this improvement in our prospects, 'Much obliged to you sir'; whereunto the brown forester (waving his hand, and still walking up and down as before) replied, 'No you an't. You're none o' my raising. You may act for yourselves, *you* may. I have pinted out the way. Down Easters and Johnny Cakes can follow if they please. I an't a Johnny Cake, *I* an't. I am from the brown forests of the Mississippi, *I* am'—and so on, as before. He was unanimously voted one of the tables for his bed at night—there is a great contest for the tables—in consideration for his public services: and he had the warmest corner by the stove throughout the rest of the journey. But I never could find out that he did anything except sit there; nor did I hear him speak again until, in the midst of the bustle and turmoil of getting the luggage ashore in the dark at Pittsburg, I stumbled over him as he sat smoking a cigar on the cabin steps, and heard him muttering to himself, with a short laugh of defiance, 'I an't a Johnny Cake, *I* an't. I'm from the brown forests of the Mississippi, *I* am, damme!' I am inclined to argue from this, that he had never left off saying so; but I could not make an affidavit of that part of the story, if required to do so by my Queen and Country.

As we have not reached Pittsburg yet, however, in the order of our narrative, I may go on to remark that breakfast was perhaps the least desirable meal of the day, as in addition to the many savoury odours arising from the eatables already mentioned, there were whiffs of gin, whiskey, brandy, and rum, from the little bar hard by, and a decided seasoning of stale tobacco. Many of the gentlemen passengers were far from particular in respect of their linen, which was in some cases as yellow as the little rivulets that had trickled from the corners of their mouths in chewing, and dried there. Nor was the atmosphere quite free from zephyr whisperings of the thirty beds which had just been cleared away, and of which we were further and more pressingly reminded by the occasional appearance on the table-cloth of a kind of Game, not mentioned in the Bill of Fare.

And yet despite those oddities—and even they had, for me at least, a humour of their own—there was much in this mode of travelling which I heartily enjoyed at the time, and look back upon with great pleasure. Even the running up, bare-necked, at five o'clock in the morning, from the tainted cabin to the dirty deck; scooping up the icy water, plunging one's head into it, and drawing it out, all fresh and glowing with the cold; was a good thing. The fast, brisk walk upon the towing-path, between that time and breakfast, when every vein and artery seemed to tingle with health; the exquisite beauty of the opening day, when light came gleaming off from everything; the lazy motion of the boat, when one lay idly on the deck, looking through, rather than at, the deep blue sky; the gliding on at night, so noiselessly, past frowning hills, sullen with dark trees, and sometimes angry in one red burning spot high up, where unseen men lay crouching round a fire; the shining out of the bright stars undisturbed by noise of wheels or steam, or any other sound than the limpid rippling of the water as the boat went on: all these were pure delights.

Then there were new settlements and detached log-cabins and frame-houses, full of interest for strangers from an old country: cabins with simple ovens, outside, made of clay; and lodgings for the pigs nearly as good as many of the human quarters; broken windows, patched with worn-out hats, old clothes, old boards, fragments of blankets and paper; and home-made dressers standing in the open air without the door, whereon was ranged the household store, not hard to count, of earthen jars and pots. The eye was pained to see the stumps of great trees thickly strewn in every field of wheat, and seldom to lose the eternal swamp and dull morass, with hundreds of rotten trunks and twisted branches steeped in its unwholesome water. It was quite sad and oppressive, to come upon great tracts where settlers had been burning down the trees, and where their wounded bodies lay about, like those of murdered creatures, while here and there some charred and blackened giant reared aloft two withered arms, and seemed to call down curses on his foes. Sometimes, at night, the way wound through some lonely gorge, like a mountain pass in Scotland, shining and coldly glittering in the light of the moon, and so closed in by high steep hills all round, that there seemed to be no egress save through the narrower path by which we had come, until one rugged hill-side seemed to open, and shutting out the moonlight as we passed into its gloomy throat, wrapped our new course in shade and darkness.

We had left Harrisburg on Friday. On Sunday morning we arrived at the foot of the mountain, which is crossed by railroad. There are ten inclined planes; five *a*scending, and five *de*scending; the carriages are dragged up the former, and let down the latter, by means of stationary engines; the comparatively level spaces between, being traversed, sometimes by horse, and sometimes by engine power, as the case demands. Occasionally the rails are laid upon the extreme verge of a giddy precipice; and looking from the carriage window, the traveller gazes sheer down, without a stone or scrap of fence between, into the mountain depths below. The journey is very carefully made, however; only two carriages travelling together; and while proper precautions are taken, is not to be dreaded for its dangers.

It was very pretty travelling thus, at a rapid pace along the heights of the mountain in a keen wind, to look down into a valley full of light and softness; catching glimpses, through the tree-tops, of scattered cabins; children running to the doors; dogs bursting out to bark, whom we could see without hearing; terrified pigs scampering homewards; families sitting out in their rude gardens; cows gazing upward with a stupid indifference; men in their shirt-sleeves looking on at their unfinished houses, planning out to-morrow's work; and we riding onward, high above them, like a whirlwind. It was amusing, too, when we had dined, and rattled down a steep pass, having no other moving power than the weight of the carriages themselves, to see the engine released, long after us, come buzzing down alone, like a great insect, its back of green and gold so shining in the sun, that if it had spread a pair of wings and soared away, no one would have had occasion, as I fancied, for the least surprise. But it stopped short of us in a very business-like manner when we reached the canal: and, before we left the wharf, went panting up this hill again, with the passengers who had waited our arrival for the means of traversing the road by which we had come.

On the Monday evening, furnace fires and clanking hammers on the banks of the canal, warned us that we approached the termination of this part of our journey. After going through another dreamy place—a long aqueduct across the Alleghany

River, which was stranger than the bridge at Harrisburg, being a vast low wooden chamber full of water—we emerged upon that ugly confusion of backs of buildings and crazy galleries and stairs, which always abuts on water, whether it be river, sea, canal, or ditch: and were at Pittsburg.

Pittsburg is like Birmingham in England; at least its towns-people say so. Setting aside the streets, the shops, the houses, waggons, factories, public buildings, and population, perhaps it may be. It certainly has a great quantity of smoke hanging about it, and is famous for its iron-works. Besides the prison to which I have already referred, this town contains a pretty arsenal and other institutions. It is very beautifully situated on the Alleghany River, over which there are two bridges; and the villas of the wealthier citizens sprinkled about the high grounds in the neigh-bourhood, are pretty enough. We lodged at a most excellent hotel, and were admirably served. As usual it was full of boarders, was very large, and had a broad colonnade to every story of the house.

We tarried here, three days. Our next point was Cincinnati: and as this was a steamboat journey, and western steamboats usually blow up one or two a week in the season, it was advisable to collect opinions in reference to the comparative safety of the vessels bound that way, then lying in the river. One called the Mes-senger was the best recommended. She had been advertised to start positively, every day for a fortnight or so, and had not gone yet, nor did her captain seem to have any very fixed intention on the subject. But this is the custom: for if the law were to bind down a free and independent citizen to keep his word with the public, what would become of the liberty of the subject? Be-sides, it is in the way of trade. And if passengers be decoyed in the way of trade, and people be inconvenienced in the way of trade, what man, who is a sharp tradesman himself, shall say 'We must put a stop to this'?

Impressed by the deep solemnity of the public announcement, I (being then ignorant of these usages) was for hurrying on board in a breathless state, immediately; but receiving private and con-fidential information that the boat would certainly not start until Friday, April the First, we made ourselves very comfortable in the meanwhile, and went on board at noon that day.

CHAPTER XI

FROM PITTSBURG TO CINCINNATI IN A WESTERN STEAMBOAT. CINCINNATI

THE Messenger was one among a crowd of high-pressure steamboats, clustered together by a wharfside, which, looked down upon from the rising ground that forms the landing-place, and backed by the lofty bank on the opposite side of the river, appeared no larger than so many floating models. She had some forty passengers on board, exclusive of the poorer persons on the lower deck; and in half an hour, or less, proceeded on her way.

We had, for ourselves, a tiny state-room with two berths in it, opening out of the ladies' cabin. There was, undoubtedly, something satisfactory in this 'location,' inasmuch as it was in the stern, and we had been a great many times very gravely recommended to keep as far aft as possible, 'because the steamboats generally blew up forward.' Nor was this an unnecessary caution, as the occurrence and circumstances of more than one such fatility during our stay sufficiently testified. Apart from this source of self-congratulation, it was an unspeakable relief to have any place, no matter how confined, where one could be alone; and as the row of little chambers of which this was one, had each a second glass door besides that in the ladies' cabin, which opened on a narrow gallery outside the vessel, where the other passengers seldom came, and where one could sit in peace and gaze upon the shifting prospect, we took possession of our new quarters with much pleasure.

If the native packets I have already described be unlike anything we are in the habit of seeing on water, these western vessels are still more foreign to all the ideas we are accustomed to entertain of boats. I hardly know what to liken them to, or how to describe them.

In the first place, they have no mast, cordage, tackle, rigging, or other such boat-like gear; nor have they anything in their shape at all calculated to remind one of a boat's head, stern, sides, or keel. Except that they are in the water, and display a couple of paddle-boxes, they might be intended, for anything that appears to the contrary, to perform some unknown service, high and dry, upon a mountain top. There is no visible deck, even: nothing but a long, black, ugly roof, covered with burnt-out feathery sparks; above which tower two iron chimneys, and a hoarse escape valve, and a glass steerage-house. Then, in order as the eye descends towards the water, are the sides, and doors, and windows of the state-rooms, jumbled as oddly together as though they formed a small street, built by the varying tastes of a dozen men: the whole is supported on beams and pillars resting on a dirty barge, but a few inches above the water's edge: and in the narrow space between this upper structure and this barge's deck, are the furnace fires and machinery, open at the sides to every wind that blows, and every storm of rain it drives along its path.

Passing one of these boats at night, and seeing the great body of fire, exposed as I have just described, that rages and roars beneath the frail pile of painted wood: the machinery, not warded off or guarded in any way, but doing its work in the midst of the crowd of idlers and emigrants and children, who throng the lower deck: under the management, too, of reckless men whose acquaintance with its mysteries may have been of six months' standing: one feels directly that the wonder is, not that there should be so many fatal accidents, but that any journey should be safely made.

Within, there is one long narrow cabin, the whole length of the boat; from which the state-rooms open, on both sides. A small portion of it at the stern is partitioned off for the ladies; and the bar is at the opposite extreme. There is a long table down the centre, and at either end a stove. The washing apparatus is forward, on the deck. It is a little better than on board the canal boat, but not much. In all modes of travelling, the American customs, with reference to the means of personal cleanliness and wholesome ablution, are extremely negligent and filthy; and I strongly incline to the belief that a considerable amount of illness is referable to this cause.

We are to be on board the Messenger three days: arriving at Cincinnati (barring accidents) on Monday morning. There are three meals a day. Breakfast at seven, dinner at half-past twelve, supper about six. At each, there are a great many small dishes and plates upon the table, with very little in them; so that although there is every appearance of a mighty 'spread,' there is seldom really more than a joint: except for those who fancy slices of beetroot, shreds of dried beef, complicated entanglements of yellow pickle; maize, Indian corn, apple-sauce, and pumpkin.

Some people fancy all these little dainties together (and sweet preserves beside), by way of relish to their roast pig. They are generally those dyspeptic ladies and gentlemen who eat unheard-of quantities of hot corn bread (almost as good for the digestion as a kneaded pin-cushion), for breakfast, and for supper. Those who do not observe this custom, and who help themselves several times instead, usually suck their knives and forks meditatively, until they have decided what to take next: then pull them out of their mouths; put them in the dish; help themselves; and fall to work again. At dinner, there is nothing to drink upon the table, but great jugs full of cold water. Nobody says anything, at any meal, to anybody. All the passengers are very dismal, and seem to have tremendous secrets weighing on their minds. There is no conversation, no laughter, no cheerfulness, no sociality, except in spitting; and that is done in silent fellowship round the stove, when the meal is over. Every man sits down, dull and languid; swallows his fare as if breakfasts, dinners, and suppers, were necessities of nature never to be coupled with recreation or enjoyment; and having bolted his food in a gloomy silence, bolts himself, in the same state. But for these animal observances, you might suppose the whole male portion of the company to be the melancholy ghosts of departed book-keepers, who had fallen dead at the desk: such is their weary air of business and calculation. Undertakers on duty would be sprightly beside them; and a collation of funeral-baked meats, in comparison with these meals, would be a sparkling festivity.

The people are all alike, too. There is no diversity of character. They travel about on the same errands, say and do the same things in exactly the same manner, and follow in the same dull cheerless round. All down the long table, there is scarcely a man who is in anything different from his neighbour. It is quite a relief to have, sitting opposite, that little girl of fifteen with the loquacious chin: who, to do her justice, acts up to it, and fully identifies nature's handwriting, for of all the small chatterboxes that ever invaded the repose of drowsy ladies' cabin, she is the first and foremost. The beautiful girl, who sits a little beyond her—farther down the table there—married the young man with the dark whiskers, who sits beyond *her,* only last month. They are going to settle in the very Far West, where he has lived four years, but where she has never been. They were both overturnd in a stage-coach the other day (a bad omen anywhere else, where overturns are not so common), and his head, which bears the marks of a recent wound, is bound up still. She was hurt too, at the same time, and lay insensible for some days; bright as her eyes are, now.

Further down still, sits a man who is going some miles beyond their place of destination, to 'improve' a newly-discovered coppermine. He carries the village—that is to be—with him: a few frame cottages, and an apparatus for smelting the copper. He carries its people too. They are partly American and partly Irish, and herd together on the lower deck; where they amused themselves last evening till the night was pretty far advanced, by alternately firing off pistols and singing hymns.

They, and the very few who have been left at table twenty minutes, rise, and go away. We do so too; and passing through our little state-room, resume our seats in the quiet gallery without.

A fine broad river always, but in some parts much wider than in others: and then there is usually a green island, covered with trees, dividing it into two streams. Occasionally, we stop for a few minutes, maybe to take in wood, maybe for passengers, at some small town or village (I ought to say city, every place is a city here); but the banks are for the most part deep solitudes, overgrown with trees, which, hereabouts, are already in leaf and very green. For miles, and miles, and miles, these solitudes are unbroken by any sign of human life or trace of human footstep; nor is anything seen to move about them but the blue jay, whose colour is so bright, and yet so delicate, that it looks like a flying flower. At lengthened intervals a log cabin, with its little space of cleared land about it, nestles under a rising ground, and sends its thread of blue smoke curling up into the sky. It stands in the corner of the poor field of wheat, which is full of great unsightly stumps, like earthy butchers'-blocks. Sometimes the ground is only just now cleared: the felled trees lying yet upon the soil: and the log-house only this morning begun. As we pass this clearing, the settler leans upon his axe or hammer, and looks wistfully at the people from the world. The children creep out of the temporary hut, which is like a gipsy tent upon the ground, and clap their hands and shout. The dog only glances round at us, and then looks up into his master's face again, as if he were rendered uneasy by any suspension of the common business, and had nothing more to do with pleasures. And still there is the same, eternal foreground. The river has washed away its banks, and stately trees have fallen down into the stream. Some have been there so long, that they are mere dry grizzly skeletons. Some have just toppled over, and having earth yet about their roots, are bathing their green heads in the river, and putting forth new shoots and branches. Some are almost sliding down, as you look at them. And some were drowned so long ago, that their bleached arms start out from the middle of the current, and seem to try to grasp the boat, and drag it under water.

Through such a scene as this, the unwieldy machine takes its hoarse sullen way: venting, at every revolution of the paddles, a loud high-pressure blast; enough, one would think, to waken up the host of Indians who lie buried in a great mound yonder: so old, that mighty oaks and other forest trees have struck their roots into its earth; and so high, that it is a hill, even among the hills that Nature planted round it. The very river, as though it shared one's feelings of compassion for the extinct tribes who lived so pleasantly here, in their blessed ignorance of white existence, hundreds of years ago, steals out of its way to ripple near this mound: and there are few places where the Ohio sparkles more brightly than in the Big Grave Creek.

All this I see as I sit in the little stern-gallery mentioned just now. Evening slowly steals upon the landscape and changes it before me, when we stop to set some emigrants ashore.

Five men, as many women, and a little girl. All their worldly goods are a bag, a large chest and an old chair: one, old, high-backed, rush-bottomed chair: a solitary settler in itself. They are rowed ashore in the boat, while the vessel stands a little off awaiting its return, the water being shallow. They are landed at the foot of a high bank, on the summit of which are a few log cabins, attainable only by a long winding path. It is growing dusk; but the sun is very red, and shines in the water and on some of the tree-tops, like fire.

The men get out of the boat first: help out the women; take out the bag, the chest, the chair; bid the rowers 'good-bye'; and shove the boat off for them. At the first plash of the oars in the water, the oldest woman of the party sits down in the old chair, close to the water's edge, without speaking a word. None of the others sit down, though the chest is large enough for many seats. They all stand where they landed, as if stricken into stone; and look after the boat. So they remain, quite still and silent: the old woman and her old chair, in the centre; the bag and chest upon the shore, without anybody heeding them: all eyes fixed upon the boat. It comes alongside, is made fast, the men jump on board, the engine is put in motion, and we go hoarsely on again. There they stand yet, without the motion of a hand. I can see them through my glass, when, in the distance and increasing darkness, they are mere specks to the eye: lingering there still: the old woman in the old chair, and all the rest about her: not stirring in the least degree. And thus I slowly lose them.

The night is dark, and we proceed within the shadow of the wooded bank, which makes it darker. After gliding past the sombre maze of boughs for a long time, we come upon an open space where the tall trees are burning. The shape of every branch and twig is expressed in a deep red glow, and as the light wind stirs and ruffles it, they seem to vegetate in fire. It is such a sight as we read of in legends of enchanted forests: saving that it is sad to see these noble works wasting away so awfully, alone; and to think how many years must come and go before the magic that created them will rear their like upon this ground again. But the time will come: and when, in their changed ashes, the growth of centuries unborn has struck its roots, the restless men of distant ages will repair to these again unpeopled solitudes; and their fellows, in cities far away, that slumber now, perhaps, beneath the rolling sea, will read in language strange to any ears in being now, but very old to them, of primeval forests where the axe was never heard, and where the jungled ground was never trodden by a human foot.

Midnight and sleep blot out these scenes and thoughts: and when the morning shines again, it gilds the housetops of a lively city, before whose broad paved wharf the boat is moored; with other boats, and flags, and moving wheels, and hum of men around it; as though there were not a solitary or silent rood of ground within the compass of a thousand miles.

Cincinnati is a beautiful city; cheerful, thriving, and animated. I have not often seen a place that commends itself so favourably and pleasantly to a stranger at the first glance as this does: with its clean houses of red and white, its well-paved roads, and footways of bright tile. Nor does it become less prepossessing on a closer acquaintance. The streets are broad and airy, the shops extremely good, the private residences remarkable for their elegance and neatness. There is something of invention and fancy in the varying styles of these latter erections, which, after the dull company of the steamboat, is perfectly delightful, as conveying an assurance that there are such qualities still in existence. The disposition to ornament these pretty villas and render them attractive, leads to the culture of trees and flowers, and the laying out of well-kept gardens, the sight of which to those who walk along the streets, is inexpressibly refreshing and agreeable. I was quite charmed with the appearance of the town, and its adjoining suburb of Mount Auburn: from which the city, lying in an amphitheatre of hills, forms a picture of remarkable beauty, and is seen to great advantage.

There happened to be a great Temperance Convention held here on the day after our arrival; and as the order of march brought the procession under the windows of the hotel in which we lodged, when they started in the morning, I had a good opportunity of seeing it. It comprised several thousand men; the members of various 'Washington Auxiliary Temperance Societies'; and was marshalled by officers on horseback, who cantered briskly up and down the line, with scarves and ribbons of bright colours fluttering out behind them gaily. There were bands of music too, and banners out of number: and it was a fresh, holiday-looking concourse altogether.

I was particularly pleased to see the Irishmen, who formed a distinct society among themselves, and mustered very strong with their green scarves; carrying their national Harp and their Portrait of Father Mathew, high above the people's heads. They looked as jolly and good-humoured as ever; and, working (here) the hardest for their living and doing any kind of sturdy labour that came in their way, were the most independent fellows there, I thought.

The banners were very well painted, and flaunted down the street famously. There was the smiting of the rock, and the gushing forth of the waters; and there was a temperate man with 'considerable of a hatchet' (as the standard-bearer would probably have said), aiming a deadly blow at a serpent which was apparently about to spring upon him from the top of a barrel of spirits. But the chief feature of this part of the show was a huge allegorical device, borne among the ship-carpenters, on one side whereof the steamboat Alcohol was represented bursting her boiler and exploding with a great crash, while upon the other, the good ship Temperance sailed away with a fair wind, to the heart's content of the captain, crew, and passengers.

After going round the town, the procession repaired to a certain appointed place, where, as the printed programme set forth, it would be received by the children of the different free schools, 'singing Temperance Songs.' I was prevented from getting there, in time to hear these Little Warblers, or to report upon this novel kind of vocal entertainment: novel at least, to me: but I found in a large open space, each society gathered round its own banners, and listening in silent attention to its own orator. The speeches, judging from the little I could hear of them, were certainly adapted to the occasion, as having that degree of relationship to cold water which wet blankets may claim; but the main thing was the conduct and appearance of the audience throughout the day; and that was admirable and full of promise.

Cincinnati is honourably famous for its free-schools, of which it has so many that no person's child among its population can, by possibility, want the means of education, which are extended, upon an average, to four thousand pupils, annually. I was only present in one of these establishments during the hours of instruction. In the boys' department, which was full of little urchins (varying in their ages, I should say, from six years old to ten or twelve), the master offered to institute an extemporary examination of the pupils in algebra; a proposal, which, as I was by no means confident of my ability to detect mistakes in that science, I declined with some alarm. In the girls' school, reading was proposed; and as I felt tolerably equal to that art, I expressed my willingness to hear a class. Books were distributed accordingly, and some half-dozen girls relieved each other in reading paragraphs from English History. But it seemed to be a dry compilation, infinitely above their powers; and when they had blundered through three or four dreary passages concerning the Treaty of Amiens, and other thrilling topics of the same nature (obviously without comprehending ten words), I expressed myself quite satisfied. It is very possible that they only mounted to this exalted stave in the Ladder of Learning for the astonishment of a visitor; and that at other times they keep upon its lower rounds; but I should have been much better pleased and satisfied if I had heard them exercised in simpler lessons, which they understood.

As in every other place I visited, the Judges here were gentlemen of high character and attainments. I was in one of the courts for a few minutes, and found it like those to which I have already referred. A nuisance cause was trying; there were not many spectators; and the witnesses, counsel, and jury, formed a sort of family circle, sufficiently jocose and snug.

The society with which I mingled, was intelligent, courteous, and agreeable. The inhabitants of Cincinnati are proud of their city as one of the most interesting in America: and with good reason: for beautiful and thriving as it is now, and containing, as it does, a population of fifty thousand souls, but two-and-fifty years have passed away since the ground on which it stands (bought at that time for a few dollars) was a wild wood, and its citizens were but a handful of dwellers in scattered log huts upon the river's shore.

CHAPTER XII

FROM CINCINNATI TO LOUISVILLE IN ANOTHER WESTERN
STEAMBOAT; AND FROM LOUISVILLE TO ST. LOUIS IN AN-
OTHER. ST. LOUIS

LEAVING Cincinnati at eleven o'clock in the forenoon, we embarked
for Louisville in the Pike steamboat, which, carrying the mails,
was a packet of a much better class than that in which we had
come from Pittsburg. As this passage does not occupy more than
twelve or thirteen hours, we arranged to go ashore that night: not
coveting the distinction of sleeping in a state-room, when it was
possible to sleep anywhere else.

There chanced to be on board this boat, in addition to the usual
dreary crowd of passengers, one Pitchlynn, a chief of the Choctaw
tribe of Indians, who *sent in his card* to me, and with whom I had
the pleasure of a long conversation.

He spoke English perfectly well, though he had not begun to
learn the language, he told me, until he was a young man grown.
He had read many books; and Scott's poetry appeared to have left
a strong impression on his mind: especially the opening of The
Lady of the Lake, and the great battle scene in Marmion, in which,
no doubt from the congeniality of the subjects to his own pursuits
and tastes, he had great interest and delight. He appeared to understand correctly all he had read; and whatever fiction had en-
listed his sympathy in its belief, had done so keenly and earnestly.
I might almost say fiercely. He was dressed in our ordinary everyday costume, which hung about his fine figure loosely, and with indifferent grace. On my telling him that I regretted not to see him
in his own attire, he threw up his right arm, for a moment, as
though he were brandishing some heavy weapon, and answered, as
he let it fall again, that his race were losing many things besides
their dress, and would soon be seen upon the earth no more: but he
wore it at home, he added proudly.

He told me that he had been away from his home, west of the
Mississippi, seventeen months: and was now returning. He had
been chiefly at Washington on some negotiations pending between
his Tribe and the Government: which were not settled yet (he said
in a melancholy way), and he feared never would be: for what
could a few poor Indians do, against such well-skilled men of business as the whites? He had no love for Washington; tired of

towns and cities very soon; and longed for the Forest and the Prairie.

I asked him what he thought of Congress? He answered, with a smile, that it wanted dignity, in an Indian's eyes.

He would very much like, he said, to see England before he died; and spoke with much interest about the great things to be seen there. When I told him of that chamber in the British Museum wherein are preserved household memorials of a race that ceased to be, thousands of years ago, he was very attentive, and it was not hard to see that he had a reference in his mind to the gradual fading away of his own people.

This led us to speak of Mr. Catlin's gallery, which he praised highly: observing that his own portrait was among the collection, and that all the likenesses were 'elegant.' Mr. Cooper, he said, had painted the Red Man well; and so would I, he knew, if I would go home with him and hunt buffaloes, which he was quite anxious I should do. When I told him that supposing I went, I should not be very likely to damage the buffaloes much, he took it as a great joke and laughed heartily.

He was a remarkably handsome man; some years past forty I should judge; with long black hair, an aquiline nose, broad cheek-bones, a sunburnt complexion, and a very bright, keen, dark, and piercing eye. There were but twenty thousand of the Choctaws left, he said, and their number was decreasing every day. A few of his brother chiefs had been obliged to become civilised, and to make themselves acquainted with what the whites knew, for it was their only chance of existence. But they were not many; and the rest were as they always had been. He dwelt on this: and said several times that unless they tried to assimilate themselves to their conquerors, they must be swept away before the strides of civilised society.

When we shook hands at parting, I told him he must come to England, as he longed to see the land so much: that I should hope to see him there, one day: and that I could promise him he would be well received and kindly treated. He was evidently pleased by this assurance, though he rejoined with a good-humoured smile and an arch shake of his head, that the English used to be very fond of the Red Men when they wanted their help, but had not cared much for them, since.

He took his leave; as stately and complete a gentleman of Nature's making, as ever I beheld; and moved among the people in the boat, another kind of being. He sent me a lithographed portrait of himself soon afterwards; very like, though scarcely handsome enough; which I have carefully preserved in memory of our brief acquaintance.

There was nothing very interesting in the scenery of this day's journey, which brought us at midnight to Louisville. We slept at the Galt House; a splendid hotel; and were as handsomely lodged as though we had been in Paris, rather than hundreds of miles beyond the Alleghanies.

The city presenting no objects of sufficient interest to detain us on our way, we resolved to proceed next day by another steamboat, the Fulton, and to join it, about noon, at a suburb called Portland, where it would be delayed some time in passing through a canal.

The interval, after breakfast, we devoted to riding through the town, which is regular and cheerful: the streets being laid out at right angles, and planted with young trees. The buildings are smoky and blackened, from the use of bituminous coal, but an Englishman is well used to that appearance, and indisposed to quarrel with it. There did not appear to be much business stirring; and some unfinished buildings and improvements seemed to intimate that the city had been overbuilt in the ardour of 'going ahead,' and was suffering under the reaction consequent upon such feverish forcing of its powers.

On our way to Portland, we passed a 'Magistrate's office,' which amused me, as looking far more like a dame school than any police establishment: for this awful Institution was nothing but a little lazy, good-for-nothing front parlour, open to the street; wherein two or three figures (I presume the magistrate and his myrmidons) were basking in the sunshine, the very effigies of languor and repose. It was a perfect picture of Justice retired from business for want of customers; her sword and scale sold off; napping comfortably with her legs upon the table.

Here, as elsewhere in these parts, the road was perfectly alive with pigs of all ages; lying about in every direction, fast asleep; or grunting along in quest of hidden dainties. I had always a sneaking kindness for these odd animals, and found a constant source of amusement, when all others failed, in watching their proceedings. As we were riding along this morning, I observed a little incident between two youthful pigs, which was so very human as to be inexpressibly comical and grotesque at the time, though I dare say, in telling, it is tame enough.

One young gentleman (a very delicate porker with several straws sticking about his nose, betokening recent investigations in a dunghill) was walking deliberately on, profoundly thinking, when suddenly his brother, who was lying in a miry hole unseen by him, rose up immediately before his startled eyes, ghostly with damp mud. Never was pig's whole mass of blood so turned. He started back at least three feet, gazed for a moment, and then shot off as hard as he could go: his excessively little tail vibrating with speed and terror like a distracted pendulum. But before he had gone very far, he began to reason with himself as to the nature of this frightful appearance; and as he reasoned, he relaxed his speed by gradual degrees; until at last he stopped and faced about. There was his brother, with the mud upon him glazing in the sun, yet staring out of the very same hole, perfectly amazed at his proceedings! He was no sooner assured of this; and he assured himself so carefully that one may almost say he shaded his eyes with his hand to see the better; than he came back at a round trot, pounced upon him, and summarily took off a piece of his tail; as a caution to him to be careful what he was about for the future, and never to play tricks with his family any more.

We found the steamboat in the canal, waiting for the slow process of getting through the lock, and went on board, where we shortly afterwards had a new kind of visitor in the person of a certain Kentucky Giant whose name is Porter, and who is of the moderate height of seven feet eight inches, in his stockings.

There never was a race of people who so completely gave the lie to history as these giants, or whom all the chronicles have so cruelly libelled. Instead of roaring and ravaging about the world, constantly catering for their cannibal larders, and perpetually going to market in an unlawful manner, they are the meekest people in any man's acquaintance: rather inclining to milk and vegetable diet, and bearing anything for a quiet life. So decidedly are amiability and mildness their characteristics, that I confess I look upon that youth who distinguished himself by the slaughter of these inoffensive persons, as a false-hearted brigand, who, pretending to philanthropic motives, was secretly influenced only by the wealth stored up within their castles, and the hope of plunder. And I lean the more to this opinion from finding that even the historian of those exploits, with all his partiality for his hero, is fain to admit that the slaughtered monsters in question were of a very innocent and simple turn; extremely guileless and ready of belief; lending a credulous ear to the most improbable tales; suffering themselves to be easily entrapped into pits; and even (as in the case of the Welsh Giant) with an excess of the hospitable politeness of a landlord, ripping themselves open, rather than hint at the possibility of their guests being versed in the vagabond arts of sleight-of-hand and hocus-pocus.

The Kentucky Giant was but another illustration of the truth of this position. He had a weakness in the region of the knees, and a trustfulness in his long face, which appealed even to five-feet nine for encouragement and support. He was only twenty-five years old, he said, and had grown recently, for it had been found necessary to make an addition to the legs of his inexpressibles. At fifteen he was a short boy, and in those days his English father and his Irish mother had rather snubbed him, as being too small of stature to sustain the credit of the family. He added that his health had not been good, though it was better now; but short people are not wanting who whisper that he drinks too hard.

I understand he drives a hackney-coach, though how he does it, unless he stands on the footboard behind, and lies along the roof upon his chest, with his chin in the box, it would be difficult to comprehend. He brought his gun with him, as a curiosity. Christened 'The Little Rifle,' and displayed outside a shop-window, it would make the fortune of any retail business in Holborn. When he had shown himself and talked a little while, he withdrew with his pocket-instrument, and went bobbing down the cabin, among men of six feet high and upwards, like a lighthouse walking among lamp-posts.

Within a few minutes afterwards, we were out of the canal, and in the Ohio river again.

The arrangements of the boat were like those of the Messenger, and the passengers were of the same order of people. We fed at the same times, on the same kind of viands, in the same dull manner, and with the same observances. The company appeared to be oppressed by the same tremendous concealments, and had as little capacity of enjoyment or lightheartedness. I never in my life did see such listless, heavy dulness as brooded over these meals: the very recollection of it weighs me down, and makes me, for the moment, wretched. Reading and writing on my knee, in our little cabin, I really dreaded the coming of the hour that summoned us to table; and was as glad to escape from it again, as if it had been a penance or a punishment. Healthy cheerfulness and good spirits forming a part of the banquet, I could soak my crusts in the fountain with Le Sage's strolling player, and revel in their glad enjoyment: but sitting down with so many fellow-animals to ward off thirst and hunger as a business; to empty, each creature, his Yahoo's trough as quickly as he can, and then slink sullenly away; to have these social sacraments stripped of everything but the mere greedy satisfaction of the natural cravings; goes so against the grain with me, that I seriously believe the recollection of these funeral feasts will be a waking nightmare to me all my life.

There was some relief in this boat, too, which there had not been in the other, for the captain (a blunt good-natured fellow) had his handsome wife with him, who was disposed to be lively and agreeable, as were a few other lady-passengers who had their seats about us at the same end of the table. But nothing could have made head against the depressing influence of the general body. There was a magnetism of dulness in them which would have beaten down the most facetious companion that the earth ever knew. A jest would have been a crime, and a smile would have faded into a grinning horror. Such deadly leaden people; such systematic plodding weary insupportable heaviness; such a mass of animated indigestion in respect of all that was genial, jovial, frank, social, or hearty; never, sure, was brought together elsewhere since the world began.

Nor was the scenery, as we approached the junction of the Ohio and Mississippi rivers, at all inspiriting in its influence. The trees were stunted in their growth; the banks were low and flat; the settlements and log cabins fewer in number: their inhabitants more wan and wretched than any we had encountered yet. No songs of birds were in the air, no pleasant scents, no moving lights and shadows from swift passing clouds. Hour after hour, the changeless glare of the hot, unwinking sky, shone upon the same monotonous objects. Hour after hour, the river rolled along, as wearily and slowly as the time itself.

At length, upon the morning of the third day, we arrived at a spot so much more desolate than any we had yet beheld, that the forlornest places we had passed, were, in comparison with it, full of interest. At the junction of the two rivers, on ground so flat and low and marshy, that at certain seasons of the year it is inundated to the house-tops, lies a breeding-place of fever, ague, and death; vaunted in England as a mine of Golden Hope, and speculated in, on the faith of monstrous representations, to many people's ruin. A dismal swamp, on which the half-built houses rot away: cleared here and there for the space of a few yards; and teeming, then, with rank unwholesome vegetation, in whose baleful shade the wretched wanderers who are tempted hither, droop, and die, and lay their bones; the hateful Mississippi circling and eddying before it, and turning off upon its southern course a slimy monster hideous to behold; a hotbed of disease, an ugly sepulchre, a grave uncheered by any gleam of promise: a place without one single quality, in earth or air or water, to commend it: such is this dismal Cairo.

But what words shall describe the Mississippi, great father of rivers, who (praise be to Heaven) has no young children like him! An enormous ditch, sometimes two or three miles wide, running liquid mud, six miles an hour: its strong and frothy current choked and obstructed everywhere by huge logs and whole forest trees: now twining themselves together in great rafts, from the interstices of which a sedgy lazy foam works up, to float upon the water's top; now rolling past like monstrous bodies, their tangled roots showing like matted hair; now glancing singly by like giant leeches; and now writhing round and round in the vortex of some small whirlpool, like wounded snakes. The banks low, the trees dwarfish, the marshes swarming with frogs, the wretched cabins few and far apart, their inmates hollow-cheeked and pale, the weather very hot, mosquitoes penetrating into every crack and crevice of the boat, mud and slime on everything: nothing pleasant in its aspect, but the harmless lightning which flickers every night upon the dark horizon.

For two days we toiled up this foul stream, striking constantly against the floating timber, or stopping to avoid those more dangerous obstacles, the snags, or sawyers, which are the hidden trunks of trees that have their roots below the tide. When the nights are very dark, the lookout stationed in the head of the boat, knows by the ripple of the water if any great impediment be near at hand, and rings a bell beside him, which is the signal for the engine to be stopped: but always in the night this bell has work to do, and after every ring, there comes a blow which renders it no easy matter to remain in bed.

The decline of day here was very gorgeous; tinging the firmament deeply with red and gold, up to the very keystone of the arch above us. As the sun went down behind the bank, the slightest blades of grass upon it seemed to become as distinctly visible as the arteries in the skeleton of a leaf; and when, as it slowly sank, the red and golden bars upon the water grew dimmer, and dimmer yet, as if they were sinking too; and all the glowing colours of departing day paled, inch by inch, before the sombre night; the scene became a thousand times more lonesome and more dreary than before, and all its influences darkened with the sky.

We drank the muddy water of this river while we were upon it. It is considered wholesome by the natives, and is something more opaque than gruel. I have seen water like it at the Filter-shops, but nowhere else.

On the fourth night after leaving Louisville, we reached St. Louis, and here I witnessed the conclusion of an incident, trifling enough in itself, but very pleasant to see, which had interested me during the whole journey.

There was a little woman on board, with a little baby; and both little woman and little child were cheerful, good-looking, bright-eyed, and fair to see. The little woman had been passing a long time with her sick mother in New York, and left her home in St. Louis, in that condition in which ladies who truly love their lords desire to be. The baby was born in her mother's house; and she had not seen her husband (to whom she was now returning), for twelve months: having left him a month or two after their marriage.

Well, to be sure, there never was a little woman so full of hope, and tenderness, and love, and anxiety, as this little woman was: and all day long she wondered whether 'He' would be at the wharf; and whether 'He' had got her letter; and whether, if she sent the baby ashore by somebody else, 'He' would know it, meeting it in the street: which, seeing that he had never set eyes upon it in his life, was not very likely in the abstract, but was probable enough, to the young mother. She was such an artless little creature; and was in such a sunny, beaming, hopeful state; and let out all this matter clinging close about her heart, so freely; that all the other lady passengers entered into the spirit of it as much as she; and the captain (who heard all about it from his wife) was wondrous sly, I promise you: inquiring, every time we met at table, as in forget-fulness, whether she expected anybody to meet her at St. Louis, and whether she would want to go ashore the night we reached it (but he supposed she wouldn't), and cutting many other dry jokes of that nature. There was one little weasen, dried-apple-faced old woman, who took occasion to doubt the constancy of husbands in such circumstances of bereavement; and there was another lady (with a lap dog) old enough to moralise on the lightness of human affections, and yet not so old that she could help nursing the baby, now and then, or laughing with the rest, when the little woman called it by its father's name, and asked it all manner of fantastic questions concerning him in the joy of her heart.

It was something of a blow to the little woman, that when we were within twenty miles of our destination, it became clearly nec-essary to put this baby to bed. But she got over it with the same good humour; tied a handkerchief round her head; and came out into the little gallery with the rest. Then, such an oracle as she be-came in reference to the localities! and such facetiousness as was displayed by the married ladies! and such sympathy as was shown by the single ones; and such peals of laughter as the little woman herself (who would just as soon have cried) greeted every jest with!

At last, there were the lights of St. Louis, and here was the wharf, and those were the steps: and the little woman covering her face with her hands, and laughing (or seeming to laugh) more than ever, ran into her own cabin, and shut herself up. I have no doubt that in the charming inconsistency of such excitement, she stopped her ears, lest she should hear 'Him' asking for her: but I did not see her do it.

Then, a great crowd of people rushed on board, though the boat was not yet made fast, but was wandering about, among the other boats, to find a landing-place: and everybody looked for the husband: and nobody saw him: when, in the midst of us all— Heaven knows how she ever got there—there was the little woman clinging with both arms tight round the neck of a fine, good-looking, sturdy young fellow! and in a moment afterwards, there she was again, actually clapping her little hands for joy, as she dragged him through the small door of her small cabin, to look at the baby as he lay asleep!

We went to a large hotel, called the Planter's House: built like an English hospital, with long passages and bare walls, and sky-lights above the room-doors for the free circulation of air. There were a great many boarders in it; and as many lights sparkled and glistened from the windows down into the street below, when we drove up, as if it had been illuminated on some occasion of rejoic-ing. It is an excellent house, and the proprietors have most bounti-ful notions of providing the creature comforts. Dining alone with my wife in our own room, one day, I counted fourteen dishes on the table at once.

In the old French portion of the town, the thoroughfares are narrow and crooked, and some of the houses are very quaint and picturesque: being built of wood, with tumbledown galleries before the windows, approachable by stairs or rather ladders from the street. There are queer little barbers' shops and drinking-houses too, in this quarter; and abundance of crazy old tenements with blinking casements, such as may be seen in Flanders. Some of these ancient habitations, with high garret gable-windows perking into the roofs, have a kind of French shrug about them; and being lop-sided with age, appear to hold their heads askew, besides, as if they were grimacing in astonishment at the American Improve-ments.

It is hardly necessary to say that these consist of wharfs and warehouses, and new buildings in all directions; and of a great many vast plans which are still 'progressing.' Already, however, some very good houses, broad streets, and marble-fronted shops, have gone so far ahead as to be in a state of completion; and the town bids fair in a few years to improve considerably: though it is not likely ever to vie, in point of elegance or beauty, with Cincinnati.

The Roman Catholic religion, introduced here by the early French settlers, prevails extensively. Among the public institutions are a Jesuit college; a convent for 'the Ladies of the Sacred Heart'; and a large chapel attached to the college, which was in course of erection at the time of my visit, and was intended to be consecrated on the second of December in the next year. The architect of this building, is one of the reverend fathers of the school, and the works proceed under his sole direction. The organ will be sent from Belgium.

In addition to these establishments, there is a Roman Catholic cathedral, dedicated to Saint Francis Xavier; and a hospital, founded by the munificence of a deceased resident, who was a member of that church. It also sends missionaries from hence among the Indian tribes.

The Unitarian church is represented, in this remote place, as in most other parts of America, by a gentleman of great worth and excellence. The poor have good reason to remember and bless it; for it befriends them, and aids the cause of rational education, without any sectarian or selfish views. It is liberal in all its actions; of kind construction; and of wide benevolence.

There are three free-schools already erected, and in full operation in this city. A fourth is building, and will soon be opened.

No man ever admits the unhealthiness of the place he dwells in (unless he is going away from it), and I shall therefore, I have no doubt, be at issue with the inhabitants of St. Louis, in questioning the perfect salubrity of its climate, and in hinting that I think it must rather dispose to fever in the summer and autumnal seasons. Just adding, that it is very hot, lies among great rivers, and has vast tracts of undrained swampy land around it, I leave the reader to form his own opinion.

As I had a great desire to see a Prairie before turning back from the furthest point of my wanderings; and as some gentlemen of the town had, in their hospitable consideration, an equal desire to gratify me; a day was fixed, before my departure, for an expedition to the Looking-Glass Prairie, which is within thirty miles of

THE LITTLE WIFE

the town. Deeming it possible that my readers may not object to
know what kind of thing such a gipsy party may be at that distance from home, and among what sort of objects it moves, I will
describe the jaunt in another chapter.

CHAPTER XIII

A JAUNT TO THE LOOKING-GLASS PRAIRIE AND BACK

I MAY premise that the word Prairie is variously pronounced
paraaer, parearer, and *paroarer.* The latter mode of pronunciation
is perhaps the most in favour.

We were fourteen in all, and all young men: indeed it is a singular though very natural feature in the society of these distant settlements, that it is mainly composed of adventurous persons in the
prime of life, and has very few grey heads among it. There were
no ladies: the trip being a fatiguing one: and we were to start at
five o'clock in the morning punctually.

I was called at four, that I might be certain of keeping nobody
waiting; and having got some bread and milk for breakfast, threw
up the window and looked down into the street, expecting to see
the whole party busily astir, and great preparations going on below. But as everything was very quiet, and the street presented
that hopeless aspect with which five o'clock in the morning is familiar elsewhere, I deemed it as well to go to bed again, and went
accordingly.

I awoke again at seven o'clock, and by that time the party had
assembled, and were gathered round, one light carriage, with a
very stout axletree; one something on wheels like an amateur carrier's cart; one double phaeton of great antiquity and unearthly
construction; one gig with a great hole in its back and a broken
head; and one rider on horseback who was to go on before. I got
into the first coach with three companions; the rest bestowed
themselves in the other vehicles; two large baskets were made fast
to the lightest; two large stone jars in wicker cases, technically
known as demi-johns, were consigned to the 'least rowdy' of the
party for safe-keeping; and the procession moved off to the ferry-
boat, in which it was to cross the river bodily, men, horses, carriages, and all, as the manner in these parts is.

We got over the river in due course, and mustered again before a
little wooden box on wheels, hove down all aslant in a morass,

with 'MERCHANT TAILOR' painted in very large letters over the door. Having settled the order of proceeding, and the road to be taken, we started off once more and began to make our way through an ill-favoured Black Hollow, called, less expressively, the American Bottom.

The previous day had been—not to say hot, for the term is weak and lukewarm in its power of conveying an idea of the temperature. The town had been on fire; in a blaze. But at night it had come on to rain in torrents, and all night long it had rained without cessation. We had a pair of very strong horses, but travelled at the rate of little more than a couple of miles an hour, through one unbroken slough of black mud and water. It had no variety but in depth. Now it was only half over the wheels, now it hid the axle-tree, and now the coach sank down in it almost to the windows. The air resounded in all directions with the loud chirping of the frogs, who, with the pigs (a coarse, ugly breed, as unwholesome-looking as though they were the spontaneous growth of the country), had the whole scene to themselves. Here and there we passed a log hut: but the wretched cabins were wide apart and thinly scattered, for though the soil is very rich in this place, few people can exist in such a deadly atmosphere. On either side of the track, if it deserve the name, was the thick 'bush'; and everywhere was stagnant, slimy, rotten, filthy water.

As it is the custom in these parts to give a horse a gallon or so of cold water whenever he is in a foam with heat, we halted for that purpose, at a log inn in the wood, far removed from any other residence. It consisted of one room, bare-roofed and bare-walled of course, with a loft above. The ministering priest was a swarthy young savage, in a shirt of cotton print like bed-furniture, and a pair of ragged trousers. There were a couple of young boys, too, nearly naked, lying idly by the well; and they, and he, and *the* traveller at the inn, turned out to look at us.

The traveller was an old man with a grey gristly beard two inches long, a shaggy moustache of the same hue, and enormous eyebrows; which almost obscured his lazy, semi-drunken glance, as he stood regarding us with folded arms: poising himself alternately upon his toes and heels. On being addressed by one of the party, he drew nearer, and said, rubbing his chin (which scraped under his horny hand like fresh gravel beneath a nailed shoe), that he was from Delaware, and had lately bought a farm 'down there,' pointing into one of the marshes where the stunted trees were thickest. He was 'going,' he added, to St. Louis, to fetch his family, whom he had left behind; but he seemed in no great hurry to bring on these incumbrances, for when we moved away, he loitered back into the cabin, and was plainly bent on stopping there so long as his money lasted. He was a great politician of course, and explained his opinions at some length to one of our company; but I only remember that he concluded with two sentiments, one of which was, Somebody for ever; and the other, Blast everybody else! which is by no means a bad abstract of the general creed in these matters.

When the horses were swollen out to about twice their natural dimensions (there seems to be an idea here, that this kind of inflation improves their going), we went forward again, through mud and mire, and damp, and festering heat, and brake and bush, attended always by the music of the frogs and pigs, until nearly noon, when we halted at a place called Belleville.

Belleville was a small collection of wooden houses, huddled together in the very heart of the bush and swamp. Many of them had singularly bright doors of red and yellow; for the place had been lately visited by a travelling painter, 'who got along,' as I was told, 'by eating his way.' The criminal court was sitting, and was at that moment trying some criminals for horse-stealing: with whom it would most likely go hard: for live stock of all kinds being necessarily very much exposed in the woods, is held by the community in rather higher value than human life; and for this reason, juries generally make a point of finding all men indicted for cattle-stealing, guilty, whether or no.

The horses belonging to the bar, the judge, and witnesses, were tied to temporary racks set up roughly in the road; by which is to be understood, a forest path, nearly knee-deep in mud and slime.

There was an hotel in this place, which, like all hotels in America, had its large dining-room for the public table. It was an odd, shambling, low-roofed out-house, half-cowshed and half-kitchen, with a coarse brown canvas table-cloth, and tin sconces stuck against the walls, to hold candles at supper-time. The horseman had gone forward to have coffee and some eatables prepared, and they were by this time nearly ready. He had ordered 'wheat-bread and chicken fixings,' in preference to 'corn-bread and common doings.' The latter kind of refection includes only pork and bacon. The former comprehends boiled ham, sausages, veal cutlets, steaks, and such other viands of that nature as may be supposed, by a tolerably wide poetical construction, 'to fix' a chicken comfortably in the digestive organs of any lady or gentleman.

On one of the door-posts at this inn, was a tin plate, whereon was inscribed in characters of gold, 'Doctor Crocus'; and on a sheet of paper, pasted up by the side of this plate, was a written announcement that Dr. Crocus would that evening deliver a lecture on Phrenology for the benefit of the Belleville public; at a charge, for admission, of so much a head.

Straying upstairs, during the preparation of the chicken fixings, I happened to pass the doctor's chamber; and as the door stood wide open, and the room was empty, I made bold to peep in.

It was a bare, unfurnished, comfortless room, with an unframed portrait hanging up at the head of the bed; a likeness, I take it, of the Doctor, for the forehead was fully displayed, and great stress was laid by the artist upon its phrenological developments. The bed itself was covered with an old patch-work counterpane. The room was destitute of carpet or of curtain. There was a damp fire-place without any stove, full of wood ashes; a chair, and a very small table; and on the last-named piece of furniture was displayed, in grand array, the doctor's library, consisting of some half-dozen greasy old books.

Now, it certainly looked about the last apartment on the whole earth out of which any man would be likely to get anything to do him good. But the door, as I have said, stood coaxingly open, and plainly said in conjunction with the chair, the portrait, the table, and the books, 'Walk in, gentlemen, walk in! Don't be ill, gentlemen, when you may be well in no time. Doctor Crocus is here, gentlemen, the celebrated Dr. Crocus! Doctor Crocus has come all this way to cure you, gentlemen. If you haven't heard of Dr. Crocus, it's your fault, gentlemen, who live a little way out of the world here: not Dr. Crocus's. Walk in, gentlemen, walk in!'

In the passage below, when I went downstairs again, was Dr. Crocus himself. A crowd had flocked in from the Court House, and a voice from among them called out to the landlord, 'Colonel! introduce Doctor Crocus.'

'Mr. Dickens,' says the colonel, 'Doctor Crocus.'

Upon which Doctor Crocus, who is a tall, fine-looking Scotchman, but rather fierce and warlike in appearance for a professor of the peaceful art of healing, bursts out of the concourse with his right arm extended, and his chest thrown out as far as it will possibly come, and says:

'Your countryman, sir!'

Whereupon Doctor Crocus and I shake hands; and Doctor Crocus looks as if I didn't by any means realise his expectations, which, in a linen blouse, and a great straw hat, with a green ribbon, and no gloves, and my face and nose profusely ornamented with the stings of mosquitoes and the bites of bugs, it is very likely I did not.

'Long in these parts, sir?' says I.

'Three or four months, sir,' says the Doctor.

'Do you think of soon returning to the old country?' says I.

Doctor Crocus makes no verbal answer, but gives me an imploring look, which says so plainly, 'Will you ask me that again, a little louder, if you please?' that I repeat the question.

'Think of soon returning to the old country, sir!' repeats the Doctor.

'To the old country, sir,' I rejoin.

Doctor Crocus looks round upon the crowd to observe the effect he produces, rubs his hands, and says, in a very loud voice:

'Not yet awhile, sir, not yet. You won't catch me at that just yet, sir. I am a little too fond of freedom for *that*, sir. Ha, ha! It's not so easy for a man to tear himself from a free country such as this is, sir. Ha, ha! No, no! Ha, ha! None of that till one's obliged to do it, sir. No, no!'

As Doctor Crocus says these latter words, he shakes his head, knowingly, and laughs again. Many of the bystanders shake their heads in concert with the doctor, and laugh too, and look at each other as much as to say, 'A pretty bright and first-rate sort of chap is Crocus!' and unless I am very much mistaken, a good many people went to the lecture that night, who never thought about phrenology, or about Doctor Crocus either, in all their lives before.

From Belleville, we went on, through the same desolate kind of waste, and constantly attended, without the interval of a moment, by the same music; until, at three o'clock in the afternoon, we halted once more at a village called Lebanon to inflate the horses again, and give them some corn besides: of which they stood much in need. Pending this ceremony, I walked into the village, where I met a full-sized dwelling-house coming down-hill at a round trot, drawn by a score or more of oxen.

The public-house was so very clean and good a one, that the managers of the jaunt resolved to return to it and put up there for the night, if possible. This course decided on, and the horses being well refreshed, we again pushed forward, and came upon the Prairie at sunset.

It would be difficult to say why, or how—though it was possibly from having heard and read so much about it—but the effect on me was disappointment. Looking towards the setting sun, there lay, stretched out before my view, a vast expanse of level ground; unbroken, save by one thin line of trees, which scarcely amounted to a scratch upon the great blank; until it met the glowing sky, wherein it seemed to dip: mingling with its rich colours, and mellowing in its distant blue. There it lay, a tranquil sea or lake without water, if such a simile be admissible, with the day going down upon it: a few birds wheeling here and there: and solitude and silence reigning paramount around. But the grass was not yet high; there were bare black patches on the ground; and the few wildflowers that the eye could see, were poor and scanty. Great as the picture was, its very flatness and extent, which left nothing to the imagination, tamed it down and cramped its interest. I felt little of that sense of freedom and exhilaration which a Scottish heath inspires, or even our English downs awaken. It was lonely and wild, but oppressive in its barren monotony. I felt that in traversing the Prairies, I could never abandon myself to the scene, forgetful of all else; as I should do instinctively, were the heather underneath my feet, or an iron-bound coast beyond; but should often glance towards the distant and frequently-receding line of the horizon, and wish it gained and passed. It is not a scene to be forgotten, but it is scarcely one, I think (at all events, as I saw it), to remember with much pleasure, or to covet the looking-on again, in after life.

We encamped near a solitary log-house, for the sake of its water, and dined upon the plain. The baskets contained roast fowls, buffalo's tongue (an exquisite dainty, by the way), ham, bread, cheese, and butter; biscuits, champagne, sherry; lemons and sugar for punch; and abundance of rough ice. The meal was delicious, and the entertainers were the soul of kindness and good humour. I have often recalled that cheerful party to my pleasant recollection since, and shall not easily forget, in junketings nearer home with friends of older date, my boon companions on the Prairie.

Returning to Lebanon that night, we lay at the little inn at which we had halted in the afternoon. In point of cleanliness and comfort it would have suffered by no comparison with any English alehouse, of a homely kind, in England.

Rising at five o'clock next morning, I took a walk about the village: none of the houses were strolling about to-day, but it was early for them yet, perhaps: and then amused myself by lounging in a kind of farm-yard behind the tavern, of which the leading features were, a strange jumble of rough sheds for stables; a rude colonnade, built as a cool place of summer resort; a deep well; a great earthen mound for keeping vegetables in, in winter time; and a pigeon-house, whose little apertures looked, as they do in all pigeon-houses, very much too small for the admission of the plump and swelling-breasted birds who were strutting about it, though they tried to get in never so hard. That interest exhausted, I took a survey of the inn's two parlours, which were decorated with coloured prints of Washington, and President Madison, and of a white-faced young lady (much speckled by the flies), who held up her gold neck-chain for the admiration of the spectator, and informed all admiring comers that she was 'Just Seventeen'; although I should have thought her older. In the best room were two oil portraits of the kit-cat size, representing the landlord and his infant son; both looking as bold as lions, and staring out of the canvas with an intensity that would have been cheap at any price. They were painted, I think, by the artist who had touched up the Belleville doors with red and gold; for I seemed to recognise his style immediately.

After breakfast, we started to return by a different way from that which we had taken yesterday, and coming up at ten o'clock with an encampment of German emigrants carrying their goods in carts, who had made a rousing fire which they were just quitting, stopped there to refresh. And very pleasant the fire was; for, hot though it had been yesterday, it was quite cold to-day, and the wind blew keenly. Looming in the distance, as we rode along, was another of the ancient Indian burial-places, called The Monks' Mound; in memory of a body of fanatics of the order of La Trappe, who founded a desolate convent there, many years ago, when there were no settlers within a thousand miles, and were all swept off by the pernicious climate: in which lamentable fatality, few rational people will suppose, perhaps, that society experienced any very severe deprivation.

The track of to-day had the same features as the track of yesterday. There was the swamp, the bush, and the perpetual chorus of frogs, the rank unseemly growth, the unwholesome steaming earth. Here and there, and frequently too, we encountered a solitary broken-down waggon, full of some new settler's goods. It was a pitiful sight to see one of these vehicles deep in the mire; the axle-tree broken; the wheel lying idly by its side; the man gone miles away, to look for assistance; the woman seated among their wandering household goods with a baby at her breast, a picture of forlorn, dejected patience; the team of oxen crouching down mournfully in the mud, and breathing forth such clouds of vapour from their mouths and nostrils, that all the damp mist and fog around seemed to have come direct from them.

In due time we mustered once again before the merchant tailor's and having done so, crossed over to the city in the ferry-boat:

passing, on the way, a spot called Bloody Island, the duelling-ground of St. Louis, and so designated in honour of the last fatal combat fought there, which was with pistols, breast to breast. Both combatants fell dead upon the ground; and possibly some rational people may think of them, as of the gloomy madmen on the Monks' Mound, that they were no great loss to the community.

CHAPTER XIV

RETURN TO CINCINNATI. A STAGE-COACH RIDE FROM THAT CITY TO COLUMBUS, AND THENCE TO SANDUSKY. SO, BY LAKE ERIE, TO THE FALLS OF NIAGARA

As I had a desire to travel through the interior of the State of Ohio, and to 'strike the lakes,' as the phrase is, at a small town called Sandusky, to which that route would conduct us on our way to Niagara, we had to return from St. Louis by the way we had come, and to retrace our former track as far as Cincinnati.

The day on which we were to take leave of St. Louis being very fine; and the steamboat, which was to have started I don't know how early in the morning, postponing, for the third or fourth time, her departure until the afternoon; we rode forward to an old French village on the river, called properly Carondelet, and nick-named Vide Poche, and arranged that the packet should call for us there.

The place consisted of a few poor cottages, and two or three public-houses; the state of whose larders certainly seemed to justify the second designation of the village, for there was nothing to eat in any of them. At length, however, by going back some half a mile or so, we found a solitary house where ham and coffee were procurable; and there we tarried to await the advent of the boat, which would come in sight from the green before the door, a long way off.

It was a neat, unpretending village tavern, and we took our repast in a quaint little room with a bed in it, decorated with some old oil paintings, which in their time had probably done duty in a Catholic chapel or monastery. The fare was very good, and served with great cleanliness. The house was kept by a characteristic old couple, with whom we had a long talk, and who were perhaps a very good example of that kind of people in the West.

The landlord was a dry, tough, hard-faced old fellow (not so

very old either, for he was but just turned sixty, I should think),
who had been out with the militia in the last war with England,
and had seen all kinds of service,—except a battle; and he had
been very near seeing that, he added: very near. He had all his
life been restless and locomotive, with an irresistible desire for
change; and was still the son of his old self: for if he had nothing
to keep him at home, he said (slightly jerking his hat and his
thumb towards the window of the room in which the old lady sat,
as we stood talking in front of the house), he would clean up his
musket, and be off to Texas to-morrow morning. He was one of the
very many descendants of Cain proper to this continent, who seem
destined from their birth to serve as pioneers in the great human
army: who gladly go on from year to year extending its outposts,
and leaving home after home behind them; and die at last, utterly
regardless of their graves being left thousands of miles behind, by
the wandering generations who succeed.

His wife was a domesticated kind-hearted old soul, who had
come with him, 'from the queen city of the world,' which, it
seemed, was Philadelphia; but had no love for this Western country, and indeed had little reason to bear it any; having seen her
children, one by one, die here of fever, in the full prime and beauty
of their youth. Her heart was sore, she said, to think of them; and
to talk on this theme, even to strangers, in that blighted place, so
far from her old home, eased it somewhat, and became a melancholy pleasure.

The boat appearing towards evening, we bade adieu to the poor
old lady and her vagrant spouse, and making for the nearest landing-place, were soon on board the Messenger again, in our old
cabin, and steaming down the Mississippi.

If the coming up this river, slowly making head against the
stream, be an irksome journey, the shooting down it with the tur-
bid current is almost worse; for then the boat, proceeding at the
rate of twelve or fifteen miles an hour, has to force its passage
through a labyrinth of floating logs, which, in the dark, it is often
impossible to see beforehand or avoid. All that night, the bell was
never silent for five minutes at a time; and after every ring the
vessel reeled again, sometimes beneath a single blow, sometimes
beneath a dozen dealt in quick succession, the lightest of which
seemed more than enough to beat in her frail keel, as though it had
been pie-crust. Looking down upon the filthy river after dark, it
seemed to be alive with monsters, as these black masses rolled upon
the surface, or came starting up again, head first, when the boat, in
ploughing her way among a shoal of such obstructions, drove a few

among them for the moment under water. Sometimes the engine stopped during a long interval, and then before her and behind, and gathering close about her on all sides, were so many of these ill-favoured obstacles that she was fairly hemmed in; the centre of a floating island; and was constrained to pause until they parted, somewhere, as dark clouds will do before the wind, and opened by degrees a channel out.

In good time next morning, however, we came again in sight of the detestable morass called Cairo; and stopping there to take in wood, lay alongside a barge, whose starting timbers scarcely held together. It was moored to the bank, and on its side was painted 'Coffee House'; that being, I suppose, the floating paradise to which the people fly for shelter when they lose their houses for a month or two beneath the hideous waters of the Mississippi. But looking southward from this point, we had the satisfaction of seeing that intolerable river dragging its slimy length and ugly freight abruptly off towards New Orleans; and passing a yellow line which stretched across the current, were again upon the clear Ohio, never, I trust, to see the Mississippi more, saving in troubled dreams and night-mares. Leaving it for the company of its sparkling neighbour, was like the transition from pain to ease, or the awakening from a horrible vision to cheerful realities.

We arrived at Louisville on the fourth night, and gladly availed ourselves of its excellent hotel. Next day we went on in the Ben Franklin, a beautiful mail steamboat, and reached Cincinnati shortly after midnight. Being by this time nearly tired of sleeping upon shelves, we had remained awake to go ashore straightway; and groping a passage across the dark decks of other boats, and among labyrinths of engine-machinery and leaking casks of molasses, we reached the streets, knocked up the porter at the hotel where we had stayed before, and were, to our great joy, safely housed soon afterwards.

We rested but one day at Cincinnati and then resumed our journey to Sandusky. As it comprised two varieties of stage-coach travelling, which, with those I have already glanced at, comprehended the main characteristics of this mode of transit in America, I will take the reader as our fellow-passenger, and pledge myself to perform the distance with all possible despatch.

Our place of destination in the first instance is Columbus. It is distant about a hundred and twenty miles from Cincinnati, but there is a macadamised road (rare blessing!) the whole way, and the rate of travelling upon it is six miles an hour.

We start at eight o'clock in the morning, in a great mail-coach, whose huge cheeks are so very ruddy and plethoric, that it appears to be troubled with a tendency of blood to the head. Dropsical it certainly is, for it will hold a dozen passengers inside. But, wonderful to add, it is very clean and bright, being nearly new; and rattles through the streets of Cincinnati gaily.

Our way lies through a beautiful country, richly cultivated, and luxuriant in its promise of an abundant harvest. Sometimes we pass a field where the strong bristling stalks of Indian corn look like a crop of walking-sticks, and sometimes an enclosure where the green wheat is springing up among a labyrinth of stumps; the primitive worm-fence is universal, and an ugly thing it is; but the farms are neatly kept, and, save for these differences, one might be travelling just now in Kent.

We often stop to water at a roadside inn, which is always dull and silent. The coachman dismounts and fills his bucket, and holds it to the horses' heads. There is scarcely ever any one to help him; there are seldom any loungers standing round; and never any stable-company with jokes to crack. Sometimes, when we have changed our team, there is a difficulty in starting again, arising out of the prevalent mode of breaking a young horse: which is to catch him, harness him against his will, and put him in a stage-coach without further notice: but we get on somehow or other, after a great many kicks and a violent struggle; and jog on as before again.

Occasionally, when we stop to change, some two or three half-drunken loafers will come loitering out with their hands in their pockets, or will be seen kicking their heels in rocking-chairs, or lounging on the window-sill, or sitting on a rail within the colonnade: they have not often anything to say though, either to us or to each other, but sit there idly staring at the coach and horses. The landlord of the inn is usually among them, and seems, of all the party, to be the least connected with the business of the house. Indeed he is with reference to the tavern, what the driver is in relation to the coach and passengers: whatever happens in his sphere of action, he is quite indifferent, and perfectly easy in his mind.

The frequent change of coachmen works no change or variety in the coachman's character. He is always dirty, sullen, and taciturn. If he be capable of smartness of any kind, moral or physical, he has a faculty of concealing it which is truly marvellous. He never speaks to you as you sit beside him on the box, and if you speak to him, he answers (if at all) in monosyllables. He points out nothing on the road, and seldom looks at anything: being, to all appearance, thoroughly weary of it and of existence generally. As

to doing the honours of his coach, his business, as I have said, is
with the horses. The coach follows because it is attached to them
and goes on wheels: not because you are in it. Sometimes, towards the end of a long stage, he suddenly breaks out into a discordant fragment of an election song, but his face never sings along
with him: it is only his voice, and not often that.

He always chews and always spits, and never encumbers himself
with a pocket-handkerchief. The consequences to the box passenger, especially when the wind blows towards him, are not
agreeable.

Whenever the coach stops, and you can hear the voices of the
inside passengers; or whenever any bystander addresses them, or
any one among them; or they address each other; you will hear
one phrase repeated over and over and over again to the most extraordinary extent. It is an ordinary and unpromising phrase
enough, being neither more nor less than 'Yes, sir'; but it is
adapted to every variety of circumstance, and fills up every pause
in the conversation. Thus:—

The time is one o'clock at noon. The scene, a place where we
are to stay and dine, on this journey. The coach drives up to the
door of an inn. The day is warm, and there are several idlers
lingering about the tavern, and waiting for the public dinner.
Among them, is a stout gentleman in a brown hat, swinging himself to and fro in a rocking-chair on the pavement.

As the coach stops, a gentleman in a straw hat looks out of the
window:

STRAW HAT. (To the stout gentleman in the rocking-chair.)
I reckon that's Judge Jefferson, an't it?

BROWN HAT. (Still swinging; speaking very slowly; and without any emotion whatever.) Yes, sir.

STRAW HAT. Warm weather, Judge.

BROWN HAT. Yes, sir.

STRAW HAT. There was a snap of cold, last week.

BROWN HAT. Yes, sir.

STRAW HAT. Yes, sir.

A pause. They look at each other, very seriously.

STRAW HAT. I calculate you'll have got through that case of
the corporation, Judge, by this time, now?

BROWN HAT. Yes, sir.

STRAW HAT. How did the verdict go, sir?

BROWN HAT. For the defendant, sir.

STRAW HAT. (Interrogatively.) Yes, sir?

BROWN HAT. (Affirmatively.) Yes, sir.

BOTH. (Musingly, as each gazes down the street.) Yes, sir.

Another pause. They look at each other again, still more seriously than before.

BROWN HAT. This coach is rather behind its time to-day, I guess.

STRAW HAT. (Doubtingly.) Yes, sir.

BROWN HAT. (Looking at his watch.) Yes, sir; nigh upon two hours.

STRAW HAT. (Raising his eyebrows in very great surprise.) Yes, sir!

BROWN HAT. (Decisively, as he puts up his watch.) Yes, sir.

ALL THE OTHER INSIDE PASSENGERS. (Among themselves.) Yes, sir.

COACHMAN. (In a very surly tone.) No it an't.

STRAW HAT. (To the coachman.) Well, I don't know, sir. We were a pretty tall time coming that last fifteen mile. That's a fact.

The coachman making no reply, and plainly declining to enter into any controversy on a subject so far removed from his sympathies and feelings, another passenger says, 'Yes, sir'; and the gentleman in the straw hat in acknowledgment of his courtesy, says 'Yes, sir,' to him, in return. The straw hat then inquires of the brown hat, whether that coach in which he (the straw hat) then sits, is not a new one? To which the brown hat again makes answer, 'Yes, sir.'

STRAW HAT. I thought so. Pretty loud smell of varnish, sir?

BROWN HAT. Yes, sir.

ALL THE OTHER INSIDE PASSENGERS. Yes, sir.

BROWN HAT. (To the company in general.) Yes, sir.

The conversational powers of the company having been by this time pretty heavily taxed, the straw hat opens the door and gets out; and all the rest alight also. We dine soon afterwards with the boarders in the house, and have nothing to drink but tea and coffee. As they are both very bad and the water is worse, I ask for brandy; but it is a Temperance Hotel, and spirits are not to be had for love or money. This preposterous forcing of unpleasant drinks down the reluctant throats of travellers is not at all uncommon in America, but I never discovered that the scruples of such wincing landlords induced them to preserve any unusually nice balance between the quality of their fare, and their scale of charges: on the contrary, I rather suspected them of diminishing the one and exalting the other, by way of recompense for the loss of their profit on the sale of spirituous liquors. After all, perhaps, the plainest course for persons of such tender consciences, would be, a total abstinence from tavern-keeping.

Dinner over, we get into another vehicle which is ready at the door (for the coach has been changed in the interval), and resume our journey; which continues through the same kind of country until evening, when we come to the town where we are to stop for tea and supper; and having delivered the mail bags at the Post-office, ride through the usual wide street, lined with the usual stores and houses (the drapers always having hung up at their door, by way of sign, a piece of bright red cloth), to the hotel where this meal is prepared. There being many boarders here, we sit down, a large party, and a very melancholy one as usual. But there is a buxom hostess at the head of the table, and opposite, a simple Welsh schoolmaster with his wife and child; who came here, on a speculation of greater promise than performance, to teach the classics: and they are sufficient subjects of interest until the meal is over, and another coach is ready. In it we go on once more, lighted by a bright moon, until midnight; when we stop to change the coach again, and remain for half an hour or so in a miserable room, with a blurred lithograph of Washington over the smoky fireplace, and a mighty jug of cold water on the table: to which refreshment the moody passengers do so apply themselves that they would seem to be, one and all, keen patients of Dr. Sangrado. Among them is a very little boy, who chews tobacco like a very big one; and a droning gentleman, who talks arithmetically and statistically on all subjects, from poetry downwards; and who always speaks in the same key, with exactly the same emphasis, and with very grave deliberation. He came outside just now, and told me how that the uncle of a certain young lady who had been spirited away and married by a certain captain, lived in these parts; and how this uncle was so valiant and ferocious that he shouldn't wonder if he were to follow the said captain to England, 'and shoot him down in the street wherever he found him'; in the feasibility of which strong measure I, being for the moment rather prone to contradiction, from feeling half asleep and very tired, declined to acquiesce: assuring him that if the uncle did resort to it, or gratified any other little whim of the like nature, he would find himself one morning prematurely throttled at the Old Bailey: and that he would do well to make his will before he went, as he would certainly want it before he had been in Britain very long.

On we go, all night, and by and by the day begins to break, and presently the first cheerful rays of the warm sun come slanting on us brightly. It sheds its light upon a miserable waste of sodden grass, and dull trees, and squalid huts, whose aspect is forlorn and grievous in the last degree. A very desert in the wood, whose growth of green is dank and noxious like that upon the top of standing water: where poisonous fungus grows in the rare foot-print on the oozy ground, and sprouts like witches' coral, from the crevices in the cabin wall and floor; it is a hideous thing to lie upon the very threshhold of a city. But it was purchased years ago, and as the owner cannot be discovered, the State has been unable to reclaim it. So there it remains, in the midst of cultivation and improvement, like ground accursed, and made obscene and rank by some great crime.

We reached Columbus shortly before seven o'clock, and stayed there, to refresh, that day and night: having excellent apartments in a very large unfinished hotel called the Neill House, which were richly fitted with the polished wood of the black walnut, and opened on a handsome portico and stone verandah, like rooms in some Italian mansion. The town is clean and pretty, and of course is 'going to be' much larger. It is the seat of the State legislature of Ohio, and lays claim, in consequence, to some consideration and importance.

There being no stage-coach next day, upon the road we wished to take, I hired 'an extra' at a reasonable charge, to carry us to Tiffin; a small town from whence there is a railroad to Sandusky. This extra was an ordinary four-horse stage-coach, such as I have described, changing horses and drivers, as the stage-coach would, but was exclusively our own for the journey. To ensure our having horses at the proper stations, and being incommoded by no strangers, the proprietors sent an agent on the box, who was to accompany us the whole way through; and thus attended, and bearing with us, besides, a hamper full of savoury cold meats, and fruit, and wine; we started off again in high spirits, at half-past six o'clock next morning, very much delighted to be by ourselves, and disposed to enjoy even the roughest journey.

It was well for us, that we were in this humour, for the road we went over that day, was certainly enough to have shaken tempers that were not resolutely at Set Fair, down to some inches below Stormy. At one time we were all flung together in a heap at the bottom of the coach, and at another we were crushing our heads against the roof. Now, one side was down deep in the mire, and we were holding on to the other. Now, the coach was lying on the tails of the two wheelers; and now it was rearing up in the air, in a frantic state, with all four horses standing on the top of an insurmountable eminence, looking coolly back at it, as though they would say 'Unharness us. It can't be done.' The drivers on these roads, who certainly get over the ground in a manner which is quite miraculous, so twist and turn the team about in forcing a passage, corkscrew fashion, through the bogs and swamps, that it was quite a common circumstance on looking out of the window, to see the coachman with the ends of a pair of reins in his hands, apparently driving nothing, or playing at horses, and the leaders staring at one unexpectedly from the back of the coach, as if they had some idea of getting up behind. A great portion of the way was over what is called a corduroy road, which is made by throwing trunks of trees into a marsh, and leaving them to settle there. The very slightest of the jolts with which the ponderous carriage fell from log to log, was enough, it seemed, to have dislocated all the bones in the human body. It would be impossible to experience a similar set of sensations, in any other circumstances, unless perhaps in attempting to go up to the top of St. Paul's in an omnibus. Never, never once, that day, was the coach in any position, attitude, or kind of motion to which we are accustomed in coaches. Never did it make the smallest approach to one's experience of the proceedings of any sort of vehicle that goes on wheels.

Still, it was a fine day, and the temperature was delicious, and though we had left Summer behind us in the west, and were fast leaving Spring, we were moving towards Niagara and home. We alighted in a pleasant wood towards the middle of the day, dined on a fallen tree, and leaving our best fragments with a cottager, and our worst with the pigs (who swarm in this part of the country like grains of sand on the sea-shore, to the great comfort of our commissariat in Canada), we went forward again, gaily.

As night came on, the track grew narrower and narrower, until at last it so lost itself among the trees, that the driver seemed to find his way by instinct. We had the comfort of knowing, at least, that there was no danger of his falling asleep, for every now and then a wheel would strike against an unseen stump with such a jerk, that he was fain to hold on pretty tight and pretty quick, to keep himself upon the box. Nor was there any reason to dread the least danger from furious driving, inasmuch as over that broken ground the horses had enough to do to walk; as to shying, there was no room for that; and a herd of wild elephants could not have run away in such a wood, with such a coach at their heels. So we stumbled along quite satisfied.

These stumps of trees are a curious feature in American travelling. The varying illusions they present to the unaccustomed eye as it grows dark, are quite astonishing in their number and reality.

Now there is a Grecian urn erected in the centre of a lonely field; now there is a woman weeping at a tomb; now a very commonplace old gentleman in a white waistcoat, with a thumb thrust into each arm-hole of his coat; now a student poring on a book; now a crouching negro; now, a horse, a dog, a cannon, an armed man; a hunch-back throwing off his cloak and stepping forth into the night. They were often as entertaining to me as so many glasses in a magic lantern, and never took their shapes at my bidding, but seemed to force themselves upon me, whether I would or no; and strange to say, I sometimes recognised in them counterparts of figures once familiar to me in pictures attached to childish books, forgotten long ago.

It soon became too dark, however, even for this amusement, and the trees were so close together that their dry branches rattled against the coach on either side, and obliged us all to keep our heads within. It lightened too, for three whole hours; each flash being very bright, and blue, and long; and as the vivid streaks came darting in among the crowded branches, and the thunder rolled gloomily above the tree-tops, one could scarcely help thinking there were better neighbourhoods at such a time than thick woods afforded.

At length, between ten and eleven o'clock at night a few feeble lights appeared in the distance, and Upper Sandusky, an Indian village, where we were to stay till morning, lay before us.

They were gone to bed at the log Inn, which was the only house of entertainment in the place, but soon answered to our knocking, and got some tea for us in a sort of kitchen or common room, tapestried with old newspapers, pasted against the wall. The bed-chamber to which my wife and I were shown, was a large, low, ghostly room; with a quantity of withered branches on the hearth, and two doors without any fastening, opposite to each other, both opening on the black night and wild country, and so contrived, that one of them always blew the other open: a novelty in domestic architecture, which I do not remember to have seen before, and which I was somewhat disconcerted to have forced on my attention after getting into bed, as I had a considerable sum in gold for our travelling expenses, in my dressing-case. Some of the luggage, however, piled against the panels, soon settled this difficulty, and my sleep would not have been very much affected that night, I believe, though it had failed to do so.

My Boston friend climbed up to bed, somewhere in the roof, where another guest was already snoring hugely. But being bitten beyond his power of endurance, he turned out again, and fled for shelter to the coach, which was airing itself in front of the house. This was not a very politic step, as it turned out; for the pigs scenting him, and looking upon the coach as a kind of pie with some manner of meat inside, grunted round it so hideously, that he was afraid to come out again, and lay there shivering, till morning. Nor was it possible to warm him, when he did come out, by means of a glass of brandy: for in Indian villages, the legislature, with a very good and wise intention, forbids the sale of spirits by tavern-keepers. The precaution, however, is quite inefficacious, for the Indians never fail to procure liquor of a worse kind, at a dearer price, from travelling pedlars.

It is a settlement of the Wyandot Indians who inhabit this place. Among the company at breakfast was a mild old gentleman, who had been for many years employed by the United States Government in conducting negotiations with the Indians, and who had just concluded a treaty with these people by which they bound themselves, in consideration of a certain annual sum, to remove next year to some land provided for them, west of the Mississippi, and a little way beyond St. Louis. He gave me a moving account of their strong attachment to the familiar scenes of their infancy, and in particular to the burial-places of their kindred; and of their great reluctance to leave them. He had witnessed many such removals, and always with pain, though he knew that they departed for their own good. The question whether this tribe should go or stay, had been discussed among them a day or two before, in a hut erected for the purpose, the logs of which still lay upon the ground before the inn. When the speaking was done, the ayes and noes were ranged on opposite sides, and every male adult voted in his turn. The moment the result was known, the minority (a large one) cheerfully yielded to the rest, and withdrew all kind of opposition.

We met some of these poor Indians afterwards, riding on shaggy ponies. They were so like the meaner sort of gipsies, that if I could have seen any of them in England, I should have concluded, as a matter of course, that they belonged to that wandering and restless people.

Leaving this town directly after breakfast, we pushed forward again, over a rather worse road than yesterday, if possible, and arrived about noon at Tiffin, where we parted with the extra. At two o'clock we took the railroad; the travelling on which was very slow, its construction being indifferent, and the ground wet and marshy; and arrived at Sandusky in time to dine that evening. We put up at a comfortable little hotel on the brink of Lake Erie, lay there that night, and had no choice but to wait there next day, until a steamboat bound for Buffalo appeared. The town, which was sluggish and uninteresting enough, was something like the back of an English watering-place, out of season.

Our host, who was very attentive and anxious to make us comfortable, was a handsome middle-aged man, who had come to this town from New England, in which part of the country he was 'raised.' When I say that he constantly walked in and out of the room with his hat on; and stopped to converse in the same free-and-easy state; and lay down on our sofa, and pulled his newspaper out of his pocket, and read it at his ease; I merely mention these traits as characteristic of the country: not at all as being matter of complaint, or as having been disagreeable to me. I should undoubtedly be offended by such proceedings at home, because there they are not the custom, and where they are not, they would be impertinencies; but in America, the only desire of a good-natured fellow of this kind, is to treat his guests hospitably and well; and I had no more right, and I can truly say no more disposition, to measure his conduct by our English rule and standard, than I had to quarrel with him for not being of the exact stature which would qualify him for admission into the Queen's grenadier guards. As little inclination had I to find fault with a funny old lady who was an upper domestic in this establishment, and who, when she came to wait upon us at any meal, sat herself down comfortably in the most convenient chair, and producing a large pin to pick her teeth with, remained performing that ceremony, and steadfastly regarding us meanwhile with much gravity and composure (now and then pressing us to eat a little more), until it was time to clear away. It was enough for us, that whatever we wished done was done with great civility and readiness, and a desire to oblige, not only here, but everywhere else; and that all our wants were, in general, zealously anticipated.

We were taking an early dinner at this house, on the day after our arrival, which was Sunday, when a steamboat came in sight, and presently touched at the wharf. As she proved to be on her way to Buffalo, we hurried on board with all speed, and soon left Sandusky far behind us.

She was a large vessel of five hundred tons, and handsomely fitted up, though with high-pressure engines; which always conveyed that kind of feeling to me, which I should be likely to experience, I think, if I had lodgings on the first-floor of a powder-mill. She was laden with flour, some casks of which commodity were stored upon the deck. The captain coming up to have a little conversation, and to introduce a friend, seated himself astride of one of these barrels, like a Bacchus of private life; and pulling a great clasp-knife out of his pocket, began to 'whittle' it as he talked, by paring thin slices off the edges. And he whittled with such industry and hearty good will, that but for his being called away very soon, it must have disappeared bodily, and left nothing in its place but grist and shavings.

After calling at one or two flat places, with low dams stretching out into the lake, whereon were stumpy lighthouses, like windmills without sails, the whole looking like a Dutch vignette, we came at midnight to Cleveland, where we lay all night, and until nine o'clock next morning.

I entertained quite a curiosity in reference to this place, from having seen at Sandusky a specimen of its literature in the shape of a newspaper, which was very strong indeed upon the subject of Lord Ashburton's recent arrival at Washington, to adjust the points in dispute between the United States Government and Great Britain: informing its readers that as America had 'whipped' England in her infancy, and whipped her again in her youth, so it was clearly necessary that she must whip her once again in her maturity; and pledging its credit to all True Americans, that if Mr. Webster did his duty in the approaching negotiations, and sent the English Lord home again in double quick time, they should, within two years, sing 'Yankee Doodle in Hyde Park, and Hail Columbia in the scarlet courts of Westminster!' I found it a pretty town, and had the satisfaction of beholding the outside of the office of the journal from which I have just quoted. I did not enjoy the delight of seeing the wit who indited the paragraph in question, but I have no doubt he is a prodigious man in his way, and held in high repute by a select circle. There was a gentleman on board, to whom, as I unintentionally learned through the thin partition which divided our state-room from the cabin in which he and his wife conversed together, I was unwittingly the occasion of very great uneasiness. I don't know why or wherefore, but I appeared to run in his mind perpetually, and to dissatisfy him very much. First of all I heard him say: and the most ludicrous part of the business was, that he said it in my very ear, and could not have communicated more directly with me, if he had leaned upon my shoulder, and whispered me: 'Boz is on board still, my dear.' After a considerable pause, he added, complainingly, 'Boz keeps himself very close'; which was true enough, for I was not very well, and was lying down, with a book. I thought he had done with me after this, but I was deceived; for a long interval having elapsed, during which I imagine him to have been turning restlessly from side to side, and trying to go to sleep; he broke out again, with 'I suppose *that* Boz will be writing a book by and by, and putting all our names in it!' at which imaginary consequence of being on board a boat with Boz, he groaned, and became silent.

We called at the town of Erie, at eight o'clock that night, and lay there an hour. Between five and six next morning, we arrived at Buffalo, where we breakfasted; and being too near the Great Falls to wait patiently anywhere else, we set off by the train, the same morning at nine o'clock, to Niagara.

It was a miserable day; chilly and raw; a damp mist falling; and the trees in that northern region quite bare and wintry. Whenever the train halted, I listened for the roar; and was constantly straining my eyes in the direction where I knew the Falls must be, from seeing the river rolling on towards them; every moment expecting to behold the spray. Within a few minutes of our stopping, not before, I saw two great white clouds rising up slowly and majestically from the depths of the earth. That was all. At length we alighted: and then for the first time, I heard the mighty rush of water, and felt the ground tremble underneath my feet.

The bank is very steep, and was slippery with rain, and half-melted ice. I hardly know how I got down, but I was soon at the bottom, and climbing, with two English officers who were crossing and had joined me, over some broken rocks, deafened by the noise, half-blinded by the spray, and wet to the skin. We were at the foot of the American Fall. I could see an immense torrent of water tearing headlong down from some great height, but had no idea of shape, or situation, or anything but vague immensity.

When we were seated in the little ferry-boat, and were crossing the swollen river immediately before both cataracts, I began to feel what it was: but I was in a manner stunned, and unable to comprehend the vastness of the scene. It was not until I came on Table Rock, and looked—Great Heaven, on what a fall of bright-green water!—that it came upon me in its full might and majesty.

Then, when I felt how near to my Creator I was standing, the first effect, and the enduring one—instant and lasting—of the tremendous spectacle, was Peace. Peace of Mind, tranquillity, calm recollections of the Dead, great thoughts of Eternal Rest and Happiness: nothing of gloom or terror. Niagara was at once stamped upon my heart, an Image of Beauty; to remain there, changeless and indelible, until its pulses cease to beat, for ever.

Oh, how the strife and trouble of daily life receded from my view, and lessened in the distance, during the ten memorable days we passed on that Enchanted Ground! What voices spoke from out the thundering water; what faces, faded from the earth, looked out upon me from its gleaming depths; what Heavenly promise glistened in those angels' tears, the drops of many hues, that showered around, and twined themselves about the gorgeous arches which the changing rainbows made!

I never stirred in all that time from the Canadian side, whither I had gone at first. I never crossed the river again; for I knew there were people on the other shore, and in such a place it is natural to shun strange company. To wander to and fro all day, and see the cataracts from all points of view; to stand upon the edge of the great Horse Shoe Fall, marking the hurried water gathering strength as it approached the verge, yet seeming, too, to pause before it shot into the gulf below; to gaze from the river's level up at the torrent as it came streaming down; to climb the neighbouring heights and watch it through the trees, and see the wreathing water in the rapids hurrying on to take its fearful plunge; to linger in the shadow of the solemn rocks three miles below; watching the river as, stirred by no visible cause, it heaved and eddied and awoke the echoes, being troubled yet, far down beneath the surface, by its giant leap; to have Niagara before me, lighted by the sun and by the moon, red in the day's decline, and grey as evening slowly fell upon it; to look upon it every day, and wake up in the night and hear its ceaseless voice: this was enough.

I think in every quiet season now, still do those waters roll and leap, and roar and tumble, all day long; still are the rainbows spanning them, a hundred feet below. Still, when the sun is on them, do they shine and glow like molten gold. Still, when the day is gloomy, do they fall like snow, or seem to crumble away like the front of a great chalk cliff, or roll down the rock like dense white smoke. But always does the mighty stream appear to die as it comes down, and always from its unfathomable grave arises that tremendous ghost of spray and mist which is never laid: which has haunted this place with the same dread solemnity since Darkness brooded on the deep, and that first flood before the Deluge—Light —came rushing on Creation at the word of God.

CHAPTER XV

IN CANADA; TORONTO; KINGSTON; MONTREAL; QUEBEC; ST. JOHN'S. IN THE UNITED STATES AGAIN; LEBANON; THE SHAKER VILLAGE; WEST POINT

I WISH to abstain from instituting any comparison, or drawing any parallel whatever, between the social features of the United States and those of the British Possessions in Canada. For this reason, I shall confine myself to a very brief account of our journeyings in the latter territory.

But before I leave Niagara, I must advert to one disgusting circumstance which can hardly have escaped the observation of any decent traveller who has visited the Falls.

On Table Rock, there is a cottage belonging to a Guide, where little relics of the place are sold, and where visitors register their names in a book kept for the purpose. On the wall of the room in which a great many of these volumes are preserved, the following request is posted: 'Visitors will please not copy nor extract the remarks and poetical effusions from the registers and albums kept here.'

But for this intimation, I should have let them lie upon the tables on which they were strewn with careful negligence, like books in a drawing-room: being quite satisfied with the stupendous silliness of certain stanzas with an anti-climax at the end of each, which were framed and hung up on the wall. Curious, however, after reading this announcement, to see what kind of morsels were so carefully preserved, I turned a few leaves, and found them scrawled all over with the vilest and the filthiest ribaldry that ever human hogs delighted in.

It is humiliating enough to know that there are among men, brutes so obscene and worthless, that they can delight in laying their miserable profanations upon the very steps of Nature's greatest altar. But that these should be hoarded up for the delight of their fellow-swine, and kept in a public place where any eyes may see them, is a disgrace to the English language in which they are written (though I hope few of these entries have been made by Englishmen), and a reproach to the English side, on which they are preserved.

The quarters of our soldiers at Niagara, are finely and airily situated. Some of them are large detached houses on the plain above the Falls, which were originally designed for hotels; and in the evening time, when the women and children were leaning over the balconies watching the men as they played at ball and other games upon the grass before the door, they often presented a little picture of cheerfulness and animation which made it quite a pleasure to pass that way.

At any garrisoned point where the line of demarcation between one country and another is so very narrow as at Niagara, desertion from the ranks can scarcely fail to be of frequent occurrence: and it may be reasonably supposed that when the soldiers entertain the wildest and maddest hopes of the fortune and independence that await them on the other side, the impulse to play traitor, which such a place suggests to dishonest minds, is not weakened. But it very rarely happens that the men who do desert, are happy or contented afterwards; and many instances have been known in which they have confessed their grievous disappointment, and their earnest desire to return to their old service if they could but be assured of pardon, or lenient treatment. Many of their comrades, notwithstanding, do the like, from time to time; and instances of loss of life in the effort to cross the river with this object, are far from being uncommon. Several men were drowned in the attempt to swim across, not long ago; and one, who had the madness to trust himself upon a table as a raft, was swept down to the whirlpool, where his mangled body eddied round and round some days.

I am inclined to think that the noise of the Falls is very much exaggerated; and this will appear the more probable when the depth of the great basin in which the water is received, is taken into account. At no time during our stay there, was the wind at all high or boisterous, but we never heard them, three miles off, even at the very quiet time of sunset, though we often tried.

Queenston, at which place the steamboats start for Toronto (or I should rather say at which place they call, for their wharf is at Lewiston, on the opposite shore), is situated in a delicious valley, through which the Niagara river, in colour a very deep green, pursues its course. It is approached by a road that takes its winding way among the heights by which the town is sheltered; and seen from this point is extremely beautiful and picturesque. On the most conspicuous of these heights stood a monument erected by the Provincial Legislature in memory of General Brock, who was slain in a battle with the American forces, after having won the victory. Some vagabond, supposed to be a fellow of the name of Lett, who is now, or who lately was, in prison as a felon, blew up this monument two years ago, and it is now a melancholy ruin, with a long fragment of iron railing hanging dejectedly from its top, and waving to and fro like a wild ivy branch or broken vine stem. It is of much higher importance than it may seem, that this statue should be repaired at the public cost, as it ought to have been long ago. Firstly, because it is beneath the dignity of England to allow a memorial raised in honour of one of her defenders, to remain in this condition, on the very spot where he died. Secondly, because the sight of it in its present state, and the recollection of the unpunished outrage which brought it to this pass, is not very likely to soothe down border feelings among English subjects here, or compose their border quarrels and dislikes.

I was standing on the wharf at this place, watching the passengers embarking in a steamboat which preceded that whose coming we awaited, and participating in the anxiety with which a sergeant's wife was collecting her few goods together—keeping one distracted eye hard upon the porters, who were hurrying them on board, and the other on a hoopless washing-tub for which, as being the most utterly worthless of all her moveables, she seemed to entertain particular affection—when three or four soldiers with a recruit came up and went on board.

The recruit was a likely young fellow enough, strongly built and well made, but by no means sober; indeed he had all the air of a man who had been more or less drunk for some days. He carried a small bundle over his shoulder, slung at the end of a walking-stick, and had a short pipe in his mouth. He was as dusty and dirty as recruits usually are, and his shoes betokened that he had travelled on foot some distance, but he was in a very jocose state, and shook hands with this soldier, and clapped that one on the back, and talked and laughed continually, like a roaring idle dog as he was.

The soldiers rather laughed at this blade than with him: seeming to say, as they stood straightening their canes in their hands, and looking coolly at him over their glazed stocks, 'Go on, my boy, while you may! you 'll know better by and by'; when suddenly the novice, who had been backing towards the gangway in his noisy merriment, fell overboard before their eyes, and splashed heavily down into the river between the vessel and the dock.

I never saw such a good thing as the change that came over these soldiers in an instant. Almost before the man was down, their professional manner, their stiffness and constraint, were gone, and they were filled with the most violent energy. In less time than is required to tell it, they had him out again, feet first, with the tails of his coat flapping over his eyes, everything about him hanging the wrong way, and the water streaming off at every thread in his threadbare dress. But the moment they set him upright and found that he was none the worse, they were soldiers again, looking over their glazed stocks more composedly than ever.

The half-sobered recruit glanced round for a moment, as if his first impulse were to express some gratitude for his preservation, but seeing them with this air of total unconcern, and having his wet pipe presented to him with an oath by the soldier who had been by far the most anxious of the party, he stuck it in his mouth, thrust his hands into his moist pockets, and without even shaking the water off his clothes, walked on board whistling; not to say as if nothing had happened, but as if he had meant to do it, and it had been a perfect success.

Our steamboat came up directly this had left the wharf, and soon bore us to the mouth of the Niagara; where the stars and stripes of America flutter on one side and the Union Jack of England on the other: and so narrow is the space between them that the sentinels in either fort can often hear the watchword of the other country given. Thence we emerged on Lake Ontario, an inland sea; and by half-past six o'clock were at Toronto.

The country round this town being very flat, is bare of scenic interest; but the town itself is full of life and motion, bustle, business, and improvement. The streets are well paved, and lighted with gas; the houses are large and good; the shops excellent. Many of them have a display of goods in their windows, such as may be seen in thriving country towns in England; and there are some which would do no discredit to the metropolis itself. There is a good stone prison here; and there are, besides, a handsome church, a court-house, public offices, many commodious private residences, and a government observatory for noting and recording the magnetic variations. In the College of Upper Canada, which is one of the public establishments of the city, a sound education in every department of polite learning can be had, at a very moderate expense: the annual charge for the instruction of each pupil, not exceeding nine pounds sterling. It has pretty good endowments in the way of land, and is a valuable and useful institution.

The first stone of a new college had been laid but a few days before, by the Governor General. It will be a handsome, spacious edifice, approached by a long avenue, which is already planted and made available as a public walk. The town is well adapted for wholesome exercise at all seasons, for the footways in the thoroughfares which lie beyond the principal street, are planked like floors, and kept in very good and clean repair.

It is a matter of deep regret that political differences should have run high in this place, and led to most discreditable and disgraceful results. It is not long since guns were discharged from a window in this town at the successful candidates in an election, and the coachman of one of them was actually shot in the body, though not dangerously wounded. But one man was killed on the same occasion; and from the very window whence he received his death, the very flag which shielded his murderer (not only in the commission of his crime, but from its consequences), was displayed again on the occasion of the public ceremony performed by the Governor General, to which I have just adverted. Of all the colours in the rainbow, there is but one which could be so employed: I need not say that flag was orange.

The time of leaving Toronto for Kingston is noon. By eight o'clock next morning, the traveller is at the end of his journey, which is performed by steamboat upon Lake Ontario, calling at Port Hope and Coburg, the latter a cheerful thriving little town. Vast quantities of flour form the chief item in the freight of these vessels. We had no fewer than one thousand and eighty barrels on board between Coburg and Kingston.

The latter place, which is now the seat of government in Canada, is a very poor town, rendered still poorer in the appearance of its market-place by the ravages of a recent fire. Indeed, it may be said of Kingston, that one half of it appears to be burnt down, and the other half not to be built up. The Government House is neither elegant nor commodious, yet it is almost the only house of any importance in the neighbourhood.

There is an admirable jail here, well and wisely governed, and excellently regulated, in every respect. The men were employed as shoemakers, ropemakers, blacksmiths, tailors, carpenters, and stone-cutters; and in building a new prison, which was pretty far advanced towards completion. The female prisoners were occupied in needlework. Among them was a beautiful girl of twenty, who had been there nearly three years. She acted as bearer of secret despatches for the self-styled Patriots on Navy Island, during the Canadian Insurrection: sometimes dressing as a girl, and carrying them in her stays; sometimes attiring herself as a boy, and secreting them in the lining of her hat. In the latter character she always rode as a boy would, which was nothing to her, for she could govern any horse that any man could ride, and could drive four-in-hand with the best whip in those parts. Setting forth on one of her patriotic missions, she appropriated to herself the first horse she could lay her hands on; and this offence had brought her where I saw her. She had quite a lovely face, though, as the reader may suppose from this sketch of her history, there was a lurking devil in her bright eye, which looked out pretty sharply from between her prison bars.

There is a bomb-proof fort here of great strength, which occupies a bold position, and is capable, doubtless, of doing good service; though the town is much too close upon the frontier to be long held, I should imagine, for its present purpose in troubled times. There is also a small navy-yard, where a couple of Government steamboats were building, and getting on vigorously.

We left Kingston for Montreal on the tenth of May, at half-past nine in the morning, and proceeded in a steamboat down the St. Lawrence river. The beauty of this noble stream at almost any point, but especially in the commencement of this journey when it winds its way among the thousand Islands, can hardly be imagined. The number and constant successions of these islands, all green and richly wooded; their fluctuating sizes, some so large that for half an hour together one among them will appear as the opposite bank of the river, and some so small that they are mere dimples on its broad bosom; their infinite variety of shapes; and the numberless combinations of beautiful forms which the trees growing on them present: all form a picture fraught with uncommon interest and pleasure.

In the afternoon we shot down some rapids where the river boiled and bubbled strangely, and where the force and headlong violence of the current were tremendous. At seven o'clock we reached Dickenson's Landing, whence travellers proceed for two or three hours by stage-coach: the navigation of the river being rendered so dangerous and difficult in the interval, by rapids, that steamboats do not make the passage. The number and length of those *portages,* over which the roads are bad, and the travelling slow, render the way between the towns of Montreal and Kingston, somewhat tedious.

Our course lay over a wide, uninclosed tract of country at a little distance from the river side, whence the bright warning lights on the dangerous parts of the St. Lawrence shone vividly. The night was dark and raw, and the way dreary enough. It was nearly ten o'clock when we reached the wharf where the next steamboat lay; and went on board, and to bed.

She lay there all night, and started as soon as it was day. The morning was ushered in by a violent thunderstorm, and was very wet, but gradually improved and brightened up. Going on deck after breakfast, I was amazed to see floating down with the stream, a most gigantic raft, with some thirty or forty wooden houses upon it, and at least as many flag-masts, so that it looked like a nautical street. I saw many of these rafts afterwards, but never one so large. All the timber, or 'lumber,' as it is called in America, which is brought down the St. Lawrence, is floated down in this manner. When the raft reaches its place of destination, it is broken up; the materials are sold; and the boatmen return for more.

At eight we landed again, and travelled by a stage-coach for four hours through a pleasant and well-cultivated country, perfectly French in every respect: in the appearance of the cottages; the air, language, and dress of the peasantry; the sign-boards on the shops and taverns: and the Virgin's shrines, and crosses, by the wayside. Nearly every common labourer and boy, though he had no shoes to his feet, wore round his waist a sash of some bright colour: generally red: and the women, who were working in the fields and gardens, and doing all kinds of husbandry, wore, one and all, great flat straw hats with most capacious brims. There were Catholic Priests and Sisters of Charity in the village streets; and images of the Saviour at corners of cross-roads, and in other public places.

At noon we went on board another steamboat, and reached the village of Lachine, nine miles from Montreal, by three o'clock. There, we left the river, and went on by land.

Montreal is pleasantly situated on the margin of the St. Lawrence, and is backed by some bold heights, about which there are charming rides and drives. The streets are generally narrow and irregular, as in most French towns of any age; but in the more modern parts of the city, they are wide and airy. They display a great variety of very good shops; and both in the town and suburbs there are many excellent private dwellings. The granite quays are remarkable for their beauty, solidity, and extent.

There is a very large Catholic cathedral here, recently erected; with two tall spires, of which one is yet unfinished. In the open space in front of this edifice, stands a solitary, grim-looking, square brick tower, which has a quaint and remarkable appearance, and which the wiseacres of the place have consequently determined to pull down immediately. The Government House is very superior to that at Kingston, and the town is full of life and bustle. In one of the suburbs is a plank road—not foot-path—five or six miles long, and a famous road it is too. All the rides in the vicinity were made doubly interesting by the bursting out of spring, which is here so rapid, that it is but a day's leap from barren winter, to the blooming youth of summer.

The steamboats to Quebec, perform the journey in the night; that is to say, they leave Montreal at six in the evening, and arrive

at Quebec at six next morning. We made this excursion during our
stay in Montreal (which exceeded a fortnight), and were charmed
by its interest and beauty.

The impression made upon the visitor by this Gibraltar of America: its giddy heights; its citadel suspended, as it were, in the air;
its picturesque steep streets and frowning gateway; and the splendid views which burst upon the eye at every turn: is at once unique
and lasting.

It is a place not to be forgotten or mixed up in the mind with
other places, or altered for a moment in the crowd of scenes a
traveller can recall. Apart from the realities of this most picturesque city, there are associations clustering about it which
would make a desert rich in interest. The dangerous precipice
along whose rocky front, Wolfe and his brave companions climbed
to glory; the Plains of Abraham, where he received his mortal
wound; the fortress so chivalrously defended by Montcalm; and
his soldier's grave, dug for him while yet alive, by the bursting of
a shell; are not the least among them, or among the gallant incidents of history. That is a noble Monument too, and worthy of
two great nations, which perpetuates the memory of both brave
generals, and on which their names are jointly written.

The city is rich in public institutions and in Catholic churches
and charities, but it is mainly in the prospect from the site of the
Old Government House, and from the Citadel, that its surpassing
beauty lies. The exquisite expanse of country, rich in field and
forest, mountain-height and water, which lies stretched out before
the view, with miles of Canadian villages, glancing in long white
streaks, like veins along the landscape; the motley crowd of gables,
roofs, and chimney tops in the old hilly town immediately at hand;
the beautiful St. Lawrence sparkling and flashing in the sunlight;
and the tiny ships below the rock from which you gaze, whose distant rigging looks like spiders' webs against the light, while casks
and barrels on their decks dwindle into toys, and busy mariners
become so many puppets; all this, framed by a sunken window in
the fortress and looked at from the shadowed room within, forms
one of the brightest and most enchanting pictures that the eye can
rest upon.

In the spring of the year, vast numbers of emigrants who have
newly arrived from England or from Ireland, pass between Quebec
and Montreal on their way to the backwoods and new settlements
of Canada. If it be an entertaining lounge (as I very often found
it) to take a morning stroll upon the quay at Montreal, and see
them grouped in hundreds on the public wharfs about their chests

and boxes, it is matter of deep interest to be their fellow-passenger on one of these steamboats, and mingling with the concourse, see and hear them unobserved.

The vessel in which we returned from Quebec to Montreal was crowded with them, and at night they spread their beds between decks (those who had beds, at least), and slept so close and thick about our cabin door, that the passage to and fro was quite blocked up. They were nearly all English; from Gloucestershire the greater part; and had had a long winter-passage out; but it was wonderful to see how clean the children had been kept, how untiring in their love and self-denial all the poor parents were.

Cant as we may, and as we shall to the end of all things, it is very much harder for the poor to be virtuous than it is for the rich; and the good that is in them, shines the brighter for it. In many a noble mansion lives a man, the best of husbands and of fathers, whose private worth in both capacities is justly lauded to the skies. But bring him here, upon this crowded deck. Strip from his fair young wife her silken dress and jewels, unbind her braided hair, stamp early wrinkles on her brow, pinch her pale cheek with care and much privation, array her faded form in coarsely patched attire, let there be nothing but his love to set her forth or deck her out, and you shall put it to the proof indeed. So change his station in the world, that he shall see in those young things who climb about his knee: not records of his wealth and name: but little wrestlers with him for his daily bread; so many poachers on his scanty meal; so many units to divide his every sum of comfort, and farther to reduce its small amount. In lieu of the endearments of childhood in its sweetest aspect, heap upon him all its pains and wants, its sicknesses and ills, its fretfulness, caprice, and querulous endurance: let its prattle be, not of engaging infant fancies, but of cold, and thirst, and hunger: and if his fatherly affection outlive all this, and he be patient, watchful, tender; careful of his children's lives, and mindful always of their joys and sorrows; then send him back to Parliament, and Pulpit, and to Quarter Sessions, and when he hears fine talk of the depravity of those who live from hand to mouth, and labour hard to do it, let him speak up, as one who knows, and tell those holders forth that they, by parallel with such a class, should be High Angels in their daily lives, and lay but humble siege to Heaven at last.

Which of us shall say what he would be, if such realities, with small relief or change all through his days, were his! Looking round upon these people: far from home, houseless, indigent, wandering, weary with travel and hard living: and seeing how patiently they nursed and tended their young children: how they consulted ever their wants first, then half supplied their own; what gentle ministers of hope and faith the women were; how the men profited by their example; and how very, very seldom even a moment's petulance or harsh complaint broke out among them: I felt a stronger love and honour of my kind come glowing on my heart, and wished to God there had been many Atheists in the better part of human nature there, to read this simple lesson in the book of Life.

We left Montreal for New York again, on the thirtieth of May; crossing to La Prairie, on the opposite shore of the St. Lawrence, in a steamboat; we then took the railroad to St. John's, which is on the brink of Lake Champlain. Our last greeting in Canada was from the English officers in the pleasant barracks at that place (a class of gentlemen who had made every hour of our visit memorable by their hospitality and friendship); and with 'Rule Britannia' sounding in our ears, soon left it far behind.

But Canada has held, and always will retain, a foremost place in my remembrance. Few Englishmen are prepared to find it what it is. Advancing quietly; old differences settling down, and being fast forgotten; public feeling and private enterprise alike in a sound and wholesome state; nothing of flush or fever in its system, but health and vigour throbbing in its steady pulse: it is full of hope and promise. To me—who had been accustomed to think of it as something left behind in the strides of advancing society, as something neglected and forgotten, slumbering and wasting in its sleep —the demand for labour and the rates of wages; the busy quays of Montreal; the vessels taking in their cargoes, and discharging them; the amount of shipping in the different ports; the commerce, roads, and public works, all made *to last;* the respectability and character of the public journals; and the amount of rational comfort and happiness which honest industry may earn: were very great surprises. The steamboats on the lakes, in their conveniences, cleanliness, and safety; in the gentlemanly character and bearing of their captains; and in the politeness and perfect comfort of their social regulations; are unsurpassed even by the famous Scotch vessels, deservedly so much esteemed at home. The inns are usually bad; because the custom of boarding at hotels is not so general here as in the States, and the British officers, who form a large portion of the society of every town, live chiefly at the regimental messes: but in every other respect, the traveller in Canada will find as good provision for his comfort as in any place I know.

There is one American boat—the vessel which carried us on

Lake Champlain, from St. John's to Whitehall—which I praise
very highly, but no more than it deserves, when I say that it
is superior even to that in which we went from Queenston to
Toronto, or to that in which we travelled from the latter place to
Kingston, or I have no doubt I may add to any other in the world.
This steamboat, which is called the Burlington, is a perfectly exquisite achievement of neatness, elegance, and order. The decks
are drawing-rooms; the cabins are boudoirs, choicely furnished and
adorned with prints, pictures, and musical instruments; every nook
and corner in the vessel is a perfect curiosity of graceful comfort
and beautiful contrivance. Captain Sherman, her commander, to
whose ingenuity and excellent taste these results are solely attributable, has bravely and worthily distinguished himself on more
than one trying occasion: not least among them, in having the
moral courage to carry British troops, at a time (during the Canadian rebellion) when no other conveyance was open to them. He
and his vessel are held in universal respect, both by his own countrymen and ours; and no man ever enjoyed the popular esteem,
who, in his sphere of action, won and wore it better than this
gentleman

By means of this floating palace we were soon in the United
States again, and called that evening at Burlington; a pretty town,
where we lay an hour or so. We reached Whitehall, where we were
to disembark, at six next morning; and might have done so earlier,
but that these steamboats lie by for some hours in the night, in
consequence of the lake becoming very narrow at that part of the
journey, and difficult of navigation in the dark. Its width is so contracted at one point, indeed, that they are obliged to warp round
by means of a rope.

After breakfasting at Whitehall, we took the stage-coach for Al-
bany: a large and busy town, where we arrived between five and
six o'clock that afternoon; after a very hot day's journey, for we
were now in the height of summer again. At seven we started for
New York on board a great North River steamboat, which was so
crowded with passengers that the upper deck was like the box
lobby of a theatre between the pieces, and the lower one like Tot-
tenham Court Road on a Saturday night. But we slept soundly,
notwithstanding, and soon after five o'clock next morning reached
New York.

Tarrying here, only that day and night, to recruit after our late
fatigues, we started off once more upon our last journey in America. We had yet five days to spare before embarking for England,

and I had a great desire to see 'the Shaker Village,' which is peopled by a religious sect from whom it takes its name.

To this end, we went up the North River again, as far as the town of Hudson, and there hired an extra to carry us to Lebanon, thirty miles distant; and of course another and a different Lebanon from that village where I slept on the night of the Prairie trip.

The country through which the road meandered was rich and beautiful; the weather very fine; and for many miles the Kaatskill mountains, where Rip Van Winkle and the ghastly Dutchmen played at ninepins one memorable gusty afternoon, towered in the blue distance, like stately clouds. At one point, as we ascended a steep hill, athwart whose base a railroad, yet constructing, took its course, we came upon an Irish colony. With means at hand of building decent cabins, it was wonderful to see how clumsy, rough, and wretched, its hovels were. The best were poor protection from the weather; the worst let in the wind and rain through wide breaches in the roofs of sodden grass, and in the walls of mud; some had neither door nor window; some had nearly fallen down, and were imperfectly propped up by stakes and poles; all were ruinous and filthy. Hideously ugly old women and very buxom young ones, pigs, dogs, men, children, babies, pots, kettles, dunghills, vile refuse, rank straw and standing water, all wallowing together in an inseparable heap, composed the furniture of every dark and dirty hut.

Between nine and ten o'clock at night, we arrived at Lebanon: which is renowned for its warm baths, and for a great hotel, well adapted, I have no doubt, to the gregarious taste of those seekers after health or pleasure who repair here, but inexpressibly comfortless to me. We were shown into an immense apartment, lighted by two dim candles, called the drawing-room: from which there was a descent by a flight of steps, to another vast desert, called the dining-room: our bed-chambers were among certain long rows of little white-washed cells, which opened from either side of a dreary passage; and were so like rooms in a prison that I half expected to be locked up when I went to bed, and listened involuntarily for the turning of the key on the outside. There need be baths somewhere in the neighbourhood, for the other washing arrangements were on as limited a scale as I ever saw, even in America: indeed, these bedrooms were so very bare of even such common luxuries as chairs, that I should say they were not provided with enough of anything, but that I bethink myself of our having been most bountifully bitten all night.

The house is very pleasantly situated, however, and we had a good breakfast. That done, we went to visit our place of destination, which was some two miles off, and the way to which was soon indicated by a finger-post, whereon was painted, 'To the Shaker Village.'

As we rode along, we passed a party of Shakers, who were at work upon the road; who wore the broadest of all broad-brimmed hats; and were in all visible respects such very wooden men, that I felt about as much sympathy for them, and as much interest in them, as if they had been so many figure-heads of ships. Presently we came to the beginning of the village, and alighting at the door of a house where the Shaker manufactures are sold, and which is the head-quarters of the elders, requested permission to see the Shaker worship.

Pending the conveyance of this request to some person in authority, we walked into a grim room, where several grim hats were hanging on grim pegs, and the time was grimly told by a grim clock, which uttered every tick with a kind of struggle, as if it broke the grim silence reluctantly, and under protest. Ranged against the wall were six or eight stiff high-backed chairs, and they partook so strongly of the general grimness, that one would much rather have sat on the floor than incurred the smallest obligation to any of them.

Presently, there stalked into this apartment, a grim old Shaker, with eyes as hard, and dull, and cold, as the great round metal buttons on his waistcoat; a sort of calm goblin. Being informed of our desire, he produced a newspaper wherein the body of elders, whereof he was a member, had advertised but a few days before, that in consequence of certain unseemly interruptions which their worship had received from strangers, their chapel was closed to the public for the space of one year.

As nothing was to be urged in opposition to this reasonable arrangement, we requested leave to make some trifling purchases of Shaker goods; which was grimly conceded. We accordingly repaired to a store on the same house and on the opposite side of the passage, where the stock was presided over by something alive in a russet case, which the elder said was a woman; and which I suppose *was* a woman, though I should not have suspected it.

On the opposite side of the road was their place of worship: a cool, clean edifice of wood, with large windows and green blinds: like a spacious summer-house. As there was no getting into this place, and nothing was to be done but walk up and down, and look at it and the other buildings in the village (which were chiefly of wood, painted a dark red like English barns, and composed of many stories like English factories), I have nothing to communicate to the reader, beyond the scanty results I gleamed while our purchases were making.

The people are called Shakers from their peculiar form of adoration, which consists of a dance, performed by the men and women of all ages, who arrange themselves for that purpose in opposite parties, the men first divesting themselves of their hats and coats, which they gravely hang against the wall before they begin: and tying a ribbon round their shirt-sleeves, as though they were going to be bled. They accompany themselves with a droning, humming noise, and dance until they are quite exhausted, alternately advancing and retiring in a preposterous sort of trot. The effect is said to be unspeakably absurd: and if I may judge from a print of this ceremony which I have in my possession; and which I am informed by those who have visited the chapel, is perfectly accurate; it must be infinitely grotesque.

They are governed by a woman, and her rule is understood to be absolute, though she has the assistance of a council of elders. She lives, it is said, in strict seclusion, in certain rooms above the chapel, and is never shown to profane eyes. If she at all resemble the lady who presided over the store, it is a great charity to keep her as close as possible, and I cannot too strongly express my perfect concurrence in this benevolent proceeding.

All the possessions and revenues of the settlement are thrown into a common stock, which is managed by the elders. As they have made converts among people who were well to do in the world, and are frugal and thrifty, it is understood that this fund prospers: the more especially as they have made large purchases of land. Nor is this at Lebanon the only Shaker settlement: there are, I think, at least three others.

They are good farmers, and all their produce is eagerly purchased and highly esteemed. 'Shaker seeds,' 'Shaker herbs,' and 'Shaker distilled waters,' are commonly announced for sale in the shops of towns and cities. They are good breeders of cattle, and are kind and merciful to the brute creation. Consequently, Shaker beasts seldom fail to find a ready market.

They eat and drink together, after the Spartan model, at a great public table. There is no union of the sexes, and every Shaker, male and female, is devoted to a life of celibacy. Rumour has been busy upon this theme, but here again I must refer to the lady of the store, and say, that if many of the sister Shakers resemble her, I treat all such slander as bearing on its face the strongest marks of wild improbability. But that they take as proselytes, persons so young that they cannot know their own minds, and cannot possess much strength of resolution in this or any other respect, I can assert from my own observation of the extreme juvenility of certain youthful Shakers whom I saw at work among the party on the road.

They are said to be good drivers of bargains, but to be honest and just in their transactions, and even in horse-dealing to resist those thievish tendencies which would seem, for some undiscovered reason, to be almost inseparable from that branch of traffic. In all matters they hold their own course quietly, live in their gloomy silent commonwealth, and show little desire to interfere with other people.

This is well enough, but nevertheless I cannot, I confess, incline towards the Shakers; view them with much favour, or extend towards them any very lenient construction. I so abhor, and from my soul detest that bad spirit, no matter by what class or sect it may be entertained, which would strip life of its healthful graces, rob youth of its innocent pleasures, pluck from maturity and age their pleasant ornaments, and make existence but a narrow path towards the grave: that odious spirit which, if it could have had full scope and sway upon the earth, must have blasted and made barren the imaginations of the greatest men, and left them, in their power of raising up enduring images before their fellow-creatures yet unborn, no better than the beasts: that, in these very broad-brimmed hats and very sombre coats—in stiff-necked solemn-visaged piety, in short, no matter what its garb, whether it have cropped hair as in a Shaker village, or long nails as in a Hindoo temple—I recognise the worst among the enemies of Heaven and Earth, who turn the water at the marriage feasts of this poor world, not into wine but gall. And if there must be people vowed to crush the harmless fancies and the love of innocent delights and gaieties, which are a part of human nature: as much a part of it as any other love or hope that is our common portion: let them, for me, stand openly revealed among the ribald and licentious; the very idiots know that *they* are not on the Immortal road, and will despise them, and avoid them readily.

Leaving the Shaker village with a hearty dislike of the old Shakers, and a hearty pity for the young ones: tempered by the strong probability of their running away as they grow older and wiser, which they not uncommonly do: we returned to Lebanon, and so to Hudson, by the way we had come upon the previous day. There, we took the steamboat down the North River towards New York, but stopped, some four hours' journey short of it, at West

Point, where we remained that night, and all next day, and next night too.

In this beautiful place: the fairest among the fair and lovely Highlands of the North River: shut in by deep green heights and ruined forts, and looking down upon the distant town of Newburgh, along a glittering path of sunlit water, with here and there a skiff, whose white sail often bends on some new tack as sudden flaws of wind come down upon her from the gullies in the hills: hemmed in, besides, all round with memories of Washington, and events of the revolutionary war: is the Military School of America.

It could not stand on more appropriate ground, and any ground more beautiful can hardly be. The course of education is severe, but well devised, and manly. Through June, July, and August, the young men encamp upon the spacious plain whereon the college stands; and all the year their military exercises are performed there, daily. The term of study at this institution, which the State requires from all cadets, is four years; but, whether it be from the rigid nature of the discipline, or the national impatience of restraint, or both causes combined, not more than half the number who begin their studies here, ever remain to finish them.

The number of cadets being equal to that of the members of Congress, one is sent here from every Congressional district: its member influencing the selection. Commissions in the service are distributed on the same principle. The dwellings of the various Professors are beautifully situated; and there is a most excellent hotel for strangers, though it has the two drawbacks of being a total abstinence house (wines and spirits being forbidden to the students), and of serving the public meals at rather uncomfortable hours: to wit, breakfast at seven, dinner at one, and supper at sunset.

The beauty and freshness of this calm retreat, in the very dawn and greenness of summer—it was then the beginning of June—were exquisite indeed. Leaving it upon the sixth, and returning to New York, to embark for England on the succeeding day, I was glad to think that among the last memorable beauties which had glided past us, and softened in the bright perspective, were those whose pictures, traced by no common hand, are fresh in most men's minds; not easily to grow old, or fade beneath the dust of Time: the Kaatskill Mountains, Sleepy Hollow, and the Tappaan Zee.

CHAPTER XVI

THE PASSAGE HOME

I NEVER had so much interest before, and very likely I shall never have so much interest again, in the state of the wind, as on the long-looked-for morning of Tuesday the Seventh of June. Some nautical authority had told me a day or two previous, 'anything with west in it, will do'; so when I darted out of bed at daylight, and throwing up the window, was saluted by a lively breeze from the north-west which had sprung up in the night, it came upon me so freshly, rustling with so many happy associations, that I conceived upon the spot a special regard for all airs blowing from that quarter of the compass, which I shall cherish, I dare say, until my own wind has breathed its last frail puff, and withdrawn itself for ever from the mortal calendar.

The pilot had not been slow to take advantage of this favourable weather, and the ship which yesterday had been in such a crowded dock that she might have retired from trade for good and all, for any chance she seemed to have of going to sea, was now full sixteen miles away. A gallant sight she was, when we, fast gaining on her in a steamboat, saw her in the distance riding at anchor: her tall masts pointing up in graceful lines against the sky, and every rope and spar expressed in delicate and thread-like outline: gallant, too, when, we being all aboard, the anchor came up to the steady chorus 'Cheerily men, oh cheerily!' and she followed proudly in the towing steamboat's wake: but bravest and most gallant of all, when the tow-rope being cast adrift, the canvas fluttered from her masts, and spreading her white wings she soared away upon her free and solitary course.

In the after cabin we were only fifteen passengers in all, and the greater part were from Canada, where some of us had known each other. The night was rough and squally, so were the next two days, but they flew by quickly, and we were soon as cheerful and snug a party, with an honest, manly-hearted captain at our head, as ever came to the resolution of being mutually agreeable, on land or water.

We breakfasted at eight, lunched at twelve, dined at three, and took our tea at half-past seven. We had abundance of amusements, and dinner was not the least among them: firstly for its own sake; secondly, because of its extraordinary length: its duration, inclusive of all the long pauses between the courses, being seldom less than two hours and a half; which was a subject of never-failing entertainment. By way of beguiling the tediousness of these banquets, a select association was formed at the lower end of the table, below the mast, to whose distinguished president modesty forbids me to make any further allusion, which, being a very hilarious and jovial institution, was (prejudice apart) in high favour with the rest of the community, and particularly with a black steward, who lived for three weeks in a broad grin at the marvellous humour of these incorporated worthies.

Then, we had chess for those who played it, whist, cribbage, books, backgammon, and shovelboard. In all weathers, fair or foul, calm or windy, we were every one on deck, walking up and down in pairs, lying in the boats, leaning over the side, or chatting in a lazy group together. We had no lack of music, for one played the accordian, another the violin, and another (who usually began at six o'clock A.M.) the key-bugle: the combined effect of which instruments, whey they all played different tunes in different parts of the ship, at the same time, and within hearing of each other, as they sometimes did (everybody being intensely satisfied with his own performance), was sublimely hideous.

When all these means of entertainment failed, a sail would heave in sight: looming, perhaps, the very spirit of a ship, in the misty distance, or passing us so close that through our glasses we could see the people on her decks, and easily make out her name, and whither she was bound. For hours together we could watch the dolphins and porpoises as they rolled and leaped and dived around the vessel; or those small creatures ever on the wing, the Mother Carey's chickens, which had borne us company from New York bay, and for a whole fortnight fluttered about the vessel's stern. For some days we had a dead calm, or very light winds, during which the crew amused themselves with fishing, and hooked an unlucky dolphin, who expired, in all his rainbow colours, on the deck: an event of such importance in our barren calendar, that afterwards we dated from the dolphin, and made the day on which he died, an era.

Besides all this, when we were five or six days out, there began to be much talk of icebergs, of which wandering islands an unusual number had been seen by the vessels that had come into New York a day or two before we left that port, and of whose dangerous neighbourhood we were warned by the sudden coldness of the weather, and the sinking of the mercury in the barometer. While these tokens lasted, a double look-out was kept, and many dismal tales were whispered after dark, of ships that had struck upon the ice and gone down in the night; but the wind obliging us to hold a southward course, we saw none of them, and the weather soon grew bright and warm again.

The observation every day at noon, and the subsequent working of the vessel's course, was, as may be supposed, a feature in our lives of paramount importance; nor were there wanting (as there never are) sagacious doubters of the captain's calculations, who, so soon as his back was turned, would, in the absence of compasses, measure the chart with bits of string, and ends of pocket-handker-chiefs, and points of snuffers, and clearly prove him to be wrong by an odd thousand miles or so. It was very edifying to see these unbelievers shake their heads and frown, and hear them hold forth strongly upon navigation: not that they knew anything about it, but that they always mistrusted the captain in calm weather, or when the wind was adverse. Indeed, the mercury itself is not so variable as this class of passengers, whom you will see, when the ship is going nobly through the water, quite pale with admiration, swearing that the captain beats all captains ever known, and even hinting at subscriptions for a piece of plate; and who, next morn-ing, when the breeze has lulled, and all the sails hang useless in the idle air, shake their despondent heads again, and say, with screwed-up lips, they hope that captain is a sailor—but they shrewdly doubt him.

It even became an occupation in the calm, to wonder when the wind *would* spring up in the favourable quarter, where, it was clearly shown by all the rules and precedents, it ought to have sprung up long ago. The first mate, who whistled for it zealously, was much respected for his perseverance, and was regarded even by the unbelievers as a first-rate sailor. Many gloomy looks would be cast upward through the cabin skylights at the flapping sails while dinner was in progress; and some, growing bold in ruefulness, predicted that we should land about the middle of July. There are always on board ship, a Sanguine One, and a Despondent One. The latter character carried it hollow at this period of the voyage, and triumphed over the Sanguine One at every meal, by inquiring where he supposed the Great Western (which left New York a week after us) was *now*: and where he supposed the 'Cunard' steampacket was *now*: and what he thought of sailing-vessels, as compared with steamships *now*: and so beset his life with pestilent attacks of that kind, that he too was obliged to affect despondency, for very peace and quietude.

These were additions to the list of entertaining incidents, but there was still another source of interest. We carried in the steerage nearly a hundred passengers: a little world of poverty: and as we came to know individuals among them by sight, from looking down upon the deck where they took the air in the daytime, and cooked their food, and very often ate it too, we became curious to know their histories, and with what expectations they had gone out to America, and on what errands they were going home, and what their circumstances were. The information we got on these heads from the carpenter, who had charge of these people, was often of the strangest kind. Some of them had been in America but three days, some but three months, and some had gone out in the last voyage of that very ship in which they were now returning home. Others had sold their clothes to raise the passage-money, and had hardly rags to cover them; others had no food, and lived upon the charity of the rest: and one man, it was discovered nearly at the end of the voyage, not before—for he kept his secret close, and did not court compassion—had had no sustenance whatever but the bones and scraps of fat he took from the plates used in the after-cabin dinner, when they were put out to be washed.

The whole system of shipping and conveying these unfortunate persons, is one that stands in need of thorough revision. If any class deserve to be protected and assisted by the Government, it is that class who are banished from their native land in search of the bare means of subsistence. All that could be done for these poor people by the great compassion and humanity of the captain and officers was done, but they require much more. The law is bound, at least upon the English side, to see that too many of them are not put on board one ship: and that their accommodations are decent: not demoralising and profligate. It is bound, too, in common humanity, to declare that no man shall be taken on board without his stock of provisions being previously inspected by some proper officer, and pronounced moderately sufficient for his support upon the voyage. It is bound to provide, or to require that there be provided, a medical attendant; whereas in these ships there are none, though sickness of adults, and deaths of children, on the passage, are matters of the very commonest occurrence. Above all it is the duty of any Government, be it monarchy or republic, to interpose and put an end to that system by which a firm of traders in emigrants purchase of the owners the whole 'tween-decks of a ship, and send on board as many wretched people as they can lay hold of, on any terms they can get, without the smallest reference to the conveniences of the steerage, the number of berths, the slightest separation of the sexes, or anything but their own immediate profit. Nor is even this the worst of the vicious system: for, certain crimping agents of these houses, who have a percentage on all the passengers they inveigle, are constantly travelling about those districts where poverty and discontent are rife, and tempting the credulous into more misery, by holding out monstrous inducements to emigration which can never be realised.

The history of every family we had on board was pretty much the same. After hoarding up, and borrowing, and begging, and selling everything to pay the passage, they had gone out to New York, expecting to find its streets paved with gold; and had found them paved with very hard and real stones. Enterprise was dull; labourers were not wanted; jobs of work were to be got, but the payment was not. They were coming back, even poorer than they went. One of them was carrying an open letter from a young English artisan, who had been in New York a fortnight, to a friend near Manchester, whom he strongly urged to follow him. One of the officers brought it to me as a curiosity. 'This is the country, Jem,' said the writer. 'I like America. There is no despotism here; that's the great thing. Employment of all sorts is going a-begging, and wages are capital. You have only to choose a trade, Jem, and be it. I haven't made choice of one yet, but I shall soon. *At present I haven't quite made up my mind whether to be a carpenter— or a tailor.*'

There was yet another kind of passenger, and but one more, who, in the calm and the light winds, was a constant theme of conversation and observation among us. This was an English sailor, a smart, thorough-built, English man-of-war's-man from his hat to his shoes, who was serving in the American Navy, and having got leave of absence was on his way home to see his friends. When he presented himself to take and pay for his passage, it had been suggested to him that being an able seaman he might as well work it and save the money, but this piece of advice he very indignantly rejected: saying, 'He'd be damned but for once he'd go aboard ship, as a gentleman.' Accordingly, they took his money, but he no sooner came aboard, than he stowed his kit in the forecastle, arranged to mess with the crew, and the very first time the hands were turned up, went aloft like a cat, before anybody. And all through the passage there he was, first at the braces, outer-most on the yards, perpetually lending a hand everywhere, but always with a sober dignity in his manner, and a sober grin on his face, which plainly said, 'I do it as a gentleman. For my own pleasure, mind you!'

At length and at last, the promised wind came up in right good earnest, and away we went before it, with every stitch of canvas set, slashing through the water nobly. There was a grandeur in the motion of the splendid ship, as overshadowed by her mass of sails, she rode at a furious pace upon the waves, which filled one with an indescribable sense of pride and exultation. As she plunged into a foaming valley, how I loved to see the green waves, bordered deep with white, come rushing on astern, to buoy her upward at their pleasure, and curl about her as she stooped again, but always own her for their haughty mistress still! On, on we flew, with changing lights upon the water, being now in the blessed region of fleecy skies; a bright sun lighting us by day, and a bright moon by night; the vane pointing directly homeward, alike the truthful index to the favouring wind and to our cheerful hearts; until at sunrise, one fair Monday morning—the twenty-seventh of June, I shall not easily forget the day—there lay before us, old Cape Clear, God bless it, showing, in the midst of early morning, like a cloud: the brightest and most welcome cloud, to us, that ever hid the face of Heaven's fallen sister—Home.

Dim speck as it was in the wide prospect, it made the sunrise a more cheerful sight, and gave to it that sort of human interest which it seems to want at sea. There, as elsewhere, the return of day is inseparable from some sense of renewed hope and gladness; but the light shining on the dreary waste of water, and showing it in all its vast extent of loneliness, presents a solemn spectacle, which even night, veiling it in darkness and uncertainty, does not surpass. The rising of the moon is more in keeping with the solitary ocean; and has an air of melancholy grandeur, which in its soft and gentle influence, seems to comfort while it saddens. I recollect when I was a very young child having a fancy that the reflection of the moon in water was a path to Heaven, trodden by the spirits of good people on their way to God; and this old feeling often came over me again, when I watched it on a tranquil night at sea.

The wind was very light on this same Monday morning, but it was still in the right quarter, and so, by slow degrees, we left Cape Clear behind, and sailed along within sight of the coast of Ireland. And how merry we all were, and how loyal to the George Washington, and how full of mutual congratulations, and how venturesome in predicting the exact hour at which we should arrive at Liverpool, may be easily imagined and readily understood. Also, how heartily we drank the captain's health that day at dinner; and how restless we became about packing up: and how two or three of the most sanguine spirits rejected the idea of going to bed at all that night as something it was not worth while to do, so near the shore, but went nevertheless, and slept soundly; and how to be so near our journey's end, was like a pleasant dream, from which one feared to wake.

The friendly breeze freshened again, next day, and on we went once more before it gallantly: descrying now and then an English ship going homeward under shortened sail, while we with every inch of canvas crowded on, dashed gaily past, and left her far behind. Towards evening, the weather turned hazy, with a drizzling rain; and soon became so thick, that we sailed, as it were, in a cloud. Still we swept onward like a phantom ship, and many an eager eye glanced up where the Look-out on the mast kept watch for Holyhead.

At length the long-expected cry was heard, and at the same moment there shone out from the haze and mist ahead, a gleaming light, which presently was gone, and soon returned, and soon was gone again. Whenever it came back, the eyes of all on board, brightened and sparkled like itself: and there we all stood, watching this revolving light upon the rock at Holyhead, and praising it for its brightness and its friendly warning, and lauding it, in short, above all other signal lights that ever were displayed, until it once more glimmered faintly in the distance, far behind us.

Then, it was time to fire a gun, for a pilot; and almost before its smoke had cleared away, a little boat with a light at her masthead came bearing down upon us, through the darkness, swiftly. And presently, our sails being backed, she ran alongside; and the hoarse pilot, wrapped and muffled in pea-coats and shawls to the very bridge of his weather-ploughed-up nose, stood bodily among us on the deck. And I think if that pilot had wanted to borrow fifty pounds for an indefinite period on no security, we should have engaged to lend it to him, among us, before his boat had dropped astern, or (which is the same thing) before every scrap of news in the paper he brought with him had become the common property of all on board.

We turned in pretty late that night, and turned out pretty early next morning. By six o'clock we clustered on the deck, prepared to go ashore; and looked upon the spires, and roofs, and smoke, of Liverpool. By eight we all sat down in one of its Hotels, to eat and drink together for the last time. And by nine we had shaken hands all around, and broken up our social company for ever.

The country, by the railroad, seemed, as we rattled through it, like a luxuriant garden. The beauty of the fields (so small they looked!), the hedge-rows and the trees; the pretty cottages, the beds of flowers, the old churchyards, the antique houses, and every well-known object; the exquisite delights of that one journey, crowding in the short compass of a summer's day, the joy of many years, with the winding up with Home and all that makes it dear; no tongue can tell, or pen of mine describe.

CHAPTER XVII

SLAVERY

The upholders of slavery in America—of the atrocities of which system, I shall not write one word for which I have not had ample proof and warrant—may be divided into three great classes.

The first, are those more moderate and rational owners of human cattle, who have come into the possession of them as so many coins in their trading capital, but who admit the frightful nature of the Institution in the abstract, and perceive the dangers to society with which it is fraught: dangers which however distant they may be, or howsoever tardy in their coming on, are as certain to fall upon its guilty head, as is the Day of Judgment.

The second consists of all those owners, breeders, users, buyers and sellers of slaves, who will, until the bloody chapter has a bloody end, own, breed, use, buy, and sell them at all hazards; who doggedly deny the horrors of the system in the teeth of such a mass of evidence as never was brought to bear on any other subject, and to which the experience of every day contributes its immense amount; who would at this or any other moment, gladly involve America in a war, civil or foreign, provided that it had for its sole end and object the assertion of their right to perpetuate slavery, and to whip and work and torture slaves, unquestioned by any human authority, and unassailed by any human power; who, when they speak of Freedom, mean the Freedom to oppress their kind, and to be savage, merciless, and cruel; and of whom every man on his own ground, in republican America, is a more exacting, and a sterner, and a less responsible despot than the Caliph Haroun Alraschid in his angry robe of scarlet.

The third, and not the least numerous or influential, is composed of all that delicate gentility which cannot bear a superior, and cannot brook an equal; of that class whose Republicanism means, 'I will not tolerate a man above me: and of those below, none must approach too near'; whose pride, in a land where voluntary servitude is shunned as a disgrace, must be ministered to by slaves; and whose inalienable rights can only have their growth in negro wrongs.

It has been sometimes urged that, in the unavailing efforts which have been made to advance the cause of Human Freedom in the republic of America (strange cause for history to treat of!), sufficient regard has not been had to the existence of the first class of persons; and it has been contended that they are hardly used, in being confounded with the second. This is, no doubt, the case; noble instances of pecuniary and personal sacrifice have already had their growth among them; and it is much to be regretted that the gulf between them and the advocates of emancipation should have been widened and deepened by any means: the rather, as there are, beyond dispute, among these slave-owners, many kind masters who are tender in the exercise of their unnatural power. Still, it is to be feared that this injustice is inseparable from the state of things with which humanity and truth are called upon to deal. Slavery is not a whit the more endurable because some hearts are to be found which can partially resist its hardening influences; nor can the indignant tide of honest wrath stand still, because in its onward course it overwhelms a few who are comparatively innocent, among a host of guilty.

The ground most commonly taken by these better men among the advocates of slavery, is this: 'It is a bad system; and for myself I would willingly get rid of it, if I could; most willingly. But it is not so bad, as you in England take it to be. You are deceived by the representations of the emancipationists. The greater part of my slaves are much attached to me. You will say that I do not allow them to be severely treated; but I will put it to you whether you believe that it can be a general practice to treat them inhumanly, when it would impair their value, and would be obviously against the interests of their masters.'

Is it the interest of any man to steal, to game, to waste his health and mental faculties by drunkenness, to lie, forswear himself, indulge hatred, seek desperate revenge, or do murder? No. All these are roads to ruin. And why, then, do men tread them? Because such inclinations are among the vicious qualities of mankind. Blot out, ye friends of slavery, from the catalogue of human passions, brutal lust, cruelty, and the abuse of irresponsible power (of all earthly temptations the most difficult to be resisted), and when ye have done so, and not before, we will inquire whether it be the interest of a master to lash and maim the slaves, over whose lives and limbs he has an absolute control!

But again: this class, together with that last one I have named, the miserable aristocracy spawned of a false republic, lift up their voices and exclaim 'Public opinion is all-sufficient to prevent such cruelty as you denounce.' Public opinion! Why, public opinion in the slave States *is* slavery, is it not? Public opinion, in the slave States, has delivered the slaves over, to the gentle mercies of their masters. Public opinion has made the laws, and denied the slaves legislative protection. Public opinion has knotted the lash, heated the branding-iron, loaded the rifle, and shielded the murderer. Public opinion threatens the abolitionist with death, if he venture to the South; and drags him with a rope about his middle, in broad unblushing noon, through the first city in the East. Public opinion has, within a few years, burned a slave alive at a slow fire in the city of St. Louis; and public opinion has to this day maintained upon the bench that estimable Judge who charged the Jury, impanelled there to try his murderers, that their most horrid deed was an act of public opinion, and being so, must not be punished by the laws the public sentiment had made. Public opinion hailed this doctrine with a howl of wild applause, and set the prisoners free, to walk the city, men of mark, and influence, and station, as they had been before.

Public opinion! what class of men have an immense preponderance over the rest of the community, in their power of representing public opinion in the legislature? the slave owners. They send from their twelve States one hundred members, while the fourteen free States, with a free population nearly double, return but a hundred and forty-two. Before whom do the presidential candidates bow down the most humbly, on whom do they fawn the most fondly, and for whose tastes do they cater the most assiduously in their servile protestations? The slave owners always.

Public opinion! hear the public opinion of the free South, as expressed by its own members in the House of Representatives at Washington. 'I have a great respect for the chair,' quoth North Carolina, 'I have a great respect for the chair as an officer of the house, and a great respect for him personally; nothing but that respect prevents me from rushing to the table and tearing that petition which has just been presented for the abolition of slavery in the district of Columbia, to pieces.'—'I warn the abolitionists,' says South Carolina, 'ignorant, infuriated barbarians as they are, that if chance shall throw any of them into our hands, he may expect a felon's death.'—'Let an abolitionist come within

the borders of South Carolina,' cried a third; mild Carolina col-
league; 'and if we can catch him, we will try him, and notwithstanding the interference of all the governments on earth, including
the Federal government, we will HANG him.'

Public opinion has made this law.—It has declared that in
Washington, in that city which takes its name from the father of
American liberty, any justice of the peace may bind with fetters
any negro passing down the street and thrust him into jail: no
offense on the black man's part is necessary. The justice says,
'I choose to think this man a runaway': and locks him up. Public
opinion impowers the man of law when this is done, to advertise
the negro in the newspapers, warning his owner to come and claim
him, or he will be sold to pay the jail fees. But supposing he is
a free black, and has no owner, it may naturally be presumed that
he is set at liberty. No: HE IS SOLD TO RECOMPENSE HIS JAILER.
This has been done again, and again, and again. He has no means
of proving his freedom; has no adviser, messenger, or assistance
of any sort or kind; no investigation into his case is made, or
inquiry instituted. He, a free man, who may have served for
years, and bought his liberty, is thrown into jail on no process,
for no crime, and on no pretence of crime: and is sold to pay
the jail fees. This seems incredible, even of America, but it is
the law.

Public opinion is deferred to, in such cases as the following:
which is headed in the newspapers:—

'Interesting Law-Case

'An interesting case is now on trial in the Supreme Court, arising out of the following facts. A gentleman residing in Maryland
had allowed an aged pair of his slaves, substantial though not
legal freedom for several years. While thus living, a daughter was
born to them, who grew up in the same liberty, until she married
a free negro, and went with him to reside in Pennsylvania. They
had several children, and lived unmolested until the original owner
died, when his heir attempted to regain them; but the magistrate
before whom they were brought, decided that he had no juris-
diction in the case. *The owner seized the woman and her children
in the night, and carried them to Maryland.*'

'Cash for negroes,' 'cash for negroes,' 'cash for negroes,' is the
heading of advertisements in great capitals down the long columns
of the crowded journals. Wood-cuts of a runaway negro with
manacled hands, crouching beneath a bluff pursuer in top boots,

who, having caught him, grasps him by the throat, agreeably diversify the pleasant text. The leading article protests against 'that abominable and hellish doctrine of abolition, which is repugnant alike to every law of God and nature.' The delicate mama, who smiles her acquiescence in this sprightly writing as she reads the paper in her cool piazza, quiets her youngest child who clings about her skirts, by promising the boy a whip to beat the little niggers with.'—But the negroes, little and big, are protected by public opinion.

Let us try this public opinion by another test, which is important in three points of view: first, as showing how desperately timid of the public opinion slave owners are, in the delicate descriptions of fugitive slaves in widely circulated newspapers; secondly, as showing how perfectly contented the slaves are, and how very seldom they run away; thirdly as exhibiting their entire freedom from scar, or blemish, or any mark of cruel infliction, as their pictures are drawn, not by lying abolitionists, but by their own truthful masters.

The following are a few specimens of the advertisements in the public papers. It is only four years since the oldest among them appeared; and others of the same nature continued to be published every day, in shoals.

'Ran away, Negress Caroline. Had on a collar with one prong turned down.'

'Ran away, a black woman, Betsy. Had an iron bar on her right leg.'

'Ran away, the negro Manuel. Much marked with irons.'

'Ran away, the negress Fanny. Had on an iron band about her neck.'

'Ran away, a negro boy about twelve years old. Had round his neck a chain dog-collar with "De Lampert" engraved on it.'

'Ran away, the negro Hown. Has a ring of iron on his left foot. Also, Grise, *his wife,* having a ring and chain on the left leg.'

'Ran away, a negro boy named James. Said boy was ironed when he left me.'

'Committed to jail, a man who calls his name John. He has a clog of iron on his right foot which will weigh four or five pounds.

'Detained at the police jail, the negro wench, Myra. Has several marks of LASHING, and has irons on her feet.'

'Ran away, a negro woman and two children. A few days before she went off, I burnt her with a hot iron on the left side of her face. I tried to make the letter M.'

'Ran away, a negro man named Henry; his left eye out, some

scars from a dirk on and under his left arm, and much scarred with the whip.'

'One hundred dollars reward, for a negro fellow, Pompey, 40 years old. He is branded on the left jaw.'

'Committed to jail, a negro man. Has no toes on the left foot.'

'Ran away, a negro woman named Rachel. Has lost all her toes except the large one.'

'Ran away, Sam. He was shot a short time since through the hand, and has several shots in his left arm and side.'

'Ran away, my negro man Dennis. Said negro has been shot in the left arm between the shoulder and elbow, which has paralysed the left hand.'

'Ran away, my negro man named Simon. He has been shot badly, in his back and right arm.'

'Ran away, a negro named Arthur. Has a considerable scar across his breast and each arm, made by a knife; loves to talk much of the goodness of God.'

'Twenty-five dollars reward for my man Isaac. He has a scar on his forehead, caused by a blow; and one on his back, made by a shot from a pistol.'

'Ran away, a negro girl called Mary. Has a small scar over her eye, a good many teeth missing, the letter A is branded on her cheek and forehead.'

'Ran away, negro Ben. Has a scar on his right hand; his thumb and forefinger being injured by being shot last fall. A part of the bone came out. He has also one or two large scars on his back and hips.'

'Detained at the jail, a mulatto, named Tom. Has a scar on the right cheek, and appears to have been burned with powder on the face.'

'Ran away, a negro man named Ned. Three of his fingers are drawn into the palm of his hand by a cut. Has a scar on the back of his neck, nearly half round, done by a knife.'

'Was committed to jail, a negro man. Says his name is Josiah. His back very much scarred by the whip; and branded on the thigh and hips in three or four places, thus (J M). The rim of his right ear has been bit or cut off.'

'Fifty dollars reward, for my fellow Edward. He has a scar on the corner of his mouth, two cuts on and under his arm, and the letter E on his arm.'

'Ran away, negro boy Ellie. Has a scar on one of his arms from the bite of a dog.'

'Ran away, from the plantation of James Surgette, the following negroes: Randal, has one ear cropped; Bob, has lost one eye; Kentucky Tom, has one jaw broken.'

'Ran away, Anthony. One of his ears cut off, and his left hand cut with an axe.'

'Fifty dollars reward for the negro Jim Blake. Has a piece cut out of each ear, and the middle finger of the left hand cut off to the second joint.'

'Ran away, a negro woman named Maria. Has a scar on one side of her check, by a cut. Some scars on her back.'

'Ran away, the Mulatto wench Mary. Has a cut on the left arm, a scar on the left shoulder, and two upper teeth missing.'

I should say, perhaps, in explanation of this latter piece of description, that among the other blessings which public opinion secures to the negroes, is the common practice of violently punching out their teeth. To make them wear iron collars by day and night, and to worry them with dogs, are practices almost too ordinary to deserve mention.

'Ran away, my man Fountain. Has holes in his ears, a scar on the right side of his forehead, has been shot in the hind parts of his legs, and is marked on the back with the whip.'

'Two hundred and fifty dollars reward for my negro man Jim. He is much marked with shot in his right thigh. The shot entered on the outside, half way between the hip and knee joints.'

'Brought to jail, John. Left ear cropt.'

'Taken up a negro man. Is very much scarred about the face and body, and has the left ear bit off.'

'Ran away, a black girl, named Mary. Has a scar on her check, and the end of one of her toes cut off.'

'Ran away, my Mulatto woman, Judy. She has had her right arm broke.'

'Ran away, my negro man, Levi. His left hand has been burnt, and I think the end of his forefinger is off.'

'Ran away, a negro man, NAMED WASHINGTON. Has lost a part of his middle finger, and the end of his little finger.'

'Twenty-five dollars reward for my man John. The tip of his nose is bit off.'

'Twenty-five dollars reward for the negro slave, Sally. Walks *as though* crippled in the back.'

'Ran away, Joe Dennis. Has a small notch in one of his ears.'

'Ran away, negro boy, Jack. Has a small crop out of his left ear.'

'Ran away, a negro man, named Ivory. Has a small piece cut out of top of each ear.'

While upon the subject of ears, I may observe that a distinguished abolitionist in New York once received a negro's ear,
which had been cut off close to the head, in a general post letter.
It was forwarded by the free and independent gentleman who had
caused it to be amputated, with a polite request that he would
place the specimen in his 'collection.'

I could enlarge this catalogue with broken arms, and broken
legs, and gashed flesh, and missing teeth, and lacerated backs, and
bites of dogs, and brands of red-hot irons innumerable: but as
my readers will be sufficiently sickened and repelled adready, I
will turn to another branch of the subject.

These advertisements, of which a similar collection might be
made for every year, and month, and week, and day; and which
are coolly read in families as things of course, and as a part of
the current news and small-talk; will serve to show how very
much the slaves profit by public opinion, and how tender it is in
their behalf. But it may be worth while to inquire how the slave
owners, and the class of society to which great numbers of them
belong, defer to public opinion in their conduct, not to their slaves
but to each other; how they are accustomed to restrain their
passions; what their bearing is among themselves; whether they
are fierce or gentle; whether their social customs be brutal, san-
guinary, and violent, or bear the impress of civilisation and refinement.

That we may have no partial evidence from abolitionists in
this inquiry, either, I will once more turn to their own newspapers, and I will confine myself, this time, to a selection from
paragraphs which appeared from day to day, during my visit
to America, and which refer to occurrences happening while I was
there. The italics in these extracts, as in the foregoing, are my
own.

These cases did not ALL occur, it will be seen, in territory
actually belonging to legalised Slave States, though most, and
those the very worst among them, did, as their counterparts constantly do; but the position of the scenes of action in reference to
places immediately at hand, where slavery is the law; and the
strong resemblance between that class of outrages and the rest;
lead to the just presumption that the character of the parties concerned was formed in slave districts, and brutalised by slave
customs.

'Horrible Tragedy.

'By a slip from *The Southport Telegraph,* Wisconsin, we learn that the Hon. Charles C. P. Arndt, Member of the Council for Brown county, was shot dead *on the floor of the Council chamber,* by James R. Vinyard, Member from Grant county. *The affair* grew out of a nomination for Sheriff of Grant county. Mr. E. S. Baker, was nominated and supported by Mr. Arndt. This nomination was opposed by Vinyard, who wanted the appointment to vest in his own brother. In the course of debate, the deceased made some statements which Vinyard pronounced false, and made use of violent and insulting language, dealing largely in personalities, to which Mr. A. made no reply. After the adjournment, Mr. A. stepped up to Vinyard, and requested him to retract, which he refused to do, repeating the offensive words. Mr. Arndt then made a blow at Vinyard, who stepped back a pace, drew a pistol, and shot him dead.

'The issue appears to have been provoked on the part of Vinyard, who was determined at all hazards to defeat the appointment of Baker, and who, himself defeated, turned his ire and revenge upon the unfortunate Arndt.'

'The Wisconsin Tragedy.

'Public indignation runs high in the territory of Wisconsin, in relation to the murder of C. C. P. Arndt, in the Legislative Hall of the Territory. Meetings have been held in different counties of Wisconsin, denouncing *the practice of secretly bearing arms in the Legislative chambers of the country.* We have seen the account of the expulsion of James R. Vinyard, the perpetrator of the bloody deed, and are amazed to hear, that, after this expulsion by those who saw Vinyard kill Mr. Arndt in the presence of his aged father, who was on a visit to see his son, little dreaming that he was to witness his murder, *Judge Dunn has discharged Vinyard on bail.* The Miners' Free Press speaks *in terms of merited rebuke* at the outrage upon the feelings of the people of Wisconsin. Vinyard was within arm's length of Mr. Arndt, when he took such deadly aim at him, that he never spoke. Vinyard might at pleasure, being so near, have only wounded him, but he chose to kill him.'

'Murder.

'By a letter in a St. Louis paper of the 14th, we notice a terrible outrage at Burlington, Iowa. A Mr. Bridgman having had a difficulty with a citizen of the place, Mr. Ross; a brother-in-law of the latter provided himself with one of Colt's revolving pistols, met Mr. B. in the street, *and discharged the contents of five of the barrels at him: each shot taking effect.* Mr. B., though horribly wounded, and dying, returned the fire, and killed Ross on the spot.'

'Terrible Death of Robert Potter.

'From the "Caddo Gazette," of the 12th inst., we learn the frightful death of Colonel Robert Potter. . . . He was beset in his house by an enemy, named Rose. He sprang from his couch, seized his gun, and, in his night-clothes, rushed from the house. For about two hundred yards his speed seemed to defy his pursuers; but, getting entangled in a thicket, he was captured. Rose told him *that he intended to act a generous part,* and give him a chance for his life. He then told Potter he might run, and he should not be interrupted till he reached a certain distance. Potter started at the word of command, and before a gun was fired he had reached the lake. His first impulse was to jump in the water and dive for it, which he did. Rose was close behind him, and formed his men on the bank ready to shoot him as he rose. In a few seconds he came up to breath; and scarce had his head reached the surface of the water when it was completely riddled with the shot of their guns, and he sunk, to rise no more!

'Murder in Arkansas.

'We understand *that a severe rencontre came off* a few days since in the Seneca Nation, between Mr. Loose, the sub-agent of the mixed band of the Senecas, Quapaw, and Shawnees, and Mr. James Gillespie, of the mercantile firm of Thomas G. Allison and Co., of Maysville, Benton County, Ark., in which the latter was slain with a bowie-knife. Some difficulty had for some time existed between the parties. It is said that Major Gillespie brought on the attack with a cane. A severe conflict ensued, during which two pistols were fired by Gillespie and one by Loose. Loose then stabbed Gillespie with one of those never-failing weapons, a bowie-knife. The death of Major G. is much regretted, as he was a liberal-minded and energetic man. Since the above was in type, we have learned that Major Allison has stated to some of our citizens in town that Mr. Loose gave the first blow. We forbear to give any particulars, *as the matter will be the subject of judicial investigation.*'

'Foul Deed.

'The steamer Thames, just from Missouri river, brought us a handbill, offering a reward of 500 dollars, for the person who assassinated Lilburn W. Baggs, late Governor of this State, at Independence, on the night of the 6th inst. Governor Baggs, it is stated in a written memorandum, was not dead, but mortally wounded.

'Since the above was written, we received a note from a clerk of the Thames, giving the following particulars. Gov. Baggs was shot by some villain on Friday, 6th inst., in the evening, while sitting in a room in his own house in Independence. His son, a boy, hearing a report, ran into the room, and found the Governor sitting in his chair, with his jaw fallen down, and his head leaning back; on discovering the injury done to his father, he gave the alarm. Foot tracks were found in the garden below the window, and a pistol picked up supposed to have been overloaded, and thrown from the hand of the scoundrel who fired it. Three buckshots of a heavy load, took effect; one going through his mouth, one into the brain, and another probably in or near the brain; all going into the back part of the neck and head. The Governor was still alive on the morning of the 7th; but no hopes for his recovery by his friends, and but slight hopes from his physicians.

'A man was suspected, and the Sheriff most probably has possession of him by this time.

'The pistol was one of a pair stolen some days previous from a baker in Independence, and the legal authorities have the description of the other.'

'Rencontre.

'An unfortunate *affair* took place on Friday evening in Chatres Street, in which one of our most respectable citizens received a dangerous wound, from a poignard, in the abdomen. From the Bee (New Orleans) of yesterday, we learn the following particulars. It appears that an article was published in the French side of the paper on Monday last, containing some strictures on the Artillery Battalion for firing their guns on Sunday morning, in answer to those from the Ontario and Woodbury, and thereby much alarm was caused to the families of those persons who were out all night preserving the peace of the city. Major C. Gally, Commander of the battalion, resenting this, called at the office, and demanded the author's name; that of Mr. P. Arpin was given to him, who was absent at the time. Some **angry words** then passed with one of the proprietors, and a challenge followed; the friends of both parties tried to arrange the affair, but failed to do so. On Friday evening, about seven o'clock, Major Gally met Mr. P. Arpin in Chatres Street, and accosted him. "Are you Mr. Arpin?"

' "Yes, Sir."

' "Then I have to tell you that you are a—" (applying an appropriate epithet).

' "I shall remind you of your words, sir."

' "But I have said I would break my cane on your shoulders."

' "I know it, but I have not yet received the blow."

'At these words, Major Gally, having a cane in his hands, struck Mr. Arpin across the face, and the latter drew a poignard from his pocket and stabbed Major Gally in the abdomen.

'Fears are entertained that the wound will be mortal. *We understand that Mr. Arpin has given security for his appearance at the Criminal Court to answer the charge.*'

'Affray in Mississippi.

'On the 27th ult., in an affray near Carthage, Leake county, Mississippi, between James Cottingham and John Wilburn, the latter was shot by the former, and so horribly wounded, that there was no hope of his recovery. On the 2nd instant, there was an affray at Carthage between A. C. Sharkey and George Goff, in which the latter was shot, and thought mortally wounded. Sharkey delivered himself up to the authorities, *but changed his mind and escaped!*'

'Personal Encounter.

'An encounter took place in Sparta, a few days since, between the barkeeper of an hotel, and a man named Bury. It appears that Bury had become somewhat noisy, *and that the barkeeper, determined to preserve order, had threatened to shoot Bury,* whereupon Bury drew a pistol and shot the barkeeper down. He was not dead at the last accounts, but slight hopes were entertained of his recovery.'

'Duel.

The clerk of the steamboat *Tribune* informs us that another duel was fought on Tuesday last, by Mr. Robbins, a bank officer in Vicksburg, and Mr. Fall, the editor of the Vicksburg Sentinel.

According to the arrangement, the parties had six pistols each, which, after the word "Fire!" *they were to discharge as fast as they pleased*. Fall fired two pistols without effect. Mr. Robbins' first shot took effect in Fall's thigh, who fell, and was unable to continue the combat.'

'*Affray in Clarke County.*

'An *unfortunate affray* occurred in Clarke county (Mo.), near Waterloo, on Tuesday the 19th ult., which originated in settling the partnership concerns of Messrs. M'Kane and M'Allister, who had been engaged in the business of distilling, and resulted in the death of the latter, who was shot down by Mr. M'Kane, because of his attempting to take possession of seven barrels of whiskey, the property of M'Kane, which had been knocked off to M'Allister at a sheriff's sale at one dollar per barrel. M'Kane immediately fled, *and at the latest dates had not been taken.*

'This *unfortunate affray* caused considerable excitement in the neighbourhood, as both the parties were men with large families depending upon them and stood well in the community.'

I will quote but one more paragraph, which, by reason of its monstrous absurdity, may be a relief to these atrocious deeds.

'*Affair of Honour.*

'We have just heard the particulars of a meeting which took place on Six Mile Island, on Tuesday, between two young bloods of our city: Samuel Thurston, *aged fifteen*, and William Hine, *aged thirteen* years. They were attended by young gentlemen of the same age. The weapons used on the occasion, were a couple of Dickson's best rifles; the distance, thirty yards. They took one fire, without any damage being sustained by either party, except the ball of Thurston's gun passing through the crown of Hine's hat. *Through the intercession of the Board of Honour,* the challenge was withdrawn, and difference amicably adjusted.'

If the reader will picture to himself the kind of Board of Honour which amicably adjusted the difference between these two little boys, who in any other part of the world would have been amicably adjusted on two porters' backs and soundly flogged with birchen rods, he will be possessed, no doubt, with as strong a sense of its ludicrous character, as that which sets me laughing whenever its image rises up before me.

Now, I appeal to every human mind, imbued with the commonest of common sense, and the commonest of common humanity; to all dispassionate, reasoning creatures, of any shade of opinion; and ask, with these revolting evidences of the state of society which exists in and about the slave districts of America before them, can they have a doubt of the real condition of the slave, or can they for a moment make a compromise between the institution or any of its flagrant fearful features, and their own just consciences? Will they say of any tale of cruelty and horror, however aggravated in degree, that it is improbable, when they can turn to the public prints, and, running, read such signs as these, laid before them by the men who rule the slaves: in their own acts and under their own hands?

Do we not know that the worst deformity and ugliness of slavery are at once the cause and effect of the reckless license taken by these freeborn outlaws? Do we not know that the man who has been born and bred among its wrongs; who has seen in his childhood husbands obliged at the word of command to flog their wives; women, indecently compelled to hold up their own garments that men might lay the heavier stripes upon their legs, driven and harried by brutal overseers in their time of travail, and becoming mothers on the field of toil, under the very lash itself; who has read in youth, and seen his virgin sisters read, descriptions of runaway men and women, and their disfigured persons, which could not be published elsewhere, of so much stock upon a farm, or at a show of beasts:—do we not know that that man, whenever his wrath is kindled up, will be a brutal savage? Do we not know that as he is a coward in his domestic life, stalking among his shrinking men and women slaves armed with his heavy whip, so he will be a coward out of doors, and carrying coward's weapons hidden in his breast, will shoot men down and stab them when he quarrels? And if our reason did not teach us this and much beyond; if we were such idiots as to close our eyes to that fine mode of training which rears up such men; should we not know that they who among their equals stab and pistol in the legislative halls, and in the counting-house, and on the market-place, and in all the elsewhere peaceful pursuits of life, must be to their dependants, even though they were free servants, so many merciless and unrelenting tyrants?

What! shall we declaim against the ignorant peasantry of Ireland, and mince the matter when these American taskmasters are in question? Shall we cry shame on the brutality of those who ham-string cattle: and spare the lights of Freedom upon earth who notch the ears of men and women, cut pleasant posies in the shrinking flesh, learn to write with pens of red-hot iron on the human face, rack their poetic fancies for liveries of mutilation which their slaves shall wear for life and carry to the grave, breaking living limbs as did the soldiery who mocked and slew the Saviour of the world, and set defenseless creatures up for targets! Shall we whimper over legends of the tortures practised on each other by the Pagan Indians, and smile upon the cruelties of Christian men! Shall we, so long as these things last, exult above the scattered remnants of that race, and triumph in the white enjoyment of their possessions? Rather, for me, restore the forest and the Indian village; in lieu of stars and stripes, let some poor feather flutter in the breeze; replace the streets and squares by wigwams; and though the death-song of a hundred haughty warriors fill the air, it will be music to the shriek of one unhappy slave.

On one theme, which is commonly before our eyes, and in respect of which our national character is changing fast, let the plain Truth be spoken, and let us not, like dastards, beat about the bush by hinting at the Spaniard and the fierce Italian. When knives are drawn by Englishmen in conflict let it be said and known: 'We owe this change to Republican Slavery. These are the weapons of Freedom. With sharp points and edges such as these, Liberty in America hews and hacks her slaves; or, failing that pursuit, her sons devote them to a better use, and turn them on each other.'

CHAPTER XVIII

CONCLUDING REMARKS

THERE are many passages in this book, where I have been at some pains to resist the temptation of troubling my readers with my own deductions and conclusions: preferring that they should judge for themselves, from such premises as I have laid before them. My only object in the outset, was, to carry them with me faithfully wheresoever I went: and that task I have discharged.

But I may be pardoned, if on such a theme as the general character of the American people, and the general character of their social system, as presented to a stranger's eyes, I desire to express my own opinions in a few words, before I bring these volumes to a close.

They are, by nature, frank, brave, cordial, hospitable, and affectionate. Cultivation and refinement seem but to enhance their warmth of heart and ardent enthusiasm; and it is the possession of these latter qualities in a most remarkable degree, which renders an educated American one of the most endearing and most generous of friends. I never was so won upon, as by this class: never yielded up my full confidence and esteem so readily and pleasurably, as to them; never can make again, in half a year, so many friends for whom I seem to entertain the regard of half a life.

These qualities are natural, I implicitly believe, to the whole people. That they are, however, sadly sapped and blighted in their growth among the mass; and that there are influences at work which endanger them still more, and give but little present promise of their healthy restoration; is a truth that ought to be told.

It is an essential part of every national character to pique itself mightily upon its faults, and to deduce tokens of its virtue or its wisdom from their very exaggeration. One great blemish in the popular mind of America, and the prolific parent of an innumerable brood of evils, is Universal Distrust. Yet the American citizen plumes himself upon this spirit, even when he is sufficiently dispassionate to perceive the ruin it works; and will often adduce it, in spite of his own reason, as an instance of the great sagacity and acuteness of the people, and their superior shrewdness and independence.

'You carry,' says the stranger, 'this jealousy and distrust into every transaction of public life. By repelling worthy men from your legislative assemblies, it has bred up a class of candidates for the suffrage, who, in their every act, disgrace your Institutions and your people's choice. It has rendered you so fickle, and so given to change, that your inconstancy has passed into a proverb; for you no sooner set up an idol firmly, than you are sure to pull it down and dash it into fragments: and this, because directly you reward a benefactor, or a public servant, you distrust him, merely because he *is* rewarded; and immediately apply yourselves to find out, either that you have been too bountiful in your acknowledgments, or he remiss in his deserts. Any man who attains a high place among you, from the President downwards, may date his downfall from that moment; for any printed lie that any notorious villain pens, although it militate directly against the character and conduct of a life, appeals at once to your distrust, and is believed. You will strain at a gnat in the way of trustfulness and confidence, however fairly won and well deserved; but you will swallow a whole caravan of camels, if they be laden with unworthy doubts and mean suspicions. Is this well, think you, or likely to elevate the character of the governors or the governed, among you?'

The answer is invariably the same: 'There's freedom of opinion here, you know. Every man thinks for himself, and we are not to be easily overreached. That's how our people come to be suspicious.'

Another prominent feature is the love of 'smart' dealing: which gilds over many a swindle and gross breach of trust: many a defalcation, public and private; and enables many a knave to hold his head up with the best, who well deserves a halter; though it has not been without its retributive operation, for this smartness has done more in a few years to impair the public credit, and to cripple the public resources, than dull honesty, however rash, could have effected in a century. The merits of a broken speculation, or a bankruptcy, or of a successful scoundrel, are not gauged by its or his observance of the golden rule, 'Do as you would be done by,' but are considered with reference to their smartness. I recollect, on both occasions of our passing that ill-fated Cairo on the Mississippi, remarking on the bad effects such gross deceits must have when they exploded, in generating a want of confidence abroad, and discouraging investment; but I was given to understand that this was a very smart scheme by which a deal of money had been made: and that its smartest feature was, that they forgot these things abroad, in a very short time, and speculated again, as freely as ever. The following dialogue I have held a hundred times: 'Is it not a very disgraceful circumstance that such a man as So-and-so should be acquiring a large property by the most infamous and odious means, and notwithstanding all the crimes of which he has been guilty, should be tolerated and abetted by your Citizens? He is a public nuisance is he not?' 'Yes, sir,' 'A convicted liar?' 'Yes, sir.' 'He has been kicked, and cuffed, and caned?' 'Yes, sir.' 'And he is utterly dishonourable, debased, and profligate?' 'Yes, sir.' 'In the name of wonder, then, what is his merit?' 'Well, sir, he is a smart man.'

In like manner, all kinds of deficient and impolite usages are referred to the national love of trade; though, oddly enough, it would be a weighty charge against a foreigner that he regarded the Americans as a trading people. The love of trade is assigned as a reason for that comfortless custom, so very prevalent in country towns, of married persons living in hotels, having no fireside of their own, and seldom meeting from early morning until late at night, but at the hasty public meals. The love of trade is a reason why the literature of America is to remain for ever unprotected:

'For we are a trading people, and don't care for poetry': though we *do,* by the way, profess to be very proud of our poets: while healthful amusements, cheerful means of recreation, and wholesome fancies, must fade before the stern utilitarian joys of trade.

These three characteristics are strongly presented at every turn, full in the stranger's view. But, the foul growth of America has a more tangled root than this; and it strikes its fibres, deep in its licentious Press.

Schools may be erected, East, West, North, and South; pupils be taught, and masters reared, by scores upon scores of thousands; colleges may thrive, churches may be crammed, temperance may be diffused, and advancing knowledge in all other forms walk through the land with giant strides: but while the newspaper press of America is in, or near, its present abject state, high moral improvement in that country is hopeless. Year by year, it must and will go back; year by year, the tone of public feeling must sink lower down; year by year, the Congress and the Senate must become of less account before all decent men; and year by year, the memory of the Great Fathers of the Revolution must be outraged more and more, in the bad life of their degenerate child.

Among the herd of journals which are published in the States, there are some, the reader scarcely need be told, of character and credit. From personal intercourse with accomplished gentlemen connected with publications of this class, I have derived both pleasure and profit. But the name of these is Few, and of the others Legion; and the influence of the good, is powerless to counteract the moral poison of the bad.

Among the gentry of America; among the well-informed and moderate: in the learned professions; at the bar and on the bench: there is, as there can be, but one opinion, in reference to the vicious character of these infamous journals. It is sometimes contended—I will not say strangely, for it is natural to seek excuses for such a disgrace—that their influence is not so great as a visitor would suppose. I must be pardoned for saying that there is no warrant for this plea, and that every fact and circumstance tends directly to the opposite conclusion.

When any man, of any grade of desert in intellect or character, can climb to any public distinction, no matter what, in America, without first grovelling down upon the earth, and bending the knee before this monster of depravity; when any private excellence is safe from its attacks; when any social confidence is left unbroken by it, or any tie of social decency and honour is held in the least regard; when any man in that free country has freedom of opinion, and presumes to think for himself, and speak for himself, without humble reference to a censorship which, for its rampant ignorance and base dishonesty, he utterly loaths and despises in his heart; when those who most acutely feel its infamy and the reproach it casts upon the nation, and who most denounce it to each other, dare to set their heels upon, and crush it openly, in the sight of all men: then, I will believe that its influence is lessening, and men are returning to their manly senses. But while that Press has its evil eye in every house, and its black hand in every appointment in the state, from a president to a postman; while, with ribald slander for its only stock in trade, it is the standard literature of an enormous class, who must find their reading in a newspaper, or they will not read at all; so long must its odium be upon the country's head, and so long must the evil it works, be plainly visible in the Republic.

To those who are accustomed to the leading English journals, or to the respectable journals of the Continent of Europe; to those who are accustomed to anything else in print and paper; it would be impossible, without an amount of extract for which I have neither space nor inclination, to convey an adequate idea of this frightful engine in America. But if any man desire confirmation of my statement on this head, let him repair to any place in this city of London, where scattered numbers of these publications are to be found; and there, let him form his own opinion.[1]

It would be well, there can be no doubt, for the American people as a whole, if they loved the Real less, and the Ideal somewhat more. It would be well, if there were greater encouragement to lightness of heart and gaiety, and a wider cultivation of what is beautiful, without being eminently and directly useful. But here, I think the general remonstrance, 'we are a new country,' which is so often advanced as an excuse for defects which are quite unjustifiable, as being, of right, only the slow growth of an old one, may be very reasonably urged: and I yet hope to hear of there being some other national amusement in the United States, besides newspaper politics.

They certainly are not a humorous people, and their temperament always impressed me as being of a dull and gloomy

---

[1] NOTE TO THE ORIGINAL EDITION.—Or let him refer to an able, and perfectly truthful article, in *The Foreign Quarterly Review,* published in the present month of October; to which my attention has been attracted, since these sheets have been passing through the press. He will find some specimens there, by no means remarkable to any man who has been in America, but sufficiently striking to one who has not.

character. In shrewdness of remark, and a certain cast-iron quaintness, the Yankees, or people of New England, unquestionably take the lead; as they do in most other evidences of intelligence. But in travelling about, out of the large cities—as I have remarked in former parts of these volumes—I was quite oppressed by the prevailing seriousness and melancholy air of business: which was so general and unvarying, that at every new town I came to, I seemed to meet the very same people whom I had left behind me, at the last. Such defects as are perceptible in the national manners, seem, to me, to be referable, in a great degree, to this cause: which has generated a dull, sullen persistence in coarse usages, and rejected the graces of life as undeserving of attention. There is no doubt that Washington, who was always most scrupulous and exact in points of ceremony, perceived the tendency towards this mistake, even in his time, and did his utmost to correct it.

I cannot hold with other writers on these subjects that the prevalence of various forms of dissent in America, is in any way attributable to the non-existence there of an established church: indeed, I think the temper of the people, if it admitted of such an Institution being founded amongst them, would lead them to desert it, as a matter of course, merely because it *was* established. But, supposing it to exist, I doubt its probable efficacy in summoning the wandering sheep to one great fold, simply because of the immense amount of dissent which prevails at home; and because I do not find in America any one form of religion with which we in Europe, or even in England, are unacquainted. Dissenters resort thither in great numbers, as other people do, simply because it is a land of resort; and great settlements of them are founded, because ground can be purchased, and towns and villages reared, where there were none of the human creation before. But even the Shakers emigrated from England; our country is not unknown to Mr. Joseph Smith, the apostle of Mormonism, or to his benighted disciples; I have beheld religious scenes myself in some of our populous towns which can hardly be surpassed by an American camp-meeting; and I am not aware that any instance of superstitious imposture on the one hand, and superstitious credulity on the other has had its origin in the United States, which we cannot more than parallel by the precedents of Mrs. Southcote, Mary Tofts the rabbit-breeder, or even Mr. Thom of Canterbury: which latter case arose, some time after the dark ages had passed away.

The Republican Institutions of America undoubtedly lead the

people to assert their self-respect and their equality; but a traveller is bound to bear those Institutions in his mind, and not hastily to resent the near approach of a class of strangers, who, at home, would keep aloof. This characteristic, when it was tinctured with no foolish pride, and stopped short of no honest service, never offended me; and I very seldom, if ever, experienced its rude or unbecoming display. Once or twice it was comically developed, as in the following case; but this was an amusing incident and not the rule, or near it.

I wanted a pair of boots at a certain town, for I had none to travel in, but those with the memorable cork soles, which were much too hot for the fiery decks of a steamboat. I therefore sent a message to an artist in boots, importing, with my compliments, that I should be happy to see him, if he would do me the polite favour to call. He very kindly returned for answer, that he would 'look round' at six o'clock that evening.

I was lying on the sofa, with a book and a wine-glass, at about that time, when the door opened, and a gentleman in a stiff cravat, within a year or two on either side of thirty, entered, in his hat and gloves; walked up to the looking-glass; arranged his hair; took off his gloves; slowly produced a measure from the uttermost depths of his coat pocket; and requested me, in a languid tone, to 'unfix' my straps. I complied, but looked with some curiosity at his hat, which was still upon his head. It might have been that, or it might have been the heat—but he took it off. Then, he sat himself down on a chair opposite me; rested an arm on each knee; and, leaning forward very much, took from the ground, by a great effort, the specimen of metropolitan workmanship which I had just pulled off: whistling, pleasantly, as he did so. He turned it over and over; surveyed it with a contempt no language can express: and inquired if I wished him to fix me a boot like *that?* I courteously replied, that provided the boots were large enough, I would leave the rest to him; that if convenient and practicable, I should not object to their bearing some resemblance to the model then before him; but that I would be entirely guided by, and would beg to leave the whole subject to, his judgment and discretion. 'You an't partikler, about this scoop in the heel, I suppose then?' says he: 'we don't foller that, here.' I repeated my last observation. He looked at himself in the glass again; went closer to it to dash a grain or two of dust out of the corner of his eye; and settled his cravat. All this time, my leg and foot were in the air. 'Nearly ready, sir?' I inquired. 'Well, pretty nigh,' he said; 'keep steady.' I kept as steady as I could, both in foot and face; and having by this time got the dust out, and found his pencil-case, he measured me, and made the necessary notes. When he had finished, he fell into his old attitude, and taking up the boot again, mused for some time. 'And this,' he said, at last, 'is an English boot, is it? This is a London boot, eh?' 'That, sir,' I replied, 'is a London boot.' He mused over it again, after the manner of Hamlet with Yorick's skull; nodded his head, as who should say, 'I pity the Institutions that led to the production of this boot!'; rose; put up his pencil, notes, and paper—glancing at himself in the glass, all the time—put on his hat; drew on his gloves very slowly; and finally walked out. When he had been gone about a minute, the door reopened, and his hat and his head reappeared. He looked round the room, and at the boot again, which was still lying on the floor; appeared thoughtful for a minute; and then said 'Well, good arternoon.' 'Good afternoon, sir,' said I: and that was the end of the inter-view.

There is but one other head on which I wish to offer a remark; and that has reference to the public health. In so vast a country, where there are thousands of millions of acres of land yet unsettled and uncleared, and on every rood of which, vegetable decomposition is annually taking place; where there are so many great rivers, and such opposite varieties of climate; there cannot fail to be a great amount of sickness at certain seasons. But I may venture to say, after conversing with many members of the medical profession in America, that I am not singular in the opinion that much of the disease which does prevail, might be avoided, if a few common precautions were observed. Greater means of personal cleanliness, are indispensable to this end; the custom of hastily swallowing large quantities of animal food, three times a day, and rushing back to sedentary pursuits after each meal, must be changed; the gentler sex must go more wisely clad, and take more healthful exercise; and in the latter clause, the males must be included also. Above all, in public institutions, and throughout the whole of every town and city, the system of ventilation, and drainage, and removal of impurities requires to be thoroughly revised. There is no local Legislature in America which may not study Mr. Chadwick's excellent Report upon the Sanitary Condition of our Labouring Classes, with immense advantage.

I HAVE now arrived at the close of this book. I have little reason to believe, from certain warnings I have had since I returned to England, that it will be tenderly or favourably received by the American people; and as I have written the Truth in relation to the mass of those who form their judgments and express their opinions, it will be seen that I have no desire to court, by any adventitious means, the popular applause.

It is enough for me, to know that what I have set down in these pages, cannot cost me a single friend on the other side of the Atlantic, who is, in anything deserving of the name. For the rest, I put my trust, implicitly, in the spirit in which they have been conceived and penned; and I can bide my time.

I have made no reference to my reception, nor have I suffered it to influence me in what I have written; for, in either case, I should have offered but a sorry acknowledgment, compared with that I bear within my breast, towards those partial readers of my former books, across the Water, who met me with an open hand, and not with one that closed upon an iron muzzle.

POSTSCRIPT

At a Public Dinner given to me on Saturday the 18th of April, 1868, in the City of New York, by two hundred representatives of the Press of the United States of America, I made the following observations among others:

'So much of my voice has lately been heard in the land, that I might have been contented with troubling you no further from my present standing-point, were it not a duty with which I henceforth charge myself, not only here but on every suitable occasion, whatsoever and wheresoever, to express my high and grateful sense of my second reception in America, and to bear my honest testimony to the national generosity and magnanimity. Also, to declare how astounded I have been by the amazing changes I have seen around me on every side,—changes moral, changes physical, changes in the amount of land subdued and peopled, changes in the rise of vast new cities, changes in the growth of older cities almost out of recognition, changes in the graces and amenities of life, changes in the Press, without whose advancement no advancement can take place anywhere. Nor am I, believe me, so arrogant as to suppose that in five-and-twenty years there have been no changes in me, and that I had nothing to learn and no extreme impressions to correct when I was here first. And this brings me to a point on which I have, ever since I landed in the United States last November, observed a strict silence, though sometimes tempted to break it, but in reference to which I will, with your good leave, take you into my confidence now. Even the Press, being human, may be sometimes mistaken or misinformed, and I rather think that I have in one or two rare instances observed its information to be not strictly accurate with reference to myself. Indeed, I have, now and again, been more surprised by printed news that I have read of myself, than by any printed news that I have ever read in my present state of existence. Thus,